THE
KNIGHT'S
Bride

THE KNIGHT'S Bride

Chivalry Lives in Six Stories from the Middle Ages

TRACIE PETERSON
DIANNE CHRISTNER, PAMELA GRIFFIN,
YVONNE LEHMAN, JILL STENGL

BARBOUR BOOKS
An Imprint of Barbour Publishing, Inc.

Where Angels Camp ©2002 by Dianne Christner
A Legend of Mercy ©2005 by Pamela Griffin
The Stranger's Kiss ©2001 by Yvonne Lehman
A Kingdom Divided ©1995 by Tracie Peterson
Alas, My Love ©1996 by Tracie Peterson
A Child of Promise ©1998 by Jill Stengl

Print ISBN 978-1-63409-565-5

eBook Editions:
Adobe Digital Edition (.epub) 978-1-63409-392-7
Kindle and MobiPocket Edition (.prc) 978-1-63409-393-4

Published by Barbour Books, an imprint of Barbour Publishing, Inc., P.O. Box 719, Uhrichsville, OH 44683, www.barbourbooks.com

Our mission is to publish and distribute inspirational products offering exceptional value and biblical encouragement to the masses.

Member of the
Evangelical Christian
Publishers Association

Printed in the United States of America.

Contents

Where Angels Camp

Dianne Christner

Dedicated to my brother Bruce,
who traipsed through Germany with me.
What fun it was to explore Dinkelsbühl together!
To my sister-in-law, Teri, for her support,
and my loving husband, Jim, for making the trip possible.
Your love and encouragement inspire me above all else.
To those who made this writing project such a pleasure—
my coauthors and editors.
To Dinkelsbühl, such a sweet city!
And to my Lord, Creator of all the above.

The angel of the Lord *encampeth round about them
that fear him, and delivereth them.*
Psalm 34:7

Chapter 1

Dinkelsbühl, Germany, 1632

The hinges on the large, plank door creaked as *Graf* Christian von Engel peered into the armory. An elbow-cop, hung in an amusing manner, hailed him. Inside, the tang of metal and smoke instantly filled his nostrils. The unattended shop contained many things to interest a man, even if the idea of going to war did not.

He caressed the smooth surface of a breastplate, then stepped up to examine an odd-shaped helm. An army wearing such a headpiece would frighten the enemy to death. He turned it this way and that, then slipped it over his head.

The rusty visor snapped closed. Christian gave it a jerk. Stuck tight. Sucking in a breath of hot, moist air, he fumbled with the lock, but the visor would not budge. He tried to shove off the infuriating chunk of metal. The helm clamped itself around his throat. In his shuffling about, his feet bumped something, and he nearly lost his balance.

"Be still. You'll hurt yourself."

Every muscle in his body tensed at the soft musical voice. Hot coals of embarrassment burned the pit of his stomach.

"Stand still, now. Let me help," the female voice insisted.

"I need no help." The helm's ventail, with only narrow slits for breathing, muffled his words. He felt a light touch on his shoulder and stilled. The working of the visor's spring pin pressed the helm against his cheek.

"There. Now it should open."

Christian jerked the visor. Fresh air cooled the top segment of his face. A pair of soft blue eyes gazed up at him. Surrounding her face was hair the color of golden grain. The eyes twinkled, and the woman's lips curved. She averted her gaze to the arming-nail, glancing up at him once or twice while she unfastened a clasp by his neck. Christian did not stir.

"You may remove it now," she said and stepped back.

Slowly, he lifted. It slipped off.

"The helm is a relic." She cocked her head and studied him. "Perhaps you should consider keeping a squire."

"The land is too dangerous for a squire's travel," Christian grumbled as he replaced the helm in its proper place.

"Ja, it is that," a deep masculine voice boomed. Christian jerked his gaze away from his lovely rescuer-tormentor and spun around to get his first look at the German craftsman. The stocky armorer had bushy, light curly hair, wrinkles, and a stern face.

Christian exhaled deeply, like one who had discovered a rare treasure. "I have traveled a long distance to meet the armorer over whom the entire kingdom raves."

Gerrard Trittenbach's expression softened, and they exchanged introductions. "If you heard that I am a man who takes pride in his craftsmanship, then you have heard no falsehood."

From the corner of his eye, Christian noticed the lovely Fräulein slip away. "I need a new suit of armor. My entire armory is in disrepair." The man did not reply, only leveled a penetrating gaze. Unsure of how to persuade him, Christian foolishly rambled, "Cleaning, buckling, leathering..."

"Oh? Are you preparing to go to war?"

"Nein." Christian shook his head. "Only to defend my land. The Swedes are ravaging nearby estates. It is only a matter of time until—"

Gerrard's eyes lit. "So your loyalties are with the emperor?"

"I would prefer to remain neutral." He shrugged. "The Swedes and French who invade our German lands disregard such a stand. In their eyes, if you do not join up with them, you are considered their enemy. I suppose it is the same with the emperor."

"Ja. No middle ground." The armorer's expression darkened. "Let me show you a few pieces."

Christian followed Gerrard about the workshop as they discussed details.

"We must fit you," Gerrard said. "Come. Stand here and remove your outer clothing."

Christian did as the older man bade and dispensed with his doublet. The armorer took measurements. A small boy peeked out from an open doorway that led to a rear shop door. But what really bothered Christian was that the Fräulein remained in the room in a far corner, sewing. Although she paid him no attention, her presence unsettled him. With his arms suspended over his head and the armorer poking about his body, he wondered what one was supposed to do with his gaze in such a circumstance. More to the point, how could he keep it off the Fräulein? He glanced at Gerrard. A scowl darkened the older man's face.

Finally, with a grunt, Gerrard dismissed him. Christian instantly lowered his arms and snatched his clothing.

"Where are you staying tonight?" Gerrard asked.

Christian tugged at his doublet. "My men and I intend to camp outside Dinkelsbühl."

"As you implied, the countryside is not safe. We will find you beds inside the city wall. How many men?"

"Sechs."

Gerrard glanced over his shoulder and softened his voice. "Amelia, Daughter, can you come here a moment?" So the Fräulein was his daughter.

She crossed the room and stood before the armorer. "Ja?"

"Would you run to Watchman Hurtin's house and see if we can find lodging for Graf von Engel and his six men?"

Amelia gave Christian a brief saucy glance, then nodded respectfully at her father and departed.

"Thank you for your kindness, Herr Trittenbach. I'll see to my men and return." As Christian left the shop, he heard the clatter of small feet. A boy's voice could be heard through the open window.

"Who was that, Papa?"

"Why, that was Graf Christian von Engel of Engelturm."

"Where is that, Papa?"

Christian couldn't help but smile. So what if he had made a fool of himself? He had met the respected armorer and had taken care of a necessary task. He had secured safe lodging for his men. Best of all was the armorer's daughter. He strode down the narrow, cobbled street. As he passed by the colorful shops—each topped with an orange-tiled, steeply pitched roof—he thought, *Dinkelsbühl. A sweet city.*

Hours later, Amelia fiddled with the black velvet lining, irritated with her crooked stitches. Father, her only living parent, valued her work as an integral part of their armor merchandise. But ever since Graf von Engel had entered their workshop, she had torn out rows of uneven stitches. When the count had opened his visor and gazed into her eyes, weakness and desire swept over her in one warm rush. Her face felt hot even now in remembrance.

Many men frequented her father's workshop. But none had ever interested her nor earned her father's approval. She had even traveled with her father to other villages and castles. But never had she recalled meeting anyone who stirred her like this.

The familiar sound of the shop's creaky door hinges drew her gaze. There stood the object of her thoughts. The count shifted his stance and scrutinized her with sky-colored eyes.

She pushed aside her work and squirmed to her feet. "Good news. We found you lodging."

A smile softened his lean, angular face. "You are too kind. Is it far?"

Amelia gestured toward the watchman's home. "Nein. Just beyond the *Tor.*"

The count nodded. His center-parted, brown mane brushed against the shoulders of his doublet; its full curls cascaded down his upper back. He glanced out the shuttered window to the gate. "Could you take me there?" His eyes teased. "Otherwise, I might take a wrong turn. The countryside is very dangerous."

With her father occupied in the back room, she pretended to consider. "Since you paid Father such splendid praise, ja. I will go with you."

Christian swept open the door. She brushed by him, and they stepped out onto the cobblestones. They had not walked far before the count spoke. "You are quite charming."

"How can you say so? I took advantage of your moment of weakness."

"Indeed you did. But if you had not come to my rescue, I might still be stumbling in circles."

Amelia's laughter bubbled forth. "Where is Engelturm?"

"On the edge of the Black Forest. West, not far from the River Rhine."

"Oh, I have seen the Rhine. How lovely it is."

"I am glad you liked it. You travel often?"

"Ja. But look, here we are." A round-faced woman stuck her head out an opened window of a house built into the city's wall.

Graf von Engel hung back and frowned. "So soon. I am disappointed."

"Come," Amelia urged. "I will introduce you."

Amelia left the count and returned to the workshop, humming. When she entered, her father was seated at a workbench.

"Where have you been, Amelia?"

"Why, the count returned. I took him to the watchman's house."

His eyes darkened. "I wish you wouldn't associate with him."

Amelia was shocked at her father's blunt remark. Was he not the one who had suggested they find the count and his men lodging? "Why would you wish such a thing?"

"Our kingdom is at war. It is not a good time to fall in love."

"Love?" Amelia gasped, even more shocked. "Don't be absurd. We just met."

"I saw the way you looked at each other. For all we know, he could be a spy."

Amelia just gaped at him.

Her father sighed heavily and stretched forth his stocky arm. "Come." She crossed the room to him. "If he hurts you, my own heart will break."

Amelia's eyes stung, and she nodded. It was her greatest pleasure to serve her family. Although she did not understand why her father was concerned about the count, she certainly could not deny her attraction, nor was there any reason not to trust her father's judgment and abide by his request.

The next morning, Christian entered the armory and watched in amusement as the armorer's little son galloped about the room. In his make-believe, his hands grasped an air bellows—the reins and neck of his horse—which he brought to a halt before a standing suit of armor. "You! Draw your sword and defend yourself!" He laid the bellows aside. "Wait here, Beauty," he commanded, then turned back to the faceless helm. "You, sir, are a coward!"

"*Gut! Sehr gut!*" Christian clapped. "Good! Very good!"

The boy ran up to Christian, his eyes bright. "Are you a knight?"

"My *Opa* was," Christian spoke fondly of his grandfather. "Are you?"

"I hope to be. But Father says that the knights are fading out." He pointed to the empty suit of armor. "My papa made him."

Christian knelt down beside the lad and held back a chuckle. He touched the boy's shoulder. "What is your name, son?"

"Nicolaus."

"How old are you?"

"I'm five!"

"Hello, Graf von Engel," Gerrard greeted.

Christian straightened. "I was just getting acquainted with Nicolaus."

"I hope he has been minding his manners."

Christian glanced into Nicolaus's pleading eyes. "Indeed, he has."

The boy beamed and turned back to his father. "May I play?"

"*Ja.* Run along."

"A fine lad." Christian's gaze swept across the room in search of the armorer's daughter. "I wanted to thank you for all your kindness."

"*Ach*, think nothing of it."

"Will you come to Engelturm and set my armory in order?"

"I have not decided. I shall have an answer upon your return."

"Do consider it," Christian said before he opened the door and strode out.

"Humph!" Christian whooshed—the breath being knocked from his chest. When he could breathe again, he muttered, "Of all the clumsy—"

"Me? Clumsy?" Amelia fumed from the ground.

"Nein. Me. I am the clumsy one. Here, let me help." She eyed him warily and rejected his outstretched hand. He apologized as she stood and brushed off her long skirt. "Truly, I am sorry."

Amelia nodded. "We are even now. You have seen me in an embarrassing situation, and I have seen you—"

"Stop!" He held up his hands in defense. "Enough." They looked at each other and burst into laughter. The count shook his head. "You are a delight."

Her brows arched. "Am I?"

He softened his voice. "I wish I didn't have to go. But my men await."

A glimmer of alarm passed over Amelia's face. "May I pray for your safety?"

Christian's heart swelled. "I would welcome it above any other thing." He boldly stated, "Upon my return, may I see you?" Her face paled. Christian frowned. "You are not spoken for?"

"Nein. But, of course we shall meet again. You have dealings with Father. Godspeed."

"Farewell," he tried to say, but she was already gone. Pondering her abrupt behavior, he strode away in search of his men.

Chapter 2

The silk lining was flawless, a labor of devotion. Someday Graf von Engel would wear it over his heart. As Amelia stitched, she also prayed for his protection.

"Finished?" Gerrard asked.

"Ja. I think I need a stretch."

"Go. You work too hard."

"No more than you." Amelia rose from the heart-shaped, wooden chair and left the stifling shop, smoky from the fire needed to work the metal. She had not walked far alongside the street named *Unterer Mauerweg* when two small bodies darted from behind a cart.

"Nicolaus! Heidi!" Amelia shouted for them. *"Anschlag!"*

The two little bodies jerked, and their feet stopped churning. Their faces slowly turned toward Amelia. She crooked her finger, beckoning them. Their tiny shoulders instantly sagged, and their hands stole behind them. Amelia smelled mischief as the two dawdled forward.

"What is behind your backs?"

Heidi thrust forward her arm. "Buttercups for you!"

Nicolaus joined in the false tale. "Ja. We know how you like them."

Amelia stifled her amusement and accepted the bouquet. "And aren't they a lovely gift?" The hills beyond the city were clad in brilliant yellow. She cast a dreamy gaze toward the wall. Somewhere out there was the count.

"Can we go play now?" Nicolaus tugged on Amelia's sleeve.

The children were forbidden to go outside the city wall since Swedes had been reported to be in the vicinity. The sad restriction was for their safety. "Where did you find these? From someone's window box?"

Heidi's face paled. Nicolaus's mouth formed a pout. Amelia accusingly arched a brow. Nicolaus set his hands on his hips. Heidi pointed toward the wall.

With a sigh, Amelia knelt down. "You did a very dangerous thing. The enemy's army would like nothing better than to catch *Kinder*, to whisk children up onto their horse and carry you off to their camp. Then they would barter you Kinder to capture the entire city. You would not want that to happen, would you?"

"Oh, nein. There was nobody out there." Heidi's braids whipped from side to side as she shook her head.

"There was not even one horse." Nicolaus clearly did not display any signs of regret.

"They could be hiding and gallop out in an eye blink to snatch you up before you could run to safety." Amelia watched Heidi's eyes widen as the child scratched her arms. Hopeful she had instilled a measure of caution into the children, Amelia gentled. "Let's take half of the flowers to Heidi's mother so she can share the beauty. Shall we?"

Amelia touched their shoulders and urged them forward. "And you know, Kinder, buttercups are poisonous. We'll have to scrub."

Nicolaus straightened his arms toward the cobblestones and clenched his hands into fists. "Ugh!"

Amelia stifled a giggle.

Frau Hurtin had a houseful of daughters. The oldest, Lore, looked up from her weaving as Amelia paraded the children through the room and deposited them with Frau Hurtin. In this warm household, it was easy to see why Nicolaus loved to come and play. Lore, who had listened to the children's chatter, left her work to cross the room to Amelia.

"Are there really enemy soldiers beyond the wall?"

"Don't worry, dear. Our walls are thick and strong."

Lore nodded, but her expression remained doubtful.

Nicolaus reappeared, his face scrubbed red. "Frau Hurtin says that Heidi cannot play anymore today."

Amelia gave Lore a parting smile and drew Nicolaus away. "Nor can you. Let's go home." He shrugged away from her touch but obeyed.

At bedtime, Amelia listened to Nicolaus's rote prayers. He hugged her neck as she leaned over him to adjust his feather coverlet. She kissed his cheek and smiled.

"Can we pray for Count von Engel?"

Amelia blinked. "You met him?"

"Ja. He was nice to me. He's very tall and brave."

"Brave? How do you know?" She fastened her gaze on Nicolaus's carved headboard, hoping that her cheeks would not give away her emotions.

"Because he's out beyond the wall. And he's getting fitted for war."

"Oh. Ja. Let's pray for him."

Nicolaus scooted out from his feather coverlet and knelt on the floor. "God. Keep Count von Engel safe so I can see him again."

These were the very words she had been praying every day this past week.

⌒

Christian paused outside a brass-studded door, selecting a key from a large metal ring. The lock needed working, but it released. Inside Engelturm's armory, a gray blur scurried across the floor, through a leg greave, and disappeared beneath a knee-cop. As Christian's gaze meandered over the room laden with sword and rivet, its neglect embarrassed him. The servant, who had lagged behind, now drew up alongside and followed his master's stare.

"Set this place in order." Christian ignored the servant's dour expression and crossed the room, swiping a cobweb from his pathway. He opened an arched window. Sunlight caught the dancing dust particles he had just roused.

The servant sneezed hard, twice.

"Ja. Bring the maids to dust. And ask the steward to take inventory."

Since his journey to Dinkelsbühl, Christian had brimmed with plans for the armory. He had witnessed, firsthand, the remains of ruined castles and burned villages. Cousin Leopold was a gifted scout. Otherwise, they surely would have skirmished with the small clusters of soldiers that roamed the countryside.

Christian was not a coward. He was trained at arms, but his heart was not in warring. How could God condone such a thing? Nor did Christian fear death. When his own father died, there was peace in the aged eyes. During his father's long illness, many matters at Engelturm had fallen into neglect. Now it was Christian's responsibility to protect the people within his castle and those who lived in the nearby village of Engelheim.

Beautiful Engelturm stood like a sentry atop a magnificent cliff that seemed to reach up to heaven itself. Below, the River Wurm meandered through a lush green valley. Christian gazed out across the bailey, reminiscing his childhood.

Suddenly Nicolaus came to mind. The child had wormed his way right into Christian's heart. As had Amelia. He must persuade Herr Trittenbach to put Engelturm's armory in order. Not only would he make ready his defense, but also he would see the lovely Fräulein again.

He turned from the window to his servant, who now held a small cloth over his long bulbous nose. "Let's go see how the upper chambers fare."

Weeks passed. Amelia combed through her wet, waist-long tresses. Water from the moat powered her father's grindstone and glazing wheel. Reluctantly, she left the refreshing stream's edge, proceeding past their home and into the back entrance of the shop.

"Count von Engel!"

"Fräulein Trittenbach." His face shone with pleasure. "What good fortune that we should meet."

His gaze roved over her hair. Amelia tossed it behind her back and felt an uncustomary warmth creep up her neck. "I assume you had safe travel?"

"Ja. *Danke schön* for your prayers."

"Father has been expecting you. I am sorry, but he is running errands." He looked pleased. "I am in no hurry."

"Would ye care for a drink?"

Christian smiled at her. "Ja. If it's not too much trouble."

Moments later, Amelia leaned against the closed door of her living quarters and fanned her face with her hand. Next, she hurriedly knotted her hair at the back of her neck, and then she crossed the room to a jug and poured water into a flowered cup. Some sloshed over the side onto her puffed sleeve. She snatched a cloth. After drawing several deep breaths, she returned to the shop. The count's back was toward her. He was inspecting his finished armor.

"Perhaps you should try on the helm."

He flinched, but when he turned, his eyes twinkled. "Once caught, but not twice."

She handed him the drink and nodded. "Wise, indeed." Amelia watched him empty the cup. He handed it back to her, and she withdrew a few steps. "I will go find Father."

"Please, stay." His voice was gentle. "My arrival is no secret. With my men at large in the city, your father should come bounding through that door any moment. And I had hoped—"

"Ah, Graf von Engel. I see you have found your suit." Her father's voice sent a rush of relief through Amelia.

Christian arched a brow at her, then shifted his gaze onto the approaching armorer. "Herr Trittenbach. It is ready, then?"

"Ja. Try it on."

"First I would discuss Engelturm with you."

"Come and sit." Gerrard motioned toward two brightly painted benches. Grateful, Amelia slipped away.

"Herr Trittenbach. I see no hope for my armory unless you agree to come to Engelturm." Gerrard crossed his fingers in front of his belly as if he had not fully discarded the idea, so Christian continued to persuade him. "I brought a dozen men. Enough for a safe journey."

Gerrard tapped his chin. "I have no other pressing commitments. Truth is, I am only a short while from having to make candlesticks. I loathe the idea. But one day soon it will be the fate of every armorer." Gerrard brightened and brushed away the topic with a sweep of his hand. "But that is not your problem. Should I agree, I would need to take a wagon full of supplies, perhaps two." Gerrard drummed his fingers on the table. "Seems I have no choice but to agree."

Chapter 3

Amelia looked up from her dusting and frowned at Valdemar, the mercer. She always dreaded his visits to their shop, especially his forward behavior.

"You are not happy to see me?" Valdemar strode forward.

"What can I do for you, Herr Valdemar?" her father asked.

As soon as Valdemar turned to acknowledge him, Amelia tactfully removed herself from that part of the room, but not before hearing Valdemar's next remark. "You have to tell her sometime." Curious now, she paused—just out of sight—to listen.

"Keep your voice down," Father warned. "What do you want now?"

"Your name rests upon the lips of the band of strangers roaming our city's streets."

"The matter is my affair."

"Ever since I discovered that you supplied the French with armor, everything about you concerns me. Next you will be aiding the Swedes. I have every right to keep a sharp lookout over your affairs. And if you are not cooperative, I may let my tongue slip. It would be a shame for the city council to learn about the French."

"Graf von Engel's hired me to put his armory in order."

"And you remember our agreement?"

"Ja, I remember."

"Then leave the boy."

Amelia heard her father sigh, then soon after that the clatter of Valdemar's boots as he departed. What kind of agreement did they have? And how was Nicolaus involved? Hurrying across the shop, she saw her father's flushed face. "Father? What is it? Are you ill?"

"Nein. Sit and let's talk. We are going to Engelturm."

"But I thought you did not want us to associate with the count."

"I understand your surprise. My feelings on the matter have not changed. Graf von Engel has a large armory. The job will give us needed income." While Amelia digested this news, he added, "We will leave Nicolaus with Frau Hurtin."

"But why? What agreement was Valdemar talking about?"

She saw a flicker of surprise in Father's eyes, but he waved his hand. "Just business. About Nicolaus, I heard him coughing this morning."

Amelia nodded. "Ja. I did, too, but I hate to leave him."

"We prepare today and tomorrow. The next day we shall leave. First, you must speak with Frau Hurtin. I will start making arrangements for supplies."

Amelia stood. "Are you sure you are feeling all right, Father?"

"Ja. Run along, now. There is much to do."

Seeing it would do no good to argue, Amelia hurried from the shop and gazed up and down Unterer Mauerweg, hoping to catch sight of her little brother. The boy was not in view, but she noticed several strangers. Most likely the count's men from Engelturm. This made her errand seem all the more urgent. She hurried toward Frau Hurtin's cottage. Perhaps Nicolaus was playing with Heidi.

"May I join you?" The count's familiar voice jolted her. It was as though he appeared from nowhere. Before she could reply, he had swept off his large plumed hat and fallen into step beside her.

Do not associate with the count. Picking up her pace, she replied, "I am not out for a pleasure walk. I have errands to run. If you will pardon me." She caught a blur of his swinging arm and hat from the corner of her eye. If she looked straight ahead, perhaps he would catch the hint and leave.

The count was not that easily dissuaded. "Would these errands have anything to do with a journey you will be taking?"

Clearly, this was a man used to having his way. She gestured with her hand. "There are several men about this city who seem to be under your command. Surely you have more important matters to consider."

"I presumed your errands were on my account; therefore, I hoped I could—"

"Please. I do not wish to be rude, but I must go." She brushed past him. Pride forbade her to look back until she reached the Hurtins'. By then, the count was gone.

❧

Two days later, a small group of people gathered at the *Wörnitz Tor* to bid farewell to Amelia and her father. Nicolaus begged to go along.

Father squatted down to address him. "We discussed all of this already. The journey will be hard. We cannot risk your health."

"And who would play with Heidi if you go?" Amelia asked.

Nicolaus's mouth drooped; he shrugged his thin shoulders.

"You are young. There will be many other castles." His father opened his arms.

A choking clutched Amelia's throat as she watched them embrace. She could cry after they had left the city, not now. Her father's knees creaked as he rose. She forced a smile and hugged Nicolaus tight. "You be good for Frau Hurtin."

He ignored her cursory remark. "I want to hear all about the count's castle. I. . ." He covered his mouth to muffle a spasm of coughing. Amelia gently set Nicolaus at arm's length and cast a glance over at the count. Nicolaus followed her gaze and pulled loose. "Godspeed, Sister." He tossed the flippant farewell over his shoulder and hurried off to where the count stood next to his tall brown steed.

Without releasing the reins, Christian knelt down, his expression tender. "If you do all that your father and sister have asked, when I return, I shall take you for a ride on Champion. Would you like that?"

Nicolaus nodded. "Ja. And will you have on your new armor?" His eyes lit up as he glanced at the gleaming blade strapped to Christian's side. "And can I hold your sword?"

Christian appeared to consider the request. "Many brave men fight in battles. But the sword should be one's last recourse." Nicolaus screwed up his face in confusion. The count ever so lightly patted the boy's shoulder and rose.

Nicolaus shrugged and ran off to join Heidi, whose fist bunched up a wad of her mother's skirt. With her other hand, the little girl reached out and clasped Nicolaus's hand. Frau Hurtin smiled reassuringly at Amelia and her father.

Amelia felt a touch and turned with a start. "Herr Valdemar."

"Have a good journey. I will be anxious for your return."

Pulling away, she frowned. "Danke schön. I do not know when we shall return."

Father cleared his throat. "Ready?" Amelia let him hoist her up onto the first of two wagons. The wagon sagged beneath her father's weight. The count's men mounted their horses. Watchman Hurtin opened the Wörnitz Tor, and the traveling party proceeded out of Dinkelsbühl, wheels clattering across the moat's bridge.

The wagon fell into a rhythmic sway. Amelia clasped the seat beside her. Ahead, the count's brown steed trotted through the tall grass and buttercups. They crossed the River Wörnitz and entered the open countryside.

Amelia cast a final backward glance. The gates of Dinkelsbühl were already closed tight.

⌒

Shortly before dark, Christian gave orders to prepare camp in the shelter of a wooded area while he and Leopold rode ahead to do a routine scout. They had not ridden far when Christian reined in Champion. "Didn't we pass by here on our way to Dinkelsbühl?"

"Ja." Leopold nodded. "The road is just beyond. Why?"

Christian pointed through a thick copse of trees to a small meadow. "Look, there." The tall grass was tramped down. They dismounted to examine the area. Cold ashes indicated the source of three separate campfires. Christian removed his wide, feathered hat and mopped his brow.

"Looks like they camped here while we were in Dinkelsbühl."

"I pray we don't run into them," Christian replied, replacing his hat. "Let's turn back before it gets dark."

At camp, Christian saw Herr Trittenbach preparing a bedroll beneath the wagon. Amelia was headed toward the stream. Christian dismounted. "Herr Trittenbach. All is well, I hope?"

"I was about to ask you the same."

"No sign of trouble," Christian said, believing he spoke the truth. "Do you have everything you need?"

Gerrard chuckled. "My only needs are a meal and a bed. Both seem to be shortly forthcoming."

"Gut."

Christian led Champion to the stream to tether alongside the other horses while his gaze searched the predusk area for intruders or anything that might harm Amelia. She had not sought a private place, so he observed her from a distance. Her hand dipped into the water, then patted her face. Next, she seated herself on a rock in the midst of a bed of cuckoo flowers with clusters of funnel-shaped white blossoms.

Thoughts of her had been swirling in his mind for days, like a corralled horse circling the same territory. Why was she avoiding him when flames of desire leapt forth from her eyes? He often caught her watching him. If he approached her now, would she rebuff him? Or would her eyes reveal interest? Finding out was worth the risk of another rejection. He strode toward her. "It's beautiful, isn't it?"

Her chin was propped in her palms, and her face turned toward the pink-and-gold horizon. "Ja. This is a peaceful spot."

"The sunsets are spectacular at Engelturm." He studied her a moment. "Is there anything I can do to make this journey more comfortable for you?"

She straightened and gave him a half smile. "I am a bit hungry."

"And I'm starved. Come, let's go get something to eat." He extended his hand to help her off the rock. "Careful."

At the camp's entrance, the armorer called out, "Over here, Amelia."

"I hope you weren't worried, Father. I couldn't take my gaze off the sunset."

Christian was so stricken at the fierce look the armorer leveled at him that he continued to worry over it until they had finished their meal. He could only assume that it concerned Amelia. His opportunity to clear up the matter came when the armorer drew away from the campfire.

"Herr Trittenbach. May I have a word with you?" Christian asked.

The armorer hesitated, then followed Christian to a private spot. "Ja?"

"I felt your displeasure when Amelia and I returned from the stream. I assure you that it is my utmost concern to make sure that no harm comes to your daughter."

"I do not fear for her personal safety as much as I fear for her heart." The armorer's tone contained a dagger's warning and certainly cut straight to the core of the matter.

"I understand your concern, but. . ." Christian suddenly wondered if Amelia's behavior was linked to her father's attitude. "Have you warned her away from me?"

"Ja. And now I am warning you away from her. I trust you will take heed."

"I intend to do all in my power to make your stay at Engelturm comfortable and enjoyable. But most of all, I shall prove to you that I am honorable and trustworthy."

The armorer gave a gruff humph and strode back to his place by the fire.

Things were more complicated than Christian had expected. First, the father must be won. He was proving to be a pigheaded man, but surely with time he could be persuaded to think differently.

Chapter 4

The next day, a wall of clouds shut off the sun. Everything that was not tied down or close-fitting flapped and billowed. Huddled against her father, Amelia pushed away strands of hair that whipped her eyes to tears.

"This makes me glad we did not bring Nicolaus along," Father said.

Amelia spit the corner of her square collar out of her mouth and secured the fluttering cloth with her hand. "I suppose we did the right thing."

The traveling party entered a more sheltered stretch of road skirted at both sides with tall trees. Amelia shivered from the deepened shade and cast an apprehensive glance at the slit of menacing sky.

The count rode up alongside their wagon, his long hair streaming away from his lean face. One hand secured his hat. "I'm taking Leopold to scout ahead and see what the weather holds," he shouted.

Father nodded. Graf von Engel hugged his horse's flanks with his cuffed, high-topped boots, yelled orders to one of his men, then rode off with his cousin.

The incident made Amelia wonder. Had the count finally lost interest in her? Breaking camp that morning, there had been a perfect opportunity for him to speak with her in private. Instead, he had gone to help her father secure the canvas on the supply wagons. All day he had been courteous, but not the persistent, charming pursuer she had come to expect. Was it the result of her efforts to discourage him? Or was it her father's doing?

"Warm enough?" Father asked, giving her a quick hug.

"Ja, Father. I am fine."

⁓

"It looks like we'll stay dry as long as we keep moving," Christian shouted to Leopold.

"Ja. But once we make camp, the rain will surely catch up with us."

"We'll need shelter." Christian considered the landscape beyond.

"Isn't there a rock outcropping this side of the River Neckar?" Leopold asked.

Christian nodded with enthusiasm. "East of Stuttgart. Ja. That will be perfect."

With that settled, Leopold remarked, "This stretch of road would make a good place for an ambush."

"Ja. I was thinking the same thing. Let's scout the area."

Christian and Leopold left the trail and entered the thick, dark green forest, not going far until Leopold gestured. Christian also saw it. Four tethered horses. Off to the right were two soldiers with their backs turned toward them. Another leaned up against a tree, and one soldier stretched out on a fallen log, his eyes closed. The yellow-edged blue bands around their hats identified them as Swedes.

Communicating with hand gestures, Christian and Leopold eased their mounts slowly forward until, with swords and pistols drawn, they were close enough to charge.

"Drop your weapons!" Christian shouted as they broke into the camp.

The soldier by the tree jerked rigid, his gaze darting back and forth. The one on the log jumped up into a half crouch. The other two Swedes had wheeled about, their arms spread.

"Now!" Christian demanded. But the soldiers remained frozen and did not drop their weapons.

"Perhaps they don't understand German," Leopold suggested.

"Dismount and collect their arms," Christian said while keeping his pistol leveled at the Swedes.

Leopold slid from the saddle and went to the nearest soldier. He nudged him with the tip of his sword. One of the other soldiers uttered a string of foreign words. Instantly, all their weapons thudded to the ground.

The foreigner glared at Christian and, to Christian's great surprise, said in stilted German, "As you wish."

"Move in closer to each other," Christian said. The Swede's eyes darkened with resentment, but he interpreted the command for his comrades. Soon Leopold had them penned in like cattle. Their expressions were cold and full of hatred, and the gleam of fear in their eyes indicated they expected to be slaughtered like livestock, too.

It would be a senseless killing. But Christian couldn't take them as prisoners either. That would endanger Amelia and her father. Anyway, stashing them in his dungeon would only incite the enemy into a full-scale battle at Engelturm, where he had the villagers to protect.

Christian kept a steely edge to his voice. "I apologize for this intrusion. We are scouts with a group of travelers who wish you no harm. I do not care to kill a man for no good reason. If you agree to a peaceable parting, we will unhand you."

The German-speaking Swede looked surprised, even relieved. He quickly replied, "I give you my word." When he passed the information along to his soldiers, they seemed just as amazed and confused.

"Mount up," Christian told Leopold, then added quietly for his cousin's ears only, "We'll test them. Turn slowly and retreat. But be prepared for action. Better they challenge us now than later with their many reinforcements against our few men."

If matters had not been so dire, Christian would have chuckled at Leopold's expression, which clearly indicated that although he would obey the command, he thought Christian had lost his mind.

"Guten Tag!" Christian shouted and wheeled his mount around, Leopold following suit. They slowly retreated in a deliberate act of trust, their ears in tune for the slightest sounds of resistance. Christian's heart galloped, and time seemed to suspend until, at last, he felt confident that the Swedes did not intend to attack. He reined Champion back around to face the enemies.

The Swedes had retrieved their weapons and stood in a defensive position. The German-speaking soldier saluted.

Christian smiled and returned the gesture. When he turned back to Leopold, he said, "We can go. They mean no harm." They urged their horses onward through the heavy woods until they reached the road. When the danger was far past and they were riding abreast, Christian warned Leopold, "Let's keep this matter to ourselves."

That evening, Amelia busied herself stirring a pot of the cook's thick beef stew. They had camped beneath a protruding rock ledge. Beyond her, Father waited to speak with the count, who was busily instructing his men. When Graf von Engel had finished, he gave the armorer his attention.

"This is an excellent encampment," Father said.

"Ja. It will protect us from the wind and rain."

"If you run your castle as efficiently as you do this troop, I will enjoy my work at Engelturm."

"I only hope my armory doesn't reflect badly on Engelturm."

"There is no fault in a man who sees a need and fixes it."

"And I, for one, am most happy with our arrangement. With my own father deceased, I can hope to learn from you, Herr Trittenbach."

Amelia bit back a smile. Had the count changed tactics? He was certainly lavishing his charm on Father. Dare she hope that in time her father would relinquish his admonitions against the count? It was still a puzzle. Father liked the count. So why forbid her to associate with him? War seemed like a flimsy excuse. The German lands had been at war since she was a child.

"I'm going to check on my supplies before it gets dark," Father said.

Amelia watched his retreating back. The count caught her gaze. The intensity in his blue eyes deepened. He started toward her.

She stared into the pot of beef stew and gave it several good rounds with the spoon.

"Smells good. Was your day gut?"

Her stirring paused as she looked up. "Ja, but it feels good to be out of the wind. I couldn't help but overhear, and I agree with Father. This is a good encampment."

"Engelturm is built into rock much like this ledge."

"You often speak of Engelturm. You must love it very much."

"Ja, I do." He gave her a warm smile. "I hope you do, too."

"Oh? Well. . ." She gave a hesitant glance toward their wagons.

"Your father has asked me not to pursue you."

So she had not imagined the count's reformed behavior. Now he seemed to be waiting for her to express her intentions. "Graf von Engel. I do not like to do anything against my father's wishes. I love him very much."

"Please. Call me Christian."

Amelia frowned. "Why? Don't you understand what I just said? We cannot be friends."

Christian gave a confident smile. "But we already are. And I intend to become much more than mere friends. May I call you Amelia?"

"But you just said you spoke with Father."

"I did not agree to his terms. Do you think I can win him over, Amelia?"

"I shall have no part in your scheme. I fear you are on your own, Christian." Amelia saw his face light up at the familiar form of his name. She chided herself. Why had she done that?

"It is enough for now." He leaned close to her. "I have enjoyed our conversation. But I must go lest I bring you trouble and defeat my purpose. It has been a pleasure, Amelia."

She cocked a brow at him and fought the urge to smile.

"Better not let the cook come back and find you burned our meal. By the way, did I tell you that I like the way that fire lights up your hair?"

"Oh!" She gasped, turning quickly back to the bubbling kettle. She was glad he could not see her broad smile.

Chapter 5

The sandstone castle that crowned the top of a craggy height above the River Wurm came into view, pink and glowing. "Oh my." Amelia tugged on her father's arm, then pointed. "Look!"

"Ja. It looks aflame."

Together they watched the magical spectacle, straining for fleeting glimpses along the climbing, winding forest road. After the sun dropped off behind the cliffs, Engelturm lost its shine. But even weary as Amelia was from another full day of travel, this first encounter with the castle deeply stirred her.

Soon a wall and moat appeared. Christian had ridden ahead with Leopold, so the drawbridge was already lowered. Torches lit their way. The wagon rattled across, and Amelia bent over the side to peer down. It was too dark to see, and she could only imagine the depth of the moat and ravine. Inside the bailey, servants swarmed to welcome them.

Christian appeared at her father's side with a lighted torch in his hand. "We will wait until daylight to unload the wagon except for any personal things you want removed tonight."

Father pointed out the vicinity of one small trunk that would suffice, then helped Amelia down. Her father's hand at her elbow, they followed Christian and a servant through the bailey. A stone arch provided entrance to the castle. Christian explained, "A private *Sittingraum* separates your bedchambers, which are located directly above the armory. My own chambers are in the same tower on yet an upper level."

"Perfect," Father replied.

"I know you are fatigued. You have only to tell the servants your wishes. A bath? A meal? My staff will gladly serve you. In the morning, someone will bring you to *Frühstück*, and we will plan our day while we eat this meal."

"Thank you for your kindness," Father said.

"Engelturm is lovely. I see why you adore it," Amelia added, ignoring her father's frown.

Two servants preceded them through the south wing corridor to their tower bedchambers.

Amelia's chamber was comfortable with a large fireplace. She bathed, ate a meal, then fell into a large canopy bed, feeling as if she had gone to heaven.

In the morning, Amelia blinked at the unfamiliar wall paintings, wrapped a blanket around herself, and shuffled across the room to peer out an arched window. Swallows swooped to and fro. To the east, the view contained a river valley and a village of orange-tiled rooftops. There were fields and meadows, each appearing the size of a *Taler*—only square instead of round like the German coin. Farther beyond was the dark green forest.

If only Nicolaus were here to see the way the moss-covered castle wall plunged eternally downward. Her heart gave a sad tug. She could only imagine how thrilled her little brother would be to explore Engelturm. Homesick as she already was for him, nothing could squelch her own excitement. Amelia hurried to a handsome, carved wardrobe and threw open its double doors. A servant had unpacked her small trunk. Amelia quickly slipped into a blue, high-waisted gown and joined her father, who was lounging in the adjoining Sittingraum.

"I heard you stirring."

"Thank you for waiting, Father. Do you have a window in your chamber?"

"Ja. Magnificent view."

They chatted amiably and followed a servant down a winding staircase, through a corridor, and into a great hall with a large, ornate table. Frühstück, a light morning meal consisting of *Brot*, *Wurst*, and *Käse*, was served. Christian and Leopold instantly stood to greet them. Amelia hoped no one heard the rumble of her stomach. As she ate her portion of the bread, sausage, and cheese, she listened to the ensuing conversation.

"I can show you the armory first. Later, the wagon can be unloaded under your supervision."

Amelia beamed at Christian. He did seem—what was the word her father had used that night at the rock-ledge encampment? *Efficient*. Ja. Christian seemed very efficient and capable in any situation. The count openly returned her smile.

Father cleared his throat.

Instantly, Amelia lowered her gaze.

"Ja. That is a sound plan," Father said.

Elated to have such special guests at Engelturm, Christian could have skipped down the corridor as he led Herr Trittenbach and Amelia from the hall to the armory. A servant opened its great door, and a rustle could be heard as a gray rat scurried across the floor. Christian grimaced. He had told the servant to set traps and had hoped they would be rid of all their rodent tenants by now.

Gerrard seemed not to mind as he stepped into the room. "Ah." He nodded. "I see there will be plenty of room to work. The light from that window is good." The armorer examined the area with its shelves of weapons and armor. "Do you have a list of the men you will outfit?"

"Ja. I will get that at once. Is there anything else you need?"

Gerrard shook his head.

"See that Herr Trittenbach has everything he needs until I can come and help," Christian told a servant.

To Christian's pleasant surprise, Gerrard smiled and gestured with his hand. "Enough formality. *Bitte.* Please," he repeated, "call me Gerrard."

"I would be honored. And you will return the favor?"

Gerrard nodded again.

Christian gave Amelia a half smile, then left them alone with the servant. Time passed quickly. When the morning was half spent, Christian returned to the armory, hoping that Gerrard would not consider him a pest. Alone in the room, Amelia stood staring out the armory window.

"I hope you grow as fond of that view as I am."

She spun. "Graf von Engel. You startled me." Amelia studied him a moment. "Why do you hope that?"

"So that you will never want to leave."

"You intend to lock me in the dungeon?"

He shook his head. "What a delight you are."

She gave him a teasing frown. "Ja. You said that once before."

Christian advanced toward her—so close, he could have touched her rosy cheek. "I remember. In Dinkelsbühl." He paused. "The day we met, when I caught my first glimpse of you through the slit in that rusty visor, I was spellbound. Your own gaze spoke volumes. You were witty and coy, but our souls meshed. Do not deny it. But then your manner toward me changed. I was crushed and returned to Engelturm, questioning every word I had spoken to you, every action that passed between us. I tried in vain to figure out what I had done to cause you to withdraw." She quietly listened, her face vulnerable. "Then on our journey, when your father told me he feared for your heart, I hoped that it was only his warning that had changed your mind about me. Was it?"

Amelia nodded.

"Then I ask that you give me a chance to prove to him that I would never hurt you."

Amelia hesitantly touched his arm. "I wonder why Father is so adamant about us."

"I intend to find out." An intimate moment of silence passed between them. "What does he think of my armory? Did he say?"

"It is the perfect challenge for him. In need of work but not a total disaster."

Christian released a sigh. "Gut. That is good."

"It did not take Father long to begin its organization. Until this moment, he has been directing the men, coming and going with loads of leather, metal, and tools."

"Amelia." They turned their gazes to the door as Gerrard's voice preceded him into the armory. Two bolts of material were draped over his arm, and a troop of servants trailed after him, equally laden with cloth. "See what I have? Where would you like to set up your work area, by that window?"

"Oh, ja." When she blushed, Christian knew she was remembering his earlier comment about the view.

Gerrard dropped the bolts near the count's feet. "You can arrange the cloth and your supplies as you wish."

"Certainly, Father. I'd be happy to."

"Is there anything I can do?" Christian offered, while handing over the list of men he needed to outfit.

Gerrard stuffed it into his pocket. "Everyone is so helpful. I suppose you have other affairs you should be managing?"

"Well, ja. But I'd be happy to assist here."

"Nein, Christian. See to those other things. If you have time, when you are done. . ." Gerrard's voice dwindled off, and he crossed the room to inspect a stack of metal sheets.

Christian cast a final glance around the room, pleased that all was going so well. Then reluctantly, he left.

That night, Christian entertained Amelia, Gerrard, and several of his men over a meal. They dined on boiled pork and dumplings with cherry cake for dessert. It turned into a merry gathering with everyone joking and sharing stories of their recent journey from Dinkelsbühl.

Keeping with the general high spirits, Amelia remarked, "And to think we worried about running into the Swedes."

An eerie quietness befell the room until Leopold said, albeit too exuberantly, "Ja. To think that!"

Gerrard's eyes widened. "Christian? Did you come across some Swedes?"

Christian cleared his throat. "Why, ja, Gerrard, we did. But I didn't want to frighten Amelia."

She pointed at him. "You saw the Swedes? Where?"

"Ja, where?" Gerrard echoed.

Waving his knife in the air and trying to keep the incident trivial, Christian replied, "Remember that second day when Leopold and I went scouting?"

"Ja. Go on."

"We scared up a few Swedes." Christian took a bite, thoroughly chewing his meat, then waved his knife again. "Disarmed them, rounded them up in a little huddle, and talked some sense into them."

"Did your sword do the speaking?" Amelia asked.

Christian toyed with another bite. "We came to a peaceable agreement. Didn't we, Leopold?"

"Indeed, we did. To my surprise."

Amelia gasped. "Did you kill them?"

"Daughter!" Gerrard scolded. "It is not in our place to—"

"Nein!" Christian hurried to dispel Amelia's worry. He softened his voice and met her gaze. "We did not kill them. We let them go."

"It seems you can accomplish most anything," Gerrard muttered, his eyes twinkling with amusement. He shook his head. "Are you sure you even need me here, Christian?"

"I most certainly do need you here. As I told you before, I hope the war never reaches Engelturm, but that's almost too much to wish for. Ja. I need you. Now, enough about the Swedes." Christian's mind groped for another topic. "Did I show you the chapel, Gerrard?"

"Nein. I have not seen it."

"You must. Feel free to use it whenever you wish. We do not have a priest here at Engelturm, but there is one in Engelheim."

"Danke, Christian."

He nodded, then glanced at Amelia. Her hands were primly folded in her lap, and she gazed at him with an expression close to adoration. His heart leapt.

When the meal was cleared away, Christian rose. "Would you care to see the chapel now? Or perhaps I can challenge you to a game of chess?"

"I prefer to retire to my chamber," Gerrard declined.

"We are very pleased with everything at Engelturm. I'll go with you, Father. *Guten Abend.*"

"Good night," Christian replied with the others, everyone scrambling to their feet.

Once his guests had departed, Christian gazed across his assembled men. "Which one of you wishes to challenge me to a game?"

"I will," Leopold answered.

Several plays into the chess match, Christian lingered too long over his next move.

"I believe my friend is in love," Leopold said.

Christian jerked up his head. His cousin appeared to be serious. "That is yet to be determined. But I can guarantee you it shall not interfere with my chess abilities."

Leopold chuckled. "We shall see."

Christian was wrong. He could not concentrate at all.

Chapter 6

From the armory window, Amelia and her father watched Christian and his musketeers practice. Some used flintlock pistols. In the few weeks that had lapsed, Christian had recruited all of the physically capable men at Engelturm, as well as those from the village of Engelheim, for routine training.

She remembered Christian's advice to Nicolaus. *Many brave men have fought battles, but the sword should be one's last recourse.* Yet, Christian was arming his people. She also recalled the incident during their travel to Engelturm when Christian had released the Swedish soldiers unharmed. Most men whom her father armed were eager to greet action. Christian was, indeed, proving to be a man of honor. Surely he would not break her heart. Why then did her father distrust him?

"Watching them makes me long for a bit of practice myself. The metal I brought from Dinkelsbühl was a new batch. We shall have to proof it soon, before we progress much further. Would you care to help?"

Amelia brightened. "You know I would."

That afternoon, Christian entered the tower in time to see Amelia descending. He halted at once. "What a pleasant surprise."

"How are your drills going?"

Christian shrugged. "Some of the men are skilled. But those from the village still need much practice. I detest the idea of matching them against Swedish soldiers or those of the Imperial army."

"It is commendable that you possess such a passion for your people."

Wishing to extend his time in her presence, Christian grasped at the first idea that came to mind. "Have you had a tour of the inner courtyard?" When Amelia shook her head, he gave a swooping arm gesture. "May I?"

First she cast a hesitant, backward glance, then smiled. "I am in need of exercise and fresh air. That would be nice." They passed through the gallery and to a door that led outside. "It's lovely. I often wished to come here, but I didn't want to intrude."

"It is my personal courtyard. But you are most welcome to come any-time you wish."

The square courtyard in the center of the castle was unlike the bailey and outer courtyards, where all the work of the castle took place. This one was designed purely for pleasure. They walked among plantings of plum, apple, and pear trees. The cobblestone path was edged with flowers and plants. Stone benches and statues added elegance.

"I have watched men prepare for war. You are different. Why do you care about your enemies?"

"Jesus Christ loved to the point of death. When I ponder this, I know that He would want me to love my fellow man."

"Love? I am also a Christian. But I don't *love* everyone."

"I don't always feel loving, but I try to act with compassion." He saw that her expression remained puzzled; but before he could further explain, a fish broke the surface of a small pond, and the moment was lost when Amelia giggled and started toward it.

At the pond's edge she paused and asked, "How did Engelturm get its name? Angel Tower seems such a curious name."

"You are full of questions. But I am happy to oblige you. There are times, especially at sunset, that the cliff almost glows."

"Ja. I saw it the first night we arrived. Father and I watched in amaze-ment."

Christian shared her enthusiasm. "So you understand. A tale goes that angels make their camp on this mountain. So when the castle was built, it was fittingly named Angel Tower."

"That's beautiful."

"The Württemberg dukes built Engelturm to use as a hunting castle. When Frederick the First knighted my Opa, the duke also gave him En-gelturm. Opa gave the castle a verse."

"He was a poet?"

Christian smiled. "A Bible verse, Psalm 34:7. 'The angel of the Lord encampeth round about them that fear him, and delivereth them.' Opa made sure we all memorized his verse, giving God the glory. Castle walls alone do not protect those within. God is in control. Grandfather said that even angels are not to be praised, for they are merely God's messengers."

"I believe that is a lovely story and a most appropriate name for your castle. As to your faith, I must add that it does not hurt if the walls are made strong."

With a chuckle, Christian said, "I agree. Strong walls and strong faith make the best defense."

They moved away from the pond. "After watching your men train this morning, I am eager to do some shooting myself."

"You want to learn to shoot?" Christian stammered, his steps faltering. "I—I don't think you understand. The muskets are much too heavy, and the pistols misfire so easily that—"

"Christian, I can shoot."

He stared, his mind churning. "Your father taught you, didn't he?"

"Ja. We proof our own armor. I can fire a flintlock. I have used a matchlock musket, but you are right. It is too heavy and awkward. And I can wield a sword."

"Once again, you amaze me." He shook his head. "You and your father duel?"

Amelia laughed. "I'm not very good. But I enjoy it."

"Are you bored here, Amelia?"

"Nein. I am enjoying myself at Engelturm."

"Gut." After a moment of silence, Christian said, "Now let me show you something else that is marvelous about Engelturm."

He led her to a stone bench. "Sit. Close your eyes. And wait just a moment." He returned. "No peeking. Keep your eyes closed."

"I am."

Christian knelt, his *Hosen* scraping the cobblestones as he faced her. "Open your mouth."

Amelia's lips parted, and Christian swallowed twice, wondering what it would be like to kiss her.

"Christian?"

He plopped the plump berries on her tongue before he lost control.

Amelia's eyes flew open. "Mm! Delicious!"

"I must confess, in season, I sneak in here to rob these bushes every chance I get."

"So you do have a weakness after all."

He tenderly took hold of her hand, giving her an intimate look. "Many weaknesses."

After a moment, Amelia drew her hand away. "Which reminds me of Father. I must be getting back before he comes searching."

Once they finished the berries, Christian reluctantly returned her to the tower. But their time together left him brimming with a multitude of emotions. Feeling the urge to expel some of his nervous energy, Christian headed to the stables to fetch Champion. He spoke to the groom, then departed through the castle gates and over the drawbridge. The road hugged lush, green, sloping hills and at one point cut into thick, evergreen forest—teeming of birdcalls and rambling bush. It emerged at a solitary lookout point, where he dismounted, tethered Champion, and strode to the rock ledge that he often visited to sort out his life. He had come here when his father was ill and again after his father died. Settling in among a patch of bugleweed, he gazed beyond their blue flower spikes to the surrounding German countryside.

So much was on his mind these days. His loyalties and sympathies did not match. He owed his loyalties to a prince who supported the emperor. If Christian were pressed into this war, he was obligated to fight the Swedes. But he did not agree with imperial politics. His sympathies lay with the protestant princes in league with the Swedes and the French. "Lord, help me to do what I have to do," he prayed.

Next he prayed for Amelia. Gerrard was doing wonders with the armory. He could sense the man's attitude warming. Soon Christian hoped to obtain his approval to pursue Amelia. Even though Gerrard was occupied, he kept a strict watch over his daughter. There had only been a few instances since her arrival that Christian had been alone with her.

Today in the courtyard he had wondered if Amelia were a true believer. If not, perhaps he could lead her to God's truth. He hoped that wasn't the only reason that God had brought her into his life. Each moment spent with her excited him as nothing had ever done before. Such abilities. She could sew, stir a pot, and help Gerrard with his armor. He envisioned her shooting or wielding a sword—just the capable, spunky sort of countess his castle needed.

His thoughts turned to the village sprawled out below and to his father's dying words. *"Be iron-fisted in protecting your lands but allow Christ's love to guide you."* Christian bowed his head to conclude his prayer before he returned to the castle.

The next afternoon, after military exercises had finished, Christian accompanied Gerrard and Amelia to the practicing field. Two servants carried several breastplates to set up against stationary targets. Gerrard wished to test the metal with the sword stroke and firearms.

Hoping to impress Amelia, Christian gave the sword stroke his best. Gerrard was pleased when their blades easily glanced off the armor. Next they backed off the appropriate distance and brought out a German flint-lock pistol. Christian continued to enjoy the practice until Amelia's turn came. Then his emotions began to do strange things. A protective impulse rose so strong that he could not help but fret for her safety.

He sucked in a deep breath as she took the flintlock from Gerrard. She loaded the pistol herself. It took several maneuvers—first she brushed the pan free from the last shot, then placed a few grains of priming powder into the pan, closed the frizzen, and cocked.

Christian held his breath again when Amelia fired at the target. Her shot hit the breastplate. She brought her arms down and gave him a lopsided grin. "Your turn, Christian."

He exhaled and carefully took the gun, his chest bursting with admiration.

After the round was completed, they examined the targets and inspected the armor. Christian ran his finger over the marks, which, though visible, had barely dented the breastplate, and nodded his approval.

"The finely tempered German metal is superior over any other," Gerrard boasted.

"I noticed your work lacks ornamentation compared to others. There must be a reason that you keep the rivet plain."

"A very intelligent observation. Weapons glance off smooth surfaces easier than those that are embellished."

Christian's heart soared with hope under the other man's praise. They returned to their shooting positions. The gun was wiped down with a cloth before they started another round. The proofing was such a pleasant experience that Christian was sorely disappointed when it was time to return to the castle.

"I am pleased with what you have already accomplished, Gerrard. Now that you are settled in, perhaps you would like to take a tour of Engelturm. I have tomorrow afternoon free."

"Settled, perhaps, but my work has just begun."

"Another time, then." Christian turned to Amelia. "What about you, Amelia? Would you have time for a tour?"

"I would enjoy that very much." She turned to Gerrard. "Father, could you spare me for a while in the afternoon?"

Gerrard's mouth drooped, and his eyes saddened.

Christian quickly added, "Of course, a servant will accompany us."

Amelia cast him a conspiratorial grin, then turned to Gerrard. "Father?"

"Ja. A short tour. There is much to do."

Christian bit back a triumphant smile.

Chapter 7

When Amelia saw the count's fine breeches and sapphire-blue doublet, she was glad that she had donned her favorite, pale blue gown for their planned tour of Engelturm. With such luxuriant ringlets, Christian had no need of a wig like so many other men wore.

"Amelia. You look lovely." He offered her his arm.

Embarrassed that she had been caught admiring him, she replied, "And you look as though you are expecting the emperor."

"I hoped to make a good impression." They left Amelia's Sittingraum, and a servant fell into step behind them at the appropriate distance. "I feared your father would find some excuse to keep us apart."

"Do not be surprised if the castle comes crumbling down around us from all his pacing."

"I know that you are a prize, but I do believe he is overly protective."

"Ja. But it is not like him. That's why it perplexes me so."

"Might I hope it is your fondness for me that worries him?"

"A lady would never answer such a question."

Christian chuckled. They stepped into the gallery. Although Amelia had passed through this wide passageway before, she did not know the history of its many exhibits. Along one wall, windows revealed the inner courtyard. Opposite, several openings and an arched doorway displayed the great hall. Otherwise the massive walls exhibited portraits. Amelia removed her hand from the crook of Christian's arm to caress a sculpture, then studied a man in an ornate, gold-gilded portrait.

"That is Württemberg's Duke Frederick the First. My ancestors are at the far end of the gallery."

In slow progression along the gallery, Amelia marveled over the noblemen and women, intrigued by their antiquated fashions and weapons. Christian respectfully gazed at a portrait of a white-haired man.

Amelia readily discerned the family resemblance. "Your father?"

"Opa. I am the last of the family line. There are cousins, of course. Leopold you have met."

"Your grandmother was beautiful." Amelia moved farther down and stared at a painting two spaces over. "And so was your mother." Beneath her portrait was a wooden chest, intricately carved with flowers and birds. Amelia stooped down and felt the inlaid jewels on its lid. "How lovely."

Christian knelt beside her. "There is a family of wood-carvers in the village, the Linders. Father refurbished the castle and Herr Linder did much of the ornate woodwork. He presented this gift to my mother. Father provided the jewels. I am told that she loved it. Herr Linder also fashioned my cradle, which remains in the nursery. Mother died soon after I was born."

"I'm sorry you did not get to know her. That is the way it was for Nicolaus."

Christian laid his hand upon Amelia's. "Nicolaus is fortunate that he has a sister like you. Do you miss him?"

"Very much. I was surprised Father did not bring him along. We usually do. He had a cough, but. . .I don't know." She shrugged. "Father is acting strange lately. But let's not talk about Father."

"I agree." Christian's hand still covered Amelia's, atop his mother's wooden chest. "I always intended to give this chest to my bride as a wedding present." Amelia felt a flutter of excitement in her breast. "That is why I am so glad that you like it." Christian stood, drawing her up with him. He caressed the tops of her fingers with his thumb. "Someday, I'd like to speak of this again."

Amelia glanced at the servant at the far end of the gallery and withdrew her tingling hand, placing it back beneath his arm. "Perhaps someday, Christian."

He smiled at her, and they continued their tour. The gallery extended to the northwest tower. On the ground level was the chapel. It was a room of splendor with its stained-glass window and intricate altar hangings, but all Amelia could see was the count.

When they returned through the gallery, Christian stopped at one of the windows that overlooked the inner courtyard and placed his hand at the back of her waist. "I enjoyed our interlude in the courtyard the other day. We could meet there again."

She fingered her lace collar, struggling with the idea of going against her father's wishes. Her own will, however, waged stronger. "Tomorrow I could slip away about midday for just a few moments."

"Stolen moments I will treasure. But now, I must return you to Gerrard."

"Ja. We must return."

That night, Christian had felt bolstered by the secretive smiles he and Amelia had exchanged over the evening meal. As usual, once they had finished eating, Gerrard had whisked her away to the privacy of their Sittingraum. Since the Trittenbachs' arrival at Engelturm, Christian and Leopold had whiled away most of their evenings with chess. This evening was no different.

"She seems to have fallen under your charm at last," Leopold said.

"It is the strangest thing. As if some natural force is drawing us together, as if there is nothing we could do to stop it even if we wanted to."

"Hm." Leopold studied the chessboard. "Definitely not your charm."

"I think not. I'm hoping it is God's work."

"I do not think it is anything new. Probably just common, old-fashioned love. But since God is love, then in a way. . ." Leopold shrugged.

"Have you ever been in love?"

"Nein!" Leopold splayed both hands to ward off such an odious idea. "One lovesick person in this castle is enough. I have more important matters to consider."

Christian tilted his head and wrinkled his brow thoughtfully. "I don't think there is anything more important than love."

"Ach! You have it bad. So when are you going to approach Gerrard? He looks and acts like an angry bull every time he sees you watching Amelia."

"Did he do that again tonight?"

"Ja. And if you aren't careful, he's liable to sweep her up and away from Engelturm just to separate you."

Christian shook his head. "I don't think so. He enjoys working in the armory. But I do mean to have a talk with him. When the time is right." He moved his chess piece. "Checkmate! I believe, Cousin, you have missed your calling."

Leopold scowled. "How is that?"

"You are a natural counselor. You should have been a priest."

The next day, Amelia stepped into the inner courtyard, and instantly Christian appeared.

"I'm so glad you came. Shall we walk or sit?"

"Let's walk. Oh look!" Amelia pointed at a flock of swallows overhead, their songs filling the courtyard. "I saw their nests outside my window. I've watched them swoop down to the river."

"And have you seen our stag? He appears near twilight to drink from the river. I think you could see it from your chambers."

"I have not, but I shall look for him."

"He has appeared for several years. I have forbidden any of my men to shoot him."

Amelia saw the awe in his expression. "Is he special?"

Christian shrugged. "Like any other deer, I suppose, only older, wiser, wild, and very protective."

"Protective? How is that?"

"At certain times of the year I see him with several doe. He lifts his antlered head to sniff for danger and stamps the ground with his front hooves. He is a fearsome sight."

"He sounds much like you."

"A frightening sight?"

Amelia's laughter tinkled throughout the garden. "You are protective of those in your charge."

"Perhaps you are right. When Father died, I thought it could not be. I did not want to take on the responsibility of the castle and the village. I had been living a very carefree life."

"I suppose there are many things we wouldn't do if there weren't others depending upon us."

"Meeting you has helped me."

Astonished, Amelia asked, "How? I have done nothing." She shook her head, "I do not understand."

"Why, you've given me a purpose, Amelia. I'll admit I've been a bit wild in my growing-up years. Father had so much patience. But now, since I've met you, I don't resent being master of Engelturm. Rather, I get the urge to see that everything runs smoothly, to improve the conditions of the castle, to protect, to settle down and live with. . ."

Amelia released a whoosh of air. "I fear you misplace the source of your inspiration. I certainly deserve no credit for your behavior, good or bad." Christian frowned, and Amelia rambled on, "Though I believe it seems to be mostly good. At least from what I have observed. . ."

His frown turned to a smile, and he gazed at her with adoration in his eyes.

Amelia returned to the armory, practicing in her mind how she would bring up the subject of Christian. Her father sat on the stone window seat, hunched over a barrel filled with sand and vinegar. He had been cleaning some of Engelturm's rusty plate armor. When he heard her enter, he looked up, his eyes bright.

"Come look, Amelia! See what I have found!"

She crossed the room and joined him on the bench. "What is it, Father?"

With a cotton cloth, he quickly hand-polished a small area and exclaimed, "See this armorer's mark?"

Amelia leaned forward to inspect the tiny mark. It was a small side view of a helm with a star at the top. She ran her finger over it. "I like it."

"It is the mark of either Desiderius or Coloman Colmon. The son and father used the same mark." His voice held awe.

"Who are they?"

"They came from a family of armorers that have been around since the thirteen-hundreds. They served many of the emperors."

"How old do you think this piece is?"

"If it is the father, it would be one hundred years old. If the son, perhaps half a century. Fascinating." Father mumbled to himself as he rose to rummage through some similar pieces of plate armor.

"Father, about Christian. Do you like him?"

He came hustling back to the bench. "I'll bet this is yet another piece of their work." He plopped it into the barrel.

Amelia sighed. It seemed that this was not going to be a good time to discuss Christian. She would let it drop for now.

Chapter 8

Christian paced beneath the pear tree—his rendezvous spot with Amelia. He was nervous because, after three weeks of meeting her like this, today he planned to confess his feelings of guilt. And he did not know how she would react to this news. But it was wrong to go behind Gerrard's back. Possibly everyone else in the castle knew what had been transpiring. At first, it had seemed like a good idea; but Christian had felt farther from the Lord each day this facade had continued.

That morning, a Bible verse had struck him hard, admonishing "whatsoever is not of faith is sin." What he was doing reeked of sin. He was not trusting God but making things happen on his own. In doing so, he had dishonored God to the servants—who did not miss a lick of gossip—to Leopold, and to Amelia. And he was undermining the trust of the very man he hoped to win over.

He glanced up at the sun. What was keeping her? She was never this late. His concern and impatience grew, until in his agitated state, he resolved to find her. Although he had already asked God for forgiveness, he would not find peace unless he also asked for Amelia's.

Quickly he covered the passageways that led to the southwest tower and the armory. Amelia and Gerrard instantly looked up at him, then Amelia let out a little gasp and glanced at the window. "My, the time has slipped by this morning, has it not, Father? I was so busy, I hadn't noticed."

Gerrard chuckled and said to Christian, "She has always enjoyed painting."

At that moment a servant knocked, then entered. "The additional leather has arrived, Herr Trittenbach."

"Wonderful. Just on time. Will you excuse me?" Gerrard hurried from the room. The door closed.

"I missed you in the courtyard."

Amelia wiped her hands and placed the brush in a barrel. "I am sorry. I did not do it intentionally."

"I am glad it happened. Even though I cherish the time I spend with you, it has been wrong."

She frowned. "Please explain."

"I was wrong to suggest something your father forbids. Wrong not to trust God in this matter."

"Oh." Amelia looked contrite. "I confess it has bothered me, too."

Christian released a breath of relief. "Can you forgive me for persuading you to go against your father's wishes?"

"Of course. I was just as much in the wrong as you."

"We must make things right. I will talk to Gerrard at once. Then"—he paused and shrugged—"we will go from there."

"I will also speak with Father, though I have been trying to do so for quite some time."

"As have I." Christian gave her a crooked grin, wondering how he could have doubted her sweet-spirited reaction.

The door opened, and Gerrard directed several servants with bundles of leather. Christian watched him for a moment, then loudly cleared his throat.

Gerrard glanced sideways at him. "Did you want something, Christian?"

"Ja. I would have a word with you as soon as you are available." Christian forced himself not to glance at Amelia, lest he give away his intentions without a word in his own defense.

"I suppose we could meet after supper. Is that soon enough?"

"That would be fine," Christian said, happy to have the time to form his address.

Christian faced Gerrard. "Would you care for a drink?"

"Nein." Gerrard yawned. "I'm a bit tired."

Whether or not the yawn was feigned, Christian chose to ignore manners and press forward. He seated himself close to Gerrard and fastened his gaze on the older man. "I would like to bring up the subject of your daughter, Amelia."

"I believe I know my daughter's name," Gerrard grumbled.

"Very well. At one time you told me you did not want her heart broken. I have no intentions of doing so."

"Gut!" Gerrard said, rising from his chair. "Glad that's settled. If that is all—"

"Nein!" Christian said, his voice rising. "It is not! Please be seated."

Gerrard raised a brow at Christian but reseated himself, clamping his teeth together.

"I would like to ask for Amelia's hand in marriage. I love her."

The older man's jaw slackened. He closed his eyes, then opened them. "It is not possible."

"Your answer is not enough for me. I need a reason."

Gerrard narrowed an angry gaze at Christian. "If you had only listened. It was never possible. Amelia is spoken for."

"What? But that cannot be. I would know if Amelia—"

"Amelia does not know yet!" Gerrard ground out as he jumped to his feet and pointed his finger at Christian's face. "And now because you would not listen and have won her heart—for I assume you have or you would not be addressing me—you will also break it. You have done the very thing I warned you against."

Christian fumbled to his feet. His face burned. Through an escalating dizziness, he repeated, "Amelia is spoken for?"

"I realize that you are the master of Engelturm, but I am your elder, and as I am Amelia's father, you should have respected my wishes."

In agony, Christian pressed his eyes shut. "The heart does not listen well."

"But it will mend. Keep away from her." Gerrard turned abruptly and strode from the room.

When silence surrounded him, Christian slumped down into a chair and stared at the hearth.

After an immeasurable period of time, he heard the whispering of his name. "What?" he croaked.

"I asked if I may come in."

His eyes still glassy, Christian gave Leopold a weak wave.

His cousin took the chair that Gerrard had abandoned. "I'm sorry. It looks as though your audience with Gerrard did not go well."

"Amelia is already spoken for."

Leopold's brows slanted. "What is the situation?"

Christian's face scrunched up in a distasteful scowl. "Gerrard did not explain anything. He only cursed my clumsy behavior. I must withdraw my attentions."

"But why would Amelia lead you on? Perhaps she does not want this arranged marriage."

"She does not know about it."

"Whew!" Leopold exclaimed. "He is selling his daughter."

Christian clenched his teeth, imagining what Amelia might have to endure. "If I am not in God's will with this, then I will only make matters harder for Amelia if I pursue her."

"I thought we had decided love is a matter of the heart."

Confused, Christian reasoned with himself. Hadn't he just this day turned the matter over to God? Might God be punishing him for going behind Gerrard's back? Nein. God forgave him. "I do not like it. But I have no choice right now. I must wait on God."

Leopold also scowled, and they spent the remainder of the evening staring into the hearth fire.

Amelia waited impatiently in her Sittingraum, though it was not long until her father appeared. She noted his unusually red face but refused to let this perfect opportunity to speak with him about Christian slip away. "Father. I wish to speak with you."

"Not tonight," he grumped.

"Ja. Tonight. I want to speak about Christian. I have a right to know what has passed between you."

Father folded his hands in front of his stomach and rocked on his heels as if he were forming an explanation. "We will speak of this in the morning."

Amelia stood, emboldened by her desire. "I will not let you push the matter away."

He stepped forward and squeezed her shoulder. "I need time to think. You are right. We need to discuss the matter. Only give me until tomorrow morning."

"All right, Father. Tomorrow."

He nodded, released her, and crossed the room to his chambers. Unable to fight back the emotions that overwhelmed her, Amelia hurried to the privacy of her own chamber and allowed her tears to freely fall. As she lay on her bed, she determined not to let him evade the issue tomorrow. She barely slept at all and was up early, waiting for her father in the Sittingraum. When his bedchamber door opened, she jutted out her chin. "Father!"

He joined her on a settee. "You are up early."

"I did not want to miss you. We have something to discuss." Father gestured with his hand for her to begin, so she said, "I have tried to ask you a question for many weeks. Do you like Christian?"

"I like Christian very much."

The answer startled Amelia. Dare she hope? "You find him honorable?"

"I do."

Her heart raced faster. "Then why forbid me to see him? I find your protective behavior ill-placed."

He placed his hands in a prayerful position and tapped them against his chin. "I only wanted to spare you from hurt." He drew them down. "The truth is, I have already promised your hand in marriage to another."

At first this preposterous explanation left Amelia speechless. Of course, she had known that someday her father might bring someone around for her to look over, but to think that he had arranged such a thing behind her back absolutely infuriated her. Anger began to course through her already pulsing veins. She and Father worked so closely, shared intimate thoughts. . . . She just always assumed he would want her to be happy, that he would take into consideration her own desires. How could he do this? Christian. He would know what to do. "Did Christian ask for my hand?"

"Ja. But I have promised another."

"But I want to marry Christian." Amelia strove to keep her voice calm. "Father, I never thought you would do such a thing behind my back."

"I did not want to."

Once again Amelia's mouth fell open, and her calm dissolved. "But I love Christian."

"This is not about love."

She no longer cared about keeping her voice low. "Tell me. What is this about? And who is this chosen man?"

"It is the mercer."

Her arms gestured wildly, and she paced. "Herr Valdemar? Ach! I cannot stand him! How could you?"

Her father's voice became stern. "I want you to listen well. There are times when we must do things we do not especially want to do. This is one of those times."

She glared at him. "And why?"

"Do you remember when I took the commissions for the French?"

Amelia jerked a nod.

"Valdemar found out and has threatened to tell the city council. With the way the war has been going, I would be a traitor. Our entire family would be in serious danger. Valdemar has had his eye on you for a long time. Because he loves you, he will look aside. I believe he will treat you kindly. But if you turn him down, he will ruin us."

"Ach!" Amelia said again, only this time with even more distaste. "I am already ruined if I marry him."

Father's voice took on a harsher, authoritative tone. "You must grow up. You have until your birthday. Then you will obey your father, who has provided for you all of these years. And you will marry Valdemar."

"I shall never!" Amelia spat back at him. Father flinched. She did not care, but filled with fury, she turned her back to him and flew into her chambers.

Chapter 9

Christian fasted and prayed. But regardless of his good intentions to trust God with his heartache, he fell into bouts of self-pity. Frustrated at his lack of faith, he sought the privacy of his inner courtyard. He meandered about, sending prayers heavenward, then sat on a stone bench. He heaved a great sigh, absentmindedly plucking berries off a nearby bush and plopping them onto his tongue, remembering another time and Amelia's red, juice-stained lips. He bowed his head to the Father.

"Christian?"

His head jerked up. It was Leopold. He rose. "Ja?"

"I thought you would want to know that Amelia is out on the practicing field by herself with a pistol."

"Ach! Of all the insane things." He strode toward the castle, giving Leopold a nod. "Danke."

Amelia had spent the morning in her bedchamber. By afternoon, her grief gave way to anger until it became a mighty river of rage. She stomped into the armory and grabbed one of the flintlock pistols off the shelf.

Her father quickly asked, "What are you going to do with that?"

"Shoot it," Amelia snapped, helping herself to the ammunition that she would need.

He stepped forward. "You're not going to do anything foolish?"

"I'm not putting it to my head, if that's what you mean. Let me pass!" Amelia had never spoken in such a disrespectful manner, and she half expected him to reach out and slap her. But he did not. He looked so sad. She was glad, for she was still very angry with him for ruining her life.

Withdrawing from the armory, she marched out to the field with the large pistol, all the while trying to come up with a logical solution to her problem—like pointing the pistol at Valdemar, or perhaps a Frenchman, or a Swede. But she knew that was not an option.

Targets still remained in their places from morning exercises. Amelia stomped to the location where she had earlier helped to proof armor and tried to dismiss memories of that charming day from her mind. She prepared her firearm, and with both arms extended, she raised it up and aimed.

"Amelia!"

Her arms jerked, the gun went off, and she missed the target entirely. Trembling from head to toe, she spun around. "See what you made me do!"

"I'm sorry," Christian said. "But what are you doing here alone?"

Amelia tried to rein in her anger. "What does it look like, Christian? I'm shooting."

"You're ferocious."

Her chest heaved. "I have every right to be. Aren't you? Or are you relieved that I am promised to another?"

Christian ventured closer. "You know about it, then?"

"I just found out. It does not please me at all." One corner of Christian's mouth tipped up, and Amelia noticed his red-stained lips.

He stepped forward. "I wish there was something I could do. I don't want to hurt you."

"Sometimes I have dreams of what I'd like to do. But I always push them aside for Father's sake. But this time..." her voice grew cold, "I do not care about disappointing him."

"What is it that you would like to do?"

She glanced over at the armory. Her father watched them from the window. It angered her anew. "I should like to do this." The pistol slipped to the ground, and she stepped forward. Christian blinked. She rose on tiptoes, wrapped her arms around his neck, and kissed him full on the mouth. At first his lips were firm and unsuspecting, but it did not take long for him to respond. Amelia felt her body melt and knew that she must pull away. Her hands splayed against his chest, she gave him a reckless smile. His features still displayed shock.

Amelia tapped his lower lip with her forefinger. "You had berries on your lips. Anyway, Father was watching from the armory window. I wanted to spite him." Christian jerked. "Do not look," she warned and stooped to pluck up the pistol. "My anger is gone now."

"I rather liked you angry," he teased.

Together, they walked back toward the castle. "I told Father I would never marry Valdemar."

Christian took hold of her hand. "I love you."

Amelia returned to the armory the next day. An unspoken truce of sorts had been struck with her father, enough so that they could continue their work.

Once, Christian stuck his head inside the room. Amelia admired him for venturing into such hostile territory. What a mess they had gotten themselves into. She motioned to him with a black, paint-speckled hand.

"How do you fare today, Amelia?"

"Better. Work helps."

"I agree. Prayer is also good. After I quit feeling sorry for myself, I found peace."

"When did you quit feeling sorry for yourself?"

"When you kissed me yesterday."

Amelia blushed. Now that her insane anger was spent, she was embarrassed over her behavior. "I apologize for my forwardness. You must think I'm a—"

"I think you are a passionate woman. I was walking around in a daze until that kiss. But I still believe that we must give God a chance to work in this. I thought perhaps we could pray together."

"Now?"

He shrugged. "Such opportunities seldom arise." Christian tentatively reached out to touch her puffy sleeve. She gave him a nod, and Christian prayed. "Father. We have gone about things our own mindful way. Only because we love each other." He looked up from his prayer. "At least, I love you."

"I love you, too," she whispered, feeling her face heat.

His face broke into a wide grin. Finally, he closed his eyes to continue. "We love each other and ask for Your forgiveness for our actions in the past. But please, Father, change Gerrard's heart. We need a miracle so that we can be married. We place our faith in You. Amen." Christian looked at her, then encircled her waist in his hands and whispered, "Have faith, Amelia."

She nodded and gave him a quick hug. "Ja. I'll try."

Christian released her. "I must go. I love you."

"I love you," Amelia said, embarrassed at the newness of the spoken words.

She watched him go. Her mouth dropped open in horror. The door closed. She swallowed. Two black handprints splayed across the back of his doublet.

Christian left the castle and went to the practice field.

"You seem in a good mood," Leopold greeted.

"I'm at peace," Christian said.

"Faith?"

"Ja. It's hard, but God is my only hope." Christian turned away to assist in an exercise detail.

"Uh, Christian?"

He looked over his shoulder. "What?"

Leopold crooked his finger. "Come here." Christian backtracked. "I believe you have Amelia-prints on the back of your doublet. Unless you want Gerrard and every man here to know you've been embracing, I would suggest you remove your doublet."

Christian remembered Amelia's hug, and his face burned. But before he could do anything about the situation, his attention was riveted to yet another distraction. The watchman hollered, "Riders approaching!" Christian and his men hurried as one body toward the entrance gate. "It is William from the neighboring castle."

"Lower the bridge. Let them in!" Christian yelled.

Three riders crossed the bridge and entered the bailey, reining in next to Christian. "Welcome," Christian said to his neighbors.

"We do not stay. But bring news."

Christian motioned his men away, except for his select few. "Tell us."

"We know that you keep the Dinkelsbühl armorer. He will want to know. Dinkelsbühl has been under siege by the Swedes for weeks."

Frowning under the terrible news, Christian thanked them for their trouble. As they rode away, he turned to his remaining men. "Assemble in the chapel. Leopold, come with me." They strode toward the armory. "Gerrard won't take this lightly with Nicolaus remaining in Dinkelsbühl. This may be the spark that starts the war we've been dreading."

When they reached their destination, Gerrard already stood in the open doorway, a wary expression on his face. Christian glanced at Amelia across the room. "I must speak with you in private."

"Is it about the riders?"

"Ja. And it concerns you."

Amelia rushed forward. "Something about the Swedes?"

"Tell us," Gerrard urged.

Giving Amelia another glance, Christian said, "Very well. The riders were from a neighboring estate. They say that Dinkelsbühl has been under siege by a very large company of Swedes for several weeks."

Amelia gasped and closed her eyes. Gerrard's face paled, and his hands formed fists at his side. "Nicolaus!"

"My men are assembling in the chapel. Will you join us?"

Gerrard huffed. "I need to leave. I must save Nicolaus."

"We need to work together." Christian usurped the right of command. "We will pray first. Then we will draft a plan. This is how we do things at Engelturm." Instantly, Christian felt a pang of guilt. He had not handled his situation with Amelia that way. But God had forgiven him for that. Today was another day. He was thankful that God provided for new beginnings. His voice softened. "Will you join us?"

"Father?" Amelia urged.

Gerrard gave a jerky nod and strode silently after Christian and Leopold.

When they reached the chapel, Christian explained the situation to those he kept in confidence. "Let's pray. Search your own hearts and listen for counsel." He removed his hat and went to the altar to kneel down. Everyone followed suit and prayed in silence.

Time passed. With a semblance of peace about the situation, Christian stood and turned to face his men. He looked over the tiny assembly, forming his words when his gaze rested on Leopold. His cousin did not seem to be taking the matter seriously. It was not like him to act so foolish. His face was contorted, his mouth stretched to one side, and his head ticked hard against one shoulder. Next he gazed heavenward, frowned, and wagged his brow.

Christian frowned back. By now he was totally distracted. "You wish to speak?"

"Nein," Leopold replied, shaking his head.

Christian bit his lip in frustration. Then his gaze swept across the chapel, and he noticed a red-faced epidemic. He narrowed his brow in thought, then all of a sudden he comprehended the situation. With the serious nature of their problem, he had forgotten about Amelia's handprints on his doublet, which by now, every person in the room had discovered. He gave an expression that dared anyone to make a remark, removed and folded his doublet, and laid it over a stone bench. Leopold visibly relaxed. Christian did not chance a look in Amelia or Gerrard's direction. "I have a plan." Faces returned to normal hue, and a murmur spread through the chapel.

Christian continued, "We are far outnumbered. It would mean defeat to attack the Swedes, but if we could sneak into the city, we might be able to rescue Nicolaus. Once Nicolaus is safe, we will offer our services to the city's defense."

"Through the wall?" Gerrard's voice sounded rusty.

Christian nodded. "Ja. You have told me how you used water power."

Gerrard's face became animated. "My shop has access to the moat!" Amelia's eyes also lit with hope.

But the plan was fallible. Christian hoped for everyone's sake it did not fail. "We could sneak troops in but not horses. While some men would remain to aid the city, the rest would bring the Trittenbachs back to Engelturm for safekeeping. Reinforcements seem impossible. I cannot knock on castle doors, not knowing each man's stand. The neighbors that were kind enough to bring us the message did not even volunteer their help."

Ideas interchanged for the next hour. When they had discussed all that was necessary, Christian ordered, "Quickly, prepare for travel." His men filed out of the chapel, and Christian told Gerrard, "I am sorry this has happened. I am also sorry for the misunderstanding between us."

Gerrard dipped his head. "Everything seems hopeless."

"There is hope with God."

"Many people die in war. Faith is no guarantee."

"Ja. But I would rather face the worst with God. Without Him. . ." Christian shook his head. When Gerrard did not reply, Christian instructed, "We'll take the armor and weapons that are ready. We ride in the morning. I must go. There is much to do."

"I will be in the armory getting things ready."

"I'll send you help."

"I'm going, too," Amelia said.

"Nein!" both men wheeled about and shouted simultaneously.

"I am sorry to have become such a rebel, Father. But you cannot stop me." She turned to Christian. "If you all die, I do not want to live. I'm going."

Christian opened his mouth to speak, but Gerrard said, "I can use your help, then. Let's go get started."

Christian watched them depart, Amelia's back straight as an arrow. Such courage. He wished his faith were as large as he professed it to be. In reality, their situation looked about as hopeless as jumping out of one of the castle windows that overlooked the cliffs and expecting a soft landing. But he reminded himself of Opa's verse, "The angel of the Lord encampeth round about them that fear him, and delivereth them."

Chapter 10

How are you faring, Amelia?" Christian asked on the second night of their journey.

She drew her gaze away from the campfire and gave Christian a weak smile. "I give it no thought. My mind is so occupied with Nicolaus. . . and prayer."

"I admire your courage."

"Why? It is by your example I have discovered a strength in the Lord."

Christian's gaze swept across the camp: twenty-four men, thirty horses, and one supply wagon. "When this is over, I plan to tell you many things that are on my heart. But now is not the time for it. You do better to dwell on Christ. I hope you can get some sleep tonight."

"You, too, Christian. Danke."

Her brave, grateful attitude clutched Christian's heart and rekindled his mind to the urgency of their mission. Leaving Amelia by the fire, he searched out Gerrard and addressed him in a low, confidential tone. "Would you come with me?"

Gerrard gave a nod and followed. They rounded up Leopold and a few others and assembled on the far side of the supply wagon. "As you know, we will arrive at Dinkelsbühl tomorrow. Let's go over our plans. Leopold, you will scout out the Swedes' camp and report back. I will take three men with me to slip into the city."

"Take me!" Gerrard said. "As your guide. We will have to find Nicolaus quickly. I know the city."

"Very well. And I will need two others." Several of the men volunteered, including Leopold. Christian shook his head at his cousin. "Not this time, my friend. You must stay back. If something happens to me, Engelturm is your responsibility. And I am placing Amelia under your protection."

Leopold reluctantly agreed. Christian chose two of his most trusted men from the other volunteers, then turned to Gerrard. "Do you have any advice for us?"

"Only that the opening in the wall is small. Are your men swimmers?"

The matter was discussed, and once all their plans were laid, Christian dismissed everyone to get some rest.

The next day, they rose early and arrived at their destination in good speed. As planned, Leopold rode off to scout while everyone else occupied a wooded hill near Dinkelsbühl to wait. Finally Leopold returned, riding into the assembly, winded, and reining in his steed. The beast snorted, his muscles quivering as he settled under Leopold's control.

"The Swedes and city—over the next two rises. Something is happening. They're assembling now—at the Wörnitz Gate—to attack."

"Take charge here as we discussed," Christian grimly ordered.

Gerrard and those who would accompany Christian stepped forward. Amelia also rushed forth. She kissed her father on the cheek, and he embraced her. Next she turned to Christian. "Bring my brother back. I will pray for your safety."

"The Lord's will, we shall do it," Christian said, rallying his men. "Let's go." They mounted and galloped their horses nearly to the top of the next rise, then Christian turned one man back with their animals and they proceeded on foot.

Stealthily crouching ahead, while keeping under cover, they topped the hill and also climbed the next. On the crest, everyone lay flat and panted, peering below. The Swedish tents remained intact, but the camp was deserted. Beyond, just as Leopold had reported, mounted soldiers and foot soldiers alike were assembling outside the Wörnitz Tor. Christian could only imagine the carnage that would take place once the Swedes broke through the gate and into the city. He glanced at Gerrard. The armorer's face was drawn tight. With each passing moment, the chances of rescuing Nicolaus or even escaping with their own lives intact grew slimmer.

Christian pointed out the way, and everyone hunkered down to sneak past the enemy camp. At one point they had to drop to their bellies and crawl through the tall grass. They swam across the river, climbing out and over a muddy bank, then went back on their bellies to slither through the grass like snakes. When they came to the moat, they slid in quietly, keeping beneath its surface as much as possible. Gerrard led them to the arched opening behind his shop. Christian sucked in a deep breath, ducked under the water, and swam beneath the wall. His lungs felt like they might burst until he reached the other side. Gasping, he hoisted his chest up onto dry ground, wiped his eyes, and looked around. Not a person was in sight.

Fortunately, he heaved himself the rest of the way out of the water and lay on his side, taking deep drafts of air while he waited for the others.

Gerrard soon drew up beside him, even more winded and weak. "We made it," he sputtered. "Give me a little time—take you inside."

"We don't have much time," Christian reminded.

It was enough. Gerrard stood up on wobbly legs, still breathing heavily, and motioned them to follow him as he staggered toward the door that led into his personal quarters.

"Dry clothes," Christian mumbled, shivering. Gerrard hastened to a wardrobe and, with trembling hands, brought back several sets of clothing. But only he and Christian would leave the premises in search of Nicolaus.

When they stepped out into the street, Christian saw that with all the activity, no one would notice them. A loud upheaval sounded from the Wörnitz Tor. They fell into step with others hurrying in that direction. The city's soldiers lined the street. The council stood just inside the gate. Worming their way through the crowd, Christian and Gerrard caught bits and pieces of conversation.

"Council members now insist on surrender. . . ."

Two citizens argued loudly. "I still say we must remain true to the emperor. Surely he'll be sending troops. . . ."

"There is not enough time. The Swedes are restless, and if we do not surrender, they will burn the city, kill the women and Kinder, and imprison. . ."

The other man cursed. "They will do so anyway. We must fight."

"The city council has already decided, all three mayors. . . ."

A hush fell over those gathered as one of the mayors gave an order. Christian panicked. They must find Nicolaus now, for they were opening the gate! But it all happened too fast. The great Wörnitz Tor opened wide, and instantly, enemy troops poured inside.

Gerrard nudged Christian in the ribs and pointed frantically. "Nicolaus!" Christian saw him, too. He rushed forward, but Nicolaus disappeared behind the crowd. They stopped and scanned the area. Something strange was happening. The Swedish troops had come to a halt. All eyes were riveted in one direction. On Nicolaus! And a throng of Kinder. Singing children! Everyone watched the scene unfold, too shocked to prevent it from happening.

A Swedish officer rode to the front of the procession. He reined in and gazed over the city's elite. Squinting his eyes, he scanned the area to see who mocked them with song. But when he saw it was the children, he nearly lost his seat. A young girl led the choir of many who were not much more than infants.

"It's Lore Hurtin," Gerrard whispered and lunged forward in another desperate attempt to go after Nicolaus.

But Christian locked his arms beneath the older man's. "Wait! Not yet!" He felt Gerrard relent but continued to hold him fast. "What are they doing?" He watched in puzzlement over Gerrard's shoulder.

"Flowers," Gerrard croaked, breaking free from Christian. "They're giving the commander flowers." He placed both hands to the sides of his face, moaning. "Ach, Nicolaus, nein, Nicolaus, nein."

"Look at the colonel," Christian urged.

The colonel slowly dismounted and waited for Dinkelsbühl's tiny intercessors. They marched right up to the officer, singing, encircling him, their arms extended with fists of bouquets. Fräulein Hurtin curtsied and offered him her flowers. "Welcome. We beg your mercy." Each child filed past with his or her colorful gifts.

Gerrard gasped. Nicolaus stood straight and tall, looking up at the commander. "What is your name?" The officer asked in Swedish, but his German interpreter had taken position beside him to give aid.

"My name is Lore," the young girl replied.

"And yours?"

"My name is Nicolaus."

"I am Colonel Sperreuth, and I will do what you request." Christian heard the quick intake of gasps among the townsmen. The colonel then spoke something that only Nicolaus could hear and strode directly to his field commander. He swatted him in the chest with a bouquet of flowers. "Here. From the children." The interpreter translated the colonel's deep, gruff, "In memory of my own son, I urge you to take a gentle approach with these people."

"Yes, sir," the flustered field commander replied.

A glad murmur spread among the German people. The town bells pealed, and the head mayor stepped forward to face the colonel. He bowed low. "May God repay your human kindness. All we can do is to thank you, to. . ."

Christian lost the rest of the mayor's address when someone from the crowd reached out and snatched one of the children to safety. Soon the little ones were all being drawn into the protective circle of their fellow Germans. "Quick, over there!" Christian tugged Gerrard's sleeve, and they made their way to the children. Nicolaus was one of the last to leave the street, but when he did, Christian clasped him tight about the waist and whisked him up into his arms. He covered the boy's mouth with his hand. "Be quiet!" he whispered and hurried back through the crowd toward Gerrard's shop.

Christian glanced down once. Nicolaus's eyes were wide and round. He smiled and removed his hand, shifting him onto his hip. The boy's legs clasped around him, and his hands clung to Christian's clothing. When they reached the armory, the shop door swung open, and the three of them hurried through. Christian set Nicolaus down in the midst of his men.

Gerrard snatched him to his chest and hugged him so hard, Christian thought the poor boy couldn't breathe. "Son. Ah, Son. Right in the midst of it you had to be." Tears washed down the father's creased face.

"When did you return, Father? Did you see me speak to the colonel?"

Christian hated to disrupt their reunion, but he knew the Swedes could come bursting through the door any moment.

"We're taking you to Engelturm, Nicolaus. Are you up to it?"

"Ja. But I didn't see your horse."

"He's waiting for us outside the city. Ready, Gerrard?"

The armorer nodded. "Ja. Of course, we must not delay." He pulled Nicolaus toward the back of the house, then stopped. "I must write a note to Frau Hurtin so she knows Nicolaus is with us."

"Hurry," Christian said impatiently.

Gerrard hastened to get paper, scribbled something, and left it on their table. "Will she find it here?"

"Ja, Father. Let's go," Nicolaus urged. "I want to see Christian's castle."

Christian chuckled. Pounding shook the shop door, and instantly he sobered. As it opened, creaking filled the room. "Go!" He pushed Gerrard. "I will detain them. Be off, and hurry!" Christian's men quickly obeyed and swept Gerrard and Nicolaus out the back. Christian strode toward the shop.

"Halt!" a Swede ordered.

Christian froze. But when he looked closer, he recognized the face. The other man's expression also shone with recollection. "Ah! We meet again," he said in German. "Who do you have back there?"

Another Swede pushed Christian aside and started forward. An argument erupted between the two soldiers. Christian watched for a chance to flee, yet he didn't wish to lead them to the others. Would they be outside the wall yet? Finally the argument stopped, and the one soldier stomped off and left the shop entirely. "Seems you got your way," Christian said, giving the remaining soldier a lopsided smile.

"He thought you were hiding someone and wanted to take you prisoner. But I wish to repay a debt. Once you trusted me. So now I return the favor." He shrugged. "After this, I cannot promise your safekeeping."

"It is enough."

The soldier gave a stiff nod, pivoted, and strode from the shop before Christian could even thank him. And Christian fled out the back.

Amelia paced. What was taking so long? Leopold had sent out a scout, but even he had not returned. She should have managed to go with them, somehow. What if they had all been captured? She would not even entertain the thought that something worse might have occurred. She jerked her head up when she saw Leopold charge forward. Ja! It was a rider! She scrambled after Leopold. But it was only the scout. Still, his face was flushed with excitement.

"They come! They come!"

"Nicolaus?" Amelia asked, straining toward man and beast. "Do they have Nicolaus?" Leopold stretched forth an arm to keep her a safe distance from the high-strung horse.

"Easy, Amelia."

"Ja! The boy is along!" the scout shouted gleefully. "I'll go back with their horses!"

"Quick, then!" Leopold ordered. "Everyone mount! Let's ride." He grabbed Amelia's arm, pulled her along toward the wagon, and helped her aboard. She looked back over her shoulder. "Don't worry. They'll catch up." Soon he urged the freshly harnessed team forward. Their wagon led the pace of the party's departure.

Even as Amelia rejoiced over Nicolaus's liberation, she worried about all of her friends and loved ones who still remained in Dinkelsbühl. She breathed up a prayer for them. Her world, of late, had been tipped, but she was holding steady, for she had discovered a relationship with Jesus. So many things had gone wrong, but finding Jesus was right. As her thoughts ran to and fro, the whirl of passing trees, the bumpy gait—too fast for a wagon—and the deep longing for Nicolaus all blended together to encase her in a haze. She did not know how much time passed before she heard the men cheering.

Leopold slowed the wagon just enough so that Christian could deposit Nicolaus with Amelia. She leaned forward and scooped him into her arms and squeezed. "Oh, Nicolaus! I am so relieved—so happy to have you here." She did not loosen her grip until he began to squirm.

His eyes shone bright. "I got to ride Champion! And I spoke to the colonel. He was not even scary."

Amelia gave him another squeeze. "Let's get you out of your wet clothes and wrap you in this blanket. Then you can tell me all about it."

Nicolaus was still chattering about his adventure at the evening meal, where Gerrard had invited Christian to sit with them, apart from the others.

"And we had to swim under the wall. I always wanted to do that, but Father would never allow it. And Count von Engel kept his promise, too. He let me ride Champion."

"Ja. The count kept his promise to me, too," Gerrard interrupted.

"What promise is that, Father?" Amelia asked.

"More than one, actually. He promised from the beginning that he only meant to watch out for your welfare, Amelia. And that he would prove himself worthy of my respect. Now, I owe him beyond what can ever be repaid."

Christian cast a longing look at Amelia. She was all he wanted.

Gerrard arched a brow. "Matters have changed, you know. Since the city's surrender, Valdemar no longer has any hold over us. You once asked me for Amelia's hand."

"You mean we c–can. . . ?" Christian stammered.

"Ja. I give you my blessing. But now you must ask her."

Nicolaus's eyes narrowed. "What does Herr Valdemar have to do with anything?" Suddenly his face lit with understanding. "Are you going to marry my sister?"

"I hope so," Christian said, his gaze feasting on Amelia. "First I must ask her."

Gerrard cleared his throat. "Come, Nicolaus, let's go see how Leopold and the others fare."

"Ja. Let's tell him about the army, and. . ."

Once they were left alone, Christian closed the distance to Amelia. They stood facing each other, and he enveloped her hand. "I did not plan to ask you here like this. I wanted to wait until we were at Engelturm, to take you on a stroll through the gallery, pausing by Mother's wooden chest. It seemed appropriate."

"And what would you say, Christian?"

"I would say that I love you above all others. That I want you to be my wife, to hold and cherish forever. I would ask you to be my countess."

"I remember the chest, Christian. Ja, perhaps we should wait until we get to Engelturm. Of course, there's always the chance that Father might take back his blessing, and. . ." Her eyes twinkled.

Christian leaned forward. "Enough! Will you marry me?"

"Ja. You know I will." Amelia hugged him in such wild abandonment that Christian nearly lost his balance.

He clamped his eyes closed for a moment in a heartfelt prayer of thanks. When he opened them and looked down into hers, her loveliness stirred him, just as it had at their first meeting. Only there was no rusty visor to separate their faces. He tilted his lowered head and tasted her lips.

"Amelia!" Nicolaus shouted. They drew apart. "Does this mean I'm going to live at Engelturm?"

"One thing at a time, Son," Gerrard said, appearing out of the shadows from behind Nicolaus. "And the next thing that I must do is ask your sister to forgive me. Will you, Amelia?"

She went to her father. "I already have."

Christian gently touched the child's shoulder. "And I have not yet thanked Nicolaus for saving the city." He felt Nicolaus shrug beneath his hand.

"At first I did not think Lore's idea was worth a rat's whisker. But then Lore explained to me what you meant when you said the sword should be one's last wreck horse." Nicolaus smacked his forehead with his small hand. "But I can't believe it worked."

"Wreck horse?" Gerrard asked.

"Recourse," Christian clarified. Everyone laughed until their sides hurt. "Nicolaus, what exactly did Colonel Sperreuth say to you?" Christian asked.

"He said that I reminded him of his little boy. He just died, and the colonel is sad."

"That explains things," Gerrard said. "It was a miracle that he spared the city and did not harm its citizens. God has been good to us this day."

Christian scooped Nicolaus up into his arms. "When we return to Engelturm, I shall throw a party to celebrate Nicolaus's bravery and to announce our wedding plans. What do you think?"

Nicolaus pumped his arm into the air. "Ja!"

Christian chuckled and slipped his other arm around Amelia's waist so he could whisper into her ear. "And as soon as we are alone, my dear, I have many wonderful things to discuss with you."

Dianne Christner and her husband make their home in Scottsdale, Arizona, where Dianne enjoys the beauty of the desert. They have two married children and five grandchildren. Her first book, *Proper Intentions,* was published in 1994, and she has fourteen novels to her credit. Visitors are welcomed at her web page: www.diannechristner.net

A Legend of Mercy

Pamela Griffin

Special thanks to my critique partners in this project: Linda W., your help was above and beyond, your patience as pure as gold, your friendship highly treasured. Ditto, Tamela H.M. and Vickie M.—I couldn't have done it without either of you. To my friend Robin B., a big thank-you for fulfilling my dream of going to Scarborough Faire and discovering the medieval world. And to my sons, Brandon and Joshua, whose enthusiasm to hear Ardghal's story spurred me on—I cherish you, two of my most encouraging and loving supporters.

Dedicated to my Lord and Savior, whose mercy is as far-reaching as the widest rainbow, as refreshing as the mist that waters the land, as timeless as the green hills of Erin. To You, my Lord, I give my all.

Blessed are the merciful: for they shall obtain mercy.
Matthew 5:7

Prologue

Ballymara, Ireland, 1359

A cold shiver of air whispered down from the distant Wicklow Mountains. It stirred the treetops as though to tell of ancient secrets and chilled the three who trekked near the forest edging the castle on the highest hill. Eight-year-old Breanda grew even colder when she caught sight of a boy lying on the snow-covered ground.

"Is he alive, m'lord?" she asked in shock.

Before the earl could answer, Breanda slipped her hand out of his soft one and ran toward the boy, who lay huddled against a huge rock.

"Breanda—wait, lass!" Lord Garland called. "He could be dangerous."

More troubled about the boy's health than with obedience at the moment, she dropped to her knees beside him to see his face better. He appeared not to be breathing. Fearful, she brushed a damp chunk of his black hair away. He was so pale. No pink colored his cheeks, and his lips were blue. She frowned. She had seen that look before on the face of a poor tenant who'd caught his death from winter's cold.

All at once, the lad grasped her wrist hard, and his eyes shot open. Breanda drew back in surprise. His eyes shone a deep, dark blue and held an uncertain look that captured her young heart.

"Wh–who are you?" His voice shook. "What d' ye want?"

"I'm Breanda. Be ye ill?" Strangely, she was not afraid that he held her captive, though his skin felt like ice. The coarse fur wrap he wore made it clear that he must be one of Ballymara's tenants. She'd thought him younger, huddled up as he was, but when he released his hold and awkwardly tried to stand upon Lord Garland's approach, she saw that his limbs were longer than hers and he must be older.

The boy fell back against the rock. "C–cold," he whispered, his voice hoarse. "I no longer f–feel me legs."

"Who are you?" The earl moved closer. "Why have you come to the castle grounds?"

"I—I am Ardghal. I seek Lord Garland."

The earl's bushy brows lifted higher. "I am he."

Ardghal sighed in relief. He reached inside his tunic and pulled out a silver amulet hanging from a thick chain around his neck. A red stone glimmered from its center as if lit with a hidden flame. "I was told to give ye this."

At sight of the medallion, the earl's ruddy skin lost color above his pointed brown beard. He crouched low to study what the boy held. "Who gave this to you? Speak, child."

"Me *máthair*." Tears glistened in Ardghal's eyes, but he brushed them away with a grimy fist. "Afore she died this week past, she told me to c— come here. I journeyed two days from the mountains."

"In the cold?" Breanda thought of the wind and rare snow that had chilled the area.

"Aye."

"Have you no father?" Lord Garland's voice was quiet.

"Me *athair* died of the Black Death. Years ago."

"There is no one else?"

The boy studied the earth below him. "No one, m'lord."

The strange bond that Breanda felt ever since Ardghal opened his eyes and looked at her strengthened. She, too, had lost her parents to sickness. Not four moons after she'd come to live with Lord and Lady Garland as their ward, when she was seven, her own mother and father died. She looked toward her guardian. "May we take him to the castle?"

Lord Garland peered closely at Ardghal. "What is your age, lad?"

"I've lived on the earth one and ten winters, m'lord."

The earl shut his eyes.

"Father?"

Both Breanda and Lord Garland turned to look at ten-year-old Cormac. Upon spotting Ardghal, Breanda had forgotten all about Lord Garland's only son, who often straggled behind like a shadow. From his place on the path where they'd been walking, the skinny boy with flaxen hair curiously stared at Ardghal, Breanda, and Lord Garland in turn. "Should we not return to the castle? The light wanes, and Mother will wonder what keeps us."

"Aye." With a determined look, Lord Garland lifted the shivering Ardghal into his arms. "We shall see you fed and warm, lad. You shall have a home at my castle."

Ardghal's expression filled with relief. "The amulet, m'lord," he reminded, offering it to him.

Lord Garland gave the silver disk a fleeting glance. "Keep it. Perhaps one day it will bring you good fortune."

Breanda fell into step beside Lord Garland, every so often casting a shy glance at Ardghal, who watched her. It pleased her when he returned her smile with a faint one of his own. Quickly, they made their way up the snow-crusted hill toward the stone castle, which now shone ghostlike against a darkening sky.

Chapter 1

Ardghal stood on a grassy knoll, his unbound hair whipping about his face. He watched the beautiful maiden in the churchyard below him. Unaware of his presence and with no one else in sight, she continued her graceful dance beside the narrow round tower. With eyes closed, she lifted the skirts of her blue cotehardie and twirled about the area. Even from this distance, he could see her smile. Brown silken locks flowed past her hips, unencumbered by braids or coils. A flower garland adorned her hair, which captured the sun's fire, dazzling the curly strands into ruby and dark gold brilliance.

Ardghal smiled and stooped to pluck a shamrock from the ground. Descending the hill, he had almost come upon her, when she opened her lovely green eyes.

"Oh!" Her face was flushed from her exertions. "Ardghal. I did not expect to see you this morn. I supposed that you would lie in repose before the tournament."

"Disappointed?" He raised his brow, his smile never faltering.

"Nay, merely startled. I came to speak with Father Stephen."

"And is this what has you so joyful, my lady?"

Breanda bridged the short distance between them. " 'Tis much more. After what was said between us last night, I thought you would know—" Sudden shyness cloaked her, and she glanced away, though they'd been friends for years and shared many secrets.

"Aye." He lifted her chin with a curled finger. "And I meant every word."

Since they were children, Ardghal had loved Breanda, but only last night had he dared act upon that knowledge and told her so. Today was the sixteenth anniversary of her birth, and he fully intended to query Lord Garland on a most important matter.

"Fair Breanda," he murmured, "how long have I loved you? Forever, perhaps?"

Her luminous eyes answered in kind as she lifted her smooth palm to his cheek. He grasped her wrist and kissed the palm, his heart aching with the love he felt for her. "Come," he said, relaxing his hold and slipping his fingers through hers. "I've something of import to say, and only one place is worthy enough in which to speak it."

He led her to the stone arch fronting the church. Generations ago, 'twas said that his ancestor Conn, the holy man who brought Christianity to Ballymara, and his wife, Sorcha, first pledged their love at that same stone, now part of the entryway. Damaged during battle years ago, one of five stained-glass windows depicting shepherds had been replaced by Lord Garland and dedicated to Conn.

Once beneath the arch, Ardghal lifted her hand. With care he wrapped the shamrock he'd earlier plucked from the hillside around her finger. The stem was too short to tie, so he held it in place, looking beyond the splendor of her eyes to the sweetness of her soul.

"Breanda. . .as sure as the shamrock is green, as sure as Three are in One, our love shall be redeemed by the Father, Spirit, and Son."

His voice was soft, yet fierce with sincerity. Once, when they were very young, he'd recited those same words to her, though neither of them understood the full significance at the time. Now he spoke the words with all his heart. The ancient pledge etched beneath Conn's window was sacred, not one to be given in haste, and a vow a man would only give to the woman with whom he wished to share his life.

Breanda's eyes widened. "You. . .I. . ." She shook her head, dazed. "You are certain?"

"Aye. With all that I am I wish to make you my wife."

Joy blossomed upon her face, rivaling the beauty of any flower. "You'll ask Lord Garland? Today?"

"After the tournament ends, two days hence, I shall speak with him. I only hope he considers the match between us a worthy one."

"He will agree, Ardghal; he must. He holds you in high regard. You're one of his most trustworthy knights." A faint crease marred her smooth brow.

"Something ails you?" His hand tightened around hers.

" 'Tis nothing." She gave a slight shake of her head as if to dislodge a thought. "A foolish premonition clouded my joy for a moment, but it will soon pass."

"An omen?"

"Ardghal, I'm not one to put my faith in such things. You know this. Perchance, I simply cannot trust this abundance of joy that is now mine, a joy I've so long coveted. I fear 'tis only a dream, and when I awaken, it shall all be stolen from me."

He smiled wide in an effort to recapture her happiness. "Ah, Breanda. What can steal such joy away? Nothing on the earth, if you will it, nor in the heavens above. 'Tis yours to keep, and I'll wield my sword against any fiend who dares attempt t' take it from you."

Twirling the shamrock near her lips, she giggled as he waved an imaginary sword. Then, swinging her up into his arms as if to rescue her from a foe, much in the manner in which they'd played as children, he dashed with her toward the trees and the glimpse of the river beyond. Yet children they were no longer. And Ardghal again became conscious of the manifest difference between present and past, her soft, womanly form no longer the girl's he remembered. The lighthearted mood drifted beyond him as surely as dew fades from the grass.

Gently, he set her upon her feet. "Forgive me. I should not have—"

"Ardghal." She laid her palm against his linen surcoat where his heart now fiercely pounded. "We've no need for such words between us. I've always loved you; I always shall."

Their eyes met...and held. Like a prisoner long denied refreshment, he drank in the nectar of her words.

"Wilt thou favor me with a kiss, my lady fair?" His own words were husky as he gave voice to the question never before asked in all their childhood play.

"Aye," she whispered, lashes fluttering downward as she slowly lifted her face to his.

His lips were but a breath from hers when a thick shadow blanketed them. At the sudden absence of light and a shrill horse's whinny, Ardghal turned to look skyward. An ominous cloud had swallowed up the sun, casting the countryside in darkness.

" 'Tis Cormac," Breanda murmured.

Indeed, Lord Garland's son sat on his mount atop the hill, watching them—always lurking in the background like some oppressive phantom. He remained that way awhile longer, motionless, then pulled his steed's head around and disappeared from sight.

Breanda stiffened beside Ardghal. The shamrock flew from her fingers, swept away by a sudden strong gust of wind. If he didn't know better, Ardghal would believe Cormac to be a sorcerer, such dread came over his beloved's face.

"Breanda?"

"You must ask Lord Garland with all haste. Do not delay. Promise me."

Her urgency infected him. "As soon as the opportunity presents itself, I will."

She looked at him a moment longer before delivering a fleeting kiss to his jaw. Then, as swift as the wind that tore through the trees, she picked up her skirts and ran up the hillock to the milk-white mare tied beside his black stallion. Mounting her horse with the aid of a rock for a stepping stone, she turned the mare toward the path edging the forest and galloped toward the castle on the highest hill.

Ardghal watched her retreat. Was he unwise to elevate her hopes in view of the prince's recent edict? Yet most assuredly he could sway the earl to resist the intolerant decree. Both in battle and in peace, Ardghal had proven his merit, also demonstrating good stewardship. All of Ballymara respected him. Surely the earl would deem him capable of managing the land left to Breanda by her father; or he might instead issue him a small tract of land for his services, on which to live with a wife and raise a family. 'Twas the earl, himself, who'd knighted Ardghal, once he served his apprenticeship as a squire to Sir Rolf. The earl had even gifted him with plate armor and a fine warhorse.

This time, too, Ardghal was sure to win his favor.

Within the large stretch of land known as the Pale, the sole part of Ireland under English rule, and at a meeting point between the two noblemen's castles, Lord Garland's knights battled against the knights of Lord Roscoe. The reason for the tournament was twofold: to celebrate Breanda's birthday and to entertain an emissary of Prince Lionel, Earl of Ulster, whom King Edward III appointed as viceroy years ago.

Breanda fanned herself with her stiff imported silk and looked toward the tromped field of grass. At a distance, two knights on powerful steeds faced each other within the list, the low fenced area used for the joust. In their coats of armor, glinting silver in the hazy afternoon light, the knights were barely distinguishable from one another. Only by their coat of arms on their shields and surcoats and by the colorful cloth trappers their horses wore could Breanda tell which contender was Ardghal. That, and by her blue veil with which she'd favored him before the heralds had lauded their knights and the trumpets' blasts had announced the start of the joust. Ardghal wore her veil fastened around his arm.

Heart brimming with love, she studied her valiant champion. He had bested each of Lord Roscoe's knights who earlier competed with him in the events of wrestling, ax throwing, and sword fighting. Accomplished at the joust, he would likely prove himself in the next competition as well.

Breanda thought back to this morning. She had been disappointed when the fulfillment of their first kiss was waylaid. Often of late, she wondered how it might feel to have Ardghal's lips touch hers and hoped the chance would soon revisit itself. Her face warmed at the prospect, and she fanned it more violently, bringing the fan closer and accidentally striking her nose. She sneezed.

"Have ye caught a chill, m'lady?" her lady's maid, Elaine, asked.

"Nay, I am well."

Rubbing the bridge of her stinging nose, Breanda determined to rein in her thoughts before she did herself true bodily harm. Along with other onlookers seated on the elevated stand built for ladies and important guests, she watched from beneath a fluttering crimson canopy that made a *thwupping* noise as the wind tried to tear it from its stakes. A flag bearer stood to one side of the list. He lifted a flag high, then let it down with a mighty sweep.

Both horses charged toward one another as the knights held their lances ready. More than the length of a man, the narrow weapons were fashioned of hollow wood and blunt steel at one end; still, Breanda knew they could inflict damage. Pressing her hand to her bodice, she held her breath as the knights came abreast of one another. A dull clang of metal on armor made Breanda gasp, then exhale in relief when she saw Ardghal was unharmed. His contender remained seated on his horse but was unsteady. The knights turned around to face off for a second charge.

Out of the corner of her eye, Breanda glimpsed Cormac riding toward her. He stopped near where she sat with her lady's maid on the third row. Seated on his horse as he was, they were almost eye-to-eye. He leaned over his mare's neck, closer to her.

"Breanda, have I told you how lovely you look?" His words were low, meant for her ears alone. "Your face shines as brightly as the noonday sun."

Thinking the flattery odd, since a thick cloud had recently swallowed that great orb of light, which rarely made its presence known anyway, Breanda kept her focus on Ardghal. She paid little heed to Cormac but perceived his continued stare. Of late, his attentions toward her had been a source of discomfort, and she was still angry with him about his conduct this morning.

On the tourney field, Ardghal and his opponent again raced toward one another. This time Ardghal's lance knocked the other knight off his horse. From the stand above, Lord Garland cheered, loudly proclaiming Ardghal's prowess to Lord Lumpston, the viceroy's visiting emissary.

"He makes a fine warrior," Breanda murmured to Elaine. "Does he not?"

"Indeed he does, m'lady."

"I know what you must be thinking," Cormac said testily, his voice low. "But you realize a union between the two of you will not be permitted?"

Breanda's focus snapped his way. He had removed his helmet, and his tawny locks blew over his armor. Ruddiness washed his cheeks, a sure sign of his anger.

"If you'll excuse me, m'lord," she said, not really caring if he excused her or not. "Come, Elaine."

'Twas best that she seek temporary respite in the thicket, so as not to shame her guardian by a display of temper toward Cormac. With her tongue seized between her teeth lest it yield to temptation, Breanda drew her cloak about her and left the stands. As she moved toward the privacy of a copse of trees, she lifted her eyes to the rounded, smooth peaks of the distant mountains, praying for calm.

Cormac's gray steed cut her off before she could reach her destination.

"You cannot escape the truth, Breanda. Since the Statutes of Kilkenny have been enacted, we're forbidden to continue with Gaelic customs, dress or otherwise, as well you know. Why do you suppose that the tourney today is focused on the matches exercised in England? To appease the emissary who's been sent as a spy to see that all the king's subjects uphold the new law, of course."

She blew out a short breath. "Your reasoning?"

"'Tis simple. Your father was a baron and a subject of the king, as is my father. You and I both possess Anglo blood, while Ardghal's blood runs as Gaelic as the Wicklow Mountains, with nary a drop of Anglo to it."

Ire rising, Breanda addressed Elaine. "Leave us. I will return anon."

Once her lady's maid retraced her steps, Breanda turned on Cormac. "I have yet to understand why you deem yourself an authority to interfere in my affairs. Aye, we've shared friendship these past years, Cormac. But that does not give you license to tell me what I may or may not do, or with whom I may do it. Your father is my guardian, and to him only will I answer. Ardghal may have been born to clan members, but Lord Garland reared him. He looks upon him with favor, as well you know. In truth, Ardghal may possess the wild Gaelic in his veins, but he's become one of us."

"'Tis of little matter." Cormac's thick brows beetled together. "First and foremost, my father is a subject of the king. He'll not risk being demoted and having his lands stripped away—all to appease the whims of a foolish young lass who acts with her heart and not her head. The statute decrees that any alliance with the Gaelic-Irish by marriage shall be punishable as high treason."

She was aware a statute had recently been decreed, though she knew little about it. She'd only been instructed by the earl to dispense with any Gaelic form of dress or music. Nor was she to speak the language.

The uncertainty Breanda experienced at the church revisited her, but she tried to mask it. "Why do you speak thus, Cormac? Why do you seek to wound me with your words?"

His blue-green eyes gentled a fraction, and he dismounted to stand before her. "From the day you came to the castle, Breanda, when you were but seven, it has been understood that you and I would wed once you came of age."

"I knew of no such arrangement."

"Nevertheless, 'twas understood."

She studied his face. He was a handsome man, and once she considered him a friend and as close as a brother. But the lust for power had changed him, and sometimes his brash actions caused her to regard him as a stranger. His cruelty toward the serving wench at table this morning when she spilled his wine and the heated altercation Breanda and Cormac shared afterward were two reasons she had avoided him all day.

"You speak in truth when you say I act with my heart," she admitted quietly. "I've loved Ardghal for many years. And if what you say is true and I cannot have him for my husband, then I should prefer to remain cloistered the rest of my days."

"He's not worthy of your undying affections, Breanda," Cormac growled, taking a step closer until little space separated them. "I'm as great a warrior as he! What traits does he possess that I lack? Why have you always favored him over me? Indeed, I can give you so much more—anything you desire—since all that my father has will one day be mine." He grabbed hold of her hand and kissed it.

His emphatic declaration reminded her of something he might have said in their youth; indeed, he was acting childish. Did he think her so shallow that the promise of greater wealth or lands would sway her to accept his offer? Did he suppose it was merely Ardghal's strength and courage in battle that drew her to him?

"It grieves me to learn that you think so little of me, Cormac." She pulled her hand free of his tight grasp. "I seek no excess of earthly riches, and I cannot marry you. Indeed, a similar vow I've already given. This morning, I pledged myself to Ardghal." Too late, she realized she should not have uttered the last until Ardghal had spoken with Lord Garland.

"He's taken you from me!"

"Cormac, no. What nonsense do you speak? I was never yours for the taking." She gentled her demeanor, knowing she'd unintentionally hurt him. "I hold affection for you in my heart as I would toward my brother if he were alive. To be sure, you and Lord Garland are all the family I have left aside from a distant cousin."

"I want you for my wife, not my sister, Breanda."

"In good faith, Cormac, I cannot give you what you ask."

A nerve pulsed near his jaw. His eyes glinted with dangerous fire. "We shall see—as we shall see who is the better man."

"What do you mean?"

He stormed away from her and mounted his horse.

"Cormac!"

He wrenched his horse's head in the direction of the joust and galloped toward the others.

Fear clutching her heart, Breanda lifted the skirts of her cotehardie and ran after him. Breathless upon reaching the stands, she saw an intermission was underway. Across the field, Cormac rode to where Ardghal had dismounted. Ardghal's helmet was absent, his raven-black curls glistening with sweat from his recent victory.

"Ardghal!" Cormac shouted, his hand going to the hilt of his sword. "Before all gathered here today, I challenge you. Let us see if the hand of a cur can successfully wield his blade against mine."

Dear Father in heaven, no! Breanda's blood froze in her veins. The crowd of onlookers quieted, then began to murmur. A challenge issued in such a manner meant one thing.

The fight would be to the death.

Chapter 2

Ardghal peered into eyes filled with hate. His friendship with Cormac had disintegrated since they'd grown into men. Glancing toward Lord Garland, he caught sight of Breanda beside the stands. Her face was tense, white. She clutched the scaffold as if it were her only support. Any simpkin could see that Cormac now knew they had pledged their troth. And Ardghal was no fool. Still, he sensed the challenge was over more than Breanda, though jealousy must have spurred it. Ardghal had discerned the younger man's affection for their lady friend, though he doubted it could compare with the love he himself felt for her.

"Cormac, my son." The earl stood and pressed his fingertips together near his waist, then spread his hands wide in a gesture solely his. Ardghal had seen him use it often when addressing a difficult issue brought before him by his tenants. "Today is a day for merriment, not for blood to be spilt. Whatever slight you deem Ardghal has inflicted, whatever ill will has sprung between you, let the matter be settled in a match—a joust—but let it be *à la plaisance*."

À la plaisance. Of peace.

Cormac's stare hurled daggers through Ardghal. Tense seconds elapsed, but he finally called out, "Yea, Father. It shall be as you will it. But let the victor claim the prize of the loser's battle horse."

"So let it be done," the earl approved.

Relieved that he would not be forced into a situation that could result in his taking the life of his benefactor's son, Ardghal inclined his head toward Cormac. "I accept your challenge, my lord."

Cormac opened his mouth to respond, then shut it and jabbed his heels into his destrier's sides. Ardghal turned to the young squire who helped him suit up.

"Padrac, my armor."

"Aye, Sir Ardghal."

Within a short time, Padrac again laced the protective armor of greaves to Ardghal's legs, placed the gauntlets to his hands, and outfitted him with the coat of plates for his torso. Ardghal pulled on his helmet, impairing his vision to what could be seen through the two slits. He swung atop his battle horse, its head and chest also protected with armor, and resumed his position at one end of the list. Padrac handed his shield and lance up to him. With his steel glove, Ardghal held the weapon horizontally under one arm.

His armor of chain mail and steel plate was the weight of a robust lad. Moreover, after contending in three matches and taking a hard blow during the last, Ardghal was weary. Nonetheless, Cormac was not as adept at the joust as he was at swordplay, a fact Ardghal ascribed to his own favor.

Ash-dark clouds rolled across the gray firmament. Rainfall would impair his vision all the more, but there was little to be done if it did rain. Sitting tall in his high-backed saddle, he impatiently waited for the flag to drop. To be done with this match was his sole desire.

At the signal, he urged his destrier to charge. Horse hooves pounded, jarred him, as Ardghal worked to keep his lance steady, aiming for Cormac's breastplate. As they drew alongside each other, their lances made contact. The agonizing force of a blow to his chest knocked the breath from Ardghal, and he barely kept his seat. 'Twas the second time today he'd been hit in that spot. While the crowd cheered, he and Cormac turned their horses about for a second charge. This time, only Ardghal's lance made contact, the wood shattering upon impact. Cormac almost fell from the blow.

Padrac handed up a fresh lance to Ardghal just as the clouds opened and drops blew at a vicious slant toward him. He grimaced. A third charge was made, and he struggled to see past the blur of rain. Cormac's lance struck his helmet. Lights flashed inside Ardghal's head. Thrust backward from the blow, he lost his grip on the reins, crashing to the earth.

The next thing Ardghal became aware of was the roar of the crowd in his ears and Padrac kneeling beside him. "Are ye injured, sir?" the boy asked as he helped to pull off Ardghal's helmet.

Pain mixed with heaviness made it difficult to move. Trying to rid himself of the wooziness, Ardghal shook his head. "No blood is apparent. I'm able to bend my limbs." He sat up stiffly. With the way his right shoulder throbbed, he must have landed on it first.

Suddenly Breanda knelt in the mud beside him, her cloak's hood fallen back from her hair. Her face was flushed, wet from the rain. Her eyes shimmered with anxiety. "Are you hurt?"

"Nay. Merely winded." Unease filtered through him that she should see him in a weakened position, one he rarely suffered. "You should not be here.

You'll ruin your new gown."

"I care not for the gown. I care only for you." She looked at Padrac. "Is he hurt?" she asked, as though not believing Ardghal's assurances.

With the aid of the boy, Ardghal stood to his feet, keeping his gauntlet on Padrac's shoulder until the dizziness abated. Breanda stood as he did.

"Behold." Ardghal kept his voice light. "I am unscathed, my lady. You must return to the stands. We will talk later, at the banquet."

"Aye." Her eyes told him what her lips could not say since they shared the company of others. Indeed, he felt her love so strongly, it was difficult to refrain from taking her in his arms.

As he watched her hurried retreat, Ardghal reveled in the knowledge that he possessed the love of a virtuous woman, the favor of the earl, and a promising future. To be sure, the man he once considered a friend seemed bent on making life wretched.

However, Cormac had just bested him and won Ardghal's powerful destrier. At least Ardghal owned another, swifter horse, one he used outside battle and had gained during a prior tournament with a contending knight. He harbored little doubt he would win additional horses in future tourneys. Yet for the present, let Cormac reign as conqueror. Perhaps he would be satisfied with his small triumph, and this would be the end of the discord between them.

From beneath the hood of her velvet cloak, Breanda stared at the mist that fell from a twilight sky. 'Twas fine weather for ducks but little else. Thrice, this day, the dismal clouds had wept over Erin's sod. Earlier, Breanda had escaped the gala at the castle, secretly hoping Ardghal would seek her out and they could talk, but now she retraced her solitary steps.

To her left, the narrow river wound like a silver veil billowing in a gentle breeze. Beyond Ballymara Castle, the timeworn Wicklow Mountains sloped toward the heavens as if presiding over the area, ancient lords to the grounds beneath them. Thin bands of receding sunlight escaped their imprisoning gray clouds and caught myriad droplets that misted the air, transforming them into iridescent jewels that bedazzled the eye.

Breanda stared at the many-colored rainbow shimmering a stone's throw away. She thought of the first rainbow, given along with the Almighty God's promise that He would not flood the earth again to destroy it.

Lord, wilt Thou allow my heart to be flooded with this pain it now carries? For surely it shall be Thy servant's destruction. Wilt Thou guide me and reveal to me a fitting solution? Is there one?

Again, Cormac's bitter words resounded in her mind, and she cast her gaze upon the path before her feet. To him she'd shown a measure of bravado, implying she would prevail. To herself, she knew she could not act in a manner that would reflect badly upon Lord Garland. As was often the case with noblemen's children, she'd been sent to live with a family of higher nobility when she was very young. During her past nine years at Ballymara Castle, she'd developed affection for the earl. She would do whatever he asked. She would make her requests known to him, yea, and if he refused her, she would appeal to be sent to a nunnery.

"Why do you tread the grounds and with such downcast countenance? Surely this is a day for rejoicing?"

Startled, Breanda looked up into the dear craggy face of her guardian. Since his wife had died two years past, a stoop had claimed his broad shoulders, and he exhibited greater tolerance toward her than when she was a child. Though he'd always been kind.

"My lord." She sought for appropriate words. "Might I speak with you about a matter that concerns me?"

"Let us converse as we return to the castle." He held out his hand. "The mist falls more heavily, and I would not wish you to catch a chill."

Breanda left the path she had traversed along the river's edge and looped her fingers around his. Glistening blades of lush grass swept against the hem of her cloak and dampened her thick hose. Thorny shrubs of yellow-flowered gorse grew in abandon over the emerald green hills that were speckled with all manner of wildflowers.

"Do you recall when we walked in such a manner when you were but a child?" Lord Garland's fond words stirred Breanda's memory. "You with your little hand in mine?"

"Aye. And 'twas during such a walk that we found Ardghal."

"Ah, yes. Ardghal." He chuckled. "You were his champion, rushing to his side even then—much as you did today, when he was knocked from his horse. The speed with which you reached him amazed even Lord Lumpston. I've never seen a lady leap over a fence so gracefully, and in full skirts as well."

Heat singed her face; the cooling mist did little to help. She slipped her hand from his. "My lord, if I displeased you with my behavior, I ask pardon. Verily, I gave little thought to what I was doing—"

He raised his ringed hand to stop her apology. "Breanda, I'm not angered. You've had lads as companions and no mother or other woman to instruct you in a lady's ways when you came of the age to be taught. Any fault is mine, not yours, to bear. I should have looked to your future after my wife died, and found you a suitable mentor. Perhaps I should have sent you to your cousin's for a season. But alas, those things that should have been cannot be recaptured."

She could not bear to look at him. "Then I *have* displeased you."

"Nay. I admire your spirit and strength. Those twin traits will serve you well in the future. However, a word of counsel. You've come of the age to marry, but you must curb your willfulness, at least before the wedding takes place. A man likes to think he'll receive a wife who's submissive and meek, not one who'll clash with him at every turn."

At his light words, a second wave of heat rushed over her face. Had he seen her confrontation with Cormac during the joust or heard their heated words that morning? Was he referring to his son when he spoke thus?

"As to the matter of marriage, it is on this subject I wish to speak," she said quickly before she lost all nerve. "I've chosen the man I wish for my husband."

"Indeed? *You* have chosen?"

"Aye." She swallowed over a dry throat. "It is Ardghal."

"And why does such a revelation not surprise me?"

She twisted her head his way, gratified to see him smiling.

"Even before this, had I not seen the brightness in your eyes when he walks into a room, your behavior at the tournament made it clear, and not only to me."

She looked away toward the square castle of pale stone with its crenellated curtain wall and round towers abutting it. "Cormac."

"Aye, Cormac. And every other guest in attendance today."

She closed her eyes in a brief moment of contrition.

"Be not dismayed, child. I'll admit, when you first came to Ballymara, I had thought that when you reached the age to marry, Cormac would make a fitting choice. Yet I deem Ardghal just as worthy."

"Truly? But Cormac said—" She cut off her flow of words. She could not betray her friend to his father by revealing those things he spoke in what she assumed to be confidence. True, he had angered her, but she was loath to slight Cormac by revealing to another his profession of feelings toward her. Feelings of which his father must be unaware, contrary to what Cormac had implied, since her guardian had just stated that he approved of a match between her and Ardghal.

Lord Garland's brows almost met. "What exactly did Cormac say?"

Breanda nipped in her bottom lip, thinking of what to disclose. "He told me that, because of the prince's new statute, a match between Ardghal and me would not be permitted since he is Gaelic and I am Anglo. He said that for me to wed Ardghal would cause you to lose favor with the king.

That it would be considered high treason."

The earl ceased walking though they'd reached the barbican. Two guards stood at attention on each side of the keep's entrance. Lord Garland grew silent, his focus going beyond them and to the inner courtyard, where Breanda could see people milling about. Most were servants tending to their duties. Others were guests and visiting knights, the ribald actions of the latter displaying their continued merriment.

Breanda returned her gaze to the earl. His face was ashen.

"My lord?" Concerned, she gripped his arm to support him. "Are you ill?"

'Twas a moment before he spoke. "Tonight, after the banquet, I wish to speak with you and Ardghal privately. I fear the time has at last come upon me. . . ." His final words trailed away, as elusive as the mist. He speared her with a sober gaze. "You will tell Ardghal? I must see to Lord Lumpston before he takes offense."

"I will tell him." Breanda's anxious thoughts took free rein as she trod quietly beside him and into the castle yard.

Chapter 3

After the feasting ended and many had slipped away to bed for the night, Ardghal proceeded to the earl's private chamber in the solar. Earlier, Breanda had whispered that Lord Garland wished to speak to both of them after the banquet. Before Ardghal could inquire further, a lady guest requested Breanda's audience, and Ardghal's curiosity as to the reason for the meeting went unquenched.

Nearing the entrance, he glimpsed Breanda standing in the light of several candles that lit the wide corridor. The muted glow from the thick beeswax pillars could not hide the apprehension on her face.

"Breanda?"

"Lord Garland ordered me to wait. He seemed upset."

As though he heard them, the earl cleared his throat from within the chamber whose door stood ajar. "Breanda, Ardghal. Come."

They exchanged glances before Ardghal led the way inside. Lord Garland stood with his back toward them, staring out a glazed window that overlooked the river. Hands clasped behind him, his stance appeared resigned, his shoulders slumped.

" 'Twas there, near the forest, I met your mother," he said as if to himself. He turned to Ardghal, his gaze solemn. "The time has come for you to know. . .I am your father."

Ardghal felt as if he'd been struck by another lance's blow. "My lord?"

"I met your mother while I was out riding. My father was then overlord, and a fine thing, too. I was young, imprudent, as yet unmarried." He shook his head in self-rebuke. "Your mother was gathering herbs when I crossed her path. She'd wandered far, and a storm was brewing. She accepted my offer of a ride home but would not give her name. Before we could reach her dwelling, she urged me to stop, dismounted, and ran from my sight. After that, I saw her thrice more before the fair, always alone, in the forest. She'd become a mystery to me, an intrigue. I was besotted."

He looked away, as if caught in the past. Ardghal could only wait for the earl's next words. His own voice seemed to have abandoned him.

"At the fair, my father at last persuaded the clan O'Cullen to sign a treaty of peace. For years, they had remained obstinate, refusing to serve as tenants though the king gave my father authority over them and the lands on which they lived. They agreed to wage no further war and to pay taxes in return for promises made by my father, and a pact was made. I knew little of this at the time. My sole desire was to indulge myself, and I did. Freely." He winced.

"I found her—your mother—and together we partook of the festivities. I learned her name—Maggie—but knew little else about her. Her mystique allured me, and I was enamored. The rich wine and music intoxicated me but no more than her beauty. I had to have her. She did not protest."

Ardghal focused on the waving treetops. He clenched his jaw, tamping down fierce emotion.

"More than a moon elapsed before I encountered her again," the earl continued after a moment. "She seemed removed, anxious—though she'd set out to find me—and she told me she carried my child. I was stunned but assured her I would care for her and the babe in whatever way I could. My oath did little to appease her. She broke from my embrace and said I must never see her again if peace was to remain in Ballymara. 'Twas then she told me that she was a daughter of the O'Cullen chieftain. I made her vow that if ever she was in trouble to send me her amulet—the one you now wear—and I would come for her. With tears in her eyes, she kissed me one last time and fled into the forest. I desired to go after her, to pledge that we would find a way to be together. But we both knew that my father would never allow me, a nobleman, to wed a woman from a clan who'd been a thorn in his side for years. Nor would her father allow it."

The earl heaved a deep sigh. "Later, when I thought I might die from her absence, I attempted to seek her out. In the village, I learned that the clan had been torn asunder due to a disagreement. Half the tribe moved beyond the Pale into Wicklow Mountains. Your mother had married and left with them—but you are the child that resulted from our union. You are *my* son."

Ardghal managed a curt nod. His mother had borne only one babe. The man he'd thought was his father had hurled cross words at her, calling her cursed because she could only give him one son. Had he suspected

Ardghal was not his son? Was that why he often exhibited violence toward them before the sickness took his life?

"I blame you not for despising me, Ardghal. When I made peace with God, I realized the wages of my sin, my selfishness, and how it had wounded both your mother and me. But I never stopped loving her. And though I endeavored to show affection toward my wife, a piece of my heart always remained with my Maggie." The earl seemed to come to himself and shook his head. "But you have no need to hear all of what went on before. I took you into my castle so that I might atone for my grievous wrong. I've come to regard you as my firstborn, and I wish to give you all that is within my power to give."

He looked at Breanda. "I recognize that you have deep affection for my ward, who's become as a daughter to me. Due to the statute issued by the viceroy, Breanda feared a match between you would be considered unlawful. 'Tis for this reason I've chosen to divulge the truth. Your blood is as Anglo as mine, Ardghal. No opposition will come from those loyal to the crown. If you wish to wed Breanda, you have my blessing."

"Thank you, my lord." Ardghal could not look at him, could not give explanation for the sudden distance and anger he felt toward the man. "I do wish it."

"So let it be done. I shall announce your betrothal and post the bans once the emissary leaves and upon Breanda's return from visiting her cousin next week. I will host a feast then."

Ardghal watched as the earl embraced Breanda.

"Thank you, my lord." She pulled away, clasping his hands. "You've given me great joy."

Lord Garland approached. Casting his gaze to the floor, Ardghal still felt unable to meet his eyes. An uncomfortable silence ensued before the earl stepped back to the window.

"You may go."

As he turned, Ardghal glimpsed a shadow slip away from the flagstones near the chamber exit. He hastened to the area, but no one was in sight. Looking to where the corridor angled off in another direction, he strode that way. Did a spy lurk in their midst?

Breanda's light footsteps hurried up behind him. She put a hand to the sleeve of his tunic. "Ardghal, I see that you're troubled. Will you not talk to me?"

He turned and, sensing her distress, took a steadying breath. "In truth, I know not what to speak or think or feel. Once I can make sense of this matter, then I may seek your company." He touched his fingers to her silken cheek "You've always been an encouragement, Breanda. And I shall count myself blessed to have you for my wife." Feathering his fingers down to her jaw in caress, he dropped his hand away, preparing to go.

"Before you retire," she hastened to whisper, "I—I believe you owe me a kiss. Or perhaps 'tis I who owe you one?"

"A kiss?" He lifted his brow at her swift change of topic.

"Aye." She quietly cleared her throat. "Earlier, this morn, we. . .we were interrupted. I should like that kiss now, if you would be so inclined to give it. As a token of your affection."

Ardghal grinned, all former stiffness vanishing. "Indeed. I can think of nothing that would please me more."

He lifted his hands to cradle her blushing cheeks. In the candlelight, her eyes shone like jewels, and he gazed a moment longer into their jade-green depths before lowering his mouth to hers. Brushing his lips lightly, slowly over hers, he thrilled in their softness, their sweetness. Her breath was fragrant and warm as it mingled with his. Her hands, so soft and gentle, touched his upper arms, then slid up to clasp his shoulders and move to his back, as she leaned into him and freely returned his affection. Her response ignited a blaze within, so fierce, he wanted nothing more than to crush her to him and deepen their kiss. Never stop kissing her, never stop holding her. . . .

Heart pounding so loudly he could hear it, Ardghal pulled back. Her eyes were luminous, marveling, questioning. He laid a forefinger against her lips when she opened her mouth to speak.

"There shall be opportunity for us to fully share our devotion, Breanda. Once we are wed." His words were husky. "Until that day, let us exercise caution. The hour is late. We should retire to our chambers."

Disappointment tinged her eyes, but she nodded. "You are wise, Ardghal. If you count yourself blessed to have my love, I count myself doubly blessed to have yours. May the Lord smile upon you and give you a sleep that is sweet," she added, as she'd said to him each night for eight years, since the evening he'd first come to the castle.

"And may it be returned to you a hundredfold, dear Breanda."

She offered a parting smile. He watched until she disappeared from sight.

A sudden scraping—what sounded like a shoe against flagstone—broke Ardghal from his tender thoughts, reminding him of his suspicion that he wasn't alone. He hastened in the direction of the sound. Yet when he reached the bend of the corridor and looked its length, again he saw no one there.

A sennight had passed since Lord Garland divulged the truth of Ardghal's parentage. In those seven days, Ardghal was distant, though he assured Breanda that he, too, was overjoyed that the earl gave his blessing. Why, in all these years, had she never guessed at the relationship between the men? Both possessed eyes of the same dark blue, and both carried themselves in a similar noble manner, though Ardghal's stance seemed prouder, stronger.

Breanda fidgeted against the bench of the closed, horse-drawn chariot that transported her to her cousin's and the wedding of her only relation to be held on the morrow. Yet again, she relived the kiss she and Ardghal had shared and felt the blush rise to her face. Never had she dreamt a kiss could be so tender, so poignant, so powerful. . . .

Faith, was she wicked to dwell on that kiss? With no one to ask, Breanda decided it best to steer her thoughts onto safer ground, befitting a maiden, and returned her attention to the landscape. Beyond the square window opening, forested hills in every hue of green occupied her sight. As the carriage jounced and rolled within the heather- and gorse-covered granite mountains around her, Breanda observed that fewer sheep dotted the grasses of the valley here than in Ballymara. On occasion, she spotted a Celtic high cross through lush foliage.

Another jolt shook her as the wheels rolled over an obstacle. Her body ached from the bruises she was certain she'd acquired due to the constant bouncing as they traveled over rough terrain. She missed the company of her lady's maid, who'd taken to her pallet with fever. A good thing she'd not had to endure this vexing ride, which lasted the greater part of the day.

Breanda didn't often venture from Ballymara and hoped she wouldn't appear plain to her elegant cousin. Taking inventory of her simple gown in deepest blue, she noticed dirt sullied its lap. Frowning, she brushed it away. The scoop-necked bodice hugged her to the waist, as all her cotehardies did, and ended in full skirts that hid her pointed-toe slippers. At least *they* were embroidered. No embellishment adorned the gown, but she did wear an ornamented girdle slung above her hips and, concealed within it, a small, jeweled dining dagger. Bandits were known to attack travelers, and though she had an escort of four worthy knights, Ardghal among them, she was grateful for the weapon which would serve a dual purpose, if need be.

In the distance, a round tower loomed near a thick copse of trees, snagging her attention. Ballymara's own belfry had been hit by lightning five years past, and the earl had used stones from its damaged side to build onto the village church. She preferred that church to the stuffy castle chapel, especially since the lovely and peaceful church site included the pledging stone arch. And near it the round tower. Such remains, once used as hideouts for priests during Viking raids centuries ago, were now used only for storage, if they were used at all.

Father Stephen's tales of how priests would gather their gold and enter the tower from the outside high window—higher than the church itself—spawned hours of adventurous play for Breanda, Ardghal, and Cormac as children. Pretending they, too, were under attack from Vikings, they gathered stones as treasure to take with them while they ascended the rope ladder, afterward drawing up the ropes to protect their cache—until the day they were caught during one such escape. A wistful smile curled Breanda's lips at the memory of how Ardghal had championed her, taking the brunt of the blame. Nevertheless, Father Stephen had scolded them all soundly and sent them running home to Ballymara Castle.

The sudden clamor of approaching horses startled Breanda. Twisting toward the noise, she peered out the window. Eight mounted men galloped from the cover of trees.

Stunned, Breanda watched as one man aimed a crossbow behind the chariot. Its arrow whizzed past. A strangled cry came from one of the knights, followed by the sound of a body thudding to the earth.

Shouts rent the air. Ardghal sped into her line of vision on horseback, brandishing his sword as he charged toward the bandits. The alarming clang of steel striking steel rang within her ears. A second mounted knight appeared, his gleaming blade raised high as he targeted one of the fiends. Terrified, Breanda watched yet another bandit race up behind the knight, his weapon held ready for attack.

Save us, heavenly Father!

Everything was happening so quickly, she could scarcely think. *Escape!* her mind screamed. But no—she'd been forewarned to stay inside the chariot in the event of danger.

The chariot's driver plummeted to the ground, a crossbow's arrow protruding from his back. A bandit jumped atop the chariot, causing it to shudder. Dropping her hand to her dagger hilt, Breanda threw open the door. Stay or flee—she would not be taken without a fight!

Before she could jump down, the horses pulling the chariot took off with a jolting start. She braced her hands to the sides where the door had been fastened. It swung wildly, banging against the outside of the hurtling chariot. Breanda nearly flew headlong into a massive tree. Struggling for balance, she dared to peer past the jamb and spied Ardghal fighting off a bandit. Another raced up behind him.

"Ardghal!" she yelled as loudly as she could in warning.

He turned, and in that instant, a bandit's sword plunged into him. He toppled from his horse.

"No!" Breanda screamed.

The wheel hit something hard. Legs buckling, she fell, striking her head on the bench. Darkness blotted out the sun as her world went black.

Chapter 4

Breanda awoke with a start. Her head throbbed. Carefully, she touched the back of it, discovering a lump. A canopy of dirty canvas stretched above her. Pushing herself up to sit, she noticed the sides of her world were round and similar in color. She lay in a tent on a sour-smelling bed of rushes.

Memory flooded her mind, increasing the pain.

Ardghal!

Quickly, she rose. Dizziness swept over her, a merciless bird of prey. She grabbed the center stake that held the tent upright. Somehow, she must find him, tend his wound, do what she could to help. He *must* be alive.

Her vision clearing, she spotted the tent's opening. She felt for her dagger, surprised to find it. Her abductors must not have searched her. Grateful for that small miracle, she wrapped her fingers around the dagger hilt, unsheathing the weapon. Hiding it in her skirts, she moved toward the flap and pulled the canvas aside.

A bearded giant blocked her way. With a beefy hand thickly sprinkled in black hairs, he motioned her to return to her prison. Beyond him, men gathered around a fire in a clearing surrounded by a dense thicket. Her sentry roughly grabbed her arm when she did not budge.

"Unhand me, knave, or live to regret it." She raised the double-sided weapon chest high, pointing it toward him. The emeralds embedded in the silver hilt gleamed in the murky light, but no more so than the wicked point of her blade.

"Threaten me not, woman." His reply came in swift Gaelic. His eyes closed to slits, and his grip on her tightened.

She slashed the blade's point along his knuckles.

Yanking his hand from her arm, he cursed and wiped a thin line of blood onto his tunic against the red shield emblazoned there. 'Twas then that she noticed the O'Cullen crest. The guard took a menacing step closer.

Again, she pointed the dagger toward him.

He ceased his advance and swore again. "Get back in there afore we both live to regret it."

"Who are you, and why have I been taken? What plans have you for me?"

"'Tis not for me to say."

She tried once more. "Where are my escorts? What have you done with them?"

"All dead. Enough! Test not me patience."

Catching her unawares, he covered the scant distance and grabbed her wrist, wresting the dagger loose from her fingers. With a harsh thump of his massive palm against her shoulder, he forced her back into her prison. Her feet flew from under her, and she landed hard on the ground. He leered, then wrenched the tent flap closed.

Alone again, Breanda pushed herself up on one elbow but could scarcely think. Dead? They were *dead*? Baldric. Gaston. Leonard. . .Ardghal. It could not be. It must not be. The ache of her bruised body paled in comparison with the anguish that ripped through her heart.

The dank smell of wet earth and the twittering of birds aroused his senses, and Ardghal opened his eyes. He lay stomach-down on the ground. Sharp pebbles dug into his cheek. When he forced himself to move, his left side burned as though impaled with a flaming torch. He clenched his teeth to keep from crying out. The pain brought with it the memory, and he examined the wound in his shoulder.

Fortunately, the cut wasn't near his heart. The lesion had stopped bleeding but appeared deep. Apparently, the thick patch of black mud in which he'd fallen had acted as a poultice and quenched the blood's flow. His left arm useless, he relied on the aid of his right arm to help him stand.

The sight of his three friends and fellow soldiers lying in the grass, along with four lifeless bandits and the chariot driver, sickened him. But the absence of the chariot and horses had him falling to his knees. *Breanda. . .*

"Dear God, help me to find her."

Stunned to see the O'Cullen crest on the brigands' tunics, he tried to make sense of the matter. His mother's clan had attacked. Why? For what purpose would it serve to break a treaty of peace?

Ardghal's heart weighed heavy as he lumbered to each of Ballymara's knights in turn and found all of them dead. He paused a moment in prayerful silence over each man. Then, swiping at the moisture that rimmed his eyes, he collected his sword from the ground and blew out a shrill whistle that caused the birdcalls to fade then increase in intensity.

From a distance, the pounding of hooves struck the earth. Ardghal sheathed his blade and turned. A fine black steed burst through the trees, coming to a stop beside him. With a muffled snort in greeting, the animal tossed its raven-black mane.

Ardghal reached up to stroke his stallion's glossy neck. "Faithful Destroyer. Always you are near when I have need of you." Using his one good arm, he mounted the powerful beast and took the reins, guiding his horse to the twin trails the chariot's wheels had made.

Paramount to all else, he must find Breanda. And quickly. There was no time to return to Ballymara and enlist the aid of fresh troops. He assumed Padrac, who was fleet of foot, had escaped the bandits and returned with news of the ambush, heeding an instruction Ardghal had earlier given. Urging Destroyer into a gallop, he winced, pressing his left arm to his side.

The sun had dropped a notch in the heavens before he approached a stream. Besieged with light-headedness and pain, he dismounted, knowing he must rest. He stretched out on his stomach beside the stream to drink his fill, then dunked his head beneath the icy water. It chilled his teeth and bones, but he hoped it would keep the dizziness at bay. Groping to a kneeling position, he shook his head like a dog, sending drops of spray everywhere.

Something scraped on the rocks behind him. A plunking of pebbles hit the earth.

Ardghal hastened to his feet as fast as he was able, grabbing the hilt of his sword as he spun around. Atop a low rock cliff, three bearded men circled, brandishing weapons. Their tunics bore the same crest as those who'd killed his friends and had taken Breanda. The shorter of them, obviously the leader, wore a sapphire-blue cape.

Ardghal held his sword aloft, waiting, assessing. His fighting arm was not the one stabbed; yet that shoulder still ached from the fall he'd taken at the tourney.

Letting loose a fearsome shout, the wiry man in the cape leapt down from the rock shelf and rushed forward. Ardghal met the assault with all he had in him. The clash of steel rang in his ears, seeming to echo in his mind.

Vision swimming, he broke away and gasped for breath. A second man drew close through the blur. As if sensing Ardghal's strength abandoning him, the first brigand advanced, slicing his blade downward. Almost caught unawares, Ardghal swivelled, managing to parry the blow. The second man cried out in Gaelic.

"Fearghus, look. The amulet!"

Sword positioned, the first attacker stared at Ardghal's surcoat over its chain mail. Blades at the ready, the others crowded close, gathering in for the kill.

Ardghal wielded his sword in defense, but it grew heavy in his hand. A dense blackness descended like a shroud of death over his eyes. Stumbling to his knees, he lost his hold on the weapon and crumpled to the earth.

Nightfall swept its mantle of darkness over the land, as if to hide men's evil deeds. The only sounds to disrupt the silence were those of a crackling fire and voices murmuring outside the tent. On occasion, the buzz of an insect or the rustle of a nocturnal animal could be heard outside the cloth wall. A tear in the canvas roof revealed a sharp slice of moon piercing the sky. Few stars shone. Breanda hoped there would be enough light to track her whereabouts, for she was certain someone must come.

After her altercation with the ogre guard, a lad with ruddy curls had brought her a hunk of bread and some pottage. He remained mute to her demanding questions, however, and had regarded her fearfully, as though he thought she might actually bite him. Good. With her dining dagger gone, little damage to his person could be achieved, but 'twas best these ruffians know she wasn't a woman to be trifled with. She could almost hear Ardghal chuckle as he had in their youth when he called her wild and un-broken—"worse than a mare with a thorn under her saddle." At the time she had growled in indignation to be compared to a horse and, waving an upraised fist, chased him over the hill abloom with wild orchids while he eluded her, laughing.

Breanda bit into the stale bread, surprised to find it salty, then real-ized it was her tears that seasoned it. She swiped them from her cheeks and raised her chin. 'Twould not do to show any sign of weakness to these ruffians.

Ardghal could not be dead. Surely the Lord would not allow it, as of-ten as she'd prayed for his safety. Yet Breanda knew that the Almighty did allow tragedies to enter one's life. Her own parents had died shortly after she'd gone to live at the earl's castle. The sickness had stolen their lives, and her brother had died in battle. She would never visit her family or again see them on this earth. Father Stephen once tried to console her, attributing such circumstances to God's omnipotence, but Breanda barely listened at the time. In truth, she barely sat still long enough to pray, except when to do so involved something she desired.

A wisp of guilt unfurled within her, but she smothered it. Were her prayers even heard? Or were they wasted on the heavens above that could hear nothing? The winds blew, the clouds produced rain, the sun and moon and stars gave off light. Yet they did not speak to her or reassure her. They were nothing. Acts of nature that had no voice...

Angered shouts broke the stillness, startling Breanda from her bitter ruminations. The murderous clangs of steel upon steel rang through the air. Eyes going wide, she hurried to the flap to see.

Chapter 5

Ardghal opened his eyes. He lay inside a wattle and daub hut on a mat of straw. The sky he discerned through the cracks of the thatched roof was black as pitch, but a fire nearby crackled close enough to produce a harsh yellow glow, also drowning him in heat. Sweat streamed off his face, into his ears, and over his scalp. He dragged his hand to his chest and found it bare. All his armor and the quilted garments he wore underneath had been removed. A rough fur blanket covered him to the waist. Something bulky and weighty wrapped his throbbing arm and shoulder. A poultice of some sort, if the stench coming from the cloth was anything to go by.

A figure came into his line of vision. By the outline against the fire, he assumed his visitor to be a woman.

"So, ye be awake," a feminine voice said. He placed it at no less than forty years. "The devil will not have ye, then."

"Where am I?" Ardghal asked, astonished at the raspy sound in his own throat.

"Ye be with the clan O'Cullen. And a fine thing it is that the amulet you were wearing."

The amulet! He slapped a hand to his neck but found no chain there. His swift action brought a ripping pain to his shoulder, as if ground glass had been smashed into his wound, and he groaned.

"Have a care, man. Are ye daft? Lie still. The fever is not gone from you, and the cut may flow a second time, though 'twas necessary to cauterize it."

Ardghal shut his eyes, remembering the searing pain, though he had trouble recalling how he'd gotten there.

"Aye. Sleep while ye may. The chieftain will soon be wantin' a word with you."

"Chieftain?"

She drew herself up proudly. "Niall O'Cullen. Me brother."

Ardghal stiffened in recognition. Niall O'Cullen. The man about whom his mother had warned him with her last breath.

While she lay on her deathbed, she made Ardghal vow that after her demise he would leave their clan and seek out Lord Garland. She stressed that he should not remain in the camp. Anxious to calm her, Ardghal had agreed. Had the chieftain suspected that Ardghal was the son of an Anglo and not sired by a member of their clan, as had always been believed? Otherwise, why would his mother have feared him so?

The hulking, dark shape of a man entered the hut and came to stand beside the woman.

"Niall," she murmured. "If it is well with you, I'll take me leave."

"It is well." The newcomer's voice was gruff.

Ardghal steeled himself not to look away, though he could see little of the chieftain's face. The chieftain, this man. . .his grandfather.

Breanda's heart pounded fierce and without mercy as she stood with the tent flap parted and watched the battle. Along with several other knights, a flaxen-haired man wielded his sword against her abductors and guards. As he turned toward the firelight, his visage became clear.

Cormac! He had come to rescue her. . .yet there was a strangeness about the manner in which the rogues fought. Those who'd taken her didn't fight as fiercely as they had during the ambush. Was it the lateness of the hour that made them weary, the unexpectedness of the attack that made them sluggish, or her own weariness that prompted what was only her imaginings? Whatever the reason, Breanda was relieved when Cormac reached her prison of canvas and grasped her above the elbow. His eyes darted around the area, his sword held aloft to fight any who would try to stop them. The ogre guard seemed to have disappeared.

"Are you hurt?" he asked.

"Nay."

"Then let us be away from this place."

Cormac need not have spoken. Breanda was already running beside him toward a patch of murky white near the trees that proved to be Cormac's stallion. He mounted, swung her up behind him, and prodded the horse into a hard gallop, leaving the other knights to continue the battle. Behind, Breanda heard shouts; yet after a lengthy span of hard riding, it was evident no one followed.

Cormac soon brought his mount to a slow trot as they approached a deep glen. One of the cliffs descended at a slant, providing an overhang. Cascades of water shimmered over rocks nearby, emptying into a dark lake.

"We shall await the morning here," Cormac said. "The night is too dangerous for travel."

Breanda loosed her arms from about his waist and wearily dismounted. "Is it wise?" She watched him slide off after her. "Will they not pursue us?"

"I appear to have convinced them such a course would be folly."

"I fear for Ardghal." Despite what the ogre guard had told her, her heart refused to believe her beloved was dead.

Even in the scant moonlight, she noticed Cormac's scowl. "Must you always think of him? 'Twas I who saved you from those brigands!"

"Aye, and you have my gratitude. Yet Ardghal attempted the same and was wounded for his loyalty." The sudden desire for truth made Breanda clutch his sleeve. "Tell me. He is alive? For surely you must have come upon the place of ambush to learn I was in peril. Did he tell you?"

Cormac's lips thinned as he twisted his arm from her hold. His visage haughty, he lifted his head. "Your faith is misplaced, Breanda. You speak of loyalty, but a cur such as Ardghal knows no such word or deed." He moved to the lake and knelt to drink.

Resentment simmered within her as she followed. "How dare you speak ill of one who was willing to sacrifice his life for me!"

"Sacrifice his life?" Cormac let out a sneering laugh as he shook the water from his hand and stood to face her. "My dear, misguided Breanda. 'Twas a message delivered to the castle that informed us of your peril. I knew of no ambush."

"A message?"

"Aye. Signed by Ardghal himself. He conspired with the lot of his worthless clan to kidnap you for ransom. Two hundred pieces of gold was the price for his loyalty."

Chapter 6

In the heavy gray light before daybreak, Cormac and Breanda resumed their journey homeward along with the other knights who'd earlier caught up to them. She found it curious that Cormac wasn't as hurried as he'd been last night. Did he not fear that the bandits might try to recapture her now that morning had dawned?

Twice during their sojourn, Cormac spoke of Ardghal, inferring that his knowledge of his illegitimacy and subsequent anger regarding the earl's duplicity must have sparked his rebellion. Breanda was astonished he knew the truth. To her knowledge, the earl hadn't disclosed it to anyone, save her and Ardghal. When Cormac made his disparaging remarks, she turned a deaf ear to him, as she'd done last night when he first laid the blame on Ardghal. Each time, she didn't miss Cormac's reddened face or the infuriated sigh he heaved.

Let him be irate and think her a fool. She wouldn't believe evil of Ardghal. She had seen him wounded in his efforts to protect her. That he instigated her abduction or had taken part in it was folderol. The supposed letter of ransom had to be forged; surely the earl must know this.

The sky glowed a fiery red gold by the time Ballymara Castle came into view. Seeing its high, curtained wall and round towers, Breanda relaxed. Tears sprang to her eyes, and she wiped them away. Oh, to be home again. Safe. She would speak to Lord Garland, and all this nonsense would be swept away like the rubbish it was. Ardghal would be found, and life, as she'd known it, would resume.

Once they dismounted in the lower bailey's courtyard, Breanda spied her maid hurrying toward her.

"Oh, mistress." Tears washed Elaine's cheeks as she flung her arms around Breanda's shoulders. " 'Tis glad I am ye be safe! Curse the sickness that kept me from your side. Would that I'd been with ye, where I belong, this mightn't have happened."

Breanda drew away, attempting a smile. "And what do you think you, a mere maid, could have done that four armed knights could not?" She sobered at the reminder of the lost noble soldiers. "I'm glad to see you recovered but relieved you were absent from me. I might have lost you to a brigand's sword as well."

Breanda turned to find herself encased in velvet as Lord Garland embraced her. "Breanda, child, you're home."

"'Tis thankful I am to be home, my lord." She pulled from his embrace, alarmed at how lined his features appeared. Overnight, he'd aged into an old man. "If I may confer with you, I wish to speak of Ardghal."

Pain misted his eyes, and his jaw trembled. "Later. You must rest after your ordeal."

Breanda was weary from a full day of riding, but a sense of urgency prompted her to converse on the matter that had beset her ever since Cormac touted his lies. She parted her lips to speak, but caught Cormac's slight shake of the head. Tempted to ignore him, she gave the issue further thought. Perhaps it would be in her best interest to air her concerns when she and Lord Garland could speak privately.

She led the way to the inner bailey and the solar, where the family quarters were located, and ascended the spiral stairway to her chamber. Elaine followed and drew the heavy curtains back from the wooden frame bed.

Gladly, Breanda lay on the cool bedding. She shook her head when Elaine approached to help remove her soiled gown. Even to wash the dirt from her face and hands and neck seemed too much of a task. She inhaled the sweet scent of tansy, earlier sprinkled on her feather mattress to keep the fleas away and on the stone floor to freshen the air when crushed underfoot. . .so much nicer than her prison tent. She closed her eyes, her last thought drifting to Ardghal and his avowal of love at the pledging stone. A tear slid down her cheek.

When Breanda awoke from her slumber, a patch of inky darkness tinted the window. How much time had elapsed? Had the earl retired for the night? Without waking Elaine, who slept on a straw pallet nearby, Breanda quickly freshened herself, attempting to smooth the frizz that had come loose from her plaited hair. She dared not take the precious time to comb it out. The urgency to speak with Lord Garland about Ardghal prompted her to hasten toward the earl's chamber. Muted voices emptied out into the candlelit corridor. Breanda halted, surprised.

"I fear you are right, Cormac." Lord Garland's sorrowed words were low. "And it grieves me to air the edict that will most surely seal Ardghal's fate. Nonetheless, justice shall be met, and you'll be rewarded for your bravery."

"I ask only one reward, Father. Give to me Breanda. In marriage."

Breanda clapped her hand over her mouth to muffle a gasp. She leaned close to the chamber entrance, not wanting to miss the earl's reply. When it came, it chilled her very soul.

"Aye," he said quietly. "So let it be done."

When next he woke, Ardghal felt lucid. His wound didn't ache as much, and he struggled to a sitting position. The air held a chill that made him shiver. Through the hut's opening, a pale sun shone beneath a white strip of cloud. Daylight. But how many days had passed? He recalled little of the conversation with his grandfather or how long ago it had taken place. The fever stole his consciousness during that first meeting, but he did remember the words Niall O'Cullen spoke before the world faded: "So, ye've come back."

Come back? His presence in their camp wasn't by his will. He'd been captured, though no fetters bound his hands or feet and no one seemed to be guarding him. Ardghal studied the area outside the hut. People moved about, but none took notice of him, save for some children who stood whispering in a group, a stone's throw away.

He frowned when he saw a child with hair the color of Breanda's. Had she been brought to this place as well? He must find her.

Awkwardly, he pushed himself to his feet, holding the fur coverlet against him. He staggered and waited until a wave of dizziness passed.

A lass of approximately six years separated from the children and moved toward the hut. Her big inquisitive eyes, a hue of blue lighter than his own, studied him. He clutched the fur cover more securely about his waist, feeling like a turtle stripped of its shell.

She smiled, giggled, and ran off, shouting in Gaelic for her mother. Ardghal tensed. What malady would the child now bring upon his head?

The girl returned, followed by a plump woman with red braids and wearing a green gown of fine cloth. Ardghal was grateful that she carried his clothing and armor, evidently cleaned, but his sword and dagger were absent. She handed over his things, seeming embarrassed and amused at the same time.

"I'm Alma, the chieftain's daughter. Ye must dress, and I will bring food. Me athair will then speak with ye."

"How long have I remained here?"

"Five days."

Five days? What had become of Breanda?

The child continued to stare at Ardghal after her mother left the hut. The woman looked over her shoulder. "Isabel, come!"

"Aye, Máthair." The girl hurried to obey but not before giving Ardghal another big, close-lipped smile. He watched her scamper off before he turned to the task of dressing, favoring his injured shoulder as he did. So Isabel was his cousin. A fair and fetching lass, and at such a tender age. And Alma was his aunt. He had failed to recognize her, but then he'd only been a lad when last he'd seen her.

Once Ardghal wolfed down a bowl of vegetable pottage and tore his teeth into a hunk of wild boar—the first food he'd eaten in days—a short, wiry man entered the hut, announcing he was to take Ardghal to the chieftain. The man's tunic bore a red shield with a white chevron, three hands raised in pledge, two black shamrocks, and a shaft of wheat. The O'Cullen shield. Upon second glance and noticing the mole on his cheek above a sparse brown beard, Ardghal realized that this was the swordsman with whom he'd fought near the stream after the ambush.

Wary, Ardghal walked with his guard past other huts scattered within the confines of the rath. A sense of familiarity struck as he recognized areas of the wooden fortress.

"I've heard it said ye be Ardghal," his guard muttered.

"Aye."

"I am Fearghus. You and I hunted together as lads."

"Fearghus. . ." Ardghal recalled his boyhood friend, a snaggle-toothed lad who possessed a comic mischief. A chuckle escaped. "And do you still sling rocks at the crows that perch along the rath's outer wall?" He motioned to the sharp, pointed tips of the tall wooden wall that enclosed the compound, noticing a few of the black birds there now. For the first time, he wondered why the chieftain had built a rath of wood, as in ancient days, instead of a sturdier fortress of stone.

Fearghus's jaw clenched. "Why did ye side with the enemy?"

"I heeded a deathbed promise, asked me by my mother. But Lord Garland is no enemy, Fearghus. He took me into his castle and cared for me when I might have died." He spoke the words, though bitterly. What would Fearghus say if he knew Ardghal was the earl's son?

"Ye speak as the Anglo nobles do," Fearghus shot back as though he'd heard nothing said. "Ye dress like an Anglo, as well. Ye've become one of them. 'Tis surprised, I am, that ye be keepin' yer máthair's amulet."

"Where is it? And my sword and dagger?"

"I gave 'em to yer *seanathair*." Fearghus stressed the word for grandfather, spearing him with an accusatory glare, as if again to remind him of his supposed betrayal.

They approached the inner bailey, which housed the chieftain's quarters. Ardghal grabbed hold of Fearghus's upper arm before they went farther. "With all that I am, I vow to you that I mean no harm, Fearghus. To you nor any of the clan."

"Why then were ye on our land, if not sent as a spy?"

Ardghal chose not to remind Fearghus of the verity they both knew, that the English Crown ruled much of eastern Ireland. But he did speak of what lay deepest in his heart. "The woman I guarded—Lady Breanda—is she here?"

"Think ye that we abducted the earl's ward?"

"Men bearing the O'Cullen colors ambushed our party."

"'Tis a lie! Niall would not break a treaty of peace. Our number is few compared to the earl's army—of which ye appear t'belong. Would be to our destruction to raise his ire against us."

His words made sense. Ardghal continued to walk with Fearghus and caught sight of some children nearby. Their clothes were ragged, their eyes soulful, as if begging him for something, though they spoke not a word. "Who are these children?"

"Pitiful waifs, are they not? They scavenge what food they can find and keep to themselves. They have no parents. We lost both men and women during a clan war with the Byrnes two years past."

"Women?"

"Aye, they fought as well. Anyone who could raise a sword did so in defense."

Pity surged through Ardghal for the orphans. He wished he had the means to give them what they needed.

In a dim corridor, Fearghus halted in front of a chamber. Before they could enter in, Ardghal spoke. "You've become a fierce warrior, Fearghus, one I do not wish to clash swords with again. Let us not be enemies, when once we were friends."

"Ye made your choice eight years past. To be enemies is all that's left to us now." Fearghus turned on his heel and left Ardghal to weather the storm alone.

Who is in the whirlwind or the storm? Who is in the fire? In the midst of one's distress, does a lone voice cry out to be heard? If so, from whence does it come? No, a thousand times no. There is no voice of comfort, no relief from one's distress. There is only the whirlwind, only the storm, only the fire. . . .

Breanda laid down her quill next to the vial of ink and studied what she had written. Lady Garland, when she was alive, had kept records of her daily activities. Since the day she'd reached the age of six and ten, Breanda had chosen to do the same on scrolls of parchment she kept safely hidden in a trunk in the wardrobe. Yet this day, the words that came to the shaved nib of her quill troubled her soul.

She turned her head in the direction of the window to stare out at the pearl-gray sky. A peregrine falcon sailed past her line of vision. Drawn to the stirring sight, she rose from her bench at the small writing table and moved closer, placing her palm against the rock wall. Filmy white clouds brushed the horizon. In the distance, gently sloped hills of emerald green rose beyond Ballymara's forest.

"I am not in the storm, nor in the fire, nor in the whirlwind, daughter. Hearken unto Me, for I am the still, small voice inside your spirit."

The gentle thought flitted through her mind, taking roost in her heart. It reminded her of a lesson Father Stephen once taught about the prophet Elijah, when God hid him in the cleft of the rock until the storms passed him by. And at last she began to comprehend.

Despite the whirlwind of Cormac's accusations. . .despite the storm resulting from the earl's belief in what surely must be lies. . .despite the agonizing fire that scorched Breanda at the very thought of becoming Cormac's bride—she recognized truth. God was in none of those things. He was the still, small voice that whispered to her heart. The voice that assured her of Ardghal's innocence.

She bowed her forehead to the cold stone. "Almighty Father, I seek forgiveness. I've been neglectful in my prayers and in seeking Thy face. I've yet to understand why this happened, but Thou perceive and understand all things. Protect Ardghal. Keep him safe. I beg Thee, let not Cormac's plan for vengeance come to fruition. Hide Ardghal in the cleft of the rock till the storms pass him by."

She shuddered at the thought of his possible capture. Four days now, the earl's soldiers had been searching for Ardghal, with Cormac leading the men. The earl commanded that he be brought back alive, but at the memory of Cormac's murderous eyes at the tournament, Breanda feared for Ardghal's life.

Her gaze lifted to the heavens and a flock of birds in the distance. "Where is he, Lord? Why has he not sent word to me by messenger? I believe he's alive. For surely, if he were not living, I would feel it within my heart."

Watching the birds, she thought of the pigeons the earl used to deliver urgent messages to remote districts. The birds flew to their original nest, in this case what used to be her parents' manor, and from there, another pigeon was sent to carry the message to another castle. . . .

Elaine stepped into her chamber. "Pardon, m'lady, but Padrac, Sir Ardghal's squire, wishes to speak with ye."

"The lad?" She furrowed her brow. "Very well. I shall meet him in the courtyard."

"He asked the meeting be private."

"Near the dovecote, then. No one should be there this time of day." She assumed the reason she named the location was because she'd been thinking of the birds.

Within a short time, Breanda joined Padrac. Loud cooing could be heard from beyond the round timbered walls of the structure where hundreds of birds were kept. The squire, who was four and ten, raked a nervous hand through his dirty brown hair. His eyes darted about the area, as though fearful someone might see them.

"You wish to speak with me?" Breanda prodded.

"Aye, m'lady. On the day of the ambush, I ran with news to the castle as Sir Ardghal told me to do. But in the forest I came upon the men who'd attacked us. I hid close enough to hear them. Another man was there. He asked if the deed was done, and they said yea, that they'd left only my master, Ardghal, wounded, so he could not give chase. But that he was alive. The man said 'well done' and handed over a coin pouch."

Excitement tingled through Breanda to hear testimony that her beloved was indeed alive. "This man—can you describe him?"

"He stood taller than the others and was slight of build. Dressed in fine linens. But there's more."

"Go on."

"The bottom half of his ear was missing as though it had been shredded by a wild animal."

"Have you told the earl this?"

"Oh no, m'lady. His lordship mightn't give heed to a simple squire like me. But I knew you would listen. Sir Ardghal spoke well of you often."

"You've done a good service for your master, Padrac. I shall see that you are rewarded."

"I speak not for the reward, Lady Breanda, but for Sir Ardghal himself." He looked down as though ashamed. "I delayed coming forward because I feared Lord Cormac, but I speak now. I would do anything to help my master."

Breanda smiled. "As would I. Now, go, fetch the keeper of the dovecote.

Your words have given me a plan." She lifted her gaze beyond him, to the round building.

The boy scurried off, and Breanda mentally formed the message she would send. Surely, 'twas not coincidence that she'd been thinking of the pigeons and told Padrac to meet her here. Peace enveloped her, and she sensed God's guidance for the first time since the day of the ambush.

At last, she could do something to help Ardghal.

Chapter 7

Ardghal faced down his grandfather, who stared at him with the disgust one would show vermin. Graying brown hair hung to the shoulders of his crimson cloak trimmed in squirrel. His visage was lined with age, but his form appeared sinewy and muscular, and he stood tall, taller than Ardghal.

"Why are ye here?" Niall O'Cullen asked, pressing his palms to the long table that stood between them. "What curse has come upon me that ye bring the wrath of the Anglos upon our head?"

"The choice is not mine to be here. I seek Lady Breanda. She was abducted by men bearing the O'Cullen colors."

"No clansman of mine did such a deed."

"Someone did. We were ambushed."

Niall narrowed his eyes. "And so the lofty Lord Garland exacts vengeance upon us, even laying the blame at his own whelp's feet."

"*What?*"

"Your father seeks your capture and ours." Ardghal blinked, stunned, as the man continued, "Aye, I ken the devil who sired you. Me daughter was foolish in thinking she could hide it. She made haste in taking for herself a husband and clansman whom afore she could not abide. She should have drowned ye at birth, and I might have done the deed meself had I known the trouble you'd cause."

Ardghal fought the fierce emotion that threatened, both at the knowledge that the earl had declared him an adversary and that his grandfather knew his parentage. He struggled to keep his voice level. "If the earl has sent soldiers, they are strong in number. 'Twould mean war against your clan. You cannot survive such an attack."

"A conclusion I'd already reached."

Ardghal thought quickly; only one solution seemed apparent. "Niall O'Cullen, whatever our differences, we must put them aside and aid one another. Give me your word that you had no hand in this matter, and I shall do all within my power to return you to the earl's good graces. Give me Fearghus and other strong fighting men to accompany me, and we will find those responsible."

Niall scoffed. "Ye think me a fool that I would send me warriors with you and leave the rath at the mercy of the earl's soldiers?"

"Then give me Fearghus only. I give you my word; I mean no harm. I loved my máthair and would not hurt her people. Keep in mind the risk is also my own. Lady Breanda is pledged to me. My future hangs in the balance until I can find her *and* prove my innocence."

As though no longer concerned, the chieftain sank to his high-backed chair and plucked up a roasted leg of mutton from his wooden trencher. He took a bite, chewing as if his meal was of greater importance, though Ardghal sensed his tension. Niall peered at him with half-closed lids. "Me messenger gave word the girl's been found. By your half brother on the day of her capture."

Cormac? Ardghal digested the news. *How could he have found her so quickly?*

"I also heard the earl intends to give your betrothed to him in marriage. The announcement's to be made at a feast nigh unto a week."

The news struck Ardghal a mighty blow. *Breanda to marry Cormac? No! Does she, too, doubt my loyalty?* Working to keep his expression blank, Ardghal returned the chieftain's calculating stare with a steadfast gaze.

As if coming to a decision, the man grunted. "Take Fearghus. Find those responsible. Me word I've given, and we're none of us to blame. But heed this warning, Ardghal. If ye do anything to bring harm to our clan, I'll see you dead." He pulled a silver disc from his robe and tossed it across the table. It hit the wood with a clunk and shimmered in the firelight. The amulet.

"Fearghus will return your sword and steed. Go."

Ardghal retrieved the amulet and wasted no time in doing just that.

Having supped, Breanda prepared to leave the spacious great hall.

"A word with you before you retire to your chamber," Lord Garland said.

Tensing at his somber tone, she waited. Except for a few servants removing the remnants of dinner from the low trestle tables, they were alone. The knights had quit the building and headed for their sleeping quarters.

"I understand you made a visit to the dovecote today."

Breanda stiffened. The keeper must have revealed her plan. He hadn't been keen on her idea, without first gaining permission. Her duties as lady of the castle, a title gained upon her fourteenth year after Lady Garland's death, included overseeing the servants of Ballymara. Not issuing urgent messages to outlying regions.

"Aye, my lord."

He released a heavy sigh and drained what was left in his chalice. "Ardghal's treachery is hard to accept—how well I know! Had I not seen the message or learned of the ambush, I would believe his innocence. The revelation that I'm his father was difficult for him to bear. 'Tis time for you to release fruitless hopes grounded in wishful fantasies."

"I cannot, my lord." A mist of tears veiled her eyes, but she lifted her chin in defiance to them. "His squire witnessed a meeting between those rogues in the forest, as I've told you."

Her guardian scoffed. "A lad given to wild tales."

"I believe him."

"Aye. But you've a gentle heart, often perceiving good that's truly absent. Ardghal wasn't among the dead, and he's not made contact with me. What else am I to surmise but that he's rebelled? Padrac reveres the ground upon which Ardghal walks. Is it so astonishing that the boy would concoct such a story to help his master?"

Breanda shot to her feet, but other than stiffening her shoulders and staring down into his shocked countenance, she did not move. "Perhaps not. Yet what I do find astonishing is how swift you are to accuse Ardghal, the man whom you've treated as a son for eight years. The man who *is* your son. And in that time, he's shown you nothing but selfless service and undying loyalty."

Working to rein in her anger, she gentled her voice. "Forgive me for speaking harshly, my lord, and I beseech you to grant me this petition. Delay the announcement of my betrothal to Cormac until a thorough search has been made for the evil men about whom Padrac spoke. Send soldiers to hunt them down." She inhaled a steadying breath. "And if they've not been found four weeks hence, I shall do as you say and marry Cormac."

His jaw tensed. "Matters of war are not for a maiden's shoulders to bear."

"But surely you do not wish to start a battle that should not be!"

"Breanda! Curb your tongue." Rare anger swept across his face as he upbraided her, startling her into silence. "You *must* accept the truth. Ardghal's heart has turned from us. He has sided with the O'Cullens, who've broken the treaty of peace. Cormac rescued you from those who would harm you, and it is to him I owe my good faith." He rose from the table, his expression grave, resolute. "The announcement will be given on the morrow, and the bans made. The wedding will take place *one* week hence when the nobles assemble here for talk of warfare. What I have decreed shall be so."

Helplessness gnawed at Breanda. Sinking to her chair, she watched him leave the great hall. Alone, she buried her face in her crossed arms and silently wept.

Ardghal, my beloved, I know you're not what he says, what any of them say. Prove them all wrong, and return to me. I've done all I know to do.

Ardghal and Fearghus rode past a thundering waterfall and along a narrow path that led out of the copse of thick trees. They approached Glendalough's monastery. Beyond the nearest wooded hill, the glowing orb of the moon rose, and Ardghal's thoughts flew to his beloved. *My dearest Breanda, what must you be thinking. If only you knew how my heart yearns for you, how I long to hold you in my arms and kiss away your every fear. . . .*

"Someone comes," Fearghus said, breaking into Ardghal's reverie.

A monk in a cowl shuffled from the lit doorway of one of the stone buildings, cupping a candle with his hand.

"My sons. All is well?" he asked.

Ardghal reined in his mount. "We seek a place to rest for the night."

"Come, come. Have you eaten?" The man motioned to a small building near the church. "Stable your horses and share me table."

Within a short span, Ardghal and Fearghus sat across from their host, who introduced himself as Brother Cleary. His age-spotted hands were stained with red and blue ink at the fingertips, doubtless from the illuminated manuscripts such monks were noted for composing, detailed paintings accompanying scripture verses. His tonsured hair was almost white. A spiderweb of lines stretched across his round face, but his blue eyes were merry. Chin to his chest, hands folded in prayer, he said a litany of grace over the meal. Fearghus squirmed, restless, but Ardghal put in his own quiet petition.

After spooning a thick brown pottage into his mouth, Brother Cleary looked up. "Have we met? I sense a familiarity about your face."

"I am Ardghal of Ballymara, but, no, we've not met."

"Ballymara?" The monk straightened in surprise. Peering more closely at Ardghal, his gaze fell to the amulet. "I've seen that before."

Ardghal fingered the ruby in its center. "My mother gave it to me the night she died."

The monk sank back in his chair as if struck with a revelation. "Her name was Maggie, was it not?"

Ardghal's eyes widened. "You knew her?"

"Only twice did I look upon her face, when she sought my counsel." He grew thoughtful. "Such a comely lass but so weighted with sorrow. The Lord has blessed me with a keen mind, and she was not easy to forget."

Ardghal tore a hunk off the bread, stuffing it into his mouth. He didn't want to hear again how the earl had wounded his mother.

"I see you've not forgiven him."

"Who?" Ardghal looked up.

"Your father."

The bread went down with difficulty. "You know?"

"Aye. 'Twas for that reason your mother sought me. She could not conceive after she bore you and judged that she was being punished for her past sin. She made confession and sought the Lord's forgiveness the second time she visited." He thought a moment. "Nigh unto ten years past."

Ardghal blinked in surprise. "I never knew. 'Twas shortly thereafter she took sick and died."

"I'd heard of her death." The monk leaned forward, his expression compassionate. "My son, you must release this anger you hold toward your father."

He did not ask how the monk could know such things. He was a man of God after all.

"I've tried but cannot. And now he seeks my life."

Ardghal sensed Fearghus's body jerk as the man swung a look his way.

"Pride is a terrible thing," the brother commiserated. " 'Tis the root of a man's destruction. Your father's sins are his own; they're not yours to bear, nor must you regard them as grounds for punishing him. Make not the mistake of confusing sinful pride for righteous anger. 'Twill do you naught but harm. Rather, show those who've wronged you mercy, as our heavenly Father has shown you mercy by sending His Son to absolve your sins."

Astounded by the monk's perception, Ardghal choked down the emotion that rose to his throat with the last morsel of bread. "I fear my destruction is already upon me if I cannot find those responsible for laying the blame at my feet. Even Breanda, the woman dearest to my heart, doubts my fealty and love. Why else would she agree to marry my half brother, when she'd given her pledge to me?"

"Lady Breanda of Ballymara." The monk actually smiled. "Of course. Please, wait here."

Bewildered, Ardghal watched the elderly man shuffle from the room.

"So the earl be your athair?" Rancor seethed from Fearghus's tone.

Ardghal released a weary breath. "Be assured, the knowledge brings me little pleasure."

"Yet ye swore ye would help us try to prevent a war. Why?"

Ardghal seethed in incredulous anger. "D'ye think me so heartless I would not help me own clan? I'm an O'Cullen, too, remember!"

When Ardghal slipped into his old way of talking, Fearghus grinned for the first time since Ardghal's capture. "Aye, ye may be at that."

Yet another ember of truth branded itself deep into Ardghal's soul. "And I am Anglo."

Fearghus sobered. "Aye." He returned his attention to his pottage.

While Ardghal waited for the monk's return, he thought more on the holy man's words. He *was* prideful. Taking glory in his prowess of being one of Ballymara's most accomplished knights and in defeating his opponents while giving none of the glory to God. Smug in the fact that the earl had always highly favored him. He'd even borne a prideful attitude that Breanda returned his love and had chosen him above all others. And now all had been stripped from him. His good name, the earl's favor, Breanda. He took a long swig from the chalice set before him.

Aye, he was incensed with the earl for his delay in speaking the truth and in taking advantage of his mother. But his affection for the man had not waned. In the last village he and Fearghus came to, Ardghal surreptitiously heard word that he was suspected of being a threat to the earl. As if he could harm the man who'd once saved his life and reared him! He held back a dry chuckle at the irony. Lord Garland and his men assumed him eager to take the earl's life, thinking that he'd sided with the O'Cullen clan for war. While the chieftain, his grandfather, believed that Ardghal strove for the clan's demise. How fearsome he must seem!

He gave way to a humorless bellow, aware of Fearghus's odd look toward him. The man must deem him as mad as a swineherd. Ardghal merely shook his head and bowed it into his hand.

Although the royal blood of two nations coursed within his veins, he had no home, no family to call his own. He was lost in a web he himself had helped to make.

Almighty Father, I've been brought low by my sinful pride. I humble myself before Thee now and ask Thee to forgive my foolishness. A strange calm filtered through Ardghal at the prayer that filled his heart, allowing him to relax and finish his meal.

The monk soon returned, a slip of curled parchment in his hand. His thin lips stretched into a smile as he handed it to Ardghal. "I received this message by pigeon today, which by now most assuredly has been spread throughout the region. Perhaps it will help put your mind at ease over your lady love."

Ardghal knit his brows at the peculiar statement but unrolled the minute scroll, penned in Latin. His heart leapt with astonished exhilaration at the news then pounded with love for the woman who'd not abandoned him:

> *Find the man with half an ear. He alone knows who was behind the ambush in Wicklow Mountains. Ardghal is innocent.*
> *Lady Breanda of Ballymara*

Chapter 8

M'lady? Ye must dress. Many have gathered for the feast."

Breanda looked with disinterest at the splendid cote-hardie of green silk, its sleeves and neckline richly embroidered in gold. She waved her maid away and again scratched words onto the parchment with her pen.

"Ye've grown pale these past days." Elaine's voice quavered. "Ye be slippin' away from us, and that's the truth."

"'Tis only my heart that's ill. Fear not, I shall play the role of the obedient ward and do as I'm told," Breanda replied in quiet monotone. "Yet how can I be expected to find even a morsel of pleasure in this matter when my heart belongs to Ardghal?"

Elaine broke down, and Breanda swung her gaze to her bowed head in surprise. "Elaine?"

"I beg pardon, m—m'lady. I never woulda done such a thing had I known the trouble it would cause. Despite his threats, I never woulda done it."

"What threats? Who?"

"His lordship, m'lady. He ordered me to spy on you the night Sir Ardghal learned who truly sired him."

Breanda drew in a sharp breath, setting down her quill. "Why would Lord Garland command such a thing?"

"Not himself. 'Twas Lord Cormac gave the order."

So *that* was how Cormac had learned Ardghal was his half brother. Nonetheless, Breanda's mind was weary from lack of sleep and couldn't think past that revelation.

Elaine sniffled. "I heard him gloat to one o' the knights that soon he would control the manor and the lands left ye by yer father."

Faith, she'd been a dullard. Of course that was why Cormac was eager to marry her. His aloof yet victorious glances aimed at her since her rescue had made Breanda wonder what he might be plotting. His first love was power, his second greed. Still, there was little to be done in any case. Many men married for land and, with it, the power they could attain. Such was the way of things; there was no law against it.

Breanda managed a smile for her distraught maid. "Be at peace, Elaine. I do forgive you, though your part in the deception didn't bring me to this moment. And I know how formidable Lord Cormac can be." She looked at the gown laid out on the bed. "Now cease your tears and help me dress. 'Tis time I made my appearance."

Yet Elaine continued to sniffle as she assisted Breanda. Staring into her round mirror of polished steel, Breanda noted the pallor of her own face beneath the complex arrangement of small plaits Elaine had earlier styled around the one thick shank twisted into a braid that traveled down her back. Her appearance was without fault; only her eyes remained haunted. As Elaine fastened a decorative chain of gold around her hips, Breanda felt shackled, a captive to her future.

Lord, grant me the courage to do what I must.

Breanda entered the great hall, well lit with copious candles impaled on iron-spiked stands and a ringed candelabra hanging from the lofty, timbered ceiling. The spacious room was packed with knights and other guests. They sat on benches along the tables, which were lined in rows upon the flagstone floor. These men had come from surrounding estates, accompanying their noble lords, who sat along one side of the high table and would later talk over the matter of war against the clan O'Cullen and anyone who sided with them. Her heart heavy, Breanda stepped onto the dais and took her place at the earl's long table.

"Verily, I am the envy of every man present. On the morrow, lovely Breanda, you shall be my bride." Cormac's eyes were bright. With wine or his victory, she had no way of knowing.

A page poured water from a ewer into a bowl for Breanda to wash her hands. The feast commenced as servants brought in dishes of mutton stew. Breanda had no appetite for what followed. Heaping platters of roasted venison, mutton, and boar, as well as goose, plover, and a fish pie were served to her table of honor on the dais, then to those below. Throughout the feast, she picked at her dish of mushrooms with roasted hazelnuts while watching the men at the low trestle tables as they devoured their meat, throwing their bones and rubbish to the floor, where the hounds bounded over the fresh rushes to gulp down their own feast. The crunching of bones the dogs chewed mingled with the clamor of men's voices in conversation and the sprightly notes the minstrels played in one corner.

Breanda missed the Irish minstrel who'd often visited the castle. She preferred his poetry and harp to the lute this Anglo played. She failed to understand why the viceroy would deny to the Anglos all things Irish, though the earl once tried to explain to her that the English Crown feared that the Anglos had become more Gaelic than the Irish people themselves, and the king didn't want to lose his power over Ireland.

Power. 'Tis always about power.

Frowning, Breanda quenched her thirst from her silver goblet. Dreading the passage of time that brought her closer to her wedding day, she conversed little with her cousin, the new Lady Barbour, who sat on her right. Nibbling what food she could stomach, Breanda continued her assessment of the guests. Those few ladies in attendance were dressed as splendidly as she, while many noblemen wore the popular counter-changed style of clothing, with heraldic designs and jagged edges in serrated, diverse shapes.

Weary of surveying the nobles, her attention drifted to three monks at a table near the wall. They still wore their hoods, doubtless to dispel the chill. Suddenly her heart seemed to cease beating, then hammered within her breast as she briefly caught sight of a face hidden within a brown cowl. As though he felt her intense stare, the monk slowly swung his attention her way. Their eyes met and held.

She dropped her dining dagger. It clattered to her trencher. Cormac looked at her.

"Breanda?"

Realizing the danger, she lowered her gaze but not soon enough. With a loud hiss, Cormac threw down his goblet.

Ardghal realized his folly at allowing his attention to stray and rest on Breanda the moment Cormac glowered his way. Knowing to put off the plan would be madness now, Ardghal shot up from the bench and tore back the hood that disguised him. Running to the dais and the opposite end of the table from Cormac, he further ripped the slit he'd made in the monk's cloak, to free his weapon, and tore his dagger from its scabbard.

The feasting knights, caught unawares, were still scrambling to their feet by the time Ardghal came up behind the earl. He clapped his forearm to the man's thick chest and shoulders, drawing him backward. With his other hand, he held his dagger at the earl's throat, careful not to let the blade touch skin. Cormac halted his advance, though he kept his weapon positioned.

"Come no farther," Ardghal warned him and the soldiers, who now circled the high table, their swords also raised to fight.

"You would end my life so easily?" The earl uttered the words as though torn from his heart.

"Nay, my lord," Ardghal responded just as quietly. "I seek not to take your life or your lands or your wealth. I seek only to redeem my good name and that of my clansmen and could think of no other means to gain opportunity to do so." Louder, so all present could hear, he said, "I ask only that you allow me to speak. Afterward, if you wish your guards to clap me in irons, I'll not resist."

He heard Breanda gasp. Under his taut forearm, he felt Lord Garland stiffen then relax. "Lower your swords," the earl ordered his men.

"Father—"

"Be still, my son." Lord Garland halted Cormac's protest. "Let Ardghal have his say."

Ardghal waited until his fellow knights obeyed before lowering his dagger from the earl's throat. The men closest made as if to rush forward and apprehend him, but the earl raised his hand to stop them.

"I stand before you, a man falsely accused," Ardghal began. "If I were guilty of the charges laid upon my head, think me so foolish as to enter your castle with so few men and with so many men-at-arms against me?"

The earl nodded once. "You speak wisely. Continue."

"I searched for Lady Breanda but was weakened from a wound I obtained during the ambush. The O'Cullens found me and tended to me. When I awoke, I learned I'd been blamed for the attack, I and my mother's kinsmen. Later, I came across a message of import, which led me to search for the man I bring before you today. Fearghus," he beckoned. "Bring him forward."

Still wearing the borrowed monk's cloak, with its hood now away from his face, Fearghus gripped the arm of their prisoner. He forced him to walk to the dais, then snatched off their captive's hood as well.

"The man with half an ear," Breanda gasped.

Ardghal briefly swung his attention her way, gentling his expression. "Aye. He admitted that an English nobleman hired him to arrange the ambush and abduction. He, in turn, hired a small band of deposed clansmen to do the deed—men who'd been cast from the O'Cullen tribe years ago and had become outlaws."

"Give me the name of this nobleman who instigated such a crime," the earl demanded of Ardghal's prisoner, outraged. "I'll see him punished, and you'll suffer also, if you'll not do as I say."

The man with half an ear lifted his weasel-like face, dark eyes glittering. "The name you seek, my lord, is Lord Cormac of Ballymara. Your son. He arranged the ambush and the lady's abduction to point the finger of blame at Sir Ardghal."

A pall of silence smothered the great hall. Many turned disbelieving eyes toward Cormac.

"'Tis a lie!" he spat, advancing toward his former conspirator. "I'll slay you where you stand for speaking such a falsehood."

"I'll not suffer alone for your indiscretions," the man shot back. "There are others who saw us meet. Ask them!"

"I've procured the names, if you wish them," Ardghal added.

The earl turned dismal eyes his son's way. "Why, Cormac? Why have you done this thing?"

Red suffused Cormac's face. "Always him. You always hold fast to his words—never my own." He lifted bitter eyes to Ardghal. "Well, he'll not again take what's rightfully mine!"

Cormac rushed forward, swinging his blade. Ardghal barely withdrew his sword from its scabbard in time to deflect the powerful blow. Time and again their weapons crashed as Ardghal defended himself and was driven back off the dais. Cormac's rage drove him, and he fought with passion rather than skill. Ardghal gained the initiative, fencing in Cormac. With one leap, Cormac jumped atop a table. Trenchers and goblets flew as he kicked them aside. Men scurried out of the way of the slashing blades.

Ardghal's shoulder throbbed, but he fought as fiercely as Cormac. To do less would mean to die. He could see that truth written in Cormac's eyes. As he parried each blow, the knowledge that Cormac had placed Breanda in peril with his selfish plan of abduction ignited a new blaze within. His thrusts came more swiftly. He took charge of the assault, feinting and thrusting, until Cormac fell back in retreat. Stumbling onto the flagstones, Cormac evaded Ardghal's blow, lifting his weapon high. Ardghal skillfully circled his blade round Cormac's, flinging the sword from his hand. With one step, Ardghal closed in, placing the point of his steel against Cormac's heaving chest.

Ardghal's arm shook with fury as he glared down into his half brother's eyes.

"Go on," Cormac said from between clenched teeth. "Do it."

None would blame him. Cormac had committed treason. He should die.

"No, my son, not this way. . . Grant him mercy."

Sensing the still, small voice deep within the center of his being, Ardghal gritted his teeth until his jaw hurt.

"No, Ardghal," Breanda spoke quietly. "Not this way." She stepped up beside him. Her eyes were gentle, beseeching, but understanding, as well. "Not this way."

Ardghal's entire body trembled with fierce emotion; Breanda's words were confirmation of the voice he'd heard within. And yet. . .

He swung his gaze to Cormac, whose eyes defied him, even at the point of death. "I should run you through with my sword for the harm you've caused." Ardghal sucked in a lengthy breath through his teeth. "Yet to do so, I'd be no better than you." He hurled his sword to the flagstones, where it landed with a final clang.

Cormac let out a scoffing laugh. "You're naught but a coward. I should have had them kill you, instead of sparing your life—"

His taunt cut off as he realized what he'd said, and his gaze pivoted to his father.

"So," the earl boomed, rising from his chair. " 'Tis true! You conspired against me, against all of Ballymara. Your terrible greed and jealousy nearly cost us a war." He straightened, his expression formidable. "Leave my sight; I refuse to look upon your face again. Henceforth, you are exiled to England, nevermore to return to Ballymara—to all of Ireland—for as long as you draw breath. And may God have mercy on your black soul."

Two knights grabbed Cormac's arms and hoisted him to his feet. He shook them off and glared at his father, then at Breanda and Ardghal, but said not a word.

Once the guards removed Cormac from the hall, the earl sank to his seat, his face gray, twisted in pain. A long moment elapsed before he addressed Ardghal in a low voice.

"I've done you a great disservice, you and your kinsmen." His weary glance took in Fearghus before returning to Ardghal. "Verily, you've shown me nothing but allegiance, and I've repaid your honor by wrongfully hunting you as a criminal. What recompense can I offer to atone for my folly in believing so great a lie?"

"I seek no reward, save one." Ardghal held out his hand to Breanda, and she took it, stepping close to him.

A ghost of a smile lifted the earl's lips. "Ah, yes. However, I can do much better than that. Come hither, both of you."

They did so, and the earl looked out over the great hall, at his guests. "Today, in the presence of all gathered here, I, Frederick Garland, Earl of Ballymara, Baron of Fairway, stand before you and claim Ardghal as my rightful heir. Flesh of my flesh, my son." A loud stir of excited conversation rumbled throughout the hall, but the earl raised his voice to be heard above it.

"Although English law forbids him my title, he shall have my wealth and Ballymara upon my death. Once I laud Ardghal's valor and tell of how he prevented hostilities from rising up against the English Crown within the Pale, I doubt not that good King Edward will grant his consent."

His father—now proclaimed as such to all of Ballymara—clapped both hands to his shoulders and kissed Ardghal. Stunned, he could only stare. The bitterness he'd carried for the earl had begun to dissolve after his talk with Brother Cleary, and he sensed that their relationship was on its way to being restored.

"My lord?" Breanda asked, as though prompting him.

A trace of amusement flickered across the earl's face. "Patience, lass. I've not forgotten." Again he looked over the crowd. "As a reward for his bravery in preventing what surely would have amounted to dissension and war, I give to Ardghal the hand of my ward, Lady Breanda, in marriage. Since the guests are already assembled here, let the wedding commence on the morrow! I trust there are none to object?"

A thunderous cheer arose from the men gathered. Ardghal clasped Breanda's arms, drawing her close. Her eyes shone with love for him. Suddenly realizing where they stood, Ardghal smiled at his father and said a soft, "I am overwhelmed, my lord. . .Father. Thank you."

The shimmer of moisture in the earl's eyes bespoke his great emotion.

When at last Ardghal and his bride-to-be were done with the congratulations, he led Breanda out of the great hall. Drawing her with him into an alcove, he laid his hands upon her slender waist while she wrapped her arms about his neck. "I cannot begin to tell you how wondrous it is to hold you again," he said.

"You need not tell me. I've dreamt of you here with me endless times this past fortnight." Her expression waxed serious. "I never doubted you, Ardghal. Not for a moment."

"No." He smiled. "You wouldn't. You're my dearest champion, Breanda. A lady of true valor. When I read the message you sent by pigeon, I never realized it more."

Heart overflowing with love for her—this woman he thought he might never again have the right to claim as his own dearest beloved—Ardghal brushed his lips against Breanda's in a tender, lingering kiss.

Epilogue

Fifteen Years Later

Sunlight paled and a delicate mist beaded the air as Breanda commenced a slow, joyful dance near the round tower. Here, in this silent area, she'd often experienced an intimacy with her Creator she felt nowhere else. . . .

Perhaps 'twas because here she and Ardghal were joined as husband and wife. Beside her, on bended knee, he'd spoken his vows before the priest: "I, Ardghal of Ballymara, do vow on my sword and on my name and on my honor to defend the faith and observe all the obligations of holy matrimony." Throughout the years, they'd celebrated happiness as well as endured sorrows, growing closer in their union and becoming stronger because of both. Toward Cormac, they practiced forgiveness, daily praying for their childhood companion. Of late, they had heard he'd taken a wife in England, who was, sadly, as greedy as he. . . .

Perhaps 'twas because here she and Ardghal dedicated their firstborn son, Frederick. At four and ten, he was now a squire to Sir Padrac, who himself once served as Ardghal's squire. Tilting at the quintain was Frederick's favorite exercise as knight-aspirant; indeed, he had grown accomplished at charging with his lance or sword and attacking the dummy of chain mail with shield on its post. Truly, he was his father's son. Now she and Ardghal had a quiver full of children, all with dreams of their own: their three boys to become knights of valor like their father, who'd become a legend in all of eastern Ireland; and their three girls to learn what it meant to be noble ladies of courage like their mother, so they could please the future husbands Ardghal would one day find for them. . . .

Or perhaps 'twas because here, fifteen years ago, Ardghal first pledged his love and wrapped a shamrock around her finger. Breanda laughed and twirled around, lifting her face to the mist.

"My lady fair, what has you so joyful?"

At the long awaited—albeit amused—shout, she spun around and squealed, then took off running to greet Ardghal, who galloped on horse-back down the hillside toward her. Even after so many years of wedlock, her heart never failed to leap at the sight of her husband. He dismounted and plucked her up in his arms, then swung her around and gave her a sound kiss. Pleasure burst like streams of sunshine warming within her.

"Dear wife, I have missed you."

"No more so than I." She pulled his face close again, pressing her lips against his, relishing the kiss that deepened and lengthened and caused her heart to pound with joy.

The mist fell heavier upon them. He ran with her to the stone archway fronting the church. Safely underneath, he set her on her feet and retreated a step until his shoulders hit the arch. "Let me look at you; a fortnight has never seemed so long. . . . Ah, Breanda, you are lovelier than when you were a girl, if that is possible. You are well? You should not be out in such weather."

Breanda knew by his concern that he referred to the babe she now carried. "The sun shone bright when first I came, and the mist approached me unawares, but I am strong. And I shall give you another strong son as willful as his father."

"Or a fetching lass as spirited as her mother," he teased in return.

She brushed back his damp hair that had started to silver. Apart from a few new lines that creased his face, he was the same vigorous man she'd known in spirit and in body. "And would you have me any other way, good sir?"

At her saucy smile, he let out a great bellow of a laugh. He lowered a swift kiss to her lips. "Nay, my fiery wild rose. You are most certainly the woman the Almighty designed for me."

Satisfied with his response, she switched the subject to what she'd prayed about each night since his departure. "All went well? Your grandfather was pleased?"

"Aye. The builder I found to design the stone fortress created a for-midable structure. The O'Cullens will hold out well should another clan attack." He grew thoughtful. " 'Twas the first time my grandfather actually smiled at me."

Since the earl's death four years past, Ardghal had become guardian of Ballymara, with the young king Richard's approval, and oversaw im-provements to the villages, including the construction of an orphanage nearby. Having been orphans themselves, he and Breanda considered the latter a project of the heart. Using a portion of the wealth left him by the earl, he also helped his mother's clansmen by building them a stronger defense against their enemies.

As a result, the O'Cullens now showed Ardghal respect and no longer presented a problem to the English Crown by refusing to acknowledge the king as their sovereign, though other clans beyond the Pale still resented English control. Fearghus's eldest son had come to Ballymara Castle to serve; he and Niall, Breanda and Ardghal's second son, had become close friends.

Breanda was pleased that the O'Cullens were now allies. The viceroy's edict fifteen years ago amounted to nothing; scarcely any Anglos had observed the law not to marry the Irish and to do away with Irish customs.

"Niall O'Cullen smiled?" She scoffed. "Perhaps when the great falcon makes his home 'neath the Irish Sea. Years ago, when first we met, he looked fierce, as if he would rather see my head on the end of his spear."

"As chieftain, he must show strength. Yet he's had a thorny life, Breanda. All three of his wives and his sons died. My mother and aunt were all he had left. In truth, he holds you in high esteem and thinks you 'a fine lass.'"

Breanda lifted her eyebrows.

He grinned. "I jest not. He gave me a token to give you, in gratitude for all I've done. It belonged to his head wife." Ardghal pulled something from the pouch at his waist and lifted the hand that contained her wedding band. He pushed a ring onto her forefinger.

'Twas a golden shamrock with an emerald in its center.

"Oh," Breanda murmured. " 'Tis beautiful."

"Remember the words I spoke on the day we first declared our love?" he asked softly. "As sure as the shamrock is green, as sure as Three are in One..."

"Our love will be redeemed by the Father, Spirit, and Son," Breanda finished in as sacred a whisper. "And He has redeemed it, Ardghal. He most surely has." They exchanged a kiss, slow and tender. When next they drew apart, she inhaled a wondering breath.

"Ardghal, look."

He turned, and awe slackened his expression.

A many-colored rainbow made a vivid arc in the sky, beginning above lush treetops and ending on a far-off hill. "God's promise to us," Breanda whispered. "He is so faithful. So merciful."

"Aye." Ardghal circled his arm about her waist. "He is at that."

A native of Texas, **Pamela Griffin** is a bestselling author and has contracted approximately 50 books in both contemporary and historical romance. Writing to her is more ministry than career, and it thrills her to hear evidence of God working in others' lives through her stories. She loves to hear from her readers and can be contacted at: words_of_honey@juno.com.

The Stranger's Kiss

Yvonne Lehman

Yea, though I walk through the valley of the shadow of death,
I will fear no evil: for thou art with me;
thy rod and thy staff they comfort me.
PSALM 23:4

Chapter 1

1815

Don't you know we would do our best to make a proper marriage for you after Emmie is married?" Aunt Christine snapped. "Must you take your own cousin's beaus?"

"What?" Jenny jumped up. "I would never do such a thing. How could I?" Although Jenny was three years older than Emmaline, she knew it only proper that Uncle Thomas and Aunt Christine's daughter be married before their poor relation. "I don't know what you're referring to," Jenny stammered, "or who you're talking about."

"Who?" Aunt Christine mimicked. "Don't pretend innocence with me, Jennifer. You know I mean Lord Bodley."

"What. . .what did he say?" she asked helplessly.

"What did he say?" Aunt Christine mimicked, glaring at Jenny with icy blue eyes full of venom. "Only that he wants to marry you!"

Dumbfounded, Jenny stumbled back, bruising her thigh against one arm of the chair as she sank into it. Now she understood why, from the moment she'd entered the drawing room, she'd felt like she must have unknowingly committed some dastardly deed.

Uncle Thomas stood with an arm propped on the mantel. The elegant clothes he wore gave him an air of distinction but could not hide the overweight of his middle years. His midsection protruded quite noticeably. His flushed face suggested that he and Aunt Christine had recently engaged in a heated discussion.

Aunt Christine's face had turned a deep scarlet. Her pale hair, adorned with jewels, was piled high on her head. Jenny felt her aunt overdressed for early morning, but she would have chosen her attire with Lord Bodley's visit in mind.

"I've never encouraged Lord Bodley," Jenny protested, gesturing helplessly. "I despise him. I'd rather die than marry Lord Bodley! Simply tell him that. He and Emmaline can marry. She is perfectly willing and would make Lord Bodley a fine wife."

"I'm afraid no amount of persuasion is going to change Bodley's mind. We certainly have tried." Aunt Christine lifted her hands and eyes toward the ceiling in exasperation.

Jenny stood and took a few steps toward them. "Surely Lord Bodley wants a wife equal to his social standing," she said. "I would not be acceptable in his circles."

"We exhausted every argument, Jenny," Uncle Thomas explained. "He has spoken to me about this matter on numerous occasions. It seems he is enamored not only by your looks, but also by what he calls your 'spirit' and quick tongue."

"I had hoped to put him off with that," Jenny wailed.

"Well, yes," Uncle Thomas said uncomfortably. "It has only served to entice and challenge Lord Bodley. And your background, Jenny, is as impressive as Lord Bodley's."

"Or it was," Aunt Christine interjected, "before your mother drove my brother to drink and ran off to America with that duke—"

"Christine," Uncle Thomas said in a warning tone.

Jenny gasped. "What?" Her heart began to pound. All her father had ever said while he was still living was that her mother had died and that they were never to speak of her.

Jenny touched her aunt's arm. "Did my mother die in America?"

"Never mind," Aunt Christine retorted. "It's enough to know that your mother disgraced the name of Greenough."

"Christine," Uncle Thomas implored.

Jenny's aunt sighed in exasperation.

"You see, Jenny," Uncle Thomas added calmly, "your situation of dire circumstances is not of your making. Lord Bodley understands that. He is willing to, um, look at Christine's family line, along with my own, which is not insignificant. He would not consider you an embarrassment. Any man would be fortunate. . ." His voice trailed off as he glanced toward his wife and found her glaring at him.

Jenny could not believe this. Uncle Thomas's every word, although apologetic—perhaps even complimentary—was clearing the way for her marriage with Lord Bodley to be not only acceptable but approved.

"How can I marry him?" Jenny argued. "I don't love him."

"Love?" her aunt spat. "Fiddlesticks."

Jenny glanced at Sir Thomas, who seemed busy studying the tips of his shiny black shoes. Did he wonder, as she did, if Aunt Christine had just implied that her own marriage was loveless?

Aunt Christine took a deep breath and continued in a barely controlled voice. "Few of us are so fortunate as to find love. A woman must think of her future, and it's a certainty," she said, rolling her eyes toward the ceiling again, "that you'll never get another chance like this one."

"I could never marry him," Jenny insisted. "Uncle Thomas, please. Can't you do something?"

The man shook his head. "Bodley will consider no one but you."

"But of course that's impossible," Jenny protested. "Surely you agree."

"We most certainly do not agree!" Aunt Christine answered forcefully. "You have taken your cousin's beau. The least you can do is have the decency to go through with it."

"You want me to marry him?" Jenny looked from her aunt to her uncle.

Aunt Christine lifted her head, and a gleam came into her eyes. "Since Lord Bodley insists you are the only person who interests him, and he is willing to go to any lengths to get you," she answered with a sneer, "then yes, we do insist you marry him." After a pause, she continued. "He even resorted to blackmail."

"Blackmail?" Jenny queried.

"It seems your uncle Thomas lost fifty thousand pounds to Lord Bodley at the gaming tables. Now Bodley intends to collect."

Jenny walked over to face her uncle. "Uncle Thomas. You are selling me to repay a gambling debt?"

He shifted his weight from one foot to another, obviously discomfited. "It's not like that, Jenny," he replied. "He would have found another way. It's a good opportunity. One that may never come your way again."

"But I don't even like him," Jenny protested.

"Would you rather be committed to an asylum?" her aunt snapped.

"I'm old enough to go out on my own," Jenny countered. "I can start a school."

"According to the terms of the papers establishing our guardianship, we are your legal guardians until you're married," Aunt Christine reminded her. "If you defy us and refuse Lord Bodley, we can place you in an asylum."

Jenny shuddered. She'd heard of such terrifying places, but even that threat would not deter her. "Marrying Lord Bodley would be worse than an asylum," she declared, her head held high. "I will not do it."

Aunt Christine ignored her outburst. "You will do it, Jennifer," she said with an icy calm voice. "A guardian has complete and absolute power over his ward. It is our duty to see that you marry well. Besides, what parents would allow their children to attend a school where the mistress was a disobedient young wench? An unappreciative ingrate who defied her guardians?"

"But I'm not that," Jenny protested.

Her aunt's smug smile halted Jenny's words. "Exactly," the older woman agreed. "And being a sensible girl, you wouldn't allow such implications to be made about you."

Jenny knew this was no idle threat.

"Now," her aunt continued confidently, "Lord Bodley has asked for your hand in marriage. Your uncle and I have signed the settlements. Today I shall puff it off to the papers. Do you understand?"

Jenny felt trapped. Uncle Thomas remained silent. The awful thing was, she could see that from their point of view the situation was an opportunity of a lifetime. How could she ever have thought her personal desires would matter? Her own mother had abandoned her. Could she seriously expect more consideration from an aunt and uncle? She silently nodded her head in agreement.

"It seems Bodley has been planning this for some time," Aunt Christine explained, seeing the matter as settled. "The dressmakers will arrive this afternoon. Bodley says he will spare no expense. You will have whatever gowns you wish. All you have to do is snap your fingers."

"You mean," Jenny protested, "Lord Bodley is providing my very clothes?"

"Silence, Jennifer," Christine commanded. "You must learn to behave as a lady who will be escorted in royal circles, rather than as a schoolgirl who stands around with her tongue hanging out. Now," she directed, "next week we will go to Bodley House to announce the engagement."

"A week?" Jenny gasped. "I should have a year, at least. . .to prepare."

"Really, Jennifer," her aunt chided. "You are twenty-one years old. And Bodley is a passionate man. He's very anxious for the marriage to take place. As I said, he is overcome with—"

"Oh, please," Jenny wailed, placing her hands over her ears rather than hear about Lord Bodley's passions. His wicked words and grasping hands had already given evidence enough of such desires.

Turning quickly, she raced from the drawing room. Her steps did not slow until she came face-to-face with Emmaline, who stood poised at the bottom of the main staircase.

One look at her beet-red face and hostile eyes told Jenny that Emmaline had eavesdropped. "It is not my doing, Emmie," Jenny wailed helplessly, "and I won't go through with it."

Emmaline jerked away from Jenny's outstretched hand and ignored her imploring eyes. "That's prittle-prattle and you know it," she snapped. Gathering up her pale lavender skirts, Emmaline turned with a flourish and stalked across the floor toward the drawing room.

Jenny could only race to her bedroom, but she refused to fall upon the coverlet, like one condemned to a fate mapped out for her by the likes of Ignatius, Lord Bodley.

Shivering, she looked out her windows. The pea soup fog that shrouded her view seemed to have crept inside her mind, for no clear escape from Bodley's preposterous proposal lay before her.

"You're so like your mother," Aunt Christine had often said, as if that were something to be ashamed of. Suddenly Jenny's head lifted, and she set her jaw. Perhaps that was her solution. Her mother had run away to America. Well, she could run away as well.

Determination fired her eyes. No matter what it took, she would escape marriage to Lord Bodley.

Chapter 2

For days, Jenny lived with Emmaline's acute disappointment at losing Lord Bodley to her poor cousin. Emmaline stomped instead of walked, snapped rather than talked, and threw objects all over her bedroom. She slammed doors so hard that Jenny suspected they might fall from their hinges. Any protestations Jenny made about her unhappiness with the engagement fell on decidedly deaf ears.

One morning a seamstress arrived to measure Jenny for gowns and have her select materials. As she stood near the end of her bed, surrounded by the chattering woman and her imperious aunt, Jenny noticed her cousin pause at the open doorway.

"Don't stand out there gawking, Emmaline," Aunt Christine chided. "The seamstress will measure you for new gowns, too."

"To soothe my ruffled feathers?" Emmaline snapped. She turned in a huff and headed toward her own bedroom.

At the end of the week, Emmaline's anger was further fueled by the arrival of an entourage of Bodley's servants to be at Jenny's disposal. They numbered more than the entire Cottingham household servants put together.

"The house is so overrun with servants, there's scarcely room enough to breathe," Aunt Christine complained whenever her daughter was within earshot, but Jenny observed that as soon as Emmaline left, Aunt Christine's face colored with excitement. The woman obviously relished giving orders right and left.

Perhaps it was because his gambling debt was canceled by Bodley that Uncle Thomas strode around so importantly. He tried to suppress his pleasure when near Emmaline, but the look of satisfaction on his face was unmistakable. Jenny thought he smiled at her approvingly when the others weren't looking.

"I'll end up on the shelf," Emmaline wailed, one night at dinner. "My only prospect will be some dried-up old man with half a fortune."

"Don't be such a ninny," her mother chided. "As soon as this matter is settled, we can concentrate upon finding you a suitable husband."

Emmaline pushed her chair back from the table and stood up. "It was my understanding that's what we were doing all along," she countered viciously. "It was all a trick, wasn't it, Jenny? You were very clever when you pretended you hadn't set your cap for Bodley. You must have pinched your cheeks and bit your lips to make them rosy."

She threw her napkin onto her plate of half-eaten food and stalked away before Jenny could reply.

Although accustomed to Emmaline's tantrums and moods, Jenny regretted that she could not tell the sullen girl what was in her heart. She and Emmie had shared many good times when they had lived at their country home and ridden horses together across the meadows. They'd dreamed of their future. But after they moved to the London town house, Jenny began to feel the difference in their social standing.

Now with Bodley's proposal, everything had turned upside down. Instead of being a companion to Emmaline, Jenny had become the center of attention. She looked over at her aunt, who shook her head while chewing a bite of food. She knew Aunt Christine and Uncle Thomas would prefer this frantic activity to be centered on their daughter.

Aunt Christine took a sip of water. "At least," she said, stabbing another bite of food with her fork, "Bodley's money will be in the family."

When the day of the engagement party arrived, Emmaline's anger had receded into a sullen, stony silence. Jenny knew she could say nothing to redeem herself in her cousin's eyes. In all honesty, Jenny couldn't say she didn't enjoy the change of routine and status. It was almost a fairy tale existence—except for Bodley, whose likeness fell far short of the handsome prince in such fantasies. Jenny could visualize his swarthy face. She'd seen his jiggling movement, especially when he swung his cane forward when he walked. When she'd accompanied him and Emmaline on an outing, she'd watched the movement of his arms, revealing the fur lining of his cape. A top hat had covered the almost naked crown of his head, while wisps of thin brownish hair curled above his ears and at the back of his snowy white neckcloth.

He cannot buy me. But it was necessary that Aunt Christine, Uncle Thomas, and Lord Bodley believe she had accepted the proposed marriage as her destiny.

Aunt Christine's words, about Jenny's mother running away to

America, kept racing through Jenny's mind. The more she thought of the idea, the more it intrigued her. But any means of escape would be useless unless she had convinced everyone that she had agreed to this outrageous charade. Until such a time, her aunt and uncle would certainly continue their ever-watchful attendance.

"You look lovely, m'lady," said one of the attendants, bringing Jenny's thoughts back to the task at hand.

"Thank you, Mindy," Jenny murmured, staring at her reflection. She wore cheek rouge and powder. Her dark hair was arranged fashionably with several dark curls gracing her fair, clear complexion and the back of her long, graceful neck. Yet another curl fell along the front of one shoulder, where the lace of the dress ended and the satin began. The rest of her raven hair was piled high on her head. For the first time, her lips were painted a rosy red.

Jenny had decided that this one evening she would dress as she liked. After the event was over, she must drop out of sight, perhaps even change her name, in order to start a life of her own. She was not concerned with public approval, for those above the class of governess, companion, or tutor had never recognized her in social circles, nor had Emmaline required her friends to include Jenny as an equal.

The time came to go to Bodley House. Jenny had not allowed the Cottinghams to see her dress during its making. Now, Uncle Thomas, Aunt Christine, and Emmaline stood at the foot of the stairs as Jenny descended. She rather hoped her aunt and uncle would consider her choice of color scandalous and not allow the engagement party to take place.

Jenny's deep burgundy gown was cut fashionably low in front. Unaccustomed to exposing her skin, as did the parading debutantes, Jenny had insisted upon an inlay of sheer burgundy lace, in a rose pattern, to form a high scalloped neckline. Three gathered ruffles fell gracefully over her shoulders, forming the illusion of puffed and gathered sleeves. The hemline draped into folds, exposing light rose-colored ruffles, the peaks adorned with burgundy satin roses.

The ruffles matched the color of her evening gloves. Bodley, having discovered the color of her dress from a servant, had sent jewels for her to wear. Clusters of roses, set with diamonds and rubies, graced her earlobes and left wrist.

Looking distinguished in his evening clothes and graying hair, Uncle Thomas stared at Jenny. His face paled. Without a word, he turned and headed for the front door.

Emmaline, wearing a dazed expression, forgot she was not speaking to Jenny except to ridicule or snap. "You look different," she said.

Jenny could have replied that she hadn't chosen to grow up overnight. She preferred to be that young girl who had ridden through the park with Emmaline not long ago and giggled about the eligible young men.

"It's a lovely dress," Aunt Christine admitted stiffly. "But you might have picked something less flamboyant for an engagement party. Something white." She sighed with resignation. "On second thought," she murmured, "that's exactly what Bodley would want. His tastes have apparently been tainted by the world."

Jenny inwardly winced at the insult, but she had already determined that, degrading as it was to have to go to such a party and pretend she liked the idea of being bought by Ignatius, Lord Bodley, she would bide her time. Soon, she would bear no more insults.

Jenny knew she looked more fetching than ever in her life. She had always detested the pale colors that Emmaline wore, which complimented her cousin's fair skin, light hair, and gray eyes. Emmaline looked attractive in them, but they did nothing for Jenny's dark coloring and deep blue eyes.

"You look lovely, Emmie," Jenny complimented, admiring her cousin's pale yellow gown with white lace ruffles. The younger girl would have no trouble attracting young men, now that they knew Lord Bodley's attentions were directed elsewhere.

"Thank you," Emmaline said stiffly and then hurried toward the door. Aunt Christine, dressed in blue satin, followed her daughter.

Lord Bodley had sent his own carriage pulled by four black horses to convey Jenny to his house that evening.

"You girls ride in Bodley's carriage," directed Uncle Thomas. "Lady Cottingham and I will take ours."

Emmaline hesitated, then grudgingly obeyed. Jenny tried to make conversation, but Emmaline pretended not to hear and looked into the darkness outside the windows of the carriage.

"I'm not going through with this, Emmie," Jenny said doggedly. She watched as Emmaline's reserve wavered. Finally her cousin looked at her.

"You know there's no way out, Jenny. Once my mother has made up her mind about something, there's no changing it."

"But there has to be a way." Jenny leaned forward. "Help me, Emmie," she pleaded.

"What can I do, Jenny?" Emmaline asked miserably. "Bodley wants you. And from the fuss he's made, nothing will change his mind."

Jenny's eyes flashed as she spoke excitedly. "We'll have you marry him.

You can wear a heavy veil so he won't know. Then he can later be surprised that it was you instead of me."

Emmaline broke out in the first genuine laugh Jenny had heard from her in days. "Oh, Jenny. Your fantasies again. It would be funny if it were not so serious. Bodley deserves to have something like that done to him." Her voice dropped. "Only if it were someone else instead of me."

"Maybe if you told him of your love, Emmaline."

Emmaline stared at her in wonder. "Love, Jenny? I have never loved Ignatius Bodley."

Jenny gasped. "But you said you wanted to marry him."

"I'm more realistic than you, Jenny, even if I am younger," Emmaline replied. "To have married Ignatius, with all his connections, was beyond even my wildest dreams. Now, to think he courted me just to get to you." She clenched her gloved hands. "It's humiliating, but I have to go tonight and pretend I don't care in front of all those people who suspect I do. Frankly, I'd rather see Ignatius, Lord Bodley in his grave!"

"Oh, Emmie," Jenny gasped. She quickly looked away from Emmaline's distraught face. Then she admitted quietly, "I, too, would rather see Lord Bodley in his grave than in my marriage bed."

Through the carriage window, she glimpsed the lamps illuminating the front of Lord Bodley's London home. Unless her plans were successful, that home would soon become her prison.

Chapter 3

The Cottinghams and Jenny joined other guests alighting from their carriages and stepping down onto red carpet, which stretched from the sidewalk to the main steps in honor of the occasion. The soft glow of candlelight illuminated every window in the impressive mansion, one of Bodley's many residences scattered across England.

When shown to her private suite on the second floor, Jenny thought of the many times she had been separated from the Cottinghams at fine houses. Whereas then she had been placed with other companions, now Bodley had elevated her position. She wished she might discover that she was wrong about his character and find he had some redeeming qualities she could learn to love.

But as she descended the main stairs, feeling all eyes upon her, a sudden wave of distaste swept over her. She recalled the party at Lady Cramerson's two weeks earlier. During one of Jenny's unguarded moments, Bodley had maneuvered her to a spot behind a potted palm.

Such shenanigans had been a game of his since she had first made an appearance when the season had begun. He had played not only hide-and-seek, but also touch-and-grin. Such behavior was often tolerated by servants, whose livelihood depended upon their jobs, but she was in no such position.

"I'm Emmaline's companion," she'd reminded him staunchly. "Not in your class, my lord." It had taken every ounce of her self-control not to tell him what she really thought about his ungentlemanly behavior.

"If Lady Emmaline were to become my wife, would you accompany her to my household as companion or milady's personal maid?" he'd asked, a sly grin upon his face.

"I would not," she retorted, forgetting for a moment that Aunt Christine had warned her not to do anything that might harm Emmaline's chances with Lord Bodley. Her dark eyes flashed fire. "Already I have assisted in the schoolroom," she informed him. "I will become a teacher. Or," she added, inching away from him, "I might even take a job in a factory."

He threw back his head and laughed. "Ah, my little spitfire. You do not belong in a factory." He leered and thrust forth a sweaty hand.

Gasping, Jenny swatted at his hand. "I'll scream," she warned.

"And I'll say you saw a mouse," he answered with a triumphant smile.

Now, as Jenny descended the stairs, she felt like a mouse caught in Lord Bodley's trap. There was nowhere to hide. Forcing a neutral expression onto her face, she extended her hand to Bodley's outstretched one. He bent down and planted a slobbery kiss upon the back of it. Jenny forced her lips to curve in a slight smile.

Leading her to the entrance of the great ballroom, Bodley himself, with Uncle Thomas and Aunt Christine in close pursuit, introduced her to his guests. The experience simply reinforced her opinions of those who looked down their aristocratic noses at the lower social classes.

"Oh, I had no idea that Emmaline had such a delightful cousin," one grand lady exclaimed, although she had often visited the Cottinghams' London home.

"I did not know Sir Thomas and Lady Cottingham were blessed with such a lovely niece," other guests murmured.

Jenny knew they had seen her at other events when she had served as Emmaline's companion. Or perhaps they had not seen her but had taken her for granted as a necessary convenience, like a piece of furniture.

Jenny could not dwell long upon the hypocrisy of so many of the guests, for she was obligated to dance with her intended. She attempted conversation, but he only praised her beauty and complimented her on her choice of gown. He held her much too tightly, despite her protests. Any faint hope of a decent life with Bodley became more unlikely with each passing moment.

Jenny had been dancing for almost an hour when she noticed the man. He stood at the top of the staircase, leaning against the banister. She thought him quite handsome and wondered if he were evaluating the young ladies from that vantage point, wondering if any present might make him a suitable wife. Then she blushed at the thought, for his eyes seemed to follow her wherever she went.

Despite all attempts not to do so, Jenny found herself looking for the man, who changed positions every so often. She wondered if he would ask her to dance, but he did not. When other men danced with her, she pretended they were the stranger—so incredibly handsome, tall, elegant, and mysterious.

Smiling, she allowed herself to glide over the dance floor, except when Bodley held her so tightly she could scarcely breathe. She avoided his leering gaze but could not escape the uncomfortable feel of his hot, raspy breath on her neck. He was not much taller than herself, she realized. And he was overweight. His ruddy face did not help matters, nor his lewd remarks about what they would do once they were married.

She began to realize the advantages of being plain and wished she had not dressed up so much. But, she told herself, it wouldn't have mattered. He had made his advances even when she'd worn youthful garments and her hair had been braided in a style appropriate for a prim young companion.

The stranger knew he must remain as inconspicuous as possible, without raising suspicion that he was deliberately doing so. And it was not difficult to remain at the top of the staircase under the circumstances.

His eyes could not get their fill of her. They gazed upon Jenny, followed her every step, assessed her every move. He had become mesmerized—spellbound by her beauty, her grace, and what appeared to be playful attempts at assuaging her ardent admirer, soon to become her husband. She was Bodley's intended! That thought wrenched his heart. How could she be attracted to such a bloke as Bodley? But of course, he knew. Bodley had been the highest bidder for her hand, what else?

But now that I've found her, how can I let her go? That was impossible. Now that he had found her, saw her, he must meet her, speak with her. With the dark thoughts that penetrated his mind, a shadow passed over his countenance as he contemplated in his heart and mind what he must do.

Jenny did not see the stranger during the seven-course dinner. Sir Thomas's formal announcement of the engagement at the end of the meal received applause. After the requisite toasts, the ladies rose to leave the men in private for their customary drinks and conversations. As Jenny started toward the door, the handsome stranger passed by her. He paused briefly, only long enough to make eye contact, and she saw that his eyes were a dark brown, almost black. His eyes gleamed as he looked on her with apparent approval. He seemed different from the other men she had met at Bodley's party, but although she intended to look at him boldly and flash him a charming smile, she instead found herself suddenly quite shy.

Jenny reprimanded herself for the blush she felt on her cheeks. She lowered her eyelids and felt a quickening of her breath. When she looked up again, he nodded politely, then turned away and moved swiftly toward Bodley's table.

While throughout the evening all of the ladies had indicated a willingness to accept Jenny's newfound position, they did not push their attentions upon her as the ladies broke into smaller groups and strolled the huge formal gardens. For the most part, they left her alone. She had been the poor relation of Emmaline's, and although she knew of no enemies among the aristocracy, neither had she formed any close friendships with this privileged group.

Jenny walked through the gardens, along a narrow path for some distance, then came to a small glade in the midst of trees and fragrant blooming shrubs. Beneath a tree sat a small table and two chairs. A warm breeze stirred the tender green leaves, gently lifting them. The full moon's silvery sheen filtered down between the branches, creating an ethereal setting.

Surrounded by such enchantment, Jenny did not want to think of her predicament or of her future. For the moment, she preferred to escape with her fantasies. Lifting her face to gaze through an opening in the canopy of tree limbs, she glimpsed the shimmering stars. If one wished hard enough, surely dreams would come true.

In the dining room, the gentlemen raised their voices to a loud and boisterous pitch. They made comments and joked in a way that could not be done in the presence of ladies. Bodley himself poured drinks for everyone. Then Sir Thomas, reveling in his position as guardian of the bride-to-be, took a pinch of snuff from his silver box, as was the mark of a fashionable gentleman, and offered to pour the next round of drinks. He graciously handed Bodley his drink, then proceeded around the table, toasting the forthcoming marriage. After these were downed, another gentleman offered yet another toast.

The stranger inched his way back until he reached the doorway, slipped from the room, and hastily exited. Outside, he looked around but could not find the one he sought. Thinking himself unobserved, he slipped around to the darkest part of the garden, found a path, and followed it into the more heavily wooded area.

Hearing footfalls, Jenny's heart began to pound, fearing it might be Bodley. Bringing her hand to her throat, she gasped as a gentleman stepped into the glade. He stood still a moment, not taking his eyes from her, then set his drink on the small table. He coughed lightly and seemed about to speak.

Jenny felt a sudden instinct to lower her eyes and run because of the quivery feeling his presence evoked. But no, she told herself, she would not be shy. She might be forced to spend the rest of her life with the grasping arms and the slobbering mouth of Lord Bodley. This might be the only chance she'd ever have for a moment like this. If forced into the arms of Bodley, she would dream of this encounter. She wanted to be like a heroine in a novel and rush into the stranger's arms. With one quick step, she moved toward him, but just as they were close enough to touch, she turned away quickly and stumbled. Reaching out her hand, she caught hold of the table.

Embarrassed by her forward actions, Jenny felt her face growing warm. She had made a goose of herself. She was about to turn and run when his voice stopped her.

"Wait," he implored, and she stopped, not looking at him. He wasn't touching her, but his voice held her captive. She didn't really want to go.

After what seemed an eternity, she shyly lifted her eyes to his. She thought his eyes would be laughing or mocking, but they were not. He seemed concerned.

"Why are you crying?" he asked, and she realized a tear had slipped down her cheek.

Because she was not adept in the art of lying, she simply told the truth. "I wanted to be near somebody...attractive. Just once in my lifetime. Something I could always remember."

His eyes held an element of surprise. "But you're engaged to be married," he said.

"I was forced into it," she said desperately. "I can't go through with it. I can't bear the thoughts of his. . ." She lowered her eyes and swallowed hard. "His kissing me or even touching me."

"I see," the gentleman said finally. He stepped closer. She felt his hand at the side of her waist. She lost her breath when he lifted her chin with his fingers, tilting her head back.

The silvery moon highlighted his handsome face. Time stood still while something deeper than moonlight burned in his dark eyes as they caressed her face. An eternity passed before his lips parted and she felt the warmth of his breath against her face. Instinctively, she leaned forward and closed her eyes. Her mouth trembled beneath his touch, as his lips moved, caressed, and gently explored her lips.

Jenny felt limp, despite his supporting arm. Then, surprised at her own boldness, she lifted her arms and wrapped them around his neck. He did not protest but pulled her tightly against himself. His lips took control of hers in a demanding, lingering kiss.

Suddenly, he stopped. A low moan escaped his throat, and he held her head against his chest. His fingers caressed a curl, and their touch thrilled the skin at the nape of her neck. She wondered if it were her heart, or his, that was thundering so. Her whole being felt alive as never before. She felt safe and protected and wished she never had to move.

"My!" he said finally, shakily. "I feel rather faint."

Jenny turned her head to look up into his handsome face. A strange expression hovered about his dark eyes.

"I think," Jenny said low and breathlessly, "in the novels, it is the lady who feels faint."

He chuckled and moved back, holding her away by the shoulders. "That was your first kiss?" he asked with incredulity.

"Well, Lord Bodley has moved his slobbery lips past mine, but I never let them stay," she affirmed. She hesitated and spoke low. "Now I am glad."

"Was it all you expected?" he asked seriously.

Jenny closed her eyes and hugged her arms to herself. "Oh, so much more. I shall always remember it. No matter what. I have something to dream of for the rest of my life." She suddenly looked at him with tenderness. "Thank you," she said. "Thank you so very much."

The stranger took a deep breath, then smiled. "My pleasure, I assure you, my lady." He reached for her hand, turned it over, and gently placed his lips on its palm.

"I would do anything to get out of this coil I'm in," she said suddenly, as he let go of her hand.

"Anything?" he questioned, raising his expressive eyebrows.

Jenny was not quite sure she knew what she meant by that statement. After a few moments, she nodded. "Yes, I think so."

He started to say something when they heard someone calling, "Jenny! Where is my sweet Jenny?"

Jenny stiffened. Fear filled her heart.

A look of distress crossed the gentleman's face. "I must go," he said hastily. "Don't worry. I will come for you tomorrow. But do not mention having seen me or anything about me. All right?"

Jenny didn't understand; nevertheless, she nodded. The stranger disappeared into the woods, just as Lord Bodley entered the glade. She looked around for the stranger, but he was gone. She wondered if she had imagined the whole thing. She had read that people did that sometimes when situations were unbearable. But she could not have imagined the tingling sensation his kiss had awakened on her lips and throughout her being. She detested the thought of Bodley intruding upon that emotion.

"Ah, there you are, my pretty," Bodley said, holding a glass. He took a big swallow and set the goblet on the table. "I thought you would be waiting here for me."

Bodley reached for her, and she barely managed to dodge his hands. He smelled heavily of strong drink. With a strength unknown to her, she pushed Bodley away. He swayed back a little, laughed, picked up a goblet from the table, and drank from it.

Jenny asked quickly, "Do you know I have no dowry?"

He shook his head. "Don't care," he said. "I have enough for both of us. You'll never want for anything. I knew you were beautiful, but tonight is more than I egs...espec...ecs..."

He shook his head as if trying to clear it, laughed, and emptied the contents of the goblet down his throat. Then he awkwardly set the goblet down and drank from the other one.

He started toward her. Jenny put out her hand.

"Did you know," she asked firmly and loudly, hoping to penetrate his mind if it was still functioning, "that my mother was an immoral woman?"

His eyes opened wide momentarily. "No," he droned, rather taken aback.

"Yes," Jenny said with renewed bravery. "She caused a terrible scandal, and when it is known, you will be a laughingstock."

"Ah, ha!" he said, and a lecherous expression crossed his face. He raked her body with his eyes. "I knew there was something different about you," he slurred. "A doxy, eh? I like that, by George. I really like that."

Jenny realized her confession had only served to incite him further. He staggered nearer.

"I don't love you, Lord Bodley," she said firmly.

"You'll learn, my sweet," he said with confidence and again drank from the goblet.

Jenny felt helpless. She couldn't bear to be alone with such a disgusting man for even a few minutes. How could she spend a lifetime with him? She moaned, lifted her skirt, managed a sidestep away from the drunken man, and ran from the glade, uncomfortably aware that while she had temporarily made her escape, she had also succeeded in becoming more of a challenge to him.

Lady Christine and Emmaline were standing by a fountain in the garden near the back of Bodley House when suddenly Jenny ran up to them from the path. She looked at Emmaline. "He won't listen to reason," she wailed. "But somehow I will get out of this. I promise, Emmaline, if it's the last thing I do."

Several women standing nearby turned their heads and stared at the distraught young woman as she ran into the house.

Speaking in a whisper so that others would not hear her, Lady Christine said to her daughter, "That girl's going to get a thrashing if she upsets these plans. Go talk to him, Emmaline. Soothe his ruffled feathers."

Seeing the hesitation in Emmaline's eyes, Lady Christine murmured, "Even if they go through with this marriage, she will end up like her mother, and he will be on the market again. It wouldn't hurt, my dear, for you to be gracious and compliant. When his ardor has abated, then he will see you for the lady that you are."

Emmaline still didn't look pleased with the situation, but she nonetheless made her way to the glade. Almost immediately she returned. "He just sits there drinking and mumbling, shaking his head," she reported to her mother. "Jenny must have really upset him. He didn't even realize I spoke to him."

"Perhaps we can get him to come back inside. I'll see what I can do." Lady Christine headed for the glade. A few minutes later, she returned. "Lord Bodley has fallen to the ground," she announced with alarm. "He's thrashing about. Oh, I'm afraid he's quite ill."

She rushed to the back door. "Please help," she said to a gentleman inside. "Lord Bodley needs assistance."

Several gentlemen followed Lady Christine to the glade.

Inside the house, Jenny descended the main stairs, carrying her wrap and evening bag. Upon rushing in a few minutes earlier, she had pled with her uncle to take her home. He had, to her surprise, agreed to do so immediately.

Now, she and Sir Thomas stared as men carried in the trembling Bodley, mumbling incoherently. His eyes rolled back into his head.

"Too much to drink," said one gentleman uneasily, while another laughed nervously.

"Our apologies, ladies," said another.

"Get him to his bedroom," suggested a perturbed guest.

With extreme effort, several men managed to hoist the uncooperative Bodley up the stairs.

"We should indeed leave," Sir Thomas said, as if mortified at Bodley's condition. Other guests expressed similar sentiments.

Just then Sir James Crittenbough came down the stairs, his face pale. "I say, Sir Thomas," he said, "could you ensure that a doctor is summoned?"

"A doctor?" Sir Thomas questioned.

"Indeed," Sir Crittenbough replied, glancing toward the ladies as if concerned that he would alarm them. "I suspect Sir Bodley needs a doctor immediately."

"Very well," Sir Thomas replied. "I will fetch him myself."

Crittenbough turned to the ladies. "You will perhaps be more comfortable in the drawing room," he said unevenly.

"What is it?" Lady Christine ventured to ask.

"Too much drink, I'm sure," Crittenbough replied, but his voice revealed the concern he attempted to conceal.

The merriment of the occasion had already died away, and silent gentlemen stood back from the elegant staircase. Other gentlemen lined the elaborate hallway above. The ladies gathered in the drawing room where they exchanged a few words in quiet tones.

Finally the doctor arrived and hurried up the stairs, followed by Sir Thomas.

Soon Sir Thomas descended the stairs and came into the drawing room. Several other men followed and walked over to their ladies.

"Lord Bodley has. . .expired," Sir Thomas said, his last word barely audible.

Lady Christine put her hand to her throat and drew herself up. Emmaline let out a startled scream, then stifled it with her hand. The first thought that entered Jenny's mind was that she would not have to marry Bodley, but the situation seemed so unreal that she felt numb, experiencing neither joy nor regret. Looking up to find her uncle staring at her, Jenny wondered if he expected her to collapse.

"Let us leave, Thomas," Lady Christine said, picking up her skirts to move forward.

"I'm afraid, my dear," he said pointedly, "such action is not recommended."

The women stared at him questioningly.

"You see," he explained, "the doctor is asking guests kindly not leave the premises. He has summoned the magistrate."

The magistrate, after consulting with the doctor and learning about both Bodley's convulsions and his loss of control of bodily functions, agreed that the symptoms were more extreme than would usually be expected from drunkenness. However, he announced that he would leave the determination of cause of death to the coroner. In the meantime, he asked the exquisitely attired guests to volunteer any information that might shed light on the regrettable situation. Everyone agreed that Bodley had an incredible tolerance for drink and had actually imbibed less than usual that evening, because he had been preoccupied much of the time with his lovely intended.

The magistrate's suspicions increased by the moment, however, when he heard the remarks of the three ladies who, one at a time, had been alone with Lord Bodley in the glade. According to them and the doctor, Lord Bodley had progressed from seeming drunkenness, to incoherence, stupor, convulsions, coma, and then ultimately to death.

Immediately, the magistrate determined he would visit the glade. "Bring me lanterns," he commanded the servants, who hurried to obey. When the magistrate reached the glade, he muttered, "Now, that's odd." Lifting the goblet toward the brilliant moonlight, he saw dregs of something in the bottom of the glass. "Well, well," he added as he observed a faint ring of fine white dust near the rim of the glass.

The magistrate allowed the guests to return to their homes, but he sternly advised them to stay in London. He took the goblet with him, along with a guest list he obtained from the butler. Clearly, this was not the end of the matter.

Later that night, the coroner determined what the doctor and the magistrate had suspected. Lord Bodley had been the victim of arsenic poisoning. The victim's excessive drinking had hastened the effects of the poison.

Arsenic could be found in the pantry of any household, even the magistrate's, because it was used to kill rats. The most amateur killer would have easy access to the poison. The magistrate shrugged in resignation. The next day, he would begin the difficult task of questioning members of the aristocracy with due sensitivity.

The next morning, Jenny ate breakfast in her room. The Cottinghams had been pointedly silent on the ride home the night before, she assumed because their dreams of further social prestige had died with Bodley.

At midmorning, the magistrate arrived, and a servant soon notified Jenny that she was wanted for questioning in the parlor. She entered the room, and the magistrate motioned for her to shut the door. Jenny complied and quietly took a seat.

"Did Lord Bodley's drinking habits repel you?" the magistrate asked.

"Yes," Jenny replied, determined to answer truthfully.

"And you were unhappy about your engagement to Lord Bodley," he quietly stated.

Jenny wondered where he had learned that fact. "I did not love him," she replied softly, reluctant to speak ill of the deceased.

"Now about last evening," the magistrate continued, "when Lord Bodley met with his untimely death."

After reviewing the information she had given him the night before, the magistrate dismissed Jenny—for the moment. Soon he asked her down again to answer questions about her situation with the Cottinghams. Jenny readily praised her relatives for their kind and generous care for her during the past eight years. Once again she was dismissed.

But that afternoon, she was called into the parlor for a third time. Immediately, she recognized that the magistrate's tone had changed. For several long moments, he simply looked at her.

Then he asked sternly, "Are you positive that you have nothing, nothing more to relate?"

She could think of nothing more.

"Very well," he said and took his leave.

"Perhaps that's the end of the matter," Aunt Christine said, as soon as the front door closed behind the magistrate. "Surely he's aware we've told all we know."

"It would seem so," Uncle Thomas replied. "Please—enough unpleasantness. Let us speak of other matters."

"I think he's going to accuse someone," Emmaline said, her fair skin paler than usual. "Isn't that the purpose of the entire investigation?"

No one replied. Throughout the rest of the day and into dinner that evening, Jenny noticed that everyone seemed to be lost in their own thoughts. Even the servants performed their tasks with bland faces and downcast eyes.

Jenny picked at her food, feeling a strange queasiness in her stomach. The evening before at Bodley's house, she'd felt the magistrate had regarded her with respect as Bodley's intended. Yet today his words had held elements of accusation. Much as she tried to shrug off her concerns, Jenny knew in her heart that something was decidedly wrong.

The following day, the magistrate, accompanied by two Bow Street runners, requested that the Cottinghams, including Jenny, accompany him to a London courtroom.

The four members of the family stood in front of the chief magistrate, who questioned them extensively but uncovered no new information. At last he asked the Cottinghams to wait in a small room while he consulted with the other magistrates.

"I don't like this," Uncle Thomas stated as soon as the door was shut. "I don't like this one bit. There is no reason for us to be called down here unless they suspect one of us committed the dastardly deed."

Jenny's stomach suddenly felt hollow. She thought she would be sick. She had done nothing wrong, but why did she have this sense of foreboding?

"They need to take some action quickly," Uncle Thomas continued, apparently unaware of Jenny's nervousness. "The public demands swift justice in such cases because such a poisoning could happen to anyone—the poison being so readily available."

After what seemed like hours, the Cottinghams were finally summoned back to the courtroom. Jenny was instructed to stand before the chief magistrate.

"The evidence weighs heavily," he announced gravely. "The motive is clear." His eyes bore into Jenny's. "Did you not make the statement many times that you would not go through with the marriage to Lord Bodley?"

"Yes, but. . ."

He held up his hand, halting her words. "The motive is clear," he continued. "The accessibility to the poison posed no problem. Only one goblet had any trace of arsenic in it, and it was discovered in the glade where Bodley had taken ill. Numerous eyewitnesses have given identical accounts of who had gone toward and who had run from the glade where Ignatius, Lord Bodley became ill and thereafter expired."

Jenny was stunned. Did these men seriously think she had poisoned Bodley?

"Apparently, this is the work of an amateur, an emotional female who had not thought through her actions," the chief magistrate asserted. "Yet, the deed itself must be judged premeditated. The engaged couple spent considerable time in the glade. Only two others had gone to the glade after Miss Cottingham had run into the garden, quite distraught, affirming her intentions of not going through with the marriage. Her statements had been overheard by several witnesses.

"I and my colleagues have questioned you several times," he added pointedly, his voice becoming stronger by the moment. "We felt you held something back and hoped our suspicions would prove to be unfounded. However, the evidence is overwhelming."

The chief magistrate took a deep breath and announced in a dispassionate voice, "Miss Jennifer Cottingham, regretfully we have no alternative but to accuse you of the premeditated murder of Ignatius, Lord Bodley." Jenny had never fainted in her life, but upon hearing those words, darkness enveloped her, blocking out all reality.

Chapter 4

When Jenny regained consciousness, the first thing she saw was the incredulous, horrified faces of the Cottinghams. "You will immediately be placed in custody. Please follow the matron," the chief magistrate ordered. A large-boned, middle-aged woman helped Jenny to her feet and began to escort her out of the courtroom by a side door. As Jenny looked back at the Cottinghams, who seemed stunned into silence, she felt as if she had already been condemned. Her last sight before walking through the door and into a waiting coach was of Emmaline burying her face in a lace-edged handkerchief.

At least she was taken to a house, rather than to Newgate Prison, Jenny consoled herself. Her room was on the third floor, with walls covered in peeling gray paint, a bed for herself, a cot for the matron, a straight chair in front of a small dresser, a rocking chair, and a chest. When Jenny approached the small open window, the matron, who had introduced herself as Mrs. Millet, hurried to close it a tad, and Jenny knew the woman feared her prisoner might jump through it in an attempt to escape.

None of Jenny's personal items had been brought to her, and she still wore her plain gray dress. Attempted conversation failed completely. Jenny did not like the silent speculation of the matron, who seemed wary and watchful, lest Jenny attempt some dastardly deed.

"May I have something to read?" Jenny asked.

"We shall see," the matron replied, then asked the woman who brought the supper tray to look into the matter. Over an hour later, the woman tapped on the door and mentioned the vicar. After closing the door, the matron handed Jenny a Bible.

Jenny lay on the bed, propped up against a pillow, and tried to read. She had read some scripture before, and wanting to rid herself of fearful thoughts about her uncertain future, she turned to the love story of Ruth and Boaz. She loved the story of the poor young woman who had won the favor of a wealthy, kind man. She'd often dreamed that such a fate would befall her, but she wasn't sure about that anymore. She had met such a man, yet he had instructed her not to mention his presence and disappeared into the night. Then Bodley had died, and she now stood accused of murder.

She shuddered, unable to concentrate on the pages. She believed in God, of course, and had prayed to Him in the past—when she needed her mother and wanted her father to stop drinking. But God hadn't answered those prayers. If He cared about her, would He have allowed this to happen? She thought not. She closed the book. Never had she felt so frightened or alone.

The following morning, Jenny's fears increased. "You think I killed him," Jenny accused her aunt Christine, who had brought some of her personal items. "How could you think that about me?"

"Oh, Jenny. We don't know what to think," her aunt said uncomfortably, sitting on the edge of the bed near Jenny and twisting her handkerchief. "I should have realized how desperate you were. We really thought it best. I should have recalled. . ."

Aunt Christine stopped as if it were useless to continue, and Jenny knew she was about to refer to her mother. Her mother had been desperate enough to abandon her husband and child. Did Aunt Christine really believe Jenny had been desperate enough to commit murder?

"What will happen to me?" Jenny whispered.

Aunt Christine hesitated before saying, "We've only been told that you will soon be removed."

"Removed?" Jenny questioned, bewildered. She did not like the sound of that.

Aunt Christine nodded, and Jenny asked what that meant.

"I don't really know," Christine replied. "Your uncle Thomas has been asked to relinquish his guardianship, and someone, I don't know who, will provide you with legal assistance."

"How can that be?" Jenny cried. These were her relatives. Her only flesh-and-blood relatives. "To. . .a stranger? Who? Why? What does it mean?"

Aunt Christine stood and paced the floor, fanning her face as if the surroundings suffocated her. Finally she turned toward Jenny.

"No doubt someone who read of your plight in the newspapers took pity on you. An unidentified person sent a representative to Sir Thomas and paid him a considerable sum to do this. Your uncle admits this is highly irregular; however, it has been done legally and with the approval of the authorities. Already, you have gained the sympathy of the courts, and this person, whoever he may be, is apparently much better able to help you than our family. It is for your own good."

For her own good? It had been for her own good that she had been promised to Bodley. Now, Uncle Thomas had relinquished his responsibility to someone else, at a time when she needed help so desperately.

"But I'll never see you again. I'll be taken to prison. Oh, Aunt Christine." Jenny reached out her arms. Christine sat down on the edge of the bed beside her and hugged her close, visibly shaken.

"There's hope, Jenny," the woman finally said, untangling herself from Jenny's arms. "The chief magistrate has already exercised judicial leniency on your behalf."

"What does that mean?" Jenny questioned, bewildered.

"I don't know the details," her aunt replied. "Except it means a delay in your being formally charged. And, Jenny, were it not for this benefactor of yours, Sir Thomas would be obligated to hire attorneys, and to be honest..."

Aunt Christine lowered her voice after a quick glance at the matron, who seemed concerned only with her knitting. "We haven't the means we've sometimes led others to believe," she murmured. "I hope you understand, Jenny."

"Of course," Jenny replied in a small voice, glancing up at her aunt, who smiled faintly. Suddenly it seemed to Jenny that she was just going through the formalities until she would be...hanged? She felt helpless in the face of forces that seemed determined to bring her personal destruction.

"Is Uncle Thomas coming to see me?" she asked.

"He cannot even leave the house without being mobbed, Jenny. You can't imagine what a stir this has caused. And he's been so busy with the legal proceedings. As I said, these transactions are highly irregular. And now, since he is no longer your legal guardian, he may not be allowed to see you." She stood quickly, adding, "But Emmaline is waiting outside."

Aunt Christine seemed eager to get away, and Jenny couldn't blame the woman. Her aunt did kiss her cheek and say, "If you're innocent, Jenny, then you have nothing to worry about."

It was the "if" that stuck in Jenny's mind, and she was hardly aware of her aunt leaving and Emmaline entering the room until her cousin sat beside her and took her hand. Emmaline seemed sympathetic. "There are probably women all over Europe who admire you for this, Jenny. Those stuck in marriages they abhor and can do nothing about. You've probably given them ideas."

"You believe I did it, Emmaline?" Jenny asked desperately. "How can you?"

"Didn't you? Oh, Jenny, all the evidence. . ." Emmaline's voice trailed off, and a pained expression appeared in her eyes.

"But the evidence shows I had everything to gain, Emmaline. A title. Great wealth. Why should I kill him?"

"Because of your views on love, Jenny. You said that wealth and titles mean nothing to you."

Jenny was momentarily flabbergasted. "You told those things to the magistrate?"

Emmaline looked guilty. "I had to, Jenny. The truth must come out at times like this."

"You yourself said you would like to see him in his grave, Emmaline."

"But that was merely an expression, Jenny."

"I know, Emmaline. That's why I didn't mention your words to the magistrate. Or how upset your parents were when Bodley asked for my hand. Or you! I would not try to implicate any of you."

Emmaline looked distressed. "Well, Jenny, if you didn't kill Ignatius, who did?"

Jenny did not reply. Emmaline stared at her for a while, then attempted further conversation, but Jenny remained silent. Finally, Emmaline left the room. The matron closed the door behind the visitor and returned to her knitting.

Who did? Those words kept running through Jenny's mind. She had obeyed the stranger who said not to mention he had been there. She had not mentioned him for he seemed so far removed from such a matter. He was someone to think about when she was alone. He was the only man who had ever taken her in his arms and kissed her as if she were the most wonderful person in the world. She had felt protected and had wanted to stay in his arms forever. She had not wanted to tell those things to the magistrate.

She hadn't believed anyone would accuse her of murder. Now it was too late to say anything. To whom could she speak, anyway? There was only an uncommunicative matron nearby. Anything she might say now would appear to be a made-up story and make her look either more guilty or insane. Even her own relatives had doubts about her innocence, so how could she expect strangers to believe her?

On impulse, she had given her heart to that stranger in the glade. He had said, "I will come for you tomorrow," and she had believed that. What a gudgeon she was.

That evening when it was time to retire, a guard locked the door to the room so that Jenny could not escape after the matron fell asleep. The small action made Jenny feel even more like a prisoner. She became more aware of her surroundings—the stark, bare walls, the skimpy furnishings, and the matron now lying on the cot near the door.

A chill crept over her. It would be much better to be put to death than to be thrown in a prison with even more deplorable conditions. Then she remembered the day one of the Cottingham servants had come in wide-eyed and declared, "Ah seen a mon hanged, ah did!"

Jenny had listened to the exciting details with great interest, even to the man's swinging from the gallows and the hangman pulling his feet from below to ensure the noose was tight enough to break his neck or choke the life out of him.

She pulled the blankets closer around her but could not still her shaking. She covered her head lest her chattering teeth disturb the matron. During the long night, Jenny could find no escape into her fantasies. Reality was much, much too insistent.

The elegance of the coach that appeared at the front door the next morning astounded Jenny. It was white, trimmed in gold, and drawn by four magnificent horses. The dour-faced matron even registered surprise as she appraised the red velvet lining of the interior—hardly the usual mode of transportation for prisoners.

An officer of the law presented official papers to the skeptical Mrs. Millet, who wore a brown woolen shawl around her shoulders. The matron was simply dressed in a dark blue skirt and muslin blouse.

Mrs. Millet's black eyes darted from the papers to the officer. "Everything seems to be in order, however odd the situation may be," she said with a skeptical lift of her eyebrows.

The officer, Mrs. Millet, and Jenny climbed inside the carriage, and the officer sat opposite Jenny and the matron. His sympathetic eyes moved toward Jenny, and he spoke kindly. "Sometimes ladies are given special privilege," he said in partial explanation of the unusual turn of events.

Although they talked little, Jenny learned that the officer was a family man and had known the matron's late husband. Mr. Millet had been an officer, killed in the line of duty.

"We helped many a wayward youngster in our day, we did," Mrs. Millet assured him, and the officer nodded after a glance at Jenny and changed the subject.

The carriage sped far outside the city of London, over beautiful countryside, in the direction of Cornwall. Finally they came to a lovely village near the sea, and high atop a hill, far in the distance, gleamed a castle with golden-trimmed turrets that glistened in the sunshine.

They passed the village, where heads turned to view the magnificent carriage and horses. Jenny wondered what the villagers would say if they knew the carriage carried an accused murderess. She shuddered at the thought.

They turned onto a long winding road and traveled higher and higher, ever nearer the castle. Only after they were inside the great iron gates did Jenny speak. "That can't be a jail, can it?"

The matron looked confused. "No, it's not," she said, looking around nervously.

"Is the jail near here?" Jenny asked.

"None exists that I know of," Mrs. Millet replied, looking at the officer questioningly.

He shrugged. "Just following orders." He assured her that the other officer, riding with the coachman, was a fellow worker and a personal acquaintance of his for several years and could be trusted implicitly.

Soon the carriage stopped in front of the castle. The officer sounded the large knocker on the front door, and a butler responded. As if on cue, he was immediately flanked by footmen in uniform. Other servants lined the great foyer.

A distinguished gray-haired man, wearing a gray suit, strode from the study. Bowing low, he said, "Welcome to Withington Castle, Lady Jennifer."

Jenny curtsied, feeling quite bewildered by the unexpected turn of events. Might this be ridicule? Might it be punishment for having spent the past week being waited on by servants and attending the engagement party while, as everyone seemed to believe, she actually had a murderous heart?

This gentleman would certainly know she had no claim to be called "lady." She looked at Mrs. Millet and the officer. They appeared as puzzled as she.

The gentleman handed Mrs. Millet documents from the court, stating that, due to an appeal from the Crown, Jenny would be confined to the castle until the time a formal charge was made and she was brought to trial. The papers outlined Mrs. Millet's duties.

Jenny wondered if she would be imprisoned in the dungeon or a tower.

"Lady Jennifer," the gentleman said.

Jenny swallowed hard. It was difficult not to respond to his pleasant, courteous manner. At the same time, however, his dark gray eyes penetrated hers, as if he were trying to read her mind. He appeared to be in charge.

"I am Silas Bingham, of Bingham, Bingham, and Chadwick, attorneys-at-law," he said.

Mrs. Millet gasped audibly. Jenny had heard her uncle Thomas speak of this man. The famous Bingham, with a reputation known throughout Europe, stood before her. He did not look at all like the ogre he was portrayed to be in newspaper caricatures. He could get anyone free or convicted, depending upon his whim, they said. Few individuals, however, could afford his fees.

The officer stepped forward and bowed deeply. Silas Bingham nodded, then again turned his attention to Jenny.

"I am your attorney, my lady, employed by the illustrious Tilden Withington, the latest duke from a long line of Withingtons who, incidentally, laid the very foundations of this castle. We," he said, making a sweeping gesture with his hand that included the retinue of servants, "are at your service."

The servants introduced themselves, bowing or curtseying, and explained their positions in the household. Jenny had never known there could be so many servants in one place, but to run a castle, she supposed it necessary.

"Might I speak with you, sir," Jenny asked hesitantly, "before anything else?" She felt terribly self-conscious about being treated royally by servants dressed better than she. Was this a farce? Or an asylum?

Silas Bingham smiled. "I anticipated that," he said. "Please come with me."

He turned to Mrs. Millet. "I'm sure you would like to see your rooms, Mrs. Millet. The servants will show you. You will act in the capacity of chaperone to Lady Jennifer. That is a stipulation of the court."

Mrs. Millet followed the servant up the wide staircase to the south wing of the second floor.

After Bingham dismissed the officer, wishing him well on his return to London, he led Jenny to the study.

"Sit here, please." He indicated a large velvet chair near a huge marble fireplace and then sat across from her.

"You did not expect this, did you, Lady Jennifer?" he asked gently.

"No, sir," she replied and faintly returned his smile.

"You are here by royal appeal, in the custody of His Grace, Tilden Withington. He personally approached the king, making an appeal on your behalf, which was granted. This is your home for the present."

Bingham walked over to the desk, picked up some papers, and brought them over to Jenny. "As you will see, there are official seals on the papers. Sir

Thomas Cottingham has relinquished all his rights as legal guardian, and you are now the ward of Tilden Withington."

"His. . .his ward?" Jenny asked with incredulity.

"Not in the sense of your aunt and uncle," Bingham explained. "But the duke is responsible for your welfare during this period of, shall we say, confinement. He must personally escort you to London for formal charges and the trial at the proper time."

"Am I supposed to know him?" Jenny asked.

"Not necessarily," Bingham replied. He leaned back in the comfortable chair and eyed her with frank and intelligent scrutiny. "You might say he is a distant relative."

She knew of no relatives. "How does he know me?"

Silas Bingham leaned forward. "My dear Lady Jennifer," he began.

"Please call me Jenny," she requested, the title making her uncomfortable.

"Jenny," he said. "We have been searching for you since you were five years old. Since your father held legal custody of you, we could do nothing but make our report of your whereabouts. But whenever we located you, by the time our report reached the appropriate persons, you were whisked off to France, Italy, or another confounded place. His Grace has personally searched for you for several years, giving up only after you were legally placed in the custody of the Cottinghams."

Astonished, Jenny's questions tumbled forth. "Why would anyone search for me? Who is Duke Withington? Why am I in a castle with servants, when I should be in jail?" So many questions. She put her hand to her forehead, feeling she must be dreaming.

Silas Bingham spoke kindly. "We will have plenty of time to talk, Jennifer. We must prepare for the trial."

"Am I a. . .prisoner here?" she asked, thinking she would like to remain one if this were her punishment.

"As far as the court is concerned, yes. But while you are here, just ask for what you want, and it will be yours."

"Does this happen often?"

"No," Bingham replied. "Fortunately, His Grace has influential friends in royal circles."

Jenny's deep blue eyes widened. "Oh, I won't do anything to break that trust or cause him undue concern. I won't run away or anything like that. I am very grateful."

Silas Bingham nodded. "The servants know you are not to leave the grounds. They would notify the appropriate authorities immediately if that were attempted. However, you may walk or ride on the grounds. You may be almost alone, Jenny, but there will always be those to, shall we say, protect or accompany you."

"I know I must be dreaming," Jenny said.

"We will do everything in our power to make the months before the trial as comfortable as possible. The duke has ordered everyone to give you the respect and attention that you deserve. Also, if you will forgive me for mentioning such a personal issue, it is clear that you did not arrive with enough clothing for an extended stay. As His Grace's ward, you will be expected to have new gowns fashioned for your use. Our housekeeper will arrange the necessary details with you."

Jenny blushed, but she understood the necessity of expanding her wardrobe. Aunt Christine had only brought a couple of her old dresses to her the day before. She looked across at Bingham quite suddenly. There were so many questions on the tip of her tongue, but before she could ask, Silas Bingham caught her quite off guard.

He stood, studying her with hard eyes, and asked in a stern voice, "Miss Jennifer Cottingham, are you guilty of the crime of which you are accused?"

"Oh no," she replied, jumping to her feet, immediately placing her hand against her thundering heart. "I am innocent."

"Rum!" he exclaimed, his eyes glittering with pleasure. He went to the study doors and opened them. "We will talk tomorrow morning at nine, if that pleases you."

Jenny agreed to the appointment, then walked over and stood in front of him. The eyes she had thought were gray were actually light blue. His smile softened the lines of what had momentarily seemed quite a stern countenance. His gray hair gave him the appearance of someone's very nice father. She would never, at that moment, have believed he was known as the horror of the courts.

Bingham took her hand, lifted it to his lips, and gently kissed the back of it.

Jenny curtsied, feeling like a grand lady, although dressed in one of her plainest gowns and wearing her hair twisted into that horrid coil. She turned and saw that servants waited to escort her to her room.

It was not a room to which they took her, however, but a suite of rooms with an ancient elegance fit for a queen. Jenny gasped as she walked through the bedroom, dressing room, drawing room, private dining area, and a Roman bath that her personal maid said had been added by His Grace only the year before. There were several other baths throughout the castle.

This was a hundred times more elegant than the suite of rooms Jenny had used that terrible evening at Bodley House. Most impressive was the bedroom, aglow from the light of a dancing fire that warmed away the coolness of the spring evening.

"We thought you'd like a fire, m'lady," the maid said as Jenny walked toward the hearth, holding out her hands to warm them. "It takes awhile for the stones to warm after a cold winter so near the sea."

Jenny smiled. "What is your name?"

"Nellie," the girl replied.

"Are you employed at the castle year-round?" Jenny asked the girl, who obviously was so eager to please her. The girl couldn't have been more than a few years younger than Jenny, and her dark eyes filled with speculation and excitement whenever she looked at her new mistress. She wore a dark blue dress with a white apron and cap.

"Not I, except upon special occasions," Nellie replied. "But my mother and father are. We live in a cottage on the castle grounds. My mother tells stories of the grand balls the old duke, God rest his soul, used to give. Ladies and gentlemen came from all around and dined by the light of hundreds of candles. Why one time, the king himself did attend." She sighed. "But that was years ago—when I was a wee babe. Then the duke sailed abroad, and he returned to England only a couple times before he died. The new duke lives at the castle now, but we only see him for a few months at a time. Most of the year he is abroad on business."

"And does he have grand parties?" Jenny asked excitedly, eager to learn any bit of information about this mysterious situation and the Withington family.

"He hasn't thrown any grand parties," Nellie replied, hanging the last of Jenny's plain gowns in the closet. She turned toward her, adding, "But he has attended them. He did, of course, receive a personal invitation from the king when he threw that private birthday party." Nellie covered her mouth with her hand. "Oh, but I've said too much. My family has been loyal to the dukes for many generations. We will be loyal to you, as well."

Perhaps, Jenny thought, she and the Withingtons could trust Nellie and her family to be loyal. And yet, Jenny knew she was providing Nellie with the kind of personal story that would be talked about for generations to come. Although loyal, the servant girl would tell her children and grandchildren that she had been a personal maid to an accused murderess who was, for a while, treated like a grand lady in the castle before she was. . .what? Released? Hanged?

Shivering, Jenny moved closer to the fire.

Nellie took extra quilts from a closet and spread them across the bed.

"You will need these during the night."

Jenny's wish to dine alone in her suite was granted. She didn't want to take the offered hospitality so far as to sit in a formal room and have servants cater to her every whim. Deep inside, she feared some kind of mockery underfoot, like giving a convicted man a sumptuous meal before snuffing the life out of him. Why was she being given this taste of heaven? Was it a sign of impending, inevitable doom? Did her gracious benefactor suspect that her young life was near an end and feel pity for her?

The dining area in Jenny's suite looked too lonely with its view of the nighttime darkness, so Jenny chose to sit in front of the fire in the bedroom. She hardly noticed what kinds of food she was served, but realizing she was quite hungry, she ate it all.

After a long, sublime soaking in a tub filled with warm water and fragrant with a scent that Nellie had added, Jenny slipped into a comfortable nightgown. Then she propped up on fluffy pillows at the head of the half-canopy bed and tried to concentrate on Jane Austen's *Mansfield Park*, a book she'd asked Nellie to bring from the library.

Apparently satisfied that Jenny had everything that she needed, Nellie blew out the candles in the wall niches and curtsied at the door. "Mrs. Millet told me to remind you that she is directly across the hall, should you need her for anything," she said before leaving.

Jenny suspected that this message was Mrs. Millet's method of reminding her that she was a prisoner. Whether Silas Bingham labeled her a chaperone, companion, or guest of the castle, Mrs. Millet remained an employee of the court, and the legal papers stipulated that she remain in the castle with Jenny.

Unable to concentrate on the book, Jenny laid it on the bedside table and blew out the candles. The fire burned low, and Jenny pulled the covers closer to her chin and closed her eyes, suddenly aware of an overwhelming need for sleep.

She didn't know what awakened her during the night. For long minutes, she lay perfectly still, listening. An eerie wind from the sea rattled the windows, and from somewhere along the castle wall came the sound of something scratching the stone.

Outside, the moonlight threw trees into silhouettes against the silk curtains at her window. The limbs stretched toward her and seemed to be reaching inside the room, down onto the floor, and across the bed. The moving shadows crept along the walls, turning the niches into dark caverns and the fireplace into a black forbidden hole. The carved ceiling changed into monstrous images. Even the half canopy woven in rich colors of blue, red, and gold velvet showed only varying shades of gray. The protective bed curtains now resembled arms, hovering, waiting.

With an exclamation of fear, Jenny bolted upright in bed, threw back the covers, and stepped out onto the floor. With shaking fingers, she lighted the candles on the bedside table. Immediately, the leaping flames dispelled the shadows, and a golden glow once again played about the room and across the stone walls.

An illusion, Jenny told herself, with a sigh of relief. No encroaching evil lurked to overtake her. But while the shadows and the wind held no threat, evil was present in the world. Its nearness to her was no illusion. She trembled.

Jenny sat on the edge of her bed, staring at cold ashes where a warm fire had burned several hours before. Over the past three days, one question continued to plague her: Who killed Lord Bodley?

Suppose she had run away before the engagement party? Would Bodley have been murdered? Was it someone angry about the engagement? She shut her eyes against the possibility of the evil deed being committed by one of the Cottinghams, her only relatives. She was ashamed to even consider such a possibility.

The magistrate had implied the action was that of an unthinking, distraught female. But had she premeditated murder, wouldn't she also have had the presence of mind to attempt to cover her tracks? She would not have left a glass of poison on a table. Even if she'd heard people coming, she would have thrown the goblet into the trees where it would have been more difficult to find.

Only two other ladies were in the glade, according to witnesses. Suppose, just suppose, Aunt Christine had been upset enough to eliminate Bodley. Jenny shook her head disparagingly and sighed. She could not envision Aunt Christine leaving a glass with poison on the table. The woman would have had greater presence of mind in such a situation.

What about Emmaline? Jenny's cousin could be impulsive, even irrational at times, but of course her rash acts had never approached something this drastic. Emmaline was the type to plan an action without thought to the consequences. But a murder?

Jenny reproached herself for even considering that her cousin could be capable of such an act. Yet the fact remained: someone had murdered Lord Bodley. The magistrates had accused Jenny. Why had they not felt Emmaline's motives were greater than her own? It was Emmaline who had been jilted. It was to Aunt Christine's great humiliation that Bodley had chosen Jenny instead of Emmie.

Had social standing influenced the magistrates? Why did she look more like a killer than her relatives? Had the Cottingham family plotted to avenge their embarrassment and place the blame on Jenny? Is that why Emmaline had told the investigators that Jenny had made a threat against Bodley's life? Or did Uncle Thomas and Aunt Christine suspect that Emmaline might have committed the act? Were they trying to steer the blame away from their daughter?

"I don't know," Jenny whispered in the darkness.

Or did an answer exist—one that she simply refused to accept?

Chapter 5

Jenny awoke with a start at the sounds of heavy knocking on the door and of Nellie frantically calling her name. By the time Jenny opened the door, Mrs. Millet had hurried from her room, tying the sash of her heavy robe. Her flushed face and anxious eyes indicated grave concern.

Jenny realized they thought she might have harmed herself. Strange, that had not occurred to her. And yet, wouldn't that be the simplest, most natural way out of an unbearable situation?

Jenny knew if she took such drastic action, it would look as if Mrs. Millet had shirked her official duty, and Nellie would feel that she had failed the dukes whom her family had served for generations.

Nellie began to fuss about Jenny, straightening her bed, asking if she wanted her breakfast in her room, could she draw another bath, or was there anything at all she might do for her.

Jenny asked about riding horses and within the hour sat atop a chestnut mare with which she had a delightful affinity from the onset. Garbed in her simple but adequate riding outfit, she followed a groom, who offered to show her the most desired route to take, instructing her which path from the woods led into the open countryside and which led to dangerous cliffs above the sea.

As soon as they emerged from the wooded path, Jenny felt the open spaces beckon to her. With the groom ahead of her and another servant a respectful distance behind, she quelled the temptation to ride on forever. The early morning adventure proved to be invigorating, and much of her tension evaporated like the dew upon the spring grass once it is touched by the gentle rays of morning sun.

Wanting the grooms to know she could be trusted not to leave the grounds, nor to gallop at a high rate of speed and throw herself over the cliffs and into the sea, Jenny kept her emotions in tight rein. The mare sensed and respected her wishes. Jenny suspected her mount would have been happier to be swept away in a fast gallop, and she herself thought such a ride would provide a wonderful escape from life's concerns.

But Jenny was extremely grateful for even a small amount of diversion from the matters pressing on her mind. However, she knew she had to return to the stables, for her appointment with Bingham must neither be missed nor delayed.

A short while later, Jenny had bathed and enjoyed the light breakfast Nellie had brought to her room. Promptly at nine o'clock, Jenny descended to the study, where she met Bingham, who was sitting at the huge mahogany desk.

Jenny's blue eyes sparkled with excitement as she related to Bingham the enjoyment of her morning ride on the chestnut mare. Bingham delighted in her asking him to ride with her in the mornings.

"Thank you, gracious lady," he responded with apparently genuine admiration. "That would be delightful, but there is much work to do, and so little time in which to do it."

With that, their conversation turned to the serious matter at hand. Bingham's next words astounded Jenny. "Your mother is concerned about your situation."

"That cannot be," Jenny stammered, her eyes wide in confusion. "My mother is dead."

"Why do you think your mother is dead, Jennifer?"

Jenny noticed that his face revealed no shock at her claim. She clasped her hands on her lap and leaned toward Bingham, while he took notes. Her heart seemed about to flutter out of her chest. Her weak and shaky voice answered his question. "My father," she said. "He told me that my mother died. Uncle Thomas and Aunt Christine never refuted that."

"Your mother is alive. At present, she is mourning the loss of her husband. She is in America. That is where Tilden has gone. To fetch her."

Jenny could scarcely breathe. Her mother, of whom she had heard such terrible stories and whom she had thought quite dead, was really alive. "How can I believe these things?" Jenny said. "Why would Tilden Withington fetch her? I don't understand."

"You have never heard of the Withingtons before coming here, Jenny?"

She paused to consider his question. "No, sir," she replied, wondering why she would be expected to know the family.

"You've never heard the name of the man your mother ran away with?"

"Only that he was a duke," Jenny replied.

Silas Bingham shook his gray head. "The duke was Stanford Withington, Jenny."

Jenny stared at him wide-eyed. It was difficult to take it all in. Quite impossible, really.

"Duke Stanford died over a year ago," Bingham said.

"But you said my mother is in mourning."

A distressed look passed over Bingham's eyes. "Yes, Jenny, I did." He cleared his throat before continuing. "The loss of Duke Stanford has been almost more than Lady Diane can bear. She and the duke sacrificed everything because of their love for each other."

Even her child? Jenny wondered.

"You can well understand, I am sure," he continued, "how the two of them would cling to each other so entirely, having lost so much else. Stanford's title became virtually ineffective because of his living in America. You well know the reputation of a woman who leaves her husband. She becomes a woman scorned, an outcast of society, publicly ostracized, regardless of private opinion. 'Ladies,'" he said, emphasizing the word, "would not be allowed to associate with her."

Jenny lowered her head to hide her expression from Bingham. Another illusion shattered. Running away with the man she loved had not brought her mother all the happiness she had sought.

"You know nothing of your mother, Jennifer?" Silas Bingham asked kindly.

Saddened, she shook her head. "My aunt said we would never discuss my mother under her roof. But she often remarked that I would turn out to be like my mother. She did not mean it kindly."

"Tell me about it, Jenny," Bingham encouraged gently. "Not just the facts, but your feelings and impressions. As far back as you can remember."

Jenny paused to gather her thoughts. Then she explained to Bingham how her early recollections were hazy. There seemed to be a time when she was happy and felt secure and loved. Then she had a recurring dream. She was in a small enclosure, like a pantry. She had been very sleepy, but frightened, and made a sound. A hand came over her mouth. She could not scream, and because she began to cry, her nose stopped up and she could scarcely breathe.

Afterward, she'd been taken to her room and had called for her mother, but she never saw her mother again. Then her life became a steady succession of new homes, moving from one place to another, one country to another, with her father.

When old enough, she began to ask why she had no mother. "Is she in heaven?" the little Jenny had asked.

"No, she is not in heaven. Now get out of my sight," her father would reply in a drunken rage. "You have no mother. The sooner you realize that, the better off you will be."

Jenny had learned to talk with him only when he was sober, which was seldom. Often he would moan, "I have no friends; money comes only by selling my possessions; and it's all because of that. . ." Then he would refer to Jenny's mother in very vulgar terms.

When he made such accusations against her mother, Jenny would run and hide and put her hands over her ears to keep out the words. She pretended her mother would come and rescue her.

Her father went away for long periods of time, leaving Jenny in the care of a series of governesses. Some of the young women were terrible bores. Others were extremely intelligent and sensitive. They talked to Jenny about life and tried to make her understand that her father drank because he was heartbroken that he had no wife and she had no mother. They introduced her to books, and in them she found a sense of security.

There had been no time for close attachments. She'd been sad when they had to leave a place and those she loved. She seemed forever trying to find her mother in each new governess, each new servant.

Jenny had always longed for her father to return. When he was drinking, he wanted nothing to do with her. When he wasn't, he sometimes embraced her.

When Jenny reached the age of twelve, her governesses began to be of poorer quality. They did not know as much as she had gleaned from her books, always hoping to impress her father with her knowledge. Jenny pretended that each new place, whether in Russia, France, or Scotland, would be her permanent home. She made attempts to learn each country's language and history. Her father gave her a new name in each place they lived.

"I don't even know if Jenny is my real name. Do you know?" she asked Bingham.

"Yes," Bingham replied. "Your real name is Sarah Jennifer Greenough."

"Cottingham," Jenny finished.

"No," Bingham replied. "You were never legally adopted by the Cottinghams. They had you take on their name so no one would know you were a Greenough. Your father was Sir William Greenough, the brother of your aunt Christine Greenough Cottingham."

Jenny leaned back, expectantly waiting for some kind of explanation to help fill the vacant spots in her life. She knew so little. And now, looking back on it, it seemed her father and she had been hiding or running from someone or something.

"Our hands were tied," Bingham said. "Your father had legal custody of you, and when we found you or the place of your father's residence, we could only report to Duke Stanford. However, your father believed that Duke Stanford would whisk you away upon the first opportunity, which is exactly what the duke had in mind."

The duke wanted to kidnap her? For her mother? It was almost more than Jenny could do not to interrupt Bingham and ask the numerous questions whirling around in her head.

"Sometimes your father returned to his houses and sold the furniture and paintings," Bingham said. "But you were never with him. You were thirteen when your father died," he went on. "We didn't know that for a while, for he had been living under an alias. When we did learn of his passing, we couldn't do anything legally, for so many years had passed since his death and your father had signed papers, giving the Cottinghams legal custody of you. Our office contacted Sir Thomas as soon as we discovered your father had died, but we could not reach you personally with your mother's letters."

Jenny gasped. "My mother tried to reach me? I never knew that."

Bingham threw his pen down on the papers piled neatly on the desk and with great vigor pushed his chair back and jumped to his feet. He paced the floor, obviously disgruntled. "Ah, if only foresight were as obvious as hindsight," he said fiercely.

After taking a deep breath, he continued calmly. "Sir Thomas had complete charge of all your father's holdings. In spite of the fact that your father died from drinking too much alcohol, he had insight enough to draw up a contract, giving your aunt and uncle complete control of any assets he had. They would become your legal guardian and were to insure that you received further education and were given a substantial amount of money each year."

"I was allowed to be tutored along with Emmaline," Jenny said in her aunt and uncle's defense, not mentioning that she had already known most of the material. She had never lacked for enough to eat. "I didn't think my father had very much money when he died."

"He had most of it invested in property and some in banks. It was simply that a couple of years before his death he apparently stopped caring about anything but gambling and drinking."

"I never knew my mother was alive. There were never any letters for me," Jenny said with a desolate note in her voice.

"We suspected as much," Bingham replied. "The Cottinghams kept a close watch on you so that none of our spies could get near enough to even speak with you. Lady Diane's letters returned unopened. Then your aunt wrote that you detested your mother and wanted no contact with her."

Jenny could only shake her head. "I wish your office or someone could have made contact with me," she said sincerely. "I've always wanted to be with my mother."

Bingham nodded. "Until you went to live with the Cottinghams, Lady Diane wanted us to find you so that Tilden could kidnap you. Of course, our own office could have no part in such an action."

"And after the Cottinghams took me in?" Jenny asked.

"Eight years had passed, Jenny, since you had had any contact with your mother. We all knew it was too late for a kidnaping of a thirteen-year-old girl. Lady Diane believed your life at the Cottinghams would be a reasonably happy one, but she wanted you to know she loved you. Although she suspected someone else was responsible for her letters being returned unopened and for the notes declaring that you wanted no contact with her, she believed that you might bear resentment against her."

With a great sigh, Silas Bingham returned to his chair. "Over a year ago," he said, "Duke Stanford Withington died of a fever he contracted during an epidemic. He never gave up hope of reuniting you and your mother. His brother, Tilden, who spent his time in both America and England, managed much of Stanford's business affairs. Tilden is extremely fond of Lady Diane. Through the years, he has been obsessed with the idea of finding you and returning you to her. As he grew older, and you grew older, the idea had to be abandoned, of course. Then after Stanford's death, Tilden could not leave Lady Diane's side for many months. She was utterly bereft. In recent months, Tilden has again become determined to find you. He promised your mother he would force you to see her, to let her explain things to you. He promised to do that even if he had to take you by force."

Jenny's surprised eyes met Bingham's. "He...sounds very determined."

"Yes, he is," Bingham said and smiled. "He would do anything to reunite you and your mother. He has been greatly touched by her suffering all these years."

Jenny looked down. Duke Tilden must love her mother. She wondered if he would now step into his brother's place in her mother's heart. Her mother must be an easy person to love.

"What is my mother like? How does she look? Why did she abandon me? How could she?" The questions poured forth.

Bingham stood. "Those are questions Lady Diane must answer, Jenny.

You and I must be about the business of saving you from the gallows."

Jenny stood and wrapped her arms around herself to hide the shudder that traveled through her frame. Preoccupied with the news about her mother, she had forgotten that horrible indictment hanging over her head.

Bingham looked at the watch he took from his vest pocket. "I have an appointment, Jenny, and will be away during the weekend. I will return around ten o'clock on Monday morning."

He stepped forward and grasped her by the shoulders. "I know it will take awhile for you to absorb what I've told you this morning. But I want you to think carefully about this horrible accusation that has been made against you. When I return, we must go over every detail of this affair, omitting nothing."

Over the next couple of days, Jenny came to realize that life at the castle would have been perfect if she didn't have an accusation of murder hanging over her head. She was grateful when Mrs. Millet, somewhat at a loss over what to do, struck up a friendship with Nellie's mother, the head housekeeper. Jenny was careful not to speak frankly about anything personal to anyone, for Bingham had warned her that one could never be sure when words might be misconstrued, as had her exaggerated remarks about wanting Bodley dead.

Most of the castle had been closed off and not used for many years, Nellie told Jenny, as she unlocked the door to the picture gallery with keys her mother had loaned her. The walls were lined with paintings of generations of Withingtons and their duchesses—all lovely, elegant women, each with a look of strong will and determination in their expressive eyes.

There were no paintings of Duke Stanford, nor of her mother, for they had spent their married life in America rather than at the castle. Nor were there any of the present Duke Tilden.

"This is Duke Stanford and Duke Tilden's father," Nellie explained. "My mother described him as a terror to his enemies but a wonderfully straightforward and fair man toward those he liked and trusted."

"Did he die in battle?" Jenny asked.

"Oh, no," Nellie replied. "He spent most of his younger years fighting for the king. My mother says women were wild for him, but he did not marry until well into his forties. These paintings were done by a very famous artist shortly following the wedding of the elderly duke Withington and his young bride, whom he loved dearly. My mother said," Nellie continued, "that the dukes always had a rather wild streak in them, and could not settle down until their adventurous nature had been abated. She called it a thirst for blood and said it was only too marvelous that the king needed men like that in his service—otherwise all the dukes would have been atrocious villains."

Jenny smiled, while staring at the painting of the earlier Duke Withington, while in his forties. He was a strong, incredibly handsome man, and his penetrating eyes bore into hers from the painting. She thought he could subdue an enemy with a single glance. Yet a rather rakish look about him reminded her of the stranger in the glade.

Having seen enough, Jenny turned to leave the gallery. She did not wish to think of the stranger in the glade. She should forget that he ever existed, as he apparently had forgotten her. She often wondered if he had been real or simply a figment of her imagination.

That night, however, she dreamed of the stranger who had held her in his arms and kissed her. He appeared as some kind of hero who promised to rescue her from an impending, disastrous marriage. Then she awakened in a cold sweat, as if, even in her dreams, she would not allow those additional, threatening, excruciatingly painful thoughts into her mind.

On Monday morning, during her consultation with Bingham, Jenny had to face the facts.

"You are holding something back," he said. "You must not do that but must tell me everything, no matter how insignificant it may seem."

"It will not be believed and will make me appear foolish or deranged," she replied.

"No matter," he assured. "It is my job to help you, not condemn you. But you must trust me. Now out with it, child."

Jenny told him about the stranger. Bingham's penetrating stare compelled her to tell him everything, from the words they said to the kisses they shared. "I was just young and foolish and frightened," she said, hoping that would be a suitable explanation for her actions. "Do you believe me?"

"I believe you," Bingham replied. "There were two glasses in the glade. Young ladies do not ordinarily go about after dinner with goblets in their hands. I had known all along there must be someone else, but your not telling me that could well imply that you are guilty and had an accomplice."

"Oh, Mr. Bingham, you don't think I'm guilty?" Her voice choked, and she felt close to tears. She could almost think of this man as a loving father, were it not that she had allowed the absent Duke Tilden Withington to occupy that space in her mind and heart. And Bingham had often told her that their relationship must remain somewhat formal so that he could be completely objective.

"This is difficult," he had said once, "because you are so beautiful and as sweet a girl I would want my own daughter to be, if I had one." He did not, however, but had one son, Edgar Bingham, a partner in the law firm. "I do have a granddaughter. And a mighty fine one," he had added upon that rare time when he spoke personally.

Now he was speaking of the stranger. "Was he a rogue and a rake sort of fellow?"

"Oh no," Jenny replied immediately. "He was definitely a gentleman. The finest-looking man I have ever seen. He looked exquisite in his formal evening clothes, and his cravat was tied to perfection. Apparently he was very wealthy, for I feel certain that was a diamond pin he wore on the cravat, and he wore rings with jewels on his fingers."

Her heart beat faster just remembering the stranger who had kissed her and her ardent response. Now she looked down at her fingers. "But one cannot tell by outward appearance, can one?" she added in a small voice.

When Bingham did not answer, she finally looked over to find a contemplative expression in his eyes. "The thing we have to discover, Jenny," he said distantly, "is not only that you did not murder Lord Bodley, but we have to discover who did."

Jenny rose from the chair. She walked around the room, touching objects, looking at paintings on the walls, gazing into the fireplace where no fire glowed. Emmaline had asked once, "If you didn't kill Ignatius, who did?"

"Maybe he killed himself," she said now. "He knew I didn't love him and never would. Perhaps he realized how hopeless—" Her words stopped in the face of Silas Bingham's slowly shaking head.

"Bodley did not commit suicide," he said gently. "Someone murdered him."

Jenny spread her hands helplessly and turned her back on Silas Bingham again.

"We will talk more tomorrow," he said finally. "Edgar will be here this afternoon to discuss the case with me."

For the rest of the day, Jenny tried to dismiss the question of who had murdered Bodley. The answer, however, appeared in the form of a dream. The stranger held her, kissed her, and spoke beautiful words of love. Then his countenance changed, and in a violent temper he struck Lord Bodley about the head. He became a monster, and Jenny awakened screaming.

Mrs. Millet could not console her, nor could Nellie, but the poor girl stayed near Jenny's bed until her sobs and shaking subsided.

Jenny could not bring herself to tell Mr. Bingham of such a dream. It seemed impossible that the stranger, who had awakened in her the first stirrings of love, could be a murderer. And yet, it also seemed impossible that she herself could be accused of murder, and that had happened.

Her affection for the stranger slowly began to be transferred to the unseen Duke Tilden Withington. As the days passed, the dreams of the monstrous stranger became less frequent, less violent. Now she dreamed of the elderly Withington, the fatherly figure who was bringing her mother back into her life.

She continued to question Bingham about her mother, but he would tell her little. "That must come from your mother," he insisted repeatedly.

"Did she not love me?" she asked.

"Your mother loved you more than anything in the world, Jenny. And you were not abandoned in the sense you have been led to believe. She has spent all these years suffering over the loss of you. The letters stating you wanted nothing to do with her simply broke her heart. She gave up hope after Duke Stanford died. That is when Tilden promised he would find you and force you to have a confrontation with your mother."

"Will she come?" Jenny asked.

"She will come," Bingham replied. But on the question of when, he remained silent.

Chapter 6

Finally the day arrived. Jenny's mother had been ill during the voyage and begged to become more presentable before seeing Jenny. Bingham said, however, that the duke would receive Jenny within the half hour.

Jenny washed her face, flushed with excitement. Her blue eyes sparkled. Would the duke be pleased with her? Would he like to have a girl like her for a daughter?

She repaired a few curls that hung way past her shoulders and brought several forward to lie against the front of her dress. Her black hair contrasted beautifully with the deep rose-colored gown which showed her trim figure to advantage. Tiny pink rosebuds graced the front of the fashionable gown, and her waist was naturally slim. She'd had the gown made for the particular occasion of coming face-to-face with the duke who was making her lifelong dream of meeting her mother a reality.

Only for an instant did Jenny think of the stranger in the glade. She admitted to herself that it had been he who caused her present distressful predicament. She had been foolish to think she had fallen in love with the stranger. It was simply that the men in her life, other than Bodley, had been limited to. . .zero.

Now, a different kind of man had come into her life. One who had unselfishly devoted months and years of his life to reuniting a mother and daughter. She loved him for that and would be eternally grateful. She admired and respected the man who had sent her to his home, used his influence with royal personages to keep her from jail, and had her treated like a lady. Perhaps she would be executed or banished for the crime of murder. But until that time, she would be brave. She would earn the respect of Duke Tilden Withington.

Before the half hour ended, Jenny tapped on the study door, wondering which sound was louder—the knock or the pounding of her heart.

Silas Bingham opened the door. "Come in, Jenny, and meet Duke Tilden Withington," he said. After she stepped through the doorway, Bingham entered the hallway, closing the study door behind him.

Jenny looked at the floor in front of her feet lest she stumble and fall. The figure of a man moved toward her. With bowed head, she curtsied low. Duke Tilden Withington bowed.

She lifted her eyes to his. Her words of heartfelt gratitude stuck in her throat. "Y...you!" she stammered. Her mouth would not close, nor her eyes. Her heart no longer thudded against her chest, for it apparently had ceased to beat.

He was no middle-aged, fatherly figure of a man. Instead, she faced the most handsome, rakish-looking man, with delight twinkling in his eyes and a half smile gracing his lips. His eyes took in her appearance, and she blushed at what appeared to be his unmitigated admiration.

He should like her attire, she told herself. After all, hadn't he left orders that she should have whatever she wished? She had thought nothing of accepting such a generous gesture from her mother's wonderful friend. Now, she realized that he had financed every stitch of clothing she wore, just as Bodley had furnished her with silks, satins, laces, and servants.

Her experience with Bodley had led to disastrous events. Now, Jenny felt even more naive and gullible. A sense of helplessness stole over her. She quickly glanced around the room and turned her head toward the door, seeking some escape. But no escape existed. What force had sought her out to torture and twist her young life into such knots of confusion and hopeless, unavoidable disaster?

The two men in her life were indeed one: Duke Tilden Withington was both her beloved stranger in the glade and the murderer in her nightmares.

The shocked, bewildered, even fearful expression on Jenny's face was not what Tilden had longed for. "You did not expect me?" His voice almost failed, for he stood so close to her. The fragrance of wild roses assailed his nostrils.

"No," she finally managed to gasp, taking a step back.

This was not the encounter he had expected. Until he had observed Jenny at her engagement party and then spoken with her in the glade, he had never found a love so binding as that shared by his brother, Stanford, and Lady Diane. But Tilden knew, from the very first moment, that he would never allow Jenny to become a victim of Ignatius Bodley's lewd and vile character, an infamous topic in society's circles.

After many years of indulgence, Tilden had committed himself to

Christian living. He repented of his past and allowed the Spirit of the living Jesus to abide in his heart. It wasn't the easy way, but he knew it to be the best way. He'd longed for one woman's love to fill his life. He'd never found such a woman until his encounter in that shady glade with Jennifer. This sweet, wonderful girl had tempted him beyond any of the experienced women he had known in past years. Her eagerness for love and affection tore his emotions. The remembrance of her soft and yielding lips against his own haunted his dreams. Since then, any thoughts of romancing a woman had been accompanied by the image of the lovely Jenny.

For many years his top priority had been to find and kidnap Jenny for her mother. As they all grew older, managing at least a confrontation between mother and daughter had become his obsession. Now that he had encountered Jenny in person, had held her warm and tender body in his arms, he knew that he needed Jenny for himself and would be satisfied with nothing less.

But now Jenny—the girl who had been in his heart and mind so many years, the young woman he'd finally found after so many years of wondering and searching—was accused of murder. Surely they would not hang such a one as young Jenny.

Was the thought of a hanging what caused Jenny's present discomfort and fear? He could only surmise that the accusation of murder had disoriented her. How could it be otherwise? That, and that alone, must be why she gazed at him with fear in her eyes.

He deliberately spoke softly. "I told you I would come for you. However," he said, turning toward a chair and motioning for her to sit, "due to the unexpected turn of events, my coming was delayed."

"I. . .don't understand," Jenny whispered. Near to fainting, she sat in the chair, not taking her eyes from him as he lowered himself into a chair across from her.

Her heart and mind had become such foreign creatures of late, for even in this crisis she could not help but be aware of how devastatingly attractive he looked in his formal dinner clothes—the champagne-colored pantaloons and darker coat. The white lace of his shirt was in evidence at his wrists and throat. Yet she remembered Nellie's comment about the blood-thirsty Withingtons. This man had promised to take her away from all her misery. How had he succeeded in doing that? Could her rescuer also be the murderer?

Jenny had read of characters who accused a murderer to his face, and in so doing ensured their own doom. She mustn't do that. She must remember what she had learned years ago—that she must live by her wits, not by trusting or counting on anyone else.

With that resolve, she moved her hand to her slender throat, swallowed convulsively for a moment, then breathed deeply. "I'm. . .I'm sorry," she stammered. "This is a shock."

Tilden rose quickly from the chair and walked to a closet along the far wall, near the desk where Mr. Bingham had sat so often during the past weeks while he and Jenny discussed the case. "It's quite unbelievable that Bingham has not told you of my identity," he said, opening the doors. He took out two crystal goblets and poured tonic water in each.

"Your name, yes," she replied, her voice slightly stronger. "But you did not tell me your name that night. I had no idea who you were."

He stood over her, holding out the glass. Their fingers touched as she reached for it, and her voice lowered to a whisper as she finished her thought. "Or even if you were real."

Their eyes met, and neither said anything. Jenny felt as if his gaze penetrated her, and a strange tingling began to fill her being. She did not want to think that the two men she loved were one and the same. Love? No, she mustn't love him for many, many reasons. Feeling fear gathering in her throat again, she lowered her eyes and gulped the tonic water, then coughed.

Although concerned for Jenny's well-being, Tilden noticed the color in her cheeks and thought it most becoming. Naturally she was upset, having no idea he was the man she had met in the glade. She must have had some very hard thoughts about a man who would kiss and run, then be such a coward as to never show his face again. She must have thought him a bit of a rip, and of no higher moral character than Ignatius Bodley. That is, if she had thought of him at all.

"You are the girl I have been looking for since you were five years old," Tilden said, in a reminiscent tone.

Jenny raised her eyes to his. Noting her interest, Tilden continued. "I was in on the plans the night your mother and my brother slipped away to board the ship to America. I witnessed their sorrow, even felt it myself, that you were not with us." He shook his head sadly, feeling deeply the experiences of the past. "Lady Diane's suffering touched my heart."

Jenny leaned forward to hear the story. "What happened that night?"

Tilden hesitated, turning the glass in his fingers. "I think it best if Lady Diane tells you about that. It is very personal." He smiled suddenly. "The important thing is," he said softly, "that I found you."

Jenny's heart began to race again, and she almost forgot the terrible suspicions she had harbored against the stranger. "Then you were looking for me when you came to the party?" She recalled how he had been staring at her no matter where she stood in Bodley's house.

"Yes," Tilden said, his gaze penetrating. "'I have finally found her,' I kept saying to myself. I had not seen you since I was fifteen and you were five. I had taken a message to your mother, and you had stood at the door, holding onto her skirts. Your small face seemed to be all eyes, blue and inquisitive, as you stared up at me."

"You remembered me for all those years?" Jenny asked in wonder.

"I remembered you as a child," he replied. "But when I saw you at Bodley's, I recognized you instantly. You were so like your mother when she was your age. You even had the same kind of brave sadness about you that Lady Diane had when she was married to your father and then again when she lost you."

Jenny's heart lifted at his words. Her mother had not deliberately abandoned her as she had been led to believe. Tears came to her eyes. "Now you have reunited us," she said softly. For the moment, her thoughts were most congenial toward Duke Withington, her kindly benefactor.

"It is something I have long looked forward to," he replied.

Jenny smiled, feeling a warmth from him that she had never experienced before. It was all-encompassing and much like the feeling she had experienced in the glade when he had kissed her—as if they were the only two people in the world.

Tilden saw the gratitude in her eyes, the tender expression in the most beautiful face he'd ever seen. He longed to touch her raven curls and to taste the sweet lips beneath his. The temptation was almost more than he could bear.

A pink flush graced her cheeks, and he wondered how often, if ever, she thought of their kiss. Or had she dismissed it as she had that night: simply a desperate attempt to create a pleasant memory to cling to after marriage to Ignatius Bodley? And to think, that night he had been amused when she had said she would do anything to get out of the situation.

Tilden suddenly stood and walked over to the fireplace. He propped one foot on the hearth and rested an arm on the mantel. "Have you been..." He started to say "happy," but one awaiting trial for murder could hardly be happy. He began again. "Have you been pleased with your surroundings?"

"Oh, Duke Withington," Jenny began, moving forward to sit on the edge of the chair.

"Tilden," he interrupted, slightly irritated with her formality.

"Tilden," she said in a small voice.

"Yes, Jenny?" he questioned, and she could no longer meet his eyes.

They were so penetrating and made her want to rush into his arms and tell him of her love. This man, who had thought of her for at least sixteen years, had approached the king on her behalf, acquired Mr. Bingham for her defense, established her in a majestic castle, and reunited her with her mother—this man could not possibly be a murderer. She refused to consider Nellie's comment about how adept the Withingtons were at eliminating their enemies.

Instead, she would now say the words she had originally planned to say upon entering the study. "You have made me the happiest girl in the world, considering my circumstances. This is a most beautiful place. You have given me more than I should dare ask for." She could not say all he had given her. A first kiss. A first love. An awakening to her own being.

"In addition to all that," she continued, "you brought my mother to me." She paused and looked up at him. "How can I ever thank you?" she asked softly.

He stared at her for a long time. She shifted her gaze, rose from the chair, and turned her back to him while taking a final sip of the tonic water and then setting the glass on the table by the chair. She inhaled deeply and walked around the room, pretending to look at the paintings. Then she stood by the window.

Jenny parted the white silk panels, flanked by gold velvet curtains, and realized that darkness approached. That wasn't all. The carpet muted his steps, but she felt his nearness. If he took her in his arms, she would be helpless to resist. More than anything at that moment, she wanted to be in his arms. It seemed, with the shadow of death hanging over her, everything in life had become so precious—the fragrance of a flower on a spring morning, a cool breeze, a ride on the chestnut mare. Even her fantasies became more meaningful, for she wanted to experience life and all its joys, not just its heartaches.

She turned to face him. Her eyes traveled along the lace ruffles on his shirt, past his throat, along his strong square jawline, and lingered momentarily upon his full lips that parted with his audible intake of breath. Then her eyes met his, and she felt mesmerized, having no will of her own. Such intense emotions in conflict with deeper instincts tugging at her consciousness warned her of danger and caused her great pain.

As he bent his head toward her pink, softly parted lips, Tilden glimpsed her troubled expression. Rather than take advantage of the situation, he cradled her in his arms, acutely aware of her. She had asked how she might repay him. He mustn't exploit her sense of gratitude by implying he sought his rewards in the same manner as the likes of Ignatius Bodley. Might she mistake his ardor for the kind of lust that she so resented in Bodley?

He should not reveal the depths of his feelings for her while so many serious matters weighed heavily upon this household. One issue, and one only, must be uppermost in their minds until this horrendous affair was settled.

Realizing how tightly he held her close, he released her, then deliberately turned and sat on the side of the heavy desk, his hands grasping the edges for support. He watched as Jenny returned to the high-backed armchair in which she had sat a short while ago. Did she wonder why he had let her go? Or did she wonder why he had held her at all? She bowed her head to focus upon her hands, clasped demurely against the rose-pink of her dress. There was only one subject he must discuss with her at this moment.

"Jenny," he said.

She lifted her deep blue eyes to his. Was it some mysterious emotion of her own that brought into them that guarded expression, or was it simply the natural dimness of the room affected by the fading light of day?

"Jenny," he said her name again. "When I saw you so distressed over the prospect of marrying Bodley, it brought back the agony Lady Diane had lived through. I know the results of a loveless marriage, Jenny. I could not bear that happening to you. The moment I saw you, my heart went out to you. I knew I would go to any lengths to prevent your marriage to Bodley."

Jenny shivered, knowing what he meant. Tilden was forcing her to believe what she so desperately wanted not to believe. He had killed Bodley to prevent her marriage. Her initial suspicions had been correct. Her dreams had accurately identified the murderer. But she was the accused. Grateful now for the near darkness, she asked, "Do you think I will be convicted?"

When he reached out for her, she drew back so suddenly, he quickly withdrew to his original position at the desk edge. "I will do everything in my power to prevent such a thing. Silas Bingham is the finest attorney in all of Europe, perhaps the world. Oh, Jenny, Jenny. I cannot bear to even think of such a thing. We will do, are doing, everything possible to prevent that."

Jenny searched his face, now in shadows. "Suppose it's not enough?" she whispered. Would he take the blame then? Would it be too late? Her body trembled with desperation.

"It must be," Tilden said, his voice deep with emotion. "It must be enough."

Jenny saw him move like a shadow, as if coming near her. She stood quickly and stepped around to the other side of the chair, as if it would fend him off should he pounce.

The movement of his head and his outstretched hand in the now-darkened room seemed so much like her nightmares. All the horrible things she had refused to admit were coming true. Each time something good and beautiful came to her, it turned out to be an illusion, bringing sure destruction instead.

The Cottinghams had not accepted her but merely tolerated her. The stranger in the glade had come, not for love, but for murder. And now her imagined, kindly benefactor was the stranger who had kissed, then murdered. Had he brought her here, not for her protection, but to ensure her conviction?

Her wits! Whatever had happened to them? "I. . .won't tell," she managed to say, and his progress toward her stopped. Turning, she almost lost her balance. She placed her hand to her mouth, lest she scream, and then ran for the door and wrenched it open.

"Jenny?" she heard him call, but she would not answer. The sound of his footsteps echoed in the hallway below her as she ran up the stairs, tripping several times on the steps.

After lifting her skirts and racing down the long hallway, she ran into her bedroom, slammed the door, and stood with her back against it. "I love him," she sobbed. "The man I love is a murderer. And he did it for me or my mother. His motives were noble. He could not bear for my mother to suffer any longer. He as much as admitted it."

Falling upon the bed, she grasped the covers in her hands and moaned into the comforters. She knew how she would pay for what he had given her. If his attorney could not prove her innocence, she would pay with her life.

Chapter 7

With a great shudder, Jenny rose from the bed. The near darkness enveloped her mind as well as the room. Lighting the candles, she reminded herself she had no one she could rely upon. Her mother was within the castle walls, but Nellie had informed Jenny that a doctor had been summoned to attend the grieving woman.

Jenny felt more alone than ever. She must find a course of action to take. And the first would be to rid herself of the notion that she was in love with that stranger who had kissed her in the glade. He was no longer a stranger, nor a fantasy, but a reality she had no idea how to deal with.

She barely responded when Nellie came in and offered to lay a fire. Jenny sat huddled in the big armchair with a comforter around her, as if she were freezing, staring at the ashes in the fireplace.

After the fire was glowing cozily, Nellie begged, "Oh, please, my lady, you must let me have the duke summon a doctor for you."

"No, no. Not that," Jenny finally responded, much to Nellie's relief. "It's just that I've had so many surprises today, Nellie. Having my mother so near yet I still can't see her. . . And the duke."

Nellie smiled, and her worried expression eased. Jenny then realized she must be careful not to let anyone suspect what she knew about Tilden. Putting her hand to her head, she gave Nellie a sidelong glance. "I shouldn't confide like this, Nellie," she began. Nellie walked closer in eager anticipation. "But my encounter with the duke was so exhilarating and my gratitude for all he's done for me so overwhelming, well, I'm afraid it has all quite gone to my head."

Jenny thought that as good an excuse as any and would perhaps explain her actions, had anyone seen her run from the study to her room. Nellie seemed eager to accept her explanation and agreed that Jenny should rest.

The servant prepared the bed and fussed with the covers after Jenny climbed between the sheets. Jenny closed her eyes, pretending to sleep, but after Nellie tiptoed from the room, she opened her eyes and reviewed the events of the day.

It seemed an eternity ago that she had worried about being engaged to Ignatius Bodley. That concern paled when compared to the present situation. At least she had understood why her engagement had taken place. This situation baffled her.

What kind of man was Tilden Withington? Certainly he was no typical murderer. One couldn't call him deranged, for even Silas Bingham spoke of him with respect and knew him to be a fine and intelligent man. But why would he murder Bodley to save her from a loveless marriage and then let her take the blame?

She tried to recall everything Tilden had said to her. He, and even Mr. Bingham, had stated that Tilden's goal for many years had been to find her and force a confrontation with her mother. Before she knew Tilden Withington, she had thought him in love with her mother and suspected that he might step into his brother's place as her mother's husband. Perhaps she had been correct in that assumption, even though he was younger than her mother.

Then again, he might not have expected Jenny to be accused of the murder. And now he might think the courts would be more lenient with a young woman than with a man of his age.

But. . .she could not love a murderer, could she? Even if he did the horrible deed for her? Wasn't there some way to excuse it? Justify it? She shook her head in bewilderment.

What a terrible, terrible injustice she was doing him, if he were innocent. But if he hadn't committed the murder, who had?

That haunting question, first asked by Emmaline, brought her cousin to mind. Jenny didn't want her relatives to be guilty of the crime, but she must consider every possibility. Her life was at stake. The time of her trial grew closer. She would prefer the culprit be some irate father or intended of a young girl whom Bodley had wronged, but in her heart, Jenny knew nothing like that had arisen as a result of the magistrate's thorough questioning. The most likely candidate was someone much closer to her.

She shuddered. Uncle Thomas and Aunt Christine, particularly her aunt, were angry enough to have done it. But Emmaline, much as Jenny hated to admit it, was impulsive enough to have acted before giving the deed any thought. Perhaps in this setting, now that some time had passed, she and the Cottinghams could discuss the matter. Surely after having lived with them for eight years, she would be able to detect some kind of remorse or guilt on their faces.

Hastily, she went to the desk and scribbled a note to Bingham. *Am I allowed visitors? Could I see Sir Thomas, Lady Christine, and Emmaline?* After folding the note and sealing it, she summoned Nellie.

A short while later, Nellie brought Bingham's reply. *Lady Jenny. Your request will be presented to His Grace,* Bingham wrote. *You shall be informed of his response.*

Jenny realized anew how much control Tilden had over her life. A great shiver ran through her with the realization that even Bingham, whom she thought would be a confidante, was subject to the wishes of the duke.

She could not face Tilden again that evening and asked Nellie to convey her regrets and explain that she was exhausted and could not possibly dine in company.

A short while later, a knock sounded on her door. Would Tilden insist she come down for dinner? Would he accept no as her response? Jenny caught her breath when the door opened and the most beautiful woman she'd ever seen stepped inside.

"Jenny," the woman said, and her voice broke. Then she managed to whisper, "I am. . .your mother."

Jenny rose and walked toward her. She could only stare at the trim lady of about her own height. The woman's black hair was sprinkled with gray and arranged in beautiful curls on top of her head. She wore no jewels around her neck. A single black curl trailed from the back of her head, around her lovely white neck, and onto the front of her soft blue gown, on which she wore a diamond broach. The blue of her dress matched the color of her eyes.

Forgetting all else, Jenny made the first move. "Mama," she breathed and took a step closer.

Her mother's eyes closed, and tears trickled down her pale cheeks. She swayed slightly. "Jenny," she said, her voice broken by a sob. "My baby."

Jenny rushed into her arms. "Oh, Mama. Is it really you?"

The woman could only moan, "My baby, my baby," over and over as she hugged Jenny, held her away and looked at her face, then drew her near again and touched her hair and her shoulders. "At last. At last. Oh, you don't hate me, do you, my darling?"

Jenny stepped back. "I could never hate you, Mama. I've always loved you. I couldn't remember what you looked like. No one would talk to me about you. But I often felt you were near. Nothing could make me happier than for you to be here. But. . .sit down. I was told you were ill."

She led her mother to a chair, then sat on the edge of her own chair, unable to take her eyes from the woman she'd thought was dead but was here, facing her.

"Oh, ships make me so ill," her mother explained. "But I'm feeling much better now, and that dreadful headache is subsiding. I'm so sorry I couldn't see you the moment I arrived. But I could not let you see me feeling so miserably. I was afraid you might not want to see me at all."

Before Jenny could protest, her mother smiled through her tears. "But you, my darling. Nellie said you aren't feeling well."

"I'm much better now," Jenny assured her, reaching over for her hands. "Now that you are here."

Jenny's own face became moist with tears born of strong emotion. At least before she would be hanged, she had seen her mother.

"I will wait until you feel like eating," her mother said, dabbing at her eyes with a lace-trimmed handkerchief. "Then we shall dine together."

Wanting to spend time with her, Jenny's answer was forthright. "We can have dinner in my own dining area," she said, gesturing toward the room adjoining her bedroom. "I would be so happy if you would join me."

Over dinner, Jenny apologized to her mother. "I'm sure you would want to be with the duke in the dining room," she said reluctantly, wishing she did not have such an ache in her heart. Should she confide her suspicions to her mother, or even warn her that Tilden could be a murderer?

The older woman reached over and grasped Jenny's hand. "I only want to be with you, Jenny," she said sincerely. "Tilden understands this. He wants us both to be as happy as possible and looks for this unpleasantness to end."

Yes, Jenny thought. *But what happens when it's over? Will I have a life? Will I be imprisoned? Will I be hanged?*

"Do you want to tell me about it, Jenny?" her mother asked softly.

Jenny felt sure that this was partly what mothers were for—to listen to their daughters. What would happen if she told her mother of Tilden's presence in the arbor the night of Bodley's murder? Suppose Tilden denied it? Would her mother think her a liar? Or if she believed her, would her mother, who had already endured great suffering, find this unbearable?

After careful deliberation, Jenny shook her head. "I think it's enough that I tell Mr. Bingham." She picked at her food, then looked across at her mother's concerned face. Forcing herself to put thoughts of Tilden aside and concentrate on the wonder of having her mother with her, Jenny said, "I want to hear about you, Mama."

Jenny concentrated on her mother's story of sailing across the ocean to the New World and a new life. She didn't explain why she didn't take Jenny.

She simply said the situation had become unbearable. "Without Stanford, I could not have endured the loss of you. Sometimes I think I must know how God felt to have given up His only Son. Nothing. . .nothing could be so distressing."

Jenny's questions remained unanswered as she watched the distress upon her mother's face and heard it in her voice.

"I counted my blessings. I had five wonderful years with you. My beautiful Jenny with the long black curls and huge blue eyes and loving arms." She blotted her tears again. "There was always a shadow on my happiness with Stanford. Then we came to understand the error of our ways. We had not known God when we ran away together, but once we came to understand His love for us, we experienced God's forgiveness." She reached over and grasped Jenny's hands. "I deeply regretted the pain my actions may have caused you and always prayed that God would watch over you."

Jenny looked down. Were the prayers not heard? She was accused of murder. She looked up to ask why she had been left behind. But her mother got a wistful look in her eyes. "I had sixteen years with Stanford, and our love never faltered," she said. "He gave me a wonderful life in America. He built me a Gothic Revival mansion on the Hudson River that was a model of one he sold in London."

Jenny smiled, glad that the conversation had turned more positive.

"His business ventures and intelligence made him a very influential man, constantly admonished to run for public office. He would not," she added, a look of regret crossing her face. "He feared the scandal would be uncovered and bring greater distress to me."

Scandal! That's what Aunt Christine had constantly alluded to. Jenny would not ask for details. She would accept whatever her mother wanted to tell her.

"We had a perfect life, with one exception," her mother continued. "That was my loss of you. After Stanford's death, I thought you were lost to me forever. Now, Tilden has found you for me."

Jenny nodded. "I'm glad," she could say honestly, despite whatever had happened in the past. "Mama, I need you."

As they sipped their tea after dinner, a beautiful smile spread across the older woman's face. "My prayers that I might at least see you again have been answered," she said softly.

Jenny thought about those words. "Would your prayers help me, Mama?"

Her mother gazed down at her teacup for a long moment before answering. Finally she looked at Jenny and told her about her belief in God and how His Spirit had given her hope and strength. "Without God," she said earnestly, "I don't believe Stanford's and my love could have survived."

God helped love survive? "Does He always make things turn out right, Mama, if you pray?" Jenny asked wonderingly.

Her mother answered quietly. "Not in this life, Jenny. Not always. But sometimes our difficulties would be too much to bear without His presence."

"That sounds very nice, Mama, but I have so many things cluttering my mind." Jenny sighed. "Oh, but of course I believe in God," she added quickly, seeing the concern that the woman could not keep from her eyes.

"Even Tilden found that he needs God. He was very worldly as a young man, and he had everything this world considers important." Jenny's mother quickly named his extraordinary good looks, charm, wealth, intelligence, education, title, and place in royal circles. She talked of how Tilden had grown from a lad into a most responsible and respected man.

"He's very important to you, isn't he, Mama?"

A beautiful expression crossed the woman's face as she nodded and looked out beyond Jenny. "Next to Stanford, Tilden has been the most important person in my life, Jenny. You have always been in my heart and mind, darling," she assured hastily, "but I am speaking of those who were around me. Yes, I love Tilden with all my heart. One of the great joys of my life is that he has become a Christian."

So the two were in love, Jenny realized. Each had admitted it. Jenny's mother was not yet forty, and Tilden was in his early thirties. But a greater age difference lay between Jenny and Tilden. If only she had never kissed Tilden that night in the glade, things would be so much easier. She must forget. She must come to want Tilden and her mother to find happiness together. If only she could stop that silly heart of hers from longing for what could not be, from allowing unrealistic fantasies.

Suddenly, a new thought occurred to Jenny. "Mama," she said, moving to the edge of her chair. "You said Tilden is a Christian?"

"Yes, darling."

"Christians could not commit murder, could they?"

Jenny's mother carefully considered her response. Her daughter had asked a difficult question, and she had no idea why the young woman had raised such an issue. Her daughter knew so little about life and people, and no wonder, being whisked all over the country by her father, then becoming a part of the Cottingham household at a young age.

How could she tell Jenny that Christians could sin, that good persons

187

could make terrible mistakes and commit dastardly deeds, without giving the impression that she condoned such actions? Could she tell Jenny that even murder could be forgiven? Or that all killings are not necessarily murder—but that some are acts of self-defense?

She set her cup down too close to the side of the saucer. It overturned. "Oh, I've made a mess," she said, exasperated.

"You're tired, Mama. We've talked for hours." Jenny went over to her mother and hugged her shoulders. "We've said it all tonight," she said. "Tomorrow there will be nothing to talk about."

The older woman laughed, grateful for the overturned cup. She'd rather blunder with tea than with the important issue Jenny had raised.

"Yes, I am tired, Jenny." She stood and put her hands on her daughter's shoulders. "Let's think on tonight's conversation, and perhaps tomorrow we will talk and walk in the woods, or across the meadow, along the lake, or down by the sea. Our minds will be clearer."

Jenny nodded. They lovingly embraced, then parted for the evening.

For a long time, Jenny's mother sat in the first chair she came upon in her bedroom. She felt a chill deep into her bones. What had prompted that difficult, disturbing question Jenny had raised?

The following morning, more questions developed in Jenny's mind.

"His Grace feels, and I concur," Bingham said, "that it would not be wise for the Cottinghams to visit."

"But they are my relatives," Jenny countered.

"True," Bingham agreed, "but as you yourself have told me, Lady Cottingham is not particularly fond of your mother. Even if your mother wished to receive her, Lady Cottingham might refuse. Tilden feels this would bring greater stress upon you both."

Jenny lowered her eyes to her hands. "I did not think of that."

"And, too," Bingham added, "we do not wish to chance your saying anything that might disadvantage our case."

"Oh, but I wouldn't—"

"Not intentionally," Bingham replied. "But the slightest remark, or even silence, can tell another much about ourselves. Your face, my dear, is most expressive." He smiled in that fatherly way. "We do not want to chance anything hampering our chances for you, Jenny."

Jenny managed a trembling smile. Bingham kept referring to "we." Apparently, Tilden worked on the case, too. He wouldn't want to do anything to upset Diane further—or to place suspicion on himself.

"Is there another suspect?" Jenny asked hopefully.

"As we have discussed, Jenny," Bingham reminded her, "we must have motive, opportunity, and evidence. There certainly are others who are more suspect than you, in my opinion," he added, with a contemplative expression in his eyes. "But I do not reveal too much, even to my clients, before we are in the courtroom."

"Do you talk over everything about the case with Duke Withington?"

"Everything that I feel is pertinent, Jenny."

Jenny looked away from his penetrating gaze. Did that mean Mr. Bingham was completely on her side in this—or did his primary obligation belong to Duke Tilden Withington, whose primary concern was his future with Lady Diane?

Cool breezes blew across the meadow, where fragrant flowers had vanished, leaving behind a rich verdant green carpet of grass. Jenny knew that the cool English fog would soon be upon them, but for now she would enjoy the summer's warmth.

She and her mother rode through the forests and fields, then came upon a lake where they spread out the cloth for their picnic supper. They were laughing when Tilden rode up to them from the woods.

Jenny saw the delightfully startled look on her mother's face and detected the lilt in her voice when she exclaimed, "I feel like a child, doing this."

Tilden laughed, too, equally joyful, then dismounted and tied his horse to a tree, several yards away. He returned to them and asked playfully, "What's this about a child?"

Jenny glanced at him and felt her cheeks grow suddenly hot. She quickly knelt and began to take items from the basket.

Her mother laughed again and held out her hands to him. "A child," she repeated. "I feel so wonderful."

Tilden laughed with her, holding her hands. "Ah, Diane. To hear the sound of your laughter again is music to my ears. And you look like a young girl. You two could be sisters."

"You flatterer," the older woman accused, then her voice softened. "Tilden. I'm so grateful to you. I never thought I would have reason to smile again. You have made it possible for me to have so much."

Jenny heard the warmth in his reply. "And I hope to give you even more."

"I know," her mother whispered. Jenny felt like an intruder. They must surely be speaking of marriage later on. The only thing which prevented it now was the upcoming trial. Everything must wait for that.

"Join us, Tilden," Jenny's mother implored, her voice light and excited again.

A brief silence ensued before he replied. Jenny sensed they were looking at her. She held her breath lest he say he would join them.

"Another time, perhaps," he said. "I came to tell you that Bingham and I must go to London for several days. There is much to discuss with his partners."

Jenny still did not look up when he walked around and stood facing her. She could see his riding breeches and shiny black boots. Then he knelt in front of her. Looking around, she saw that her mother had gone to pick wildflowers near the edge of the wooded area.

"It's wonderful, Jenny," he said, "seeing you and Lady Diane like this."

Jenny could think of nothing to say, except, "Thank you." She glanced up quickly to find him staring at her intently. His eyes held an expression she felt should be reserved only for her mother after the things he had said to her. His smile was beautiful, and she could not keep from remembering how his lips had felt on hers that night in the glade. Quickly she looked down to his arms that rested upon his bent legs. His hands were almost near enough to touch her.

"No need to thank me, Jenny," he said with meaning. "I would do anything possible for you. Anything."

Even murder? Why? Because her mother had so desperately wanted to find her? Jenny found breathing difficult and put her hand to her slender neck. Her heart and mind were in such terrible conflict. Perhaps she should save them all a great deal of grief and simply ride the chestnut mare over the cliff and into the sea, rather than wait for the ordeal of a trial. That way, her mother and Tilden could find happiness together and Jenny would not have to fear blurting out the awful truth. "Good-bye," she whispered.

Suddenly Tilden reached out and grasped her hand. Jenny closed her eyes against the feeling when he lifted her hand to his lips and she felt the gentle pressure of his kiss. Then he squeezed her hand gently. "Take care," he said, and she felt it sounded like a warning. He rose quickly and walked over to her mother.

Jenny watched as her mother put her arm through Tilden's and together they walked over to the duke's horse. Jenny turned her head and gazed out upon the water where fish dimpled the surface, making circles that appeared, expanded, then faded. That is what any personal thoughts of Tilden must do, she determined. Fade from her mind.

After Tilden mounted his horse and rode away, Diane walked over to the area where Jenny sat, apparently lost in thought. Diane sat gracefully at one edge of the cloth, beneath the shade of a tree, determined to enjoy this time with Jenny and share these invaluable moments.

"What were you like when you were young, Mama?" Jenny asked. "I would love to hear it all."

Looking into her past, Diane began talking about her early childhood that had been so happy. She had been the product of her parents' middle age, and their only child. Her father was Russian and her mother English. Their home life had been one of love and security.

Diane's parents had both Russian and English friends, as well as homes in both countries. At age fifteen, Diane had been informed by her parents that her marriage with Lord Greenough had been arranged. He and his first wife had visited their home many times when Diane was just a child. Later, in his widowed state, he had not visited as often. Diane had scarcely known him. Then, they were to be married.

"I don't mean to make your father out to be an ogre, Jenny," Diane said with difficulty. "He wasn't that at all. Nor were my parents unfeeling. They wanted the best for me and believed the marriage would provide that." Her voice grew sad. "I didn't know about love, Jenny. I had never loved any man except my father. William Greenough reminded me of him."

William was forty and Diane sixteen when they married. He was a polite, charming, handsome man with a title and wealth. But she had not understood her wedding night, after Lord Greenough had too much to drink. Diane had been terrified of him, but in his drunken state he had begun to insist upon his rights as a husband.

Later, she learned he had been devastated when he lost his first wife. He had taken to drinking and gambling. "If he had been more understanding of my innocence," Lady Diane said in defense of him, "or if I had known more about men, perhaps it would have been different. But that does not excuse what he did. Other men have faced disappointment without abusing their wives."

Because Diane feared him, he drank. When he drank, he became a forceful, violent figure who frightened her even further. But Diane determined to make the best of it. She learned to use her beauty and charm to induce him not to drink. She learned she could get her way by pretending to care for him more deeply than she did. But he always sensed her reluctance when he came near her.

A year passed. He drank more heavily and became insanely jealous. When they entertained or visited their friends, he proudly showed her off. She wore beautiful clothes and jewels, and he could not praise her enough. He caused all eyes to look at her. Then when they were alone, he condemned her for the admiration she had received from the other men and accused her of seeking their attention.

Another year passed, and Jenny was born. Diane poured the love that she could not give to her husband on her child. After she regained her figure, William proclaimed her more beautiful and desirable than before. Diane stopped trying to defend herself when he made his unfounded accusations. She simply turned her attention to her daughter. At that time, her parents were quietly living out their lives in their grand home in Russia.

Jenny was two years old when Diane met Duke Stanford Withington at a royal ball given at Withington Castle. The Greenoughs were announced, but before she could be personally introduced to the duke, she saw him from across the room. Later, when he asked her to dance, she politely told him she never danced with anyone but her husband.

He merely nodded, and she vowed she would never look at the man again, for strange, forbidden things were happening within her mind and heart. In spite of her resolve, during the course of the evening, her eyes continued to meet his.

That night, William Greenough struck her for the first time. His rage had been aroused when Stanford had asked her to dance. The fact that she refused made no difference. Diane said she would never go out in public again, but that did not please him. He wanted the world to know he had a young, beautiful wife.

On several occasions after that, she saw Stanford but refused to look at him. Then at one party, Lord Greenough was caught up at a gaming table, and Diane walked away from the other ladies. She stepped into the darkness and leaned against a tree. She had not wanted to think of seeing Stanford at the party for it caused only distress.

Suddenly he stood before her. He apologized for approaching her that first night, for since then he had heard of her husband's terrible jealousy. "I understand his feelings," he said, "for you are the most beautiful woman I have ever seen. And your actions prove you to be a wonderful lady. I will never approach you again."

Before she could speak, he turned to walk away. Just as he did, Lord Greenough appeared. Stanford attempted to dodge the blow, but Lord Greenough's fist made contact with his jaw. Stanford lost his balance and lay sprawled on the ground.

Then Lord Greenough's open hand whipped across Diane's face. Stanford jumped to his feet, but Diane feared for him more than for herself. "How dare you interfere," she said forcefully to Stanford, in an effort to reassure her husband of her loyalty. She caught Lord Greenough's arm and began walking with him toward the house. Even so, Lord Greenough began making ugly accusations that Diane knew Stanford could hear.

After they returned home that evening, William said he regretted Diane's undisciplined nature and was forced to teach her a lesson. He used a whip which made welts on her back, buttocks, and legs. After only a few lashes, he flung the whip away and began to sob, begging Diane's forgiveness. Diane cradled his head against her chest. He seemed like a sick child. He confessed that he had lost a huge sum of money at the gaming table and that loss had caused his violent outburst.

Diane forgave him. They both had been done a terrible injustice by the arranged marriage. The rising welts on her body did not hurt as much as the knowledge that her heart could never belong to her husband. They were past any form of reconciliation. It was then she asserted herself, telling him he must never again strike her or she would leave.

He apparently believed it, for he did not strike her again for a long time, but his accusations continued, and he threatened that if she attempted to leave him, he would take Jenny from her. She became terrified.

On one occasion when Lord Greenough seemed not to be around, Stanford came near Diane again. "Can you not even speak to me?" he asked.

"No," she replied desperately.

"Then leave him," he implored. "I will take care of you. You must know."

"He will take my child if I even arouse his suspicions. Please go away."

Stanford did go away. But that did not stop Lord Greenough's jealousy. His gambling and drinking worsened. He lost most of both their fortunes.

During the year that Jenny turned three, Diane's parents died.

"You were four the night everything changed," Diane said. Lord Greenough had lost a huge sum and began making accusations again. They argued violently. He shouted that he was well aware that Duke Withington left any gathering the moment they arrived. Diane insisted that his actions proved that nothing was going on between them. Jenny awakened and began to cry. William Greenough yelled for her to be quiet, and when the frightened child continued to scream, he jerked her up and spanked her bottom.

Diane said nothing that night. For the next several weeks, Lord Greenough drank very little and gambled not at all. Diane knew he was making an effort to change, but it was too late.

When he had to be away for a few days, Diane visited a sympathetic friend who knew something of Diane's difficulties. Diane sent a note to Stanford, then met him in a wooded area near the friend's country home.

When Stanford arrived, Diane asked him if he would help her and

Jenny get away from Lord Greenough. "Yes," he said, then took Diane in his arms and kissed her.

"He told me," Diane said to Jenny, while tears streamed down her face, "that we would not have a clandestine rendezvous and he would not kiss me again until I was free to love him as he loved me."

Jenny's heart ached for her mother.

"Oh, Jenny. I don't mean to imply that your father was a terrible man. He was a lonely, middle-aged man when he married me. I was too young and innocent for him. I can see these things upon looking back, but then, I wasn't mature enough to understand his nature and his problems. Then, too, he could have chosen to act differently. Instead, he did the very things that would cause what he feared most—that I might someday leave him."

"I know, Mama," Jenny assured her. "I loved my father. I knew much of his drinking was his way of numbing his pain. I felt sorry for him."

"I hope you weren't the target of his violent rages," her mother said. "That always worried me."

"He wasn't home much, Mama, and I learned not to go near him when he drank."

"If I had not fallen in love with Stanford, perhaps things would have been different. Maybe I could have established a separate household somehow to protect both you and me, but it didn't seem possible at the time because your father controlled all our money. And then I did fall in love. I didn't want to, but I couldn't help it. Later, both Stanford and I learned about God's love for us and repented of our sins."

"I don't blame you, Mama," Jenny said and looked down.

"I never knew a man could be so loving and yet so gentle with a kiss, until Stanford kissed me," Jenny's mother explained. "It was the kind of kiss that should have been my first one, not after so many years of marriage to another man."

Jenny reached over and held her mother's hands. She could understand. She knew that Tilden's kiss was exactly what a first kiss should be. But it should never have happened. Now she wondered if she had so reminded Tilden of her mother that he couldn't resist the kiss. He probably regretted it and hoped she would not tell her mother. And of course she wouldn't. No one else knew Tilden came to the glade that night. Now it was too late to tell anyone. Who would believe her if he denied it?

"Mama," she said quietly. "Could you love a murderer?"

Diane tried not to show her surprise at Jenny's unexpected question. Why would she ask it? But she mustn't avoid the question either. The best example she could think of was King David.

"You know about King David in the Bible, don't you, Jenny?" she asked.

"I've heard of him."

The words tugged at Diane's heart. Her dear child's education in the scriptures had been sadly neglected. She gave a little background on the shepherd boy who became king.

"It all started when he gazed upon the beautiful Bathsheba from his rooftop, as she bathed," Diane said, trying to answer Jenny's question. "He did not turn away, as a gentleman should, but rather watched and desired her. Although he was a great and good man all of his life, he committed adultery with her. They fell in love, and King David caused Bathsheba's husband to be murdered so he could take her as his own wife." Diane concluded sadly, "He was punished and suffered for it."

She watched her daughter's troubled eyes. Her answer had caused Jenny pain. "But God forgave him," Diane hastened to add. "He can forgive. . .even murder."

"His wife," Jenny asked falteringly. "She lived with him after that? Did she love him?"

"From all indications," Diane admitted, "Bathsheba loved King David in spite of what he did."

Jenny's reaction indicated to Diane that her response had not satisfied her daughter. Diane shivered and realized the sun had disappeared from the sky and the air had grown cool.

"Darkness will be upon us soon," she said, beginning to gather the remains of the picnic. "Let's head back to the castle."

Jenny's sense of maturity and probing mind gave Diane reason to be careful in forming answers and advice for her daughter. She wasn't quite sure how to tell Jenny she had always loved her and always would. Yes! Even if she were a murderer.

Chapter 8

During the next several days, rain fell. Diane asked that a fire be laid in the drawing room where she and Jenny ate supper. After their dishes were removed, the two women remained, sipping tea and having their evening talks. The conversations remained light. Jenny did not ask the questions that lay heavy upon her heart. She did not want to believe that Tilden Withington would murder anyone. But if he had, her mother would still love him.

Then Tilden returned to the castle. Silas Bingham remained in London to work with his partners on the trial, which was fast approaching. During dinner, Jenny's mother and Tilden attempted to draw her into the conversation, to little avail. She dared not look at or speak to Tilden.

Then the two talked about something that had happened in America and referred to a previous conversation, of which Jenny had no part. But then, didn't people in love have their own private communication? She wasn't sure about anything anymore. During that moment in the glade, she had felt there was an understanding between herself and Tilden, one that went deeper than words.

Now, she knew that experience had been one-sided. She, only, had felt that special something that awakened her to love—that painful thing that tugged so at her heart. Obviously, Tilden had not shared her feelings. He had already fallen in love with her mother.

"You've eaten so little, Jenny," she heard her mother say.

"Oh," Jenny said, looking up. She felt guilty meeting her mother's warm, tender expression. How would her mother feel if she knew Jenny had kissed Tilden?

Jenny was glad when they had finished dinner.

"Join Tilden and me in the library, Jenny," her mother invited. "We will have coffee or tea."

"I beg you to excuse me," Jenny said. "I've just finished reading a novel and would like to start another." Fearful that her mother would think she did not enjoy her company, she hastened to add, "The reading takes my mind off things."

"I understand, darling," her mother replied, though obviously disappointed.

"What were you reading, Jenny?" Tilden asked.

"Moll Flanders," she replied. "I've never had so much time to read and think, and I suppose I'm overdoing it." She hoped she sounded convincing. It was true, but she would much rather spend a part of her evening with the two people she loved if the situation were different.

"Ah, but surely you can spare us a moment of your time, Jenny," Tilden said good-naturedly. He took her arm and led her away from the dining room and down the long hallway toward the library.

Tilden's eyes focused on Jenny while he asked, "You have read the book, Diane?"

"Enjoyed it immensely," she replied with a light laugh. "What is it about human nature that enjoys such debauchery?"

"Debauchery?" Tilden asked. He arrived at the library door and held it open while the two ladies walked past him. He followed. "Defoe has stated quite clearly that his purpose was to point out the evil in it." His tone held mock humor. "And you enjoyed it, Diane?"

Jenny's mother laughed. "A slip of the tongue on my part, Tilden," she said and winked at Jenny, who could not help but smile at her mother.

Jenny sat near the glowing, cozy fire that fought the coolness so common during late summer evenings. Tilden and her mother sat on a nearby couch.

"Fire feels good," Tilden said, and Jenny's mother agreed while pouring the coffee that a servant had brought in and set on the low table in front of the couch. Tilden leaned over to hand a cup to Jenny. "We'll turn you into a coffee-loving person yet," he quipped.

"I do like it," she responded, "but not as much as tea."

"Shall I get tea for you?" he asked.

"Oh no," she replied quickly and looked over at him, then back at the cup, for she felt a trembling in her hands when their eyes met. Would she forever be foolish like this? If she had known that one kiss with a stranger in a glade could be such a world-shattering event, she would never have done it. Never! Maybe with time, it would fade from her life. But it did not seem likely.

"We didn't get your opinion of the book, Jenny," her mother observed.

Jenny's mind had to work quickly to realize just what her mother referred to. After a sip of coffee, she set the fine china cup in the saucer. "I liked it. And I think the heroine rather enjoyed her debauchery."

"Most of the characters did," her mother agreed. "Until they were caught in their crimes."

She cleared her throat, and to Jenny, the sound seemed nervous. Did her mother also believe that she had murdered Bodley? The cracking of the fire filled the silence.

Tilden felt it important that Jenny talk—whatever the subject might be. But she didn't want to talk with him. What had he done to cause her to withdraw from him? At least they were in the same room, and she seemed receptive to a discussion about the book.

"Diane," he said, "do you feel genuine repentance occurred in the characters?"

Although Jenny did not look at them, he saw her chin lift slightly and knew she listened. It took all his willpower not to stare at her lovely profile aglow in the firelight. She seemed such a sweet, delicate creature, and he seriously wondered if a court of law could truly believe her capable of murder.

And yet, Jenny's young mother had been a beauty in both appearance and spirit, but the world had taken delight in condemning her, just as surely as if they had sentenced her to the gallows. Bingham often said that nothing could save Jenny from conviction except discovering who other than the girl had killed Bodley. With considerable effort, Tilden forced his attention back to Diane.

"For some of the characters," she said in response to Tilden's question, "their repentance became a last resort. One would have to see a change that took place in order to judge correctly."

"Wasn't Moll Flanders's repentance the reason she was deported rather than hanged?" Jenny asked.

A long moment passed before anyone spoke.

"Her semblance of repenting and talking with the minister and having him speak well of her surely played a part in it," Diane finally said in agreement.

"But her repentance apparently went no deeper than her words," Tilden added seriously. "Defoe, in his introduction, said there is no true repentance apart from divine intervention."

"I skipped the introduction," Jenny admitted, looking at him and seeming interested in his words.

Tilden smiled. "That's to be expected," he said. "However, Defoe is saying that one may wish to repent, even try, but sometimes be unable to do so."

"Are you saying that Moll Flanders was unable to repent?" Jenny asked, wide-eyed.

Tilden found his mind and emotions in terrible conflict and struggled to remind himself that he was not simply dealing with the young girl who had so desperately clung to him in that glade, whose lips had sought his, whose warmth he could feel close to him even while he reminded himself he was much too mature and sensible for such thoughts.

Unable to look upon her any longer, he set the near-full cup of coffee on the table, stood, and walked over to the fireplace, where he propped a foot on the hearth. How he would like to take Jenny by the shoulders and shake her until she revealed what lay in her heart and in her mind. He longed to know, but she kept herself far removed from him. He had to stand and pretend interest in a discussion of that book.

"It seems to me," Tilden managed to say in a normal tone after a much-needed deep breath, "that she used anything and anyone—whatever seemed advantageous at the moment."

"Would not anyone do the same when fighting for his life?" Jenny asked in a small voice, her eyes fastened on the cup she held.

In carefully chosen words, Tilden replied, "The instinct for survival is that strong. Yes."

Diane's voice sounded unnatural. "But Tilden and I have heard so many sermons on repentance, Jenny. You have not had the opportunity, have you, dear?"

Jenny shook her head.

"We will have to correct that," Tilden said suddenly, removing his foot from the hearth and facing Jenny. "Sunday we will have the minister come and deliver his sermon on 'Repentance.' And afterward, if we wish, we shall discuss Defoe's book with him."

He deliberately lowered his voice an octave and spoke with mock gravity. "For teaching purposes only. The minister would not enjoy the debauchery."

When Jenny laughed with him and Diane, Tilden felt exultation flow through his veins. Her laughing eyes met his before she lowered them to her cup. He wanted more of these discussions, but on less morbid subjects. He walked over to a shelf, took a book from it, and returned to Jenny.

"Have you read this one?" he asked.

Jenny carefully put the cup and saucer on the table, then glanced at her mother. Tilden noticed a questioning look in Diane's eyes that was quickly replaced by the warm expression she always had when looking at Jenny. Although a servant would have done it at a moment's notice, Diane began to stack the cups and saucers onto the tray.

Jenny stood to take the book from him. *"Emma,"* she said with a sense of awe. "No, I haven't read it. But I have often heard it spoken of. Aunt Christine and Uncle Thomas's friends have discussed it, but of course I wasn't allowed to enter the discussion. I must confess, I often listened to conversations outside closed doors."

"Oh, Jenny," Diane said, her voice choked. "You always had such an inquisitive mind, a quick mind, even when you were little. If only you could have been with me and Stanford. You should never have had to seek information from behind closed doors."

Jenny stared at the book cover, looking uncomfortable. "Mama," she said softly. "Mama, these past days with you have been wonderful. I'm glad that I can talk to you, and be near you, and love you. It really has been the happiest..." Her voice trailed off as she turned to look at her mother's tear-streaked face.

"I know," Diane said in a whisper, walking near. "I know what it's like to be happy and yet so desperately miserable."

Jenny nodded and, grasping the book tighter in her hands, turned from both Tilden and her mother and ran out the door.

"I'm sorry," Jenny heard her mother say, but she had not moved quickly enough, for out of the corner of her eye she saw her mother turn toward Tilden with a cry upon her lips, and then Tilden's arms reached out and enveloped her.

Jenny ran up the steps and into her bedroom. She wished she could pour out her fears and longings to her mother. They had wonderful conversations about so many things, but never about Jenny's innocence or guilt. Diane often said that Jenny was brave, but Jenny knew it wasn't bravery on her part. It was fear. Fear that if she talked about it to her mother, then she would have to express her doubts about Tilden.

Jenny did not know how to tell her mother that she suspected Tilden was a murderer. Perhaps her mother already knew. But that would not stop her from loving Tilden. Even such a thing as that did not always destroy love. She knew. Yes, she knew, for her mother had said Bathsheba loved David even after she knew he had murdered her own husband. And Jenny knew she would always love her mother—no matter what. Besides, if she talked about that night, she would have to confess that Tilden had been in the glade with her. She must remain silent.

Forcing herself to begin reading *Emma* after slowly moving her fingers over the cover where Tilden had touched it, Jenny soon realized she was beginning to read a story about a girl who would most likely fall hopelessly in love. Had that been Tilden's intent when giving her the book? Perhaps to impress upon her the hopelessness of anything? He had made it possible for these past weeks to be both her happiest and, as her mother had said, most miserable.

Chapter 9

Rain fell all day Sunday, but the lighted candles lent a cozy glow to the little chapel. A warm fire sent dancing lights along the shadowed stone walls. Diane sat on the wooden bench between Jenny and Tilden. Several of the servants attended, as did Tilden's valet and secretary. Nellie, her mother, and Mrs. Millet occupied the back row.

The minister, a small man with thinning hair that was streaked with gray, had piercing dark eyes under bushy eyebrows. Jenny had thought he could do with the eyebrows on his head and smiled at the thought. His pale skin caused Jenny to wonder if he were ill, but after he began to speak, his face took on color, his eyes glowed, and his voice reflected the seriousness of his message.

She felt uncomfortable when he quoted, "All have sinned, and come short of the glory of God," however her spirits lifted when he said Jesus came and died to save mankind from their sins, to forgive, and give them eternal life.

Jenny liked the sermon, feeling it adequately defined repentance, clarifying some of the points about the novel that she, Tilden, and her mother had discussed. She felt particularly comforted when the minister quoted a wonderful verse: "Come unto me, all ye that labour and are heavy laden, and I will give you rest."

She did not take her eyes from the minister but became so engrossed in his words that she even forgot her first impression of him as a rather homely man. Jenny knew he spoke primarily for her benefit, for he seldom glanced at the others. She only regretted that she must sit and listen, rather than comment and ask questions about his fascinating, intelligent, and emotionally moving dissertation.

Then, as if sensing her undivided attention and reveling in it, he spoke of God's willingness to forgive even the most heinous of crimes, adding that one must believe in Jesus as the Son of God and invite the Spirit of that living Jesus into one's heart.

She began to wonder just why Tilden had invited the minister. Was it to convince her that he had been forgiven, even though she would have to pay for his crime? Was it so Jenny could pretend to receive forgiveness so she might be deported rather than hanged? Would his conscience be free if she were allowed to live? Her thoughts went round and round, and suddenly she realized her hands were pressed against her cheeks.

Then she heard the minister's voice near her ear. He stood in front of her. "Would you like to accept this living Jesus into your life?" he asked.

Jenny looked at him in horror. He believed she was guilty! The chapel no longer seemed warm and cozy. It had become a place where she was expected to confess to a crime she had never committed and find forgiveness.

If she said she would like to accept this forgiveness, wouldn't it be like admitting murder to a room full of witnesses? Wouldn't it simply further ensure her being found guilty? How could Tilden do such a thing?

But wouldn't a murderer do anything? Didn't he say that one would do almost anything when it came to survival?

A cry escaped her lips as she ran past them all and tore out of the chapel. Finding a door, she flung it open and rushed out into the torrential rain, her shoes becoming soaked from the muddy streams rushing over the courtyard. Within seconds, her clothes clung to her body like skin, and the icy lash of the deluge stung her face like whips, as if nature itself forbade any escape.

Having never before come into the courtyard from the direction of the lower floor, Jenny looked around helplessly. By that time, Nellie grasped one of her arms and Mrs. Millet the other.

"Let her go," a stern voice commanded. Then Tilden addressed her from the doorway. "Come inside before you catch your death of cold."

Jenny felt the hands release her arms. Released, also, was the possibility of her rushing down to the sea and flinging herself from a cliff. No one would allow her the luxury of hastening her inevitable fate. Mrs. Millet, seemingly unobtrusive, always stood nearby, on guard.

Then Jenny remembered Bingham saying that the servants would prevent her leaving. And whatever had happened to her wits? Or her courage? Or her gratitude not to have been incarcerated in a prison? Or concern for her mother's feelings?

Her mother stood just inside the doorway, her face a mask of concern. The minister stood behind her. Tilden stepped out into the rain, and Jenny could not bear his coming to force her inside. She must do that on her own. She had nowhere else to go anyway. Nowhere!

Bravely she lifted her chin, welcoming the cold pelting rain that served as a slap upon her face, reawakening her realization that she must not allow such impulsive emotions to overtake her. "I'm sorry," she said, looking toward the drenched Nellie and Mrs. Millet, standing on either side of her.

"Let me help you change and get you warm," Nellie pled.

Jenny nodded, then felt the comforting hand on her arm.

"I'll be all right," Jenny said and began to walk toward the doorway. She did not look at Tilden, standing in the rain.

But his hand shot out and grasped her arm. "Leave us," he said to the others.

"No," Jenny exclaimed, more terrified now than she had been at the minister's words. Looking around, she saw the uncertainty on each of their faces, but they had to obey the duke. His word was law. They quickly retreated into the castle.

"I'm. . .wet," Jenny stammered, looking down at the clothes plastered to her skin. She trembled, not only because she felt cold, but also because of the nearness of Tilden.

"So am I," he replied. "But that can be remedied. Now tell me, where were you going, Jenny?" he asked, his face a strange mask. She felt herself shaking uncontrollably.

"To. . .to the sea," she gasped. "Let me end it now. I can't bear this waiting any longer. I can't." She tried to sidetrack him but succeeded only in turning far enough to feel the stone walls behind her. There was no escape, for Tilden restricted her retreat from the front.

Her breath caught in her throat, and she had to part her lips to take in enough air. His arm came up, and she felt the wetness of his coat sleeve where it pressed against her own bare flesh above the drape of her soggy gown. She became quite unaware of the cold, for his hand cradled the back of her neck. Her eyes closed against the bending of his head toward her. Momentarily everything was forgotten in her great desire to be lost in his arms.

As if with a will of their own, her arms came up to embrace him. She felt the press of his sleeve against her soft flesh and the sweet roughness of his face against her cheek, the feel of his breath, hot against her ear. She felt as if she were drowning as surely as if she had plunged from the cliff. A delicious fear traveled throughout her body, rising as a wave that grew higher and higher.

"I cannot let you go, Jenny," he said, his voice raspy with emotion. "I will have you watched more closely to prevent your doing something drastic. We cannot lose you. I cannot."

The difficulty with which he spoke the words and the desperation in his voice reached her, dispelling the warmth and plunging her into icy depths.

Her arms fell to her sides. Realization swirled around her like the cruel wind. Cold and hard, the stone wall dug into her back. Wet and cold, his sleeve now chilled her body.

How could she have imagined his hand on her neck could be a caress? Was it not, instead, a grasp that could easily choke the life from her? Were not his words both a threat and a warning? And worse, was she not totally deranged for wanting to be in the arms of such a man?

What were Nellie's words? The women were wild for the Withington dukes. But the men of the family had that blood-thirsty, adventurous streak in them. Tilden wasn't in battle for a king. But the same loyalty and devotion he felt toward her mother would cause Tilden to see this situation through to the end—no matter what. Even if it meant taking the life of Ignatius Bodley—and allowing Jennifer Greenough to be hanged.

"Please, I..."

Sensing her helplessness, Tilden moved away from her. He had hoped to quell her desire to fling herself into the sea, to impress upon her that such a move would be folly, and bring acceptance to her mind. He apparently had failed in his efforts, however, for now she seemed like a caged animal, fearful and longing to retreat from its captor.

He regretted the words he had felt compelled to say to her, but he must give instructions for her to be guarded more carefully lest she harm herself. Watching her creep along the stone wall, inching away from him, holding onto the wall for support, he recalled his first sight of her from the top of the staircase. *I have found her,* he had thought. He had been unable to take his eyes from her but had watched her every move. Her beauty had captivated him. He would have known her anywhere, for she was a younger version of the lovely Diane. If only he could tell her how he truly felt. But for now, he let her disappear up a flight of stone steps.

Suddenly Tilden became aware of his wet clothing and shivered in the cold. If only the trial were over. Then he could speak his mind freely. Bingham had reported that he had very strong suspicions about the murder of Bodley and that it could be linked to another murder. The lawyer would say no more, but Tilden knew it would be a grave error in the eyes of all concerned if another tragedy occurred, such as Jenny's untimely death. Yes, he would increase his servants' watch on her.

Jenny fled to her bedroom and locked the door. As she reviewed the tumultuous events of the day, she had no choice but to accept the fact that she would not be allowed to take her own life. No, her fate was a dishonorable death by a hangman's noose. The closer the approaching trial came, the more she realized how slim her chances of acquittal. Hadn't her guilt already been decided when the official accusation had been made against her? Wasn't Bingham chasing a phantom stranger, supposed to have been in the glade that night?

If Bingham discovered the identity of that stranger, would he believe that Jenny's benefactor was trying to send her to the gallows rather than save her from them? Of course not! The idea was preposterous, even to herself. And Duke Tilden Withington would be quite aware of his power over Bingham.

If only she could talk with someone about it. But there was no one, not even her mother.

Much later, a servant brought her dinner.

"Do you mind if I join you?" Jenny's mother asked, stepping inside the room.

Jenny shook her head but resolved not to discuss the chapel incident. The two women ate in silence for a while, then engaged in safe and guarded chatter.

Suddenly the conversation took an unexpected turn. "Jenny," said her mother, "I must make you believe that neither Tilden nor I expected the minister to speak directly to you, and we are sorry."

Jenny looked at her mother's distressed face, not knowing what to say. "To repent, Mama," she asked, "would have done what? Would it have gotten me deported? Or would it make me appear guilty? Shouldn't I wait until after I'm convicted?"

"Oh, Jenny!" Her mother gasped and stood. "We had no thought of such a thing." She spread her hands helplessly. "We were only concerned about your eternal soul. We would have done the same if there were no charge lodged against you. Oh, please, believe me."

Jenny stood and allowed her mother to embrace her. She reveled in having her mother's arms around her. Suddenly she realized she could tell her mother anything without risking losing her love. But she would not tell her mother anything that might cause her more pain than she had already experienced. She knew her mother was happy to be with her but always miserable because of the threat that hung over them. It must have been that way when she was married to Stanford—happy, yet miserable.

"Mama," she said finally, moving back and taking her handkerchief to wipe away the tears that streaked her cheeks. "I wonder if maybe I could go into the city."

"Into the city? Darling, you know you can't leave here."

Jenny stepped back and began to slowly pace the floor. "Yes, I know. But I thought it might be possible for me to see Bingham. I need to talk to him."

"Well, we can send for him," her mother said confidently. "He would come immediately."

"I know," Jenny said, realizing her mother would not understand. She could not confess to her mother the unbearable prospect of facing Tilden again. His presence completely disoriented her and made her inadequate to cope with the issues that Bingham had said she must try to be clear headed about. "I feel a need to talk to him. I mean, away from here. I have imposed upon Duke Withington enough already."

"Imposed? Whatever do you mean, child?"

"Well," Jenny tried to explain, gesturing helplessly. She had never been good at lying. She was simply trying to find a way to escape the castle, Tilden, and the accusations that seemed to weigh heavily upon her. But such an explanation would never be understood. "I have accepted Duke Withington's generosity and am unable to reciprocate graciously. I really don't like being beholden."

Her mother sank slowly into the nearest chair. "What do you mean, his generosity?"

"Well, Mama," Jenny said. "Everything! His house. His servants. His money bought the dress I'm wearing. Even the food I eat—"

"You don't know?" her mother interrupted.

"Know what, Mama?"

"Bingham didn't tell you? I assumed during all those weeks before Tilden and I came, he would have told you."

"Told me what, Mama?"

"Sit down, Jenny," she said. Jenny obediently sat in a chair across from her.

"As you must know, Jenny, Stanford was a very wealthy man. I shall never want for anything that money can buy. He left the controlling interest of the businesses in America to Tilden. But Stanford always considered you his child, because you were mine.

"Of course he knew better," she added quickly. "But he loved you because you were mine. Jenny, this castle is half mine. The other half belongs equally to you and Tilden. Stanford also left a considerable sum of money that only you can touch."

Jenny stared at her mother, trying to comprehend her words.

"Jenny," she assured, "you have taken nothing from Tilden financially.

Oh, he might pay for items from his own money, but you could easily repay him. You are a very wealthy woman."

The news was quite shocking. But with the realization of her wealth, an unwanted thought pierced her heart with the force of a dagger.

She must try to remain calm. Plan something. She would send a servant for Bingham. Or perhaps she would ask a servant to ready a carriage to take her into London. Perhaps Nellie. But Tilden had increased the guard on her. That wouldn't work.

"This does put a new light on things," Jenny said carefully. Then she rubbed her temples. "But, Mama, I am afraid the emotional events of this day have left me with a frightful headache. Would you mind if I lie down and rested for a bit?"

"Not at all," her mother said, concern in her eyes. "I'll send Nellie right away with some cool cloths." After giving Jenny a gentle kiss on her brow, she left the suite.

Jenny allowed Nellie's faithful ministrations, then listened to the wind howling against her windows, as if to warn her that even nature was set against her. Somehow she had to talk to Bingham and tell him of her suspicions. Shivering beneath the covers, she waited until near dawn. The rain had stopped and the wind had abated. Looking down onto the courtyard far below, her heart seemed to stop, for something moved. Then she breathed more easily. It was only a shadow made by a sudden gust of wind through the branches of the trees, or else it had been a reflection of the moonlight peeping through the clouds that raced across the sky.

If she could reach the chestnut mare, she could make it. No one would expect her to try anything so soon after Tilden's warning against an escape attempt. There were no windows in the dressing room, so no one would see the glow from the single candle she lit. Hurriedly dressing in her riding habit, Jenny felt mounting excitement stirring within. This was the sort of thing she should have done instead of attending Bodley's engagement party. How differently everything would have turned out.

Or would it? Duke Tilden Withington would have found her, somewhere, anywhere, regardless of what she had done, for he had been so determined. She would have remained unsuspecting. At least now she knew of the danger.

Holding her breath, she crept along the silent, cold stone walls until finally reaching the courtyard. Safety! Almost! If she could get to the distant tree. Oh! That wasn't a tree. The shadow she had seen from the window was indeed a person. Tilden. Her heart sunk into her stomach. Failure. Failure again!

Tilden called her name and held out his hands toward her. He moved forward.

Helplessness, like a shadow, stole over her. For the second time in her life, she felt a welcomed darkness begin to descend upon her. Before she completely lost consciousness, his strong arms came around her, lifting her. As her cheek touched his shoulder, she had but one thought. *I am in the arms of my beloved enemy.* Then there was only darkness.

Chapter 10

Two days later, Silas Bingham arrived. Tilden had sent a servant to London to summon the lawyer after Jenny had explained her reason for being in the courtyard the morning she had encountered Tilden.

"Couldn't you tell me you wished to see him?" Tilden had asked. Jenny had not answered, afraid to admit that she couldn't trust him.

Silas Bingham had a way of calming her, assuring her that the real murderer would be apprehended.

"Do you mean," she asked fearfully, "that you have discovered the whereabouts of the stranger in the glade with me that night?"

Bingham focused his stern eyes on her for so long, she had to escape his gaze by looking down at her hands. She took his silence for denial that the stranger had been found. And of course, she knew he could not have been, unless they had apprehended some innocent person.

It was the time to tell Bingham, to disclose all she had suspected and to expose Tilden. But as she tried to speak the words, they stuck in her throat. What would her life be like if she condemned the man she loved? How could she send Tilden to the gallows? How could she and her mother ever have a loving relationship if Jenny were the cause of Tilden's arrest? Her mother would certainly understand, but the gulf would be there, just the same.

Jenny looked across at Mr. Bingham, who patiently observed her, waiting for whatever she might disclose. Her lips trembled as she slowly shook her head. The words would not come. She could not accuse Tilden of murder.

"I'm sorry, Mr. Bingham. What seemed so urgent was only a foolish notion. There is nothing more I can tell you. Please forgive me for taking you away from your responsibilities in London. All we can do at this point is hope for the best."

No amount of persuasion on Bingham's part could induce her to reveal what lay at the base of her fears and frustrations. "Do you have any other suspects?" she asked, with only a minute hope that she was wrong in what seemed daily to become more and more a reality.

"None, Jenny, other than those I've had all along. And suspicions are not enough. In court, Jenny, we must have more than even certainty. We must present motive, opportunity, and evidence, either literal or circumstantial."

Jenny felt as if a weight were pressing on her chest. She could see how a prosecuting attorney would present her motive and opportunity, along with the evidence of arsenic in a glass. No matter what she might say, she could see the accusing finger pointing nowhere else but at her.

"What did she say?" Tilden asked Bingham anxiously after Jenny left the study and went riding.

"Very little," the lawyer replied, wearing a worried look. "What happened while I was away, Tilden?"

Tilden shook his head. "Lady Diane told her of the inheritance, and the news had a strange effect on Jenny. She attempted to run away. Then she was so frightened, she fainted. Perhaps I am imagining things," Tilden added, "but I think she has withdrawn from me since the first day her mother and I arrived from America. Something I said, or did, has alienated her from me."

"Can you supply a reason, Tilden?" Bingham asked, his voice heavy with accusation.

Tilden turned toward the window, where he could look out at the trees, golden, brown, and red in the warm afternoon sunshine. The rain had stopped yesterday. It would be wonderful to ride about the grounds with Jenny and to watch her long black hair bounce in the wind, and see the golden glow the warm sun would bring to her face. There was so much he would like to do.

"I suppose it's natural for her to be afraid, and more so as the time for the trial draws nearer," Tilden said finally.

"But she remained optimistic before you and Lady Diane arrived, Tilden. Something has changed."

Tilden turned toward Bingham, knowing the man would be honest. "You believe in her innocence, don't you?"

The attorney remained silent.

"Bingham!" Tilden almost shouted, staring fiercely at the man.

Bingham stood and lightly tapped the side of his cheek with his finger.

"Has it occurred to you, Tilden," he asked, pointing that finger at Tilden, "that Jenny might have a mental lapse about that night?"

Tilden swallowed hard and shook his head. "It's impossible that she—"

"No, not impossible," Bingham interrupted. "She knows something she is not telling. Something that has bothered her since you and Lady Diane arrived."

Tilden stared at Bingham. "I don't understand."

"Neither do I," Bingham replied. "But I intend to. After dinner tonight, we'll talk. You and I and Jenny. Here in the study."

"How do you propose to get her here with me?" Tilden asked skeptically. "She avoids me now."

"I shall demand it," Bingham replied. "And you will accuse her of murder."

"What?" Tilden stormed. "Have you gone mad?"

"It must be done. That is exactly what will happen in the courtroom."

"Bingham, don't you know how devastating that will be for Jenny? To think that everyone, including me, believes she murdered Bodley?"

"It must be done, Tilden. Her mother cannot, so it must be you who accuses her. We must shock her into disclosing whatever she has shut up in her mind—these things that frighten and confuse her."

Tilden opened his mouth to protest, but he saw the wisdom of Bingham's words and intentions. He turned to face the window again.

"You must!" Bingham repeated.

Jenny felt braver with Bingham in the castle and consented to eat dinner in the formal dining room. The conversation remained light and centered on happenings in the city. With summer nearing an end, the weather became a topic, and Jenny's mother noted how the leaves were changing so quickly even on the cliffs near the sea.

For the present, Jenny did not fear for her life. All Tilden had to do was wait, and the court would handle the rest.

After dinner, Jenny asked Bingham to linger in the dining room for a moment. The others left them in privacy. "I wish to leave the castle," she asserted. "Even if I am to be placed in a prison while awaiting trial."

Bingham sighed heavily and looked down at the toes of his shoes. "Let's discuss it in the library, Jennifer." He took her by the arm and led her into the hallway, where her mother and Tilden waited.

"Come with us, Mama," Jenny said when they neared the study.

"I don't believe Mr. Bingham wants me there, darling," she replied.

The lawyer did not contradict her, so Jenny nodded and followed him into the library. To her shock, Tilden followed and stood with his back against the closed door, blocking any escape.

"I thought we would be alone," she said, turning toward Bingham, her discomfiture obvious.

"The three of us should discuss this." Bingham held out his hand, indicating that Jenny should sit in the chair near the fireplace.

She sat, wondering if Bingham realized that Tilden was involved. Surely a famous attorney with his reputation would know such things. But perhaps Bingham saw Tilden simply as his client. After all, hadn't Tilden approached him about taking this case? Wouldn't Bingham's primary obligation be to the duke rather than to her?

Tilden sat on the couch across from her. Bingham took a chair at the side of the fireplace, in the shadows. It seemed to Jenny that only she and Tilden were in the room, making her uncomfortable. She sank back against the chair.

Bingham outlined the case, making it clear that their only defense was lack of motive on Jenny's part. She had everything to gain by Bodley's staying alive.

"I had nothing to gain," Jenny protested.

"Ah, but by the standards of society, Jenny, you had everything to gain married to a man who could give you all the world's goods and escort you into royal circles."

"I'd rather. . ." She hesitated, then added, "die."

"How did you do it, Jenny?" Tilden asked suddenly. "How did you manage to sneak the arsenic into the glass without Bodley or someone else knowing?"

Hearing her gasp and seeing the devastation shrouding her face, Tilden stood and walked over to the fire, his back to Jenny. He shot a murderous glare at Bingham. How could this possibly do anything for Jenny? He'd only hurt her further.

Glancing back at Jenny, he saw the horror in her eyes. Misery rested upon her countenance as she lowered her eyes to her lap. Her chin began to tremble.

Tilden could bear it no longer. With a fierce glare at Bingham, he turned and strode over to Jenny, knelt in front of her, and took her cold fingers in his hands.

"Forgive me, Jenny. I know you didn't kill Bodley. I've never believed that. Please say you forgive me?"

She would not look up or speak. "If I had stayed that night, Jenny," he said low, "perhaps you would not be on trial. But I was in such a state over having found you. Years of searching had been futile. Then, there you were, a beautiful picture. I wondered if you were a figment of my imagination."

Jenny did not understand. He had just accused her of murdering Bodley, yet now he admitted in front of Bingham that he'd been there that night. She shook her head in confusion. "If you had stayed, then we both might have been accused of murder," she said with some difficulty.

She felt his hands stiffen against hers but knew she could not back down now. "Or," she said almost under her breath, "it might have been you who was implicated and not me at all."

"I don't understand, Jenny. Please explain." His voice held authority, and she feared looking into his eyes. She pulled her hands away, and he stood.

"All right," she said with a sense of determination. "I cannot keep this to myself any longer. You told me not to mention that you were there."

"But that was before the murder, Jenny. When I said that, I didn't know the murder was going to take place."

Jenny wanted desperately to believe that, but the evidence she had kept to herself was overwhelming. And if a person would murder, there was nothing to stop him from also telling a lie.

"It might have been your glass that had the poison in it," she protested.

Tilden stooped down again and took her by the shoulders, shaking her gently. "What are you saying, Jenny?"

A sob escaped her throat. She felt his hands pressing into her shoulders but could hold back no longer. He became more insistent and shook her harder. "What do you mean, my glass?"

"The one you brought to the glade and set on the table," she said accusingly.

Tilden made a noise much like a snort. "I forgot that I took a drink to the glade. I didn't want it, but I hadn't wanted to make myself conspicuous by refusing."

Jenny recalled that Bingham had said many times something seemingly insignificant always tripped up the criminals. Is this what would trip up Tilden?

"That night," Tilden said emphatically, "there were much more important things on my mind, Jenny, than a drink. When I think of it, and I assure you I do quite often, it is not a drink I remember."

Jenny could not stop the sudden emotion that flooded her being. Warmth flooded her face, and she knew Tilden would notice.

"So you think I killed Bodley," he said in a tone that frightened her.

"I didn't want to think it. But what else could I think? A stranger.

One who kissed me and held me the first time he saw me. Then...then...
telling me to say nothing. What else could I think? I knew it was in the
newspapers, and I felt if the stranger were innocent, he would come to
my rescue. I even dreamed he would." Unable to hold in her doubts any
longer, she continued. "I wondered why he did not come and proclaim
me innocent. Then. . ." She hesitated and would not meet his eyes. "I
realized he could not."

"Why could he not?" Tilden asked.

"Because instead of proving me innocent, he might be letting himself
in for arrest as an accomplice, or. . ."

"Or?" he asked, urging her on.

Her voice became a whisper. "Or he might even be suspected of
murder."

Tilden let go of her shoulders, stepped back, and almost lost his balance. "You honestly think I killed Bodley?"

She drew in her breath. She knew it was dangerous to tell a murderer
that she knew what he had done, but she could not hide the secret any
longer. "I no longer think you tried to kill Lord Bodley."

Just as a sigh of relief escaped his throat and a light gleamed in his eye,
she lifted her chin courageously and looked past him, toward the fire. After
a moment of hesitation, she continued. "I think...that you might have been
trying to kill me."

"What?" he shouted fiercely.

Jenny looked up into his glaring eyes and covered her mouth with her
hand to stifle a scream.

"Why would I want to kill you?" he demanded.

Tears formed in her eyes. He waited, then asked in a calmer tone,
"Could you tell me how I attempted to...murder you?"

"The drink," she said.

"The drink?"

"Yes," she replied. "The drink you set on the table. If you wanted to
murder me, then you would expect or hope that I might drink it after
you left."

"How can you be sure he drank from my glass?" Tilden asked.

"I have pictured it over and over and over," Jenny replied. "Lord Bodley came into the glade, weaving back and forth and holding a goblet. I
remember distinctly that he drained it and set the empty glass on the table.
Then a while passed as he came at me, and I pushed him away. He made
crude remarks, then sat at the table and talked about our wedding day when
I would behave more favorably toward him. He picked up your glass and

began to drink from it. Not long after that, he died."

No one spoke. Jenny felt she must continue. "So, perhaps the poison was not intended for Bodley after all. Perhaps it was intended for me."

With a cry, Bingham jumped to his feet. Jenny had forgotten he was there, but now he and Tilden faced each other. An expression of shock rested on both their faces.

"This is a development I had not anticipated," Bingham remarked in a disgusted tone. "If I am indeed the best lawyer in Europe, then God pity the poor souls at the mercy of lesser attorneys." He shook his head dejectedly.

"And why, Lady Jennifer," he asked pointedly, "why would Duke Tilden Withington wish to murder you? Would it not make more sense for the culprit to be someone in the Cottingham family? Were they not all terribly distraught when Bodley sought your hand in marriage, rather than Lady Emmaline's?"

"They certainly perceived that as an insult," Jenny said. "But what the Cottinghams wanted most was Bodley's money and access to royal circles. They were quite angry at the onset; however, that anger abated and they accepted, even wanted, my marriage to Bodley after being convinced he would not marry Emmaline. My death, or Bodley's, would be the last thing any of them would want."

"Motive, motive," Bingham almost shouted. "Why would Duke Withington want your death?"

Tilden had walked to the other side of the fireplace. She felt slightly braver with Bingham between them. "For two reasons," she replied. "One, because he did not wish to share the inheritance that his brother left to both of us. After all, I am an outsider, not blood-related to my mother's late husband. Another reason is because. . ."

When she hesitated, Bingham stepped closer. "Because?"

"Because I would just be in the way. He is in love with my mother. He found me for her. That endears him to her. But now, I am a nuisance with whom his money, and her attentions, must be shared."

"Very good motives," Bingham said finally.

Jenny tried to keep the tears from leaking out, but soon they moved unchecked down her cheeks. A small hiccup escaped her throat. She returned to her chair, lest she fall.

Tilden took out a clean folded handkerchief from his inner pocket and knelt beside her. Gently, he wiped her tears.

"Jenny," he whispered, and she looked at him. She could not bear the beautiful smile on his lips or the warmth in his eyes. He should not look at her that way, but he was a rake who had plotted her death.

He lifted her hand and touched it with his lips.

For a moment, Jenny stared at him. She had accused him of things he didn't deny, and yet he kissed her hand. He was so confident. And why not? The court had accused her. She would die for the crime. She had hoped that somehow she might be wrong, that Tilden would say she was mistaken about his trying to murder her. But he made no denial.

Perhaps he knew she loved him enough to want him to live and be happy with her mother, rather than see him swing from the gallows.

"I will not say these things in a courtroom," she said and, with that, looked beyond Tilden to Bingham.

Tilden's fingers touched her face. "Oh, my dearest Jenny. What you must be going through."

She could bear his touch no longer, lest she beg him to hold her, to kiss her again, to lie and say he loved her. "How demented I must be," she cried aloud. "Oh, please, I must go."

Tilden rose and stepped aside. Standing before him, she could see the longing in his eyes. Perhaps his actions that night had been rash and he regretted it. But it was too late, all too late. With a cry, she turned and ran from the room.

Staring at the still-open door, Tilden contemplated Jenny's accusations. He thought of all the remarks he had made about Diane. He had said he would do anything for her. He had explained that his search for Jenny had been for Diane's sake. He had often spoken of Diane's beauty and of his admiration for her. He could readily see why Jenny concluded he was in love with her mother.

"She does not seem to realize, Tilden," Bingham said after a moment of quiet, "that you could have simply forgotten about her. No one else would have searched for her, and my firm would have done nothing without your prompting."

"So there goes my motive for attempting to murder Jenny?" Tilden asked, a wry grin playing about the corners of his mouth.

"Oh, we could press the point," Bingham replied. "A jury might even believe her to be right."

"As you have often said," Tilden commented, "the simplest, obvious things are usually the most generally overlooked."

Bingham nodded. "We're ready to go to trial," he announced.

"You are ready?" Only that morning, Bingham had told him that he had not discovered the information he needed to properly defend Jenny.

"Yes," Bingham replied. "Tonight's conversation brought out things

I should have anticipated."

"You do not mean, Bingham," Tilden asked, "that you believe I tried to murder Jenny?"

"You know that if I did, I would certainly present such evidence."

"That I know," Tilden remarked. "You can't actually believe. . . ?"

A slow smile graced Bingham's lips, and a wizened look came into his eyes. "The evidence weighs heavily against you, Tilden. I think if these things came to light in a courtroom, as they did tonight, you most assuredly would be convicted."

Tilden stared. Finally a full smile spread across Bingham's face. "However, the important thing, Tilden, is what we have discovered tonight. The missing link. The key. The detail I've been looking for. That one piece of evidence."

"What is that?" Tilden asked, feeling strangely implicated.

"The poison was not intended for Lord Bodley. That is the only thing that can clear Jenny. We do not have to prove her innocence. We simply have to prove that the poison was not intended for Bodley."

"Even if the evidence is against me?"

"You hired me to clear her name, to prove her innocence, and that I shall do," Bingham said with a confidence Tilden had not detected before in this case. "Don't look so glum, old chap. If you didn't put the poison in the goblet, you have nothing to fear."

Astonished, Tilden inquired, "You think I did?"

"We must think as we would in a court of law, Tilden. As we did here tonight. You're a rising young attorney. Now, how does it look to you?"

Tilden snorted. "It looks as if I enticed Lady Jenny, kissed her to divert her attention, and gave her a poisoned drink so I could inherit all the duke's fortune and marry her mother." He half laughed with incredulity. "That is what the prosecuting attorney would point out, isn't it?"

"Exactly."

"And how do we answer?" Tilden asked.

"Simple," Bingham replied. "If you didn't do it, we quit trying to defend Jenny and begin to incriminate the real culprit."

"But as she said," Tilden pointed out, "no one else had a motive for wanting Jenny dead." He sat down and slumped in the chair, his forearms on his thighs, then straightened. "Bingham," he said slowly. "If Jenny really believes I tried to kill her, then why did she not mention it to you?"

Bingham smiled wryly. "To her, Tilden, you represent two persons. Her first encounter with you was when you were simply a stranger, a knight in shining armor who offered her a means of escape from the intolerable present and hope for something other than an unbearable future. Then, when the stranger did not appear after she had been accused of murder, she believed the stranger had killed Bodley."

"But I did come to her, Bingham," Tilden replied. "Through you."

"She has not thought of it in that way, Tilden. She expected you personally. She never told me that you were the stranger."

"I am rather surprised at that," Tilden said.

Bingham shook his head. "No, Tilden. The stranger gave her a moment in her life that she had longed for and never had before. A moment to remember. I'm sure it has taken her a long time to face the facts that the stranger had not, shall we say, cared for her but was furthering his own selfish motives."

"I can see how it would look that way," Tilden said, beginning to understand. "Did she tell you those things about. . .a special moment in her life?" he asked, attempting to make his voice indifferent.

"No," Bingham said kindly. "It is something I have surmised by what she didn't say. Instinct, you might say."

"Instinct?"

"Yes, the same way I knew Jenny has been holding back something. As if protecting someone."

"Me," Tilden replied. "But why would she protect a murderer she felt was putting the blame on her or may even have tried to kill her?"

"As I stated, Tilden, you represent two people to her. You have been responsible for giving her the only sense of freedom she has ever had. She was hidden by her father and relatives. Here, she rides the grounds, sleeps when she wants, skips meals if she wishes, eats in her room, reads books without being ridiculed. She has servants rather than being one. Most important, you have reunited her with her mother. She cannot hate you. And she cannot publicly accuse you. I do think she would rather have her own life taken. I think if you tried to strangle her, she would not utter a single protest."

Surely Bingham exaggerated, and yet something about his words touched Tilden in a way nothing ever had. But he did not want some kind of unfounded gratitude from Jenny. He wanted much more. "I should go and talk to her," Tilden said, starting toward the doorway.

"Duke Tilden Withington!" Bingham's voice resonated in his most stern manner, and Tilden stopped short of the doorway. "Where were you the night Ignatius, Lord Bodley was murdered?"

Tilden stiffened, and his gaze rested upon the door without seeing it. Instead, he saw possibilities that staggered his imagination with both horror and exhilaration.

"You know, Bingham," he replied levelly, neither his gaze nor his voice faltering, his back turned to Bingham.

"I've known all along," Bingham replied. "But why did you not tell me? Why did you allow so many weeks to pass without any word of your being in the glade with Jenny that night?"

Tilden had had many things on his mind the day after the murder. His first thoughts had been to prevent Jenny from being detained in a prison. Then he had been consumed with the idea of bringing Diane to her daughter. He had expected that Jenny herself would inform Bingham of all the events of that evening, including his having been there. He hadn't realized that he'd not told his name to Jenny. However, Bingham would have known who the stranger in the glade had to be. And regardless of what Jenny had said, there was no way of knowing if the arsenic had been in his glass or in Bodley's.

Bingham had asked his question the way it would be offered in the courtroom. He expected Tilden to give an accounting now, as he would later be forced to do in court.

"Why didn't I tell you, Bingham?" Tilden repeated after a long silence, feeling the attorney's eyes boring into his back. "Surely you cannot suspect that I would attempt to harm sweet Jenny."

Tilden turned, and his level gaze met the eyes of Silas Bingham. "There's only one reason, of course, that I followed Jenny into the glade that night," he confessed. "I'd searched for Lady Jenny for many years. Then when I found her, the most beautiful woman in the world, and discovered her engaged to that wretch, Bodley, I had no alternative. It was I who murdered Ignatius, Lord Bodley."

"That's ridiculous," Bingham said. "All you would have to do was whisk Jenny away from that party. She would have gone willingly. You had much more to offer than Bodley. You have no believable motive for murdering Bodley."

"Ah," Tilden said with a wry grin, "but you know the legends and myths surrounding the blood-thirsty Withingtons."

Chapter 11

Jenny heard the news from Lady Diane. She had just finished breakfast in her dining area when Diane knocked, then burst in without waiting for an answer.

"Jenny," she said, rushing over to her. "Silas just told me. Tilden has confessed."

"Confessed?" Jenny rose to her feet, almost knocking over the small table. He admitted he tried to kill her? "You mean—?"

"Yes, yes, darling. He says he murdered Bodley."

Jenny's thoughts were in turmoil. She had decided the poison had been intended for her and that Tilden had done it for the inheritance. Putting her hand to her head, she sank back into the chair.

"Oh, Mama, do you believe it?"

"Of course not, Jenny. Not any more than I believe you did it. I have come to the conclusion that you were framed. And Tilden?" She scoffed. "Why, he had no motive. He could buy and sell Bodley ten times over."

"Then why did he confess?" Jenny cried in desperation.

"For you, Jenny," she whispered in a shaking voice. "For you and for me."

"But you said nobody will believe him."

"Of course not! Not any more than I believe you murdered Bodley."

Jenny stared out the window. *Someone murdered him, though. The magistrate had me arrested for the murder. The court charged me with murder.*

"I must admit," her mother added, "this is a noble attempt on Tilden's part."

Jenny shook her head. Not noble, but clever. To divert attention from her accusation that she had been the intended victim, Tilden had confessed to a crime for which he knew he couldn't be convicted. And even if someone were to believe her claim—that he wanted her dead—he still wouldn't be convicted of murder because she hadn't died. His confession appeared so preposterous, she felt it made her look even guiltier.

Jenny put a shaking hand to her head. How unbearable to see her mother in such distress. Jenny realized that she alone stood in the way of her mother's happiness with Tilden. She would allow it no longer.

"I won't let him take the blame, Mama. I won't." She leaped from the chair and rushed out into the hallway, oblivious to her mother's pleas to let Bingham handle the situation.

Jenny ran to the study. Bingham wasn't there.

"Where is he?" she asked the butler.

"Who, my lady?"

"Silas Bingham!"

"In his room, perhaps," the butler replied.

Jenny didn't know which room Bingham occupied during his stay at the castle. "Please direct me to his room," she ordered the butler, who registered surprise.

From years of training, he said nothing and bowed, then led the way to the west wing of the second floor. Jenny pounded on the door the butler pointed out. Almost immediately, Bingham stood facing her.

"Protocol be hanged," he said, standing aside. "Come in."

Jenny stepped inside to find a valise on the bed.

"You're leaving?" she asked, her voice holding a note of terror.

"There's nothing more I can do here," he said resignedly, and she felt he looked a little older. But of course he would be distressed about Tilden's confession.

"You feel defeated, don't you?" she asked.

Bingham's eyes didn't meet hers, and she felt he deliberately turned away so she could not read his expression. When he turned back, he had taken a shirt from the drawer and laid it in the valise.

"Because Til. . .Duke Withington. . .has confessed," she added.

"You could hardly expect me to be exuberant over such a matter," he replied curtly.

"No, of course not," she agreed and went over to sit on the edge of the bed so she could watch his face. "But he didn't do it. I did."

He stared at her, his face inscrutable. Then his face flushed with anger. "So! Both of you want to go to the gallows!" he stormed.

She had not seen him look like that before. He seemed hard and even cruel. She felt herself shrink away as he took a step closer, bending over her. "You two are bent upon destroying each other."

"No, no. He didn't have anything to do with it," she pleaded. "He must not be accused. I did it. Only I. You don't believe we did it together, do you?"

"Neither I, nor any court of law, believe you two were in cahoots. The kind of careful watch your relatives kept over you would prevent the opportunity for such plans to be put in effect."

"But it will only make me look more guilty if he confesses to the court. It will look like he believes I did it but is willing to take the blame. You will not allow Duke Withington to go through with this, will you?"

"Can I prevent him?"

"I am the one who is charged with the murder," she said, her voice rising. "I did it alone. No one helped me, and no one else must be accused or allowed to confess. I will say it was my glass on that table beside Bodley's. I am guilty. I confess. I confess." With that, she buried her face in her hands.

A knock sounded on the door. "Pardon me," Tilden said, looking toward Jenny in surprise. He turned to Bingham. "I came to tell you the coach is ready whenever you are. Do you want to take me into town with you?"

"I take you in?" Bingham asked sullenly.

"Yes. I have confessed to murder. We need to do whatever is necessary to clear Jenny and take me into custody."

"But he can't take you in," Jenny interjected. "I have confessed to Mr. Bingham that I am guilty. We do not need to go to trial. I can be sentenced right away."

Silas Bingham shook his head. "If you two will excuse me, I will leave. There is important work to be done. But I will say, only one person is guilty of committing the crime, and I intend to reveal that person's identity in trial. Neither of you is going to deny me that opportunity."

"Then you are certain who committed the crime?" Tilden asked.

"I haven't been sitting idly by, Tilden, waiting for confessions to come my way. That is not my method of operation."

"But I thought you were completely baffled," the duke replied, "until my confession."

"It might surprise you to learn I haven't disclosed all my findings to you, Tilden. It isn't a good practice since you are emotionally involved with some of the parties in question. Also, I've been aware that you concealed some vital facts from me."

"Then you intend to expose the villain during the trial?"

"That is what I just said, Tilden, and it is my usual practice. Sometimes I feel I missed my calling. Perhaps I should have gone on the stage. I do enjoy a good drama. Especially when I have the leading role." He closed the valise with a snap. "Please! Don't try and deprive me of earning the enormous fee this is costing you." His voice held a bit of humor, and a smile hovered about his lips.

"Then you believe you know who the murderer is without a doubt?" Tilden asked.

"I know who and why," Bingham replied confidently. "Now I must discover how."

"Shall I tell you?" Tilden asked.

Bingham laughed softly and lifted a hand. "Please," he said, shaking his head. He then picked up the valise and headed for the door. "Leave a little work for me to do, Your Grace," he said mockingly. "How could I ever respect myself if my murderers tell me everything?"

He then grew serious as he studied both members of his bewildered audience. "There is something you two can do," he said. "I assure you the murderer will get his just dues, with or without confessions or protestations. So why don't you two stop trying to save each other and concentrate on telling the truth?"

Jenny didn't know the truth about anything anymore. Why did Bingham not take Tilden seriously? Were they all plotting against her—even Bingham? Or was Bingham planning a courtroom accusation of Tilden in court?

Bingham set the valise on the floor, then placed his hands on Tilden's and Jenny's shoulders. "Why don't you two concentrate on enjoying this short period of time before the trial? It begins in two weeks."

He then lifted the valise. A footman stood in the hall, ready to take it from him. As soon as Bingham was out of sight, Jenny said in a small voice, "Excuse me," and started to walk past Tilden.

His words stopped her progress. "Do you have a Bible in your room, Jenny?"

She felt her throat constricting. The question startled her as much as when the minister had asked if she wanted to repent.

Unable to speak, she took a few steps, saw Tilden's hand move in her direction, then broke into a run down the long corridor.

No one had mentioned the minister since that day when Jenny had run into the courtyard to rid herself of his words and had become drenched with the cold rain. Now, she felt drenched with the tears that had fallen down her face throughout the day. She had refused to speak to anyone, except to insist that she would eat nothing.

As the day wore on, she began to see the futility of her inaction and remembered Bingham's words, "two weeks," and Tilden's question, "Do you have a Bible?" Those words implied impending doom.

If such were her future, should she not prepare herself? Or would she remain a whimpering wench with no backbone whatsoever? No one had been able to help her overcome this charge of murder. Bingham had tried, yet he refused to consider another person's confession. Her mother's belief in her innocence was based on hope, rather than hard evidence. After a sixteen-year absence, how could her mother possibly know her true character?

No one could help her. No one—in this world.

But could God? Would God? She did not know enough about Him. She thought Him fearful. And yet her mother had spoken of Jesus as someone wonderful that had come into her life.

Jenny arose from her bed of tears, bathed her face with cold water, and summoned Nellie. A short while later in her private dining room, while forcing herself to eat some of the sumptuous meal that had been brought up, she talked with her mother.

"I would like to apologize to the minister," she said, adding, "it was not he who made me run, but the fears within myself."

"We shall have him come again if you like," her mother replied, hope shining in her eyes. "I shall instruct him to deliver his sermon on 'Love.'"

To Jenny's surprise, the minister arrived before sunset. Although the small stone chapel felt cool, evening rays of the setting sun touched the stained-glass windows and lent an ethereal glow to the small room. To her delight, the minister did not appear so ominous this time.

Sitting a few rows from the front, she did not know if anyone sat farther back, nor did it matter. She was not concerned about whether her innocence was believed; she wanted to know if she was prepared to face whatever fate awaited her.

The minister said that God loved the world so much He sent His Son, Jesus, to shed His blood and die for the sins of the world. All who believed in Him, repented of their sins, and accepted Jesus in their hearts, minds, and lives would be forgiven, would receive the Holy Spirit into their lives, and would live forever.

Jenny liked this sermon so much better than the few sermons she had heard in the past. They had made God seem so forbidding. But the minister made God seem approachable.

"We're all guilty of sin," the minister said. "Even our thoughts condemn us. But there is hope. There is forgiveness. There is a new life possible for us—if we come to Jesus."

That's what her mother had said she and Tilden had done, Jenny realized. Obviously, the experience had changed her mother's life. Although

Jenny didn't like to think her mother had abandoned her to run away with Duke Stanford, she could understand how such a thing had happened when her mother was young, distressed, and so in love. But then she had begun a new life in Christ. And her mother had shown nothing but sorrow and repentance for the hurts Jenny had experienced during their long years of separation.

Then, a great shudder traveled through Jenny as a horrible thought occurred to her. She, too, had been ready to do something reckless and sinful. During those terrible days when she was engaged to Bodley, she had been desperate enough that she herself might have been capable of murdering the man if the opportunity had arisen.

"*Even our thoughts condemn us*," the minister said. At this moment, Jenny felt condemned not by a court, but by her own conscience and by the Word of God. She wanted to run as she had before. Something was telling her to flee. The glow had faded from the windows. Shadows crept. Darkness was falling. Words seemed to echo around the stone walls. "All have sinned. All have come short of the glory of God."

This feeling of guilt had nothing to do with the accusation of murder. It had nothing to do with whether anyone believed in her innocence. It had to do with her soul. Eternity loomed large before her. A higher court than man's had condemned her, and although she closed her eyes against the scene, she could not close her heart to the minister's words.

"The Lord is my shepherd; I shall not want."

I am to follow Him? Not want for anything? In this life. . .or in the next?

"He maketh me to lie down in green pastures: he leadeth me beside the still waters."

Oh, I want the green pastures, the still waters—not this impenetrable darkness.

"He restoreth my soul: he leadeth me in the paths of righteousness for his name's sake."

I want to run and hide, but at the same time, I want to be restored. I want to be led along the right path.

"Yea, though I walk through the valley of the shadow of death, I will fear no evil: for thou art with me; thy rod and thy staff they comfort me."

I'm walking there, in the shadow of death. Not fear? Oh, I want that. I want a shepherd who will comfort me.

"Thou preparest a table before me in the presence of mine enemies: thou anointest my head with oil; my cup runneth over."

I have enemies who want to destroy me. But it is not the court of law that is my enemy. The real enemy is evil itself, is the sin that God says is in each person.

This is an entirely different matter.

Jenny slipped from the bench, fell to her knees, and laid her head on the seat while rivers of troubled waters flowed from her eyes, like a fast-rushing stream cleansing the debris from its banks.

The minister's voice came nearer, but she did not mind. She was hearing God speak through his servant. "Surely goodness and mercy shall follow me all the days of my life: and I will dwell in the house of the Lord for ever."

The minister then added, "Jesus said, 'I am the good shepherd.' And also, 'him that cometh to me I will in no wise cast out.' Jenny, do you want this Good Shepherd to be your Lord and Savior?"

Do I want?

Slowly, Jenny raised her head and her tear-drenched face. Through eyes blurred by tears, she saw the light. Had someone lit the candles in the wall niches? Or was it that her blinded eyes could now see?

With each flicker of the candle, alternating between shadow and light, her fear and doubt threatened, but she kept her eyes on the fuzzy glow and felt the words like a healing stream. "The Lord is my shepherd; I shall not want."

Do I want? Oh, I want for so much. I want the green pastures; I want the still waters; I want the restoring of my soul; I want the comfort; I want to dwell in the house of the Lord forever.

"Oh yes," she whispered. Then the flood started again, and this time it flowed until she felt free and forgiven and clean and new, and she felt as if it were Jesus who lifted her to her feet.

"Then He is yours," the minister said. "He is with you in spirit and shall always be. You don't have to want for what He offers. It is now yours, for the taking."

"Now?" she asked. "Not just. . .in eternity?"

The minister smiled. "There is more in eternity. What you have now is His presence, His guiding, His comfort."

Even though I walk through the valley of the shadow of death, He is with me.

The minister prayed, and Jenny repented of the sin in her life, of all her mean, vindictive thoughts, even those she'd had against Bodley. She confessed those times when she'd had hard thoughts against her relatives, including her mother for abandoning her and her father for deceiving her, and against some of her governesses and tutors and even life itself.

Jenny felt as if the weight of her burden no longer weighed upon her. Oh, what would it be like—this new life?

Her mother was waiting outside the chapel door. "Oh, Mama, I too have Jesus in my heart," Jenny cried. But she didn't want to talk about it just then. She wanted to think about it, absorb it, and tell this Jesus all her troubles. The minister had said Jesus would be her Friend. She'd never really had a friend before. Now she wanted to get to know Him.

Jenny had fallen asleep talking to her new Friend, after having read the first four books of the New Testament from Tilden's Bible. Her first words to her mother the following morning were, "I would like to be baptized."

"Oh, Jenny," her mother said, her eyes misty. "Nothing could be so satisfying to a mother than knowing her child has come into the kingdom of God." Jenny's mother had the minister summoned immediately.

Soon the minister, Jenny's mother, Tilden, Mrs. Millet, Nellie, Nellie's mother, and as many of the household servants as could be spared gathered in the small chapel on the castle grounds.

The morning sun shone softly on the stained-glass windows, shedding prisms of jewel tones across the stone floor. The candles burning in their niches cast a golden glow over the stone walls and the faces of those who had gathered for this important event.

Jenny and the minister, he in a black robe and she in a white dress, faced the group who had gathered near the front of the chapel. Some brushed away tears, others let their tears roll freely. Some simply looked on with curiosity. Jenny's mother and Tilden stood near each other, and when a sob escaped the widow's throat, Tilden put his arm around her shoulders and drew her near.

Jenny noticed the action, and while it brought a sudden tug at her heart, she also experienced joy that they had each other. She could live without Tilden. But she could not live without Jesus. She now knew that there was no life without Him, only survival. With a radiant face, she looked over at the minister.

He spoke briefly about what had happened to Jenny the night before and informed the audience that salvation was available to each of them. Then lifting his hand, he said, "In obedience to our Lord's command, I baptize you, my sister, Jennifer Greenough, in the name of the Father, and of the Son, and of the Holy Ghost."

Jenny felt the cleansing waters of baptism, and when the ceremony was complete, she felt clean, inside and out. Her baptism symbolized a life dead to sin and guilt and risen again to a new life.

After the service, some of the onlookers sobbed openly as Jenny and the minister rejoined them. Jenny's mother had the group join hands and stand in a circle, and she drew Jenny in between herself and Tilden. Jenny had no choice but to take Tilden's outstretched hand. How warm and strong it felt, enclosing her smaller, colder one.

I shall not want, Jenny remembered. And accompanying her longing for Tilden was a willingness to let him go. Jesus would decide her future. She belonged to Him. She smiled as her mother led them in singing "Oh God, Our Help in Ages Past," a song Jenny had heard the few times she had attended church.

Yes, she thought in wonder, *I love Him more—enough to want Tilden's happiness above my own.*

Chapter 12

Jenny left the castle in the midafternoon. She walked outside in the bright sunlight that lent a golden glow to the trees and fields. Without bothering to see if attendants followed, she walked into the woods and sat on a bench where the sun filtered down upon her through branches almost devoid of leaves. Lost in reverie, she was oblivious to the falling of an occasional leaf around her and the breeze that stirred her dark hair, haloed by the sunlight.

Sensing the presence of someone, she gave a startled glance and then quickly lowered her gaze to her hands. A whisper of wind gently caressed the leaves.

When he spoke, Tilden's voice sounded deeper and lower than she had ever heard it. A most gentle sound. "I could not be more pleased by anything, Jenny," he said, "than what has taken place in your life."

She did not protest his presence when he sat beside her. Did he mean her having been accused of the murder, or did he mean her having given her life to the Lord? She drew her shawl closer and clutched it to her chest, suddenly made aware of her secluded surroundings.

She was afraid of him, but not because she thought he was a murderer. Something else disturbed her. Her foolish heart had learned no lesson from all the instruction her mind had given. Were he to touch her now, or kiss her, she would be unable to resist responding. Two weeks, she thought, might be all the freedom she had left. Inhaling deeply, she gazed ahead of her at a falling leaf.

"No one believes you killed Bodley," she said quietly. "Mama does not. Bingham does not."

"They will," he stated firmly. "Should I make such a confession in court, it cannot be ignored. When I make it known that I attended the party, there will be those who will remember seeing me and realize my absence later in the evening. That will condemn me, Jenny."

"And what is your motive now?"

"You," he replied. "It will not be difficult at all for anyone to believe I could not bear for Bodley to have you. I could tell such a thing quite convincingly."

Jenny felt ill at ease, not wishing for anyone to commit a terrible crime, but wishing it were true that he could love her so much, he couldn't bear for Bodley or anyone else to have her. But she must stop her fantasizing and focus on reality. "Why would you do such a thing?"

He remained silent.

"How do you know I didn't kill him?" she asked finally.

"If you did," he replied, "you would not believe that I killed Bodley, nor would you have feared that I had made an attempt on your life."

"I'm. . .not sure you did it," she murmured. She heard his intake of breath but would not look at him. Her voice softened. "If you didn't, then you must despise me."

"I could never despise you, Jenny," he replied quickly, and she felt his warm breath against her cool cheek. "But I want to ask something of you."

Jenny turned her head to look at him and feared she would never look away. She became lost in his gaze, a look that she felt should be reserved for someone special. She could not even find the words to ask him what he wanted of her. Then he took her hands in his.

"I want you to grant me the privilege of your company for the next two weeks, Jenny. Surely you can find it in your heart to grant this to a man who may have only two weeks of freedom left."

How could she say that would be no sacrifice but a wonderful blessing? How could she say that she understood Bathsheba better than any other woman in the world? She could not, even when she watched Tilden's expression turn to pain. He let go of her hands, stood dejectedly, and turned away. She watched him walk several paces into the woods, with his back to her.

Wondering if she were the world's most foolish woman, Jenny stopped asking herself whether or not Tilden had a murderous heart, whether or not he had fallen in love with her mother. Whatever he had done, she forgave him, just as Bathsheba must surely have forgiven King David.

She lifted her skirt, stepped gingerly over the fallen leaves and twigs, and approached Tilden's back. If he had committed the murder, he did not do it as a cold-blooded killer but to save her from Bodley and reunite her with her mother. In the two weeks remaining of her personal freedom, she would spend time with the man she loved. God had allowed her to fall in love with him in that glade. Surely a reason existed for this, even if it were only that she know love, its joy and pain, for this short period of time. She had been at the residence of the man she loved for many weeks now. He had made them the happiest of her life. She would live in fear and sorrow no longer.

As he heard the sound of Jenny's footsteps on the leaves, Tilden held his breath. He became aware of the scent she wore, the fragrance that haunted his dreams. His muscles stiffened when she touched his arm. Afraid to look upon her, he placed his hand over hers and turned. The realization of his emotional turmoil struck him with full force.

He recalled the scripture, "For as he thinketh in his heart, so is he," and called upon the Lord's strength to keep him from yielding to this moment of dire temptation.

"Jenny, Jenny," he moaned and drew her to his chest in an embrace that he could remember when he was alone. But for now, as one who had committed his life to the Lord, he must resist. One arm encircled her waist, and the other hand spread its fingers to reach into her hair and feel the nape of her neck. Her soft skin felt warm beneath his touch.

"I do not trust myself where you are concerned," he admitted. "Despite what I might say, please have the attendants accompany us from now on. Otherwise, I fear my actions shall be most unbecoming a gentleman. Promise me that."

Jenny looked up to find his chin directly above the top of her head. His wide, full lips were tightly closed, his facial muscles taut, his eyes closed against some unwanted intrusion. His fingers moved against her neck.

She could not know if he feared he might strangle her, or if he might kiss her. She was tempted to tell him that if he must strangle her, please kiss her first. But of course, she could not say such a thing. So, because he asked, and afraid of the fierce beating of her heart, she replied helplessly, "I promise."

He seemed so distressed. Jenny moved away from him, and his arms fell to his side. In silence the couple walked through the rustling leaves, amid the gentle whisper of the wind, toward the castle.

Jenny and Tilden rode together each morning, across the fields and through the meadows, pausing by the lake to regard its beauty and the stillness of the world. Time flew. Jenny enjoyed every moment. She detected not a trace of jealousy from her mother, who seemed to encourage Jenny's activities with Tilden.

The evenings were the best. Sometimes Jenny's mother joined them in the library for discussions of whatever novel Jenny was reading, but usually she did not. She always gave excuses of having other household duties to attend to.

Many times after a fire had been lit to dispel the chill of an autumn evening, Jenny and Tilden settled by the cozy hearth and discussed books and ideas, life and death. Jenny was fascinated by the eloquent and convincing way in which Tilden stated his belief in Christianity.

"In this belief, this acceptance," Tilden said emphatically, "you have found the answer to life, Jenny. No amount of money or knowledge can buy it, nothing can compare with it, and nothing can take it away."

"Oh, thank you, Tilden," she breathed happily. "Thank you so much for having the minister come and for lending me your Bible. I shall be eternally grateful."

"Yes," he said. "You and I shall spend eternity together."

She felt eternity had arrived as they gazed at each other while the orange light of the fire leaped to dispel the shadows. Jenny realized something new had been added to her love for Tilden. She felt more depth to it—a greater love. Perhaps an unselfish love that wanted his happiness, even if it could not be found with her.

Jenny wondered what the last night before the trial would be like. Would Tilden kiss her, even in a brotherly way? Should she reveal her love for him?

A lifetime of living had been done over the past few months. She had come to accept the living Jesus in her heart. She had been reunited with her mother. She had loved a man with all the love she was capable of. She began to feel that if God wanted her to be free, she would. If not, she would try to be brave and accept the verdict. But she would not have to go to trial alone. Jesus promised His presence would always be with her. God had not spared His own Son suffering and death. He might not spare her either. But in the midst of her fear, she felt a supernatural peace.

After dinner the night before the trial, Jenny, Tilden, and her mother had tea in the library. No words were forthcoming, until Jenny's mother said she felt tired, begged to be excused, and retired to her rooms. The tension lay heavily upon Jenny's heart.

Tilden stood and walked over to the fireplace and faced Jenny. "There is so much in my heart I would like to say to you, Jenny," he began. "But it must wait. Perhaps it can never be said. Tomorrow is a day of truth. I find that most exhilarating and at the same time dreadful."

She lifted her eyes to his, and they told him she felt similar emotions about the inevitable day of truth.

"Jenny, I have become so much involved in your life that mine seems meaningless in comparison. You have always been my project. Most of my life has been taken with longing for you to be with your mother, wishing you well, searching for you, and now. . ." He paused, closed his eyes for a moment, then continued. "I struggled for a long time before I concluded that without you, my life is half a life."

"You are so noble," she whispered.

He shook his head. "No, I am a coward," he contradicted. "There is so much I wish to say to you. But I must say no more. I mustn't. Your heart is burdened with more than any young woman should have to bear. There are more pressing matters at the moment than my personal feelings. I will only say that I shall be beside you in this. I shall always be with you, even when I am not present. But I must stop. I do not trust myself to spend this evening with you. I must go."

Jenny didn't move. Tilden did not go. The moisture in his eyes matched that which raced down her cheeks.

"Please go, for I cannot," he said in a raspy voice. He was afraid to look upon her lovely countenance aglow in the firelight, yet he could not take his gaze away from her.

"Tilden," she breathed, standing, then took a step toward him.

"Please," he implored.

With a sob in her throat, Jenny turned and ran from the room. Reaching her mother's door, she knocked, and as soon as it opened, she fell into her mother's arms. Her mother led her to a couch, held her head against her heart, and stroked her hair for a very long time, just as she had done when Jenny had been a very little girl.

Chapter 13

They left the castle at dawn. Jenny, her mother, and Tilden rode in the white carriage with the golden trim, drawn by the magnificent horses. The carriage that followed them down the winding paths and through the sleepy little village held Tilden's secretary, Diane's maid, Nellie, and Mrs. Millett.

Jenny could not resist asking Tilden to have the coachman stop the carriage outside the village so she could look back at the castle. She stood for a long moment outside the carriage, Tilden beside her, and stared at the pink sky being turned to gold by the sun. There, upon the cliffs, high above the sea, she had spent the happiest moments of her life. She had gained more in the past two weeks than she could ever have imagined. Memories were something no one could take from her. Already, she had eternal life and would be with her Savior forever. And as long as she lived on earth, she would have the memories of spending time with the man, the only man, that she could ever love.

Feeling the pressure of Tilden's hand as he grasped hers, Jenny knew the time had come to go. They mustn't dally. This was the day of truth, Bingham had said.

The carriages rolled over the open countryside, and the passengers commented upon the views, enjoying the ride as if it were a wonderful outing. Jenny marveled at the courage of the human spirit, for she knew how emotionally unpredictable she had proved to be during the past months. God's Spirit within had enabled her to bear such uncertainty.

Despite their heavy burdens, the threesome spoke lightly of the beauty of London as they neared its famous bridge in the early morning light. Jenny barely glanced at the courthouse when she alighted from the carriage, concentrating instead on Bingham, who was waiting for them. He wore the traditional white powdered wig and dark robes of a barrister. She expected him to take her to a side room for instruction, but he appeared quite unconcerned, saying only, "Remember to answer truthfully, whatever questions are asked of you."

"I shall be praying for you every moment, my darling," Jenny's mother whispered as she gave her a last encouraging hug.

The courtroom began to fill. A matron escorted Jenny to the prisoner's dock, where she would stand throughout the trial. Looking straight ahead, she observed the jurors' box, where the men who would decide her fate would be seated. The judge's high bench stood against the wall to her right, and the witness box was located beside it. Bingham and the prosecuting attorneys sat at long tables across from the jury.

Jenny looked around the courtroom and noticed that Tilden and her mother sat in the front row of the public seating. They smiled encouragingly. She watched as the Cottinghams arrived and walked down the aisle. Sir Thomas's face began to redden with apparent surprise at seeing Jenny's mother. Lady Christine's face paled, as if she were seeing someone long departed.

Jenny watched her mother look at them with an air of dignity, showing no sign of the shame that might be expected from a woman who had abandoned her daughter and now watched that daughter stand accused of murder. It was the Cottingham family who appeared embarrassed and hurried past to take their seats on the left side of the courtroom.

Soon, the somber jurors filed in. Everyone stood for the judge's entrance. The day of truth had arrived.

After several witnesses gave their account of the engagement party at Bodley's, Bingham called Emmaline to the stand. Twisting a lacy white handkerchief, her cheeks the color of her pink dress, she reiterated that she didn't believe Jenny would have done those terrible things she had threatened to do, although Jenny always read novels, had a wild imagination, opposed what she called the "marriage market," swore she hadn't meant to steal her cousin's intended, and really wouldn't hurt a flea.

Emmaline presented such an impression of a pure, innocent maiden who had expected Lord Bodley to ask for her hand in marriage that Jenny felt she, herself, must truly look like a villain in comparison. Someone must have coached Emmie to pretend she loved Lord Bodley so she wouldn't be suspected of taking the rash action of a woman scorned.

The real surprise, however, occurred when Tilden was called to the stand to testify about what he had seen at the party.

"You were a friend of Ignatius, Lord Bodley?" Bingham asked.

"An acquaintance," Tilden quickly amended. "We had mutual friends, and each time I visited London, we were inevitably present at various functions."

"I believe that your mutual friends were primarily in royal circles, is that correct?"

"It is," Tilden replied.

"Why, might I ask, did you follow Miss Jennifer Greenough into the glade?"

"I sought her out to inform her of the recent inheritance that my brother, the late Duke Stanford Withington, had left to her."

"Did you so inform her?"

"No," he replied. "I promised to see her the following day but left the glade hurriedly upon hearing Bodley approach, rather than risk an unpleasant confrontation with a man I knew was already under the influence of alcohol. After all, it was their engagement party. And if I were engaged to one such as Lady Jennifer Greenough, I would not take kindly to her presence with another man in a secluded glade."

Bingham waited until a trickle of understanding laughter and comments from the onlookers dissipated before he continued. "Were you in London the night that the father of the accused, William, Lord Greenough, died eight years ago?"

"Yes, I was in London during that time, and on that particular night," Tilden admitted.

Jenny didn't understand why Bingham was referring to the night her father died and what connection it had with this trial. But Bingham had said he suspected there was a connection between the two. Before she could make any sense out of the situation, Bingham excused Tilden. Then Jenny's aunt Christine sat in the witness box.

"Would you say, Lady Cottingham," Bingham asked, "that your brother drank himself to death?"

The woman seemed uncertain how to answer. She appeared surprised to be questioned about her brother.

"Lady Cottingham, please answer the question," Bingham insisted in a quiet voice.

"That was reported as the cause of death," she replied stiffly, not meeting the eyes of anyone in the courtroom. "Sir Thomas and I spoke with him many times concerning the welfare of little Jenny. And yes, I must admit, he was gambling, wasting his money, and did indeed imbibe the spirits almost continually."

"He drank from a glass, I assume?"

Jenny's aunt lifted her chin nobly, and her lower lip quivered magnificently. "I'm afraid my brother did not bother with glasses," she said quietly.

"That will be all," Bingham said so abruptly, the entire courtroom was stunned into complete silence.

Tilden felt the tension building. With Bingham playing the leading role, this became not only a legal proceeding, but a performance as well. The spectators always expected something extraordinary from Bingham, but this case appeared impossible to figure. A total absence of anything spectacular being revealed gave the event a more ominous air. Even the prosecutor kept saying, "No questions," as if the comments of Bingham's defense witnesses were quite insignificant.

If Tilden hadn't known better, he would have suspected Bingham had lost his touch, for the famous attorney kept dwelling on an event that took place eight years ago rather than on the present tragedy. The duke knew that eventually Bingham would target the culprit, but when? And on whom?

Suddenly Bingham called Jenny to the stand.

Emmaline thought Jenny looked older than twenty-one. She supposed such experiences as her cousin had endured over the past few months matured a person, but Jenny should have remembered the oft-repeated instructions they'd received: young ladies wear pink and white. Instead, Jenny had dressed in a bright green velvet dress with a tight-fitting jacket, giving her the look of a mature woman.

The sun suddenly burst forth outside the window, as if to drive away the chill of the autumn morning. Its rays touched Jenny's hair, turning the long raven tresses to a burnished sheen of reddish gold. Jenny seemed to belong to the summer in that green dress, appearing alive and growing in the sun. Emmaline's mother had said young girls shouldn't allow the sun to touch their skin. Jenny looked as if she hadn't obeyed. Even her cheeks had the blush of the sun on them.

Emmaline shifted her gaze to Lady Diane. Right after they had taken their seats, Emmaline had asked her father, "Who is the woman who looks so much like Jenny?"

"Her mother," he replied.

Emmaline had been under the impression that Jenny's mother was dead. Now as she studied Lady Diane, Emmaline noticed the woman had a sad, sweet smile on her lips. She wore the clothes of a true lady and gazed upon Jenny as if she approved of her wholeheartedly.

Emmaline lowered her head, examining her soft white fingers. Her mother had been right. Jenny was very much like her mother.

⁓

Jenny sat in the witness box, distressed as Bingham began painting a vivid word picture of her—the poor motherless child who had been abandoned. She glanced at her mother helplessly, not wanting her to be embarrassed, but her mother's gaze showed only love, warmth, and encouragement.

At Bingham's bidding, Jenny related her loneliness and that her father had told her that her mother was dead. She told of her father's drinking and how she would hide when he drank, although she found him quite loving when he was sober.

"Do you recall the events that surrounded your going to live with Sir Thomas and Lady Cottingham?"

"Yes, sir," Jenny replied. "My father and I had recently moved to London. Uncle Thomas and Aunt Christine came to talk with my father. He had already agreed that I should go to live with my aunt and uncle. I thought he needed me, but he told me I must go and learn to be a proper lady. He cried, and I felt he really cared about me then."

Tears welled up in Jenny's eyes, but she blinked them away, sniffed, and looked at Silas Bingham.

"Continue," he demanded, and she did, although not understanding why he didn't get to the point of the trial.

"That night, Aunt Christine told me that I would be leaving to go and live with them. My father came up to my room with a bottle in his hand, drinking and mumbling something like, 'What else can I do?' He lifted his hands helplessly and then left."

Jenny swallowed hard and grew pale. "It was the next morning that I found my father in the kitchen, slumped over a table. I could not awaken him. That was not so unusual, but when Aunt Christine and Uncle Thomas came down, they summoned a doctor. Later, it was disclosed that my father had drunk himself to death."

"How old were you then, Jenny?" Bingham asked.

"Thirteen."

Bingham turned to his audience. "The records show that Lady Jennifer's father died of excessive drinking. Once they discovered that he had signed away his assets, including his daughter, to the Cottinghams in case of his demise, the authorities assumed the poor man had nothing to live for. After all, the world knew he had been deserted by one of the most beautiful women about. He had lost his seat in Parliament because of the scandal. Why shouldn't the poor man have drunk himself to death?"

Then Bingham gestured toward Jenny. "Take a look at this sweet young girl."

Jenny felt herself blush and looked down at her clasped hands resting on her green velvet dress. Bingham's words didn't sound complimentary. He had become like a total stranger, incapable of any softness. She grew quite afraid. All eyes were upon her.

"She doesn't look like a woman to be thrown into prison," Bingham continued. "She's much too lovely. A beautiful maiden. An abandoned child. One first hidden away, then thrust away by her father, who apparently preferred the bottle to his own daughter. Now, ladies and gentlemen," Bingham said in a tone of mockery, "I submit that this girl may not be all that she appears to be."

Jenny's eyes flew to Bingham in surprise. All other eyes left her and centered on Bingham. He became the sole actor on the stage. He was apparently accusing his own client of...what?

Bingham appeared to be enjoying himself. "The reports are that on the morning of the investigation of Lord Greenough's death, there was in front of him one bottle and one glass with a powdery ring around it. Dregs of a cheap beverage, perhaps?

"Yet two witnesses, one the accused, the other the sister of the deceased, have testified that Lord Greenough drank from bottles, not glasses. Would he, a defeated man on the night of having lost everything, suddenly have begun drinking from a glass? Why? To celebrate his failures? After so many years, did his adversities suddenly make a gentleman of him? Why would Lord Greenough take a glass on the night of his most dismal defeat? He drowned himself in liquor that night. Deliberately, knowing his system could take no more. Suicide, they said."

Some shook their heads, not knowing the answer but waiting for Bingham's explanation. Jenny was hearing the facts of her father's death for the first time. She, too, stared at the man before her, waiting for his answers.

"Could it be," Bingham asked in ominous tones, "that someone...someone...came down after everyone else fell asleep that night, found this man in his misery, and pretended to comfort him? Perhaps this *friend* even took a goblet and poured the poor defeated man a drink to show his sympathy. Perhaps the *friend* even slipped a little something into the goblet which left a powdery ring. Something such as. . ." Bingham paused and gazed around the assembly, making sure every eye was upon him. "Arsenic!" he finished.

No one seemed to breathe. Bingham looked at Jenny in his accusatory manner, and were she not so surprised by his behavior, she would have withered and completely disappeared.

"Could it be?" he questioned with authority, sweeping his gaze over every pair of eyes turned upon him. "Could it be that this sweet young girl, even at age thirteen, had murderous instincts? Could she, who had been abandoned by her mother, who had hidden from her father, who was now being given away like so much baggage, have put arsenic in that drink, which left a powdery ring just like that on the glass in the glade where Ignatius, Lord Bodley met his untimely death?"

Immediately the silence in the courtroom was replaced by a roar. The judge banged his gavel, but neither that action nor his threats to clear the courtroom made any impact on the commotion for several minutes. Bingham appeared to be accusing his client, not of one murder, but of two. Jenny's sweet countenance had changed to a mask of incredulity. Stunned into compliance, she dutifully allowed Bingham to take her arm and lead her back to the dock.

Chapter 14

Later in the day, murmurs sounded throughout the crowded courtroom when the beautiful, elegant Lady Diane sat in the witness box. She wasn't the picture of a woman who had lived a life of shame. Rather, she sat with dignity, as one who had endured many trials. From the moment she began to speak, she held her audience spellbound. Her words rang true.

Bingham went back further with his questioning than he had with any other witness. He asked about Lady Diane's first marriage and subsequent events. Her story flowed from her as if it had been waiting many years to be revealed.

She told about the forced marriage, the beautiful baby who gave her a reason to live, the jealous, angry husband, the love she had for Duke Stanford Withington. She told of her husband's mistreatment and ultimate abuse of Jenny. Finally, she revealed that she had signed over all her possessions to her husband in exchange for his promise of a divorce, only to discover he had no intentions of keeping his word.

She sought the duke's help, and he booked passage on a ship to America. They planned their departure during a week when Lady Cottingham, Sir Thomas, and little Emmaline were visiting the Greenoughs. Lady Diane and Jenny would sneak away in the middle of the night with the aid of a manservant.

Lady Diane recalled being surprised by how easily they had managed to get away. No one seemed suspicious of their actions that day. Lady Diane had given Jenny a small amount of sleeping draught to keep her from awakening and making noise. The manservant had taken the sleeping child, covered by a blanket, to an appointed spot in the woods where Stanford and Tilden were waiting.

Tilden had held the sleeping child in the back of a carriage while Stanford, with Diane beside him, drove the carriage to the docks where their freedom lay. Stanford, who had never before seen Jenny, tucked the child away in a reserved cabin. Then he, Diane, and Tilden kept to the adjoining cabin, alert to any disturbance that might indicate their plot had failed.

When the ship moved out onto the water, they breathed more easily. They were on their way to a new world, and a new life.

Early in the morning, Diane went in to check on the sleeping child, who still had not stirred. She screamed in agony. The child sleeping peacefully beneath the blanket was not her darling Jenny, but rather Emmaline Cottingham.

Stanford rushed into the room and unfastened the envelope tied to the little girl's dress. He had read the letter to Diane.

At that point in the proceedings, Lady Diane looked at Bingham for confirmation and then unfolded a worn piece of paper. She read it aloud to the courtroom.

> *Authorities will be awaiting this child at the next port. She must leave the ship assisted only by ship personnel, without any trouble from you, or you will be arrested and prosecuted for kidnaping. Any attempts to do otherwise will result in an extended and losing battle on your part. I do not intend to relinquish Jenny to an adulterous and conniving woman (whose sins will be known throughout Europe) nor to the good-for-nothing duke who would take advantage of another man's wife.*
>
> *I hope you understand. To disgrace you publicly as you have disgraced me would bring me great satisfaction. Any attempt to leave the ship at the next port will result in both you and the duke being prosecuted and thrown into prison.*
>
> *Your choice, my dear,*
> *Your loving husband, Wm.*

Lady Diane folded up the paper and continued her story. When she and the Withington brothers had come into port at another point along the coast of England, authorities came aboard ship, requesting that the little blond girl be released. They had been alerted that a kidnaping had taken place. The distraught parents had agreed that if the kidnapers would release the child and continue on to America, no charges of kidnaping would be lodged.

Diane and Stanford had no alternative but to return little Emmaline

Cottingham to her parents, who were watching the ship, wringing their hands, and weeping.

Diane, Stanford, and Tilden had known it would be useless to explain that they were the victims of a hoax created by Diane's husband, using the Cottinghams as accomplices. They were legally helpless to ever get Jenny. Their only hope had been to somehow find her and take her away from her father. All their efforts to that end had been futile.

Jenny looked over at the Cottinghams. Emmaline stared at her mother, her mouth agape, but Lady Christine did not reprimand her. She merely stared at the far wall. Sir Thomas took his silver snuff box from his pocket, sniffed a pinch, then replaced it.

Jenny then turned her gaze back to her mother, who had held her audience's attention, even moving them to tears. It was the first time Jenny had heard the reason she and her mother had been separated for all those years. She had forgiven her mother for whatever the reason and loved her dearly, but this turn of events made things all the more wonderful, for her mother had not willingly abandoned her.

"Mama," Jenny whispered as her mother passed by her. The woman smiled at Jenny through her tears. Looking back, Jenny saw that Tilden had time to give her mother a discreet hug around the shoulders before Bingham recalled him to the witness box.

"It would seem," Bingham began as soon as Tilden took his seat, "that the crimes and deception began long before Lord Bodley was murdered, and the evidence points to the fact that all the incidents are related to or revolve around Miss Jennifer Greenough. Could it be," Bingham asked mockingly, "that the five-year-old Jenny plotted this latest incident of which we have learned?"

A trickle of ironic laughter filled the courtroom. Bingham had asked the question in the same way he had asked if Jenny had murdered her father. He seemed to be showing the fallacy of anyone suspecting his client of murder, for she must be guilty of conspiracy in all the incidents—or in none.

"Or," he continued, as even the jurors sat on the edge of their seats, "was this young lady a victim at the age of five, when her aunt and uncle engaged in such deception, substituting their own child for Lady Jennifer Greenough?"

"Objection, Your Honor," the prosecuting attorney said, but was overruled when Bingham presented the note Diane had read. The handwriting had already been verified by an expert as the handwriting of Lord William Greenough.

"Now, I am not arguing that Lady Diane Greenough was right and Lord William Greenough was wrong," Bingham assured his audience. "The custody of the child should have been a matter for the courts. However, I think it perfectly fitting to present the case that the Cottinghams entered into a deceptive and illegal practice in substituting their child for Lady Greenough's and withholding Lady Greenough's own child from her, where the child had every right to be. It could well be the Cottinghams who might be accused of kidnaping. And I submit further, that the deception embarked upon that night has continued throughout the years when the Cottinghams repeatedly told Lady Jennifer Greenough that her mother had died."

Bingham suddenly turned toward Tilden, in the witness box. "Duke Withington, who stood to profit by the death of Lord William Greenough, if anyone?"

"Lady Jennifer Greenough stood to profit financially," Tilden answered, "until shortly before Lord Greenough's death, when he signed over his assets to Sir Thomas and Lady Christine Cottingham. They had access to the holdings of Lord Greenough and the authority to distribute his wealth as they wished as long as Lady Jennifer remained their ward."

"And in what manner was the money to be spent? Were there stipulations?" Bingham asked pointedly.

"Lady Greenough's basic needs were to be met, including her education. Also, the death of Lord Greenough came at a most convenient time for them, because his money saved Sir Thomas Cottingham from bankruptcy. Lord Greenough's assets were considerable and included the funds Lady Diane had signed over to her husband in return for the divorce he wouldn't give. The Cottinghams have lived off Lady Jenny's money for the past eight years."

Jenny's surprised glance darted toward her aunt and uncle. She had wanted many things during that time. Simple things, really. And she had longed for either a more competent tutor or the opportunity to be sent away to school.

Emmaline was biting on her nails and crying. Lady Christine's head was lowered, as if in defeat. She stared fixedly at her clasped hands. Sir Thomas appeared rather dazed, like a man humiliated, as he stared at Tilden.

"And who would gain if Ignatius, Lord Bodley were dead?" Bingham continued.

"No one, sir," Tilden replied immediately.

"And who would gain if Lady Jennifer Greenough were dead? If the poison were intended for her?"

Jenny held her breath. Was Bingham now going to accuse Tilden of trying to murder her? She could hardly believe the words Tilden said when he answered.

"No one, sir. We would all be the losers if Lady Jennifer Greenough should not grace this world with her beauty and charm."

Bingham cleared his throat as a few chuckles sounded through the courtroom. "I mean, Your Grace, who would benefit financially if Lady Jennifer were murdered?"

"I and her mother, sir, for we would inherit all of Duke Stanford's estate, rather than share it with Lady Jennifer."

A murmur traveled through the courtroom, and the judge threatened to empty it if silence wasn't restored immediately.

"Tell us, Your Grace," Bingham entreated Tilden, "how you happened to be at the party, and in the glade, the night Lord Bodley drank his poisoned drink."

Jenny's thoughts were in turmoil. It seemed that everything was leading to Bingham accusing Tilden of trying to murder her so he could get the bulk of the inheritance.

"I had spoken with Sir Thomas Cottingham a week before," Tilden explained, and Jenny again looked at her relatives. Both Emmaline and Aunt Christine appeared surprised.

"All had been settled concerning my brother's estate. I felt it time I left Lady Diane in America and tried to see Lady Jennifer. We had known for several years the whereabouts of Lady Jenny but had received letters to the effect that she did not wish to see her mother or have any contact with her. We now know these letters were forgeries, in the handwriting of Lady Christine Cottingham."

Bingham presented the bundle of letters—those written to Jenny and returned, as well as those written by Lady Christine Cottingham.

"Then when Lady Jennifer inherited part of my brother's estate," Tilden continued, "I thought it time to confront her personally, for if she still rejected her mother, surely she would not reject the money and property."

"And did you see her?"

"No," Tilden replied. "Sir Thomas informed me that she was too busy preparing for her engagement party and that she soon would be married. He invited me to the engagement party."

Sir Thomas calmly pinched his snuff from the silver box, then replaced it in his pocket.

"Most sporting of him," Bingham remarked.

"Indeed," Tilden replied.

"And did you tell Lady Jennifer Greenough of her inheritance?"

"I followed her to the glade for that purpose," Tilden replied, looking at Jenny. "But we were interrupted."

"By Lord Bodley?" Bingham asked.

After a pause, Tilden answered, "Yes."

Suddenly Bingham wore the look that Tilden, the judge, and most of the occupants of the courtroom always waited for. It indicated that the moment for his startling revelation had arrived. Tilden stared at Bingham uncomfortably and felt himself growing quite warm. It was as if he were guilty and about to be accused and convicted.

Bingham did not, however, accuse Duke Tilden Withington of murder, or even attempted murder. Instead, he simply asked the duke to step down. Then Bingham called Sir Thomas Cottingham to the stand.

Sir Thomas answered Bingham's questions in the same controlled modulated tone in which they were asked, even stopping on occasion to take a pinch of snuff. The questions were of a general nature, pertaining to his relationship with Jenny and the years of her upbringing. Sir Thomas, of course, had every legal right to her money, had provided for her basic needs, and therefore had nothing to fear from the law on that count. The fact that Jenny had been treated as a poor relation remained an ethical question, not a legal one, and was mentioned only in a passing remark by Bingham, as if it were inconsequential. The jury, however, seemed to take note of his words.

"It really isn't necessary to investigate your deceit, Sir Thomas, the night you substituted your young daughter for little Jenny. I don't believe anyone would care to press charges on that matter at this late date."

Sir Thomas had the presence of mind not to reply.

"But the matter of Lord Greenough's death is a different matter," Bingham said with concern. "There's this old doctor who said he got to thinking afterwards about that white powdery ring around that glass. He suspected it came from something other than an alcoholic beverage, but then he told himself the man no doubt committed suicide. Why, the doctor wondered, should he bring such scandal upon the poor child, on top of everything else she had to endure? But," Bingham drawled slowly, as if his words were of little importance, "it might be difficult to prove at this late date, would not you agree, Sir Thomas?"

Sir Thomas shrugged. "I certainly have no reason to believe my brother-in-law died of anything but his drinking," he replied. "However, I can see that the conditions of his life could cause him to sink to suicide."

Bingham shook his head, and Sir Thomas looked away from his eyes and fixed his stare on a distant wall. "I think murder is a more appropriate word," Bingham said simply. "More appropriate than suicide."

Suddenly he faced Sir Thomas, asking quickly, "Would you benefit by the death of Ignatius, Lord Bodley?"

"There is no reason whatsoever that I would want Bodley dead," Sir Thomas answered confidently, sitting a little straighter in the chair and looking directly at Bingham. "I, personally, would have greatly benefitted by the marriage of Bodley and my ward."

"In what way?" Bingham asked quietly, turning his back on Sir Thomas and looking out at his audience with what might be mistaken for a smug look of satisfaction.

Sir Thomas told in detail of the deal between him and Bodley. His every word seemed to exonerate him of any suspicion of his motives, had any ever existed. Legal papers had been drawn up with his and Bodley's signatures. Sir Thomas presented the papers that proved he would have benefitted more by the marriage of Bodley and Jenny than by any transaction he had ever made.

"It would certainly appear that Sir Thomas Cottingham had no motive whatsoever to murder Lord Bodley," Bingham agreed. "There isn't a shred of evidence to point in that direction."

Just as Sir Thomas got a self-satisfied look on his face, Bingham turned toward him and continued. "I believe we have every reason to suspect Sir Cottingham in the murder of Lord Greenough, but of course that is not a question for this trial."

Sir Thomas closed his eyes. He made no sound, and his face was set as in stone, revealing nothing. Lady Christine, however, looked briefly concerned, sitting near the front and studying her husband. Then she took a deep breath, straightened her shoulders, and raised her chin imperiously.

The silence in the courtroom was broken by Bingham's quiet voice. "No," he said, "I don't for a moment think you would murder Bodley. Nor do I think the poison was intended for Lady Jenny."

Sir Thomas's eyes came up to meet Bingham's.

"No," Bingham repeated, shaking his head.

Sir Thomas tried to look away, but he didn't seem able to move. "Could I have a glass of water?" he finally asked.

"That's the least we can do," Bingham replied, without taking his eyes from Sir Thomas. The witness had grown quite red, and sweat covered his forehead.

"Bring a glass of water," Bingham ordered, without addressing anyone in particular.

Complete silence permeated the room during the eternity in which the glass of water was fetched. During the silence, Jenny stared at her uncle Thomas questioningly. She could not comprehend what she knew to be taking place. She was afraid to even speculate as she watched the clerk bring the water to Sir Thomas.

Bingham waited while Sir Thomas took a swallow of water and then set the glass on the wooden railing beside him. Then Bingham began to speak clearly, loudly, and distinctly, all the while staring at Sir Thomas, who looked alternately at the glass and the floor.

"No one would have benefitted greatly by the death of either Lord Bodley or Lady Jenny," Bingham said. "That is why, Your Honor, I submit that the poison was not intended for either person. It was Duke Tilden Withington's drink that contained the poison. It was Duke Withington who took the drink into the glade and set it on the table where it was drunk, not by the duke, but mistakenly by Lord Bodley. The poison was intended neither for Bodley, nor for Jenny, but for Duke Tilden Withington."

Sir Thomas began gulping water convulsively. Jenny gasped, as did most of the other occupants of the courtroom.

"All we need to do now is discover who handed the drink to Duke Withington, and then we will know the identity of our murderer," Bingham stated simply.

"And I'm sure Duke Withington knows who handed him that drink, just as he knows who invited him to that engagement party." Bingham kept his eyes firmly on Sir Thomas, who seemed to be trying to sink into the chair. The witness licked his very dry lips and seemed to be gasping for air. He would not raise his eyes.

Bingham continued relentlessly. "It was Duke Tilden Withington who would take Lady Jennifer Greenough away and leave the Cottinghams without the financial means to which they had become accustomed. If Duke Withington took Jenny away, he would also remove the Cottinghams' entry into royal circles, for he would be taking away the money that is so much the mark of today's leisurely gentleman.

"No one would even know that Sir Thomas knew Duke Withington," Bingham continued, his voice filled with the confidence of a lawyer who knew his case was won. "So he would not be suspected. Lady Diane had been in America for sixteen years and would be informed that her daughter wanted no part of her or the inheritance. Jenny would live unhappily ever after with Lord Bodley, and the Cottinghams would live splendidly on the profits from Cottingham's sale of this beautiful, unsuspecting young lady to the infamous Lord Bodley. Was the entire family in on the deception as they were involved in the deceit the night Jenny was snatched so cruelly from her mother's arms?"

Bingham's voice had risen with that last question. For the first time in many minutes, Sir Thomas met the eyes of his accuser. Sir Thomas stood, and his eyes bulged as he looked out and pointed toward Lady Diane. "It all started with her," he accused. "I knew she was unhappy with William Greenough. I tried to console her, but no, she wouldn't confide in me. She was loyal to her husband, so I thought. But then Duke Stanford Withington changed all that. She simply preferred any man to me."

The judge ordered Sir Thomas to sit down. He staggered back into his seat and took a sip from the glass. Some of the water drooled from the side of his mouth. He didn't wipe it away.

Lady Christine buried her face in her hands. She had often accused her husband of loving Diane, but she hadn't really believed it. Everyone's eyes were fastened on Sir Thomas, and the judge did nothing to keep the man from incriminating himself.

"Jenny looked so much like Diane," Sir Thomas was saying, in a distant voice. "I really cared for that little girl. That's why I joined in on the kidnaping scheme. I didn't want Jenny taken away, too. Lord Greenough had everything, but he was too demanding, too loud, too mean for a lady like Diane. I deserved her and Jenny. I could have handled the money, but he was squandering it. I kept telling him the way he was bringing Jenny up wasn't right. I talked for years. Finally he began to relent, but by that time my finances were in disastrous shape."

Sir Thomas looked about helplessly, as if appealing for sympathy. "He was about to die anyway. He was finished." The man's shoulders slumped, and his voice became lower. "I did provide for Jenny. I used her money, yes. But my daughter and wife needed it. They needed those things to make them happy, to make them respect me."

Sir Thomas cleared his throat and in a trembling voice continued. "I loved Christine and Emmaline. It's just that this other thing is a weakness, shall we say. Then the younger brother of the man who took Diane away came to take Jenny away. Jenny would know that her mother was not dead. There would be questions. What else could I do? Let everyone know where my wealth came from? My friends? My wife? My daughter?"

He shrugged helplessly. "I knew what I had to do when I invited Duke Tilden Withington to the party. Then I saw him when he first looked at Jenny. I knew he was thinking she was as beautiful as her mother and would never let her marry Bodley if he could prevent it. And Jenny didn't want to marry Bodley."

Lady Diane wiped away the tears that streaked her face, tears shed for Christine and Emmaline. She knew so well the pain of heartbreak, estrangement from a loved one, a troubled mind, and accusations. She longed to tell Thomas that the Lord could forgive him, give him a certain kind of acceptance and peace, although he would still have to pay for the terrible things he had done.

"I knew what I had to do," Thomas said, his voice suddenly bold, but his eyes glazed. Bingham stepped back, almost behind him, allowing Sir Thomas to be the center of attention.

"I poured a round of drinks," Sir Thomas said, "and as I did, at one moment I stopped and pretended to take the snuff from my snuff box, like this." He took out the silver box and demonstrated. "Then I emptied the contents into a glass, poured several drinks, and handed them out. I gave the one with arsenic to Duke Tilden Withington, placed the snuff box that had contained the arsenic back into my inside pocket, poured other drinks, and handed them out as well. No one knew or even suspected what I had done. Upon my person, I had two of the silver tins, and I disposed of the incriminating one when I left Bodley House to fetch the doctor."

Before anyone could react, Sir Thomas emptied the contents of his snuff box into the glass beside him, stirred with his finger, and gulped it down. In shocked silence, all eyes watched as he sank dejectedly into the chair. The glass clinked to the floor.

Murmurs rose through the courtroom. Emmaline screamed. Lady Christine gasped in disbelief. The judge called for the courtroom to be cleared and for a doctor to be summoned. In the midst of the confusion, with the spectators reluctant to leave, the relentless Bingham asked one final question to the man whose physical pain now matched his emotional anguish.

"Would you have allowed Lady Jenny to take the blame for the murder of Ignatius, Lord Bodley?"

Sir Thomas's pain ceased momentarily as he stared at Bingham. He sought out Jenny's distressed face. Finally comprehension of the depths to which he had sunk entered his eyes. He would have allowed the destruction of Diane's child. That realization was more painful to him than the physical agony that now racked his body. His eyes bulged with fear at some distant image within himself, then Sir Thomas leaned forward to bury his head in his arms against the wooden railing.

The dying man looked down, and his eyes fastened upon the glass that had rolled along the hardwood floor in front of him. The last thing he saw was the white powdery ring around its inside edge.

Chapter 15

enny stood starboard, alone, looking at the white frothy foam made by the waves of the vast ocean. She would look back for only a moment, remembering the last few days and Uncle Thomas's funeral. It had been a great embarrassment to Aunt Christine and Emmaline, for no one had attended the event save family members. The Cottinghams were now social outcasts, as her mother had been for so many years.

But Jenny and her mother both found that with divine help they were able, not only to forgive, but also to share the source of strength they had received from God. They both realized that Thomas had suffered a gradual decline in character after having set in motion a chain of events that led to his eventual self-destruction.

"We are ruined," Aunt Christine had wailed desperately. "Oh, Diane, for the first time I realize what you must have gone through. How can we live with the ostracization and ridicule that will surely come?"

Jenny's mother had implored them to return to America with her. "It will be a new start for the two of you. I think you both will learn to love it." Emmaline looked forward to such an adventure, and Aunt Christine gratefully accepted the invitation.

Yes, Jenny thought as she stared out at the sea, *I have come through the valley of the shadow of death.* Only one shadow was upon her life now, and that was the impossible love she felt for Tilden. Her mother, aunt, and cousin were being so brave, enduring the harsh realities of life, so perhaps with time, she could learn to endure a life without Tilden.

She would not allow the past and its troubles to distract her now but watched the great ship steer toward the setting sun, which painted the sky in streaks of red and gold. Tomorrow, the sun would rise on a new day, a new life.

Hearing footfalls she assumed were those of her mother, Jenny turned. "Mama—"

Jenny was stunned into silence. Her mother was nowhere to be seen. Instead, Tilden walked toward her, causing her heart to leap like the frothy tips of the waves. The reflection of the water, gold from the last rays of the sun, gave her countenance an ethereal glow.

Tilden simply stared at her, and she mistook his silence for displeasure. She had done him a terrible injustice. "I'm so sorry that I ever suspected you of murdering Lord Bodley or of making an attempt on my life," she said.

"I, too, had my doubts about you upon occasion," he confessed. "I admit to having had windmills in my head."

"You. . .you forgive me?" she asked hesitantly.

"I would forgive you anything," he replied, then added, "with one exception."

"Wh. . .what?" Suddenly she found it difficult to breathe, for her chest had tightened when he came so close to her. His wonderful face bent toward hers, and his eyes held that special glow.

"I could never forgive you, Jenny, if you didn't allow me to say what I've wanted to tell you from the moment I saw you at Bodley House." He drew in his breath. "I love you, Jenny. I want to marry you. I want to live my life with you."

Her eyes danced, and inscrutable joy graced her beautiful face. "I thought. . .you and my mother—"

"You were wrong." He grasped her hands and came even nearer. "Lady Diane and I are like older sister and younger brother. But I couldn't explain that to you when you thought I was a murderer. You would have also judged me a liar and would have had no reason to believe my words. But believe me, Jenny, I've never loved any woman the way I love you. I've never wanted another to become my wife. Oh, Jenny. There will never be another. Only you, my dearest."

Jenny closed her eyes and drew in her breath as if his words were unendurable.

Not sure what she was feeling, Tilden added, "If you think you could love me, Jenny, let me know. If not, tell me and I will go away and try not to see you, for that would be torture. But please know, I love you dearly, with all my heart."

Finally Jenny found her voice. "I love you with all my heart. And I think, Tilden," she whispered, her pink lips trembling with emotion, "that you should kiss me, lest I swoon from the want of it."

The light leaped into Tilden's face. "Oh, Jenny!" He swooped her into his arms, swung her around, then set her on her feet again and tenderly drew her near. His lips found hers, and they met in a lingering, tender kiss of love, as their hearts united and they committed themselves to each other.

Finally Tilden moved his lips away long enough to ask softly, "Where did you learn to kiss like that?"

With a beautiful upturned face and eyes shining, she murmured, "There was once, in a lovely glade, a stranger—"

Tilden's arms tightened around her, and his heart raced. The brilliant red and golden glints of sun danced around them, while inside he burned with tomorrow's promise, ignited by love's eternal flame. Just before he again claimed her lips as his own, he said huskily, "Strangers no more."

Yvonne Lehman, is an award-winning, bestselling author of 56 novels, founded and directed the Blue Ridge Mountains Christian Writers Conference for 25 years, and is now director of the Blue Ridge "Autumn in the Mountains" Novelist Retreat (htp://ridgecrestconferencecenter.org/event/novelist). She has joined Lighthouse Publishing of the Carolinas as Acquisitions and Managing Editor of Candlelight Romance and Guiding Light Women's Fiction. She earned a Master's Degree in English from Western Carolina University and has taught English and Creative Writing on the college level. Recent releases are a novella in *Reluctant Brides* and *Name that Tune* in *A Gentleman's Kiss* (Barbour). Her 50th novel is *Hearts that Survive – A Novel of the TITANIC (Abingdon)*, which she signs periodically at the Titanic Museum in Pigeon Forge, TN. Her non-fiction compilations (Grace Publishing) are *Divine Moments* and *Christmas Moments* (2014), *Spoken Moments, Childhood Moments,* and *Christmas Moments Book #2* (2015). She blogs at www.christiansread.com and Novel Rocket Blog.

A Kingdom Divided

Tracie Peterson

To Steve Reginald, my editor and friend,
with thanks for the help you've offered, the direction you've given,
and the chances you've taken with my work.
Philippians 1:3 sums it up from me to you.

Chapter 1

I desire to see her," the tall man stated with an air of one used to his commands being met. His scowl deepened as he awaited an answer.

Duke Geoffrey Pemberton looked sternly at the speaker. It was difficult for him to take orders, much more so from one who was a score of years his junior. Still, the duke of Gavenshire, His Grace Richard DuBonnet, was no ordinary man, and the orders he gave were nearly the same as if they'd come from King Henry himself.

"Surely it would be a waste of Your Grace's time. She is everything your proxy must have told you. I assure you, I speak for my daughter when I say she will go into this marriage with dignity, respect, and honor," Pemberton said in a much-controlled manner and added, "Remember, sire, 'twas your choice to send a proxy to the betrothal ceremony."

Richard brought both fists down on the table. He was weary of dealing with the older man. Weary from the greed and unpleasant cruelties he'd witnessed in things Pemberton said and did.

"Don't question me," Richard said firmly. His breeding and background had given him the skills to easily fight and defeat opponents, but he recognized that the art of diplomacy was wasted on one such as Pemberton. "I want to see her now!" he exclaimed without room for argument.

Pemberton bit back a retort and called for his daughter's chambermaid. The terrified girl appeared, cringing as the duke bellowed out the order that his daughter was to be brought at once to the great hall.

The maid curtsied to both men and, gathering her skirts, lit up the stairs as though a roaring fire chased her.

Richard eased back into the nearest chair. Cupping his hand against the neatly trimmed beard he wore, Richard's green eyes never left his host.

The man was ruthless and cruel, and it showed in his dark eyes. Richard had been forewarned, not only by his men, but by the king's messengers as well. Pemberton had a reputation for a quick temper and heavy hand, which led Richard to wonder about the daughter who would soon be his wife.

Just then the frightened maid returned to curtsey again at her scowling master. "My lady is indisposed at present, sire. She begs to join you in a moment." The girl cowered, awaiting an angry strike, but Pemberton noted the frown on Richard's face and held back retaliation. Before Richard could speak, Pemberton was up the stairs, disappearing from sight.

"You may go," Richard said softly, and the girl hurried from the room, not even raising her eyes to acknowledge the duke's words.

With brush in hand, Arianne Pemberton sat quickly stroking her long hair. The duke of Gavenshire, her betrothed, sat in the great hall below. She'd never even met him before finding herself suddenly engaged. What manner of man would send a proxy for his betrothal ceremonies and leave his bride-to-be wondering at the sight and condition of the man she would vow to take to her side for life?

She hummed nervously to herself, then stopped with a frown. Her father, only moments ago, had sent the maid to fetch her. She had sent the maid back to decline, and no doubt her father would be furious. *But I have to dress my hair,* Arianne thought. *It would have been most inappropriate to have been introduced to the duke with my head bare.*

In spite of her attempts to convince herself she'd made the right decision, the one thing that kept coming back to her was the cruelty she'd known at her father's hand. He wouldn't like her defiance, just as he hadn't cared about her feelings toward the upcoming marriage. She didn't want the wedding, but he did. That put them at odds.

Arianne continued to run the brush through her hair, even while she considered the consequences of her actions. Her father was a ruthless man who ruled all around him with a mixture of injustice and self-servitude. He would not take lightly Arianne's delay.

Arianne's door slammed abruptly open, causing her to drop her brush.

"Get thee below at once!" her father raged. He gave her no chance to stand but reached out and yanked the girl to her feet and out the door.

Below in the great hall, Richard heard the commotion. Pemberton appeared at the top of the stairs, dragging behind a shapely young woman.

With hip-length auburn hair flying out behind her, Lady Arianne Pemberton was dragged down the steps and landed in an unceremonious heap at her father's feet.

"Here," her father said smugly, "is your bride. Her temper can be a bit much, but the back of your hand will easily settle her disposition."

Richard was on his feet in a heartbeat, and before Arianne could lift her face, he was helping her.

"Your Grace," she whispered and pushed back the wavy bulk of hair that kept her face from his. Dark brown eyes met angry green ones, causing Arianne to instantly realize that her worst fears had come true. She was to marry a man just like her father!

"Milady," Richard spoke softly, delivering her to a nearby chair. Turning abruptly, Richard closed the distance to where the duke stood with a haughty stare of disgust.

Balling his hand into a fist, Richard raised it to within inches of the duke's face. "Never, I repeat, never treat my wife with such ill respect again, or you will feel the consequences of your actions."

Arianne could not suppress a gasp of surprise. No one had ever dared to speak to her father in such a manner. The duke's face flamed red, but he remained silent, further surprising his daughter. He must want this match badly.

With the king's edict that she be wed to the duke of Gavenshire, Arianne couldn't imagine that her father would worry that the marriage wouldn't take place. Perhaps he was simply in awe of the younger man's position with the king. Arianne knew that position and power were the only things of importance to her father and surmised that this must, indeed, be the reason for his good manners.

Completely ignoring the indignant duke, Richard turned to take in the vision of the woman he was slated to spend all of time with. She was everything his men had related and more. They hadn't told him of the way her hair flashed glints of gold amid the deep auburn mass. No doubt they'd not seen her hair, Richard mused, for it would have been covered with a white linen wimple and mantle.

Arianne grew uncomfortable under the duke's close scrutiny. She'd had no time to plait her hair and cover her head before her father had stormed into her chamber and dragged her to meet her husband-to-be. She was most grateful that she'd dressed carefully in forest green velvet, for while it was simply adorned with a gold and jeweled belt at her waist, it was a becoming color, and Arianne did hope to meet with the duke's approval.

"Milady," Richard said, coming to greet her formally, "I am Richard DuBonnet, Duke of Gavenshire." He gave a bit of a bow before taking Arianne's hand in his own and continuing. "And you, of course, are the most lovely Lady Arianne Pemberton."

Arianne wanted to melt into the rush-covered floor. The warmth in his eyes set her heart beating faster, but the gentleness of his touch was as none she'd ever known.

"Your Grace," she whispered, getting to her feet. Even as she curtsied deeply, Richard refused to let go of her hand.

"It would pleasure me greatly, milady, if you were to call me Richard."

Arianne rose and lifted her face to his. "Richard," she whispered the name, trembling from head to toe.

"And might I call you Arianne?" he questioned. Both of them were oblivious to the older duke, staring on in complete loathing of the gentle exchange.

"But of course, Your—Richard," Arianne corrected herself. She mustn't do anything to anger this powerful man. "You may call me whatever pleases you."

A hint of a smile played at the corners of Richard's lips. "It pleases me to call you my wife," he said boldly. "The king has chosen well for me."

Arianne blushed scarlet and felt her knees grow weak. She couldn't very well reply with her true feelings toward the arrangement. Not with such gallant praise being issued on her behalf. With a quick glance past Richard to where her father stood, Arianne realized instantly that he was displeased.

Richard noticed the exchange at once and led Arianne back to the chair. "Come, we will speak of our marriage," he announced.

Pemberton could no longer remain silent. "I see no need to waste your valuable time, Your Grace. You must have many affairs to oversee. I have already assured you of my daughter's virtue, dowry—"

"Yes, yes. I know all about the business dealings of my betrothal and marriage. What I desire to know now is the heart of your daughter," Richard interrupted with a flash of anger in his eyes.

"But what woman knows her heart on any matter?" Pemberton retorted with a silencing stare directed at his daughter. "Her thoughts are nothing to you or to me. She knows how to tend a household and direct the running of an estate. She is a comely lass and no doubt will give you many fine sons. More than this is unimportant."

Arianne knew better than to cross her father. She was not yet married, and until she came under Richard's complete protection, there was always the possibility that her father would beat her for her remarks. She shuddered, knowing that she still bore lash marks from the last argument she'd had with her father regarding the upcoming marriage.

Richard took the seat beside Arianne and stared thoughtfully at the duke as if he considered his words of value. Then without warning, he turned to her. "What are your thoughts on the matter of our marriage, Arianne?"

Arianne's father seethed noticeably at the disregard of his statement. He flashed a warning to Arianne that told of trouble to come should she say anything to jeopardize her standing in this arrangement.

Arianne bowed her head slightly before speaking. "It is my honor to share vows with you." The words were barely audible.

"You know very little of me," Richard continued gently. "Is there something I might share with you regarding myself that would put to rest any questionable matter in your mind?"

"Nay, Your Grace," she replied, forgetting to call him Richard.

"Is there any matter about yourself that you would like to share with me?" he questioned.

Arianne was shaking noticeably now. On one side stood her father, threatening with his eyes to strip her of her dignity should she say anything outside of his instruction, and on the other side was Richard, who genuinely seemed to care about her feelings.

The room grew uncomfortably silent. The tension between the girl and her father was clear. Richard frowned slightly. He noticed Arianne's trembling and the duke's scowling face. So long as Arianne's father remained within sight, she would no doubt say little or nothing. Without warning, Richard stood and pointed to the door. "Leave us," he commanded the duke.

Pemberton was shocked beyond reason and enraged beyond words. He struggled for the right response, but before he could find any words, Richard called for his men and ordered them to take the duke into the outer room.

Richard knew he was making a great enemy, but he no longer cared. His real concern was for the frightened young woman who sat cringing in terror.

As his men took the duke from the room, Richard called out one final order. "We are not to be disturbed for any reason."

When the door closed behind his men, Richard turned to Arianne and smiled. "Now, Arianne, you must feel free to speak to me honestly."

Arianne's mouth dropped open slightly, and Richard couldn't help but notice her lips. Raising his gaze slightly, he stared into huge brown eyes that reminded him hauntingly of a doe about to be slain.

"I. . .I. . . ," she stammered for words.

Richard sat back down and took her hand in his own. Lifting it to his lips, he gently kissed the back. "Arianne," he whispered, "I can read things in your eyes that are not making their way to your lips. You might as well speak your heart. You aren't going to offend or injure me, I assure you. Now speak to me of this marriage. Are you truly in agreement?" he questioned gently.

Arianne could feel the warmth of his breath against her hand and pulled it back quickly. "I have never been allowed the luxury of speaking openly, sire—Richard."

"I'm certain you speak the truth," he said with a slight smile. "But your father is no longer a concern to you. You are under my protection and you will leave with me on the 'morrow, so put aside your fears and talk to me. We cannot change what the king has arranged, but we might yet come to a better understanding of it."

Arianne swallowed the lump in her throat. She lifted her delicate face to meet Richard's gentle expression. With the exception of her brother, Devon, she'd never known a man such as Richard. But Devon was hundreds, maybe even thousands of miles away doing the king's bidding, just as she was doing the royal bidding at home.

"I am against marriage to you," she said softly, then tightly shut her eyes and braced herself for his rage.

"I see," he replied without emotion. "Has another captured your affections?"

Arianne's eyes snapped open. "Nay, there is no other," she stated adamantly.

"Then what makes this arrangement so unbearable?"

"I. . .I," she stammered for a moment, then drew a deep breath. "I do not love you, Richard."

Richard chuckled.

"You laugh at me?" Arianne quickly questioned.

"Nay, dear lady. I do not laugh at you. Neither do I expect you to love me. Not yet, anyway. We've only just met, and this arrangement is new to both of us." Richard paused, getting to his feet. He paced a few steps before continuing.

"Why, in all honesty, I hadn't planned to take a wife, at least not yet. When King Henry suggested this arrangement, however, I knew it would be one that would benefit our families and fulfill his desire to see me properly wed."

Richard's words seemed most sincere, and Arianne began to relax. Perhaps the duke was not the kind of man her father was.

Arianne studied Richard for a moment. He was handsome—tall and lean with broad shoulders. His legs were heavily muscled, no doubt from many hours of supporting the chain mail hauberk and chaussures that were customary costume for men of armor. His dark brown hair had been neatly trimmed, as had been his mustache and beard. But most disturbing were his eyes; green eyes so fiery one minute and soft, almost childlike, the next. Arianne truly wished she knew more about the duke of Gavenshire.

"It is a good arrangement for my family," Arianne finally spoke. "I would never do anything to disgrace them. Neither would I do anything to bring the king's wrath upon them. It is my desire to be married to you, just as King Henry wishes."

Richard stopped in his pace and turned. "I don't wish to force an undesirable union upon you, Arianne. The church still presses its people for mutual consent to marriage. I could speak to the king, if it is your wish that we discontinue these arrangements."

"Nay!" Arianne exclaimed, coming up out of her seat. She threw herself at Richard's feet. Her father would kill her for causing the betrothal to be dissolved. Under no circumstances could she appear to be anything but congenial. "Please don't!" There were tears in her eyes. "I beg of you!"

Richard lifted her from the floor and set her down in front of him. "Arianne, you mustn't worry. I understand your circumstances. If you are truly agreed, I want very much for this wedding to take place."

Arianne nodded, unmindful of the tears that streamed down her cheeks. "I am agreed, sire. I will make you a good wife. I promise."

"I've no doubt about that," Richard stated. He reached up to wipe away the tears on her face. "I simply want you to be happy, as well."

Arianne's heart soared, and the first spark of feeling for her soon-to-be husband was born. "I will be happy, Richard, and in time, I pray it will be God's will that I grow to love you."

Chapter 2

Without a chance for her father to lay a hand to her again, Arianne found herself in a long traveling procession the very next morning. She mused over the events that had led to this day. Everyone had been stunned when the young duke himself had arrived to bring the party to his castle. But even more surprising was the way he'd taken control of His Grace, Geoffrey Pemberton. Even Arianne was amazed.

Arianne had never understood what her father expected to gain from her match with the duke of Gavenshire. Of course, it bode well to have such a powerful man in one's family lineage, but Arianne also knew that her father was giving up a great portion of estates that adjoined Richard's property. It was part of her dowry, and Arianne was hard-pressed to understand how her father would have ever conceded to such an arrangement. The king must have promised him a great deal more than what he stood to lose.

Upon her own fine mare, Arianne enjoyed the passing warmth of the afternoon sun. Soon they would stop for the night, and the next day they would make their way to Gavenshire Castle.

Absorbed in thought, Arianne did not hear the rider approach to join her. Richard held back in silence, taking in the beauty he found before him. She sat regally, he thought, and in truth, he had always wondered how a woman could sit so confidently atop a sidesaddle. Arianne, however, seemed not to consider the situation. She was like a child taking in the countryside around her. A look of awe was fixed upon her face.

"Does the ride overtax you, milady?"

Arianne jerked back on the reins without thought. "My pardon, sire. You startled me." She released the reins and allowed the horse to proceed. "What was it you asked of me?"

Richard smiled. "I asked if the ride overtaxed you."

"Nay," Arianne replied with a wistful look spreading across her face. "In truth, it is something wondrous. I have never known the land outside a half-day's ride from my home. The world is much larger out here."

Richard laughed heartily. "That it is, Arianne."

Arianne fixed her eyes boldly on Richard for a moment, and with her smile deepening added, "There is much that I have to learn." The depths of her brown eyes pulled at Richard's heart.

He leaned forward and in hardly more than a whisper spoke. "It would pleasure me greatly to be your teacher."

Arianne blushed deeply at what could seemingly have been a statement of mixed meaning. Had he thought her a flirt? Before she could speak, one of Richard's men hailed him from the front of the procession and Richard bid her farewell.

That night, it seemed Arianne's eyes had barely closed in sleep before she was being urged awake. Today they would reach Gavenshire, she thought, and hastened her steps to get dressed.

She had prepared for this day with great care. Calling the servants her father had allowed her to borrow for the journey, Arianne directed and ordered each one until everything was just as she desired. Too nervous to eat anything, Arianne sent her breakfast away without so much as touching a crumb.

Donning a delicate tunic of pale lavender silk, Arianne nodded her approval and turned to be fitted in the surcoat of samite. The samite blend of wool and silk had been dyed deep purple and trimmed in ermine. Arianne had no desire to appear a pauper before her husband's people.

Within the hour, Arianne's toilette was complete, and she was seated once again on her sidesaddle. She glanced around nervously for Richard and blushed deeply when she met his open stare of approval. With long easy strides, he came to where her mare pranced anxiously.

"Lady Arianne," he said, taking her hand to his lips, "you are the epitome of that which all English women should strive for. Your beauty blinds me to all else."

"Your Grace," she whispered, then corrected herself. "I mean, Richard." She seemed at a loss as to how she should respond to his flattery.

"I trust you slept well," the duke responded before she had a chance to concern herself overmuch.

"Aye," she said with a nod. "Albeit a short rest, 'twas quite refreshing."

"Good," Richard said with a smile. "Then we will be on our way. Gavenshire and her people await their new duchess."

Although Arianne had lived a life of ease compared to many, she was dumbly silent at the vision of Gavenshire Castle. The gray stone walls stood atop the cliffs, rising majestically above the background of the sea's churning waters.

She gasped in awe as they drew ever closer. The spiraling twin towers of the castle seemed to dwarf the village at its feet. Everywhere, brightly colored banners flew in celebration of her marriage to the duke of Gavenshire.

If the castle was not enough, Arianne was absolutely stunned when people lined every inch of the roadway in order to get a look at their soon-to-be duchess.

The crowd cheered, while peasants handed up flowers to her waiting hands. Arianne beamed smiles upon everyone, which prompted even greater response. She was a bit afraid of the sea of people at her side, but Richard had not returned to assist her and so Arianne had to believe that nothing was amiss and that she should enjoy this as her special moment with his people.

Just then a small girl darted out in front of Arianne's mare, causing the horse to rear. Arianne tightened her grip and leaned into the horse's neck. She soothed the horse into stillness, while the child's mother ran forward to claim her frightened daughter.

"A thousand pardons, milady. The child meant no harm, she's just excited by the noise and celebration," the woman stated as if fearing for the life of the child she now held. The crowd around them fell silent and waited for their new duchess to act.

Arianne smiled. "Your apology is unwarranted, madam. I myself am quite caught up in the revelry as well."

A cheer went up once again, and Arianne could feel the mare begin to shift in nervous agitation. Soothing the horse with a gentle stroke, Arianne reached down and gave the child a quick pat on the head and moved the horse forward.

Richard observed the incident from where he'd brought his mount to a stop. Arianne was truly a remarkable woman. In one simple act of kindness, she had sealed herself upon the hearts of his people.

The sun broke out from clouds overhead and flashed out across the earth, touching everything in its warmth. Arianne lifted her face for a moment to catch the rays, and as she lowered her eyes, she caught sight of Richard. The look he gave her was so intimate that she quickly looked away. What manner of man was the duke of Gavenshire that he would boldly assess his wife in public?

The days that followed did so with such momentum that Arianne was left breathless at the end of each one. There was her introduction to the castle, which though thorough, left her more puzzled than ever. She comforted herself in the knowledge that exploration and understanding would come later.

The wedding itself, planned by the duke and his household, was more elaborate than Arianne had ever dreamed. The celebrating and festivities would most likely continue for yet another week.

The day of their wedding was perfect. The church at Gavenshire welcomed the duke and his duchess and all who could crowd inside to share in the pledges of matrimony.

Arianne wore her finest clothes. A linen chemise of pale gold with an exquisite tunic of burgundy silk adorned her frame. Over this came a surcoat of dark gold velvet that had been lavishly embroidered and trimmed in fur. At Richard's request, she had left her hair unplaited, a most unusual thing but one that seemed only to enhance her beauty. On her head she wore a veil of gossamer gold that shimmered in the light when she walked. It was held in place by a narrow gold band that glittered from the three stones it held: a diamond, a ruby, and an emerald.

Richard nodded his heartfelt approval as she approached the priest with him. The priest bade them join right hands, and when Arianne touched Richard's large warm hand with her own small trembling one, peace settled over her.

They repeated their vows before God, the church, and their people and waited while the priest expounded on the virtues of religious education, a tranquil home, and a pure marriage bed.

Finally, he asked for the ring, which Richard promptly produced. The priest blessed the ring, then handed it back to Richard. Arianne noted that it looked to be a small replica of the band that held her veil in place.

"In the name of the Father," Richard whispered and slipped the ring on Arianne's index finger, "and of the Son," he continued and slipped it to the second finger. "And of the Holy Ghost." He fitted it to the third finger. "With this ring I thee wed."

Arianne thought she might actually faint. The moment was so intense, so intimate, that she could scarcely draw a breath. The ceremony continued, and finally after the nuptial mass, Richard received the kiss of peace from the priest and turned to pass it to his new wife.

Gently, he lifted Arianne's veil and smiled. Her brown eyes were huge in anticipation, melting Richard's heart and resolve. He leaned forward without reaching out to her otherwise and, for the first time, touched his lips to hers. He'd only intended to linger a moment, but it was as if he were held against his will. The kiss deepened until, without thought, Richard had gripped Arianne's shoulders.

A gentle cough by the priest told Richard that the marriage was sealed sufficiently. Sheepishly, Richard pulled back with a half-apologetic, half-frustrated look on his face before taking Arianne's hand. He led her quietly from the church to the waiting crowd. They were heralded by the people with such sincere warmth and joy that Arianne could not keep the tears from her eyes.

"What be this?" Richard questioned, reaching out to touch a single drop against her cheek. "You are not already regretting this union, are you?"

"Nay, Richard," Arianne whispered against his bent head. "I am moved beyond thought at the kindness of your people."

Richard lifted her hand to his lips and gave it a squeeze. "They do love you, Duchess."

If the revelry prior to the ceremony was impressive, then the celebration which followed in the great hall of Gavenshire Castle was extraordinary.

First there were the tables laden with food of every imaginable kind. Huge roasted legs of beef were set before them on gold platters, while baked capons, chickens, and rabbits were arranged on smaller plates. Fruits, vegetables, sweetmeats, and breads filled numerous bowls and platters in a nearly endless display of prosperity.

Arianne sat at Richard's side, sharing with him a common chalice and water bowl. When Arianne inadvertently placed her hand on the goblet at the same time Richard reached for it, the intimacy seemed too much. The warmth of his hand covered hers as he lifted the glass to her lips first and then his own. Those at the table who witnessed the act roared in hearty approval and predicted that many would be the number of sons born to this union.

Arianne grew apprehensive and could not look Richard in the eye. She hadn't wanted this marriage, yet it was impossible to deny that he was kind and gentle with her. She thought of the night to come and nearly grimaced while taking a mouthful of roasted boar. She had always hoped that she could give herself in marriage to a man whom she cared for, nay, loved. It wasn't uncommon that people sought that affection, but in a world where the destiny of one usually correlated to the desires of others, Arianne knew that she'd been most fortunate to end up married to a man such as Richard DuBonnet. She could only pray that love would come.

The festivities continued with jongleurs playing lively songs upon their lutes and viols. A man with a tabor played, while another man sang the words of a love song written on behalf of Arianne. He sang of her beauty and virtue while most of the hall fell silent in awe.

Arianne herself was moved to tears, but she quickly held them in check. She had never felt such warmth and caring from anyone in her life.

Soon the tables were moved aside and dancing took place. The people's merriment for the day was evident in the whirling and clapping that accompanied the dance. Arianne found herself passed among Richard's knights, and one after the other whirled, lifted, and paraded her across the floor with great flourish. She caught sight of her father and Richard only once, but it was enough of a glimpse to tell her that Richard was unhappy with the older man.

Finally the revelry grew somber again and the tables were set with supper. The priest blessed the meal and the house, then placed his hands upon Richard and Arianne and blessed their union once again. He added a blessing for the nuptial bed before releasing them to the feast, causing Arianne to blush deeply.

Arianne found eating impossible. She picked at a piece of chicken unmercifully until Richard finally put his hand upon hers and stilled her attack.

"I have a gift for you," he said softly. Richard turned and motioned to an older woman. Arianne lifted her face to find a radiant smile and soft gray eyes.

"This is Matilda," Richard said. "She will be your lady's maid." Without a word being spoken, Arianne immediately liked the woman. Something in her countenance bespoke loyalty and friendship, maybe even the motherly love that Arianne had been robbed of at an early age.

"Matilda," Arianne tried the name. "I am pleased to have your care."

"As am I, to care for you, milady," Matilda replied.

Before anything else was said, Richard leaned toward the two women. "Arianne, Matilda will take you to my. . .our chamber. Perhaps you will feel better away from this crowd. I will join you later."

Arianne nodded without meeting Richard's eyes. Matilda was to prepare her for her wedding bed as was the custom of the bride's mother. Gently rising, Arianne followed Matilda from the room amid the roars and calls of some of the heartier knights. Richard's men intended that he be embarrassed, but he only frowned, knowing the likely uneasiness it caused Arianne.

Upstairs, Arianne permitted Matilda's service, while the woman spoke of the castle and Richard.

"I've know him since he was in swaddling, milady," Matilda said. She gently removed the heavy belt and surcoat from Arianne. "He is a good master, and never a kinder one was born."

Arianne smiled at the woman's obvious devotion. "What of his family?" she questioned. "I've met no one who lays claim to his blood."

Matilda frowned momentarily. "His Grace doesn't allow anyone to speak of them, but I knew them well. I cared for his mother."

Arianne waited while Matilda finished removing the tunic and chemise. She accepted a soft shift of pale cream silk before speaking again to Matilda.

"Is there bad blood between Richard and his family, Matilda?"

"Nay, mistress. 'Tis no small matter to deal with either, and I would not betray my master by speaking of it." Matilda's words were firm, but she sought to ease Arianne's fearful stare by continuing with stories of Richard as a boy.

Arianne allowed the woman to direct her to a chair, where Matilda brushed her hair until each coppery lock seemed to blaze under the soft glow of candlelight. When the task was completed, Matilda stoked the fire in the hearth and built it up until it was a cheerful blaze. Then she extinguished the candles and took her leave.

Arianne drew her legs up to her chest and tucked the silken garment around her feet. She finally allowed herself to gaze around the room, taking in first the fire, then the shadowy forms of clothing chests, and finally the huge bed that she was to share with her husband.

The bed, half again as long as a man's height was nearly as wide across. Overhead the massive wood canopy was decorated with intricate carvings and rich velvet curtains. It was no pauper's bed, to be sure.

Just then the door opened, and against the dim light of the hallway, Richard's well-muscled frame stood fast. He stared at his wife. A more heavenly vision he could not imagine, but even from across the room, he could see that she trembled. He slowly closed the door and set the bar in place.

"You are beautiful, Arianne," he whispered, coming to the fireplace. "I am a most blessed man."

Arianne lifted her eyes, meeting the passionate look of her husband. Words stuck in her throat. What should she say? What could she?

Richard wished nothing more than to dispel the fear in her eyes. Fear that he knew held deep root in her heart.

"I was sorry that your brother couldn't attend the wedding," he said, taking a seat on the bed opposite where she sat. "I know very little about you," he continued. "I would be most honored if you would speak to me about your youth."

Arianne relaxed a bit. Richard seemed content to sit apart from her, and his words made her realize that he had no intention of rushing the night.

"My mother died when I was but six years old," Arianne finally spoke. "I remember only little things about her because I was quickly taken off to a convent where I was schooled and held until my father's instruction. My brother, Devon, would visit me often there. We are very close," she said with a sadness to her voice that Richard wished he could cast out.

"My father returned me home when my brother, Devon, was preparing to ride with the king's men. We shared only a few short months before Devon left, and I have not seen him since. That was five years ago."

"And in all that time he's not returned home?" Richard questioned.

"He and my father are at odds," Arianne whispered. "It seems my father finds a rival in everything."

"Aye," Richard murmured, "I can vouch for that."

"I pray my father has not overly grieved you," Arianne replied.

Richard shook his head and reached out a hand to touch her. Arianne instantly recoiled into the chair. She regretted the action but could do nothing to take it back.

Richard saw the fear return to her eyes and sighed. "Arianne, I'm no monster. I will not beat and abuse you as others must have done. You have nothing to fear from me."

Arianne tried to steady her nerves. Her heart raced at a murderous pace, and she found that fear gripped her throat.

Richard got up and pulled Arianne to her feet. "I will not press you to consummate this marriage," he said firmly. "In fact, I will not seal this arrangement until there is no longer fear in your eyes and heart toward me."

Arianne felt the warmth of his touch spread down her arms. "I will not deny you," she whispered.

"Yea, but I will deny myself," Richard replied. "I have but one request in return."

"Name it, sire."

"That you share my bed upon my honor that I will not touch you," he replied. Then with eyes twinkling and a slight smile upon his lips, he corrected himself. "Nay, I would hold you but demand nothing more."

Arianne nodded slowly, still amazed that he would do such a thing for her. She cast her glance from Richard's face to the bed and back again when a horrible thought gripped her mind.

"The virginal sheets," she whispered.

"The what? What are you talking about, Arianne?"

"The virginal sheets." Her voice trembled. "Without them, I'll be shamed and so will you."

Richard stared blankly for a moment and then recalled the barbaric custom of a bride's proof of virtue. He grimaced slightly. "I'm sorry, milady. I forgot." Then turning to the bed, he yanked down the coverlets and pointed. "Lie down."

Arianne steadied her nerves and straightened her shoulders. *This is it*, she thought, and even though Richard had promised to wait, she quietly obeyed his command.

She closed her eyes as she reclined on the cold sheets. With her fists clenched at her sides and jaws tight, Arianne waited.

Richard stared down at her shapely form with more compassion for her fear than he'd ever known for anyone. "Open your eyes, Arianne," he said after several moments.

Arianne forced herself to look at Richard. In her eyes was the look of a trapped animal, and Richard longed to end her suffering and ease her fears.

"Now, get up," he whispered and extended a hand to help her. Arianne was stunned but nevertheless scooted quickly from the bed to stand beside her husband.

With one fluid motion, Richard drew a jeweled ceremonial dagger from his belt and slashed his forearm with a small stroke.

Arianne gasped aloud at the crimson stain that appeared on Richard's arm. He never took his eyes from her face as he waited calmly for the blood to pool. Then walking to where Arianne had lain, he sprinkled his blood over the sheet.

"There," he said with a sheepish grin. "The virginal sheets."

Arianne stood open-mouthed, staring at her husband. "Why did you do this thing? Why did you shed your own blood?"

Richard sobered. "So you wouldn't have to."

Arianne's heart pounded within her. If she had never cared for this man before, she now felt a deep respect and admiration for him.

"You make this sacrifice for me—to keep me from shame?" Arianne questioned.

Richard again smiled. "Too gallant, milady?"

"No," Arianne said, shaking her head slowly. "Amazing—for you scarce know me and I do not love you."

"People didn't love our Lord Jesus, either, but He gave His blood to save them," Richard said, his green eyes darkening.

Still not knowing what to think, Arianne found her eyes upon his bleeding arm. Tenderly, she placed her hand upon Richard. "Come," she whispered. "I will care for you."

Chapter 3

The next weeks were some of the happiest Arianne had ever known. She was constantly amazed at Richard's devotion to her, all the while honoring his promise to leave her chaste.

He took time to teach her things about his home, while continuing to see to the duties that demanded his attention. She learned that he was twenty-five and held a great friendship with the king that had been firmly in place since Richard's childhood.

She also learned what had caused her father to warm so quickly to her marriage when Richard told her of a young widow who would soon be wed to her father. The arrangement would bring both wealth and property to her father. Arianne had no doubt he cared little for the huge settlement of land he'd had to sacrifice to Richard in her dowry in order to seal the arrangement. The only thing Richard ever denied her was information about his family. Whenever she questioned him concerning his parents or whether he had siblings, Richard artfully changed the subject.

They spent their days as was fitting to their station. Arianne learned the ways of the castle and found that she thrived on its running. She was quick to settle disputes between servants and relished shopping trips that allowed her to pick from among the finest furnishings to make her castle a more pleasant home.

Richard admired her abilities, and when he found her adding figures easily in her inventory of their larder supplies, he gave her a huge purse with which to run the household in full. It eased the burden of his steward and endeared Richard to Arianne's heart.

Still, at night the old fears returned and the dread of what she did not understand. Arianne fought to sort through her confused heart and still could not tell Richard truthfully that she loved him. Until then, she felt certain that the wall of apprehension would remain firmly in place between them.

Even so, she climbed into his bed each night and curled up to the warmth he offered. He spoke softly of his days at court and his accomplishments. He shared brief details of his early childhood and asked Arianne questions that sorely strained the memories she'd buried away for so long.

"Your father seems a most difficult man. Was he always so foul tempered?" Richard questioned one night.

Arianne stiffened in his arms. "Aye." The simple word sounded painful.

Richard began to rub her arm until he felt her relax a bit. "Tell me," he whispered.

Arianne hesitantly opened her mind to the memories. Cautiously, she picked her way amid the anguish and fear to pull out just the right words to share. "My mother never loved him, and he never loved her. It was an arranged marriage to benefit their families. My mother, although she would never speak an ill word of my father, was lonely and heartbroken during her life with him. She bore him two children: my brother, Devon, and myself, and died trying to bear a third. My mother's maid told me of her death and how not even upon her final breath did my father speak any word of love to her."

"And that is why it is most important to you," Richard stated simply.

"It must be," Arianne replied as though the thought were new to her. "Yea, 'tis the reason."

Richard ran his fingers through her long wavy hair and sighed. "It is easier to understand why you hold such fear in this arrangement."

"It is?" Arianne barely whispered the question.

"You long to find the love in marriage that your mother never had. You've most carefully and completely buried your heart away to protect it from the possibility that you, too, will know the feeling of being in a loveless marriage."

"I suppose what you say is most reasonable. She died so young, yet even as she lived, my mother was a broken woman. She never knew the love of her husband, only his lust. In many ways, it was most merciful that she left this earth," Arianne reasoned, "and her pain."

Richard lifted her hand to his lips and lovingly kissed each finger. "Then you will never know her pain, my sweet wife, for I already love you."

Arianne's eyes widened at his declaration. Never before had Richard mentioned love. But even as her heart told her to tread lightly, her mind reminded her of the various times Richard's actions had already spoken of his heart's true feelings.

"It is true," Richard said with a smile. "I lost my heart to you when you threw yourself at my feet and begged me to marry you."

"I did not beg," Arianne said in mock horror. "I merely insisted you keep the bargain." Her lips curled ever so slightly at the corners.

Richard laughed and held her hand to his heart. "I would never have broken that bargain," he whispered. "Nay, even if the king himself had bid me do otherwise."

Arianne could feel the rapid beat of his heart beneath her hand. Without thought, she leaned her ear to his broad chest and listened to the steady pounding.

"It beats only for you, my Arianne," Richard said, gently stroking her hair. Before long, they were both asleep, but only after Richard had spent a great deal of time in silent prayer. He longed for her heart to be healed of its pain and for her fears to be cast aside. He prayed for the day Arianne would come to him without fear in her heart.

It was on these intimate nights of long, private conversation that Richard pinned his hopes. He saw Arianne warm a little more each day to his company and began taking advantage of that warming to press her a little bit further. On many occasions he'd held her hand while they strolled the grounds, and in several daring moments he'd kissed her and found her very close to receptive. It became increasingly important to him that his wife come to love him.

"Let us ride the estate this morning," Richard suggested after they'd shared breakfast one morning.

"I'd like that very much," Arianne answered. It had been a long time since she'd ridden.

"Good," he said, pulling her along with him. "I'd like it very much, as well." His smile was boyish, and his eyes danced merrily as though they were two children stealing away from the eyes of their parents.

With Arianne secured on her sidesaddle, Richard mounted and pointed the way. "There is a path along the waterfront and I would show it to you today."

"Lead on, Your Grace," she said in a teasing tone. She often forgot to call him Richard, and at times it became quite a joke between them.

Richard pressed his horse forward, and Arianne followed at a quick pace behind him until he slowed his mount and allowed the mare to catch up. They rode in silence, each enjoying the warmth of the sun and the view of the ocean that stretched out before them. They rode for over an hour before the land began to slowly slope downward toward the sea.

Arianne thrilled to the sound of the ocean upon the rocks. The power of each swell as the water pounded toward the shoreline captivated her in a way she'd not expected. It lulled her senses, and she found herself forgetting all that had gone before.

Richard, too, seemed to find the water refreshing. He spoke very little, occasionally pointing out some feature or fascination before leading them forward. Neither one saw the rain clouds that moved in and darkened the sky before it was too late to escape the downpour.

The rain came in torrents, saturating everything in sight. When thunder began to crack overhead, Richard sought shelter among the cliffs. "I know this land well. The cliffs will yield much in the way of protection," he reasoned with Arianne. She fought to stay seated, while each crash of thunder threatened to spill her from her saddle.

Eventually, Richard found the opening he was looking for. He dismounted and pulled the horses along a slight incline and then under the shelter of a rocky archway. Securing the horses, he reached up and pulled Arianne's drenched body from the saddle. "Come," he said above the storm and pulled Arianne farther up the cliff side.

Arianne's heavy surcoat threatened to trip her as its velvet absorbed the torrential rain. Richard finally noticed her struggles and easily lifted her into his arms and carried her to the small cave.

Once inside the shelter, Arianne realized she'd wrapped her arms tightly around Richard's neck, while burying her face against his chest. She felt most reluctant to let go and so for several moments just relished the feel of his arms around her. The storm raged outside, and Arianne trembled in fear from the noise.

"You are safe, milady," Richard whispered against her ear. His warm breath caused her heart to pound harder.

Arianne forced herself to ease her hold. She felt Richard's hesitation to put her down and held her breath slightly in anticipation of what he would do.

Richard battled with his heart, mind, and soul as he held his wife. What he wanted to do was kiss her soundly and hold her. He could feel her shaking and wondered if it was the cold or her own fears that caused her to tremble. Gently, he lowered her to the ground, then bid her to sit with him on the floor of the cave where he opened his arms to hold her.

Arianne didn't hesitate to move against him. She was freezing and frightened, and time had proven Richard worthy of his promise. She had nothing to fear from this man, she reminded herself, and snuggled down against him.

The storm continued with no sign of letting up, and with each crash of thunder, Arianne buried her head against Richard's chest and prayed that it would soon be over.

Without thought, Richard reached down and cupped her chin in his hand, lifting her face to meet his. He felt such joy at her obvious comfort in him that he couldn't resist pressing his advantage. Slowly, with painstaking effort to keep from frightening her, Richard lowered his lips in a gentle, searching kiss. Arianne's response was accepting, prompting Richard to deepen the kiss.

When he raised his mouth from hers, Arianne's cheeks were flushed red. "My sweet Arianne," he whispered before kissing her again.

Arianne felt confused by his actions. His kisses were pleasant enough and his touch comforting, but she longed to know for sure that she loved him and, as of yet, her heart could not confirm that matter. Frightened that her response might prompt a more intimate reaction, Arianne suddenly pushed away.

"I," she gasped slightly, trying to speak clearly, "I'm sorry, I can't." She started to move away but found her gown caught beneath Richard's long legs.

"Don't be afraid, Arianne. I'll not harm you. I gave you my word. Now sit here with me and I will tell you more stories about my childhood."

Arianne immediately felt at ease. Richard had a way about him, and she doubted anyone could feel uncomfortable once he sought to assuage their fears. She allowed him to pull her close once again and waited for his story to begin.

"When I was quite young," Richard told her, "I was most fortunate to foster in the care of a godly man. As was the habit of fostering, I went from my parents' home at an early age and learned how to become a man worthy of knighthood.

"This man had been to the Holy Lands and told me such tales as I could scarce believe. He told me about writings that were set upon scrolls from the time of our Lord Jesus and how they told of His life. I was determined from that moment forward to one day have a closer look at those scrolls. I set out to find a way to journey to Jerusalem."

Arianne listened in fascination at the story Richard shared.

"When my guardian learned of my desire, he took me some twenty miles to a monastery, where I was allowed to study their copies of the written scriptures. It was then that my heart was filled and my eyes opened to the truth of God. Our Lord Jesus Christ came to earth as a babe to give us life everlasting through His blood. I thought to myself what a wonderful gift this was, and the good friars of the church were amazed at my enthusiasm.

"I stayed with them for several months and studied all that they would teach. My heart craved an understanding of God, and it would not be satisfied until I had read every written Word. I spent hours in prayer, which the friars found fascinating. They naturally assumed that I would put myself into the service of the church, but it wasn't the direction I felt God's voice loudest. In fact, the church itself worried me most grievously."

Arianne sat up with a questioning look. "The church?" she questioned.

"Aye," Richard replied with a nod. "The church, it would seem, had somehow added many things that I did not see within the written Word of God. It appeared to me that man had taken upon himself to correct God's oversight."

"Your Grace!" Arianne exclaimed and crossed herself quickly. "What heresy do you speak?"

Richard smiled, knowing that Arianne had been raised in a convent where the church's ways were stressed as divine. "'Tis no heresy I make but a simple declaration of insight. The church would have you believe that it is the salvation of mankind, but 'tis our Lord Jesus Christ who holds that position."

"You could be hanged for heresy or burned alive!" Arianne exclaimed with a shudder.

"I do not generally share these words with those who would see me hanged or burned," he offered with a smile. "It is only my desire to share a deep and gratifying love of our God with you, sweet Arianne."

Arianne seemed to find reason in his words. She settled back against him and pressed a question. "Would you see the church dissolved?"

"Nay," Richard answered. "I would see it remade. I would see the scriptures offered to all mankind and not only to a few pious priests. I would see that men and women of all rank and status would come to understand not only the fear of God as our judge, but the love of God for His children."

"It sounds quite wondrous," Arianne remarked. She realized that Richard's words of God had touched a deep chord within her. This man was nothing like her father. Her father also saw the church as a problem, but for reasons of greed and personal gratification, not because the souls of a nation went tended without the truth.

Richard smiled at her sudden acceptance. Most would find his words beyond consideration, but Arianne actually found them worthy of contemplation.

"Have you a heart for the truth, Arianne?" Richard questioned softly, pushing her back enough to see her face.

"Aye," she whispered, thinking not only of God's truth, but also of the truth her heart might show her about Richard.

"When we return to the castle, I will show you something most precious to me," Richard stated confidently. "'Tis a copy of the Gospel of Saint John. And a more wondrous book of wisdom you will not find."

Arianne seemed surprised that Richard's personal possessions would include a rare copy of the scriptures. "I would be most honored to view them," she said honestly. "And, perhaps you could share more about your views of God."

Richard's heart soared. He felt more confident than ever that Arianne was the proper mate for him. Now if he could only allay her fears and teach her to trust him in full.

"What of your parents?" Arianne suddenly asked. "Do they share your views on God and the church?"

Richard frowned. "Nay, they are dead." It was the first time he had spoken of them, and Arianne was taken aback by the words.

"I did not know. Has it been long?" she asked softly.

Richard shook off the question as though he'd already said too much. "Look, the storm has abated. Let's press homeward and get you dry and warm," he said, pulling her to her feet. Arianne grimaced at his evasiveness, wondering again why he wouldn't speak of his family.

They stepped out of the cave and moved slowly down the slippery pathway to where the horses stood. Looking out across the sea, they were rewarded with a priceless display of colors.

"A rainbow," Arianne said, pointing to the sky.

"God's promise," Richard whispered against her ear. "It always fills me with renewed hope." The previous discomfort was forgotten.

Arianne lifted her face to Richard's and wondered at the man she had married. There was so much more to Richard DuBonnet, Duke of Gavenshire than met the eye. And so many unanswered questions.

Richard, feeling her eyes upon him, dropped his gaze to the warm brown eyes that beheld him. He turned her in his arms and held her close. "Ah, sweet Arianne—my Arianne," he whispered before kissing her.

Arianne no longer battled her worries. She slipped her arms around Richard's neck and returned his kiss. The moment passed much too quickly for both of them, and when Richard pulled away, Arianne could barely make out his words.

"Much renewed hope," he whispered and helped her into the saddle.

Chapter 4

Upon their return to the castle, Richard and Arianne were immediately set upon by several of the knights. Richard learned that an emissary of the king had called him to bring a good number of his men to lend protection as their entourage crossed Richard's vast open lands.

Richard brooded over the message, even while ordering his men into preparation for the trip. He didn't feel comfortable leaving the castle with so few men to defend it but comforted himself with the thought that he had no known enemies who might lay siege to his home. Times were peaceful, and his people were content. Still, the summons did not sit well with him, and his mood grew uncharacteristically harsh and somber.

Arianne, too, grew somber. She knew the time would come when Richard would be called away from home, but when she learned that his absence might stretch into weeks, she became more fearful than ever. In Richard's absence, she would be in charge of the castle, and all of its problems would be hers to solve with the aid of his chamberlain and steward.

She chided herself for her misgivings, reminding herself that this was the very work she'd been trained to do most of her young life. Still, Arianne knew the task before her was a great one, and she was struggling to acquaint herself with the people whom Richard so trusted and admired.

She recognized the help she would have in Douglas and Dwayne Mont Gomeri, brothers who were Richard's highest confidants. As his chamberlain and steward, they would remain behind to offer their services to Arianne in the running of the castle and its estates.

While it was indeed rare that Richard would travel without Douglas at his side to manage his affairs, the duke felt it in the best interests of all whom he loved that his chamberlain remain behind to support the new duchess. The brothers would also tend to the men left behind and the townspeople, should problems arise, but Arianne would command a place of great responsibility.

Upon reflection, Arianne was suddenly grateful to have spent so many hours in the company of Douglas and Dwayne. They dined daily with Richard and Arianne, along with several trusted knights who comprised an inner circle from which Richard drew wisdom and advice. Because of this, Arianne felt quite comfortable taking matters to them whenever Richard was unavailable.

Nevertheless, Arianne was only becoming used to Richard's presence in her life. The thought of lonely nights without his stories and shared confidences made her heart ache. She couldn't identify this new emotion. Dare she believe it was love?

It took less than a day for Richard to prepare his men, and Arianne waited for the inevitable good-bye. She sat in their chamber, quietly working on her sewing and wondering when he would come to her.

Then suddenly, as if answering her question, loud shouting could be heard in the hall below. Richard had been a relentless force to be reckoned with, and everyone in the household was near exhaustion in the wake of his black mood. The old apprehensions threatened to dispel Arianne's calm, and even though she felt certain that Richard's heart held love for her, she was powerless to keep the fear from her eyes. When he ranted at his men, he reminded her of her father. How could she ever convince him that she wasn't afraid, when indeed she was? Richard would never have believed her had she lied and told him otherwise, for always he said her eyes betrayed her heart.

Starting when the voices suddenly sounded in the hallway outside her chamber, Arianne pricked her finger on the needle and had to put aside her work. She sat like a little girl, sucking on her wounded finger, when Richard blasted through the door.

"It is time," he nearly bellowed, his mind still in the mode of dealing with his men. He crossed the room with heavy-footed strides and threw open one of the clothing chests. The wooden lid banged heavily against the footboard of the bed, but Richard was oblivious.

Arianne, however, cringed at the loudness. He reminded her of her father when he shouted and banged things about. She suddenly wished she could be anywhere else but dealing with this raging man who would command an army to protect the king.

Richard suddenly stopped to contemplate his silent wife. As if reading her thoughts, he stepped forward to where she sat.

"You needn't fear me, milady," Richard stated firmly. "I am not your father. Now come, I would seek my pleasure upon those sweet lips before my journey takes me far from your side." His boyish grin was all that eased the tone of his words.

Arianne sat trembling and wondered if she could even rise to her feet. "I'm sorry, Your Grace," she whispered and forgot about her sore finger. She lowered her eyes to keep Richard from seeing the tears that formed there. Were they tears of fear, frustration, or coming loneliness?

"I've given you no reason to fear me," Richard said in complete exasperation before adding, "and stop calling me Your Grace. My name is Richard!"

"Aye," Arianne replied, jumping at his agitated voice.

"And stop jumping every time I speak, and look at me when I talk to you," Richard demanded. The dread of leaving his home had worn his patience quite thin.

Arianne raised her face to meet his. The tears in her eyes threatened to spill at any moment, and Richard's heart softened.

"I'm only a man, Arianne. Look at me. No monstrous form stands here prepared to devour you, and I haven't killed anyone in days!"

Arianne straightened a bit and looked Richard in the eye, catching the humor in his voice and the hint of a smile.

Before she could prevent it, a nervous giggle escaped her lips. Richard smiled broadly, quite pleased with himself. *At least she has a sense of humor*, he thought.

"That's better," he said. "Now come and give me a long kiss. I said I'd leave you chaste for a spell, but I did not say I wouldn't work hard to shorten that span of time."

He was her Richard again, and Arianne threw herself willingly into his open arms. "I wish you didn't have to go," she cried softly.

"You will miss me, then?" he asked good-naturedly.

Arianne pulled away. "Of course I will miss you. You are like no other man I've known. You give so much and expect so little in return."

"Oh, sweet Arianne, I expect a great deal in return." He chuckled softly. "It's just that I am a man whose patience to obtain that which he desires outweighs all else. I'm glad you will miss me, for I shan't sleep a single night without your name upon my lips and the thought of your softness upon my mind."

"Will it truly be so very long?" she questioned hesitantly. Her brown eyes framed by dark, wet lashes grew wider in fear.

"Don't be afraid. Remember, God is by your side, my sweet wife. You must leave my safety and yours in the hands of One who can better deal with it," Richard said, tracing the soft angle of her jaw. "Now, I would have that kiss."

When their lips met, Arianne wished that he might never pull away. In her heart was a sudden foreboding of separation that threatened to strangle the very breath from her. What would become of her if Richard fell to some assassin's sword?

She clung desperately to his neck, knowing that she might be hurting him in her urgency, but so uncertain of her emotions that she could not do otherwise.

Richard sensed all her worries and fears and chose the kiss instead of words to ease his wife's tormented mind. He kissed her purposefully, with a tenderness that seemed so right, so necessary, that it held Richard in awe as well. As he lingered, feeling the tension of her arms give way to trembling, he knew that Arianne cared for him, and it gave him all the drive and passion that he needed to go forth and do his king's bidding.

He pulled away, but not before her tears mingled with the sweat on his face. Would he ever dry those eyes once and for all, he wondered. So much pain was mirrored in their depths, and Richard knew it was only the tiniest portion of what existed inside her heart.

"Be strong, Arianne," he whispered and gently wiped her cheeks. "Be strong and know that God is at your side. I'll be back before you know it, and all will be well."

Arianne nodded and offered the faintest hint of a smile before Richard turned away. He retrieved a bag of coins from the open chest, then without a single glance back, walked from the room and Arianne's sight.

In the days that followed, Matilda was Arianne's only real comfort. She spent a good portion of each day with Arianne and often played the comforting mother that Arianne so desperately needed. Many times they took to Arianne's private solarium, the room just off her bed chamber, and spoke for hours of life at Gavenshire and Richard's childhood.

"I don't understand," Arianne said one morning. "Why won't Richard speak of his family?"

"It pains him, milady," Matilda said, offering nothing more.

"Aye, but he expects me to tell him of my woes," Arianne reasoned.

"But thou art his wife," Matilda replied. "And he is your husband and master. If 'tis a matter for you to understand, it must be His Grace that shares the story."

"You cared for his mother," Arianne continued. "Tell me of her. Was she beautiful? Was she kind? What did she like to do? Where did she come from?"

Matilda sighed. It was from bittersweet memories that she conjured the image of Richard's mother, Lady Evelyn. "She was like a breath of spring," Matilda finally said. "She was all that nobility and gentlefolk could hope to embrace and," the hesitancy was clear in the older woman's voice, "she loved her family with a love that blinded her to all else. She saw only good in people, and because there was only good within her own heart, she presumed others were the same."

"And Richard's father?" Arianne braved the question, hoping Matilda would continue.

"Richard's father was a good man. Highly admired by the king, he was often found in his court. His death was mourned by many," Matilda responded. "'Twas his close friendship with His Highness that caused Richard to be taken under King Henry's personal care."

Arianne wanted to press for more, but something in Matilda's reply told her that they'd gone as far as the older woman would allow. "Thank you for telling me about them," Arianne whispered. "It's important that I know of them to better know my husband."

It was a start, Arianne reasoned. It was more than she'd known before, and it gave her hope that she might yet learn the full story of the people her husband kept so well hidden away.

Life moved at a painfully slow pace for Arianne. She oversaw her tasks in the castle with skill and strength born of youth, but her heart was not in it and her mind was always far from her home.

Nightly, she climbed into bed and ached for the familiar warmth of her husband. She thought for hours of how they would talk of things so seemingly trivial, yet in memory, they served to give her insight into Richard's needs and desires.

He had once told her of his love for soaking in a hot bath after working hard upon the training fields. Arianne had determined then that she would see to this need and be sure that hot water always waited in their chamber when he returned at day's end.

Then, too, he'd told her of his dislikes. He despised cold food and greasy meat. He hated injustice and mock humility and found even a slightly arrogant man better than one who cowered in feigned subjection. Wool tunics chafed his neck, and he'd stubbornly clung to the same saddle for his warhorse since he'd first acquired the mount. All these things recounted themselves in Arianne's memory.

"I will line his wool tunics with silk," she mused while closing her eyes in sleep. "I will begin tomorrow, and perhaps by the time I've finished, Richard will be home." It offered slight comfort to tell herself this, but Arianne had to have something to look forward to.

After nearly two weeks had passed, a messenger came to Gavenshire Castle bearing tidings from Richard. The messenger sought out the new duchess to assure her of her husband's safety and left nearly as quickly, taking back with him two of the newly lined tunics and Arianne's fondest wishes for his speedy return.

The incident had both comforted and tormented Arianne. To ease her pain, she arranged to take a long ride. Sir Dwayne accompanied her and, much to Arianne's relief, seemed to understand that she didn't wish to talk.

They rode silently across the land. Only when Arianne reined her mare to a halt, high above the restless sea, did she speak. "He did not say when he would return?"

"Nay, milady, he did not," her companion replied.

"And what think ye on the matter, Sir Dwayne?"

"I cannot truly say, milady," the man spoke honestly, then added with a grin, "however, knowing how His Grace feels about his wife, I would say he will make haste in returning once the king has released him to do so."

Arianne smiled and nodded. "Richard may be a patient man, but that has never been one of my virtues. Let us return to the castle and see to the noon meal."

Sir Dwayne nodded and followed Arianne as she urged the mare into a trot. He admired this woman as he had no other, save his mother. She was intelligent and quick with solutions whenever crisis arose, but she was also kind and compassionate, and he felt certain she was responsible for the happiness he'd seen in Richard's eyes. Happiness that, though haunted by an untold bitter past, seemed strong enough to dispel the ugly wounds and knit together peace and healing.

Arianne never looked back as she pushed the mare home. She'd come to love her new home, Richard's home, and for reasons beyond her comprehension, Arianne found it necessary to return quickly. Perhaps Richard had returned, she dared to hope. With that in mind, she gave the mare full freedom to stretch into a jarring gallop, mindless of Sir Dwayne's surprise.

She came rapidly upon the castle and immediately spied the congregation of mounted men that stood at the gatehouse. "Richard has returned!" she called over her shoulder. Still she didn't slow, even though she thought her riding companion called back to her. She ran the mare the full length of the way and only reined back when she reached the men.

Arianne immediately felt a sense of confusion. She was still so unfamiliar with Richard's men that she couldn't find a single face that she could place with a name. Jumping from her horse, Arianne lost track of Sir Dwayne as she pushed through the crowd.

"Where is my husband?" she questioned one man who stood at the gatehouse entrance. He said nothing but pointed through the gateway.

Arianne wondered silently where Sir Dwayne was and turned to see if she could glimpse him when she walked into the solid wall of an armored man.

"Ho, wench," he said and grabbed her arm tightly. He immediately noted the richness of her garments and the ring that marked her left hand.

Arianne twisted her body to pull away from the painful grip but found it impossible to break his hold.

"I demand that you unhand me," Arianne spat defiantly. "Sir Dwayne!" she called, but silence was her only answer.

The man who held her laughed in a low, quiet way that caused the skin on Arianne's arms to crawl. She couldn't see his face for the armor he wore, but it wouldn't matter if she could. These men were strangers, and she'd managed to place herself in the middle of them.

Lifting her chin and fixing her brown eyes on the man's covered face, Arianne was determined to show no fear.

"Who are you, and why do you handle me so?" she finally questioned.

The man suddenly released her, but Arianne knew better than to move. She was pressed in by a dozen mounted men and Sir Dwayne was nowhere to be found. She waited silently while the man reached up to take the helmet from his head.

Hard and determined eyes stared back at her, and a cruel smile played upon the lips of her captor. "You must be the duchess of Gavenshire," he said in a tone akin to sarcasm.

"I am," Arianne replied, standing her ground. "What business have you here?"

The man looked away laughing, then in a flash turned angry eyes back to appraise Arianne. "You must satisfy the duke greatly," he said in a guttural way that made Arianne feel sick. "I must say, I am most pleased at this turn of events."

"I'm sure I do not understand," Arianne replied. She could feel her determination to be strong crumbling into the terror she'd known so much of her life. "I ask you again, what business have you here?"

Without warning, the man's mailed hand flashed out to strike her across the face. The blow sent Arianne sprawling to the ground, where she sat trying to focus her eyes and rid her mind of the threatening darkness.

"You will not take that tone with me," the man sneered. "I'm not in the habit of answering for my actions to stupid women."

The words infuriated Arianne. How dare he call her stupid; but then hadn't she been just that? It was her choice to ride right up into the midst of them, offering herself over as if she were glad to see them. Slowly, she got to her feet to face the man once again. She said nothing, but her angry brown eyes spoke more than words ever could. The man actually seemed taken aback, but only for a moment.

"I will answer your question, but only because it pleases me to do so. I am here today to take you as my hostage until your husband returns so that I might seek my revenge and end his worthless life."

Arianne sank to her knees, her head still aching and ringing with the words of her husband's obvious enemy. He planned to kill Richard, and he planned to use her in order to accomplish it!

Chapter 5

Arianne knew nothing except that she was being lifted up by two of the nearby men. She was half dragged, half carried through the gatehouse and into the open bailey outside the castle proper. The men who'd been left behind to defend the keep and its people drew swords and any other available weapon and stepped forward.

At the sight of the armed men, the leader raised his hand and called a halt to the thirty or so men who followed him. A half circle of Gavenshire protectors stood between the men and the castle, making their presence and intentions well known.

The enemy leader, helmet in hand, lowered his chain-mailed arm and spoke. "I am Lord Tancred," he announced. "I claim this castle for my own and its people as well. You may shed your blood here today or you may hand over your weapons in peace. Either way, you will be my prisoners until the return of your duke."

There was a murmur of voices through the crowd, but not one man offered to lower his weapons. Arianne stood proudly straight between her captors at the sight of her people. They were loyal to her and Richard and they would not bend easily.

Douglas Mont Gomeri stepped forward, sword drawn and ready to strike. He moved within ten feet of the man called Tancred before stopping. "I am the chamberlain of this castle, and in His Grace's absence, I am the protector of Her Grace and these people. We will not yield our arms to you."

"That is a pity," Tancred said and rubbed his mailed hand over his helmet, contemplating the man before him. "For you see, my foolish man, we have already captured the duchess and her guard."

At this, Arianne was pushed forward to fall in the dirt at Tancred's feet. Before she could move, Tancred dropped his helmet and pulled his own sword in one fluid motion. Grabbing a handful of Arianne's hair, Tancred yanked her to her knees and held the sword to her throat. He returned his gaze to the young knight before him with an evil grin.

"Perhaps," Tancred said in a low hush, "you would like to reconsider your position."

"Nay, Sir Douglas, he knows he cannot kill me and have Richard, too!" Arianne exclaimed. "He will not harm me." Arianne's self-confidence was quickly lost when Tancred's heavy hand slammed across her face. This time Arianne felt her body go limp as blackness covered her eyes.

"Milady," Matilda whispered overhead. A cool cloth was brought against her face as consciousness returned to Arianne DuBonnet.

"Matilda!" Arianne gasped and struggled to sit up.

"Nay, milady. Do not move. You took quite a blow and should rest," Matilda said firmly.

"Then it is all true," Arianne stated in a resigned tone. "I had prayed it was but a nightmare, and now I awaken to find that it is cruelly true."

"I am sorry, milady." Matilda had tears in her eyes. She rinsed the rag in the basin before applying it once again to Arianne's bruised face.

"What are we to do now, I wonder?" Arianne didn't expect Matilda to reply, but the older woman had no other choice.

"He is waiting," the maid said solemnly. "He demanded that you be brought to him the minute you regained your wits."

"What of our people?" Arianne questioned suddenly, remembering Sir Douglas's bold stand.

"They laid down their arms when he threatened to hurt you. He told Sir Douglas that he wouldn't kill you, but he would torture you until he yielded. No knight could allow such a thing to happen."

"Oh, Matilda," Arianne cried, "this is all my fault. If I hadn't put myself right in their midst, this wouldn't have happened."

"You cannot blame yourself," Matilda said softly. "No one expected this to happen. No one thought he would come."

Arianne caught a note of something in Matilda's voice. "No one thought he would come," she whispered. "Who is he?"

Just then the door slammed open and an armed man entered the room. "My master is awaiting Her Grace," he said gruffly. "I am to bring her to the great hall."

Matilda stood between the man and Arianne, trying for all she was worth to make her barely five-foot-high frame look menacing. "Milady is injured. Surely your master can wait!"

"Out of my way, woman," the man said, pushing Matilda to one side.

He reached down and pulled Arianne to her feet with a snarled growl.

Arianne's head reeled from the action. She felt herself sway and might have fallen except for the strong arm that steadied her and pulled her forward.

They moved down the hall and then to the stone stairs that would take them to the floor below. Arianne looked around her as if contemplating her escape. Very little had changed except for the presence of Tancred's men. She held her hand against the side of her face where the throbbing hurt most. It caused her mind to drift unwillingly to her youth and the heavy-handedness of her father.

The man at her side seemed not to notice or to care that she was in pain. He was doing his master's bidding.

Tancred sat discussing some matter with two of his men when the knight entered the room with Arianne. The men seemed anxious to be about their orders and barely acknowledged the fact that she had joined them. Tancred noted her entrance, however, and Arianne found herself forgetting about her bruised face.

For a moment she paused, noticing that Tancred had taken the coif of chain mail from his head, giving her a better view of him. He had dark, unruly hair and piercing eyes that seemed to change color even as he lifted them in greeting. There was a lifetime of anger in the eyes that met hers, and with haughty determination, Arianne met their stare straight on.

The man at her side pushed her into a chair, where Arianne made herself straighten with as much poise and dignity as she could muster. She would not back down from this man, cowering as though she were a chambermaid. Nay! She was the duchess of Gavenshire, and her position demanded that she act accordingly. To do otherwise would betray her people's trust.

She waited in silence for Tancred to speak, wondering who this man was and why he had come to kill Richard. If only she'd had a few more moments alone with Matilda. Matilda seemed to know exactly who he was; perhaps she even knew why he hated them so much. At the first possible opportunity, she would have to seek out Matilda and learn whatever she knew.

Tancred dismissed the man who'd accompanied Arianne, but he ignored Arianne. He leaned back against the chair she'd often seen Richard in and scowled at the wall across the room.

Arianne fought the urge to squirm uncomfortably. Perhaps that was what he wanted, she thought, and doubled her efforts to remain regal and still. Finally, when Arianne thought she could take no more, Tancred turned to her.

"When is your husband to return?"

"I do not know," Arianne replied honestly. For once she was glad that she didn't know Richard's plans.

"I see," Tancred said and returned to a thoughtful mode before speaking again.

"Mayhap," Tancred began, "you think this a sport. If that is your thought, madam, I assure you there is no game in this. I am here to take back what is rightfully mine and to avenge my name. Your husband's blood is the only thing that will do that."

"Nay!" Arianne exclaimed and jumped to her feet without thought. "You will not take him!"

Tancred laughed viciously and got to his feet. "You must love him a great deal," he replied in a sarcastic tone. Nevertheless, his words struck a chord in Arianne's heart.

"Given Richard's softness toward the lovely things of this world, I imagine that he, too, cares greatly for you. He yearns to be home like a wounded man longs to be rid of pain. He will make his way home quickly," Tancred continued.

"My husband has already been gone a fortnight," Arianne answered. "I don't expect him to be released from his service any time soon. Why not retreat with your men before he returns? Perhaps you will be no worse for this confrontation."

Tancred snarled and stepped so close to Arianne that she could smell the sourness of his breath. "Milady, you will afford me the respect I am due. You will address me as Lord Tancred and you will serve me as master. It is my right. You are spoils of war!"

"I serve only the risen Lord and my husband," Arianne stated angrily. "I call no man Lord and will certainly not do so for the likes of you!"

Tancred slapped her, but it wasn't anywhere near the blow that had come from his mail-covered hand. "Silence, wench! You need to learn some manners."

Arianne faced him with tears stinging her eyes. She was determined to stand her ground. "Even an animal learns more from kindness than abuse," she braved.

Tancred stepped back. His expression showed his surprise at her change of tactics. Shrugging it off, he continued as though she'd never spoken. "I care not for your devotion to God or man. I have taken this castle in an act of war, and by the rights of that capture, you are mine to do with as I choose. It is not my fault that your husband is a fool. He left a handful of bedraggled knights and peasants to defend a castle and keep. He must pay the price as would any other fool. He forfeits that which was once his."

"He will return," Arianne said suddenly, her heart speaking ahead of her mind. "But he is no fool to march into this castle to dance from a gibbet for your pleasure."

"Perhaps not," Tancred replied. "But I care not either way. I have you, and from what I know of your duke, he will die before he sees one hair on your head harmed."

Arianne began to tremble. "Who are you, and how is it that you know my husband?"

Tancred opened his mouth to speak, then abruptly closed it again. He went back to the table and took his seat. To Arianne, he looked completely burdened by the task before him.

"Who are you?" Arianne pressed, coming to stand on the opposite side of the table.

"It is of no concern to you."

"You plan to murder my husband and me. Do I not have a right to address my executioner?" Arianne asked.

He looked at her for a moment before a wicked grin spread across his face. "I have no plan to kill you, milady."

Arianne grimaced at the picture in her mind. "If you kill my husband and dare to lay a hand on me," Arianne barely whispered, "I will see to it myself."

"What? A devoted woman of God such as yourself would brave the fires of hell and take her own life?" Tancred questioned with a sardonic laugh.

"Am I not already standing amidst the flames as we speak?" she inquired, pushing her hair away from her face.

"Touché, milady." For a moment, Arianne saw a glimmer of something other than the hatred in Tancred's eyes. But just as quickly, the harshness returned. "It is true, you have no say in the matter. Once your husband clears my name, the king himself will demand his head and I will in turn be given these lands and your fair hand, if I so choose."

"Never!" Arianne spat the word and turned to go.

"Stay where you are! I did not give you leave."

Arianne turned. The rage in her eyes was nearly enough to silence her enemy, but the wildness of her appearance only enhanced her beauty.

"You will yield to my demands." Tancred's words were firm, leaving

Arianne little doubt that he would press the issue if she did not remain silent.

"Richard will be warned," she finally said. "Someone will find a way to ride to him and warn him of your presence. My husband will not be fooled into returning empty handed."

"He will also not be foolish enough to risk that which he no doubt prizes most," Tancred replied. "You forget, my dear duchess. I hold his castle and folk, but most of all, I hold you. That fact alone will drive him quite mad with worry and muddy his thinking."

Arianne began to shake. She clutched her hands together tightly to keep Tancred from seeing the effect his words had. Fearfully, she realized Tancred was probably right. Richard did love her, given his patience and gentleness regarding their marriage bed. He would no doubt be determined to protect her and free her, just as Tancred said.

Chapter 6

Arianne paced the confines of her bed chamber, fretting over how she might get word to Richard. The fear that Tancred would see her husband dead brought tears to her eyes and a tightness to her breast. Somehow she must save her husband!

The narrow window seemed to beckon her, and Arianne momentarily halted her pacing and went to view the situation from the opening. Nothing seemed amiss. There were men in the bailey below, some with their hauberks of chain mail clothing their bodies, others with simple leather tunics and woolen surcoats. It was really no different from when Richard's knights were in control, she thought.

People moved more quietly, Arianne noticed. Women seemed to go out of their way to keep from coming in contact with Tancred's men, and Arianne was certain the reason was the men's lack of respect and chivalry. Gavenshire's people were to be treated as spoils of war, hadn't Tancred said as much? No one was safe—nor would they be until Richard was reinstated.

A light knock at her chamber door brought Arianne whirling on her heel. "Who goes there?" she called.

"'Tis I, milady," Matilda replied, and Arianne quickly went to lift the bar from the door.

Arianne ushered Matilda into the room, then replaced the bar before questioning her maid. "How goes it below?"

"I cannot bear to think that His Grace will be trapped by this group of uncouth ruffians, milady. They fight amongst themselves nearly as much as they would war with our people," Matilda replied.

Arianne forgot all about asking Matilda if she knew who Tancred was and what he wanted when another knock, this one loud and demanding, struck upon her door.

"You are to take supper below with Lord Tancred," a man's gruff voice called from the other side.

Arianne rolled her eyes, and Matilda openly quaked at the command. "Very well, tell Tancred I will be there shortly," Arianne replied, refusing to call the man her lord.

Matilda reached out to take hold of Arianne's arm. "You must be careful, milady. He is evil and cares not for the welfare of you or your people."

Arianne's mind was preoccupied, however, and she barely heard the words. "Help me dress, Matilda. I daren't keep him waiting."

As Matilda helped her into a clean linen tunic of pale green, Arianne's mind already raced with how she could get a messenger to Richard. "Tell me, Matilda, what have they done with Richard's men? Where are Sir Douglas and Sir Dwayne?"

"I'm afraid they've all been locked in the west tower, milady. It's heavily guarded and no one is allowed near, not even to give them food," Matilda answered and brought out a dark green samite surcoat to go over the tunic.

Arianne frowned at this news. "Someone has to ride and warn Richard," she thought aloud.

"Yes, milady, but who can go?" Matilda questioned. She brought one of Arianne's jeweled belts and secured it around her hips before retrieving slippers from one of the chests.

"I will learn what I can while I sup with Tancred. I don't know how, but one way or another, someone will leave this castle tonight and take warning to my husband!"

Arianne walked gingerly down the stone stairway. She moved as silently as possible, hoping that it might be her good fortune to overhear Tancred or his men as they discussed their plans. Her stomach growled loudly at the rich aroma of meat as it roasted on spits in the kitchen. Arianne realized she'd not eaten since morning, but with the soreness of her bruised jaw, she wondered if chewing would be possible.

She entered the great hall hesitantly, for all was silent except for the rustling movements of servants. It was a far cry from when Richard was in charge. With Richard, the hall was full of hungry men and others who had come at his welcome to eat. How she missed him! How she feared for him!

Moving to the table, Arianne realized that the room was not as empty as she'd hoped. Tancred sat before the fireplace, deep in thought as if contemplating the fate of the world. Her foot caught on something, making a sudden sound. Tancred sprang to his feet, hand on the hilt of his sword and eyes narrowing dangerously. Seeing it was only her, Tancred relaxed his grip and gave a mocking bow.

"Your Grace, it is good of you to honor me with your presence." His words were slightly slurred, leaving Arianne little doubt that he'd had a great deal to drink before her arrival.

She nodded but did nothing more until he held out a chair and commanded her to sit. Moving in lithe silence, Arianne did as she was bid and grimaced when he took the seat beside her.

"We will speak of your husband," he said, and then, as if noticing the discoloration on her face for the first time, he frowned. "You will choose your words carefully so that this is not necessary again," he said, pointing to her jaw.

"'Twas not necessary the first time," Arianne stated with a fixed stare of hostility. "You are surely in command here. You are larger than me, more powerful, and you have a great many men to afford you aid should it be necessary to vanquish your foe. Surely one woman, such as myself, offers no real resistance to a great knight such as yourself."

"True," Tancred replied, motioning a servant forward. The boy placed a platter of roast before the man and started to leave. "Halt, serf!" Tancred called. "Bring more wine, and be quick about it!"

Arianne watched the poor boy bow quickly before running from the room. His name was Gabe, she remembered, and he had always been most congenial in his work. Funny that it should cross her mind just now. Perhaps, Arianne thought, he could be the one to get a message to Richard. It was worth considering.

When the boy returned with the wine, Tancred took it from him and poured himself a generous amount. When he reached for Arianne's goblet, she placed her hand over it.

"Nay," she spoke hesitantly. "I do not wish it."

Tancred shrugged, but Gabe paled at her protest. Arianne wished she could ease the boy's fears, but it would be necessary to ease her own before she would be of any help to others.

"I would like water, Gabe," she continued.

"Aye, milady," he replied. "I'll bring a pitcher fresh from the well." Gabe waited momentarily to receive Tancred's nod of approval.

Tancred looked first at Arianne's fixed expression and then to the boy. "Do as your lady bids," he replied and went about serving himself a huge piece of beef.

Arianne waited patiently while Tancred served himself and then, almost as an afterthought, sliced a piece of beef from his own trencher and put it on hers.

"Thank you," she replied softly.

Tancred took the acceptance of the food as a serious accomplishment and continued to fill Arianne's plate with a variety of foods after serving himself.

Gabe brought the water and Tancred dismissed him, while Arianne timidly tried to chew the meat. It was difficult but not impossible, and her hunger was all the encouragement she needed. That and the thought that she needed to stay healthy and strong for Richard.

"You are a beautiful woman, Duchess," Tancred murmured over the rim of his goblet.

Arianne's head snapped up with a look of astonishment. What game would he play now?

As if reading her mind, Tancred reached out and snatched the head covering she wore and tossed it to the floor. Arianne's copper hair was bound in a single thick braid, which seemed to intrigue Tancred even more.

"Unbind your hair," he commanded and waited while Arianne slowly reached up to unfasten the cord that held it. She ran her fingers through the mass until the braid was unwound, then returned Tancred's stare with blazing eyes.

"Might I sup now?" she questioned with more sarcasm than she'd intended. Her tone served its purpose and broke Tancred's spell.

"By my leave," he smirked. "Eat all that you will. It will not change anything, nor will it keep you from my attentions."

"Very well, sire," Arianne replied with an overexaggerated sigh and returned her attention to the meal. She felt her hand trembling as she lifted a piece of bread to her mouth and could only pray that he did not see it. She did not wish to appear weak and vulnerable to him.

The meal continued in relative silence. From time to time, Tancred would roar out an order to Gabe for a refilling of his wine cup, but other than that, he seemed content or at least tolerant to let Arianne eat in peace.

Arianne knew when she finished eating that it was a signal of sorts for Tancred to speak. She put her napkin upon the table, folded her hands in her lap, and waited for what would come.

Tancred studied her from drunken eyes. His rage toward Richard seemed muted against her beauty, and for a moment he thought of nothing but the woman beside him.

"The property of this land gives much to warm my heart," he slurred. He reached out a hand and touched the long sleeve of Arianne's tunic.

Reflexively, she jerked her arm away and gasped. "Do not touch me! For all you think you own, I belong to Richard." She regretted her harsh response, fearing another strike would be her punishment, but Tancred's laughter was all that came.

"You belong to an absent duke, eh? A man who had not the wit about him to leave his lady better guarded. Nay, milady. You belong to me, and a more pleasant arrangement I cannot imagine."

Arianne felt her heart leap with fear. Her own safety had been far from her mind in her worries for Richard. Now a terrible thought filled her mind. What if Tancred forced himself upon her and stole her virtue before Richard and she could consummate their marriage? The thought sickened her.

"I belong to my husband," Arianne stressed. "I am his wife in the eyes of God, the church, and these people. Would you impose your will upon holy bonds?"

"I would and I do," Tancred said, taking yet another deep draw of the wine.

"Is nothing holy to you, then?" Arianne questioned.

"Holy? Pray tell what should I find holy, madam?" Tancred asked, getting to his feet. He pushed the chair back abruptly, sending it backward against the floor. He staggered back a pace, steadied himself, then glared leeringly at Arianne. "Marriage vows or naught; I made but one vow—for revenge."

"Why do you hate my husband so?"

Tancred seemed taken aback by this line of questioning. He grew thoughtful, and Arianne fervently prayed that God would somehow deliver her from the lustful hands of the man before her.

"Your husband," he spoke, twisting his lips into a cruel smile, "cost me everything that was rightfully mine. He poisoned the mind of the king and the people against me, and he must pay."

"My husband would not do that without reason," Arianne replied in defense of Richard. "He is a good man, kind and virtuous, and I would not hear him defamed in his own hall."

"Ugh! Good? Kind? Virtuous? Nay, milady." Tancred staggered forward and slammed his hands to the table. The very ground around her seemed to shake, and Arianne felt her heart in her throat.

Tancred moved closer to her and reached out to hold a coppery lock. "Nay, those are the words of a loving wife—a maiden in her youth besot with her husband. True love is a rare commodity in this world. Pity you waste yours on one such as Richard DuBonnet."

Tancred's words hit harder than any slap. Arianne sucked her breath in noticeably at the statement of love. Did she love Richard? Was this the proof she'd searched her heart for? Looking deep inside, Arianne felt a warmth spread throughout her body.

Yes! Arianne nearly jumped from her seat. Yes, she loved Richard! It seemed so understandably clear. Her fears for him, the way she missed him and longed for his companionship. It had nothing to do with the lust that she saw in Tancred's eyes, and it had nothing to do with the fear that her mother had lived with every day of her married life. She loved Richard with a pure and free love that held no fear or contempt.

Tancred had no idea what thoughts raced through Arianne's head. He saw only the grace and beauty of the woman beside him. He longed for more than the brief touch of her silken hair.

With Arianne's thoughts on Richard, she missed the look of determination in Tancred's eyes. She was stunned when he yanked her up from her seat and tried to kiss her.

Arianne brought her foot down hard on his, but her slippers were no match for his booted feet. She pushed him away and was surprised when her small effort actually caused him to stumble backward.

"Please, God," she prayed aloud. "Please be the protector and companion that Richard says You are and protect me from this man!" Her eyes were lifted upward for only a moment, but when she lowered them, she found her prayers already answered. Tancred continued to stagger backward until he met the wall. From there, he slowly slid down until he landed with a thud on the floor.

"A waste," he murmured and passed out from the drink.

Arianne breathed a prayer of thanksgiving even as she bolted from the room and ran up the stairs.

Chapter 7

Reaching her chamber door, Arianne started at the sound of footsteps behind her. Turning, she let her breath out in a sigh of relief. "Matilda! Hurry, we must make plans."

"I feared for your safety, milady. Are you well?" Matilda hurried into the room behind Arianne.

"Aye, but not for long. 'Twas only the hand of God that kept me from sharing Tancred's bed this night. I cannot risk such a thing again. I will escape the castle and warn Richard myself," Arianne announced.

Matilda nodded. "I can help," she whispered. "Let me fetch less noticeable garments from my room. They will be a bit big for you, but with a belt they should do well enough." Arianne nodded and paced nervously during Matilda's absence.

"Dear God," she prayed, "I don't even know the land well enough to find my way, much less do I know where Richard might be. Help me, God. Please help me again."

Matilda returned breathless and thrust forward the simple garments. "These will do," she said and helped Arianne to doff her richer wardrobe.

Arianne pulled the thin linen tunic over her head. It was a dark gray color and had seen many washings. The woolen surcoat was nothing more than a shapeless shift of dark blue. She pulled it over her head and, with Matilda's help, tied a corded belt around her waist.

"We must hide your hair, milady, for there is no other with such a mane. Come, I will plait it down the back and we will secure it beneath a mantle. I have a dark cloak that will hide you well in the shadows. Now, have you sturdy boots?"

Arianne nodded at Matilda's words and pointed to the chest at the far side of the room. She sat obediently while Matilda dressed her hair and then pulled the boots on while Matilda retrieved the cloak.

Peering down the hallway, the women cautiously moved toward the stairs. Matilda put her hand out and stopped Arianne suddenly. "Nay, let us use the back stairs. They lead straight into the kitchen, and from there I can get you to the tunnels below."

"The tunnels?" Arianne said in shocked but grateful surprise.

Matilda nodded and pulled her lady along the dimly lit hall. They descended the stairs cautiously, and when they reached the kitchen, Matilda held Arianne back while she went alone to make certain the room was clear of any of Tancred's men.

"Hurry, milady," Matilda urged and pulled Arianne into the kitchen. "I will get you food and water. Stay over there in the shadows, and I will take you below in a moment." Arianne moved quickly as Matilda had instructed. It didn't matter that her servant was issuing orders. All that mattered was that she loved Richard and had to find him before he forfeited his life in Tancred's snare.

Matilda brought a small pack designed from one of the tablecloths and filled with provisions. She took one last glance around the room before slipping into the buttery where the wine was kept. Here she revealed a small trap door behind a stack of kegs. "We'll need the torch, milady," Matilda said with a slight motion of her head to the wall.

Arianne pulled the torch from its place and handed it to the woman. "I suppose this is the best way," she whispered apprehensively.

"'Tis the only way to escape unnoticed," Matilda replied and started down the ladder that would take them to the tunnels. "When I reach the bottom," she whispered back to Arianne, "throw down the pack and come quickly. Remember to pull the door shut over your head."

Arianne moved quickly and quietly and soon joined her maid in the damp, dank maze beneath the castle foundations. Matilda took hold of Arianne's arm after handing her back the pack of food, then holding the torch high, she moved down the narrow corridor. After they'd gone quite a ways, Matilda stopped for them to catch their breath.

"I must tell you how to leave this place," Matilda said after resting a moment. "We can speak freely here, for no one will hear us. Richard will return from the east and so you must go in that direction once you are free of the castle. This tunnel will lead to the cliff walls over the sea. You must move down toward the beach, but not too far. You will have to work your way along the cliff wall until you reach a place where their heights are half of what they are from this place. This will be the sign you are looking for. Here you will climb upward to the top. It will not be easy, milady."

"I will manage it," Arianne stated firmly. "God will be my helper."

"Aye, that He will," Matilda replied with a weak smile. "I can see you share Richard's heart toward a merciful God who stays at our sides."

"At first, I wasn't certain what to think about it all," Arianne mused. "Truth be told, it seemed to be heresy, and I told Richard so. I had been raised to believe that the church held the only true way. But, these weeks without my husband have given me much time to consider his words. I believe that God would have us worship Him and not a religion. I might be burned at the stake for such words, but it is my heart toward the matter."

"You have a good heart, Lady Arianne." Matilda responded with such love that Arianne reflexively leaned forward and embraced the woman.

"Thank you for befriending me, Matilda. I know not what I would have done without your kindness. Now, quickly tell me what I must do after I leave the cliffs."

"There is a woods near the place where you will emerge. Take your cover there. The forest runs the length of the road for several miles and it will provide you protection from Tancred's men. The road will be the one upon which Richard will return. Rest assured that you will hear his men from the woods and you can approach him before he is endangered," Matilda answered.

"What if I move beyond the trees?" Arianne asked. "What then?"

"The land beyond the trees is hilly and open meadowland. You won't find much in the way of hiding places there. It might be best if you wait for Richard to come to you. The woods are a good ways from the castle and will give him ample time to prepare for attack. All that will matter to him is your safety. After that, he will do what he must."

"Very well. Now how do I reach the opening of this tunnel?"

"You will continue down this way," Matilda motioned with the torch. "Always stay to the right of any fork and you will soon be to the end of it." Matilda turned from Arianne for a moment and raised the torch higher. Spying what she needed, Matilda left Arianne's side and retrieved an unlit torch. Setting the second piece ablaze, Matilda handed it to Arianne. "Be certain to extinguish it before you leave the tunnel. It would be a beacon to the guards as they keep watch upon the land."

Arianne nodded, tucked the food pack down the inside of the woolen garment, and took the torch. "Kneel with me, Matilda, and we will pray."

"Surely that is the very best we can do," Matilda remarked and joined Arianne on the dirt floor.

The women offered their silent prayers, then quickly got back to their feet. "God's speed, Lady Arianne."

Arianne nodded and moved quickly down the corridor. She was a woman with a mission, and that mission would save the life of her husband

and his men. No matter the cost to herself, she had to find Richard and warn him. Then another thought passed through her mind as she edged down the inky blackness.

"I have to tell him that I love him," Arianne breathed aloud. "Most merciful Father, let me tell him that I love him."

The tunnel soon opened out on the cliffs, just as Matilda had told her it would. It was well concealed, however, with a huge boulder that hid the opening from appearing too conspicuous. Arianne put out the torch in the soft sandy dirt and waited a moment while her eyes adjusted to the dark.

She swallowed back her fears and moved out of the tunnel until she stood on the cliffside. Below, the water was stilled in black oblivion. Above, the moon shone dimly in a crescent sliver that would offer little light to direct her steps. Arianne moved cautiously down the rock wall as Matilda had instructed her.

It was imperative that Arianne make the forest under the cover of darkness. She would work at it all night if necessary. She felt her tender hands being torn by the sharp rocks and more than once felt her skirt catch and tear. Her courage was quickly leaving her as she drew ever closer to the water, but just then the rocks evened out and presented a path of sorts.

Arianne moved more quickly along the flattened path but held herself back from speed, knowing that she was uncertain of each step. Hours passed before the cliff walls lowered themselves as Matilda had promised they would. Arianne gauged the heights to be half those at the castle, and summoning up the last of her determination, she began the climb to the cliff tops.

The rocks bit at her hands and knees as she inched her way upward. Silently, Arianne issued petitions to God for guidance and sure-footedness, but always she kept moving—love mingled with concern motivating her forward.

At the top, Arianne stretched out her body and lay flat on the ground. She could see very little in the darkness but knew from Matilda's instructions that the shadowy blackness to her left was the woods.

After catching her breath, Arianne struggled to her feet and took off in a slow run for the trees. She slowed her step when she put her foot in a hole and nearly fell. Knowing that she could just as easily have broken a leg or twisted her ankle, Arianne tried to be more careful.

The trees loomed just ahead, and as she drew nearer, Arianne felt truly afraid. What if some wild beast awaited her in the darkness? What if she lost her way and moved in circles? She remembered Matilda's words. The forest ran along the road. She must stay close to the forest edge and keep the skies overhead in sight. When dawn came, she would move farther into the protection of the trees.

Keeping all of this in mind, Arianne worked for hours in the darkness. She stopped after a time, pulled the pack from her dress, and opened it. She quickly quenched her thirst and ate a piece of bread. When she started to rewrap the contents, her hand fell upon something long and cold. Feeling it gingerly, Arianne realized it was a knife. She took it gratefully and tucked it into her belt. Now, at least, she had some form of protection.

The pack was hurriedly replaced inside her gown before Arianne moved out. Cold dampness permeated her bones, and Arianne ached from the demands of her journey. Never before had she been required to endure anything so difficult, and she was certain that had it been a mission of less importance, she would have given up.

The moon had moved far to the western skies when Arianne realized that she couldn't take another step. She managed to move deeper into the trees, knowing that she would soon collapse in exhaustion. Feeling her way in the darkness, Arianne found a clump of bushes, rolled herself beneath them, and succumbed to her body's demands. Her last waking thoughts were of Richard. Her last words were whispered prayers for his safety.

Chapter 8

Arianne came awake slowly, forgetting for a moment where she was and why. She stretched out her cramped limbs and wondered why her hands hurt so much. Then the pungent smells of dirt and decaying vegetation arrested her senses, and Arianne snapped instantly awake.

She tried to focus on her surroundings and found that she was well hidden beneath a huge mass of leafy brush. She listened, straining against the silence for any sound that would reveal a threat, either two-footed or four-legged, but nothing came.

Pushing out from her hiding place, Arianne wanted to cry aloud at the soreness of her body. She rubbed her aching legs with her cut and bruised hands before trying to stand. Finally she felt her muscles limber some and got to her feet.

Cautiously, Arianne looked and listened in all directions. She found herself shrouded in a misty fog, yet easily recognized where the forest edge led to the roadway and chided herself for not having gone farther before seeking her comforts in sleep. God must truly have watched over her, Arianne mused, realizing that it wouldn't have been that difficult to spot her had a patrol been on the forest's edge.

She crept through the vegetation, trying to keep her steps noiseless. The task, however, was quickly proving impossible, as her feet crunched lightly with every move. Arianne sighed and kept moving. It was the only choice she had.

After traveling for only a matter of minutes, Arianne froze at the sound of voices. She fell to her hands and knees and tried to hide herself in the underbrush of the woods.

Three men moved just outside the forest's perimeter. They were heavily armed, each sporting full chain mail hauberks and mail coifs that covered their heads. At their sides were sheathed broad swords, and mail chaussures protected their muscular legs.

Arianne's heart pounded so loudly that she was certain the men could hear its beat. She bit the back of her hand to keep from crying out in fear. Only after the men had passed and moved on a good distance did she emerge.

With Tancred's men already searching for her, Arianne doubted she would find Richard in time. She hurried, nearly running through the trees in the opposite direction of the three men. She cast a quick backward glance from beneath her hood and, when she turned, ran smack into the center of a broad, chain-mailed chest.

Huge arms encircled her, and Arianne realized she was caught. Fighting for all she was worth, Arianne began to kick and slap the man who held her. If Tancred thought she'd come back to him easily, he was a mistaken fool.

"What is this—a wood nymph perhaps?" The man laughed at her efforts and wrapped her tightly in her own cloak to still her actions. Arianne took advantage of the man's bare hands and lowered her teeth into the tender flesh of his thumb.

"Ahh!" the man cried out as Arianne's teeth found their mark. "You feisty vixen, I'll fix you for that." He pushed Arianne to the forest floor, then pulled his sword and put his foot upon her shoulder to still her.

Arianne cringed back into the folds of her hood. Would he slay her here and now before Tancred had a chance to do it himself? Instead of bringing the sword upon her, the man cut into her cloak and tore a long strip from the edge. He used it as a gag, which he forced around Arianne's mouth in spite of her protests. He then tore other pieces of material and bound her hands and feet. With this done, he resheathed his sword and with little effort lifted Arianne over his shoulder.

Arianne's mind was frantic. She had failed Richard in her mission and she had failed herself. Now he might never know of her love. She couldn't keep the deluge of tears from falling. As the massive bulk of a man carried her from the forest, Arianne sobbed loudly, nearly wailing by the time the soldier brought her to his camp.

The man seemed not to notice her condition. He was oblivious to her tears, and Arianne was just as glad. She had no desire to evoke sympathy from her husband's enemy. Let them deal with her harshly, she thought, for it made her anger keen and her desire to fight just that much stronger.

"What have you there, George?" a man called out. Arianne couldn't see the man, but apparently he thought it great sport to tease her captor. "Seems you always did have a way with the ladies."

"This baggage is no lady," George replied, and Arianne squirmed angrily at his statement. "She bit me and slapped me and would have split my skull had I handed her an ax."

The other man laughed furiously.

"Is she from the castle?" another man questioned. This one Arianne could see from the knees down. He moved forward and lifted back her hood to reveal her helmeted face.

"Aye, she must be," George responded. "Do you know her?"

"Nay," the man replied. "But he will. Best put her in the master's tent and it will be revealed soon enough."

Arianne struggled against this news, and George gave her a firm whack across her backside. "Settle it down there, wench. I've no desire to be crippled by your flailing."

Arianne ceased her struggles, but her mind raced furiously. *I must escape these men,* she thought. *I must find Richard!*

George did as he was bid and took her to a nearby tent, where he dumped her unceremoniously upon a pallet. Arianne turned questioning brown eyes upward, wondering if he would untie her. She raised her hands to emphasize her stare.

"Nay," George said and shook his head. "I'll not be turning you loose upon the men. They are needed to fight the enemy, and I'll not have you wounding them before battle."

Arianne struggled against her bonds and muttered beneath the gag that he was an ill-mannered oaf, but the man laughed and walked out of the tent.

With the soldier out of her sights, Arianne tried in earnest to free herself. She thought of the knife tucked inside her belt and tried to reach it, but found it was useless. She raised her hands to pull at the gag but discovered George had secured it too tightly and it wouldn't budge.

Refusing to give up, Arianne worked at the cloth until her wrists were nearly bleeding. She was tired and in pain by the time she gave in and rested from her efforts. Against her will, Arianne fell asleep and dreamed of running through the night mist to warn her beloved of a deadly enemy.

The sound of voices brought Arianne awake. She shook her head to clear her muddled mind and tried to focus on the muffled sound of men in conversation.

Her heart pounded harder as the voices grew louder.

"I assure you, sire, 'twas no small feat to bring the wench in," the voice of the one called George sounded out, and Arianne cringed.

The reply was too low to give Arianne understanding, but George laughed heartily at whatever comment was made. "I'd much rather feel the taste of his steel than another bite from that sly vixen. I wish you better luck in the handling of her."

Arianne began to tremble at the words. Was she to be handed over to Tancred in this manner? Was she to meet her enemy bound and gagged without even the slightest hope of preserving her purity and life?

Dear God, she prayed, blinking back tears, *help me!*

The men were directly outside the tent, and against the shadows of early evening, Arianne could make out their movements in silhouette. The heavier of the two men was no doubt George. Arianne easily remembered that barrel-like frame. The other man still wore his helmet.

"Bring us food," the man told George. Again, Arianne struggled to make out the words that the helmet so effectively muffled. *It could be Tancred,* she thought, *but why would he risk leaving the protection of the castle?*

A mailed hand reached out to pull back the tent flap, and Arianne involuntarily sunk deeper into the folds of her cape. The man entered the tent carrying a single light, which he placed on the ground opposite Arianne.

The dim glow only added to the ominous presence of the soldier. Shadows rose up from his form to make the man look like a towering sentinel. Arianne scooted away in horror, bringing his full attention to her. Pulling off his scabbard, the man gently placed his sword on the ground beside the light.

Next, he reached up and pulled the helmet from his head, but Arianne still couldn't make out his features. She wasn't sure she wanted to.

The man looked down at her for a moment, and Arianne found herself holding her breath. What torture would he use on her first?

The man stepped toward her. Arianne couldn't suppress a cry. She pushed back with her feet and found herself against the tent wall, unable to go any farther. His hand came down, and Arianne struggled valiantly against him. Finally the man had both her shoulders gripped in his hands.

Arianne paused only to give him a sense of false security. Reaching to his side, he pulled out a dagger, and Arianne feared she would faint. Her ragged breath came quicker, and her heart raced in fear as the hand was lowered to her face. She closed her eyes tightly to squeeze out the sight of her own death.

With one quick snap, the gag was broken, and Arianne began to realize he did not intend to slay her. At least not yet. The man replaced the dagger and reached forward again to push back the cloak and learn the identity of his captive.

Arianne braced herself to see her captor's face, but what she saw was barely visible. The chain mail coif and the dirt smudged against his face made it impossible to tell if it was Tancred. He pushed the hood all the way off her head and gasped at the sight of her copper hair.

The roar emitted from the man was not what Arianne had expected. It was like that of a wild beast injured in a trap or a battle cry in the stillness of the night. She pushed her bound hands at the man, swinging them back and forth like a club.

"Leave me be, you cur! My husband will have your head for this!" Arianne screamed against the man's chest. She continued her tirade even as the man sought to still her.

"Cut my bonds and give me a knife. We'll see how courageous you are against an armed enemy. I won't allow you to harm my husband without killing me first. I'll warn him of your deceit, and nothing short of death will see me do otherwise!"

Arianne had no idea where her strength was coming from. The man kept hushing her, reaching out almost as if to comfort her, but Arianne knew that couldn't be possible. She felt renewed vigor when she managed to set the man off his feet. Escape was impossible, so she assailed him with praise of Richard.

"You and all the armies of the world could not defeat my husband. You may have caught us unawares, but Richard will know. He will come and cut out your heart for this!" Arianne suddenly stopped when she realized the man was laughing. The sound of his strangely familiar laughter seemed to frighten her more than his overwhelming presence had.

Turning away, his amusement lingering in the air, the man untied his coif and pulled the mail from his head. Then turning back to face her, Arianne thought her eyes were playing tricks on her.

"Richard!" she gasped and nearly fell back against the pallet.

"The very same, milady," he chuckled. "The one whom the world's armies could not defeat."

Arianne felt the realization of safety coursing through her veins. Richard reached forward and cut the bonds from her hands and feet. Shock numbed her mind, and Arianne did nothing for a moment but stare in mute surprise.

"Are you injured, Arianne?" Richard questioned, reaching out to touch her hand. He took her fingers in his mailed hand and noticed the cuts and dried blood. He frowned, feeling an anger beyond all that he'd known before.

"What other suffering have you endured?" he questioned, praying that God had been merciful to his young wife.

Dropping her hands, Richard reached for the light and brought it closer. When it shone full upon her face, Richard could see the dark bruise on her jaw. With an anguished cry, he ripped off his mail gloves and took Arianne's face in his hands.

"What has he done to you?"

Chapter 9

The agony in his voice was enough to reach through Arianne's shock. "Oh, Richard!" she cried and threw herself into her husband's arms. "I thought they'd captured me again. I thought I'd never get a chance to warn you."

Richard crushed her against his hauberk. "I feared you were dead. A rider came to warn us. The last thing he'd seen was you at the end of Tancred's sword."

Arianne kissed his face and felt the wetness there. His tears mingled with her own as she assaulted his face with kiss after kiss. "I prayed I'd find you in time," she whispered between kisses. "I had to find you and warn you. I had to tell you—"

"It doesn't matter now," Richard whispered. He was surprised at his wife's response but knew she'd endured a great deal at the hand of his enemy.

"Yes," Arianne said and pushed away from her husband's steely chest. "Yes, it does matter. I feared I'd die before I could tell you the most important thing of all."

"Then tell me, sweet Arianne. Tell me and relieve your worried mind," he replied.

"I love you, Richard," she said and waited for his response.

Her dark eyes pierced his heart as they confirmed the words that her mouth spoke. "Are you certain?" he questioned hesitantly. "You've been through a great deal and—"

Arianne put her finger to his lips. "I love you, and I desire nothing more than for you to know the depths of that love and the warmth of hope it gives me."

Richard pulled her gently into his arms and cradled her against him. For a moment, there were no words he could speak. It was certainly not the ideal surrounding that he'd hoped, nay, dreamed, they'd share when she declared her love for him. But the words were just as tender, just as wondrous.

"I love you, Arianne," he whispered. "I thank God you found safety in His care and were able to bring this news to me. Still, there is an enemy upon us and I must see him defeated."

"Who is he, Richard? Why does he hate you so?"

"What did he tell you?" Richard questioned. Arianne slipped from his arms to study her husband.

"He said very little," she replied softly. "He told me he sought revenge for wrong done him by you. He told me little more than to say I was spoils of war, as was my home. He planned to use me to capture you. That was when I realized I could not send a messenger, but instead, must come to find you myself."

Richard grimaced. "Tancred is a problem from my past. One that I must rid myself of once and for all."

"Who is he, and what has happened between you that such hatred cries for blood?" Arianne asked, placing her hand upon Richard's arm.

"It isn't important." He shrugged.

"Not important?" she whispered. "This man holds your home and people and you plan to end his life, but it is not important?"

Richard looked at her for a moment, then, shaking his head, got to his feet and began to remove the hauberk. "I cannot tell you."

"I'm not a child, Richard. Why can you not tell me?" Arianne questioned more sharply than she'd intended.

"It is a thing between men," he replied in a curt tone that told Arianne the matter was closed. She refused, however, to be put off.

"Nay, Your Grace," she stated in a formal tone. "'Tis not a matter between only men. That man would have put himself in your place, not only before your people, but in my bed."

Richard whirled around, jaws clenched and eyes blazing. "You think I do not know what he is capable of?" The anger was apparent in his voice, and Arianne wished she'd not pressed the issue. Perhaps it was better that she not know the details of their war.

Richard struggled to rid himself of the chain mail, but it caught. He raged for a moment at it, before stalking from the tent without so much as a backward glance.

Tears flowed down Arianne's face, and her throat ached painfully. She longed for a cool drink and something to eat, but the longing in her heart was stronger yet.

"I have driven him away," she whispered to herself. "I came here to declare my love and I have driven him from me as if he were the enemy."

She fell back against the pallet and sobbed quietly. This was not what she had hoped for.

I should never have demanded that he tell me of this thing between him and Tancred, she thought. *I should have learned from our brief time together that when Richard doesn't wish to speak of a thing, he stands firm in his resolve to remain silent.*

When her tears abated, Arianne resolved not to question Richard on any matter again. She reasoned that men often found it necessary to shield their women from the harmful, ugly things of the world. Why should she expect any different from a gentle, kind man like Richard? Hadn't he already shown her every concern?

Gathering her strength, Arianne sat up and wiped her eyes. If Richard returned, she decided, she would be nothing but the dutiful, respectful wife he deserved.

In time, Richard did return. With him came a very humble George. The man brought a tray with food and drink and placed them near Arianne. Richard, with a lighthearted voice, spoke as if nothing had disturbed him from their earlier conversation.

"Sir George, I would have you meet your duchess," he said in the amused way that Arianne had come to love.

George, with a solemn look of humility, bowed before Arianne. "Your Grace," he began, "I am most sorry for my behavior. I had no way of knowing that it was you. I'm most deeply regretful."

Arianne smiled and took pity on the man. "How is your thumb, George?" she asked gently.

The man raised his head with a sheepish smile. His cheeks were stained red in embarrassment. "'Tis nothing of any matter and certainly less than what I deserved," he replied.

Arianne nodded. "'Tis well for you that my knife was out of reach, for I had full intention of slaying whatever dragon barred my way from escape."

"For certain!" Richard exclaimed. "Why, she delivered me some well-placed blows while still bound from your dealings."

At this they laughed and the matter was behind them. Arianne took the opportunity to quench her thirst, while George turned to leave. At the tent flap, he paused.

"I will happily guard your life with my own, milady," he spoke. "From this day forward, as long as I have breath in my body, I will see to your safety." He walked from the tent then, and Arianne couldn't help but be touched by the display of chivalry.

"You have a champion, milady," Richard said, coming to sit beside her on the pallet. "I dare say, by morning's light you will find George's lance and colors firmly planted outside your tent."

Arianne smiled and reached out to touch her husband's arm. "I desire but you for my champion," she whispered.

Richard's smile warmed her, and Arianne noticed that he'd washed during his absence from her. She wished she could have done the same, knowing that she must be covered in filth.

"What are your thoughts now, madam?" Richard said, noting the change in her expression.

Arianne laughed and reached for a piece of cheese. "'Twas nothing overly endearing," she replied. "I was wishing for a bath and a clean set of clothing."

Richard chuckled. "I think we can arrange both. I was gifted by the king with many trinkets, one of which was a lovely gown for you. I will have George fetch some water while I retrieve it, but only if you promise to finish this food."

"You needn't bribe me to do that, Your Grace," Arianne stated in mock formality. "I am quite famished and only sought an excuse to keep this tray all to myself."

Richard laughed and got to his feet. "Very well. I will see to your comforts while you gorge yourself."

An hour later, Arianne felt like a new person. She was no longer cold and hungry, nor dirty and poorly clothed. The tunic and surcoat gifted her by the king was indeed a richer garment than she'd ever worn. Pity, she thought, that it should be wasted in the middle of a fog-filled forest.

She whirled in girlish style and watched the material fall into place. The tunic was the softest blue silk, while the sleeveless surcoat was deep crimson, lavishly embroidered with gold and silver thread. Giggling in delight, Arianne hurried to finish her toilette.

Richard had even thought to find her a comb, and Arianne sat untangling the waist-length bulk of copper hair when he returned.

"You put all other women to shame," he said, coming to her side.

Arianne glanced up with her heart in her eyes. "The king was most gracious to send such a rich gift," she replied.

"I thanked him most heartily in your absence," Richard answered. "I also thanked him for arranging our marriage. I told him it was a most satisfying arrangement to me."

Arianne blushed, thinking that the arrangement surely hadn't been as satisfying as Richard would have liked. She concentrated on her hair and refused to look her husband in the eye for fear he would understand her thoughts.

"Come," Richard said and pulled Arianne abruptly to her feet. "I would show you off."

"But my hair—"

"Is beautiful just the way it is," Richard insisted.

Outside the tent, Arianne was surprised to find a small encampment of men. Richard's tent had been set aside from the others, just far enough to afford a margin of privacy, yet close enough to defend. Arianne noticed how calm the men were. They seemed oblivious to the danger that awaited them.

When they looked up to catch sight of her, Arianne was delighted to suddenly find herself in the midst of their pampering attention. It reminded her of her wedding night when she was handed in dance from one knight to another. She learned their names and accepted their attentions, all the while noticing the gleam of pride in Richard's eyes. When Richard finally led her back to the tent, a firmly planted lance decorated the entrance flap.

"George's?" she asked, looking up to catch Richard's smile.

"Aye," he said with a nod and pushed back the canvas for Arianne to enter.

Arianne moved ahead of her husband, then turned to stop when he entered the tent. She wanted to say so much, yet words failed her. All she could do was stare at the man she'd come to love more dearly than life.

Finally the silence grew uncomfortable, and Arianne forced herself to speak. "I am sorry for the harshness between us earlier," she began. "I know there is much that I should leave to your care."

"It matters naught," Richard whispered and stepped forward to embrace his wife. "God kept you safe from harm, and for that I praise Him. I know not how you escaped Gavenshire, but God must surely have directed your steps."

"He did indeed," Arianne nodded. "Matilda took me through the tunnels and then told me how to climb the cliffs and where to hide. She told me the road you would return by and then returned to the castle to face them in my absence."

"She has always served my family well," Richard remarked.

Arianne thought to question Richard further on this comment, but realizing his family was another of the subjects he desired not to speak of, Arianne instead took his hand.

With a questioning look on his face, Richard followed his wife to the pallet. The warmth of her hand in his was spreading like a fire up his arm.

"You have been most patient with me, Richard, but I would have this thing settled between us," Arianne spoke in a barely audible whisper. "I would not have another take that which belongs to you."

Richard reached out and smoothed back a copper curl from Arianne's shoulder. He thought his heart might burst from the wonder of the moment.

"I don't know what to say," he replied rather sheepishly. The moment he'd waited for since first making his vows to God and this woman seemed somehow lost in the fog of his mind.

"Then say nothing," Arianne said, putting her arms around his neck. "It is enough that you know I love you. It is enough that I know you love me. Whatever else comes from this," she paused, meeting his eyes, "is that which God intended and no man will put asunder."

Richard lowered his lips tenderly to hers and forgot about everything but the woman in his arms. Gone were the images of war and the horrors of battle. On the morrow, he would ride to meet his foe, but tonight he would find peace in the arms of his wife. Little else mattered.

Chapter 10

Arianne stretched slowly and then snuggled down into the warmth of the pallet she had shared with Richard. Images from the night passed through her mind in dreamlike wonder. How very precious the union God had given to man and woman through marriage. The love and tenderness she'd known throughout her weeks of marriage were only heightened by becoming Richard's wife in full.

Arianne thanked God silently for the love He'd bestowed upon her. Daily, it was becoming just as Richard had said: God was a personal friend to each and every one of His children. Richard had translated the Latin scriptures to quote to her from the Gospel of Saint John saying, "If anyone loves me, he will keep my word, and my Father will love him, and we will come to him, and will make our abode with him."

Arianne had pondered those words with great interest. God was offering the very best to His children. He would abide with them, not as a judge or condemner, but as a friend.

Arianne found that friendship a precious thing, and while she had been raised to respect and fear God through the church, she was only coming to know what it was to truly love and trust Him. All of this had been awakened in her spirit because of Richard.

As Arianne came fully awake, she opened her eyes and turned to study her husband. When she found the area next to her empty, she bolted upright and stared at the barren tent.

"Richard?" she whispered, knowing full well that no one would answer her.

She pulled on her clothes quickly, realizing while she did that Richard's armor and gear were gone. Without bothering to comb her hair, Arianne hurried barefooted from the tent to find her husband.

Instead of finding Richard, Arianne found a sober-faced George and two of the men who'd been with him on patrol when he'd taken Arianne captive. All of the men seemed thoroughly embarrassed.

Arianne glanced around and saw that all signs of Richard's other men had been removed. Gone were the tents and horses. Gone were the smiling faces and the warm campfires.

"Where is my husband?" she asked George.

George stammered and refused to look her in the eye. He shifted nervously from one foot to the other, not at all in knightly fashion.

"George?" She took another step forward. "Where is Richard?"

"Gone, milady," George finally replied.

Arianne heard one of the other men's sharp intake of breath, while George seemed to take a side step, uncertain what Arianne's response would be.

"When will he return?" Arianne questioned, still not realizing the truth of the matter.

"There is no way to tell, Your Grace," George responded and quickly added, "I have food so you might break the fast. 'Tis cold, but nourishing."

Arianne managed to nod and followed to where George indicated she should sit. "Where has Richard gone that you have no inkling of when he will return? And why did he not awaken me and bid me good day?"

George realized he would have to tell Arianne the truth. "He's gone to Gavenshire, milady. He did not wish to worry you overmuch with his departure. He bid me tell you that he will see you soon and that he—well he wanted me to say that. . ." George stammered into silence.

Arianne bit back her anger and frustration. "He wanted you to say what, George?"

"That he loves you, milady."

"Oh," Arianne replied and lowered her head. How could Richard leave her like that? Especially after all that had passed between them in the night. It was as if he couldn't trust her to have faith in him to do the right thing. But then again, hadn't she questioned him most vigorously in his dealings with Tancred?

"I'm sorry 'tis such a shock, but His Grace thought it best," George stated sympathetically.

"I'm no child to be sheltered from the truth," Arianne remarked.

"No, of course not, Your Grace," George quickly proclaimed.

"I don't wish to be treated as an addlebrained woman, either," Arianne declared, raising her darkened eyes to George.

"Never!" George stated indignantly. "Milady wounds me most grievously to declare such a possibility."

Arianne looked intently at the massive man and finally softened her glowering stare. "I apologize, Sir George. I know that you are only doing the duke's bidding. I am, well. . ." She paused, trying to come up with the right words. "I am distressed that my husband would leave without a proper good-bye."

"Mayhap it would have burdened his mind in battle," George offered without thinking.

Arianne grimaced, knowing that George was probably right. At the thought of Richard in battle, her anger faded. "Will they fight today?" She whispered the question.

George shrugged his shoulders. "'Tis a possibility, but who can say? Perhaps the enemy will give in without resistance when they see the duke's forces."

Arianne tried to reassure herself on those words, but she knew the depth of hatred between the men. She especially remembered the overwhelming desire for revenge in Tancred's voice.

"Gavenshire Castle is more than capable of keeping out unwelcome intruders," Arianne said. "Tancred will see my husband and his men as most unwelcome."

"Yea, 'tis true," George admitted. "Still, your husband has the advantage of knowing the estate more intimately. He will have a few tricks to show that man, if I know His Grace."

"Do you know this man who holds the castle? Do you have any knowledge of Tancred?" Arianne questioned.

George looked thoughtful, then shook his head. "Nay, I'm sorry, milady. In all our time at Gavenshire, I've never known your husband to have a single enemy. I'm afraid I know nothing more than I am told."

Arianne nodded her head. "It would seem we share that fate, Sir George."

They fell silent, and one of the men who lingered in the background thought it a good time to bring Arianne's food and drink. She thanked him and took the offered meal, but her stomach was disinterested. Richard was in danger. How could she eat?

The day wore on in oppressive slowness. Each minute seemed to last hours and each hour was more like a day. Arianne tried in vain to learn more from Richard's men. She wanted to know how Richard would proceed once Tancred refused to open the gates to allow him entry into the castle. The men were of no help. They either wouldn't tell her or didn't know. Either way, it left Arianne more fretful than before.

She paced the small perimeter of their camp, glancing up from time to time to meet the eyes of one of her guardians. They were sympathetic eyes, but also they betrayed an eagerness to be doing something more than playing protector to their duchess. And try though they might, Richard's men could not hide their looks of worry.

Arianne finally pled a headache and retired for a rest. A fine, misty rain had started to fall, and she was grateful for the shelter of the tent. Without chairs or furniture of any kind, Arianne took herself back to the pallet and stretched out.

Laying there, she could almost feel the comfort of Richard's arms around her. Why hadn't he said good-bye? At least if she could have told him—

The thought broke away from her mind. What was there that she could have said? She'd already given him the words he'd longed to hear. She'd declared her love for him. Never had any man seemed to find such contentment in a simple statement, but then Arianne knew that Richard understood the price at which her trust and love had come. No, there was nothing left for her to say, but perhaps it was more that she longed to hear reassurance from his lips. Reassurance that everything would be all right and that Tancred would soon be defeated.

"Oh, Richard." The moan escaped her lips, and tears formed in her eyes.

"Father in heaven," she prayed, knowing that no other comfort would be found, "You alone know my heart, and though I am but a mere woman, I have need to know that You are with my beloved Richard. He speaks Your name with the utmost of love and respect. His lips declare Your wonders, and praises are offered up from his heart to Your throne. Now, Father, Richard must face the enemy, perhaps to do battle with a man who would see him dead. I ask, although I am unworthy to make such a plea, that You would shroud him with protection and keep him from harm. Please deliver my husband from Tancred's hand and see this matter between them settled."

Arianne fell silent and wiped the tears from her eyes. Staring upward, she was consumed by the stillness that came to her heart. There came a peace so certain and complete that it nearly took her breath away. Clutching her hand to her breast, Arianne closed her eyes and smiled. *Yes, this is of God.*

When Arianne awoke, she felt refreshed and at ease. Richard was still at a task that she'd give most anything to see avoided, but she knew for certain that God was at Richard's side.

She got up and went in search of George, who in spite of the rain and the threat of enemy soldiers, had managed to cook a rabbit over a small fire.

Arianne sat with the men, trying to converse with them about the countryside and weather. She prattled on about unimportant matters, hoping to show them that her heart was confident about Richard's fate.

It was the boredom that was setting them all on edge. As soon as the meal was cooked, one of the other men allowed the fire to die out, leaving nothing but a blackened spot where the warmth had once risen. Arianne felt the gloom of the overcast day threaten to dispel her peaceful spirit. Doubts wormed their way into her mind, but her heart held fast to a newly discovered faith in God.

She sympathized with the men as they took turns pacing the camp. With the skies growing darker and the imminent coming of night, one man was posted as guard, while the others prepared to sleep. Knowing there would be little, if any, light once the sun set, Arianne bid them good night and reclaimed the confines of her tent.

There was nothing to do but wait. Wait in the darkness, in the unbearable silence, and wonder at the outcome of her husband's campaign against Tancred.

Giving her mind over to her own curiosity, Arianne tried to remember everything she knew about Tancred. She wanted to know who this man was and why he hated her husband. It was more than a simple problem between them. Arianne knew from the look in Tancred's eyes and the tone of his voice that his conflict reached deep into his very soul. What had Richard been a part of that had caused such intense bitterness?

Matilda seemed to know who Tancred was, but Arianne hadn't been able to get her to speak in any detail. George and his companions didn't seem to understand what the conflict was about, so they were of little help. The only real understanding would come from one of two people: Tancred or Richard. And neither of them seemed inclined to tell Arianne what their war was about.

Chapter 11

Something akin to desperation gripped Arianne's heart at the sound of scuffling and hushed whispers outside her tent.

"Who's there?" she whispered in a shaky voice.

"Milady, 'tis I, George."

Arianne tried to force her voice to steady. "What news have ye that cannot keep until the morn?"

"'Tis most urgent that we flee this place, Your Grace," George whispered from outside the tent. "The enemy is nearly upon us."

Arianne's heart pounded. The image of Tancred swam before her eyes, causing a convulsive shiver. She got quickly to her feet and rushed headlong between the tent flaps.

"Have you news of Richard?" she asked with a pleading voice.

"Nay, milady. There is no word. Take my hand and I'll lead you." He reached out in the darkness to offer his hand. Groping against the blackness, Arianne took hold of his arm. "Come, the horses are waiting."

Caring little for her own safety, Arianne allowed George to lead her through the darkness. Her mind forced images of heinous battlefields to mind. Would the blood shed there be that of her husband? *Dear God,* she prayed, *he must be safe. Keep Richard safe.*

They neared the horses, hearing their soft, nervous snorts and hoofed pawing of the earth. Arianne didn't utter a word when George lifted her to the saddle of his mighty warhorse, coming up with the same action behind her. She knew there was no dainty sidesaddle for convention's sake. She knew, too, that it would have been most uncomfortable, if not impossible, for her to ride astride in the gown she wore. Had Sir George been her love, it might have seemed daringly romantic, but George was not her love, and the moment was only wrought with anxiety.

"Forgive me, milady," George whispered from behind his now secured helmet.

"Forgive you?" Arianne asked in near-hushed reverence. "Forgive you for championing me and saving my frail life?" George didn't reply, but Arianne noticed that he seemed to sit a bit taller against her back.

They moved out quietly, pressing deeper into the forest in hopes of eluding the enemy. The man posted to patrol had spotted at least ten riders not far from the camp. It would be only a matter of time before they discovered the location and raided the surrounding woods.

Arianne shuddered at the thought of being once again under Tancred's control. She knew his rage and anger. What would he do after she had so completely outfoxed him? Better to pray that it did not become a possibility, Arianne surmised, for she couldn't dare to hope he would allow such a thing to go unpunished.

Rain had begun to fall again, soaking the little band as it filtered down through the trees. Arianne pitied the men who wore their mail hauberks and plated helmets. The water would make such clothing sheer misery. Arianne herself fared little better in the heavy, royal surcoat. Her hair, plastered down against her face, seemed more like a strangling rag than the crowning glory Richard so highly regarded. But hair would dry and so would clothing. Arianne wondered about her husband's condition. Spilled blood would not be remedied as easily as the drying of a garment.

With a heavy sigh, Arianne felt tears flood her eyes. She was quite grateful for the cover of darkness. She didn't wish to alarm her husband's men with foolish fears. Still, she knew they, too, were anxious to know the fate of their comrades.

Richard DuBonnet, Duke of Gavenshire, watched his castle and home from the seclusion of the nearby forest. He saw the torches that flickered boldly in the thin-slitted, first-floor windows. Windows too narrow for a man to pass through, even if they weren't barred with metal grilling. They could have been shuttered from inside the castle as well, but no doubt Tancred had put them there to mock any impending attack. He was making it clear that Richard and his men posed no real threat.

Glancing up, Richard counted a dozen or more men as they stood watch on the rampart walkway of the castle's gray stone battlements. They were unconcerned at the force Richard might bring with him. They knew full well that Gavenshire could withstand any onslaught from outside its walls.

Richard smiled to himself. What Tancred didn't expect was an assault from within. Yet, that was just what Richard planned to give him. Richard's father had once told him that a mighty castle, like a mighty man, could never be defeated from the forces outside it. With planning and prudence, both could sustain considerable exterior damage.

Yet a man and his castle were vulnerable from attacks within. A man could not ignore the attacks on spirit or heart without paying a high price. A man was almost always defeated in the realm of his mind, spirit, and heart before he gave in to an outside force. A castle was the same. If the enemy could get inside and weaken the defenses, open the doors and gates, it would only be a matter of time until the prize could be won.

Richard would divert Tancred's attentions away from the one place he would be most vulnerable. Tancred would spend so much time concentrating on the enemy outside, he would forget to keep watch from within.

Richard moved back to join his men. His mind passed quickly from thoughts of the impending battle and, instead, took him back to the pleasant times he'd known with Arianne. How he loved her! Their few weeks of married life had been the foundation for a solid friendship. Their moments together the night before left Richard only more certain that God's hand wanted to bring good to both of them from the arrangement.

Richard was lighter of heart to know that he would not have to attack the castle with Arianne inside. It was hard enough to wonder how many good friends would perish in the fight without having to fear that Tancred would use Arianne as the pawn he had first intended her to be. He was greatly relieved to know she was safe in the hands of his own men, miles from harm.

Arianne sat rigidly straight in front of George. She ached from the position but knew she must leave George free to maneuver. She also wished that there be no appearance of impropriety to shame her or Richard. George had sworn his loyalty to guard her, but Arianne knew there was a delicate balance between her position and his. She would not be the one to create mishap between them.

Her thoughts turned once more to Richard. She worried that he might be hurt or worse. She couldn't bring herself to think that something might be horribly wrong. She couldn't bear to imagine that Tancred might have already killed him. *No*, she reassured her heart, *God is Richard's guardian. No man will come between that.*

The rain clouds moved on and allowed the slight moon to shine out overhead. Darkness had been good cover for escape, but Arianne was glad for a little light. The forest had seemed so impenetrable, so foreboding. Now she could make out the trees as they stood silhouetted against the sky. Arianne was nearly lulled into believing that they would get away unscathed, when suddenly, they were surrounded by men.

"Halt or be slain," a man cried out from behind his helmet.

"Who demands this of us?" George countered.

"I am Sir Gilbert de Meré, and I act on the orders of Lord Tancred. I have been sent to retrieve the duchess of Gavenshire and take her to his lordship."

"I will not go!" Arianne exclaimed. She would have jumped from the horse, but George's hand shot out around her.

"Nay," he whispered against her ear. Arianne froze in position. She had no idea what George would do next, but she was determined not to interfere.

"If you do not yield peaceably to us, milady," the man spoke again, "I will be forced to kill these good men and take you anyway."

Arianne blanched and swallowed hard. She had not thought of the grave danger to Richard's men. Her men. Men who had sworn to protect and keep her with their lives.

As if reading her mind, George answered slowly. "We are pledged to guard the duchess with our lives. She is worth more than many hundred more. What are we three, that we should not give all that we possess to see her well kept?"

"You are dead men," Sir Gilbert replied. "Even now I see your bones rotting on the floor of this forest."

"Nay!" Arianne shouted. "It will not be so!" Turning to face George, she could barely make out the glow of his eyes from behind the helmet. "I cannot allow your blood to be shed. I will go with them."

"A noble cause, indeed," Gilbert declared as he moved his horse forward.

Arianne heard the sound of swords as they were pulled from their scabbards. The ringing held a deadly tone to her ears.

"I beg you," she stated to all who would listen. "Let there be no blood shed on my account. I will go to Tancred and beg his mercy. He daren't kill me, for he would have no power over Richard."

"Will you yield, sir knight?" the man questioned.

"Nay," George replied.

Arianne put her hand out against the sword George held in his hand. "I command, as your duchess, that you lay aside your arms. Sir George; you will obey me in this." Then in a tone heard only by George, Arianne whispered, "Please."

It seemed forever before George and his companions put down their swords. Arianne knew that it went against every code of honor they had been raised with. She was surprised that her word was heeded. Perhaps George reasoned that a better opportunity would arise in which he might defeat the enemy. Perhaps he knew it was hopeless to expect victory at this time.

Gilbert de Meré moved alongside George's warhorse and pulled Arianne roughly against him. "You are prisoners of my master," he stated. "You will be taken to Gavenshire to await your fate." With that he touched his heels to the horse's flanks and moved out ahead with Arianne held tightly against him.

On the hard ride back to Gavenshire, Arianne gave thought to throwing herself from the horse. She reasoned that even if she could break the iron hold of the man who held her, the fall would most likely kill her and leave Richard with even more hatred for Tancred. No, it was better to face the future.

As the outline of the castle came into view, Arianne bit her lower lip to keep from crying. Where was Richard? Was he already within the castle, or did he wait to strike? Would he see her now and grow careless in his fear for her safety?

Gilbert urged his mount forward and cried out for admittance at the castle gatehouse. They were quickly surrounded and escorted inside the walls. Arianne tried not to show fear. She was aware that her people watched her, and she'd not give them reason to believe she was unworthy of their trust.

The mighty oak doors of the keep opened, and with only the benefit of torch light, Arianne knew that the man in the shadows was Tancred. Gilbert halted his horse and threw Arianne to the ground.

She landed hard against her hip at Tancred's feet. Rubbing her bruised side, she dared not look up for fear he would strike her.

"Ah, Lady Arianne," Tancred said the words sarcastically. "You do me honor with your return. Come, let us speak together." He nearly growled the last few words before yanking her to her feet by her hair.

Arianne fought back tears of pain. Her rain-drenched hair made a good hold for Tancred as he dragged her into the castle.

Arianne stumbled and fell twice, but without pausing to allow her to regain her footing, Tancred hauled her up the stone stairs to the second floor.

"I should break your scrawny neck," Tancred raged as he threw her into her bed chamber. "I don't know how you escaped or who helped you, but neither matters. You were a fool to believe yourself capable of warning your husband."

Arianne paled but remained perfectly still. Her hip was bruised to the point of distraction, yet she remained fixed to the place where Tancred had put her.

"When your husband does return, you will be the only weapon I need," Tancred said with a wicked smile. Arianne's face betrayed her fear. "But worry not, milady," Tancred said, moving to the door. "I will take you for my wife when he lies dead upon this floor."

With that he slammed the heavy chamber door behind him, and Arianne heard him instruct a man to stand guard outside it. She wanted to collapse into tears, but she managed to hold them back. Getting to her feet, she moved mechanically to rid herself of the soggy garments she wore. There was no fire in the hearth, but at least she could dry off and take refuge in her bed.

"But what if he returns?" Arianne thought aloud. She hurried to don a linen tunic. *I am helpless to keep him from me,* Arianne reasoned. *I am helpless, but God is mighty and fully capable of protecting me from Tancred.*

"Father," Arianne prayed, falling on her knees and wincing at the pain in her hip, "watch over me and keep me from Tancred's plan. Protect Richard and allow him victory over this evil man. Amen."

Chapter 12

Arianne awoke nearly a half hour before the rosy glow of dawn would grace the English countryside. There was an uncomfortable silence all around her. Throwing back the covers, she leaped from bed and ran to the window.

She looked long and hard against the early morning darkness. Something had disturbed her sleep, but what? The blackness would give up none of its secrets, and feeling that nothing else could be done, Arianne stoked up the fire in her hearth and prepared to go back to bed.

Just as the coals were stirred into life, Arianne heard a trumpeting call from outside the castle. Grabbing one of the furs from the bed, Arianne pulled it around her shoulders and returned cautiously to the window.

"I have come in the name of His Grace, the Duke of Gavenshire," the man announced. "Yield the castle or meet your fate this day!"

The men on the rampart walkways laughed as though the man had said something most amusing. Looking down into the open bailey, Arianne was surprised when a small entourage of armored men appeared with torches in hand. Tancred was in their midst, barking out orders and seeing to it that each man took his post.

Tancred paused in the procession and cast an upward glance as if he knew he'd find Arianne in the window overhead. He offered her the briefest salute to let her know that he was aware of her vigil, then proceeded to the gatehouse.

Arianne waited for what seemed an eternity. Nothing was said and no one seemed at all eager to reply to the herald's challenge.

Finally Tancred's voice sounded out against the silence. "Since your master is too cowardly to appear before me himself, I will address his herald and the challenge he lays forth."

Arianne held her breath. Tancred was hoping to bait Richard with the insult. Sending a herald was the commonplace thing to do and Tancred well knew it, as did the men who listened. But there was something more in Tancred's tone that made everyone take note.

"You may tell your master," Tancred called out again, "that I refuse to yield this castle. I challenge him to present himself and yield to me his titles, his land, and his people." The words chilled Arianne. She backed away from the window.

Richard's herald acknowledged Tancred's challenge and offered only one other thing. "The duke bids you take note that this castle is surrounded by some of the finest of the king's armies. The king himself demands you yield this land."

Tancred's hearty laughter was hardly what anyone had expected. "King? What king? I have no king, or has he forgotten that he exiled me from this land? You may tell your duke to come and take this castle if he can, for I will never yield what I am entitled to."

Richard never heard the exchange of words that took place between his herald and Tancred. He counted on the fact that all attention would be drawn to the gatehouse and the surrounding walls. While the main thrust of his men, aided by many of King Henry's finest soldiers, presented a formidable force to Tancred's eye, Richard would take his most trusted and capable men through the tunnels beneath the castle. They would infiltrate Tancred's stronghold, even while he observed the forces outside the castle walls.

Halting his men, Richard raised the torch in his hand. "You know what to do. I will proceed alone, and when the appointed time comes, you will follow. The fate of Gavenshire rests on our shoulders. We will have a moment of prayer."

One by one, his knights crossed themselves and knelt in the dirt of the tunnel floor. Richard knelt. "Father, we lift up our task to You. We are but humble servants and seek Your blessing to right that which has been wronged. Go with us into battle, even as you did King David of the Bible, and deliver the enemy into our hands. As You will it."

The knights murmured agreements and got to their feet. Richard turned to the ladder that would allow him to infiltrate Tancred's stronghold.

"God's speed, Your Grace," the man nearest him offered. Richard nodded and took himself up.

Arianne knew better than to let Tancred catch her unawares. She quickly pulled on a burgundy wool surcoat over her linen tunic, then plaited her hair and covered it with a linen headpiece.

She looked regal in her attire, but it gave Arianne little pleasure. The castle was under siege by her husband. The enemy held her hostage, and everyone's fate seemed to rest in the balance of a mysterious hatred of two noblemen. Arianne shivered, still feeling the cold in her bones. She went to a large chest and drew on a fur-lined mantle, looking much as though she were ready for an early morning walk.

The loud pounding at her door caused Arianne to take a step backward. "Unbar this door, Lady Arianne, or I shall have my men render it to kindling."

Taking a deep breath, Arianne stepped forward and removed the plank. Scarcely had she done this when Tancred burst through the door. He halted for a moment at the sight of Arianne in her stately dress. She was changed considerably from the rain-drenched wretch he'd seen the night before.

Lifting her chin defiantly, Arianne met his stare. "What seek ye here?" she questioned. "Your battle awaits you below. 'Tis unseemly that you would dally your precious moments of planning in the company of a woman."

Tancred laughed in her face. "I do so appreciate a woman of high spirit. Still, it is well that you learn your place. I have not yet settled with you for your disappearance from my protection."

"Protection, bah!" Arianne spat the words. "You, sire, have brought me more harm in the few moments we've shared than I've known in all the years of my life. You beat me, press your attentions upon me, and imprison me in my home. You afford me no protection, merely grief and grave reservation."

Tancred stepped forward with a leering smile. "You would surely change your mind should I relinquish my protection and turn you over to my men."

"I fear nothing that you or your men can do. I have the protection of my God, and He will see you defeated this day," Arianne replied confidently.

Tancred drew back his hand and slapped her. It wasn't the fierce blow he'd dealt her before, but it was enough to bring tears to her eyes. Nevertheless, Arianne stood fast. "You seem to make it a habit of beating defenseless women."

Tancred clenched his hands into fists, uncertain how to deal with the woman who stood before him. He was used to people cowering before him, and he had certainly never met with the resistance this young woman offered. Choosing his words to break her spirit, Tancred finally answered her.

"Your cowardly husband will taste my steel this day. Bards will create songs that will tell of our battle and how I avenged my name with his blood on my sword." Tancred's eyes seemed to glow in consideration of this accomplishment.

"My husband is no coward," Arianne said softly. "If you have issue with him, why not sit down to a table and discuss it as reasonable men? Why does such hatred between you demand blood?"

Tancred seemed taken aback by her words. "'Tis no affair for a woman," he muttered.

"So I am told by both you and my husband," Arianne replied without thinking.

"So you did see him?" Tancred more stated than questioned. Arianne felt her stomach churn. What had she done?

"What know ye of his plans?" He stepped forward and grasped Arianne by the shoulders. "How does he plan to attack first?"

"I know nothing," she answered, fear edging her voice notably.

"You lie!" Tancred exclaimed, shaking her vigorously. The rage in his eyes exploded across his face. "Tell me what he plans, or I shall beat you most mercilessly."

"A dead man would find that task most difficult," a voice sounded behind Tancred, followed by the slamming of the chamber door. Both Arianne and Tancred looked up to find the armored man standing, legs slightly apart, sword drawn.

"Richard!" Arianne gasped, as Tancred whirled around, pulling a dagger from his belt. He dragged Arianne across the room, distancing himself from Richard, with the knife at her throat.

"Take one step and I will cut her," Tancred said in a low, menacing voice.

Richard halted, knowing the man would do just as he said. He paled at the sight of the knife at his young wife's throat. Why was she here? He had thought she'd be safely away from this matter, not plunged into the very heart of it. His calm reserve faded. The fear in Arianne's eyes blanked out all reasoning in his mind.

"Leave her be," Richard spoke in a halting voice. "Your war is with me."

"My war is with all that you hold dear. Your title, your lands, your wife. You were responsible for my losses. Now all that you possess will be mine and you will be dead."

"Nay!" Arianne cried out, struggling in spite of the dagger.

"It would seem," Tancred said, pushing the blade firmly against Arianne's throat to still her, "that your lady is quite devoted to you. Pity. No doubt, however, I will be able to change that once she is my duchess."

Richard's eyes narrowed in a hateful stare, and Arianne felt her breath catch. He took a step forward, the sword still raised. "You will not kill her," Richard stated evenly. "You will not, because it would leave you defenseless."

"I did not say I would kill her, dear Richard," Tancred venomously declared. "I will, however, cause her great pain and suffering while you watch." Tancred drew the blade along Arianne's perfect face. "Scars upon such beauty would be a shame." He edged her cheek lightly with the knife, while Arianne fought to control her weak legs.

Richard could stand no more. "Do not harm her. I will give up my arms."

Arianne began to sob. "No, please don't give in to him, Richard. He will kill you."

Tancred laughed as Richard placed his sword on the floor. "It will give me great pleasure to tell the world how a woman caused your demise. Now throw down your dagger as well."

Richard did as he was instructed while Arianne continued to cry. "Move to the bed," Tancred instructed, still holding Arianne against himself.

Richard moved slowly back, while Tancred advanced until he took possession of Richard's weapons. His hand still held Arianne's arm possessively, causing Richard to grimace.

"You are a weakling, Richard," Tancred stated.

"I yielded to protect the lady's well-being. You hide behind her skirts and deny me the chance at a fair fight. I wonder now, just which of us is the weakling?" Richard's words seemed to strike their mark.

Tancred growled and pushed Arianne from him. "I've never denied you a fair fight. You ran from it at every opportunity, until you convinced the king to exile me. Now I have the advantage and you cry foul."

Arianne was getting to her feet, tears blinding her eyes. If only she hadn't been taken hostage again, Richard would not be compromised. This was all her fault.

While the men stared at each other in silence, Arianne considered rushing Tancred. She glanced first at Richard, then turned her attention to Tancred and back again to her husband. As if reading her mind, Richard shook his head.

"You needn't concern yourself, Arianne. God is with us in righteousness and truth. Tancred knows neither and fears not God or His people." Arianne's stare was fixed on her husband. His words seemed to soothe her pain-filled heart. Tancred saw the effect but said nothing while Richard continued. "God will always deal with wickedness, and He will always prevail. You believe in His power, Arianne. Never forget that God is not mocked by any man."

Arianne nodded slowly, and even Tancred seemed a bit taken aback by this declaration.

"I love you as no man has ever loved another," Richard said with a sad, sweet smile upon his lips. "Tancred cannot change that, nor can he understand it."

"I love you, Richard," Arianne said, taking a halting step forward. "I will give my life to preserve yours."

"Nay, love," Richard replied, shaking his head. "'Tis not necessary."

"Enough of this," Tancred interrupted. "You will be taken to the dungeon or cellars or tower, it matters not. You will be held until I am able to send word to King Henry. When I am redeemed, your life will be forfeited and all that is yours will be mine as it was always meant to be. Including this fair child." Tancred stepped toward Arianne, but she darted away from his touch and pressed against the wall.

"I will die first," she spat at the man.

Tancred halted.

"Arianne," Richard called, and the look on his face was most grievous, "you must live. 'Tis not of God to take your life. He will preserve and keep you. Remember the way in which you came to me. God always provides a means, be it at the hand of a king or that of a maidservant."

Arianne stared in confusion at her husband. She opened her mouth to question him, as Tancred moved to the door to call his men. Richard shook his head and gave her one last smile. "Remember," he whispered.

Arianne could neither do nor say anything more. Tancred's men rushed into the room and took the willing Richard in hand. Tancred moved close enough to Richard that they were nearly eye to eye.

"Harm her and answer to God," Richard said in a whisper.

Tancred's eyes narrowed slightly. "I have never answered to God."

Chapter 13

Arianne opened her chamber door only enough to see that Tancred had left a man to stand guard. Silently, she closed the door and began to pace the room.

"What did he mean?" Arianne whispered aloud. "What was Richard trying to say?"

She puzzled over his words throughout the day. At noon one of the servants brought her a tray of food and drink, but no one was allowed to come within, and Arianne was not allowed to venture out.

She looked out across the fields to the cliff-edged shores. Men were taking up position in a variety of places, but Arianne couldn't tell whether they were Richard's men or Tancred's. The surcoats of both armies were so similar that Arianne thought she might go mad trying to determine which was foe and which was friend.

Twice she tried to busy her hands by spinning wool on her distaff, but both times she made a matted mess and finally gave up the task. With a heavy sigh, Arianne fell back against her chair and stared up at the ceiling.

"Remember the way in which you came to me. God always provides a means, be it at the hand of a king or that of a maidservant," Richard had said. What did it mean, and how could it help him now?

"I came to him through the king's edict," Arianne reasoned to the cobwebs overhead. "I came to him from my father's house. I came to him as part of a bargain, a settlement of the governing powers. I. . ." Again she sighed. It was no use. Nothing made sense.

She longed to go to the castle chapel and pray. She knew Richard believed that a person could pray anywhere, at any time, and for the most part, she, too, believed this was true. But the sanctuary of the chapel always made her feel closer to God. Maybe it was the extravagant stained-glass window that graced the east wall, or maybe it was the fact that there, one could shut out all other influences and turn solely to God. Whatever it was, Arianne longed for its comfort.

"Now look what you've gone and done!" A woman's shrieking voice sounded from the other side of Arianne's door.

Quickly, Arianne took herself across the room, pulling her mantle tight as though it might muffle her movement. The door creaked softly as Arianne opened it only an inch. She studied the sight before her, unable to clearly see what was happening.

"Old crone! You nearly scalded me with that slop!" the guard raged.

Arianne opened the door a bit more and could see that the woman in the hall arguing with the guard was Matilda.

"'Twas not my fault you were born blind," she countered, noting Arianne's presence with the slightest grin on her face.

"Clean up this mess, woman!" the guard roared. "My master will not find it as humorous as you seem to. Be glad I am not given to beating women."

"Beat me?" Matilda yelled back and began screeching and crying with her eyes lifted heavenward. "Help me, oh Lord," she cried out, "for the man surely means to kill me."

Arianne knew that Matilda was staging the distraction for her benefit, but she also knew there was truth in Matilda's prayer. She hastened to ease through the chamber door and secured it behind her, all the while watching the guard as he sought to settle Matilda's ranting.

"I said I would not beat you, old crone," the man muttered over and over. "Just clean up the mess and be gone." He rolled his eyes, completely baffled by the sniveling woman who now threw herself at his feet.

"You are kind, sire," Matilda moaned her exaggerated gratitude. "Thank you for sparing my worthless life. I will do your bidding and see that this floor is cleaned. Please, I beg you, do not tell the master of this, for I fear my life would be forfeited."

The man scowled, but Arianne could see from her hiding place in the shadows near the kitchen stairs that Matilda would not be harmed by the oaf.

Arianne hurried to the kitchen below, grateful that everyone moved in such hurried steps that they seemed to take little notice of one who moved with decided slowness and secrecy. She waited in the buttery, knowing that Matilda would think to look for her there.

The minutes seemed to linger, and Arianne thought more than once she'd been discovered. But to her relief, she was safe for the moment and Matilda was soon to join her with news of Richard and the siege.

"Milady," Matilda said, embracing Arianne as though they were mother and daughter instead of servant and duchess. "I feared for your life. Is it well with ye?"

"Oh, Matilda," Arianne moaned against the older woman's shoulder, "Tancred has made Richard his prisoner, and I don't know where they've taken him."

"Hush, child," Matilda soothed, "for I know of this deed as well as where they have taken your husband."

Arianne's head snapped up. "Where is he? We must free him."

"We could not do it alone, for at least two men guard him, possibly more," Matilda whispered.

"But we must help him," Arianne pleaded. "There must be a way for us to free him from his plight."

"I know of no way," Matilda said sadly. "I knew that I could detain the guard while you slipped from your room, but there would be no such distraction for the men who guard your husband. Unless you have some other thought on the matter."

"Richard was adamant that I remember something," Arianne said with a frown upon her face. "But I know naught of what he spoke."

"What did he say?"

Arianne thought for a moment. "He told me to remember the way in which I came to him. For the life of me, I can't imagine what he means. I came to him by order of the king of England. What can I make of that?"

"Did he say nothing else?" Matilda asked earnestly.

"Only that God always provides a means, be it at the hand of a king or that of a maidservant," Arianne replied. "I came to Richard by the hand of the king, that much is true."

Matilda stared thoughtfully for a moment, and then a smile began to line her face. "Ye also came to him by the hand of a maidservant," she whispered, "when I led you to the tunnels below."

Arianne's breath caught in her throat. "The tunnels! Richard must want me to go back to the tunnels. Where are they keeping him, Matilda? Can we get to him through the tunnels?" Arianne was already moving to the trap door.

"Nay, they've put him in the cellar. There is no passage to that place from the tunnels, but Richard gained entrance to the castle through the tunnels, and he would not have traveled alone. His men must await him below, milady. Richard must desire that you tell them of his plight and take refuge there until this matter is settled."

Arianne suddenly felt hope born anew. "If Richard's men are below, they will know exactly what to do. Come help me move this door and I will go to them. We both will go!"

The women moved gingerly down the ladder, noting with satisfaction that a lighted torch offered the slightest glow from the passages below. Matilda pulled the trap door closed as she hurried to follow her mistress. She was greatly relieved to leave the conflicts overhead for the sanctuary of the tunnels.

Arianne's feet had scarcely touched the damp ground when she was surrounded by men.

"Your Grace," one of the men said coming forward. "We thought you were safely away with Sir George."

"I was captured, as were the duke's men," Arianne said and quickly added, "They have also taken my husband prisoner. He bade me find you." Another man hurried to aid Matilda down the remaining steps of the ladder.

"Where have they taken your husband, milady?"

Arianne looked around her at the eager faces. These men were Richard's most loyal, or he would not have brought them with him to the tunnels. "He has been taken to the cellar and I know naught of the place, but my maid does." Arianne motioned to Matilda.

"We know of the cellars," the man replied. "We have been given tasks by His Grace. Your appearance here with this grave news gives us cause to seek them out with haste. You will remain here in the safety of the tunnels, milady, while we venture forth and see to our duties."

Arianne nodded. "Will you return and give me word of my husband?"

The man's anxious eyes scanned her face, and with a slight nod, he motioned his men to the ladder. The women could do nothing but watch as the men disappeared. Fear bound their hearts with steel bands. Perhaps Tancred had learned of the trap door and even now awaited Richard's men.

Arianne shuddered, and Matilda took it for chills. "Come, milady. We will seek a warmer place."

With a heavy heart, Arianne followed the older woman deeper into the maze. She couldn't help thinking of Richard and the suffering he would be enduring at Tancred's hands. *Because of me, Richard walked right into the trap.* Just as Tancred had hoped, Arianne had been the only bait necessary to capture the young duke.

Arianne also remembered the painful expression on Richard's face as he watched and waited while Tancred put the knife to her throat.

"Why?" she exclaimed without realizing that she spoke aloud.

"Why what, milady?" Matilda asked, suddenly turning to stop.

"Why did I have to be the reason he was taken?" Her voice betrayed her emotions and broke with a sob. "Why did God allow me to be retaken by Tancred's men? I don't understand. It's only caused more suffering, and now my husband is prisoner and this man will most likely seek to end his life."

Matilda grimaced and turned away from Arianne as though an unpleasant thought had come to mind.

"What is it, Matilda? What do you know that I do not?"

"'Tis nothing but speculation, Lady Arianne. I would not overburden your mind with such matters. Here," Matilda motioned, "this will be a good place to await the men."

Arianne would not be silenced with her maid's excuse. "Matilda, I must know what is going on. Do you have any knowledge of this battle between Tancred and Richard?"

"Aye, milady," Matilda replied in a weary voice. She allowed herself to sit before seeing to her lady's needs—a most unusual thing for a servant devoted to her job. "I know that the man blames the duke for lost title and lands. I know, too, that he blames Richard for King Henry's decision to exile him from England."

"But why, Matilda?" Arianne asked, taking a seat in the dirt beside her maid. "Why did the king exile Tancred?"

"That, I cannot say," Matilda replied.

"Cannot or will not?" Arianne questioned.

A rustling sound in the passageway caused both women to start. Matilda put a finger to her lips, grateful to silence the younger woman's questions. She felt a growing fear that she would have to explain to Arianne the matter of affairs between Richard and Tancred, and to do so would mean to break an ancient promise to the young duke. No, she decided, she mustn't be the one to break that oath.

Chapter 14

The women waited in the damp darkness for what seemed an eternity. Arianne, with her questioning mind, grew restless and prayed that the time would pass quickly and allow Richard's men complete victory. Matilda, restless for her own reasons, also prayed. She prayed for a way to stay true to her promises, while providing Arianne the comfort and protection she deemed a part of her duties.

When both women were convinced that the sounds had been nothing more than rats in the passages, Matilda was the first to speak.

"Milady," she began hesitantly and in a low whisper. "It is my desire to keep a promise to the duke. It is a promise that I have held since he was a young man. This thing between him and Sir Tancred must be revealed by him alone. I cannot break my oath, no matter how much I would like to do so."

Arianne's eyes betrayed her curiosity, but she nodded in agreement. "I will not question you again," Arianne said soberly, "but only if you can assure me that in your keeping of this promise, Richard's life will not be further jeopardized."

"Nay, milady," Matilda replied. "His life will not be further jeopardized by my keeping of this oath. Both the duke and Tancred have knowledge of my understanding and what lies between them. 'Tis nothing that will cause either one to be aided or hindered."

"Very well," Arianne said, "then I must be content until my husband feels the matter is important enough to share with me. In the meantime, there is the matter of freeing Richard."

"But, milady, you heard the duke's men. We should remain here and keep safely out of sight. Richard would be most grieved if you were to be taken again and all because you sought to free him from his confines."

"That is unquestionably true," the young duchess answered. She considered the situation for only a moment before continuing. "However, I cannot sit here in the safety of the tunnels and know that he is suffering, maybe even being beaten or starved. I cannot and will not, and that is something you and my husband must understand."

"Yes, milady," Matilda said with a slight smile. "I feel the same. What have ye in mind that two women could lay their hands to?"

Arianne smiled. "I have not yet considered that matter. Perhaps if we pray on it, the heavenly Father will put it upon our minds and show us the way."

"That is most wise, milady."

Both women fell silent, and only the clasping of their hands together broke the deep concentration of their prayers. Arianne pleaded for her husband's life and freedom and begged God to show her how she might once again do something helpful to her love.

Hours passed in the silent meditation of the women, and in the end it was Arianne's concern for whether or not Richard was being fed that opened the window of opportunity for the escape plan.

"He won't be able to maintain his strength if they do not feed him," Arianne said with her hands at the side of her head. Her temples throbbed from the worry in her heart. Richard had promised her that God would win out over evil, but the moment seemed so hopeless.

"Perhaps that is our answer," Matilda said with sudden encouragement. "I can pass throughout the castle as one of the servants and no one will question my actions because, of course, a servant would not be moving about without being directed by those in authority. I can go to the cellars with food for Richard, and perhaps when the guards open the cellar door, he could escape."

"It has possibilities," Arianne said with a nod. "But there is too much that could happen. The guards might not allow Richard any food. They might keep it for themselves. Then, too, Richard would need a weapon against armed men, and we can't simply place one upon the tray."

"True," Matilda replied. They seemed once again to come to an impasse.

Arianne sat silently considering the situation, while Matilda got to her feet and paced the floor in front of her.

"The guards wouldn't want the food," Matilda suddenly said, "if it were nothing more than slop."

"I don't believe I understand. Richard would not desire slop, either."

Matilda smiled at the duchess and nodded. "But it would be just the kind of torment Sir Tancred would be capable of. I could tell the guards that it was all that Richard was to be allowed. If I make a stinking mess of the whole mixture, I don't believe any man would come near the tray. I have herbs and all manner of thing that can make it most unappealing. I would have to be allowed to deliver it because the men would want no part of it."

Arianne jumped to her feet. "But perhaps they wouldn't allow Richard to have it, either."

"Of course they would," Matilda said with her hands on her waist. "It would give them great pleasure to see Richard eating something so utterly disgusting."

"Those men being Tancred's, I suppose you are right."

"I know I am," Matilda replied confidently.

"But what of a weapon?" Arianne questioned. "Richard must have a sword or he will not be able to control the men who guard him."

"That does pose a bit of a problem," Matilda agreed.

"What if you were to hide it in your skirts?" Arianne suddenly asked. She could well imagine the possibility in her mind.

"A man's sword would extend below my limbs," Matilda said, all the while motioning to her short legs.

"A sword would be too long," Arianne acknowledged, "but a dagger or short sword could be hung from your waist, beneath your tunic. It would have to be done so in such a way that it would be easy and quick to free for use, but concealed well enough that the guards wouldn't notice."

"I think I can do that," the older woman said thoughtfully. "I could also pull a cloth around my waist like the cooks do. It would add concealment."

"Where can we get a dagger for Richard?" Arianne questioned. "We can't very well walk into the hall and ask Tancred for one."

"That is true," Matilda responded with great thoughtfulness. "Most of the men guard well their weapons; however, if I can get to one of Richard's men, I am certain he will assist us in the effort to free the duke."

"Then we must be about it," Arianne said, starting down the tunnel.

Matilda's hand fell upon her arm. "Nay, milady. You cannot go above. 'Twould be most unwise; the men would easily recognize you."

Arianne knew that Matilda spoke truth, but she hated being left behind to do nothing. As if reading her mind, Matilda gave her a reassuring pat on the arm. "You must keep our prayerful petition before God. Knowing Richard as I do, I am certain that it is the very thing he is about, right this minute. You will stand as one in prayerful agreement before God."

Arianne immediately felt peace descend upon her troubled spirit. *Yes, it would be just like Richard to be quoting the scriptures he'd memorized and praying for God's guidance through his misery.*

"I will stay," Arianne agreed reluctantly. "But you must promise to return to me as soon as you can and let me know that all is well."

"I promise, milady. I will do all in my power, through His power," Matilda said, pointing upward, "to free Richard from Tancred's hold."

Matilda crept through the kitchens, pulling along with her the things that she needed. She sent a whispered word here and there among trusted servants and easily concocted a hideous porridge of rotten meat and garbage.

The already potent smell was enhanced by the addition of several unknown ingredients, which Matilda cautiously threw in when no one was watching. Then, just in case Tancred's men were stupid or desperate enough to want to eat the odorous mess, Matilda added enough sleeping herbs to lay out even the heartiest soul in a long, deep sleep.

Just as she finished this task, Matilda was surprised to find one of Richard's men, Sir Bryant, dressed in the clothes of a peasant and standing at her side.

"I have the dagger you need," he whispered.

"Leave it in the buttery," Matilda replied. When she glanced up to see that the man had heard her, he was already gone.

"I will return for this in a moment," Matilda told one of the cooks. "See that no one touches it." The woman nodded and took the ladle from Matilda.

Matilda slipped through the buttery door and closed it behind her. Sir Bryant waited for her in the shadows behind several kegs of drink.

"Tell me your plan, for we must do what we can to aid in freeing our duke."

Matilda shared their plans with the young knight and waited, half expecting some rebuke or condemnation. She was gratified when none came. Instead, Sir Bryant seemed to understand that this way was best.

"I will not be far away. I will have several of Richard's best men with me, and we will await word from you. Here is the weapon. Have you a way to conceal it?"

"I hadn't the chance to consider it," Matilda admitted.

Sir Bryant thought for a moment, then noticing some rope beside one of the kegs, cut off a section and came to Matilda. "This should serve the purpose. Perhaps if you tie it around your waist tight enough that the hilt will not pass through without assistance, it will remain concealed."

Matilda took the rope and motioned the young knight to afford her some privacy while she worked to secure the dagger. Once she'd let her skirts fall back into place, she asked Sir Bryant to determine her success.

"Walk to the door and back," he ordered, and Matilda quickly did as he bid.

She felt the steel slide back and forth against her leg, but with a slower step, Matilda felt certain it was not perceivable, and Sir Bryant pronounced the matter settled.

Matilda moved with great slowness as she approached the passageway to the cellar. She knew that her noises would be easily distinguished in the silence of the hall, so she began an ancient singsong tune to announce her approach.

As she came upon the guards, they were ready and waiting for her. One man advanced with his sword drawn, but then the stench of the concoction met his nose. Wrinkling his face into a grimace, the man quickly stepped back.

"What have ye there, old crone? 'Tis surely nothing fit for man."

"Fit only for one man," Matilda said with a haggard laugh. "Lord Tancred," she bit her tongue to keep from taking back the title, "bid me bring this slop to the duke. He's to have naught but this for his meals."

The other man stepped forward and peered into the bowl. "What is it? It smells like death itself."

"Most probably is," Matilda played along. "Would ye care to serve him?"

Both men took a step back at this. "I won't touch that vile mixture," the first man said, while the other just shook his head.

Matilda raised an eyebrow and suddenly thought of how to buy herself more time with Richard. "I can't be leaving the bowl and tray with the prisoner. Must I take his plight upon myself and wait in that hole while he eats his fill?"

"'Twould seem your only choice," the second guard replied. "'Tis all he's fit for anyway. The company of old women and pigs' slop. Take it to him with our finest regards for his dining."

Matilda screwed up her face to show her feigned distaste with the matter, and when the men only laughed at her circumstances, Matilda knew she'd won. Now she'd have enough time to loosen the dagger and give Richard a weapon.

The men moved to the cellar door and removed the plank that held it in place. The first man called out as the second man stood ready for action.

"It seems our master is not so hard-hearted," the man spoke into the room. "Lord Tancred has sent supper to Your Grace." At that he pushed Matilda through the door and slammed it shut behind her. Only the tiniest bit of light filtered in from the slit of a single window, high in the wall.

"Your Grace? Are ye here? 'Tis Matilda." She waited a moment while her eyes adjusted to the darkness.

A sound came from her right, and Matilda turned slightly with the tray in hand.

"Matilda? Why has Tancred sent you to me?" Richard asked from the darkness.

"He did not send me," Matilda whispered the reply. "Lady Arianne and I thought of this."

"Arianne? What of my wife? Is she safe? Has he hurt her again?" His voice grew louder as he neared Matilda. Then his tone changed from concern to disgust. "What is that stench?" Richard asked, coming to stand beside her.

Matilda laughed softly. "'Tis part of our plan, and yes, your lady is safe."

"What plan?" Richard questioned.

"We thought to free you from your prison, sire. If you will but hold this wretched brew, I will release the weapon I've brought you from beneath my skirts."

"You managed to get a weapon in here? Did not the guards search you?" Richard asked in complete amazement.

"They would not come close enough to your supper, sire. It seems they do not have a strong stomach for such matters." She gave the tray to Richard, and in spite of the dim light, Matilda turned her back to her duke and raised her skirts cautiously to free the dagger.

"Where is Arianne?" Richard whispered while waiting for Matilda to complete her task.

"She is back in the tunnels," Matilda replied, turning to hold out the dagger. "Compliments of Sir Bryant, who will be waiting just down the passageway with several of your other knights."

Matilda couldn't see his face, but she sensed Richard had a renewal of hope and strength. He took the dagger in one hand while still holding the tray in the other.

"Now what, might I ask, is your plan for getting out of here?" Richard's amusement and admiration were revealed in his tone.

Matilda took back the tray and moved toward the door. "Just follow me, sire. I plan to douse the ambitious flames of those two pups with the stench from this tray. That should give you enough time to come through the doorway, although I'm afraid your eyes will have quite an adjustment, even in the dim light of the passageway."

"I'll manage," Richard replied. "You simply lead on."

Matilda approached the door and gave her best performance yet. "Open this door. I'll not spend another moment in here. His Grace is unreceptive to your master's gift, and this stench is likely to do me harm."

Matilda and Richard both heard the rattling sound of the bar being moved. If the men were lined up as they had been when she'd entered the cellar room, Matilda would have a clear path to cover them both in the horrid concoction.

When the door opened, Matilda lost little time. She moved forward at such a pace that neither guard was prepared for the moment when she feigned a misstep and plunged the tray forward to cover them both.

"Ahhh!" the closest man cried, jumping back. The door slammed hard against the stone wall.

"Mindless crone!" the other yelled and actually dropped his sword in the attempt to rid his hauberk of the mess.

This was all the encouragement Richard needed. He rushed from the room with the dagger poised for battle, while Matilda conveniently stood with both of her feet on the discarded sword.

The entire matter took only a heartbeat, and by the hand of God and the duke of Gavenshire, both men were thrown into the cellar room and Richard was free!

Chapter 15

What is the meaning of this?" Tancred asked the surprised guard. They stood outside Arianne's empty bed chamber, each man as puzzled as the other.

"Mayhap there is a secret passageway," the guard offered. "A way that no one but the duke and his duchess is familiar with."

"Nay," Tancred said, shaking his head. "I see no sign of that." He entered the room, however, and began to run his hand along the smooth stone wall. "Nevertheless, the wench is not here and once again she has bested me. This does not bode well with me. I will give a sizable reward to the man who finds her and brings her to me." The guard nodded and waited for dismissal. "Well?" Tancred questioned. "What are you waiting for?"

The man quickly departed the company of his sour leader. He had no desire to bear the brunt of the man's ire. It was bad enough that the woman had disappeared under his watch.

Tancred stared at the room a moment longer, then took himself to the window and looked out at the gathering of Richard's army. As the hours passed, the numbers grew. Tancred understood that Richard hoped he would be intimidated by the mass. It would seem that King Henry, feeling securely delivered to London, had spared a good many of his own men to aid Richard.

"'Tis amusing to think Henry knows I am here. He thought to deny me my title and country, but I will show him how mistaken he was on the matter. Henry and Richard, together, haven't the power to drive me from England forever," Tancred mused.

Turning from the window, he scowled at the empty room. He was quite perplexed with the young duchess Richard had taken as wife. She was no woman of tender means, of that she'd proved more than once. She was intriguing, Tancred thought, and would make him a good wife after Richard was disgraced and dead.

The sound of the herald's trumpet rang out, catching Tancred's attention. Richard was locked in the cellars, and Tancred felt it to be the proper time to relay this information to his enemy's men. Defeat would be swift without their leader.

Quickly, Tancred made his way through the castle, across the bailey, to the gatehouse. Along the way he noticed several of his men thoroughly searching the yards. Word must have spread quickly regarding his reward for Arianne. He smiled to himself. It would only be a matter of time and she would be under his control once again.

"What has the herald to say?" Tancred questioned the men who kept watch. His dark scowling face caused even the bravest men to step back.

"They claim the castle for the duke and bid us open the gate. If we will not yield, they are prepared to begin the assault."

"Let them," Tancred laughed. "We have their duke in the cellar below the castle. I doubt they will be so anxious to begin their assault when news of this is given."

The surrounding men joined in their leader's laughter, while Tancred took himself up to the battlements.

Many of Richard's men sat atop their mighty warhorses, while others stood amassed on the ground. Their numbers were impressive; even Tancred couldn't deny this. He'd never anticipated this turn of events, having been confident that he could take Richard and the castle by surprise.

Taking a position of authority, hands on his hips and feet slightly apart, Tancred addressed the enemy. "It is well you know that I have taken the duke as my prisoner. I also have his fair wife and many of his men confined within these walls. Their execution will begin immediately if your numbers are not taken from this place."

"The duke gave us orders," one of Richard's knights said, urging his horse forward a bit. "We will not disgrace him by giving up our position at the sound of your idle threats. He may well lie dead at this moment, but we will do as we were bid."

"This castle can withstand your assault," Tancred declared, yet in the back of his mind came the thought that he still had no idea how Richard had managed to gain entry through the castle walls. His men were everywhere and guards were posted all along the walkways. There was virtually no way that Richard could have made his way into the castle unseen, yet that appeared to be exactly what had happened.

Tancred's men seemed to wait for instruction, watching their leader as if puzzled about what they would do next. Tancred clenched his jaw until it ached. He couldn't very well kill Richard until he had a full confession of guilt to present to the king. Even then, it might be necessary to have Richard publicly declare his guilt, and for that reason Tancred desperately needed Arianne.

"If you attack, I will kill the duke!" Tancred declared loudly.

"He will have to catch me in order to do so," Richard called from the south wall. He was surrounded by several of his men, and in the bailey below, the sound of swords at work was already ringing out to capture Tancred's attention.

Richard's men cheered from outside the walls, while Tancred drew his sword and struck a commanding pose.

"You have but a handful of men inside the walls," he announced. "My men still outnumber yours and," Tancred said, hoping that Richard was not knowledgeable of the fact that Arianne was missing, "I have your wife."

"You have nothing," Richard countered. "My wife is safely hidden. Yield to me, Tancred, and I will be merciful."

Tancred laughed. "Never! It is because of your lies to the king that I must clear my name."

Richard seemed unmoved by the words. He remained silent with a fixed stare, which caused Tancred to grow uneasy. Without another word, Tancred took himself below and ordered his men to clear the bailey of Richard's soldiers.

When Tancred emerged from the gatehouse, Richard was gone from the rampart walkway and his men were making easy task of defeating their enemy. Motioning to several of his men, Tancred avoided the open grounds and made his way back to the castle. He had to find Arianne. She was his only hope of keeping Richard at bay.

"Has she been found?" Tancred asked the man who'd earlier guarded her chamber.

"Nay, sire," he replied. "We are sorely vexed by her disappearance, as well as the other strange happenings within these walls."

"What speak ye of?" Tancred asked.

"Half of the men cannot be found," the man answered.

"Half?"

"Well, very nearly that. I searched for my brother and our cousin, but they are nowhere to be found. When I questioned some of the other men, we totaled the numbers to equal nearly half of those who entered in with us."

"That's impossible!" Tancred declared.

"I wish it were, sire," the man said apologetically. "'Twould seem a power greater than ours stands at Richard's side."

"Bah, you prattle like a woman," Tancred said and left the man to figure out what he should do next.

Tancred moved down the shadowy corridor, fearfully watching for any sign of Richard. Should he find Richard before locating Arianne, he knew his life would be forfeited. A noise in the passage to his right caught Tancred's attention, and he cautiously followed the sound.

A small woman scurried in the shelter of the dimly lit hallway. She cast a wary glance over her shoulder before hurrying down the back stairs.

Tancred followed her, immediately recognizing the woman. *Matilda!* He knew the woman well and was confident that if anyone knew where the duchess of Gavenshire had taken refuge, it would be Matilda. With a hand on his scabbard to silence any noise, Tancred moved down the stairs.

He'd barely put a foot to the bottom step when he saw the edge of Matilda's cloak disappearing around the corner. Boldly, he stepped into the kitchens, fully expecting to confront the old woman, but he was once again vexed when all he caught sight of was the overflow of her cloak as she passed from the room.

Hastening his steps, Tancred entered the buttery just as Matilda had pulled the trap door open.

"Halt!" he demanded and stepped fully into the room.

Matilda let the door drop with a resounding thud. She could only stare at the man before her.

"You were going to your duchess, were you not?" he asked, casually leaning against the wall. Matilda refused to speak, and Tancred shrugged. "It is of no matter to me whether you speak or not. I know that is where you were going, and you will take me with you."

"Nay," Matilda said, shaking her head. "I will not hand her over to you."

"I believe you will," Tancred said, slowly coming forward. "If you do not, I will slay you here and go below to find her. Don't be a fool, Matilda. Pull up that door and take yourself below."

Matilda moved in hesitant, jerky motions. She didn't know what else to do, fearing for her own life as well as Arianne's.

Before she could give her mind a chance to form a plan, they were in the tunnels. Tancred stared in appreciation of this discovery. "So this is how Richard gained entry into the castle," he muttered.

Matilda turned to run, but Tancred quickly caught her. "Where is she?"

"I'm not certain, sire," Matilda replied. "You know full well that the duchess has a mind of her own. She may not even be here."

"It is a chance we will take," Tancred replied, eyes narrowing slightly. "Take me to where you last saw her."

Matilda shook her head, raising her voice to protest. "I will not do it. Slay me now, but I will not betray my duke or his wife."

"Matilda!" Arianne's voice called out from down a long corridor. "Matilda, is that you?"

"Answer her," Tancred said with a sneer. "Answer your duchess." He drew his sword slowly so that it didn't make a single sound.

"Aye, milady," Matilda said. Tears came to her eyes before she let out a scream. "Run, Your Grace. Lord Tancred is here."

Arianne realized too late the trap that Tancred had set for her. She appeared not ten feet from where he stood.

Tancred saw immediately that Arianne intended to run. "Don't move, or I will kill the old woman," he commanded.

Arianne froze in place. Tancred stepped forward and took Arianne in hand. Turning to Matilda, he spoke. "You will go find Duke Richard and bring him here. Tell him to come alone because if anyone, even you, shows your face in this tunnel, I will put a great misery upon this woman."

Matilda cast a glance from Arianne to Tancred and back to her duchess. Arianne knew that she awaited her approval, but how could she give it?

"I would suggest, milady," Tancred said, tightening his grip, "that you release your servant to action. Otherwise, I will be forced into a most unpleasant task."

"Go ahead, Matilda, but only as protection for yourself. Tell Richard I will gladly give my life to spare his own. Once I am dead, Tancred will have no power over him."

Matilda hurried away, feeling much like a coward at leaving Arianne to Tancred's mercies.

When the trap door sounded in place, Arianne turned her glance to the man who held her. "At every moment I have been in your company," she began, "there is always the anger and resentment you bear upon yourself. It is almost as if it were an armor that encases you, but I perceive something else."

Tancred's expression seemed to soften. His brow rose curiously. "Pray tell, madam, what is it you perceive?"

"Pain," Arianne whispered, surprising them both.

Tancred's eyes narrowed again, but before he could speak, Arianne continued. "I see pain and emptiness. Perhaps desperation and even loneliness."

"You perceive what has never existed."

"Do I?" she asked hesitantly. The iron band of his hand upon her arm tightened.

"Aye, milady. You give me weaknesses better suited to your husband."

"My husband is a good man. He is fair and just, kind and gentle. But more than this," Arianne said, lifting her chin confidently, "he is a man whose faith is firmly rooted in God. Know ye of that peace?"

"God is for old men and addlebrained women," Tancred replied. "I have no time for a God who allows honest men to be usurped, while evil ones go unpunished."

Arianne sensed that she'd somehow struck a chord. "God's ways are often a mystery, but in time He reveals them to us."

"Through the collection plate of the church? Nay, mayhap God's revelations come through Rome and the papal displays of regality and authority. Better yet, King Henry—there is a man after God's own heart!"

"Nay, Tancred. God need not rely upon a sovereign or a pope. It is true He uses emissaries and heralds, just as you or Richard might, but He comes to men and women as a Father and loves them."

Tancred dropped his hand as though Arianne's arm had grown white hot. "Cease this!" he ordered. "You know only what a woman's heart tells you. You can't begin to understand what a man must do."

Arianne rubbed her arm but didn't try to move away from Tancred. She sensed that Tancred was fighting a battle of much greater proportions than his dispute with Richard.

"I might be ignorant of the affairs of men," Arianne said, her eyes gently sweeping Tancred's face, "but I believe God knows. I don't know why you were exiled or why you and my husband are at war, but God does, and He is righteous. If injustice has been done, He will right it."

"But injustice hasn't been done, has it?" The voice belonged to Richard, and Tancred jumped in surprise before taking Arianne in hand once again.

"So we finally come face-to-face. Nothing to stand in the way. No armies, no men—" Tancred's words were cut off.

"Not face-to-face," Richard interrupted. "You hide behind the skirts of my wife."

Chapter 16

ancred slowly, methodically offered a smile. "I do not trust you. You betrayed me to the king."

"I turned over evidence of a murderer's identity."

"You turned over false documentation and the sworn statements of my enemies!" Tancred countered.

"You forget," Richard said in a deadly tone. "I saw you myself." Arianne frowned. She struggled to understand the embittered war of words that raged around her.

"You saw nothing!" Tancred shouted.

"I saw you murder my father!" Richard cried out, stepping forward.

"Our father!" Tancred countered, pulling Arianne in front of him as a warning against Richard's advancement. "And I did not kill him!"

"Nay," Richard growled. "Never let it be said that we shared common parents."

"You are brothers!" Arianne gasped suddenly.

"Aye, but only because I cannot change the past," Richard replied bitterly.

Tancred threw his arm across Arianne and pulled her hard against him. He raised his sword to point at Richard's heart. "I came back to clear my name," he said in a low, even tone. "You caused me to lose my title and lands. You took lands and wealth that should have come to me, and you are responsible for sending me from my home."

"You were guilty of murder. Be grateful you were allowed to live at all," Richard declared.

"I had no part in the murder," Tancred raged. "I told you that then and I say it again."

Richard's face darkened in a rage that Arianne had never before witnessed. Forced as she was between the two angry men, she felt her knees weaken. Had Tancred not had a good grip on her, Arianne would have sunk to the floor.

"Father thought you a man of honor, but even after the deed is long past done, you cannot admit to your guilt and shame. Your blackened heart may cry out for revenge, but your soul is in need of absolution."

"My soul cries for justice," Tancred replied. "My soul cries for the years of loss and separation from all that I loved."

"Loved? What know ye of love?" Richard inquired venomously. "The mother who taught you love at her breast then bore your sword into her heart. What love could you have been capable of?"

"I should kill you for saying such a thing," Tancred spat. "Speak not of her again; better that we should have both died the day she perished."

The words surprised Richard, and his face betrayed the fact. Arianne watched as her husband struggled with his brother's declaration.

"Were it not for Henry's mercy, you would be dead, for I desired it so," Richard finally spoke.

"The mercy of Henry?" Tancred questioned sarcastically. "Spare me words of your merciful king. The man branded me a murderer, though he had no proof. I still wear his merciful scars."

"I saw you with your hand upon the knife that had been plunged into our father's back. Our mother was not yet dead in her own blood, two paces away," Richard replied coldly.

Arianne shuddered at the image he drew. Richard could not have been more than fifteen when he had witnessed that awful atrocity.

"I found them that way," Tancred said defensively. "I heard her screams, but I was too late."

Richard stared in disbelief at his brother. "You truly expect me to believe that?"

"Perhaps he speaks the truth," Arianne whispered. She wished she'd remained silent when Richard threw her a glaring stare. His eyes clearly silenced her, and Arianne hung her head in sorrow.

"See there!" Tancred jumped at this new opportunity. "Even your wife sees the possibility. You were so blinded by your hatred of me that you could not imagine I was telling the truth."

"And just what is the truth?" Richard's voice held no hint of interest.

"Just as I have told you. I did not kill our parents." Tancred's words were no longer venomous, and Arianne sensed that the tone was nearly pleading. "I've been convinced all these years that you were the one responsible for our father and mother's death. You were conveniently there when you should have been miles away. You were the one who successfully mounted a campaign against me, in spite of your youth and inexperience, and successfully saw me stripped of my title and lands."

"You were not content with the lands you'd obtained through Henry's graciousness," Richard countered. "You wanted our father's land as well. Don't seek to ease your conscience with wild tales of my guilt. I had no hand in our parents' deaths."

"I'm past caring what explanations you might offer," Tancred said, shifting his weight nervously. "I demand that you accept responsibility for the entire matter. I demand that you send a messenger to Henry and proclaim your own guilt, for there can surely be no other who was responsible."

"You were found guilty of the crime, do you forget that?"

"I had no part in their deaths! I want my name cleared of the murders, and I want my title and lands back."

"Never!" The word reverberated throughout the tunnel.

"I will hold your sweet wife captive until the messenger returns with a full pardon. Henry, by your own admission, is quite fond of you. Perhaps he will consider that you were a wayward youth and show you mercy." Tancred's words were riddled with sarcasm. "Should King Henry refuse your admission of guilt, we will prepare a request for an audience with him in which you will openly declare, in person, my innocence and your guilt. Otherwise, I will be forced to end not only your life, but hers."

Arianne lifted her eyes to meet her husband's. Tancred brought the sword against her neck. The cold metal caused Arianne to shudder, but no more so than the look of black hatred in her husband's eyes.

"This is not her battle," Richard said slowly, never taking his eyes from Arianne. At the fear he saw there, he softened a bit. "She has endured much because of our bitterness. The least you can do is fight me man to man."

Tancred laughed bitterly. "The time for that has passed. I cannot trust you to keep your word and you will not trust me for mine."

Richard stepped back with a sigh. "What is it that you would have of me?"

"I've already told you. I want to be pardoned. I want to be reinstated in my rightful place. I want. . ." Tancred's voice fell silent for a moment. He lowered the sword from Arianne's neck. "I want to come home."

The first spark of sympathy was born in Arianne's heart for the man who held her. There was such longing in those few words.

"You will not gain your home by force, Sir Tancred," Arianne said quietly. "Nor will you find relief from the bitterness that haunts you by blaming your brother for something he did not do."

Arianne's words stunned both men. Taking advantage of their silence, she continued. "The murder of my husband will not undo the murder of your parents. King Henry is a just man. Perhaps something could be done to convince him that the charges of murder were placed upon you falsely."

"There was nothing false about them," Richard spat, causing Arianne to jump ever so slightly.

"Richard," she whispered and turned tender eyes to plead with her husband, "Tancred had no reason to risk his life and return here if he is guilty. However, if he is innocent, no price would be too dear to pay in order to see his name cleared of such heinous charges."

"So you believe him?" Richard questioned.

Behind her, Tancred said nothing.

Arianne reached a hand out to Richard's arm, but Tancred pulled her back, fearing that Richard would snatch her away.

Arianne shook her head. "I don't know if he lies, but I do know that I would do most anything to keep him from harming you." There were tears in her eyes, and Richard felt his anger fading.

"And I would do anything to keep him from harming you," Richard countered.

Tancred resented the exchange that left him feeling more alienated than before.

"Enough!" he said, pulling Arianne several feet with him. "I grow uncomfortable with this scene. Will you help me of your own free will, Richard, or must I force you?"

Richard glanced hesitantly from Arianne to Tancred. He faced his brother and for the first time honestly wondered if Tancred was telling the truth about their parents' deaths. Arianne's words gave him much to consider.

"Nay," Richard finally answered. "I cannot lie to help you. I will not admit to something I had no part in, even if you have been wrongly accused."

"Not even to save her life?" Tancred asked, nodding at Arianne.

"I cannot sin one sin to cover another," Richard replied. The pain in his face was as evident as the fear in his wife's.

"You would not tell a lie to ensure that this fair lady's life be spared?"

Richard stared deeply into Arianne's eyes, and Arianne lost her fear. God was her strength and the source of hope that she prayed for. Richard had taught her that, and because of his strong convictions, he wouldn't, nay, he couldn't, cast those beliefs aside, not even for her.

She nodded ever so slightly, telling Richard with her eyes that she understood.

"I'm sorry, Tancred," Richard spoke sincerely. "I cannot break a vow to God or tell a lie, even in order to save Arianne's life. I would gladly trade my own for hers, however, and beseech you to let her go."

Arianne watched brother confront brother, wondering which would back down first. She had no doubt that Richard was completely devoted to his faith in God. Tancred, too, was devoted, but to an entirely different cause. A cause that Arianne couldn't hope to understand.

"I can see that you are going to be most difficult to deal with," Tancred finally spoke, and his words were edged with controlled anger.

"Henry would never believe that I, of my own free will, came forward to clear your name. He knows about this attack. Some of his own elite guard accompanied me to take back my castle. No matter what I say or do, Henry will know that I do only that which has been imposed upon me."

Arianne felt the heaviness of her husband's heart. The longing to free her was revealed in his eyes, and she silently prayed that God would give him direction so that the matter could be concluded without bloodshed.

"So you will not help me?" Tancred questioned slowly.

Richard shook his head. "Nay, I cannot."

"Even if it means the life of your duchess?" It was as though Tancred couldn't believe Richard would actually walk away from a chivalrous fight to defend the honor and life of one he loved.

"I did not say I would not fight for her," Richard replied, his eyes narrowing as deep furrows lined his brow. "I will give my life for hers. Let her go and face me as a man."

"I control you through her," Tancred replied, toying with the edge of the blade he held.

"Then kill her," Richard said in a cold, almost indifferent voice. "For one who declares himself incapable of murder, you certainly hide behind its threats often enough. Mercifully slay her now and be done with it."

Arianne's mouth dropped open. She stared at Richard in horror, wondering what he was about. Tancred was so shocked that he pricked his finger on the blade before drawing Arianne tightly to his side.

"What's the matter?" Richard asked his brother. "Haven't ye the stomach for the task?"

"I have no desire to slay her," Tancred replied. "I am no cold-blooded killer."

"Then let her go," Richard insisted.

"Will you assure me safe passage from this place if I do?"

Richard's face contorted in anger. "Why should I?" His words were low and even as he fought to control his rage.

"I will go back into my exile," Tancred answered. "I will seek out another way to clear my name."

"You mean that you will plot my death in another manner, don't you?"

Arianne could remain silent no longer. "Please," she said, lifting her eyes to meet her husband's. "Let him go and be done with this."

"He deserves to pay for the attack on my home and people. Not to mention that he has laid his hand upon you, causing great harm. Nay, he will not go free."

"But, Richard," Arianne's voice was filled with pleading, "he will not give himself over. Without spilling his blood and taking his life, your brother will continue this stalemate."

"Then I will end this now," Richard said, raising his own sword.

"Nay, Richard," Arianne cried out, completely ignoring the blade that Tancred held. "His soul is not safe from the fires of eternal damnation. Would you have his blood on your head, when by mercy you could let him live to accept salvation through our Lord Jesus?" By the look on Richard's face, Arianne knew her words had hit their mark.

Tancred was at a loss to understand the battle of wills that raged inside his brother. He only knew that Richard's wife seemed desirous to save his life.

"You would be no better than those who murdered our parents," Tancred offered.

Richard looked at his brother, then sheathed his sword. "I thought you believed me the culprit of that deed."

"Nay," Tancred replied with a laugh, knowing he had the upper hand. "I never thought one so soft-hearted could be capable of using a knife for much more than threats."

Richard's hand went back to the hilt of his sword, but Arianne shook her head. "He provokes you, Husband. Be not concerned with his tongue, but remember his soul."

Richard was amazed at Arianne's calm. She had learned so well his love of God and desire that all mankind would come to be saved that there was no doubt who would win this hand.

Tancred, too, sensed the control Arianne's words had upon her husband. What troubled him was the effect those soft-spoken words had upon his own heart and mind. He had to distance himself from her gentle concern. There was no room for it in this fight.

"Will you let me rejoin my ship?" Tancred finally asked.

Richard stepped back a pace. "Aye."

"And you will give me your oath on the Code of Nobles that you will do nothing to hinder me from passing from your estates?"

"I give you my word. You may leave to return to your exile," Richard promised. "Release Arianne and I will guide you through the tunnels to your ship."

Tancred shook his head, not trusting his brother. "Nay, Arianne knows the way, for obviously this is the means by which she escaped me before. She will guide me to the ship so that no harm will befall me."

Richard's clenched fists were clear signs of his displeasure, but before he could open his mouth, Arianne lifted her hand.

"I will show him the way, Richard. God will not see me suffer at his hands anymore. Put into practice that faith that so strengthens those around you." Her words were peaceful balm on the wounds of Richard's heart. God was in charge of the matter, as Arianne so simply had reminded him.

It went against everything he'd ever known, but Richard backed away and, making a sweeping bow, gave his brother what he demanded. "Arianne will lead you. I will arrange for your men to be at the ship, but mark my words, dear brother, my men will be there also." Then almost as an afterthought, Richard added, "As will I."

Tancred offered his brother a mocking salute. "I will see you at the ship, then."

Richard nodded and met Arianne's eyes. "I will come for you, my sweet Arianne. Fear naught, for God is your protector and keeper."

Arianne nodded, feeling complete peace in the matter. God would see her through this, and nothing Tancred could do or say would change how fully she had come to understand her heavenly Father's power. God was in control of the matter, she reasoned. Therefore, Tancred had no power over her life.

"Come along," Arianne bid Tancred. If they didn't move out, she feared, Richard might change his mind.

Chapter 17

he harsh dampness of the tunnels made Arianne shiver. She longed to pull the torch closer to her body for warmth, but Tancred seemed unconcerned with her plight and hurried her forward.

Nearing the tunnel opening, Arianne could hear the crashing waves on the rocks below like a great churning caldron. She wondered if the beach would be covered and if they would have to climb the rocks. Silently, she offered a prayer for strength, knowing that of her own accord she could never make it.

"We are nearly outside," Arianne whispered to the man beside her.

"Aye, I hear the sea," replied Tancred.

"It must be difficult to leave again."

"I beg your pardon?"

Arianne swallowed hard. Had she the bravery to continue this conversation? "I was only saying that it must be painful to leave your home again."

"Gavenshire is not my home. It was awarded to my brother after his faithful service to Henry. My lands were well to the south," Tancred replied with uncharacteristic softness.

"Does my husband also control those?"

"Nay, he didn't want them, so Henry took them," Tancred answered. Light from the tunnel opening guided their steps. "Hurry thy pace that we may reach my ship before Richard."

"Richard will have little trouble getting there ahead of us," Arianne replied. "We still have to climb down to the beach, or if the water is too high, we must climb up the cliffside. 'Twill be no easy matter for me, I assure you."

"You'll have plenty of time to rest once we're aboard my ship."

Arianne stopped dead in her tracks. Tancred was quite serious. "You mean to take me after giving Richard your word that you would leave me unharmed?"

"I don't intend to harm you," Tancred replied softly. He looked at Arianne with new eyes. "I am most sorry for the way I've treated you in the past, but it was necessary to take control. You must believe me. I will see my name cleared, and I will use whatever means I must in order to do just that."

"But you cannot hope to take me!" exclaimed Arianne. "Richard will never allow it."

"My brother loves you more than life," Tancred said, putting out the torch in the sandy soil of the tunnel floor. "I can count on that."

Arianne said nothing more. Tancred pulled her out into the sunlight and surveyed the scene.

"There is adequate clearance for us to take to the shore. We will be quick enough, and my ship is no more than a half a league around the bend. Come along, milady."

Arianne's mind mulled over Tancred's plan even as he assisted her down the rocky path. She was amazed at the change in his attitude toward her. Perhaps the words she'd spoken had made him think about his plight. Perhaps no one had ever cared to defend him before.

"Sir Tancred," Arianne said, fighting with the skirt of her gown, "I do not fear you any longer."

The words seemed a bold declaration under the circumstances, but Tancred was not offended. He glanced over his shoulder at her with a smile so similar to Richard's that Arianne was stunned.

"It is well that you do not," Tancred replied. "I have no need for more enemies. I perceive that you see something of value in this exiled hide of mine. I do, however, require that you replace what once was fear with a healthy respect for my will. I am not a puppet to be played with, milady, and in spite of my brother's pliability, you will not find me a character to be dallied with."

"You have much to overcome, sire," Arianne replied thoughtfully. "I must believe that you were reared to fear God as Richard was. I must further believe from the stories my husband has told that you, too, must have listened to stories at your mother's knee."

"Speak not of my mother," Tancred said in a warning tone. "I will not hear of it."

"She must have loved you greatly," Arianne dared to continue. "I have heard Matilda speak of her."

"Enough!" Tancred said harshly and yanked Arianne's arm.

Arianne remained silent while they worked their way down to the beach. Tancred handed her down onto the shore without comment and pulled her in lengthy strides along the water's edge.

Arianne was gasping for breath by the time they reached the place where Tancred's ship was anchored. On the beach, a small boat with six men awaited Tancred's arrival.

Tightening his grip on Arianne, Tancred moved forward. In a flash, Richard stepped out from behind the rocks and, with him, over a dozen of his own men.

"Halt there!" he called to Tancred. "Release my wife and take to your ship."

Tancred took two more steps then stopped, pulling Arianne to his side. "I'm taking her with me. She will be my guarantee of safety from Henry and from your wrath."

"Try to take her and you will know more of my wrath than you had ever thought possible." Richard's words held a deadly tone.

Arianne's heart pounded at the scene unfolding before her. If she could not do something to assuage the tempers of these men, she could well be a widow by nightfall.

"I beg of you, Tancred," she whispered, then turned to her husband. "Please, Richard, let this thing be at peace between you. Your brother knows naught of God and His mercy. You are God's witness to that mercy and love. If you do not show forth the light of God's truth, how will Tancred come to know it?"

"I am not his salvation," Richard replied, his eyes never leaving Tancred's stony face.

"'Tis true you are not his salvation, but you have knowledge of the way to that salvation that has been forsaken or forgotten by your brother."

Richard's face was etched in pain. The truth of Arianne's words affected him in a way he couldn't explain. For so many years he had carried blind hatred for the man before him, certain that Tancred had been responsible for the deaths of their parents. But maybe Arianne was right. Perhaps Tancred had no responsibility in the murders. Maybe it was time to let go of his hatred.

"King Henry has etched in the walls of his palaces words that are most eloquent and true," Richard murmured. Tancred and Arianne waited in silence for him to continue. "It reads, 'He who does not give what he has will not get what he wants.' I must give up my hatred in order to find the peace that I desire."

"Will you let me pass?" Tancred asked. His grip tightened on Arianne, causing her to wince painfully.

"Not with my wife. You may leave, and I freely give you your men and ship, but you will never leave English soil with Arianne. She is my wife and will remain here with me," Richard stated firmly.

Arianne held her breath, wondering what Tancred's reply would be. Without a word, Tancred pulled Arianne with him as he began to edge around Richard.

"I am no fool, dear brother. You could easily send your men to cut me down. With Arianne, I will have my assurance that you will behave in a gentlemanly manner and honor your word."

"You will not take her," Richard restated, and the sound of his sword being freed from the scabbard rang clear for all ears.

Tancred stopped as Richard raised his sword, but it was Arianne who stunned them both into silence. With a strength she'd not known she possessed, Arianne wrenched herself free from Tancred's grip and threw herself between Tancred and Richard.

"You will be no better than him," Arianne whispered desperately to her husband. "You cannot murder him, for his soul will haunt you for all eternity. You will always know that he died without God's forgiveness and that, had you been merciful, Tancred might have lived to accept God."

The tip of Richard's sword pointed to Arianne's breast. Dumbfounded at her words, he didn't know how to respond.

Tancred, too, stood frozen in place. He was mesmerized by the young woman who so gallantly defended his right to live. He was troubled by her words of God's forgiveness, but he couldn't bring himself to betray the longing they stirred within.

"Please," Arianne begged, as the wind tore at her copper hair. Several strands fell across the raised blade, bringing Richard back to his senses.

"Go," Richard told his brother, lowering the sword slowly.

Tancred reached out for Arianne, but before Richard could move, Arianne turned to face her brother-in-law.

"Nay, Tancred," she whispered. "I will not go with you freely, and you will not force me. There is something of value within you, something yet redeemable and good. You are harsh and troubled, and there is much that you must confess before God, but you have my forgiveness for the evil you have done me. Let that be your starting place. Remember Henry's words with respect for their value, even if you cannot respect the man."

Tancred stared at Arianne and saw compassion in her eyes. It was the first time in many years that he had experienced such sincerity and generosity of spirit. He quickly stepped back as though being too near her caused him greater pain. Lifting his face to meet Richard's, he saw that Arianne's words had also humbled his brother.

Arianne moved into Richard's waiting arms. She relished the warmth and safety found there and sighed with relief as he pulled her close.

"And what of you, Brother?" Tancred suddenly found his tongue. "Have I your forgiveness as well?"

"Do you seek it?" Richard questioned without sarcasm.

Tancred was taken aback only for a moment. Richard's forgiveness was something he desired almost more than the reinstatement of his land and title. How could he have been so blinded by fury and hatred to have expected his brother to lie, even give his life up, in order to free him from exile?

"I came here to seek my freedom," Tancred answered, and the sadness in his voice was not lost on the young couple before him. "I know naught of the peace you know in God. Mayhap in time it will be shown to me in the same manner it has been revealed to you. Mayhap I will lay to rest the demons from the past." He paused and shook his head. "I know naught what manner of woman you have married, Brother, but she is like none I have ever known. Do not consider her lightly, for there are few like her."

Richard smiled down at the woman in his arms. "Aye," he whispered, "I know it well."

Tancred turned to leave and then, remembering his brother's question, paused. "I did not slay our parents. Perhaps my negligence of them somehow aided in the deed, but not because I chose it to be so. I did not kill them."

Richard sobered and nodded. "I believe you." Deep peace filled his heart as Richard realized he meant the words in full.

"Then will you give me your forgiveness?" Tancred questioned.

"Aye," Richard replied. "You are free from my hatred. I desire nothing more than you live out your days in peace and in the true understanding of God's love." Then Richard added, "Will you forgive me?"

Tancred said nothing for several moments. He saw a truly great man in his brother, and it was difficult for him to realize that had things been different, they might have stood side by side.

"Aye," Tancred said. "You have my forgiveness." Without another word, he turned and waded into the water. There was no fear that Richard would have him murdered or waylaid en route to his exile. After a brief salute, Tancred climbed into the boat and never looked back.

Chapter 18

That night, Arianne sat deep in thought beside the hearth in their bed chamber. Staring into the fire, she wondered at the differences between Richard and his brother. What drove men to such contrasts? A noise behind her caused Arianne to look up only to find Richard's intense green eyes watching her.

"You creep more silently than the night itself," Arianne mused, then felt a warm blush edge her cheeks. Suddenly she felt very shy. The look on Richard's face stirred her heart and quickened her breath.

Richard crossed the room and pulled his wife against him. "I've missed you more dearly than anything else these walls could offer." He lowered his face to her hair and breathed in the unmistakable scent of Arianne's favorite soap. The long coppery curls wrapped around his fingers as he plunged his hands into the bulk. "You are perfection on earth," he sighed.

Arianne lifted her face from his chest with a mischievous grin. "I was thinking much the same of you," she admitted, causing Richard to chuckle.

"'Tis most grateful I am to have married a cunning, intelligent woman. Milady, you are a most precious jewel to me, and as long as I live, I will love no other."

Arianne reached up her hand to touch the neatly trimmed beard. "My heart's true love," she whispered.

Her brown eyes held the promise of a life of love, and in their reflection Richard found all that he had ever longed for. Gently, as though afraid the spell would be broken, Richard lowered his lips to Arianne's and kissed her with all the longing that had been denied them both. With his world once again at peace, Richard intended to concentrate on the fact that he and Arianne were yet newly wed.

Weeks blended into months, and Arianne knew a peace and contentment that was like nothing she'd ever imagined possible. Life with Richard was so much more than the routine tasks of the day. She never failed to be warmed by the glint in his eyes when he lifted his gaze from the company of his men to take note of her when she entered a room. Nor could she begin to understand the wonder of lying in his arms at night, feeling the rhythmic beat of his heart against her hand as it lay in casual possession of Richard's chest.

Forgotten were the days of her father's brutality and rage, for in Richard's care, Arianne knew nothing more than the firm correction in his voice when she erred and the loving approval of his smile when she caused him great pride in something new she'd learned. There were still unanswered questions about his parents' deaths, but Arianne's only unfulfilled desire was to see her brother, Devon.

"Arianne!" Richard called from the great hall. "Arianne!"

Arianne rose from her work in the solarium and went in search of her husband. Matilda met her in the hall with a smile broader than the river that flowed nearby.

"Your Grace," she said with a light curtsey. "The duke will be most pleased to see you."

"And what has he to show me this time?" Arianne questioned with teasing in her voice. "The last time he arrived home with this much excitement, he brought me news that the king intended to receive us as guests. Pray tell, what could top that?"

Matilda smiled knowingly but said nothing as she hurried Arianne to the stone stairway. Arianne knew better than to question her maid, for when Matilda wanted to keep something to herself, she did so quite well.

Arianne lifted her skirts ever so slightly and in a most unladylike fashion hurried her descent. She hadn't reached the final step, however, before Richard reached out and lifted her into the air. Swinging her round and round until Arianne begged him to put her down, Richard couldn't contain his joy.

"What have you done this time?" Arianne asked with a grin.

"I have brought you a gift, milady," he replied, taking her hand in his own. "And I believe it will meet wholeheartedly with your approval."

"Most everything you do meets with my approval," replied Arianne.

Richard raised an eyebrow and stopped in midstep. "Only most everything?"

"Well, there was that problem with the puppies you brought into our bed chamber," Arianne laughed, remembering an incident several days past.

"Who knew they could move so fast!" Richard said in his defense. "Besides, I caught them all again, didn't I?"

"True," Arianne nodded, trying to be serious, "but not before they'd tracked mud all over the room and threatened to raise the roof with their yipping and howls."

"Well, this time there will be no tracking of mud and no yipping or howling," Richard promised, pulling Arianne along with him once again.

"We shall see," she mused with a wifely air.

Entering the great hall, Arianne could see that nothing looked amiss. She glanced up curiously to catch her husband's eye, but Richard refused to give away his secret.

"Sit here," he commanded lovingly and assisted Arianne into a chair. "Now close your eyes."

Arianne's brow wrinkled ever so slightly, and a smile played at the edge of her lips. "The last time you told me to do that—" Her words were cut off, however, when Richard insisted she be obedient.

"Hurry, now, or you'll spoil everything."

Arianne shook her head in mock exasperation but nevertheless closed her eyes.

"Are they closed tight?" Richard asked her.

"Yes," she replied. "They are closed as tight as I can close them. Now will you please tell me what's going on?"

"In a minute. I've almost got it ready," Richard answered.

"Remember your promise," teased Arianne while she waited in her self-imposed darkness.

"What promise was that, my dear?"

"No mud, no yipping, no howls," she said, laughing in spite of her struggle to remain serious.

"I promise," came a voice that did not belong to her husband. "You will get no such scene from me."

Arianne's heart skipped a beat. Her eyes flashed open wide to greet the vaguely familiar face of her brother. "Devon!" she cried and threw herself into his waiting arms.

"You are an enchanting sight for such weary eyes," Devon said, squeezing Arianne tightly. "We've been separated far too long."

"I can't believe you are truly here," Arianne replied and stepped back to search the room for Richard. He was leaning against the table with his arms folded against his chest and a broad grin on his face.

"I told you it would meet with your approval."

"Richard, you are indeed a wonder. However did you find him, and whatever possessed you to bring him here?" Arianne asked, returning her gaze to Devon.

"You spoke of him so often, I thought he might as well be here in body, as well as spirit. Henry had him in service elsewhere, but then Henry has always had a soft spot in his heart for me." Richard seemed quite pleased with himself, and Arianne broke away from Devon's side to embrace her husband.

"You are a man of many talents, Your Grace," she murmured against his ear before placing a light kiss upon his cheek.

Richard pulled her close, winking at Devon over her shoulder. "I knew this would make up for the puppies." He grinned.

Devon and Arianne both laughed at this. "I will never bring up the subject of the puppies again," Arianne promised. Her heart was overflowing with the love and happiness she felt at that moment. "How long can you stay, Devon?" she questioned, knowing that she might not like the answer.

"That depends on you," Devon replied with a knowing glance at Richard.

"On me?" Arianne's confusion was clear.

"Aye," Devon said with a nod. "How long will you have me?"

Arianne moved to her brother, pulling Richard along with her. "I'd have you here forever," she answered and looped her free arm through Devon's.

"That might be pressing it, my love." Richard's voice held a tone of teasing. "Why not just until King Henry rewards him with lands of his own for the service he's so faithfully given?"

Arianne could not have looked more pleased. "Truly?" she asked. "Truly, Henry is going to bestow a title upon him?"

"'Tis true enough," Richard replied. "But, until then, Devon is our guest and—"

Devon interrupted, "And your most humble servant, milady."

"Nay," Arianne said, shaking her head. "Never that. Just a long lost soul who has finally come home to those who love him." The pleasure on her face was clear. "And for that I truly thank God, King Henry, and my most tenderhearted husband."

Later that evening, Arianne sought out Richard in their bed chamber. He had just finished with his bath and was donning one of the lined tunics she'd made for him.

"These have worked like a wonder," he commented. "I don't think I've ever had a chance to thank you properly for the thoughtfulness of your work."

Arianne smiled. "It was a task I took to with a glad heart, for I knew it would be well received."

"Aye, that it has. I see that Devon, too, has been well received."

"Oh, most assuredly. Richard, I cannot tell you what it means to me to have him here. I have missed him sorely and look forward to rekindling our friendship. Already he has shared many great stories of his adventures."

"What of your father?" Richard asked softly. "Has he given you word of him?"

"Nay," Arianne replied and walked away to the window. "But, neither have I asked. 'Tis a difficult matter. I am glad my father is not alone, and I pray his new wife makes him happy. I hold him no malice. I simply wish to forget the sorrow."

"No doubt your mother's passing grieved him in a way that left him unable to deal with his children properly," Richard said from behind her.

"Mayhap he grieved that she never loved him," Arianne replied without turning. "He always knew, and in spite of the fact that he never told her, I believe my father loved my mother."

"Hopefully things will be different this time. Devon tells me your stepmother will bear him a child."

Arianne turned and stared at her husband in surprise. "Is this true?"

"Aye," Richard said. He sat down on the edge of the bed and awaited Arianne's response to the news.

"When?" she questioned so softly that Richard nearly missed the word.

"Devon tells me the babe should be born after Hocktide at the end of Easter."

Arianne completely surprised Richard as a mischievous grin spread across her face. "Good," she said, folding her arms against her body. "I shall beat her by a fortnight, at least."

Richard stared dumbly for a moment, not fully understanding the news his wife had just shared.

Arianne continued before he could question her. "Matilda tells me we should expect to become parents in the spring." Anticipation and joy radiated from Arianne's countenance.

Richard shook his head as if trying to awaken from a dream. "Parents?" he questioned, coming to his feet. "You're going to give me a child? How long have you known?"

Arianne giggled like a little girl with a secret. "I've only just learned this myself, Your Grace. But you will admit, 'tis a surprise that ranks at least as high as puppies."

At this Richard's laughter filled the chamber. He lifted Arianne in his arms and hugged her tightly. "Madam, it most assuredly surpasses all my other surprises. I am most pleased at this news. God has given me all that a man could want and then doubled it. My joy truly knows no bounds."

Arianne sighed against the warmth of her husband. "I feel the same, and had I not been forced by the king into marriage with you, I would never have known what a truly remarkable man you are. And had you been any less remarkable, I would never have known what true love was about. You have given me much, Richard. A child, a home, a loving companion for life, but even more: you opened my eyes to the love of God. A love that reigns here," she whispered and placed his hand over her heart, "because one man heard the soft call of His master's voice above the roar of men's."

"Sweet Arianne," Richard murmured, lifting his hand to cup her chin. "In the stillness of His love, we will heed His call together. All of our lives we will face the future knowing that He has seen what is to come and walks the path beside us. There will be no kingdom divided or heart destroyed, so long as we keep our steps with Him."

Tracie Peterson, bestselling, award-winning author of over ninety fiction titles and three nonfiction books, lives and writes in Belgrade, Montana. As a Christian, wife, mother, writer, editor, and speaker (in that order), Tracie finds her slate quite full. Published in magazines and Sunday school take-home papers, as well as a columnist for a Christian newspaper, Tracie now focuses her attention on novels. After signing her first contract with Barbour Publishing in 1992, her novel, *A Place To Belong*, appeared in 1993 and the rest is history. She has over twenty-six titles with Heartsong Presents' book club (many of which have been repackaged) and stories in six separate anthologies from Barbour. From Bethany House Publishing, Tracie has multiple historical three-book series as well as many stand-alone contemporary women's fiction stories and two nonfiction titles. Other titles include two historical series cowritten with Judith Pella, one historical series cowritten with James Scott Bell, and multiple historical series cowritten with Judith Miller.

Alas, My Love

Tracie Peterson

To Dr. Doug Iliff, physician extraordinaire and good friend. With thanks for his time, trouble, and good sense of humor when I call up with those pesky questions.

Chapter 1

The Middle Ages

elena Talbot held back a strangled cry as the whip came down again. Her tender skin, marred with bleeding welts, bore yet another strike. Would it never end?

Stripped to her lightest linen tunic, Helena received the punishment of her defiance without a word of protest. Twenty years old, without mother or father in this world, Helena faced her stepbrother's demands and temper.

"Will you go?" Roger Talbot questioned, and again Helena shook her head.

He grimaced and raised the whip, while Helena steadied herself as best she could. Her strength had given out hours ago, so she stood on sheer determination alone. She longed for the dizziness to overtake her and put her mind from the whip's biting edge. Even death would be a welcome relief.

"Your refusal has caused this grief," he said firmly but with a hint of gentleness to his tone. "I find no pleasure in punishment." Helena believed it to be true. At one time, she and Roger had been the closest of friends.

"I. . .I cannot." Helena wanted so very much to sound brave, but in truth her words were barely audible. Through fading consciousness, she knew his displeasure. Poor man. If not for his sister Maude, Roger would never have forced the situation. Maude's jealousy had tainted Roger's love. For over twenty years, Maude had loudly protested the interference of Helena's mother, Eleanor, and then of Helena herself. With Eleanor only days in the grave and the words of her funeral service still ringing in Helena's ears, Roger found no way to ignore Maude's demands.

"Give her over to the church," Maude had told him in a hushed whisper while Helena cried over her mother's still body. "Send her with haste."

They believed me too grieved to understand, Helena thought. Even then she'd known this would be a bitter battle to the end.

A chilled, damp wind blew across the newly plowed fields. The rich aroma of dirt assailed Helena's meager senses. Home! At least the only home she'd ever known. Now with her beloved mother and stepfather both dead, no one was left who cared for her. No one except perhaps Tanny. Images from the past flooded her mind to offer comfort.

Helena, oblivious to Roger's consternation, slumped against the whipping post. As she did, she could feel the braided hemp bite into her wrists. How long had she been there? First, Roger had made her stand for hours, bound to the post and exposed to the elements. After that, he'd deprived her of food and drink, all in hopes that she would acquiesce to his will.

Helena knew, however, that she had a most special circumstance. It was because of this circumstance that Helena remained strong in her resolve, refusing to give even the slightest consideration to her stepbrother and stepsister's plans. Helena smiled to herself, even in her half-conscious state. Her mother, Eleanor, had been second-cousin to the queen. Not only had they been related, but they had also been the dearest friends. Because of this, King Henry III would not hear the demands of Roger Talbot to force a marriage upon his young stepsister. The king had instead listened to his wife and Eleanor in their pleading to allow Helena to marry, not as customary in an arranged affair, but for love.

And Helena had loved. With all her heart, she had loved a man who barely knew of her existence. She didn't blame him, though. When last he'd seen her, she had been a mere child of nine, but her love for him was eternal.

"Tanny," she breathed the name, not realizing she'd done so aloud.

"What say you?" Roger stepped forward anxiously. "I demand you speak to me."

Helena's head bobbed and swayed in rhythm with the wind. She barely heard Roger's words. She tried to move, but the fire in her back caused her to gasp for breath before surrendering to the black oblivion her mind offered. Her fading thoughts were of her beloved. Tanny!

"Helena!" Roger rushed forward, afraid that he'd dealt her one blow too many. How many times had he hit her? Five? Six? He reached out for her crumpled form and lifted her upward in order to release her bonds from the overhead hook. God alone would be his refuge if Henry learned of this matter.

"Helena," he spoke once more, this time against her ear. Roger had no way of knowing whether she heard him.

Cursing, he called for help. "Take her to her room," he said to two men who waited nearby. Then turning to Helena's maid, Sarah, he added, "Make her comfortable and cleanse the wounds."

The woman nodded her reddened face. "Aye, milord. 'Tis my duty."

Helena writhed and moaned as Sarah gently rubbed salve into her wounds. *Thanks be to the Creator,* Sarah thought, *the cuts are not deep.* Still it grieved her, and tears rolled down her weathered cheeks.

Sarah, still crying in soft sobs, dressed the wounds as best she could. Her poor lamb did not deserve the heavy hand of her stepbrother.

"Hush now, my little one." Sarah sprinkled a concoction of herbs over the worst of the cuts and offered what consolation she could. "No one will hurt you now."

"Tanny," Helena whispered. "I. . .I want Tanny."

Sarah struggled to make out the words but knew without a doubt that Helena was speaking of her one true love.

"Just rest, milady. 'Tis sure that your love will come one day. Just rest." Sarah spoke the words even if she didn't believe them. She prayed they would comfort the young woman and give her peace of mind.

In her strange state of dreams, Helena saw the face of the man she'd loved. Gentle, dark eyes teased her with winks, and a laughing face crowded out the memory of the burning pain in her back. She imagined her beloved returning from the sea. His longing would match her own, and she would rush to his side and proclaim her love. She would write a song for him, she thought through the haze of her sleep. Yes, she would write him a love song.

For as long as she could remember, Helena had been devoted to music. She wrote songs and sang them, always finding a closeness with God when she did so. She devoted most of her music to the goodness and wonder of God and His creation. But some songs, little snippets really, were devoted to more emotional and personal matters. She'd written half a dozen songs to declare her love to a man who thought her only capable of child's play.

Smiling to herself now, Helena imagined the days when they were all together; a time when her stepfather had been alive and Tanny had fostered in their home. She had been but a tiny child then, still under her nurse's care.

"What a frightful sight you are!" It was Tanny's voice she heard, just as clearly as if it had been yesterday. She had been playing in the barn and was covered in a variety of things, some most disagreeable and odorous. Roger and Tanny had found her and knew that her nursemaid would beat her for disobeying and visiting with the animals.

"You've been to the mews as well," Roger had said, picking bird feathers from her hair. The young men agreed to clean her up and keep the nurse from learning of her actions. And that was when Helena had lost her heart. Sitting on Tanny's lap while he used a wet cloth to wipe her face, she had stared into his kind eyes and fallen in love.

A sound at the door brought Helena awake and surprisingly clear-headed. Maude and Roger entered the room, heavy in discussion on the matter of Helena's beating. Helena pretended to sleep but watched cautiously from barely opened eyes. No sense in letting them nag her just yet.

"You've softened in your old age," Maude said to Roger. "She hardly looks worse for the ordeal."

He stared at her a moment in disbelief. "Did you not see the marks?" He waved a hand over Helena. "Henry will have me swinging from a gibbet."

His frown deepened, and he moved away to the window where Helena couldn't see him. "I did as you bade me, Maude. I starved the child and forced her to endure more punishment than our father would have dealt out to a wayward villein."

"Our father was a weakling when it came to Helena. He pampered and spoiled her at every turn." Maude's gray eyes narrowed. "Have ye our father's heart?"

"Our father had no heart for unjust affairs, and neither do I. I would hardly call this a pampering."

Helena wanted to cheer Roger's retort. Maude always bullied him, and Helena hated the way he allowed her to dominate their home.

"You have endured Helena's childish demands that she be allowed to choose her own husband, but honestly, Roger." Maude paused to emphasize the emotion of the moment. "She is a woman of a full score. What man would take her now?"

Roger laughed aloud. "Helena could have any suitor she wanted. 'Tis this that grieves you most, me thinks." Helena almost giggled at this and quickly moaned and coughed to disguise her reaction.

Roger came to her bedside, but Maude remained where she stood. "Helena? Can you hear me?" Helena let out another moan but refused to offer anything more.

Let him think I'm nearly dead, she thought. *Then maybe the fear of what he's done will sink in and he'll stand up to Maude.*

Maude gave Roger no time to consider the matter, however. "Even the king cannot expect you to continue responsibility for one so wayward."

"The king will expect me to heed his wishes."

"But she is past marriageable age," Maude protested, coming within Helena's view.

"So are you, my dear sister. Or have you forgotten you hold seven years in addition to Helena's twenty? Age has not stopped you from looking for another husband."

Maude grimaced. "But I am a widow. My status is more favorable for a union."

Roger sighed. "I have done what you asked of me. I beat the child, and still she refused."

"Then have her taken away," Maude said menacingly. "Have her taken away tonight before she regains enough strength to object."

Helena felt her breath catch. Would Roger actually listen to Maude and do as she suggested? If that happened, what hope would there ever be of finding Tanny or of him finding her?

"And bear the wrath of King Henry? When he learns of this, I will be lucky to retain my life, much less my title." Helena felt Roger's hand upon her forehead. He smoothed back her hair, and Helena couldn't resist feeling some pity for him.

Maude viewed the entire matter disdainfully. She clucked her tongue. "Poor brother. The responsibilities put upon your shoulders are too great. I shall ease your burden and make the arrangements myself. She will be removed tonight."

"I am lord of this manor and you are but my sister. Bide thy tongue carefully, or it will be you who makes the journey to the abbey." With that he turned and stomped out of the room, while Maude stared after him.

"Think to threaten me, will you? Ha!" Maude stated to no one in particular. She let her gaze travel to Helena. "Precious Helena. Exalted child. You had but to crook your finger at anyone, be it man, woman, or child, and they would quickly come to do your bidding." Helena's body trembled. Maude's tone was so menacing and hate filled. Would she go so far as to see Helena permanently removed from her life?

"You are just like your mother," Maude said, her face contorted in rage. "The best of everything came to you both, even though I was here first. You stole my place and took my father's love."

Helena moaned and pretended to be struggling to wake up. She hoped Maude would see this and decide to leave before her stepsister became conscious, but it was not to be.

"Poor Helena. Do your injuries cause you pain? I pray they do. I pray you find the same pain I did. The same pain you and your perfect mother dealt me as a child of seven. I was sent away," she muttered, still staring down at Helena's pale form. "They sent me away to foster in a convent, while you remained to nibble at my father's heart until there was naught left for me. Now I will send you away, and there will be no one to mourn your passing."

"Maude!" It was Roger calling from the hall below. "Maude!"

"We will settle this matter yet," Maude whispered and withdrew from the room to leave Helena trembling and afraid.

It was as if the angry words had taken what little strength Helena had. "What am I to do, Lord?" Her whispered voice was little more than a croak.

In the hall, Maude paced out a pattern on the rush-covered floor. Fresh herbs had been mixed in with the rushes just that morning, but the damp, stale odor of the closed-up manor hung thick in the air. It only served to add to Maude's restlessness. She had come at her brother's demanding calls but found instead that he'd been distracted by a grooms-man who needed his advice regarding the saddle sores of one of his cherished horses.

"I wait to do Roger's bidding, while he concerns himself with dung heaps and festering wounds," she muttered. Then as if speaking his name could suddenly conjure his form, Roger crashed through the door. It had started to rain, and he was soaked from the exposure.

"Prepare me hot ale," he said to a waiting servant. The man nodded and hurried away to do his master's bidding. After the servant disappeared behind the screens that divided the kitchen from the great hall, Roger finally acknowledged Maude.

"'Twill be a beastly night," he remarked, casting his drenched garde-corp to a peg beside the door. Freed of this outer coat, Roger found his remaining clothes to be fairly dry.

Maude motioned him to the far side of the room as tables were brought out and set up in preparation for the supper meal. Maude spoke in a low, hushed tone. "I can arrange for Helena to be taken from this house and delivered to the convent. You are the final authority, of course," she said to placate him.

"You would send her out in this storm?" Roger questioned.

"Nay, 'tis unnecessary to endanger the horses," Maude replied. She knew the lives of his horses were of the utmost concern to her brother.

Maude noticed Roger's uneasy frown. "Fret not, brother dear," she said in feigned sympathy, "the life of a nun is quite good. Our sister will be well cared for and work only six of a day's hours. And those hours will be spent in choir practice—singing as she so loves to do. With a voice such as Helena has been given, surely she will be happy with her life there."

"'Tis not her choice," Roger spoke absentmindedly.

Maude could see that he was not giving her his total attention. "Helena should have no choice. No other woman would, but because of Lady Eleanor's constant nagging—"

"Now you insult the dead?" Roger interrupted. He paused only long enough to retrieve the drink offered him by a young boy. "'Twas my under-standing," he said, pausing to draw deeply from the tankard, "that we put Lady Eleanor to rest. Must you constantly bring her back?"

Maude scowled. "Indeed not. I seek to dismiss her presence once and for all. 'Tis you, milord, who keeps her walking the rooms of this pitiful manor. Send Helena away and bury them both."

Roger frowned into his cup. "King Henry will still question Helena's disappearance. With Eleanor gone, no doubt the queen would call for Helena to attend her in court. Would that not suffice?"

"Never!" Maude's screech caused a young woman to drop several empty mugs. The girl hastened to retrieve the still-clattering mess, while Maude lowered her voice. "Never. Helena would punish us both for what has happened. No, send her away with instructions to all that she has taken a vow of silence. Even the king will not question her choice of mourning."

"I will consider it," Roger said. The inviting aroma of beef stew, mutton pies, and roast pigeon caused him to wave away Maude's protests. "First we will sup; then we will reason out the matter of Helena."

Maude nodded, following Roger to the table. Neither one of them saw Helena's crumpled form at the top of the stairs. With barely enough strength to crawl back to her bed, Helena realized she had to make plans and make them quickly.

"Oh, God, help me," she moaned, throwing herself across the narrow bed. The fiery reminders of her brother's handiwork pierced her and caused her to cry aloud. "God, where are You?"

Chapter 2

Heavy fog blotted out the scenery surrounding the manor and left an eerie silence to engulf the land. The dampness permeated everything, including the clothes and cloak that Helena had been dressed in for her journey.

Without resistance, Helena had allowed the transfer of her body to a makeshift litter. She feigned great weakness and exhaustion while Roger ordered a blanket to be placed over her body. Only Sarah knew that her wounds were quickly healing and that the cloudiness had left her thinking. It was Helena's plan to give them no reason to think her capable of escape.

Helena observed as Roger slipped a coin into the hand of the man that waited near her litter. "Understand this, no longer is harm going to come to her. I will, myself, contact the abbess to learn of her well-being."

"As you wish it, milord," the man replied, revealing a gap where two teeth were missing.

Maude looked on in bored indifference. Helena knew that her stepsister's only concern was that they'd be on their way before Helena regained strength and offered a fight. With deep sadness, Helena closed her eyes.

"Let them be off," Maude finally said.

Helena narrowly opened her eyes to see Roger glance at Maude briefly before nodding. "Aye. Be gone, then." The man gave a curt bow, then motioned his comrade to lead his horse forward.

"I'll await your return," Roger called after the man. "See no harm comes to the horse."

Helena waited to open her eyes full until the stranger who walked at her feet moved forward to speak with his comrade. They were oblivious to her, and for this, Helena rejoiced. Jostling along on the litter, Helena contemplated the situation and wondered when opportunity would lend itself to her escape.

She could not let either the men who accompanied her or Roger know where she had gone. Roger would expect her destination to be London and so it would be. But Helena was smart enough to realize that the direct routes would have to be avoided. She could neither take to the road nor seek out help from other travelers. No, it would be necessary to travel under cover of darkness and stick to the fields and forests. As long as she continued south, all would eventually be well.

As she prayed for guidance, Helena remembered the comfort of bedtime prayers when she'd been a small child. The dark frightened her as little else did, and her mother was good to stay by her side and pray away the gloom. *Oh, Mother,* she thought, wiping out the tears in her eyes, *I'm glad you cannot see me now.*

When the morning sun rose high enough to burn off the fog, Helena remained unmoving and silent. Feigning sleep, she opened her eyes only on occasion to see her surroundings. They were traveling south, and from her brother's directions, Helena knew that the longer she stayed with the men, the closer she'd come to London. However, she also worried about her safety with these coarse, unkempt ruffians. They laughed loudly as they talked together and, from time to time, discussed the crude pleasures they would seek once they'd earned the rest of their pay.

Helena shuddered as she realized she had no protector. Why, her clothes alone could be resold for more than these two could earn in a month. Was there no one who could know her fate should they decide to do her harm? But even as fear stirred her blood, a small voice inside told her that God was her protector as He had always been. Remembering this came as a comfort, and Helena relaxed. God was her protector. It was enough.

She let them believe her asleep until they came to a halt for the night. Only then did she moan out a request for a drink of water.

"Be it well with ye, then?" one of the men asked her.

"I hurt," she managed to whisper. It wasn't a lie.

"Aye," was all he said before seeing to the horse.

After the horse was tethered and cared for, the man who'd spoken to Roger brought Helena a chunk of bread and cheese. He said nothing to her but left the food at her fingertips and took himself off to tend the fire his companion had built.

Helena struggled to sit up. She pulled her cloak tight and ate part of the food given to her. With a watchful eye, she tucked the remaining bread under the surcoat and inside her tunic. She felt strangely at peace with the arrangement. She would watch and pray for the perfect moment to escape, and when she did, she would have food to take along for her journey.

Overhead, the stars were clear and brilliant. They sparkled like diamonds. Helena studied them for a moment and thought of her love. Perhaps wherever he was, he, too, was looking at the stars and thinking of her. Shaking her head sadly, Helena knew it wasn't so. Tanny didn't know she existed. At least not as a woman. No, the Helena he knew existed only as a scrawny, tomboyish child.

"'Tis of no matter," Helena whispered to the starry night. "I hold enough love for us both."

In time, Helena felt herself grow stronger, but for the sake of her companions she continued to feign weakness. Waiting and watching, Helena's patience was rewarded when the opportunity to escape presented itself to her.

"'Tis less than a half-day journey," one of the men stated. They were watering the horse and contemplating whether or not to set up camp.

"I say we push on," the other replied. "The abbey will offer us shelter. Better to keep going and spend the night, even a small portion of it, under a roof than out here in the cold."

"It bodes well with me. We can be there before morning and enjoy a hot meal with our rest."

Helena felt her heart skip a beat. The time had come. She didn't know exactly where they were, but she knew they were well away from Roger and Maude. She contented herself with this while contemplating what to do next.

There were woods on either side of the road that would afford her cover during her escape. There was also the blessing of a cloudless night and moonlight to guide her way. The only real problem was escaping the notice of her companions, but the solution came soon enough.

With the horse slowly plodding along, the first man spoke up. "I say we go to London after the deed is done and our pay is in hand. We can buy our comforts there and gamble for even more."

"London's not fer me. Ye forget I be a marked man there. I say we sail to Normandy. Me sister be there, and we could hold up a spell with her."

"Normandy? I'll have no part of Normandy!" They argued on, their voices rising ever higher with the flaring of their tempers.

Knowing that the debate would block out any noise of her escape, Helena rolled from the litter and lay in silence at the edge of the road. A heady scent of the land rushed up to assail her senses. No doubt the soft dirt would ruin her fine burgundy velvet, but no matter. If she could escape to London, there would always be the opportunity for more velvet.

Helena's breathing quickened as she waited for what seemed an eternity, certain that at any given moment the horse would be halted and the men would come back for her. If they came back, she would simply pretend to be asleep and let them assume that she'd rolled off the litter by mistake.

She squeezed her eyes shut tightly, almost as if in doing so she could make herself invisible. They just had to keep going without her, she thought. This was her only hope. When the noisy argument faded into the distance, Helena realized they were unaware of her absence.

Gingerly sitting up, Helena untangled herself from the blanket that had covered her on the litter. She was grateful for the additional warmth as the night chill seemed to penetrate her bones. *Thanks be to God*, she thought, *that the winter was mild and spring has come early*.

Standing came with more difficulty. She had only been on her feet for short periods of time in the past days. Those times had come only out of necessity to relieve herself, and they were brief and nontaxing. Now, however, she faced the need not only to walk a great distance, but to do so quickly as well. Stretching her limbs, she began to have doubts.

"Oh, God," she whispered to the starry sky overhead, "please be with me. I beg Ye, Lord Father, give me the strength to make this journey." She felt better just in knowing that she would not travel alone.

By the end of her third day and night, Helena was far less confident. She had long since run out of food, and the only water she had was that which she found along the way. Her back, though mostly healed, was stiff and sore, and at times the scabs would rub against the rough material of her tunic.

"I must keep going," she told herself aloud. "Roger's men will find me, and I cannot let that be. I must get to London. I must find Tanny." She remembered her beloved with his dark eyes and tender words. What kindnesses he had shown to Helena as a child were indelibly fixed in her memories.

Skirting a nearby village, Helena walked across the ridges and furrows of a newly plowed field. Exhaustion washed over her like waves claiming a shore. Dropping to her knees, she felt despair claim her. *This is hopeless*, she thought. *I can't go on.*

John Tancred DuBonnet stared at the timber framework of the wattle-and-daub hovel. The wind outside shook it fiercely, and any moment he expected it to give into the force and collapse.

"So fall down upon me," Tancred said, emotion thick in his voice. "At least then my suffering would be done."

He knew deep despair, and the single-room hut with its open floor hearth did nothing to ease his miseries. With something akin to apathy, Tancred reached down to tend the fire. *Why bother*, he thought, *to resurrect a dying flame that offered little warmth and no real comfort?*

Sheltered away from the rest of the world, Tancred faced yet another year of exile from his beloved England. The home he'd once known was long since removed from his grasp, as were his family and friends. Sitting down to the poorly contrived trestle table, he absentmindedly toyed with a wooden bowl of cold pea soup and longed for home.

It had been eleven years since he'd been falsely accused of the murder of his parents. King Henry III of England had listened to the impassioned testimony of Richard, Tancred's younger brother. Richard had found Tancred standing over the bodies of their dead parents, knife in hand, the blood still wet upon the blade.

"Murderer!" Richard had shouted accusingly.

Tancred had pleaded his case, begged for understanding, then listened as his accusers found him guilty. He should rightly have been sentenced to death, but Richard had intervened. Even hatred for his brother could not bring the tenderhearted Richard to support his brother's hanging. He had, instead, encouraged Henry to be merciful. Some mercy!

"Condemned for a deed I had no part of," Tancred muttered. Tancred remembered the blind hatred he had once felt for his brother—hatred that had led him to action. Only last fall, he'd stormed Richard's home in Gavenshire, taken Richard's wife hostage, and later confronted the man who'd been responsible for his painful years of poverty. All for nothing. Tancred's exile continued.

Pushing the dish away, Tancred knew his misery had grown to a level he could no longer abide. Death would be sweet relief from the agony of facing another day. Yet, there was something that kept him from taking his own life. Something planted there in the deepest part of his heart by Richard's wife, Arianne.

"Would that the woman had kept her mouth closed," Tancred moaned, putting his head in his hands. For several minutes he did nothing, then lifting his face again, he stared upward to the hole in the thatched roof where the hearth smoke escaped into the stormy night.

"How can it be that God could care for me?" he questioned. "He leaves me here rejected of man and despised by all. And for what?" Tancred's voice rose accusingly. "For a crime I have not committed. Where be the justice in this?"

Just then a knock sounded. Tancred gazed at the door in disbelief.

"'Twould be madness to be out on this night," he announced, yet got to his feet.

Pulling the door open and feeling the wind and rain pelt his face in sheer fury, Tancred noted the battered pilgrim who stared back.

"Enter, soul," he shouted and pulled the man within the questionable comforts of the hut. Tancred wrestled the door back in place, then turned to study his visitor.

The man was at least a score of years older than Tancred's thirty-one. His stooped shoulders gave evidence to his many hours spent over a writing table, and his ink-stained fingers confirmed his occupation of scribe.

"My thanks to you," the man panted with a broad grin. "'Tis no night for casual strolls in the countryside."

Tancred nodded but did not smile. "What seek ye here?"

"Shelter, if thou wilt have me," the man replied, pushing back rain-drenched white hair.

"You are welcome to what hospitality this hovel affords. I have but the floor to sleep upon and precious little else to offer."

The man smiled. "'Tis enough."

"Very well," Tancred stated with a shrug. "Be welcomed."

The man pulled off his heavy wool cloak, revealing a large sack beneath it. "I cannot impose without sharing my own good fortune," the man said, placing the wet cloak on the empty peg beside the door.

Tancred eyed the bag with some interest but said nothing. The pilgrim smiled broadly as he opened the sack and brought out a loaf of bread. He handed it to Tancred and returned to rummage for something else.

"There is more," he said with joy in his voice. "I passed supper with a wealthy merchantman and he bade me take this for my journey." He drew out a grease-stained cloth and opened it to reveal a portion of mutton.

Tancred felt his stomach rumble. How long had it been since he'd enjoyed a fine piece of meat such as this?

"I do not require this of you," he finally told the smiling man. "You are welcome here without need to share such a treasure."

"'Tis my joy to share with you," the man stated. "I am Artimas, and the Lord is my keeper. He gives to me generously, and I in turn give to those He sends my way. Let us sup together and enjoy this feast, for on the morrow, the Lord will surely supply again."

Tancred shook his head in wonder at the man. "You have great faith indeed to wander from place to place with little more than the cloak. It is always true that God provides for your hunger?"

Artimas smiled. "Do I look underfed, my friend?"

This time Tancred did smile, for the man was rather stocky and bore the look of one who was never late to the noon meal. "You do not," Tancred finally replied.

"Then let my appearance be evidence of God's goodness. Come, we can warm this meat and reason together."

Tancred could only stare after the man as he made himself comfortable by the hearth fire. Was this some divine intervention to keep him from giving in to his despair? Surely God cared little for whether he continued to hope for redemption. Yet if not by God's hand, then from where else could Artimas have come? This hovel was well off the main roadway and of little concern to anyone for miles around.

Tancred moved to join the man at the fire. "How came ye by this way?"

"I was led," Artimas replied simply.

"Led? By whom?"

Artimas glanced upward. "By He who always leads me."

Tancred couldn't accept the deliberate confidence of the man before him. "And why would God bring you here?" he asked gruffly.

Artimas patted the beaten dirt floor. "You might best answer that question yourself."

It was some hours past their first meeting when Artimas looked up from across the fire and questioned, "So ye stand accused of something ye did not do?"

"Aye," Tancred replied with a dark scowl marring his features. "The blood of my parents is upon my head. I did not kill them, but all of England believes it so, mayhaps even all the world."

Artimas smiled indulgently. "I have seen a fair piece of this world in the last few years and I have yet to hear your name mentioned amidst the crowds."

Tancred's face relaxed, and for a moment he fell silent. "I seek the true killer," he finally said in a reserved manner.

"Ah," Artimas said with a grin, "to free your name and see justice served."

"Partly." The scowl had returned, and the deep brooding in his eyes was now intensified with bitter hatred.

"Only partly?" puzzled Artimas. "For what other purpose would you desire this madman be captured?"

Tancred met Artimas's gaze. "Revenge," he stated softly, then with more clarity repeated the word. "Revenge!"

Chapter 3

Helena awoke to find a plump young woman lingering at her bedside. She focused her eyes and realized the woman was smiling at her.

"There ye be," the woman said as if Helena had accomplished some wondrous feat. "We were beginning to fret."

"Where am I?" The stiffness in her body caused Helena to cry out in pain.

"There, there," the woman said, easing Helena back to the straw mattress. "'Tis no good your trying to move about. Rest is what you need."

"Who are you?"

The woman smiled. "I might ask you the same thing. I am Mary. My husband, Felix, found you in the field as he prepared to sow seed. He brought you to me, and I have cared for you."

"Thank you, Mary," Helena murmured, gingerly stretching her limbs. "What is this place?"

"'Tis Gavenshire." Mary's voice betrayed her surprise. "The castle lies yonder."

"I'm not familiar with it. Is it near York?"

"Not so near. Closer to Brid."

"Brid?" Helena questioned.

Mary shook her head at the strange young woman in her bed. "Ye know naught of it? How did you come to be upon these lands?"

Helena frowned. Memory served her faithfully, but a reminder of her brother's henchmen gave her reason to remain quiet. "I know naught," she finally replied. In truth, she knew naught of Gavenshire.

"You have no memory of the journey?"

Helena did not answer. She watched Mary grow increasingly uncomfortable.

The silence hung heavy between them for several moments before

Mary finally cleared her throat and asked, "What. . .what is your name?"

"Helena. That much I remember." Helena hoped it would ease the furrowed brow of her caretaker.

"'Tis something," Mary said, trying to force a smile. "I will bring you broth to warm your bones. Mayhaps with food, your memory will return."

"Mayhaps."

Helena watched as Mary bustled around the one-room house. The accommodations were poor and such that Helena instantly felt guilty for the trouble she was causing. Silently appraising Mary's meager surroundings, Helena knew that anything the other woman offered would be a sacrifice. Despite the pain, Helena forced herself to sit up.

"There's no need to put yourself out on my account," Helena stated. The drab little house seemed to grow smaller by the minute.

"'Tis no bother, Milady," Mary said, clearly acknowledging that she accepted Helena as her superior.

Helena said nothing about this. She watched as Mary put more peat on the fire before bringing her a wooden bowl filled with steaming broth.

"This will see you right," Mary said with a meager smile. "I am sorry 'tis not more."

Helena sampled the soup. "'Tis fine broth—the best I've ever known." In spite of her concern, Mary beamed at the compliment.

"Thank you, milady." She quickly went back to the fire and stoked it with a poker.

Straightening up and looking again at Helena, Mary spoke.

"Ye are gentle born, of that there is no doubting."

Helena swallowed hard and nodded. "I suppose 'tis true enough. The evidence is upon my body." She waved a free hand over her surcoat of velvet.

"Aye, that and the way you talk. Mayhaps someone at the castle knows of you." She left it at that and bustled over to the only other piece of furniture in the house, the herb-laden table.

Mary's plump frame did nothing to slow her down. Helena watched the woman dart around the room and decided to leave well enough alone. If she showed fear or objection at Mary's suggestion, it would no doubt give her further concern. Besides, Helena reasoned, no one at the castle would know her because she had never heard of Gavenshire.

Helena relaxed, drank the soup, and watched Mary at work. She was an earthy creature with a dark brown braid that hung down her back. Her coarse wool kirtle of woad blue did little to make her more attractive, yet there was kindness about Mary that made Helena feel like the shoddy one.

Mary glanced up from where she ground herbs. "Feeling better?"

"A little, thank you. I am certain that your fine care has given me health." Helena finished the broth and started to get up.

Mary rushed to her side. "Nay, stay and rest. My husband will return shortly and we will send word to the castle for your care."

Helena eased back against the straw-filled mattress with a sigh. She glanced across the room to the only window and noted the fading light. There was nothing to do but wait for Mary's husband.

Soon enough the sound of someone nearing the hovel caused Mary to perk up and cock her head. "'Tis Felix," she confirmed for Helena's benefit, then went to open the door and greet her husband.

Helena watched as a large filthy man in a ragged wool tunic entered the doorframe. The man had huge hands, which quickly wrapped themselves around Mary's stout waist.

"Wife," Felix said with a grin, "'tis the face of an angel ye have."

He gave her a quick kiss on the lips.

"Go on with ye." Mary's mock protest was given with a smile.

Felix noted that Helena was awake and dropped his hold on Mary. "So, ye have come around."

Helena nodded. "Mary tells me that you found me in the fields. I am most grateful for your care and hospitality."

Felix noted Helena's refined manner of speech with an arching of his brow and a questioning glance at his wife. Helena saved Mary the trouble of explanation.

"My name is Helena, although I can scarce offer more than this. Your wife suggested that someone from the castle might best assist me. I would be grateful if you would send word on my behalf."

Felix nodded. "Were you traveling alone?"

"I—it seems so." Helena hated being caught up in the deception, but she feared reprisal from Roger more than the consequence of her actions.

"Ye have no memory of it?"

"I—I'm confused." Helena sat up and threw her legs over the edge of the bed. "If it is too much trouble to send word, I can attempt the journey myself."

"Nay, I could not let you," Felix replied firmly. "I will find the bailiff and ask him to settle the matter."

"Thank you, Felix." Helena's voice rang sincere even if her heart questioned the sanity of her actions.

Felix was to only have been gone for a matter of minutes, but instead was gone for nearly half of the hour. Mary began to fret, and Helena worried that she'd somehow caused the man grief. When he did finally reappear, he came with a stranger by his side.

"Milady," the man said, stepping forward to offer his hand to Helena. "I am Devon Pemberton. I am the estate steward for the duke of Gavenshire."

Helena allowed him to help her to her feet and then she curtsied. "Sire, I am Helena."

Devon Pemberton was a tall, handsome man, and Helena found him most reassuring with his warm smile and bright eyes. He eyed her over from head to toe and back again before speaking. "Felix tells me you have no memory of your kin or home. Is this true?"

"My travels have exhausted me, I fear. I remember only a little of the trip, but nothing of the travelers. I'm certain I know naught of the names of those who went with me." Helena comforted herself in the fact that this was no lie.

"'Tis no matter. You are welcome at the castle, and we will search to find your family on the morrow. Be ye well enough to walk, or shall I send a cart for you?"

"I can walk," Helena said hesitantly. She avoided his searching eyes for fear she would break down in her charade. "I would like to see these people rewarded," she quickly added. "They have been most kind in caring for me and have shared their meager foods with me as well."

Devon nodded. "It will be done. Felix, come with me to the castle and I will issue you food."

Felix and Mary both gasped in surprise and exclaimed in unison, "The castle!"

"'Tis not necessary, sire," Felix protested. "We gave nothing more than the good Lord would have asked of us."

Devon smiled and took firm hold of Helena's arm. "A kindness, nevertheless, and one worthy of repayment. Come."

Helena felt the strength in Devon's hand as he pulled her forward. She was deeply aware of his presence. *He is a powerful man,* she thought. He was determined and self-assured, and the very nearness of him gave her cause to think about her beloved Tanny. Would he be as tall as this man? Would his hair be soft and brown like this?

Tanny had dark hair, she reminded herself. Rich brown hair the color of newly plowed dirt and eyes so dark they were nearly black. She could almost see him in Devon's place, and her heart skipped a beat. *Where are you, my love? Why am I not upon your arm instead of this man's?*

In the soft blue-and-purple haze of twilight, Gavenshire Castle rose beyond the village. The town was closing down for the night, and the soft glow of firelight illuminated the windows of the houses as they passed by. Helena felt a chill and gave an involuntary shudder.

"Are you cold, milady?" Devon inquired.

The silhouette of his face in the fading light caused Helena to tremble more. Fear was gnawing at her like a hound to a bone.

"Aye," she whispered, unable to offer any other explanation.

Devon removed his own cloak and placed it around her shoulders. "This should keep you warm enough."

Helena snuggled down in the warmth, grateful that Devon could not see the blush that crossed her face.

Gavenshire Castle was a grand affair, Helena decided. She reviewed the bailey as they crossed to the outer stairs and noted the large number of men who guarded the grounds. Torches had been placed strategically to offer light, and in their glow, Helena could make out stables and mews where the falcons were kept.

Devon's ever-present hand upon her cloaked arm made Helena painfully aware of her inability to escape. There was no reason to fear, she reminded herself. But her thought was not all convincing.

She turned at the stairs to find Felix's face awash in wonder.

"'Tis a fine place, is it not?" she questioned, and Felix smiled broadly.

"To be sure, milady. To be sure. I must remember every detail and tell my Mary." Devon smiled at the exchange and assisted Helena up the stone stairs.

The castle was fairly quiet, even though the evening meal was in progress. Supper was not as much of an affair as was the noon meal. Many people simply took their food to their own chamber and spent the evening in retired silence or quiet conversation.

"Would you care to dine, Helena?" Devon questioned.

"Nay." She was not anxious to be made the center of attention.

Sensing this, Devon led her to a small room off the great hall. "Wait here while I see to Felix. I will find the duke and announce your arrival."

Helena watched as Felix padded off in dumbfounded silence behind Devon. She then allowed herself to survey her surroundings, noting the red-and-blue woolen hangings that draped the walls. Seeing the way they ruffled in particular spots, Helena had little doubt they blocked out the draft and helped to keep the room warm.

The chamber looked to be a private solar of some type. Perhaps it was a place where the duke received guests privately. At this thought, Helena felt herself weaken. She sank down in the nearest chair and wondered as to what type of man the duke of Gavenshire might be. Would he find it acceptable to take in a young woman with no memory and little more than gentle speech and velvet clothing to prove her right at hospitality in his home?

It was several minutes before Devon returned. With him came a rugged-looking man whose brown beard made him look to be the senior of Devon. On his arm was a woman who was great with child. Helena instantly rose to her feet and smoothed out her skirt.

"May I present the duke and duchess of Gavenshire," Devon announced.

"Your Grace," she said, curtseying first to the man and then again to his wife.

"I am Arianne," the woman said, taking Helena's hand. "Devon is my brother, and he tells me that you are to be our guest. I am glad to receive you, for there is a definite shortage of women in this castle."

"Don't I know that," Devon said with a laugh.

"Don't mind him." The duchess instantly put Helena at ease. "Are you hungry, or would you prefer I show you to your room so you might rest?"

"Please, milady," Helena replied, "do not put yourself out on my behalf. I would not wish to overtax you. 'Tis you who should rest and care for yourself."

The duke laughed. "If you can get my wife to heed your counsel, you may have a permanent home here." Then extending Helena a broad smile, he added, "I am Richard. I will bear up with no formalities between friends. Why don't you sit and tell us how you came to be here?"

Helena swallowed hard. She had allowed the villeins to believe a lie, as had the estate steward, and now she was to lie to a duke and his wife. The moment was too much for her, and nearly before Devon could catch her and break her fall, Helena fainted dead away.

Chapter 4

Helena was treated with the utmost care, and the question of her arrival to Gavenshire did not again become an issue. She could only imagine that Devon had shared her situation with the duke and duchess and that they had all agreed the trauma to be too great for her to bear.

Whatever the reason, Helena was glad for the reprieve. She was quickly welcomed into the inner circle of the duchess, becoming fast friends with Arianne, as well as with an older woman named Matilda, who acted as the duchess's closest confidante and friend. Helena soon relaxed in the unconditional friendship offered her.

"You look quite fetching, milady," Devon offered, taking the seat beside hers at the noon meal.

Helena felt shy next to this man. She'd had so little experience with men, having stayed so close to the protection of her mother. Devon was obviously interested in her, and whether it was simply as a means of solving the mystery about her or because he was attracted to her, Helena was uncertain.

"Thank you, sire," she whispered and turned her attention to her other side, where Richard seated Arianne. The duchess was laughing about something, and Helena instantly felt a pang of envy for the happiness that emanated from her face.

She watched as the duke leaned down to whisper something in Arianne's ear and caught the look of deep love in his eyes. *Oh to be loved like that,* she thought. Turning away, almost embarrassed for having intruded, Helena caught Devon's smile of knowing.

"'Tis truly a great love affair," he whispered in her ear.

Just then the noise of the hall faded as a grave-looking man rushed to the duke's side.

"What is it, Douglas?" Richard questioned.

"There is news, Your Grace," Douglas Mont Gomeri, chamberlain to the duke, announced.

"Pray tell?"

Douglas glanced to Arianne, then beckoned Richard to join him outside.

"Nay, Douglas," Arianne stated with a fierce shake of her head. "Share your news here."

Douglas looked at Richard, who questioningly nodded. "I fear 'tis Her Grace's father and stepmother. A fever has taken them."

Arianne dropped her chalice. "They are dead?"

"Aye."

Helena watched as the color drained from Arianne's face. She heard the swift intake of breath from the man beside her and remembered that Devon and Arianne were siblings. She turned to offer her condolences and noted the shocked expression on Devon's face. Little more was said, however, as the duchess doubled over in pain and gasped her husband's name.

"'Tis the babe," she whispered.

Richard immediately pulled her from the chair and lifted her into his arms. "Douglas, get the midwife. Helena, find Matilda and send her to our chamber."

Helena nodded, watching as the duke carried his weeping wife to the stairs. Devon sat motionless, and Helena wished she could offer some comfort. Not knowing anything she could say, she placed her hand upon his arm, met his gaze with her sympathetic one, and went in search of Matilda.

Richard paced nervously in the great hall. With sidelong glances at the stone stairs that led to the upper level and the lying-in chamber where Arianne lay, he prayed fervently for his wife's safe delivery. Helena sat in silence. She no longer envied the duchess.

She knew full well that pregnancy and childbirth were frightening times for women. Should a child struggle in finding its way into the world, there was little that could be done to assist it. She knew Richard took some comfort in the fact that Matilda was assisting the midwife. Matilda had waited upon his own mother, and Richard trusted her to be honest with him about his wife's condition.

Still, it had been some time since she'd come to tell them any news, and Arianne had been confined to the room throughout the night. Now with daybreak upon them, Richard found exhaustion overtaking his weary mind.

"Dear God," he prayed aloud, "please ease her pain and deliver her safely of our child. Give life to the seed that You caused to grow from our love. 'Tis a selfish man I am, Lord," Richard continued, "but I plead for their lives and beg forgiveness for my concern."

Helena's heart ached for the man. He was clearly worried sick for his wife, and the helplessness of the matter left him frustrated and ill tempered.

"Your Grace would do well to rest," Helena said softly.

"Aye," Devon offered, coming into the room. "You will need your rest to show off that fine babe. 'Twould be a pity should the child have more strength than his father."

Richard tried to laugh, but it came out little more than a huff, and foreboding crept over the hall.

Matilda appeared nearly an hour later, shaking her head. "'Tis time it takes for these little ones to come into the world. God's timing is best."

"You will let me know as soon as something happens?" Richard asked, already knowing the answer.

"Aye, you know I will." Matilda then turned to Helena. "Her Grace would like it if you would bear this with her."

Helena's face registered surprise. "Arianne has asked for me?"

"Aye. 'Tis certain enough she would prefer her husband," Matilda said with a grin, "but the midwife will have none of that. Come."

Helena looked at Richard, who nodded. "'Twill ease my mind to know you are with her."

"Very well."

Taking a chair by the fireplace, Richard watched them go and knew that his heart went with them. He thought only to rest his eyes a moment and await word of Arianne. A storm had brewed up off the coast, and the howling wind outside made him feel even more tired. The damp chill of the room caused him to pull his chair closer to the flickering fire. He would just sit a moment and pray. Instead, he fell into a much-needed sleep and dreamed not of Arianne, but of his brother.

Helena patted Arianne's hand supportively, knowing little else she could do. She was honored that the duchess had asked for her, but she found the entire scene quite foreign and frightening.

"Milady," Matilda said to the laboring Arianne, "I've placed jasper in the four corners of the room. 'Tis a good stone to bring about the quick delivery of a child."

Arianne felt the contraction ease and relaxed against her pillow, while the midwife, an ancient woman dressed all in black, rubbed a soothing ointment on her distended abdomen.

"Aye," the midwife said with a nod. "Jasper will quicken the birth." Then turning to Matilda, she questioned, "Did ye open all of the doors and drawers within the castle?"

"Aye," Matilda responded quickly. "The cupboards and larder doors as well."

"'Tis good," the midwife stated, then glanced at Arianne as she felt the tightening of another contraction. "'Twill beckon the child out."

Matilda nodded at Arianne and Helena's questioning glances. The midwife gently kneaded the duchess's stomach and asked, "What of the knots? Be there any yet untied?"

"Nay," Matilda answered confidently. "I have overseen it myself. 'Tis sure that all knots in this castle have been undone."

The midwife nodded. "'Twill keep the cord from knotting about the child's neck," she told Arianne.

Arianne's misery and pain left her little time to consider the traditional forms of midwifery. She knew there was a knife placed beneath her mattress to cut the pain of delivery. Not that it was helping. She'd also seen Matilda sprinkle special herbs about the room, knowing that they were to give off pleasant scents and coax the baby to come with haste. But in truth, this baby was already coming in haste. It was at least a month early by Matilda's calculations, but the shock of her father's death had been too much.

"I'm glad you are here," Arianne told Helena. "I feel as though we've become as sisters these past few days. I pray I have not asked too much of you."

"Never, milady." Helena again patted the duchess's hand. "I am your faithful servant."

"Nay." Arianne's eyes were bright with pain. "You are now a most cherished friend."

Helena had just reported Arianne's progress to a sleepy Richard, when Douglas Mont Gomeri entered the room. "Your Grace, there is a messenger from the king."

Richard came instantly awake, noticing for the first time the brilliance of sunlight that flooded in from the open windows. The silence left in the passing of the storm was nearly deafening. "What be the hour?" he questioned and glanced again to the stairway.

"It is coming upon noon," Douglas replied. "Has the duchess—"

"Nay. Helena has just told me it will still be some time. Show the messenger in." His voice betrayed his concern.

Douglas nodded and returned with a weary-looking man. He wore the colors of King Henry, as well as the markings. Richard acknowledged the man with his eyes but said nothing. The man, in return, gave a deep bow and produced a wax-sealed parchment.

Richard took the message eagerly and noted that preparations were being made in the hall for dinner. "Will you take the noon meal with us?" he questioned, while breaking the seal.

"I would be most humbly grateful," the man replied.

Richard motioned to Douglas. "My chamberlain will see to your needs. Douglas, please show this man where he may wash."

Douglas led the man away while Richard scanned the words on the paper. There was joy in his heart as he realized that Henry had agreed to pardon Tancred DuBonnet.

"I pray it is not more bad news," Helena said, feeling a faint despair wash over her.

"On the contrary. 'Tis good news." Richard beckoned Helena to sit and then read, "'Upon your word and oath that your brother has been falsely accused and because of the grave injustice done him, I do hereby pardon—'" Richard's words fell away. "The king has pardoned my brother!"

Helena could only nod. She had little idea as to what the duke's brother needed pardoning for by the king, but such a matter was indeed cause for celebration. "Congratulations, Your Grace," she announced, getting to her feet. "I must return to Arianne. I will come again when there is word."

Richard barely heard Helena's words. Tancred would be pardoned!

"The babe is nearly born, milady," Matilda said soothingly to Arianne. "Just a wee bit longer and you will know such joy that pain will be forgotten."

Arianne doubted that Matilda spoke the truth, but she gave a final push to appease the midwife's demands. Suddenly it was done. The child was being pulled from her body, and the pain was taken with it.

The midwife quickly tied the cord and cut it at four fingers' length from its belly. The slightly blue-skinned baby soon colored to a hardy pinkish-red as its lusty cries filled the chamber.

"'Tis a son, milady," Matilda announced proudly, and Arianne wept for joy.

Helena could only stare in dumbfounded silence. What a wondrous event she had just witnessed. Never in her life had she imagined such a thing.

The midwife quickly took the baby to wash him in a readied tub of water. She rigorously rubbed his tiny body with salt, then took honey and rubbed it on his gums and tongue to give him an appetite. Helena left Arianne's side to watch on in amazement as the tiny infant protested such treatment.

"'Tis a fine son, Your Grace," the midwife called over her shoulder as she bound the baby tightly in a fine linen cloth. His swaddling kept him completely immobilized but did not interfere with his hearty cries.

"You must take him to Richard," Arianne stated. Helena looked up, wondering to whom she was speaking.

Matilda was weeping tears of joy and nodded to Helena. "He'll be most happy to see you with this news."

"You want me to take the baby to Richard?" Helena's obvious surprise amused Arianne. The midwife placed the bundled infant in Helena's arms before she could refuse. "But what if I stumble? I've not cared for a child before."

"Neither have I," Arianne replied. "Go, take him to his father. You will do well, of this I am certain."

Richard had heard the cries of his son. With little thought to the king's message, he had let the parchment fall to the floor in wonder of the new sounds.

He held his breath, closed his eyes, and thanked God for the child who cried so fiercely. Opening his eyes, he again found the room suddenly filled with people. Douglas came to his side, staring in wonderment at the staircase. Behind them, voices were murmuring with approval and speculation.

"'Tis a boy for sure, Your Grace," one of the knights called out.

"No other could cry with such a voice," another assured.

In a few moments, a wide-eyed Helena appeared on the stairs, a tiny white mummy in her arms. The cries grew louder as she approached, for the baby was decidedly unhappy with his new surroundings.

"Her Grace," Helena said with obvious pride in her voice, "has been delivered of a son."

A hearty cry of congratulations and approval filled the air. The word was quickly spread throughout the castle and into the surrounding village. The duke had an heir.

"What of Arianne?" Richard questioned anxiously.

"She is well, sire, and quite pleased."

Richard looked down into the face of the crying babe. Without thought, he retrieved the baby from Helena's arms and studied him closely. The infant calmed under his father's scrutiny, and Richard smiled.

"'Tis a fine son, indeed," he said to no one in particular. Then noticing the shock of burnt-red hair, Richard's smile grew broader. "And he bares the mark of his mother, I see." Those in the room drew near to catch sight of the baby.

"'Tis time I thank your mother," Richard whispered to the child.

Helena followed Richard to the lying-in chamber, where in keeping with tradition, all of the castle's finest treasures had been laid out on display. No treasure there, however, caught the duke's eye save Arianne.

She was lying back against the pillows, eyes closed and copper hair spilling out over the coverlet. The midwife was removing her things from the bedside and glanced in surprise at Richard's early entry into the room.

"You should place the babe in his cradle," she motioned to the darkened corner of the room, "where his eyes cannot be harmed by the light."

He scarcely heard her, for Arianne's eyes snapped open at the words and fixed on Richard. She noted the pride in his eyes and the pleasure that seemed to radiate from his face.

"A gift, my husband. A gift from the Lord above and from our love," she whispered tenderly.

"A most perfect gift," Richard replied and drew close to the bed. He placed the small boy at her side and watched as his son turned his face and rooted.

"'Tis hunger that causes his search," the midwife said, realizing that Richard was not going to heed her suggestion for placing the child in his cradle.

Arianne lovingly guided the baby's mouth to her breast, then started in surprise when he took hold and began to feed. Richard laughed at her expression, then placed a kiss upon her forehead.

"Love has a most unique way of surprising us, does it not, sweet Arianne?"

"Indeed," she whispered sleepily.

Helena silently backed out of the room, feeling much the intruder in this very private moment. She was filled with wonder and thanksgiving. "Oh, God," she said, closing the door to her own chamber, "what a remarkable thing You have done."

Gone were all thoughts of Roger and Maude. Gone were the concerns of being sent to the abbey and never finding Tanny. No, Helena reasoned, a God who would create such a wonderful marvel as this could surely handle the simple reunion of two people.

Chapter 5

Roger was not happy at the news of Helena's disappearance. His anger at the men who bore him the tidings was evident.

"Imbeciles!" he shouted. "I gave you a small task and you could not even see it to completion."

The men begged his forgiveness, pleading their innocence, but Roger silenced them with his raised fist. "Get out of my sight," he growled. The men quickly took their leave, and only Maude's laughter remained to prick at Roger's conscience.

"So she outwitted them, did she?" Maude could not help but take the issue further. "What will you do, brother dear, when our sister shows herself to the queen?"

"London is a far piece from these lands," Roger said, barely controlling his rage. "Helena could never make the journey. No doubt some other destination is on her mind."

"Would that you should believe it!" Maude declared. "I know well our little sister. She will see to it that you are punished for her treatment."

"Me?" Roger questioned accusingly. "Me? What of yourself, or have you forgotten your part in this matter?"

Maude shrugged indifferently and seated herself before the fire. She was mindless of the servants who rummaged about the house and completely unconcerned with Roger's tantrum.

"Helena is gone. Let it be. If she is found, you simply tell them she has gone mad because of her mother's death."

"What of the lash marks upon her back?"

Maude smiled in a twisted manner. "Flesh knits and Helena will heal. I doubt it will leave overmuch of a mark. Besides, you can always plead innocence and declare it the handiwork of someone she met on the road. Better yet, go to Henry first and weep before him with a heavy brother's heart. Tell him your precious little sister has fled and you fear for her safety."

Roger seemed to relax a bit at this. Maude was perhaps right. Appearing before the king in a fit of brotherly concern would offer his feelings for all to see. Should Helena appear to say otherwise, it would remain his word against hers, and now that the Lady Eleanor was dead, Helena's word would surely hold less weight.

"You fret over nothing," Maude assured Roger. "Concern yourself instead with a more worthy matter."

"That being?" Roger questioned, staring down at the immaculately groomed woman.

Maude toyed with the keys that hung from her girdle. "I am of a mind to marry," she stated without fanfare.

"This is not news to me," Roger replied. "Nor is it a worthy matter."

Maude laughed haughtily. "'Tis worthy enough. I desire to better my standing. Our good neighbor to the south suddenly finds himself a widower, and I seek to remedy that matter."

"Have you given him time to even bury his wife?" Roger asked angrily.

Maude stuck her nose in the air and refused to comment, making Roger laugh. "I see my point has hit its mark. There is time enough to concern yourself with such a thing. I must decide what is to be done in regards to Helena."

"I thought it was decided," said Maude with a look of reproach. "Take yourself with haste to His Majesty's fortress and tell of our deep sorrow. Our sweet little sister has run away."

Working over her needlework while the duchess nursed her son, Helena commented without thought, "You are my first true friend."

Arianne noted the sorrow in her voice. "There is no one else?"

"No."

"Mayhaps it is only that your memory fails you in this matter," the duchess suggested carefully. She was already suspicious of Helena's artful dodge regarding her family.

Helena winced and cast her gaze to the fire. "Mayhaps."

"Still," Arianne continued, feeling deeply grieved for the young woman's obvious pain, "you have a friend in me, and I would like very much for you to stay on here for as long as you like. You may be my lady-in-waiting, if it pleases you."

Helena's heart swelled with gratitude and joy. "I would be honored."

Arianne smiled. "We are quite isolated here, but the city is ever growing and drawing more people. The duke is seeking a charter for the town, and that will enable us to have a yearly fair, instead of making the journey to Scarborough or York.

"I have no other lady-in-waiting, and Matilda has been my only friend and companion these long months. The duties of my home require much of me, and you could do much to help me."

"I know naught what capacity I might assist you in," Helena responded, "but I am most humbly your servant."

"Nay," Arianne said with a shake of her head. "Never that. You will be my friend. Perhaps you would find pleasure in helping me with the babe?"

"To be certain, milady. I would find caring for your son an honor." Helena bubbled the words. "I have never been around children. I was the youngest in my family." The sudden realization of what she'd said hit Helena hard.

The intake of her breath was not lost on Arianne. "See there, a bit of your memory returns. Mayhaps it will not be long before you remember in full."

Helena knew that Arianne was being graciously generous. She offered a weak smile and nodded at the duchess's words.

"Perhaps the first place we should start," Arianne continued, "is in moving you to the chamber nearest my own. Then, too, we shall need to fit you for clothing. I presume you have little else with you?"

"Nay," Helena confirmed with a frown.

"I have fine seamstresses here and can work a stitch quite well myself. We'll have you clothed in no time. What colors do you favor?"

Helena felt her throat tighten. To admit a favorite would be to offer up yet another proof of her memory. "I. . .I am," she stammered, "uncertain."

"Of course," Arianne nodded, then appraised the girl carefully.

Helena self-consciously allowed the scrutiny. She was dressed simply, yet the velvet cloth bore the evidence of her status. She remembered having lost her head covering in the woods one night, and no one, not even Matilda, had offered her a replacement. This thought caused Helena to put her hands to her bare head, sending her needlework clattering to the floor.

"You have lovely hair," Arianne said, noting the long blond braid that hung down Helena's back. "My own, as you can see, is frightfully unsettling."

Helena shook her head. "'Tis not true, milady. It is a fine shade. It reminds me of late autumn sunsets when the sun is like a fiery red ball on the horizon. I find it most beautiful."

"Mayhaps, but I am no courtly English beauty." The baby was now sleeping, and Arianne ran a finger against his cheek. "Hair of gold and eyes of blue are what the women of England long to display. Alas, I cannot even boast the eyes, for mine are brown. Yea, you are the very image of refined womanhood, Helena."

Helena blushed at the praise, and nervously she sought to occupy herself. "May I put him in the cradle for you?" She motioned to the baby, and Arianne offered him up.

"I think crimson would do you justice. Yea, and golden yellows and silvery blues to match your eyes. I'll have the cloth brought to you and you can choose from the bounty of our storerooms."

"You are too generous, milady," Helena said, fighting to keep the tears from her eyes. She put the baby in his cradle, then turned to face the duchess.

Arianne patted the bed, and Helena sat down beside her. "It pleases me to do this." Arianne put her hand upon Helena's shoulder. "I am truthfully glad for your company. Richard is often about his work, and sometimes the loneliness does not bode well for me."

"But there are things," Helena finally said, knowing that she couldn't go on lying to Arianne, "things which you do not know about me."

Arianne smiled. "When you are ready, you will speak of them. Until then, I am content to wait. Please know this, however." Her eyes were soft and full of concern. "You are safe here, and no harm will come to you. My husband is a powerful man and good friends with King Henry. If you have fears, Helena, lay them to rest. We are happy to be your protectors with God's help."

Just then the door opened, and Richard entered with Devon at his side. "Am I interrupting?"

"Nay, but the babe is sleeping, so please do not address us as though you were barking orders to your men."

Richard eyed his wife with a grin. "I wouldn't dream of it, Your Grace." Devon chuckled from behind, while Richard gave a sweeping bow.

"Why have you come, then?" Arianne questioned in mock annoyance.

Richard straightened. "Devon has agreed to bring my brother home to England. I pray it meets with your approval."

"It does, indeed."

Helena glanced up to find Devon looking at her. His gaze only made her long for Tanny, and she quickly looked away to check on the baby.

"When do you leave?" Arianne was questioning.

"With the tide," Devon answered and crossed the room to peer over Helena's shoulder at the baby. "Has he a name?"

"Of course he has a name. Richard, have you not shared with the castle your own child's name?"

"I have been a bit preoccupied, milady."

"His name is Timothy," Helena said matter-of-factly and took her seat to begin sewing once again.

"Timothy is a good name," Devon replied. "I'm envious of you, Richard. A fine home, a good wife, albeit that she has a sharp tongue at times, and a perfect son."

"You'll no doubt be following suit quite rapidly. You are soon to inherit your father's lands and title."

The words were no sooner out of Richard's mouth than he regretted having said them. Arianne's face sobered immediately. While she had no great love for the iron-fisted man who'd been her father, she still mourned his passing.

"I'm sorry, Arianne," Richard said, taking her hand. "Forgive me."

"'Tis naught to forgive. Your words are true enough. Devon, will you soon settle down and take a wife?"

"I would be most happy to do just that, should the proper young woman present herself. Mayhaps the king will arrange a marriage for me. You seemed to have benefited greatly from such an arrangement."

Arianne smiled, the grief of the moment passing. "Indeed, I have benefited."

Helena looked up at this exchange. She had never known arranged marriages to be anything but pure misery for those involved. How often she had heard her mother discuss the unhappy unions of her friends.

Devon noted her expression and smiled. "I do not believe our guest finds truth in this matter. Mayhaps she suffered from such an arrangement."

"Nay, not I," Helena answered too quickly. Three pairs of eyes turned to gaze in surprise at her, and Helena colored crimson under the close scrutiny.

Several moments passed before Richard broke the uneasy silence. "It is settled, then. Devon will go to Bruges, and we will expect you back by Easter."

"By Easter, eh?" Devon turned from Helena with hands on hips. "I take it you will allow no complication upon the sea to slow down my trip."

Richard laughed. "None. 'Twould be most unacceptable. I will have to give the matter over to God and beg His blessings on it. I would enjoy celebrating the resurrection of our Lord with my family. All of my family."

"'Tis settled, then," Devon stated, and after briefly bowing to Helena, he touched his lips to Arianne's forehead and bid them good-bye.

"Thank you, Devon." Richard's words were clearly heartfelt, and his eyes were filled with gratitude. "'Tis a good brother you have, milady."

Richard lifted Arianne's slender fingers to his lips. "Goodness must be a family virtue." He grinned before placing a lingering kiss on the back of her hand. Helena enjoyed the tender exchange.

Timothy took that moment to let loose a cry, causing Arianne to chuckle. "Let us hope 'tis a virtue that extends to the generations."

Chapter 6

"Can it not wait?" Arianne questioned, following Richard into their bedchamber.

Helena had been caring for Timothy and got up to leave, but Richard waved her back down. "You needn't go."

"Nay," Arianne replied sarcastically, "because the duke is going instead." Helena raised questioning eyes. She'd never been in the middle of one of Arianne and Richard's squabbles, but in a castle there were few secrets.

"You would like for me to tell the king it is an inconvenient time to do his bidding?" Richard questioned with a smirking grin.

Arianne rolled her eyes. "'Tis unfair. Henry knows you have a new son. 'Tis not fitting to draw you away just now."

"Bah!" Richard said, slapping a leather tunic on top of the clothes and slamming down the lid. "The matters of state wait not for one such as Timothy. He is but one small child in the eyes of his king. Perhaps the king has need of me in ways that will affect many such as Timothy."

Helena tried to occupy herself with her needlework. It was hopelessly snagged, however, and she could only pull at the threads in a desperate attempt to free them.

"I will miss you."

Helena thought Arianne sounded close to tears. She silently wished she could slip from the room, but the duke had already instructed her to stay.

Without considering Helena's presence, Richard crossed to Arianne and pulled her in his arms. "My heart will long for you every moment of my day. Each beat will be for you alone, and each breath I breathe will whisper your name." He tilted her tearful face to his and gazed deeply into her eyes. His lips were only inches from hers, the warmth of her breath was upon his face, and her tears now fell against his fingers. "Ah, sweet Arianne." His words were nearly a moan. Slowly, with all the longing and passion that had followed him through the final months of Arianne's confinement, Richard kissed her. Arianne returned the kiss, also uncaring that Helena sat only a few feet away.

"Come below and see me off. Helena, bring Timothy and come, too."

Helena nodded and quickly retrieved the baby, grateful to be done with the emotional farewell scene.

In the bailey, Richard's men were restless to be on their way. They waited patiently while final instructions were issued and additional precautions were made against strangers approaching the castle. Hadn't it been an overtrust of this peaceful existence, Richard had told them, that had caused Arianne to fall into danger when Tancred had stormed the castle?

Helena was rosy cheeked and filled with emotion at the love she watched transpire between Arianne and her husband. *Such love only comes to a person once,* she thought as Richard bent from his horse to offer Arianne a final kiss. It was more than she could bear, and she looked away.

Clutching Timothy tightly to her bosom, Helena could not fill the ache that grew there. The most immense ocean could not fill the void that left its mark so deeply engraved upon her heart.

"Have courage, Wife," Richard was calling, causing Helena to lift her head again. "When I return, I will bring your brother and mine as well. God will it to be so!"

"Aye," Arianne said with an earnest face. "God will it to be so!"

"You will have all that you need. Seek out Sir Dwayne in any matter that you cannot resolve." Richard's words were said in the same authoritative manner he used with his men, and Helena knew all moments of tenderness between duke and duchess had passed.

"God go with you, Richard," Arianne said in parting.

"And with you, milady."

The little band watched until all riders had passed through the gatehouse and into the village. Arianne brushed away tears and noted that Helena seemed close to them herself.

"We must surely be a sight," she contended, and Helena nodded in agreement. "Come," Arianne said, taking Timothy into her arms, "let us partake of something warm to fill the chill within." But Helena knew that no refreshment would find its mark and ease what ailed them.

They climbed the stone steps to the great hall, and Arianne motioned Matilda to her side.

"We seek refreshment against the dampness and chill. Would you bring it to my solar?" Arianne requested.

"Of course, milady," Matilda said with the slightest nod.

Arianne noted two servants squabbling in the corner of the room and, without thought, handed Timothy to Helena and motioned her to the stairs. "Wait for me in my chamber," she bade. "I will see to this matter."

Helena was grateful for the reprieve. She lovingly took Timothy in hand and carefully made her way upstairs. Noting Timothy's growing agitation, Helena realized it had been some time since he'd received a changing.

Placing the babe in his cradle, Helena drew water from the ever-filled hearth pot. She tested it to make certain it was neither too hot nor too cold, then poured it into a basin and added rose oil. Her final act before retrieving the squalling Timothy was to pull out new swaddling and a fine linen drying cloth from a nearby chest. This was a procedure she repeated every three hours during the day.

Without giving thought to what she was doing, Helena began to sing a song of love. It was the first time she'd lifted her voice in song since her mother had died. Now, for a reason beyond her understanding, Helena not only desired to sing, she found that her heart demanded she do so.

The lyrical notes filled the room and joined with Timothy's cries, which immediately ceased.

"Come see, come see the tiny babe," Helena sang. "Lullay, lullay, the tiny babe. Before you now, this blessed day, Lullay, lullay, the tiny babe." It was a song from her childhood in celebration of the Christ Mass.

The silky soprano tones seemed to mesmerize Timothy as Helena unwound his swaddling bands and gently placed him in the bath. She felt her heart swell for the child whom she'd come to love as dearly as her own.

The aching that had so totally held her captive only moments before seemed somehow eased in this simple task and song. Helena washed the tiny infant, then dried him with the linen cloth and rubbed more rose oil onto his body. She carefully rewrapped him in the swaddling bands, for it was well known that until the babe was old enough to sit, this would prevent his limbs from twisting. Still, she couldn't help but like it best when Timothy was free of the binding and his soft baby fingers would wave upward to her face.

"You must await your mother," she whispered to the expectant child who even now rooted against her for satisfaction. Timothy knew full well this routine, and his mother's breast always followed his bath.

Arianne entered the room none too early. "I see you have already bathed him."

"Aye," Helena said with a warm smile. "'Tis your face he cries for now."

Arianne chuckled softly as she took the baby. "Mayhaps not so much my face, eh?" She quickly settled down to the task at hand and watched as Helena pulled back the woolen wall-hanging that hid the garderobe door.

"'Tis certain with all the rose water we dispose of here," Helena mused, "you surely have the most fragrant latrine in all the castle." She retrieved the small basin of water and emptied it into the dark hole.

"No doubt," Arianne said with a laugh. "'Twould be a finer service still to bathe the entire castle in such sweetness."

Helena replaced the basin and dropped the cloth back into place. Just then Matilda entered the room with a tray containing two steaming cups and thick slices of warm bread.

"Ah," Arianne whispered, "our refreshment."

Timothy was nearly asleep at her breast, and Helena quickly prepared his cradle before taking the offered mug from Matilda.

"Join us," Arianne said, placing Timothy in his bed.

"I cannot, milady," Matilda responded. "There is much that needs my care."

Arianne nodded and took the tray. "Thank you, Matilda." She waited until Matilda had closed the door behind her, then turned conspiratorially to Helena. "She thinks I know naught of her birthday. 'Tis but two days from now, and I have a fine warm surcoat and tunic for her gift."

"She will be pleased," Helena said, taking the chair beside Arianne's.

"I think so." Arianne put the tray on the table beside her chair and offered Helena a slice of bread. They shared the silence of the room in nibbled bites and satisfying drink.

Helena was the first to turn from their feast. She picked up her sewing, a small embroidered gown that Timothy would wear when he outgrew swaddling.

"You have a most unusual stitch there," Arianne said, leaning over to note the piece.

"My mother taught me this," Helena said proudly. "When I sat at her knee and listened to gentle instruction, I thought there surely must be no other place so perfect."

Arianne said nothing of Helena's pleasant memory. "My own mother died when I was young," she noted instead. "I was taught to sew at the convent where my father sent me. It was a good life, but none that I would have called perfect."

Helena felt a sadness wash over her. "The loss of a mother is not one easily borne by the child, at any age."

"Nay," agreed Arianne. "'Tis surely not."

Days later, Matilda was indeed proud to show off her new gift. She embarrassed at the fanfare Arianne made of her day, and when the duchess suggested Matilda take a quiet day of repose, the woman could only gasp.

"But my duties...," Matilda began to protest.

"Can wait," Arianne stated firmly. Just then the lyrical notes of Helena's nursery songs filtered down to reach their ears. Casting a glance at the stairway, Arianne shook her head. "'Tis a voice like no other. Oft I have heard her sing long into the night, and it comforts me greatly in Richard's absence."

"Aye," Matilda agreed. "Many say she is instructed by the angels."

In the solar, Helena composed a new love song for her beloved. She hummed the notes of the melody, picking and choosing each carefully, discarding those whose tones were too harsh or dour. The music always came first—notes of melodies that raced inside her head and would scarce let her rest before she'd fully composed them into song.

Timothy stared up with watchful blue eyes from his cradle. So long as Helena sang, it mattered little to him what the meaning of the words were.

"If my beloved were a king," Helena put to the melody she'd just completed. She tested the words against the notes and decided they worked well. It was to be the song she'd promised Tanny when Roger's whip had lain her ill.

"If my beloved were a king," she whispered and sighed. "Oh, Tanny, you are a king. King of my heart." Dropping to her knees, Helena prayed, "Most holy Father, You alone know where my beloved lays his wearied head. You alone see his sorrows and his needs. Go with him and send my love along. I miss him so." She felt the wetness upon her cheeks. How long would it be? How long before she saw him again?

Several nights later, Helena anxiously paced her room. There was such a restless spirit within her. She had spent hours in the castle chapel listening to the gentle words of Father Gies as he prayed for her to have the peace of God. Each morning during services, she had prayed fervently for such a peace to ease her longings, and of yet, no peace had come.

Without thought, Helena lifted her voice in a church song of scripture. The Latin words were heavy compared to the Anglo-French she more often used for song, but the words encouraged her heart.

"*Sine fide impossibile est placere Deo,*" she sang in earnest. *Without faith it is impossible to please God.*

"Oh, Father," she whispered, "my faith comes so hard these dark, lonely nights. I listen to sounds of life within the castle and know that no life stirs within my own walls. Nay, only the empty ramblings of a faithless woman.

Yet, without faith, I cannot please Thee."

"Helena?" Arianne's soft voice called from outside her door. Wiping her tears with the back of her linen robe, Helena opened the door to her duchess.

"I heard you singing," Arianne said simply. "I am about to nurse Timothy. Come sing for me."

Helena followed her into the hall, grateful for the reprieve from her lonely walls. Arianne settled down on the bed and took Timothy to her side. "It seems so dark sometimes," she said faintly as Helena took a seat on the end of the mammoth bed. The high wooden canopy created shadows against the dying firelight's glow.

"Aye," Helena whispered. "Quite dark."

Arianne reached out her hand to Helena. "Tell me of your home. Tell me of the family you have left behind."

Helena's fingers had barely touched Arianne's hand, but the words spoken caused her to jerk back as if stung. "I cannot."

Arianne pulled Timothy closer and sighed. "I do not hold you in contempt for your choice. I feel strongly that you remember full well your past and all that remains there for you."

"I cannot," Helena replied again, her voice a sob.

"Helena, I will not judge you harshly."

"I know," the sorrow-filled young woman replied. "I judge myself and the lack of faith within me."

"Then judge no more," Arianne replied. "'Tis God's job and His alone."

Helena lifted her eyes to meet Arianne's. "I remember it all," she admitted, "but 'tis nothing worth sharing with gentlefolk." Then more adamantly, Helena continued. "I love this life. Please do not send me away."

"Send you away?" Arianne gasped. "I would rather lose my arm than lose your friendship. You are welcomed here for all time, Helena. Know that here and now."

"Thank you, milady." Helena felt a world of weight eased off her shoulders. "My love of God is deep, and for all these many years, I have felt its return in only the love of my mother. Now, I see differently. I see His love in you."

"'Tis but a reflection of that which shines in you, Helena. He has not forsaken you. Be at peace and know He cares."

Chapter 7

Tancred DuBonnet leaned against the rail of the ship and stared at the filmy image of English shoreline. Home! It had come at last. After eleven years, he was going home.

"I wonder," Devon began, coming up from behind him, "if you will find it changed."

Tancred smiled weakly. "Perhaps yea, perhaps nay. The true point is that England will find me changed."

"For the better or the worse?" Devon questioned seriously. He knew all about the rough treatment his sister had suffered at Tancred's hand.

Tancred continued to stare across the waters. A light, salty mist assailed him, leaving droplets on his bearded face. "Would you have asked that but a short time ago, I might have answered strongly in the latter. I was a most bitter man."

Devon pushed back his cloak and adjusted the sword at his side. The cold steel felt good against his hand, and were this man still considered his enemy, he'd find little difficulty in challenging him to fight to the death. Thoughts of Arianne being beaten by this bitter man caused Devon to turn narrowed eyes on his companion.

"And now?" Devon's voice was low and formidable.

Tancred never broke his gaze. "Now, I am not so bitter. Perhaps now I am more thoughtful and filled with reasoning."

"Reasoning? Reasoning for what, pray tell?"

Tancred raised an eyebrow as if casually considering the matter. His camlet garde-corp, woven of the finest camel hair in Cyprus, offered him cherished warmth. It also reminded him of the giver. Artimas.

"I met a man not long ago. A pilgrim philosopher on his journey to Paris. A man of more difference and provocative thought I have ne'er met."

"A man of philosophy?" Devon asked in a tone of disbelief. "And what heresy did he preach, or did you contemplate angels and how many existed on pin-tops?"

Tancred laughed and turned to the younger man. "Nay, but my thoughts were much the same as yours, even though I had no concern of heresy. I had long ago presumed my soul unsaveable. That was, until I met your sister."

Devon's face tightened. "Yes, you were most uncharitable to her as I have learned."

Tancred nodded thoughtfully. "'Tis true and nothing of pride for me. I acted out of spite and hate and have no other excuse to offer. I posted my sincerest regret to the woman and begged her forgiveness. Richard's scribe penned me a fine letter in her name, releasing me from the debt."

"'Tis like Arianne to put aside a difference so easily. Still, I have not her ease of reconciliation."

Tancred said nothing for a moment. "Mayhaps I should seek your forgiveness as well," he paused, meeting Devon's eyes, "for the offense you still carry in her name."

Devon was clearly convicted by Tancred's words. He swallowed hard, released the sword that he'd toyed with throughout the conversation, and looked away. "Mayhaps, I should seek yours."

"Then we are in agreement," Tancred said and returned his gaze to follow Devon's. England's shoreline drew ever closer.

"Was it your philosopher who changed your heart?" Devon questioned in a voice barely audible.

"Nay," Tancred replied. "'Twas God. Artimas only assisted in pointing out the finer details."

"Such as?"

"So much was muddled in my thinking. The church had done nothing to aid me when I was accused of my parents' murder and exiled, although I had beseeched Rome on many occasions. I worked for over ten years, putting together all my worldly goods. This, in order to see my brother brought to justice for something I knew in my heart he was incapable of having done.

"I knew I hadn't killed our father and mother, but Richard was the only other person close at hand. I tried to imagine him capable of the act but knew full well it was impossible. But I came anyway and was defeated by him, as you well know. But the defeat came in so many ways far deeper than the obvious."

Tancred grew silent for a moment in memory. "Arianne prayed for me. She told me so. She told me that she saw a remnant of good left over from the past. It gave her hope that I could be changed. She pleaded with my brother for my worthless life, for she knew my soul was condemned."

Devon smiled. He could well imagine his sister's meddling. "She has a tender heart."

"Aye," Tancred responded softly. "Would that all men could know the love of one such as she."

Devon nodded. "She is more dear to me than life itself."

"Arianne's words haunted me these last months. I knew I was without hope. I could not bear to share my heart, even with the priest, for fear of hearing confirmation that I was completely unsaveable."

"And did your philosopher see the error of your thought?"

The ship pitched against the waves, and both men gripped the railing for support. Tancred could nearly smell the English soil, and all that was in him cried for the sights of home.

"Artimas," he said, fixing his eyes on the landed horizon, "told me of his own teacher. A man of great intellect. His name is Thomas Aquinas. Artimas was on his way to meet with his master when he took his comfort with me." Tancred chuckled in memory. "Of course, there was plainly little of comfort in that hovel you found me in, but Artimas made it seem unimportant.

"He asked me of my life, and I laughed at the man. I truly had no will to live and plainly told him so."

"And what did he say?"

"He told me that the will was the single strongest source of motivation to all the other powers of the soul."

"Meaning exactly what?" Devon asked, now fully curious of this man's philosophy.

"That without will, nothing can be done." Devon nodded in understanding but waited for Tancred to continue. "Artimas believes that faith is the one thing that gives power to the will."

"And where does faith find birth when a man has no desire to live?"

Tancred smiled. "Through action and reason. Faith and reason are dependent upon each other. Aquinas teaches that reason without faith is meaningless, but then so, too, is faith without reason. Faith is that substance that causes a man to say, 'Yea, I will believe even though it is impossible,' while reason finds a way to make the impossible happen."

"Spoken like a true philosopher!" Devon declared.

"In the second century after the death and resurrection of Christ, people heard Saint Justin proclaim that God had given philosophy to the Greeks even as He had given His Law to the Jewish people. I believe philosophy is not without merit."

"But what of the argument that you can either be a philosopher or a

Christian? If Christianity contains the truth, then all else must surely not contain it. I've always been given over to the thought that it is not our place to join them together but to choose one or the other," Devon said with honest interest in the matter.

Tancred nodded. "I've heard it said as well. People fear that to question and reason that which causes them difficulty might in fact nullify their faith, and faith is most necessary to please God. The scriptures make this clear."

"Sine fide impossibile est placere Deo—without faith it is impossible to please God," Devon remembered from his childhood training.

"Exactly. But man, being man, questions things quite naturally. To reason a matter seems a logical choice until another comes along and declares you a heretic for having no faith."

"A twisted matter to be sure."

"Alas," Tancred said with a look of peace so clear upon his face that Devon could not doubt the truth of his statement. "'Tis more important that God has given peace to my soul."

Devon nodded, knowing that peace for himself. "Aye. 'Tis indeed most beneficial."

In a small, unpretentious room, Richard found himself face-to-face with his king. Henry, in his surcoat of green and gold, entered the room and waived off the cleric who dogged his every step.

"I have no need of you here, man. Await me in the outer room," the king spoke, and the man quickly responded to his command.

"Richard!" Henry said with a heartiness he reserved for family. "'Tis good you are with us. There is a matter that I believe you will find much to your liking."

"You have always treated me generously," Richard replied.

"And you have served me faithfully. Therefore, I have brought you here this day to inform you of a particular matter. I am granting workers and monies to see an expansion of your harbor. You will soon have a fine place to receive goods and trade of all manner."

Richard stared in surprise. "I had no idea. I sought but a charter to give our town a fair each year. I had little reason to hope such a thing as this could be within my grasp."

Henry smiled benevolently upon the man who had once held residency with his own family after the death of his parents. "'Tis a generous act, for a good man."

"I am most humbly honored."

"There is yet another matter," the king said, pleased with the announcement he was about to make. "I have had word that your brother's ship safely entered our harbor yesterday. He and your wife's brother are making their way north to Gavenshire. I release you to join them."

Richard's face revealed his anticipation and pleasure at the news. "What of your men and the harbor plans?"

"I will send them north within a fortnight. Give it no further concern for the time," Henry replied, then lowered his voice as if to imply secrecy. "Richard, I know you seek the murderer of your father and mother. You have my leave to bring that person to justice. I pray you are successful, only make certain of the facts. A man's life is now eleven years gone, and all because we rushed to judgment. I regret that deeply and beg God's forgiveness."

"I, too," Richard admitted to the pious king he so admired. "'Tis a lesson I'll not soon forget."

"Aye," Henry answered, nodding. His face seemed to change from the sobriety, however, in a flash. "Then be off with you, man. They have a lead on you by more than a day's ride."

Richard bowed, and then the matter of Helena came to mind.

"Sire, there is a matter that I feel should be aired."

"Pray tell?"

"I have taken a young woman into the protection and care of my castle. Her name is Helena, but she claims memory of nothing more. She is gentle born and clearly a lady."

"I see," Henry said, thoughtfully stroking his chin. "No one knows of her origins?"

"Nay," Richard replied. "I sent out riders and they returned without a single word to encourage us. Helena says very little, but she is a kind and hearty soul. I gave her leave to remain with us but thought you should be made aware of the matter. There is always the possibility that someone may seek her out, and should they begin their search here, you will already be aware of the circumstance."

"I will bear it in mind."

The sound of riders caused Devon and Tancred to come to their feet. A heavy fog had just begun to cloud over the land, and what the darkness did not blot out, the misty whiteness did.

"Who goes there?" Devon called out, his hand on the hilt of his sword.

"His Grace, the Duke of Gavenshire," came the call. A look of relief crossed Devon's face, and he released the sword. Tancred, also armed, did likewise and stood with a sobering glance in the direction of the voices.

"Richard?" Devon called.

"Aye, 'tis me," Richard replied, riding into the soft glow of their campfire light. He drew his horse up and dismounted. Throwing the reins to his squire, Richard stepped forward with a determined stare and met his brother's gaze.

"Henry told me you had arrived. I found it most gratifying to spend the day in yon saddle in order to reach you by nightfall."

"Gratifying is not a word that comes to mind," Tancred replied in jest, "when thinking of a hard ride to London on a beast such as that."

Richard laughed tensely. "'Tis good to see you again."

"Better circumstances than our last meeting, eh?" Tancred's dark eyes were lit with amusement, yet there was hesitation in his manner. Would his brother truly forgive him and honor this new peace between them? Everyone seemed to watch and wait for Richard's reply.

"Aye, the matter is clearly a more pleasant one." Then with a smile, Richard stepped forward a pace and opened his arms.

"I pray it is well with thee."

Tancred hesitated for a moment, then embraced his brother. There were tears on his cheeks, and Tancred was grateful the darkness covered his embarrassment. Yet when he pulled away, he noted there were tears in Richard's eyes as well.

"We have much to discuss," Richard said in a voice none too steady.

"Aye," Tancred replied. "Eleven years' worth."

Chapter 8

Helena watched Arianne and Matilda, almost as if she were detached from the life around her. The more she kept up her deception and refused to speak of her past, the worse she felt. Now the Easter season was upon them and great preparations were underway for the celebration that would come.

The castle took on a rumbling of excitement. Servants worked a little harder and faster, while knights, clerics, and clergy anticipated the fine feasts and parties that would follow the unveiling of the cross on Easter Sunday.

But, Helena reminded herself, Easter Sunday was still several days away and there was much to be done. She tried to keep her hands busy at the tasks Arianne had assigned her, but her heart wasn't in the work. She watched Timothy, cradled at her side without a care in the world. He stared up at her with dark blue eyes as if to say, "My life and yours be not that different." Helena thought it true, whether Timothy was actually considering such a weighty matter or not.

The parish priest had stated that Easter was a matter of faith. Faith that the stone would be rolled away. Faith that the Savior would rise from the dead. Faith that in such an action, death would be defeated and all the wrongs in the world righted. But Helena felt her faith wane. It had been so long since she'd had any reason to believe that her wrongs would be righted.

There was a commotion in the kitchen, and Helena couldn't resist smiling at the way Arianne quickly settled the dispute. Arianne was quite competent, and Helena greatly admired her. Admired and was jealous of her, which Helena had sought forgiveness for on more than one occasion. It wasn't that she would wish any other life for the duchess. Nay, it was that she longed with all her heart to have a joy and happiness similar to that which Arianne called her life.

Oh, Tanny, she thought. *Would that you could take me as wife and dispel my longing and anguish. What would be the price I would pay for your return, for a single day, even an hour, to sit by your side?* Tears came unbidden to her eyes, and Helena lowered her head so that no one could see her cry.

"Oh, Father," she whispered, "I fear I cannot bear up under this burden any longer. 'Tis more than I am able to conquer." Timothy seemed to think she was talking to him and gave a gurgling sound.

Helena smiled and lifted the babe to see the activity that bustled around him. "See there, young sire," she said softly, "your mother, the duchess, is planning quite a celebration."

Arianne glanced across the room to see Helena holding Timothy. She smiled and came to extend her hands out to take her son. "What mischief are you about, my Timothy?" she questioned in amusement.

"I told him you were preparing a feast," Helena offered. "He seemed quite interested."

"No doubt," Arianne said with a laugh. "In a few years, he'll race with the other boys and tilt at the quintain. Soon enough he'll go off to foster with others and my time with him will be greatly diminished."

"But you'll have other children," Helena reminded her.

"Yea, but I'm thinking the first is something different. The firstborn gives you cause to think and remember the sheer wonder of God." She looked down at her son with such love that Helena had to lower her gaze. It hurt too much to be so near what she needed and yet know that it could not belong to her.

Why God? she wondered silently. *Why must my heart belong to one who is so very far away; one who knows not whether I come or go? One who may very well be dead.* This last thought caused Helena to shudder. If Tanny were dead, she would have no reason to go on.

"God is good, is He not?" Arianne offered softly, not knowing the gloomy thoughts of her friend.

Helena had barely heard the words and took a moment as if to translate their meaning. "Yes, He is good," she finally replied. *But not always swift,* she added to herself.

It was hoped that Richard would be home by Easter, but when Good Friday arrived and the duke was still absent, Arianne tried to make the best of it.

Throughout Lent, the observations of the season had been met with enthusiasm. The castle chapel, as well as the church in the village, found its sanctuary hung with veiling to shroud the cross and holy relics. Good Friday presented a memorial to that day when Christ had gone willingly to the cross to offer salvation to all mankind.

Leaving one of the other chambermaids to care for Timothy, Arianne and Helena led the castle procession in the "creeping to the cross."

The women bowed low and walked slowly in reverent memory of the crucifixion. Helena couldn't hold back her tears. She was deeply moved at the sacrifice her Lord had made, but so, too, was she in deep sorrow for the loss in her heart. Somehow their combination was appropriate, and she instantly felt that God would have her leave her heartache on the church steps with the cross.

Approaching the now unveiled cross, Helena rose up only slightly and kissed it, declaring to God as she did so that just as they would bury the cross until Easter Sunday, so Helena would give over her anguish to be buried as well. At least this had been her heart's desire.

If the duchess thought it strange that her lady-in-waiting sobbed openly at the symbol of Christ's sacrifice, she did not say so. Instead, as they left the steps to allow the others to come forward, Arianne simply placed her arm around Helena's shoulders.

They watched from the side as the ceremony concluded. The priest took the cross and wrapped it tenderly in white silk and placed it in a prepared sepulchre set deep inside the church wall. With this done, a veil was set over the opening, candles were set to surround the tomb, and each candle was lit as a prayer was recited.

The time that followed the ceremony was one of reflection and sobriety. The castle was strangely quiet, and even the servants worked in hushed effort. It was as though the entire community held its breath in anticipation.

Helena found it strangely comforting. She went about her duties, seeing to Timothy's needs when Arianne was busy with other tasks, and writing songs in her head when moments of inspiration came upon her.

On Easter Eve, the candles surrounding the sepulchre were extinguished. A single candle, the great Paschal candle, was lit as an all-night vigil of the clergy began. Arianne watched with Helena, deeply disappointed that Richard had not yet returned. Helena felt her lady's sorrow and reached out a hand to reassure the duchess.

They walked back to the castle in silence, a procession of knights and their families following behind. Many parted at the castle gatehouse for their own homes, while unmarried knights took refuge in the barracks provided for them within the castle walls.

To Helena, it seemed as though a great shroud had been placed upon them. The silence fell heavy in an almost smothering way. Each sound seemed magnified against the stillness; each footstep rustling against the rushes upon the floor echoed loudly within the dark, damp halls. It was a hallowed time.

Matilda handed Arianne a cresset lamp with oil. Without being told, she lit the wick and nodded, as though words would somehow have been a blasphemy of the moment. Arianne, bearing the lamp, went upstairs with Helena following closely behind her. They parted at Helena's room, Arianne placing a silent kiss upon her cheek.

"Let us pray that Richard returns soon and," she added almost as an afterthought, "that Devon will return and bring Richard's brother home."

Helena nodded and sought the refuge of her room. The fire burned low, and Helena knew it would only be a matter of time before the castle curfew or "cover fire" would be upon them and the watchman would make his rounds to stoke up the hearth fires for the night.

Feeling the cold and damp penetrate her skin, she readied herself for bed. A song came to her lips, and only when she began to sing did Helena realize it was a requiem. The mournful words flooded the room, while the haunting melody seemed to drip down from the walls and flood the stones below.

With slow, almost practiced steps, Helena went to the bed and knelt on the turned-back covers. Reaching up, she loosed the ties that held back the canopy curtains surrounding the bed and closed them around her.

Heavy brocade snuffed out the light from the hearth. It was like burying herself in the sepulchre, Helena thought. She pulled the covers high to her chin and settled upon the satin-covered pillow. Then with a will of its own, her mouth opened, and again the eerie strains of mourning filled the night's silence.

Arianne stood at the window of her bedroom. While the priests kept vigil in the church, she kept her own for Richard's return. Silently, she brushed her copper hair and with each stroke thought of her husband's absence and the longing she felt for his return. Had it only been weeks? It truly felt as though a lifetime had passed since she'd last felt his arms around her or heard his boyish laughter ringing in the halls.

Putting the brush aside, Arianne hugged her arms to her body and looked out upon the darkened lands.

"Oh, Richard," she whispered. Just then Helena's sad voice came through in a muffled song.

Arianne strained to hear the words but couldn't make them out. She thought of how blessed Helena was. The voice of an angel, Matilda had said, and Arianne thought perhaps even angels would behold Helena's voice in awe.

But tonight was different, Arianne thought. Usually Helena's songs were light, lyrical, and joyful. This was music for the dead, and Arianne knew that it came from deep within Helena's own heart. Was she wishing that she were dead?

"Dear Father," Arianne prayed in earnest, "go to her and give her peace." Then glancing out again to a world that would offer no hope of her husband's return, Arianne pleaded for the same comfort for herself.

"Bring him home, Lord," she begged. "Bring Richard home soon and with him Devon and Tancred, as well."

Timothy began to fuss, and Arianne went to the cradle and tenderly took him in hand. Taking him with her to the bed, Arianne settled down to nurse him. She took great comfort in this action. Somehow with Timothy beside her, she felt Richard's presence. Her cheeks flushed warm at the thought of Timothy's life coming out of her love for Richard. What wonders God had wrought and how inconceivable His ways, Arianne thought.

Just then Helena's singing ended, and somehow its absence made the silence seem overwhelming. Arianne cuddled Timothy closer and nuzzled his soft head with her lips.

"Dear Father," she whispered, "let this night pass quickly."

Chapter 9

Helena awoke and pushed back the bed curtains, just as the morning sun was streaking the horizon with pale, rose-colored light. Taking the fur that had been placed upon her bed for added warmth, Helena wrapped it tightly around her and stood in the open window.

As each inch of darkness yielded to the light, Helena felt a small corner of her heart yield as well. It was easier to be brave in the light, she mused. Staring out across the newly plowed fields to the forest of trees in the distance, Helena wondered how much longer she would be able to stay at Gavenshire.

"Oh, Father," she whispered in a moan, leaning heavily against the stone that framed the window opening. There was little else to say, for in her heart she had no words. Words seemed inadequate. What more could she ask of God?

From the village and bailey below her came sounds of the morning. Cocks crowed and hushed voices rose to sounds of merriment and laughter. It was Easter, and today they would celebrate the resurrection of Christ. Helena smiled sadly. She had tried so hard to bury her suffering, yet daily it seemed to come back to life with a will of its own. *What strange creatures we must seem to God,* she thought.

It wasn't long before a young girl appeared at Helena's door to help her dress for morning services. Helena felt extremely privileged as she donned a tunic of the finest pale pink silk. It felt soft and cold against her body, but Helena relished it. The neckline had been embroidered by her own hand with tiny flower buds and ivy twining. Next came a surcoat of amber velvet. Helena had never known anything so regal in all of her life.

"You look grand, milady," the girl said boldly. And indeed she was right in saying so.

Helena waited patiently while the girl dressed her hair and secured a thin white wimple to cover her head and neck. She was bringing Helena her slippers when Arianne knocked on the door.

"Good Easter morn," she announced, sweeping into the room.

She was resplendent in her sendal tunic of cream and surcoat of dark green velvet. The sendal material made a rustling sound, causing Arianne to smile. "My finery will no doubt announce me in church."

Helena laughed and curtsied. "You are truly a pleasure to behold, Your Grace. Would that your husband could be here."

"Aye," Arianne sighed. "I prayed it might be so." Her words seemed sad, but still she smiled. "The day is not yet out. Perhaps Richard will arrive after church."

"Let us hope so," Helena replied.

They made their way to the bailey below with a crowd of others following and gathering around them. Easter was quite a celebration for the people. The villeins would be given time off to enjoy a rest from their labors, knights would test their skills against each other in mock joust, and nobility would survey all from amid the revelry and deem it good.

Helena had been a part of Easter celebrations before, but never anything so grand and glorious. They made their way to the church, finding smiling faces and happy greetings wherever they went.

"I truly love this," Arianne stated as they walked. "I have enjoyed our own castle chapel, but the church in town allows me to be amidst all the people. I feel as though I've always belonged here."

Helena grimaced but did not allow Arianne to see her pain. The words only served to remind her that she did not belong here or anywhere and that only by Arianne's kindness had she been allowed to stay. What would happen when the duke returned? Perhaps he would insist Helena reveal her identity and go home. What would she do then?

The pealing of the church bells brought Helena out of her stupor. It was impossible to be lost in such gloomy thought with such glorious sounds all around her. It made Helena want to sing, and in spite of her resolve to be quiet, she began to hum to herself. If Arianne heard, she said nothing. She was too busy laughing and greeting the people around her.

"Richard told me that the priest has arranged to present the *Quem quaeritis*," Arianne said in a whisper to Helena. "It will come at the end of the mass."

"I have heard of this but never seen it," Helena replied as they walked up the steps of the church and were greeted by the priest.

Ushered inside by two of Richard's most trusted men, Arianne and

Helena stood upon the straw-covered floor and awaited the procession of the priests and choirboys. With a song of celebration, they entered the church. Helena watched in complete captivation as the cross was brought out from the mock sepulchre and laid upon the altar.

At this, they knelt in the straw and bowed their heads as the priest offered up a Latin prayer. The service progressed in a series of prayers, songs, and ceremony. At the end of the service, the priest stepped behind a screen and then reappeared with three other men for the *Quem quaeritis*, a reenactment of the resurrection story.

One priest, dressed in white vestments and holding a palm in his hand, represented the angel at the tomb. *"Quem quaeritis in sepulchro?"* he questioned. "Whom do you seek in the sepulchre?"

The others, representing the three Marys, answered in unison, "Jesus of Nazareth."

Helena's breath caught. It was a moving play, and in her mind, she could very nearly imagine it was all real and happening for the first time. "Whom do you seek?" a voice seemed to question within her soul.

Tears came to her eyes. For all of her life, she had been raised in the beliefs and understandings of the church. She had never once questioned the existence of God or of His Son, Jesus Christ. She practiced with the utmost reverence the requirements of her faith, yet in all that time she could not say in honesty that it had been God whom she sought.

"He is not here, He has risen," the angel-priest was announcing.

With this, the three Marys turned to the choir and replied, "Hallelujah, the Lord is risen today!" Then the choir joined in a chorus of praise.

The angel-priest moved to where the cross had been placed in the wall. He lifted the veil that now covered the opening and said, "Come, see the place."

The Marys crossed to peer inside, while two men representing the apostles Peter and John appeared from behind the screen. John was in white and holding a palm, while Peter was dressed in red and carrying keys.

John reached the sepulchre first, but Peter reached inside. He pulled out the gravecloth in which the cross had been wrapped on Good Friday. "He is not here."

"He is risen as He said," the angel-priest announced.

Helena felt the tears flow down her cheeks. "Quem quaeritis? Whom do you seek?" She thought of Tanny and the love that might have been given to the hope that she would one day find him. "Whom do you seek?"

She watched the play continue with the exit of two of the Marys. The third, dressed in red and representing Mary Magdalene, stood weeping. For some reason, this made Helena cry all the more.

"Woman, why weepest thou? Whom seekest thou?"

The voice went straight to Helena's heart. She knew that God had been with her through all the years of anguish and lonely heartache. Now, it seemed as though this simple trooping of the resurrection story had brought a realization to Helena's soul. God wanted her to seek Him, Him alone. Not Tanny and not a home or place where she'd feel safe. God wanted her to seek only Him.

"They have taken my Lord," the man playing Mary stated in a sobbing voice.

The miracle unfolded, and the man playing Jesus revealed himself to Mary, much as God was revealing Himself to Helena as she stood and beheld the story.

"Rabboni," Mary said, falling to the ground. "My master."

"Rabboni," Helena whispered, knowing in her heart that God had truly taken control of her life.

The performance ended with a glorious hymn sung by the choir. "*Te Deum Laudamus*—We praise Thee, God." Overhead, the bell pealed in celebratory announcement. "He is risen. He is not here."

Helena left the church a converted woman much, she imagined, as Mary must have left the garden. Just the knowledge that she was no longer bound to her fears gave Helena the first real happiness she'd known since her beloved had gone away.

All around, the revelry was evident. There was dancing and singing, feasting and gifting. The tenants of the land brought eggs in payment to the castle, while in return Arianne had planned a great feast for all the people.

Arianne acted as hostess with Helena never leaving her side except to take baby Timothy upstairs in order to remove him from the noise of the castle bailey. Helena knew that Arianne scanned the horizon constantly for some sign of her husband, and when evening was approaching, the call that she had waited for finally came.

"The duke approaches!" one of the battlement guards called out.

"The duke!" Murmurs ran through the crowd, and people stopped their feasting to line the entryway into the castle.

Arianne glanced around for Helena and then remembered that she'd gone to take Timothy for his changing. "Matilda!" she said, beckoning the woman from the crowd. "Run, get Helena and Timothy. I would present him to his father and show Richard how much he has grown." Matilda quickly went in search of Helena, while Arianne rushed forward to greet her husband.

Three horsemen appeared in front of the procession, and Arianne instantly recognized each rider. Richard rode slightly to the front, with Devon and Tancred bringing up the rear.

"Richard!" she shouted and hurried to his side.

Richard dismounted in a leap and pulled her into his arms. "I have missed you sorely, sweet wife," he whispered and kissed her boldly in front of everyone.

Cheers below went up from the crowd, and Helena could only wonder at what matter had stirred them this time. There had been such cheering and shouting all day, and at times, Helena had worried that the babe's ears would be harmed from such noise. Nestling Timothy against her tightly, Helena moved through the happy people.

She knew from Matilda that the duke had returned, and no doubt his people were simply celebrating that fact. As the crowd parted for her, however, she found herself only a few feet away from the embracing couple and instantly flushed at the scene.

Arianne pulled back and saw her. "Richard, come see your son. He has grown wondrously since you last saw him."

Richard smiled at Helena, who was now trembling. "Your Grace," she said, as Richard reached out and took the baby.

"You are looking much better than the last time I saw you," Richard said with a smile.

Helena nodded but refused to meet his eyes. Would he send her away? Again, peace washed over her, and Helena realized it didn't matter. Lifting her gaze, she smiled.

"Much better," Richard said, then smiled down at his son. "And you truly have grown."

Helena noted the two men who were dismounting but gave them little thought until Arianne went to embrace each one of them. They had their backs to her, but Helena could see the smile of pleasure and something akin to relief in Arianne's eyes.

Richard handed Timothy back to Helena and pulled her forward. "You must meet my brother," he said firmly.

"It has been a long time," Arianne was telling one of the men. "I am glad you have returned."

Helena thought little of the matter, but when her eyes lifted to meet the man whom Richard introduced, she was stunned silent.

"Helena, this is my brother, John Tancred DuBonnet."

Helena's eyes were drawn to Tancred's against her will. "Tanny," she murmured so softly that no one understood her. Her arms began to shake, and she thought for a moment she might drop Timothy. Arianne noted her state and quickly took the baby from her.

"Helena, is it well with you?" Arianne whispered against her ear. But Helena only stared dumbfounded at the man before her.

"Milady," Tancred said, with a slight bow. He was mesmerized by the huge blue eyes that refused to break their hold on him. She was clearly the most beautiful creature he'd ever beheld.

"Helena?" Richard said, noting the whiteness of her face. "Are you ill?"

"Mayhaps she's just taken in by the charming faces of these men," Arianne teased lightly. She was truly worried about her lady-in-waiting but refused to cause Helena any further embarrassment. "Helena needs to attend to Timothy's bath. Come, no doubt my son will seek his feeding as well."

Helena allowed herself to be led away by Arianne, but still she said nothing. How could it be so? Tanny, her own beloved Tanny, had come to her. Still, he knew her naught. She had been but a child when last they'd met, and now she was a grown woman. Should she go to him and reveal herself? Yet in revealing herself, she would also betray her true identity.

"Have you not heard me?" Arianne questioned with a gentle nudge.

"I am sorry," Helena whispered. "I am just a bit spent from the celebration. It has been a most taxing day."

Arianne nodded. "I asked you if there was something you wanted to tell me. Has the past somehow caught up with you?"

Helena looked panicked as her gaze met that of the concerned duchess. "May we speak of it another time?" Her voice was soft and pleading.

Arianned nodded. "Of course. Would you prefer I take care of Timothy's bath?"

"Aye," Helena replied. "I would like to lie down."

"Then do so and know that when you feel better, I will be here for you." Arianne reached out a hand to touch Helena's slender arm. "Don't be afraid, Helena. You have a home here for as long as you want one. No one will put you from Gavenshire."

Somehow she knows, Helena thought to herself. Somehow the duchess had understood a portion of her fear. *But what will the duchess of Gavenshire have to say when the entire truth is revealed?* Helena wondered.

Closing her chamber door behind her, Helena leaned heavily against the wood. He was here! Her heart quickened, and she crossed to the window, anxious to catch some sight of him in the bailey below. Darkness and shadows refused to offer up anything, however, and Helena felt cheated.

"Tanny, it is I," she said softly in the silence of her room. "'Tis your Helena, whose heart has ever been and evermore shall be yours and yours alone."

Chapter 10

Roger Talbot paced anxiously while awaiting his appointment with the king. It wouldn't be easy to explain Helena's disappearance, but if he handled the matter carefully, he was certain he could be convincing.

"The king will see you now," a pious chamberlain announced.

Roger entered a room where the king sat in conversation with two other men. The chamberlain made the introduction, and Roger waited to be acknowledged. In time the king motioned Roger forward.

"You have requested an audience with me?" Henry questioned.

"Yea, Your Majesty." Roger choked back bile. His nerves were raw, and this matter did not bode well with him.

"Then be at it, man. What matter did you wish to discuss?"

"'Tis my sister, Helena. As you will recall, her mother, Eleanor, was cousin to the queen."

"Aye, I remember it, man. I remember it well. What do you seek?"

"I seek my sister. Helena disappeared from our home, and I have not found her, though we have searched the land far and wide." Roger hoped he sounded convincingly worried.

"Helena?" The king spoke her name and instantly the memory of Richard DuBonnet entered his mind. "I believe I know where your sister is."

"You do?" Roger swallowed hard. Had Helena somehow managed to venture to London without his knowledge?

"Yes, yes," Henry nodded enthusiastically. "She is at Gavenshire. Duke DuBonnet mentioned the presence of a young woman named Helena. She has only been with him a short time and claimed no memory of her family or home."

"DuBonnet?" Roger questioned. He felt his stomach lurch again.

"Aye, Richard DuBonnet, Duke of Gavenshire. You know of the place, do you not?"

"Aye," Roger replied between clenched teeth. "I know it." The DuBonnets had long been known to him, especially Richard's brother, Tancred. "I will seek her out immediately."

"By my leave," the king said, dismissing Roger Talbot as though there was nothing more that interested him about the man.

Roger seethed at the thought of his sister under the care of a DuBonnet. Tancred DuBonnet, once his most trusted friend, had dishonored Maude and refused to marry her. A scandal of outrageous proportions had been narrowly averted only when an aging earl had agreed to make Maude his wife.

He had thought himself well rid of DuBonnets when Tancred had been convicted of killing his parents. Roger remembered with great satisfaction the day he had learned of Tancred's sentence. Would that it could have been his death rather than his exile.

With his mind made up, Roger called a messenger to him and paid the man well to take word to Maude. There was no point in putting off his journey to Gavenshire, and he had little desire to confront Maude before doing battle with Tancred's brother. Mounting his horse, Roger grimaced and took the reins in hand. "Once again the DuBonnets cause me grief. This time I shall put an end to it."

The days of Easter celebration passed in a mixture of bliss and pain for Helena. She watched with dedicated interest as Tancred moved about the castle. From behind carefully guarded eyes, Helena kept track of his every move.

From the first break of dawn and morning services, Helena's eyes seldom failed to keep Tancred in their view. When they partook of the meals, Helena tried to react in a calm and collected way, but knowing that Tancred sat on the other side of Richard made her nervous and testy. How much longer could she stand being so near him and not confide in him who she was?

It no longer worried her that she would be sent from Gavenshire. Now what concerned her was that Tancred would not return her love. Her beloved Tanny had left her childhood days as a strapping young man of twenty. Now, he was a brooding man of thirty-one years with a mission to find the true murderers of his parents.

Obviously, Helena realized, he had no time or inclination for romance. She thought of the hours she'd spent dreaming of the day they'd meet again. Now that day had come and gone, and it was nothing of what she'd dreamed about.

As they sat at supper one evening, the revelry of festivities in the village still going on in celebration, Helena picked at her food and listened to the conversation around her.

"What a difference this life must be from the one you spent the past eleven years," Richard said to Tancred.

"Aye. The food is much better, the housing much drier, and the company preferable to any that I knew abroad."

Arianne leaned forward. "Devon tells me of your philosopher Artimas. He sounds like a wonderful man. I would very much like to meet him one day."

"He was, indeed, a great man, dear sister. I found the seeds you tenderly planted in my heart grew under his careful watering."

Helena felt a twinge of jealousy rear within her heart. "Pray tell, what seeds does he speak of, Your Grace?"

Arianne smiled. "I but saw the potential in Tancred that he could not see for himself. I told him of his value in the eyes of God. Artimas apparently found a way to cultivate that meager planting."

"'Twas far from meager," Tancred said. His eyes were reflective of the deep emotion he felt. "I felt hopelessness such as I beg never to feel again, but even in the darkest moment, Arianne's word of love gave me cause to hope."

"Hope is often all that keeps us going," Helena said softly, her eyes lowered to her trencher.

"Faith," Arianne added. "Faith is hope at work."

"Very good, Sister," Tancred said with a smile.

Later that night, Tancred stood in the quiet of his chamber, undressing for bed. He thought back over the last few days, but his mind could not let go of Helena. He saw her everywhere, even when he slept. It was as though he knew her, and yet there was nothing of recollection in his mind.

"She watches me with the eyes of a hawk," he thought aloud. Yet lovelier eyes of crystal blue Tancred was sure he'd never seen. She was a most fetching woman, and he decided on the morrow he would speak to Arianne about her.

"No need for the woman to haunt my every step. At least not without my reasoning out why." He drew the bed curtains and closed his eyes in sleep. As was true for every night since having been introduced to Helena, Tancred fell asleep with the soft, tender features of her face on his mind.

"Is your husband already among his men?" Tancred asked Arianne the next morning as she sat in the counting room. A long ledger lay before her on the table.

"Aye, he's already gone. You might find him in the stables."

"What of Helena and Matilda?"

"They are upstairs with Timothy. Why do you ask?" Arianne put aside her quill and stared up at her brother-in-law.

Tancred closed the door behind him and pulled up a chair. "I have some questions to ask of you."

"I see. Pray tell, on what matter?"

"Helena."

Arianne smiled. "So she has vexed you as you have her."

"I have vexed her? How so?"

"I am uncertain that I should say. Be it simple enough to conclude she finds you most appealing to her sense. Why, my own brother, Devon, found her fascinating and paid her many compliments, but she saw him naught. She never questioned me about him, either."

"And she questioned you about me?" Tancred's dark eyes pierced Arianne. He leaned forward, intent on her every word.

"Aye." Arianne's voice was soft, and her eyes danced with amusement. "She has scarce discussed anything else."

Tancred smiled in spite of himself. "And why not?" he teased. "Am I not worthy of discussion?"

"Oh, prideful man," Arianne said with mock disdain, "thy pathway leads to destruction."

Tancred laughed aloud. "Never mind that. Tell me what she has asked of you."

Arianne grew thoughtful. "She asked me about your arrival here last year. She asked if the things we had heard about you were true."

"What things?" Tancred's eyes narrowed.

Arianne grew uncomfortable, and involuntarily her hand went to her face—to the cheek Tancred had so sorely bruised when he'd hit her in anger.

"Oh, that," he replied before she could speak. The sorrow in his eyes matched that in his voice.

"I told her you were beside yourself in hopelessness. I told her you were desperate and that you saw all that you loved taken beyond your grasp." Arianne paused and reached out to touch Tancred's arm. "I told her there was a void in you that could not be filled, and she told me that this was something she could understand."

"You are most gracious, Arianne. I do not deserve your kindness."

She smiled and squeezed his arm. "I have such happiness with Richard and Timothy. God took me from a frightful existence and no earthly love, save that of my brother, and gave me an abundance. My advice to you, Sir Tancred, is that you grasp firmly what is held within your reach. Helena is besot with you, and I believe she considers herself in love with you."

"Did she say that?"

"Nay. She didn't have to." Arianne took her quill back in hand. "Sometimes the heart speaks most loudly when the mouth says nothing at all."

Tancred took Arianne's words with him, and they only served to double his determination to seek out the alluring Helena and learn the truth from her. He had spent so much time in conference with Arianne that he was certain Helena would no longer be in the rooms with Timothy. Where she might be was a mystery to him, but experience had shown him that Helena would no doubt find him.

Coming down the outer castle stairs, Tancred could not believe his good fortune when he spied Helena planting herbs in the castle garden. He watched her for a moment, knowing that she was unaware of his presence.

There was something strangely familiar about her, and yet Tancred knew he had no recollection to their ever meeting. Perhaps that was what he should ask her first, but then again, mayhaps that would only serve to scare her off.

She was singing softly, and the sound rose up to greet him in a pleasant way. Arianne had said that Helena had the voice of an angel, Tancred remembered. It was one night after dinner when someone had mentioned hearing singing in the castle.

He couldn't make out the words, but her voice haunted him and he felt almost mesmerized by the melody. He came down the steps quietly, still studying her form as she dug at little spots of dirt and patted seed into the ground.

He was standing directly behind her, and it wasn't until Helena noticed his shadow on the ground that she started and turned to face him.

"I—I. . ." She couldn't form the words.

"Lady Helena," Tancred said, reaching his hand down to draw her up. "I wondered if we might talk."

"Talk?" She was shaking and refused to take the offered hand. *I can't let him touch me*, she thought. *He'll feel how I tremble and he'll know what I'm thinking*.

Tancred was unconcerned at her aloofness. He reached out and pulled her to her feet. "Aye, talk. Come along, there is a bench over here."

Helena felt him draw her along, and all the while her mind could scarcely take it in. This was Tanny. This was no dream, but a living, breathing man—the man she'd pledged to love for as long as she lived.

"Here," he said, allowing Helena to take a seat. For a moment, he stood towering over her, arms crossed against his leather tunic. He looked much like a father about to scold his child, and when that image filtered through to his senses, he softened and took the seat beside her.

"You have been much on my mind of late," he began. "I wonder why that is?"

Helena couldn't answer. Her throat felt constricted and her tongue too big for her mouth. Swallowing hard, she wavered between fainting and gasping for air.

"You are a comely maid, and I find that your beauty is most appealing. However, I am not used to such attention, and I feel I must ask why you have sought me out?"

"Sought you out?" Helena questioned, finally finding her voice. "But, sire, you brought me here. 'Twas your idea to talk."

"Yes, yes. But, what else could I do? You watch my every move. You peer down even from your bedchamber to watch me upon the training field. I know, for I have seen you there."

Helena paled, then blushed. "Aye, I have watched you."

"For what purpose, if I might ask?"

"I—I do not...," she stammered, then tried to get to her feet, but his hand shot out to take hold of her.

"Nay, do not leave. Answer my question."

Helena could bear it no longer. The sight and scent of him, the feel of his ironlike grip upon her wrist, even the very breath he breathed called out to be taken into account.

"Why do you watch me?" he asked softly.

"Because I love you," she declared, and the words so shocked Tancred that he dropped his hold. "Because I love you now and always have and forever will." She hurried from the bailey, running up the stairs and vanishing out of sight while Tancred sat with open mouth.

"She loves me? But she knows naught of me," Tancred said, staring at the stone stairs. What did she mean by it? The words came back to haunt him. "*Because I love you now and always have.*" Did he know her? He searched his memory for some woman named Helena and gave up without a face to set it in place.

"Helena," he murmured, and the word wrapped itself as a band around his heart.

Chapter 11

Richard was soaked in sweat from the sword fights he'd endured with his men on the training field. He was aching in several muscles, which told him he'd let himself get soft. He shook his head ruefully and determined that he would begin practicing daily. Plunging his head in the water trough, he didn't hear the first call from his sentry that a rider approached.

Richard took an offered towel from his squire and dried his face.

"Will you see the man?" the squire asked his master, knowing full well Richard had not heard the sentry's announcement.

"What man?"

"A rider has been announced." The squire motioned to the sentry on the battlement overhead.

"A single rider?" Richard questioned. The sentry confirmed this. "Admit him."

The lone horseman rode into the castle and was soon surrounded by several of Richard's knights. One held the man's horse while the stranger dismounted. Richard strode forward to meet him.

"I am the duke of Gavenshire. How might I help you?"

The man was clearly amazed at being greeted by the duke himself; nevertheless it was hostility that sounded in his voice and not surprise. "I am Sir Roger Talbot, and you have my sister."

Richard stared at the man for a moment. "I do not believe I understand."

Roger's anger surfaced more boldly, and several of the knights moved to stand beside their duke. "You have Helena!"

Richard studied the man for a moment. "There abides here a young woman named Helena; that much is true. You claim she is your sister?"

"Aye, that she is. King Henry told me himself that she was here. I've come to take her back."

"I see. Why don't you come inside with me and we will speak to Helena on the matter."

"Helena has no voice in this. She will do as I tell her." Roger was livid. His face was purplish red, and veins in his neck were engorged.

Richard narrowed his eyes. "Helena is under my protection, and I say we speak to her on the matter."

Roger gritted his teeth and realized the duke would not be bullied by him. "Very well," he muttered.

Richard motioned him to follow and called for one of the castle maids to seek out Arianne and Helena. The girl went quickly upstairs to the bedchambers while Richard took Roger to his private receiving room just off the great hall.

"Perhaps we will be more comfortable here. Will you not have a seat?"

"No." Roger's voice was clipped and cold.

"Have I offended you in some way?" Richard asked, his eyes narrowing. "You barge into my home and make demands and do so with the utmost rudeness. What is there between us that merits such action?"

Roger remembered Tancred's dalliance with his sister Maude and frowned. "Your brother was John Tancred DuBonnet, was he not?"

"He still is. What is it to you?"

"He fostered in my home when we were boys. He played false with my sister Maude and nearly ruined her, and you ask me what there is between us that merits my anger?"

"I suppose I was too young or too busy with my own fostering to worry overmuch about Tancred's deeds. Still, the past is no call for bad manners. You and I have no quarrel, so why not be civil?"

Roger eyed Richard suspiciously for a moment, then nodded. "Very well. We will be civil. I have come to take my sister home. She ran away many weeks ago, and I have been quite worried for her safety."

"I see. May I inquire as to why she ran away?"

"'Tis a family matter. The girl's mother passed away not long before, and she could scarce deal with her grief."

Just then Arianne entered the room in conversation with Helena. The two women did not look up until they were well within the room, and when Helena spied her brother, she stopped dead in her tracks.

"Helena!" Roger stated, taking a step forward.

Helena moved back a step, and Richard noted the fear in her eyes. Interceding, he introduced Arianne. "May I present the duchess of Gavenshire." Then turning to his wife, he added, "Arianne, this is Helena's brother, Sir Roger Talbot."

"I am pleased to meet you," Arianne said but realized Roger's eyes were on Helena. Arianne tried to draw Roger into conversation. "We have very much enjoyed your sister's company and would be happy if you, too, would consider yourself welcomed here."

"Helena, I've come to take you home." Roger stepped forward, rudely ignoring Arianne's statement.

Helena shook her head fiercely. "No! I am not going anywhere. The duke and duchess have opened their home to me, and I would very much like to remain here for a time."

"You are coming home," Roger stated flatly and stepped forward to take Helena in hand.

Helena did the only thing she could. She turned and ran for the door, counting on the fact that she knew the castle and Roger did not. She also planned on Richard intervening and calling his men. What she did not plan on was running into the broad, iron chest of Tancred DuBonnet.

Helena was shaking so hard that even Tancred could not mistake the trembling. He looked down at her and found frightened horror in her eyes.

"Helena, what is it?"

"Let her go, DuBonnet," Roger's voice called from behind his sister. Turning to Richard, Roger's eyes blazed. "What would Henry say if he knew you harbored a fugitive? This man is supposed to be in exile for the murder of your parents."

"Henry pardoned Tancred weeks ago. I have the writ upstairs. He is innocent of the murders."

Roger snorted. "I remember the day the king said otherwise. I do not believe him innocent nor pardoned."

"It matters little to me what you think," Tancred replied dryly. His arms engulfed Helena's small frame.

"Unhand her!"

Tancred kept a firm grip on Helena and pulled her closer. Looking past her, he met the eyes of his onetime friend, Roger Talbot.

"What is she to you, Talbot?"

"Fool, she is my stepsister, Helena. Remember? She's the one who used to pester you when you dallied with my sister Maude." Roger moved forward, but this time Richard put himself between them.

Tancred stared down in wonder at the woman in his arms. "This is that little squirt of a girl we pulled out of one scrape and then another?"

Helena was still shaking as she lifted tear-filled eyes to meet his softened expression. "Oh, Tanny," she whispered in a near-mournful tone.

"But you were just a baby," he said, still staring in disbelief. That little girl from his past was the young woman who so fiercely declared her love to him in the bailey only yesterday. It was impossible to comprehend.

"Babies grow up, Tancred. Now unhand my sister and—"

"No!" Helena raged and pushed Tancred away. "I won't go with you. Not now, not ever!" She ran from the room, leaving Tancred to stare after her and Roger to yell a stream of curses.

Helena was grateful for the festivities that still occupied the attention of most of the town. No one paid any attention to her as she ran from the protection of the castle and made her way out across the land.

Tears blinded her eyes, and her heart pounded against the reminder that her brother and Tancred had faced each other for the first time in eleven years. She knew of the past between them. She knew, too, of Maude and the lies that had passed between her and Roger regarding Tancred.

It was all too much.

Fleeing to the sanctuary of the forest, Helena collapsed into a heap on the ground and cried until she felt her heart would break. How could Tanny ever love her now—now that he knew who she was? He hated her brother and her brother hated him. How unfair it all was!

"Oh, God," she cried and hugged her knees to her breast. "Oh, God, 'tis not the way I would have it be. I love him so that I scarce can start my day without my first thoughts being of him." She buried her face against her knees. "Oh, God."

She pleaded for solace and begged for understanding, and still all she could see was the raging eyes of her brother and his determination to take her from Gavenshire. Now that he knew about Tancred, he would no doubt force the issue.

Strong arms lifted her upward, and without looking, Helena knew it was Tancred. She let him hold her while she cried uncontrollably. This would probably be the only time she'd ever feel his arms around her. She wanted to remember the comfort he offered and the way it felt to bury her face against his chest.

Tancred sat down on a fallen log and held the sobbing woman close. She was beautiful, and he could not deny the feelings she had stirred in him in her adoration throughout the week. Yet now, for reasons beyond his ability to consider, her feelings were quite precious to him. In his memories, Helena was but a child. A little girl with torn tunics from her antics and a dirt-smudged face that begged to be washed. Who was this woman who had replaced the child?

Gradually her sobs subsided, and Helena felt strengthened by Tancred's presence. Drying her face on the edge of her surcoat, she looked up at him with reddened eyes.

"I remember a time when you had fallen from the rafters in the stables," Tancred began. "You were no more than eight years and you cut your knee. Remember?" Helena nodded. "I remember holding you like this and telling you that big girls should not handle their miseries in such a fashion." His grin broadened to a smile. "I suppose the same advice would work in this situation as well."

Helena reached up her hand to touch Tancred's trimmed brown beard. She searched his eyes for some confirmation of his returned feelings.

"I have loved you since I was a child, Tanny. I cannot be untrue to my heart. When you spent so much time among us, I couldn't help but fall in love."

"But you were a child, a little girl," Tancred said softly, still not trusting the declaration.

Helena wasn't offended by his words. "Cannot a child love?"

Tancred smiled down at her. "Apparently so."

Helena nodded. "I watched Maude treat you badly. I knew she had her numerous suitors, but for a little girl of nine, there was no real understanding for the game she played. I knew, however, for I'd watched her in the stable with others, that you did nothing to steal her virtue. I hated her for setting Roger against you, but my mother told me it was a matter that had to be resolved among adults. She would not allow me to go to Roger nor to defame my stepsister."

"Your stepsister was looking to make herself a wealthy match. 'Twas not my desire to become a husband." He added with a chuckle, "At least not then."

Helena boldly threw her arms around Tancred's neck, surprising them both. "I love you. 'Tis real enough and true enough, and whether you ever love me or not, it will remain just as it is and always has been."

She sobered but kept her hold on Tancred. "I know my brother will never approve of my feelings. He hates you and has often said as much. He believes you killed your parents, but I do not. I have always known it would have been impossible for you, for your heart is rich with love and goodness.

"When they told me of the accusations, I defended you and raged at them for their pettiness. I told Roger, even though I was only nine, that he owed you his loyalties. I reminded him that he had once exchanged signet rings in bonds of friendship. I insisted that he was wrong—that everyone was wrong. I knew that you were incapable of such a disgusting act." The absolute certainty in her voice was evidence of her convictions.

Tancred stared at her with sheer gratitude in his eyes. "You are the only one who believed me innocent, and you were just a child." In his mind, she was still a child, yet the reality of the woman he held made it difficult to hold those memories in place.

"But I am no longer a child."

"I am most certain of that," Tancred stated, running his hand down her arm. "Most certain."

"And my brother seeks to put me away now that my mother is dead. Maude is jealous of me and cannot bear for me to be in the same house. They plan to put me in a convent and intend to see me remain there for life."

It was Tancred's turn to surprise them both by throwing his head back and laughing. Helena stared at him, not speaking or even blinking.

"Forgive me, love, but I can think of many far better things to do with you."

"Pray tell?" Helena eyed him suspiciously, a hint of a smile on her lips.

Tancred stood up and placed Helena on the log. "For now, suffice it to say that I am quite intrigued by your devotion. I no longer find a child before me, but a grown woman—a very beautiful grown woman."

"And what will you do with me?" Helena asked innocently.

"Well, 'tis certain my thoughts do not include a nunnery."

Chapter 12

ome." Tancred pulled Helena to her feet. "Let us go reason with your brother."

"There is no reasoning with that one."

Tancred put Helena's hand upon his arm. "Perhaps not, then again maybe there is. We've dealt him a double blow this day. First he finds you after many weeks and then he finds me not far behind. Now that he has had time to simmer, perhaps he will listen."

They walked out into the clearing, and Tancred paused. "I have known days past when your brother was a reasonable man. I trust God can give him the ability to deal evenhandedly with this, Helena."

"Roger cares naught for fairness or evenhanded dealings. He cares for Roger." She paused and let her gaze go to the open meadow where men and women laughed and cheered the children in three-legged races. "I fear him, Tanny." She couldn't help but shudder. "He hated me, mayhaps not as much as Maude, but nevertheless I was a thorn in his side. Henry would not allow him to force my hand in marriage and that angered him greatly. He could neither touch the dowry left me by my mother, nor could he benefit from a wealthy arranged union."

"You have never married?" Tancred asked in disbelief. "But you must be at least. . ." The image of Helena as a little girl faded more and more.

"I am twenty," Helena said with a frown. "And no, I could not marry when my heart belonged to you."

Tancred shook his head. "All those years spent in my miserable exile and you were here across the sea."

"I would gladly have shared your exile, Tanny. Most gladly."

Her eyes pierced his heart in the warmth of their sincerity. Her love caused him to feel strong in a way he'd not felt in years. Uncertain of what he might do should they tarry any longer, Tancred led her forward and motioned at the castle in the distance.

"My brother and I will not allow you to be taken. Roger will have little to say in the matter when Henry learns of this. But tell me, why did you refuse to tell us your story?"

Helena lowered her head in shame. "I could not admit to being Lady Helena Talbot. Richard would no doubt have sent word to Roger, and in turn my brother would have retrieved me. I could not bear the thought of another beating at his hand. Nor could I agree to his terms in regards to the abbey."

Tancred stopped abruptly. "He beat you?"

"Aye. 'Twas the reason I ran. While he was just boisterous and raging, I could handle him and Maude as well. But Maude convinced him to starve me and then put me to shame at the whipping post. I bear those lash marks even now."

Tancred's eyes narrowed in rage. "He will answer for it with marks of his own."

"Nay, Tanny," Helena begged, her hand firmly gripping his arm. "'Twould resolve nothing. I am reconciled to the matter and know that Roger would never have acted as he did, if not for Maude."

She held him in her pleading gaze, and finally Tancred nodded. "Very well, but I pledge to you that it will not happen again."

Helena smiled. "Thank you. You have always seen fit to rescue me from one bad situation or another. Many was the beating I avoided as a child because you and Roger interceded. Now I can only pray that the good Father in heaven will intercede on my behalf today."

"'Tis my way of thinking He already has."

Roger was not happy to see his stepsister enter the castle on Tancred DuBonnet's arm. He began his tirade on the bailey lawn, but Richard prevailed and suggested they return to the privacy of his chambers. Begrudgingly, Roger agreed and followed Tancred and Helena inside.

Tancred seated Helena near the fire and stood behind her in a protective fashion. He gave Roger little doubt in the menacing stare he offered that he would and could protect Helena from further attack.

Richard took his seat and motioned to Roger. "Be seated, Talbot, and let us speak as gentleborn folk."

"There is nothing gentleborn in that man's manner," Talbot said, refusing to sit. "I demand you release Helena to my care and stay out of this matter."

Helena surprised them all by speaking up. "I will not go with you, Roger. As nearly as I can understand it, you sought to send me to the convent in order to appease Maude. Her desire was that I be put from the house, and now I am. So where lies the problem?" Unafraid, her gaze met his.

"Maude's desires are not the only ones to be considered here. I would see you well cared for. You refuse to take a husband, and I—"

"I did not refuse to take any husband. I simply refused the ones you offered. You know my heart on the matter."

Roger clenched his fists. "You would throw yourself at this cur's heels? The very man who soiled your stepsister and nearly caused her complete disgrace."

"Ha! Maude caused her own disgrace," Helena declared. "You forget, I was a child then."

"What has that to do with it?"

"Much. I was able to slip into the shadows unobserved. I watched the things my stepsister played at. 'Twas not this good man who stole your sister's virtue, and this I know full well."

Roger stared at her in surprise. "What do you mean?"

Helena folded her hands and glanced up at Tancred. "Tanny never played false with her. He refused her advances, and so our dear sister sought revenge upon him. She set your mind against him, though he was not the one to be the cause of your grief."

Roger sat down and stared in silence for several moments as if trying to decide if Helena spoke the truth. He looked at Tancred, the man who had been like a brother to him. Was it possible that Maude's interference had separated him from the dearest friend he'd ever known?

"I had just received my title and lands," Tancred said, breaking the silence. "It was a most attractive package to your sister, and when she learned of it, her pursuit ensued. I'd simply have no part of it, for I did not love her."

It was too much to concede, and Roger, instead, changed the subject. "Maude is not the only issue here. What of the murder? You were convicted by your brother's own testimony." He turned to Richard. "Was this not true?"

"'Twas a mistake and one I deeply regret, for it cost my brother eleven years of his life."

"But there were witnesses to the act," Roger protested. "I know because I paid special attention to the details of the matter."

"They were false witnesses," Richard stated. "Obviously, the true murderer paid them well to sing their song. Tancred and I intend to learn the truth of the matter."

"I do not believe you," Roger said, still clearly shaken by Helena's declaration.

Tancred stepped from behind Helena's chair. "It matters little what you believe. 'Twas a time, however, when your loyalty would have remained with me. I believe the poisoning of your mind can be traced back to Maude's hard heart. If you are honest with yourself, you will agree."

"'Tis true, Roger." Helena's voice was soft and tender. "You once rode with this man at your side. How many times did you conspire with him to keep me out of trouble? How many times did you take the full punishment when our father learned of the matter?" Roger said nothing, and Helena continued. "Maude met Tancred one afternoon in the mews. She didn't realize I was there, and she began her tirade before I could take my leave."

Helena lifted her face to smile at Tancred. "Tanny knew naught that I was there watching him work. 'Twas my fondest pleasure, just to be near him. Maude came into the mews and began to weave her spell. She flattered and played at his pride until I was certain Tanny would do most anything she asked. Of course, I was enraged, knowing that only the night before she'd been with the neighboring earl's son.

"Maude pleaded her love to him and begged him to reject her naught. She concocted stories of her miseries. Her mistake came in the fact that Tanny already knew of her dalliances."

"How could he know? Did you tell him these things, and if so, why should he believe a child?" asked Roger.

"I said nothing to him. My mother would not allow me to become a part of the matter."

"I was no fool, Roger." Tancred spoke in his own defense. "Neither were you, and if you think back on the matter, you will know the fact of this."

For several moments, nothing was said. Helena felt sorrow for Roger as he reconciled himself to the truth. She could see his eyes soften for just a moment before he hardened himself again.

"It still does not excuse your actions. You refused to even defend yourself to me," Roger finally stated.

"I should not have needed to defend myself to a friend."

Again, Roger was taken aback. "Perhaps, but just because Henry absolves you of murder does not mean I do. I see no proof of your innocence."

"I intend to find it," Tancred replied. "Until then, my clear conscience is all the proof I need—that and your sister's fierce loyalty." He put his hand on Helena's shoulder.

Helena cherished the touch. She could scarcely believe that he stood at her side. Better yet, that he had not rejected her love. *Oh God*, she prayed, *please lay these matters to rest*.

Just then Arianne entered the room with Timothy. "'Tis the supper time, and I know my own hunger is great. Come to the table and resolve these issues on the morrow."

Richard went to her and took Timothy in his arms. "I believe my wife is the only one with any sense. Talbot, a room has been prepared for you. Will you stay?"

Roger got to his feet and nodded. "Aye, for this is not yet concluded, and my sister and I must talk."

Helena felt her peace dwindle. What would Roger do to force his hand in the matter? She decided then and there to not allow Roger to speak with her alone. Tancred could not follow her everywhere, and when his back was turned, Roger very well might steal her away. She was so lost in thought that she did not realize that everyone but Tancred had left the room.

"Is it well with you, Helena?"

She looked up to find his brow furrowed in a worried expression. Forcing a smile, she nodded and accepted his hand. "It has been a most taxing day."

"And a most revealing one." He smiled at her upturned face. Then surprising them both, he leaned down and placed a brief kiss upon her forehead.

"Aye," Helena murmured, her cheeks blushing scarlet.

When darkness fell upon Gavenshire, Arianne and Helena took Timothy and retired to their chamber. Helena could hear voices in the great hall as she closed her door. Would they take matters into their own hands and refuse to consider her will in the affair? She felt frightened for a moment, and then the words from the Easter sermon came back to her. *Whom do you seek?* Forcing her will to come under control, Helena realized that seeking out God first was harder than she'd believed. Still, by placing herself in God's hands, Helena knew peace.

Letting contentment replace her fear, she doffed her garments and slid into bed. Thoughts of Tancred's kiss played on her mind. She touched her finger to her forehead and frowned. Was it only a brotherly kiss? The more she considered it, the more it seemed to be the kiss of an adult to a child. Chiding herself for questioning Tancred's motives, Helena smiled.

Without further contemplation, she lifted her voice in a song of praise to God. The joyful melody filled the silence of her chamber and warmed the room with hope. For the first time in years, she snuggled down into the cover of her bed and knew a deep, heartfelt serenity. Tanny was home. It made her song just that much sweeter.

In his chamber, Tancred heard the lyrical voice and strained to catch the words. Who was it that sang with such purity and joy? He opened his door for a moment and cocked his head into the hall. Just then the watchman was making his way to stoke up the fires.

"Who is it that sings?" Tancred asked the man.

"'Tis the Lady Helena. Her voice is like no other."

Tancred nodded and closed the door with a smile on his face. Helena was a woman like none he'd ever known. It was a pleasant surprise to find her springing up from his past, yet it was a wonder to replace the image of Roger's little sister with that of the warm, shapely woman Helena had become.

Preparing for bed, Tancred remembered the way she'd defended him, nor could he put from his mind the way she'd cried in his arms and declared her love for him.

"'Tis certainly more than I expected," he said to the empty room. Then a thought of Artimas came to mind. The man had told Tancred in complete assurance that God's planning was always best and never out of time.

"If I'd remained here with my land and title," Tancred mused, "I no doubt would have married and fathered many children by now. Helena was but a child and not yet even fostered. I would never have looked to her for companionship." Somehow the idea of this gave Tancred a start. He suddenly realized just how unwelcome this thought was.

Getting into bed, Tancred smiled. "She loves me." He closed his eyes, extremely satisfied. "Someone loves me."

Chapter 13

ilady, he's asked to see you again," Helena's young maid told her.

Helena shook her head. "I cannot." She looked at the girl with sympathy. Sending her off to meet Roger's disappointment and anger wasn't an easy decision. "Tell him he can talk to me later when I am with Her Grace and young Timothy."

"Aye, milady." The girl curtsied and finished helping Helena into a samite surcoat of yellow. The shade did her pale complexion justice, and the gold threads that had been embroidered at the neckline brought out the gold of her hair. Smoothing down the richness of the wool and silk-blended gown, Helena felt the knotting of her stomach as the church bell began to peal. It was time for church, and no doubt Roger would seek to accompany her. It wouldn't matter that he couldn't speak to her at that moment. He would simply take charge and make his presence known.

Hastening her maid, Helena pulled on the pale yellow wimple and tucked all but a few wily strands of plaited blond hair beneath its covering. She wondered at her predicament when a light knock sounded on the door.

"Helena, 'tis Arianne."

The maid quickly opened the door for the duchess and took her leave. Arianne entered the room with Timothy in hand. "I thought you might like some company."

"To be sure, milady." Helena nervously slipped her feet into matching yellow slippers and stood to face Arianne. "Thank you," she whispered.

Arianne put a hand upon Helena's arm. "Richard has assured me that you will not be forced to leave this place. Your brother has much to answer for, and we will not allow him to harm you."

Gratitude flashed into Helena's eyes. "But he is my guardian."

Arianne nodded. "Aye, but Richard has Henry's ear, and before you are given over against your will, we will see it brought before him."

Helena took a deep breath. "I do not wish to be left alone with Roger. Please."

"Of course. I will see to it that one of us accompanies you at all times."

"Thank you, Arianne. I owe you much and can never hope to repay it."

Arianne smiled slyly. "I have but one question for you."

"Ask it." Helena's curiosity was piqued. What could the duchess possibly want to know? All of her secrets were in the open. Her mind raced to consider what the duchess might want to ask.

"Are you truly in love with Tancred?"

Helena's mouth dropped open, and quickly she struggled to conceal her surprise. Arianne's face was lit with amusement, and even Timothy cooed as though delighted by the aspect of Helena's answer.

"I think you just answered my question," Arianne said with a grin. "I am most gratified at this turn of events. Tancred needs a good woman at his side. A strong woman—one who can soften his roughness and strengthen him where he is weak."

"Tanny is not weak," Helena said firmly. "He is the strongest man I have ever known. He has endured so very much and yet survives to tell of it. I greatly admire him, and yes, I love him. I have since I was a small child."

"Good." Arianne shifted Timothy and took Helena by the elbow. "Then we must work hard to see you two brought together."

"'Tis no matter of hard work, Your Grace," Tancred stated from the doorway. He stood there with arms crossed, leaning against the stone wall as though he had been there for some time.

Helena blushed and refused to meet his eyes. She was confused that after all of these years of loving him, she should suddenly feel shy.

"Ah, so you are in agreement." Arianne reached out to hand Helena over to Tancred. "That saves me much time and trouble."

Tancred grinned at his sister-in-law. His dark eyes met hers. "Would that Helena have saved all of us the time and trouble. Do you know she cared for me since she was a child?"

"So she says."

"Do not talk as though I were not here," Helena protested, raising her head to meet Arianne's and Tancred's amused faces.

"I see your sudden case of vapors has passed," Tancred said and took firm hold of Helena's arm. "Come along, you two. The priest will have vapors if we keep him waiting."

After church, there was a warming breakfast with thick bowls of porridge and a special treat. Matilda had overseen the making of a special sweet bread. The delicacy was laden with almonds and raisins, and everyone at the table agreed it was a delightful surprise.

Roger had tried twice to corner Helena, once as she was coming out of the chapel and the second time as she was being seated for breakfast. Both times, either Tancred or Arianne had interceded and prevented Roger from whisking his sister away for the private discussion Helena so dreaded.

At the table, Helena found herself carefully positioned between Arianne and Devon, just as she had been since her arrival. On Devon's other side sat Roger with a scowl on his face that clearly stated his frustration. Helena glanced his way only once and shuddered at the expression she met. Arianne, noticing the problem, gave Helena's hand a reassuring pat.

Relaxing a bit at this gesture of support, Helena knew that she was truly safe. Arianne was a wise and thoughtful woman, and Richard was completely devoted to her and heeded her suggestions. Helena knew, too, that Tancred would intercede in a heartbeat, should Roger distress her with more than a glance.

Thank You, Father, she prayed silently. *Thank You for the protection and comfort I have found among these people.* Lifting her head, Helena smiled. She felt sated with reassurance, and even Roger's sour face could not distract her from feeling secure.

"I keep thinking there is something that I have overlooked," Tancred said, running his hands through his dark hair. "I have relived the night of the murders over and over until I'm nearly certain that I am there again."

"Aye, as have I." Richard's tone held only sadness. They had agreed to come together and discuss the matter of their parents' death, but now Tancred was uncertain it would do any good.

"I was excited about returning home after spending much time in London," Richard continued. "It seemed I had been gone an eternity, and I was anxious to greet our mother and know her gentleness once again."

"How came you to return home?"

"It came as a surprise, actually," Richard replied. "I was working upon the training field when a messenger arrived explaining that the king desired an audience with me. I went to Henry, and he told me that our parents had requested I return home to attend some matter. He did not say what that matter might be."

"But you arrived at the manor only moments after I did?"

"Aye, and the rest you know full well."

Tancred nodded. "I was settling down for the night on my own estate. It was still a wonder to me that I was titled and in control of such a large piece of land." Just then Helena's voice could be heard. She was singing to

Timothy, and Tancred couldn't resist pausing to listen.

"I had just put the business of Roger's sister, Maude, to rest. At least so much as I could. Maude was outraged that I could walk away from her. She was so certain that she could dupe me into marriage, and when it didn't work, she destroyed my friendship with Roger." Sadness overtook Tancred's features and softened him in a way that Richard had never seen. There were tears in his eyes when Tancred continued. "I loved him as dearly as I did you. He was a brother to me in every way. We grew up together, trained and fought together, laughed and sought entertainment together. Never was there a better friend than Roger."

"'Tis a pity that a woman should destroy that bond."

"Aye, but one very hard and embittered woman. Maude only sought to better herself, and she cared naught for whom it destroyed in the meantime. But that aside, I go back to that night and remember it early on to have passed in relative peace."

Helena's singing comforted Tancred as he recalled the latter parts of that tragic evening. The parts that offered no peace. His face grew rigid. "There came a man with a message bearing our father's seal."

"Who was this man?" Richard asked.

"I knew him naught," Tancred replied. "He was there but a moment and then gone. Before I could even break the wax, he had slipped into the shadows of the night and disappeared. I thought little of it. I presumed the letter was but our father's suggestion for resolution in a matter I had with my villeins. I took the message to the fireside and at my leisure broke the seal and read it."

"And that message called you to the manor?"

Tancred began to pace restlessly, while Richard shifted in his chair and stretched his legs. Tancred could see the message only too clearly in his mind. The words still haunted him.

"It read, 'Your assistance is needed immediately. There is grave danger this night for us.' Of course I readied my horse and went to them."

"You are certain the message came from our father?"

"Aye," Tancred said rather indignantly. "I recognized his seal, it belonged to no other."

Richard raised his hand as if to calm Tancred's growing agitation. "I simply wanted you to be sure in your mind. It might be something that would help us learn the truth."

"It bore his seal. The same that is upon the ring we three wore. There was no mistaking it."

"Very well," Richard replied, and his soft-spoken voice seemed to calm

Tancred immediately. "Pray tell, what happened then?"

Tancred finally took a chair opposite his brother at the hearthside. He stared into the flames, remembering the fire of another night. "I rode to the manor and found the barn set ablaze. The villeins were already working to put out the flames. I searched for Father but was unable to find him. One of the men told me he was in the manor house, but I could not believe that our father would allow others to do all of the work. He loved his land and his people and would have served at their side."

"This is true," Richard agreed.

"I went to the water trough, and he was not there. I searched the faces on the way to the manor and realized neither he nor our mother was among those who watched and waited." Tancred continued to stare into the fire. His mind had transported him back in time. Back to the night when his world was suddenly destroyed.

"The smoke was thick and putrid. It smelled of burnt animals and manure. It seemed a hopeless cause, but the villeins did manage to keep the fire from spreading, which was, itself, a miracle. I believed the matter to be what Father had referenced in his message. I continued my search for him and finally went into the manor house.

"It was dark inside. No fires burned in the hearth and no candles or lamps were lit to offer light. The eerie glow of the barn's fire was all that directed my steps. I called out to Father, but no one answered. I heard something at the far end of the hall. It was nothing more than a scurried scratching sound, like a rat upon the floor. It was too dark to know what the source of it was, so I went back outside and found a torch."

"You saw no one in the house?" Richard asked skeptically.

Tancred shook his head. His soul writhed in agony, pierced with the regret that if he had stayed to investigate the noise or perhaps come directly into the house upon his arrival, their parents might still be alive. "I heard voices upon my return. Muffled voices, barely audible, but nevertheless there. I called out again, but no one answered. With the torch in hand, I lit some candles and checked out the hall. There was no one. No house servants, no one at all. I knew something must be terribly wrong, and that sense of foreboding followed me through the house.

"I had come to the screens that divided the kitchen area from the hall when I saw something out of the corner of my eye. A booted foot. I came closer and saw the blood. Then the truth of the matter was clear. Our parents were there, together, dead."

His voice fell flat. "They had both been stabbed several times, and the knife was still plunged there in Father's back. I drew it out—"

"That's when I arrived," Richard stated. The memory of that night was only too clear in his mind. "I came upon you just as you had drawn it out."

"It truly must have presented a grisly picture. I cannot fault you for what your eyes must have demanded to be true."

"But I can fault myself for my lack of faith in you. I was greatly humbled by Helena's bold declaration of your innocence. She spoke with Arianne and me not long ago, and to hear her tell the tale, there was never a doubt in her mind that you might have performed the deed."

Tancred smiled, his look haunted with a bitter sweetness. "I was redeemable only in the eyes of a child."

Richard closed his eyes, and Tancred saw that he fought for control of his emotions. There were tears in the duke's eyes when he opened them to face his brother. "I wish to God most earnestly that I would never have arrived to stand as your accuser. How I have prayed a thousand times that I could take back that single night."

"'Tis no sense in living with regret of that night," Tancred said, meeting his brother's pain-filled gaze. "The matter is no longer between us. We need to combine our forces and seek out the true murderer."

"Aye," Richard said with a nod. "I have tried these long months to find the men who bore you false witness."

"And?"

"They are of no help to us, Tancred. They are dead."

"Dead?"

"Aye. Shortly after the trial was completed and you were sent into exile, both men met with untimely deaths. Both died in their beds from what their families can remember. But after eleven years. . ."

"It will not be easy to learn anything after all this time, but there must be something that will open the door for us. Even a small thing that can prove the matter in one direction or another."

"We must pray it will be so," Richard said with confidence. "God in heaven would not allow this injustice to continue. I know not what reasons He has for this matter, but I trust He will guide us to a solution."

"May it be so, Brother," Tancred replied. "May the truth be known to us both."

Chapter 14

ancred was greatly impressed by Richard's newest addition to the castle. His weapons storeroom was not large, but it was well stocked. Tancred admired the collection of swords, battle axes, and flails.

"With the town growing larger and stronger, there may not be so much to fear," Richard remarked, "but we'll be ready nevertheless."

"The tunnels you have below the castle are invaluable to you also," Tancred reminded his brother.

Richard smiled. When Tancred had taken over Gavenshire in hopes of clearing his name, Richard had used the tunnels to gain access to the castle. "Aye, the tunnels are most beneficial."

"You've done well here, Brother." Tancred could appreciate the hard work and fortune spent upon the fine arsenal.

"The men have trained throughout the winter, and I believe they'd almost relish the chance to make war upon someone."

Tancred laughed. "'Tis the way of our kind, I suppose. We make war upon things and conquer."

"I pray we might not find the need to make war just yet," Richard said earnestly. "I've only begun my home and family. I'd not relish the thought of giving up my peaceful life so soon."

"God grant us a long peace and the strength to defeat our enemies when war does come." Tancred's words were still ringing in the room when Devon appeared in the doorway.

"Richard?"

"What is it, Devon?"

"We have a visitor to Gavenshire."

"Another one? Well, let it be so. Spend as much time here as you like, Tancred, and I'll go see to our newest guest."

Tancred nodded and picked up a well-made shield. It was expensively crafted with heraldic work gracing the face with Richard's coat of arms. He paused to trace the lines of the design, but his mind was upstairs on the fair Helena. What was he to do about her? He had nothing at this point to offer her, and so marriage was out of the question. He could not subject her to his shame, and until he cleared his name once and for all, Tancred knew he would not feel comfortable even in paying her court.

With a heavy sigh, he contemplated the matter. He would have to speak to Helena and let her know how he felt, and yet, there was so much he still couldn't understand. Eleven years had passed, and throughout that time, Helena's faith had never wavered. Even when the rest of the world had condemned him as a murderer, Helena had never believed him possible of the feat. How could he now tell her that he could have no part of her until the matter was resolved?

Forgetting the shield, Tancred saw, instead, Helena's sweet face. He wanted nothing more than to go to her and proclaim his love, for if one thing was truly clear in his mind, it was that he held a deep, abiding love for her. It was hard to imagine that he was capable of such a thing after so much had happened to embitter him and harden his heart. But God had released him from that pain, and the sorrow that he'd known deep down in his soul was now only a fleeting memory.

"Ah, Helena," Tancred whispered in the shadowy privacy of the room, "I do love you. First as a tiny girl, flitting about under my feet, and now as the woman you've become."

"I would like to speak a word with my sister," Roger Talbot said. He stood just inside the common room where Arianne and her maid servants spent time sewing and spinning wool.

Arianne and Helena glanced up together, but neither one said a single word to acknowledge Roger's presence. The women working alongside the duchess cowered back a bit, but Arianne refused to be intimidated.

"I have come some distance, and I refuse to be put off any longer. I looked for your husband but was unable to locate him. In his absence, I implore you to consider my request," Roger stated, this time a bit less harsh.

Arianne glanced at Helena for only a moment before returning her gaze to Roger. "I do not believe it to be in Helena's best interest."

"Helena's best interest!" Roger bellowed. "What about my best interest? I have lands that need my attention and villeins who are most likely robbing me blind—"

"Then I suggest you return to your land and people," Arianne interjected. "No one is forcing you to stay here." She paused for a moment to make certain her words were heard. "Just as Helena will not be forced to leave."

"She is my sister, and I am her guardian."

Helena lifted her face to meet her brother's angry stare. "I will appeal to King Henry," she stated matter-of-factly. "I have that right. I am kin, and you are not."

Roger paled noticeably at this. "You have caused me nothing but grief."

Arianne's temper got the best of her. "She has caused you grief? How dare you? I have seen the marks upon her back. She certainly did not put them there of her own accord. I wonder, Sir Talbot, who might have lain a whip upon the back of the queen's own relation?"

"I am not proud of the past, neither am I content with the present." Roger paused, as though weighing the situation.

Helena forced herself to watch him. He wanted very much to frighten her because, in her fear, Roger found his power. She shuddered at this thought. Roger's power and Maude's vindictiveness were all too close in her memories. It was the reason she so adamantly pleaded with Arianne for protection. It was the reason she could not allow Roger to corner her alone.

"Your Grace, I beg your indulgence." Roger spoke to Arianne, never taking his eyes from Helena's face. "This is but a family matter. The child is grief stricken and knows not what she wants or needs. As her guardian, I am obligated to make the best possible choices for her well-being."

"And those choices include a sound lashing when she refuses to do your bidding?"

Helena felt Arianne tense beside her. She'd never seen the duchess truly angry. Timothy started to fuss, so Helena reached down to the floor where he lay and lifted him to her lap.

"This is my bidding," Roger stated angrily, waving his arm to where Helena sat with the baby. "I only wanted her to have a family of her own. She needs a good husband, one who will care for her and give her children."

"And she was to find this in a convent?" Arianne asked sarcastically.

"Nay! The convent was my last alternative. I intended to see her cared for, that is all."

"Then why not allow her to live on with you?"

Helena spoke so softly that at first Arianne and Roger seemed not to have heard her. Handing Timothy to Arianne, Helena got to her feet. Her eyes were blazing.

"I am tired of this constant battle on my behalf, with no consideration to my desire. I sit in this very room, and while I want no part of conversing with you in seclusion where you would take advantage of my weaker nature, I certainly do not wish to be discussed as though I didn't exist.

"If I were to return to the manor with you, would you swear an oath that I would be allowed to choose my own mate? Would you put Maude away from me and refuse to listen to her contrivances against me? Would you forget the foolishness of sending me to a convent? And before you answer, dearest brother, might I remind you that perjury is a mortal sin."

Roger stared blankly at her for a moment. He'd known Helena to speak up from time to time, but never to defend herself with the strength he saw here. Perhaps it was only that the duchess's presence made her brave. Perhaps it was finding DuBonnet and proclaiming her love. Whatever it was, he found it most disturbing.

Helena moved across the room to stand only inches from Roger. She was tired of cowering before him and angry for the way he continued to treat her as though she were nothing more than a serving girl. "Can you swear an oath to any of my requests, Roger?"

Roger shook his head. "I need not swear to you anything. I have a responsibility to you, and whether or not you like it, I am your guardian. It is my right to see you properly wed—"

"I intend to be properly wed," Helena interrupted. "I intend to be a wife and to keep a home and, yes, even to bear many children. But I will do so with the man I love and not with some addlebrained milk sop that you pawn me off on."

She snatched off her wimple and tossed it to the floor, where she stepped on it roughly. "I'm nothing more than this cloth to you. Something to be trampled beneath your feet, for your good pleasure and will. I refuse to be that any longer, Roger Talbot. I will not be commanded by you or your sister."

Roger was so taken aback by her actions that he was near to cowering himself. He stared in surprise at Helena as though seeing her for the first time.

Helena turned from him to face Arianne. "I most humbly apologize for my overzealous manner. My stepbrother has greatly vexed me for some time. It amazes me that one as refined as Roger can act so completely void of intelligence. He has no loyalty and no honor."

Just then a commotion arose from the door where a young serf was urgently trying to precede an overdressed woman into the room.

"I'm sorry, Your Grace," he apologized. "The duke bid her wait in the hall, but she heard the voices and—"

"I refuse to be put off any longer," Maude announced, pushing past the boy. "Roger, tell him to leave me alone and be gone."

The boy looked to Arianne for his instruction. "The matter is no longer your concern," Arianne told him. "Bid my husband to join us."

"Aye, Your Grace," he said and gave a brief bow.

"Helena, precious little sister," Maude said, reaching out to offer a kiss of greeting.

Helena pulled back, and her eyes narrowed. "Don't touch me."

Maude was notably shocked, and Roger laughed out loud. "It seems our little sister has found her voice useful for more than singing. She was just informing me of her demands."

"Demands? From her guardian?" Maude said in a snide tone that immediately set Arianne on her feet.

"This is my home, and I would know who you are. Surely you forget yourself." Holding Timothy close, she eyed Maude sternly and waited for the older woman to speak.

"I am Lady Maude Talbot. I was wife to Lord Ricbod before he died in poverty and disgrace. As sister to Roger and, of course, Helena," Maude said with contempt in her eyes, "I reclaimed my family's name."

"Very well, Lady Talbot, I am the duchess of Gavenshire," Arianne stated and did not offer to lessen the formality by giving her first name.

Maude's eyes widened for just a moment before she regained her composure and curtsied. "Your Grace." The words were muttered, but nevertheless, the title was offered.

"I am quite unused to people refusing to keep my husband's orders. This was a private conversation, and I would keep it that way."

Maude realized her opponent and changed tactics. "I beg your pardon, Your Grace."

Helena recognized Maude's plan immediately. "She begs no one for anything. She is not to be trusted, Arianne."

Maude stepped forward with her hand raised as if to slap Helena, but a firm hold on her wrist stopped any forward motion. "What in the—" She stopped in midsentence as she realized who held her. "Tancred DuBonnet. But you can't be here," Maude said, completely aghast. "The king—the king, he found you guilty of murder and exiled you."

"Aye, and that same king set me free with pardon." He released Maude's hand and went to stand beside Helena. "I suppose you have come out of deep concern for your stepsister."

Helena felt her spirits soar at the evident support that Tancred was offering her. She stepped a bit closer to her beloved Tanny and felt his arm slip around her in a protective manner.

Maude nearly blanched. "How dare you touch her?"

"He dares because I will it so," Helena declared.

Richard entered the room, with Devon not far behind. "I thought I gave you instructions to await my return." He gazed hard at Maude. It was the first time Helena had ever seen her shrink back from any man.

"I heard the voices and knew it to be my family. You must forgive me, Your Graces, but my worry for my sister was greater than my fear of reprisal. I do beg your pardons." Maude's voice was as smooth as polished silver.

Helena snorted. "Hah! She has been my misery these twenty long years. The only thing you fear, Maude, is missing out on a good fight."

Maude looked at Roger for support. "Are you going to let her talk to me that way?"

"What would you suggest I do? Challenge the men of Gavenshire to a fight? Swords at dawn? Be reasonable, woman, Helena has the upper hand here, and so long as the good duke intercedes on her behalf, we have naught a say about it."

Roger came up alongside Maude and stared past the woman to Tancred. "As for this man, our sister fancies him to be her true love." No one missed the sarcasm in Roger's voice. "She has worshipped him since she was a swaddling, or so it would be told."

"You cannot mean it," Maude said, turning to see if her brother was serious.

"Oh, but I do. Fair Helena intends to marry the fool."

Helena blushed crimson and would have turned away from Tancred to bury her face in her hands, but he held her tight and answered the assault. "'Tis my understanding that she has the king's blessing to choose her mate. A man would be a fool, indeed, were he to reject the devotions of one so innocent and pure." He reached across to caress Helena's cheek.

"You are not married yet," Roger said, his voice low and menacing. "Unhand her and treat her with more respect."

"Respect such as you would offer?"

"Stop it!" Helena exclaimed.

"Yes," Richard said, interceding. "I would see this matter concluded. Lady Talbot, you are welcome to stay. I have ordered a room to be prepared for you. If you desire, I will have one of my people show you there."

Maude looked at Roger for a moment and then at Helena. "I would be happy to take my comfort here."

"Very well." Richard motioned to one of the women. "Take Lady Talbot to her room. As for you," Richard turned to address Roger, "I will keep peace in my home. Should that not be possible with you or your sister within the walls of this castle, then you will be asked to leave."

Sometime later, Maude stood looking out her chamber window. She was seething with rage and jealousy. She hadn't missed the loving way

Tancred had rushed to Helena's defense, nor had she missed the devotion and admiration in Helena's eyes. It was surprise enough to find Helena had survived her ordeal and taken refuge with the duke of Gavenshire, but this was too much.

Tancred DuBonnet was in England. Not only in England, but here. How wonderful he looked, Maude mused. He was only better after all these years, and now, with the king's pardon, he would no doubt be reinstated with the title and lands.

"And that little baggage thinks she can snatch him away from me," Maude said venomously. "Methinks there will be no wedded bliss for you, dear stepsister. Tancred DuBonnet rejected me once. He dare not do it a second time."

Chapter 15

Tancred felt sweat run down the middle of his back as he hoisted the sword overhead. The leather tunic was newly made and not very supple, and because of this, his movements were far less fluid than he would have liked.

"You fight like a woman," Roger said smugly. He had been observing the knights in training and found it to be a most disturbing display. His own men were far from being trained as well, and even Tancred, with his years in exile, fought better than many of Roger's most trusted people.

"Then hoist up your skirts and enter the fray," Tancred replied, meeting the sword of his opponent with a dull thudding ring.

"How dare you!" Roger's face reddened as several idle men guffawed and snickered. He glared at them sharply, but to no avail. These men knew he was of little threat to their well-being.

Tancred waved his hand to call off the mock battle and approached Roger. "You have no war with me, Talbot. Be gone from this place so we can work in peace."

Roger drew his own sword with one fluid motion and pointed it at Tancred's chest. "I most certainly have a war with you. You have dallied with my sister's affections."

"Helena told you the truth about Maude."

"I speak not of Maude, but of Helena herself. You speak of her devotion and love amidst the castle's audience, yet you have no possible hope of ever returning her love."

"Why say ye this?"

"Because you are nothing, Tancred DuBonnet. You have but a name and not even that, for it bears the tainted blood of your parents. Therefore you are without even that honor. What will you offer my sister? Oh, true enough she has a fine dowry, but it does not include land, and what is a man without land and honor?"

Tancred grimaced at the words. Were they not the same ones he'd focused on throughout the night? "I need you not to explain my plight, Sir Talbot. But Helena's heart is tender, and I will not see her broken by your anger."

"Tell me naught of your concern, DuBonnet. Pick up your sword and let us clear this matter once and for all."

Tancred stared blankly at his old friend. "You wish to fight me?"

"Aye, that I do and to the death!" The words were hissed out between clenched teeth. One of the young squires went running to the great hall, but otherwise no one moved.

"I do not wish to fight you, for in spite of the wrong you have done me, you are like a brother to me. Had I said that only months ago, it would have meant little. I would have fought Richard to the death over the anguish and bitterness my soul carried into exile. Now, however, my soul is at peace with God, and therefore, I am at peace with man."

"That may well be," Roger said, raising the sword to strike, "but I am not at peace with you." He brought down the sword hard, causing Tancred to reflexively ward off the blow with his own sword. It was a simple enough way for a fight to begin.

The clanging of metal against metal rang throughout the bailey. Men moved out of the way and surrounded the two fighting knights, but instead of the usual cheering and betting that went on in most disputes, the audience was as silent as a spider spinning a web.

"I see you won't die easy!" Roger called out after deflecting Tancred's thrust.

"I seek peace with you, not blood!"

Roger swung around and pulled the sword across in a great arcing sweep. Tancred fell back a step, regained his balance, and deftly managed to ward off the attack.

"I seek revenge!" Roger bellowed against the blows.

"You seek it for a thing that never happened! You know the truth!"

Inside the castle, Helena was just descending the stone stairs when the squire appeared, proclaiming the battle on the castle grounds.

"'Tis a fight between His Grace's brother and Sir Talbot!" the boy exclaimed.

Helena's hand went to her throat, and several men who sat below in the great hall scurried for the door. She, too, had intended to follow, but her foot no sooner reached the floor when Maude appeared from nowhere.

"And where do you think that you are going?" She took hold of Helena painfully hard. "We need to talk, little sister."

Helena's surprise was so great that she could do nothing but allow Maude to pull her into the privacy of the duke's receiving room.

"What is the meaning of this?" Helena finally found her voice. Jerking away from the talon-like hands of her stepsister, Helena refused to let Maude have the advantage. "Be gone from me. I have matters that do not concern you."

"Pray tell? If you mean the matter of Tancred and Roger doing battle, then it is you who have no place in the matter. They are fighting over me."

Helena laughed. "So say you. I believe it to be otherwise, and I will go to Tanny and offer my encouragement."

Maude screeched at her with hands raised and nails bared. "You insufferable ingrate. Roger has given you everything, and you scorn him." She stopped just short of tearing at Helena's face.

Helena backed away. "I have known nothing but misery at your hands and Roger's. I wish only to be left alone."

"That is no longer possible for you. You have cost me too much, and now you must pay the price."

"I have cost you?" Helena's stunned tone did not bode well with her stepsister.

"Aye, and do not deny it. You have grieved me in every way, but especially where that man is concerned."

"Tancred?"

"Aye, your beloved Tanny." Maude's face contorted in disgust. "You, a mere child. How old could you have been? Eight? Nine? Surely not old enough to know the truth of love, yet here you stand proclaiming for the world your undying devotion to a man you scarcely know. He is a deceiver, and I would be less than a loving sister to not guide you away from his cruelty."

"He is not a deceiver!"

Maude laughed loud and harshly. "So you say. I have the painful memories to haunt me. I have the broken promises—"

"You have nothing!" Helena countered in anger. "I was there. I saw you throw yourself at him, begging for him to save you from the misery of your loveless home. I wanted to retch at the way you played him for a fool, pleading your purity and innocence, pledging your virginal love. Hah! I saw what you did, night after night. Playing many a man false, offering of yourself whatever it took to get some trinket or bauble that you took a fancy to."

"How dare you!"

"I dare because it is the truth!"

Maude's face turned reddish purple, and her eyes were narrow slits that stared evilly back at Helena. Her voice dropped to a deadly softness. "You have always come between me and my suitors. You think I could forget that? I will see you dead before you marry Tancred DuBonnet. Do you understand me?"

"You speak idle," Helena said, turning to leave.

"Do I?" Maude called, making no move to stop her. "I still have the bottle of poison I used to rid myself of your mother." Helena froze in place. She turned to see the wickedly satisfied smile on Maude's face. "That's right, I killed her. What of it?"

"I will tell my brother. I will tell the duke of Gavenshire and King Henry as well!" Helena declared. There were tears in her eyes as she thought of her mother dying painfully at Maude's hand. "Murderer!"

"Call me what you like, but you will say naught to Roger or anyone else."

"And how do you intend to stop me?" Helena questioned. She was trembling in fear but prayed silently that Maude would not see how she'd upset her.

"If you do anything to imply my responsibility in Eleanor's death, I will see to it that Tancred dies most painfully."

"He may already lie dead by Roger's hand, for all I know. You're evil, Maude, and I will have no more part in this." Helena opened the door and quickly made her way across the hall.

Maude was immediately at her heels, whispering in a hissing tone that could not be understood. "Should you seek our brother's ear on this matter, it will cost Tancred's life."

Helena paused to look at Maude. There was no doubt of her seriousness. *What should I do?* Helena wondered. *What can I do?*

"Aye, I will do the deed," Maude replied. "But if you keep your mouth closed, return home with Roger, and leave me to rekindle the flames of passion that once existed between Tancred and myself, then I will let him live. Otherwise. . ."

Helena looked away from Maude and contemplated the words. "He may well lie dead at this moment."

"Roger will not kill him. There is nothing more than a misunderstanding between them. I've been most fortunate that it's lasted eleven years. I cannot hope for it to bear through even another day. Nay, your problems do not lie with Roger."

Helena heard her name being called, and soon a young woman came through the castle's outer door. "Come, Lady Helena, Her Grace has sent me to fetch you."

Helena turned to leave, but Maude was at her heel again. "Remember what I said."

Helena said nothing. Instead, she hoisted her skirts and ran most unladylike down the stairs to the bailey. She followed the messenger at a run, and when she came upon the scene of Tancred and Roger's fight, she wanted to die a thousand deaths. Roger had Tancred on the ground, his sword poised at the hollow of Tancred's neck, ready for the kill.

Just as Helena opened her mouth to scream, Roger burst out laughing, and Tancred joined in. Helena was stunned. She wanted to sink to her knees from shock, but Arianne quickly came to her side and extended her arm.

"Remember that time when we were boys," Roger said, laughing so hard he could barely stand up. "You and I were staging a battle for my father. He was so impressed with our abilities and entered the fray himself. It wasn't long before he had both of us pinned to the ground in just this manner."

"I remember it well," Tancred replied, his laughter joining Roger's. "He said, 'Will you yield?' and instead of answering, you made a face at him."

"Aye, and it so surprised him to see his honorable son, in training to become a knight, with tongue waggling from side to side and eyes rolling in circles that he was taken unaware when you pushed him backward. He landed with a mighty thud, as I recall." Tancred remembered the moment with great pleasure.

Roger sobered for a moment, then slipped his sword into the scabbard and extended his arm to Tancred. "I have wronged you greatly. Never have I once truly believed you capable of killing your parents, yet I allowed you to bear the shame alone. I did nothing to defend you."

Tancred took the offered hand and got to his feet. "'Tis a matter for the past."

"Only if you place it there," Roger said quite seriously, "for I still carry the wrongfulness of it here." He placed his hand over his heart.

"You have my forgiveness, friend," Tancred replied. His dark eyes softened. "Have I yours?"

"Aye, that and much more!" Roger exclaimed and embraced Tancred heartily.

Helena watched the reunion as if in a dream. Only moments before she had learned that Maude was responsible for the death of her cherished mother. Now Roger and Tancred were embracing with all possible joy, and it was quickly becoming too much for Helena.

"'Tis wondrous the way that God works in our lives," Arianne whispered in Helena's ear.

Helena turned and found Maude approaching her. A low moan escaped her lips, and Arianne turned to see what the problem might be. "Come with me to the solar," Arianne suggested. "'Tis time for Timothy's feeding."

Helena could only nod and allow Arianne to lead her toward the castle. She knew that with Arianne present, Maude would say nothing, and because of this, Helena felt a false sense of security. It was a security that was quickly snatched from her, however, when Helena met Maude's hateful stare. Her eyes burned into Helena, and it was more than she could bear. Without warning to Arianne, Helena fainted dead away.

"Helena?" She heard her name being called. The voice was soft and muffled. The blackness that held her spellbound was lifting, and Helena could barely make out Tancred's face overhead.

"Helena, wake up," he commanded, and she fought hard to be obedient.

"Oh, Tanny," she whispered, reaching out to touch his face. "What happened?"

"I was to ask you the same thing. Do you not remember?"

She gave him a gentle, sleepy smile, but then the memory of Maude's threatening words came back to haunt her, and Helena abruptly pulled back her hand and tried to turn away.

"What is this?" Tancred questioned, taking hold of her shoulders.

Arianne was at her side in a moment. "What is it, Helena? What is wrong?"

Helena moaned and shook her head from side to side. She couldn't speak to either one of them. She mustn't give Maude any reason to harm yet another person. Hot tears formed in her eyes and threatened to spill.

"Please go," she finally said.

"Go?" Tancred questioned, turning her to face him. His eyes were so full of tender concern that Helena wanted nothing more than to throw herself into his arms. Instead, she forced herself to push against him.

"Yes! Go! I don't want you here!" The tears poured down her cheeks as she turned away. She wasn't quick enough to avoid seeing the hurt in his eyes. Burying her face in her hands, Helena sobbed.

Tancred looked up at Arianne, who stared thoughtfully at the young woman. With a shrug, she motioned Tancred to the door. "I have a feeling there is much we do not know. Do not be too quick to judge her in this matter. Something is amiss, and I will seek to find out what it might be.

Until then, please do not lose hope."

Tancred glanced from his sister-in-law to the sobbing woman across the room. "But I know not what I've done."

"'Tis my strong suspicion," Arianne said, with a note of anger in her voice, "that you've done nothing to bring this about." She touched his arm reassuringly. "Give us time, Tancred. Secrets have a way of coming out."

Chapter 16

In the shadowy glow of firelight, Roger, Richard, and Tancred sat discussing the death of the DuBonnets. Tancred's mind was still confused by Helena's outburst. What did she mean by pushing him away? And, too, why did she look so frightened?

"Our parents had no enemies." Richard was starting, and Tancred forced himself to pay attention. "Our mother was the local healer, with a loving hand and calm word for anyone who sought it. Our father was a fair man who allowed his villeins to earn their freedom and generously bestowed gifts upon them throughout the year. I know of no one who sought to do them harm."

Roger agreed. "I knew your parents well. They were highly regarded, even in the lake lands up north."

"So then, if not an enemy of our parents," Richard paused, looking at his brother, "then maybe one of yours?"

Tancred laughed, but there was no humor in the sound. "You could have picked from a dozen or more who would have seen me dead. But, I would not have expected a single one of them to seek their revenge in that manner. Nay, the men who would have seen me dead would have aced me themselves. My enemies were a noisy lot who had little difficulty in making themselves well known."

"But perhaps there was one," Richard suggested. "All it would take would be one."

Tancred gave it concentrated thought while staring hard into the dying fire. "There were many who envied my position and lands. It mattered little that I had earned the right to those things—jealousy would not allow some to let the matter rest."

"Perhaps one of them felt Henry had unjustly rewarded you. Mayhaps they were angry enough to seek revenge, but knowing they could not get to you in person, they sought to settle the score in another fashion."

"It is possible," Tancred admitted.

"Think, Brother. Is there not some face that comes to mind? Some name that can traverse the years to utter itself to you?"

Tancred shook his head. He stared at Roger for a moment. "Is there anyone you can think of?"

"Nay," Roger said without second thought. "I know of no one."

Moments later, Roger dismissed himself to go to bed. He was fretful and restless from the hours of conversation. He knew, too, that if he had to spend another moment contemplating the death of Tancred and Richard's parents, he very well might say things he would later regret. He stepped into the darkened great hall and let out his breath.

He only knew one person who hated Tancred enough to see him suffer to the extent he had. Maude.

"But how?" he whispered.

Maude would never have been capable of such a feat on her own, and besides, she would have been only six and ten—a tender age with romantic notions and marriage on her mind. He laughed aloud at his own foolishness. Nay, there was no point in looking to Maude for the deed. True, she had hated Tancred for spurning her love, but she quickly got over it, as Roger recalled to mind.

He made his way up the torch-lit stairs, still chuckling to himself. He no sooner reached the top when Helena appeared in her night robe.

"Why be ye here, girl?" Roger asked. "Is it well with you?"

"I. . .came. . .to. . .to seek you out," Helena said, her teeth chattering more from nerves than from the cold stones beneath her feet.

"You did not wish to talk to me privately, remember?" His voice was soft and gentle.

"I remember, but now I find I must. Please hear me out." She was shaking, and Roger motioned to her open door.

"Go back to bed. We can talk on the morrow."

"Nay!" she exclaimed a bit louder than she'd intended. "It must be done now."

"Then speak before you catch your death. If this is about Tancred, you waste words with me. I have ended my war with him, and we are at peace with each other."

Helena nodded. "I know and I am glad. Tancred was always faithful to your friendship, and he was wronged deeply by you."

"I know." Roger's eyes softened, and he suddenly saw Helena as the devoted woman she really was. "You never lost faith in him, did you?"

"I knew him incapable of hurting anyone purposefully." Helena wanted very much to end this part of the conversation. It only made what she had to say that much more difficult. "But that is in the past."

"Then what do you want of me?"

"I want to go home." The words were stated simply and echoed in the near-empty hall.

"You what?" Roger stared at her in utter amazement. "I could not have heard you correctly."

"You did," Helena replied, refusing to lower her face. "I have to go home. The sooner, the better. Please, Roger. 'Tis the reason you came here for me."

"Aye, 'tis true enough, but what of Tancred? What of your love for him?"

"It hasn't changed, but there are many problems that need to be overcome. I was only a child when Tancred left England."

"But you are no child now, neither does he see you as a child. I know the heart of men, and I know that man better than most. He cares deeply for you, Helena. If this is a matter of him not having a title or lands of his own—"

"His title, or lack of one, does not matter," Helena interrupted indignantly. "I care little for such things. I would live in a hovel with him were I only able to be his wife."

"Then why leave? The duke has bid you stay as long as you desire. Tancred and His Grace hope to resolve the death of their parents, but that may take some time. I no longer object to you marrying Tancred."

Helena put her hands to her head as if to stop the pounding against her temples. "Cease!" she demanded. "I cannot bear this much longer. I want to go home. It matters not why. Will you take me on the morrow?" She dropped her hands and reached out to Roger with pleading in her eyes. "Please."

Roger nodded. "If that is your desire."

"'Tis not a matter of desire," Helena whispered, desperately close to tears. "'Tis what must be done."

Roger stepped forward to put an arm around Helena, but before he could do so, Maude's voice sounded from behind them.

"Yea, 'tis what must be done."

Helena drew closer to Roger. She glanced up to find him frowning, then dropped her gaze to the floor. There was no way she could explain it to him. Maude knew full well the reasoning behind her sudden declaration to return home, but Helena knew she'd say nothing.

"What causes you to skulk about the halls like a rat in feeding? Are you feasting upon our private words, Maude?" Roger demanded.

"Some privacy," Maude retorted and drew closer. "I heard you in my room."

"Still, it was not your concern." Roger's mind went back to his earlier suspicions about his sister. Somehow, seeing her made his thoughts take a bit more validity. Roger's arm went protectively around Helena's shoulders. For once, he was not going to allow Maude to bully the younger woman.

"I heard her say she wants to go home. I believe this most beneficial to all concerned. With the facts before us and Tancred cleared of wrongdoings, I desire to resume our friendship. I can scarce do that with the child in my way, now can I?"

Roger laughed. "Tancred would not notice you if Helena were removed to the Holy Lands."

"How caustic your words are, dear brother," Maude said, straining to control her temper. She glared down at Helena and hated her even more. "Yours is but a childish fascination. What existed between Tancred and myself is something far more real."

Helena said nothing. She could not very well defend herself and plead with Roger to keep his word and return her to his estate. Maude's murderous threats continued to haunt her. Maude would no doubt poison Tancred's drink or food if Helena refused to leave Gavenshire.

"Mayhaps she is right, Roger. Either way, I will be ready in the morning." Helena eased herself away from Roger and stepped toward her bedchamber door. Her heart was sickened at the thought of giving her beloved Tanny over to Maude. "Please, put the matter to rest," she whispered before hurrying into her room and securing the door. Once there, Helena gave into heart-wrenching sobs that did not cease until well into the night.

Morning came too soon for Helena. She had tossed about the large bed throughout the night and had found no peace. How could she leave him when she'd only just found him? How could she allow him to believe that she no longer cared, when her heart was near to bursting for all the love she felt for him?

Getting up and washing her face, Helena no longer cared what happened. She knew that Roger was a changed man, and for that she was grateful. She had seen the softening in his eyes and known in his voice a gentleness that had been missing for eleven years. He would not hit her again. In fact, he would probably hurry to see Maude married off, even to Tancred, and allow Helena to stay at home and care for him until he found a wife. After that, Helena sighed, after that she would go to the convent. What purpose would there be to fight that move if Tanny were already married and beyond her grasp?

Without waiting for assistance, Helena found the burgundy surcoat she'd worn on her arrival to Gavenshire. It was patched and stained, a poor companion to the grand and beautiful things Arianne had made for her, but it belonged to Helena, and she would leave with nothing more. Pulling it on in the dim light of dawn, Helena could scarcely keep from crying anew.

When she stepped into the hall, Helena half expected Maude to be waiting. When she found that Maude was nowhere in sight, relief washed over her. It would be hard enough to leave without having to face Maude again. Helena's most fervent prayer was that she could somehow escape speaking with Tancred, as well.

"What would I say?" she muttered to herself. How could she declare her love one day and callously take it back the next? He would see her as deceitful and wicked, and there would be nothing Helena could say to keep him from such opinions. His anger, even hatred, might make her departure easier, Helena thought. But then, she truly doubted that anything would help.

She came upon Roger, who was talking with a stunned-faced Arianne. Richard was at her side and looked up first to spy Helena.

Arianne turned and, recognizing Helena, rushed to her side. "Is it true that you asked your brother to take you home?"

"Aye," Helena whispered. "'Tis what I desire, Your Grace. He did not force me into this."

"But you told me only yesterday—"

Helena held up her hand. "I know, but 'tis different now."

The chapel bell began to peal, calling the castle to services, and Helena relished the excuse to hasten away before anyone could question her further.

Tancred came upon his brother and a teary-eyed Arianne. He was so taken aback by Arianne's tears that he instantly scowled. "Is something amiss?" he asked Richard.

"Aye, 'tis a matter most disturbing," Richard replied in a hushed tone as they walked on toward the chapel.

"Why does she weep?" he asked, leaning in close to his brother's bearded face.

"Helena told us she's leaving with Roger. They plan to depart after we break the fast."

"What?" Tancred's voice rose, and Arianne's head shot up.

"'Tis true enough. She claims Talbot has not forced the matter, but that it is her desire to go." Arianne's words were hardly more than whispers.

"I don't believe it," Tancred stated. "I cannot believe she'd leave without word to me."

Richard shrugged. "Perhaps you are the only one who can learn the truth."

"I will learn the truth," Tancred replied between clenched teeth. "I swear it."

Tancred saw Helena flee the chapel as soon as the service was over. He stalked after her with determined steps and never noticed the look of dissatisfaction on Maude's face at his actions. Helena could not leave him now. He loved her, and though he could not declare it and ask for her hand in marriage, he was determined that she know the extent of his feelings. He would insist she wait for him. Wait at least until the matter of his parents' death was cleared. Then, if need be, he'd beg Richard for a home at Gavenshire and take Helena as his wife.

Reaching back to childhood instincts, Helena fled to the mews where the hooded falcons were kept. She had loved to venture to just such a place as a child and now it offered her a comfort of sorts. She leaned hard against the far-end wall and buried her face in her hands. Would the tears never dry up? She had cried bucketfuls in the night, and her face was red and her eyes swollen from the tirade. But still, she cried.

"Oh, Tanny," she moaned his name softly through her sobs. "Tanny."

"I am here," he said softly. Startled, she looked up and saw that he had followed her into the mews.

"No," she said and cried all that much harder. She couldn't look at him or the truth might come from her lips. She couldn't let him know her fear or the circumstances that drove her away.

Tancred pulled her shaking form against his body and held her firmly. Helena pushed away from him, but he'd have no part of it and drew her that much tighter against him.

"Why are you leaving me?" He whispered the question against her ear.

Words refused to form. Helena fell limp against him and cried. She drenched his chest with tears until the surcoat was wet and uncomfortable against her cheek. Tancred waited patiently, stroking her face gently.

"Why are you leaving me?"

Chapter 17

Roger was desperate to find Helena. He'd seen her fearful glances at Maude and could well imagine that the older woman had threatened and browbeaten the younger into submission. Why had he tolerated it all those years? Helena had never been anything but joy to him. Sadly enough, a joy he had denied himself when his heart had hardened against Tancred.

Following the path he'd seen her take, Roger came into the mews and found Tancred holding the weeping Helena.

"Is she ill?" he questioned.

"I am uncertain as to what ails her. I found her here weeping, calling my name, and yet she refuses to speak to me."

"Helena, stop up the flow and speak to me," Roger demanded.

Helena lifted her face and turned her red, swollen eyes to meet Roger's gaze. She drew a ragged breath but still could not speak. Shaking her head dispiritedly, she buried her face in her hands.

"What is this about?" Roger asked more gently. "Please tell me. I promise I am not the man I was before. I will listen and understand."

"I cannot speak of it," Helena managed to croak out between sobs.

"Pray tell, why not?" It was Tancred's turn to ask questions. "I have patiently waited for you to put your tears aside and talk to me, and now you say you cannot speak of it? Am I not worthy of an explanation?" Helena looked back to Tancred and knew she was lost.

"Oh, my love," she whispered, "you deserve more than simple words."

"I will happily settle for them alone," Tancred replied with the barest hint of a smile. "Later, however, I might well extract a heavier payment."

Helena shook her head. "I have endangered you. Perhaps you as well, Roger. Please ask nothing more of me. I cannot speak of it!" She pushed away from Tancred and turned to leave, but neither man would hear of it, and each took hold of a slender arm.

"You are no longer a child, Helena." Roger's voice was stern, yet loving. "I insist you bear the truth to me. I will protect you from whatever you fear." Helena looked up and met his gaze.

"As will I," Tancred promised.

She turned from Roger's face to Tancred's. Both men were so hopeful in their desire to help her, but memories of Maude loomed in her mind and spoiled the scene.

"Nay!" Helena shook her head violently. "You cannot take my punishment this time." She ripped away from their hold and put several paces between them before turning. "'Tis true enough I am no longer a child. In matters such as these, the stakes are much higher and I do not merit a child's punishment. Nay!" She choked back a harsh, near hysterical laugh and held up a hand to Tancred's advancing form. "'Twill be no simple denial of supper or extra hour of housecleaning. 'Tis now a matter of life and death, and I will not be the one to cause bloodshed."

"What are you saying, Helena?" Tancred's voice was soft, yet demanding. "Whose blood is to shed?" He took another step.

"Never mind." She struggled to calm her nerves.

Tancred again moved forward. "Helena, whose blood?"

"I've said too much."

"Nay, you have said too little. Whose blood is to be shed?" He was only inches away from her now.

"Yours!" Helena exclaimed, then put her hand to her mouth. Her eyes grew wide with shock at the word she'd spoken. There was no taking it back, and she knew Roger and Tancred well enough to know that this simple announcement would not go unquestioned.

Roger saved her the moment of dilemma. "Maude." He stated the simple word, knowing full well that his guess was accurate.

Helena dropped her hands and stared in wonder at her stepbrother. "I... But how...?" She couldn't answer.

"I thought as much." Roger's eyes narrowed in anger. "You will sit down and tell us all."

"But I cannot," Helena said, shifting her gaze from Roger to the face of her beloved Tanny.

"You will do as you are told," Tancred said, taking the falconer's stool and pulling Helena to his lap. "I believe we used to resolve problems just like this when you were but a child. Shall we play one of our guessing games and learn of your dark secrets?"

Helena was appalled at the amusement in Tancred's voice.

"'Tis no matter of games. She means to wed you or—"

"Or kill me?" Tancred threw back his head and roared. "She was always one to weave tangled webs. Think not much of it, nor trouble your heart on that one."

"She killed my mother!" Helena exclaimed, and tears came again to her eyes.

"What say you?" Roger stepped closer. "Can this be true?"

Helena's trembling shoulders slumped against the security of Tancred's arms. She gave only a brief nod before giving way to her sorrow.

"But how?"

"Poison," Helena finally admitted. "Oh, can you not see? My mother was a thorn in Maude's side. Mother did nothing but offer her love, and Maude cast it aside as though it were tainted. She blamed my mother and me for all of her hurts and miseries." Helena's trembling voice had steadied as she reached her real concern. "She tired of my mother's interference and poisoned her. She'll do the same to all of us, but especially to my," she paused, "to you, Tanny."

He smiled and slipped his warm fingers under her chin. "Maude is no threat to me, except that she divide us apart. I cannot cast off the devotion of one so dear and true in fear that one so evil and false would see me dead."

"Do not trifle with Maude. She is evil, Tanny," Helena said, hoping that the seriousness of the matter would settle upon him.

"Aye, I can vouch for that," Roger agreed.

"You are in as much danger as Tancred," Helena said. "Is it not true that should you die, Maude will take control of the estate? After all, there are no male heirs and not one relative beyond you two who lay claim to your father's blood."

"You are right, and the point is well taken. I had not considered Maude's limitless treachery. The matter is such that we must work together and lay a trap for this beast."

"But how? If I do not leave within the hour, Maude will know that something is amiss."

"I will state that our journey is to be delayed by a day. That should give Tancred and me plenty of time to set our plans into action."

Helena dried her eyes with the back of her well-worn tunic sleeve. "I cannot let you risk your lives. I haven't the heart for such matters, nor the faith."

"What say ye—this great woman of faith, who knew no fear of the years or miles that separated her from the love of her heart? Faith is all that we do have." Tancred stroked her cheek fondly. "Without faith, we are lost."

"Yet let us be up and about putting faith into action," Roger interrupted. "Were you not telling me of your great philosopher and his mind toward reason?" Roger smiled conspiratorially at Tancred.

"Aye, 'tis true enough. Faith and reason. The two walk as friends, hand in hand. Ye cannot be a man of faith without putting that faith to the test. And testing your faith oft pushes a man to great depths of reasoning. Still, 'tis God's reasons and faith in Him that lead us forward."

"I do not understand," Helena said, looking defensively from Tancred to Roger.

"Be of courage, Helena. That is enough of a task for you," Roger reassured. "Tancred and I can manage Maude."

Roger and Helena entered the great hall together. Helena was notably subdued and kept her head down to avoid meeting Maude's stare. Maude was already seated, impatiently awaiting the formal announcement that she'd anticipated since the night before, while Arianne and Richard shared intimate conversation with Tancred.

The priest offered a blessing on the food, and the fast was broken with warm bread and porridge. Helena had no stomach for the food. In her mind she kept imagining the death of her mother. Food had been the bearer of Maude's misdeeds, and as she thought of it, Helena choked on her porridge.

Coughing quietly into her linen napkin, Helena felt Arianne's reassuring hand on her arm. She glanced up to meet warm brown eyes that sympathetically assured her that all was well. The slightest smile touched Arianne's lips and then faded as the duchess turned to receive a question from one of the serving boys.

Devon had been called away, so Roger took the seat beside Helena. *How very different a matter of days has made*, she thought. *It was once a terrifying thought to have Roger so near, and yet now Roger offers immense comfort.*

"I am afraid I must plead the duke's indulgence," Roger announced amid the table conversation.

"By my leave," Richard replied, playing out his part.

Helena realized instantly that Richard and Arianne were well aware of their roles. It was the reason for Arianne's smile and for Richard's calm, deliberate manner. Helena wished she had some of the duke's calm assurance. The butterflies in her stomach refused to settle, even as Roger continued with his announcement.

"With your permission, sire," he began, "my sister, Lady Helena, and I will be departing for our lands."

"I beg you, no!" Richard said in a voice that hinted surprise. "My wife

481

has come to greatly depend on your sister. Might you reconsider?"

"I wish it could be so, Your Grace, but there is much amiss in my land. Only this morn, I had word of a border dispute. I must return."

"Aye, 'twould be for the sake of your people and land. I see the need, still, could Lady Helena not stay on? We have extended a home to her as long as she desires one."

"Aye," Arianne joined in, turning to Helena. "You are most welcome here. Timothy will scarce know how to fall asleep without your angelic song."

Helena smiled sadly. She was still uncertain of her own part, and for all the lives that hinged on her reactions, she was uncomfortable with the plan. "I must go," was all she managed to say.

Arianne knew the younger woman's distress and hurried to move the conversation on. "I will have Matilda see to your packing."

"Nay," Roger said with raised hand. "My sister has requested that those generous garments be left in your care."

Arianne said nothing more, and Richard picked up the conversation. "You will certainly require provisions, and with two women, you will require an escort."

"I beg Your Graces' indulgence," Maude interjected. "I should plead upon your mercy and ask that I might be allowed to remain behind. I fear I am not up to the long journey and request a few more days of respite."

"Of course," Richard replied after a quick, reassuring glance at his wife. "You are most welcome to stay with us."

"Thank you, Your Grace." Maude bowed her head in feigned humility.

"That still leaves you with Lady Helena's safety in mind," Richard continued.

"'Tis no problem, Brother," Tancred nearly roared. It was the cue he had waited for. "I would like very much to accompany Sir Roger and Lady Helena. Upon a time, their home was my own. It would give me great pleasure to once again view it. That is, should Sir Roger and his sister be in agreement with this idea."

"'Twould be my delight," Roger exclaimed as though hearing the idea for the firs time. "I pledge you shelter and comfort for as long as you desire."

Maude's head snapped up at this new development. Helena noted her disgust but continued quietly picking at a piece of bread, while Roger and Tancred played out the scene.

"By my brother's leave, I could take several of his men and accompany you," Tancred announced.

"It would be greatly appreciated," Roger replied, and both he and Tancred turned to Richard for confirmation.

"A splendid idea!" Richard's words were given in such positive affirmation that Helena nearly laughed aloud. She barely controlled the smile that played at her lips, but when her gaze fell upon Maude's pinched expression, Helena instantly sobered.

"'Tis settled, then," Tancred said after taking a long drink from his mug. "I will prepare as soon as we adjourn."

"Nay," Richard said thoughtfully. "I would ask that you spend yet another night in my care. I have need for my men until the morrow. Would another day matter, Sir Roger?"

Roger looked down at Helena. "Would the morrow be soon enough, my sister?"

Helena nodded nervously. She was twisting the dark burgundy velvet of her surcoat. "Whatever His Grace wills."

Roger added his confirmation. "We are your humble servants."

Everyone at the duke's table could clearly see Maude's irritation. She tore at her bread and crashed her cup around as though she were trying to stave off vermin.

Conversation carried them through the rest of the meal, and though nothing more was said of the Talbot's departure, Helena was certain that Maude contemplated her revenge. Helena knew that her stepsister would find a way to blame her for these developments. Of course, in this case, she would have reason to do so, but Helena would give her no satisfaction in knowing that.

When breakfast was completed, Roger helped Helena from her chair, and Richard did the same for Arianne. Servants hurried around the room to clean up the mess, while everyone else flooded into the various parts of the castle and grounds to begin their day.

The duke immediately caught Roger's attention, leaving Helena momentarily wondering what she should do with herself.

"Please say you will come and sing for Timothy," Arianne said, with a hopeful smile.

"Of course, Your Grace," Helena replied. "'Twould be my honor."

"I shall miss your voice when you are gone from this place." Arianne's words were genuine and heartfelt. "I have enjoyed not only your songs, but the words we have shared in conversation. I have no sister, and so I have but glimpsed the delights of one through our friendship."

"Sisterly delights are overly credited," Maude said in a haughty tone from across the table. "'Tis well enough to share company as grown women, but as children," she paused with a meaningful glare at her stepsister, "the matter can be quite different."

Arianne gave a brief lyrical laugh. "I would well imagine it to be so. I was not without sibling. My brother, Devon, was my fondest companion, at least while I was at home."

"Then he must know well how little sisters can play cruel jokes and spy out from their lairs. 'Tis mostly mischief and mean-spirited games that young ones have to offer."

"I cannot call you false, Lady Talbot," Tancred interrupted, "but neither can I imagine either Lady Helena or the duchess as mean-spirited. 'Twould be impossible for a cruel word to pass from either of those sweet mouths."

Helena wanted to laugh, but the sight of Maude clenching her velvet surcoat in her balled fists kept her from uttering a peep. Instead, she allowed Arianne to take hold of her arm and lead her from the room.

At the stairs, Arianne paused and turned to find Maude scowling. "You are welcome to come with us, Lady Talbot."

But Maude had already sent a serving girl to retrieve her cloak and shook her head to reject the offer. "I am afraid I require a bit of fresh air. My condition is not so that I would feel comfortable with the child."

"Very well," Arianne replied sweetly. "But surely you will come and see your nephew, Tancred?" Helena stared at Arianne's suggestion, and Maude turned red in anger. There would be no way for her to take back the declined invitation should Tancred accept.

"I would be most honored to hear Lady Helena sing. Seeing my nephew would be a fond way to pass the hour, as well." Tancred joined them at the stairs. He offered his arm to Arianne, who simply shook her head and nodded to Helena.

"I would not presume to interfere," she said with a grin.

"Nor would I presume to contradict the duchess of the land," Tancred said, flashing a charming smile at his sister-in-law.

Helena felt it was wrong to goad Maude, but a part of her delighted in the obvious attention. Arianne had made it perfectly acceptable for her and Tanny to spend time together, and Helena was not going to do a simple thing to discourage it. She turned to Tancred from the gray stone step above him. From here they were nearly eye level with each other, and Helena found the moment quite moving. Tancred put out his hand, and Helena touched her fingertips to his. For a moment, neither one did anything more. It was as if the rest of the world had completely forsaken them.

Tancred's harsh face softened as his dark eyes drank their fill of Helena. She felt a blush warm her cheek, and her heart beat faster. How she loved this man! Melodies welled up from within her soul, and Helena felt as though she might burst into song at any moment.

"And what will you sing for us, sweet Helena?" Tancred breathed the question in a hushed whisper, almost as if he had read her mind.

Helena smiled and spoke in an almost seductive way. "Mayhaps I shall sing a love song." Her eyes twinkled mischievously. "But only if I am so inspired."

Tancred stared at her quite blank faced, but his eyes sparkled in amusement. "Of course. Let us pray it is so."

They hurried up the stairs together, neither one noticing the cloaked form that stood in the shadows below. Maude's brooding glare followed them from behind the hood of her cape.

"I warned you, Helena," she murmured, but there was no one to hear her, nor to understand the danger Maude had come to represent.

Chapter 18

In the duchess's private solar, they gathered with Timothy. The baby cooed and gurgled his approval of the new company, and when Arianne handed him to Tancred, Helena laughed aloud at the expression on his face.

"He will not break," Arianne said with a smirk, while Tancred held Timothy stiffly. The look on his face said it all. "Do not tell me the great fearless lord of the land who came last year to best my husband now trembles before his son?"

Helena giggled, then cupped her hand to her mouth at Tancred's look of mock disgust.

"I thought you loyal to me," he said sternly, then softened the words with a wink.

"To find another as loyal as this one," Arianne said, taking a seat, "would be quite impossible." She watched her brother-in-law in his discomfort. "By my leave, Tancred, please sit down."

He did so in a manner that caused him to move as little as possible from the waist up. Helena could not refrain from laughing out loud.

"I heard that snickering and will deal with it later."

"Forget not, I am under the duke's protection," Helena said in a sing-song voice. "Harm me and deal with him."

"Aye," Arianne acknowledged conspiratorially. "My husband would be far from tolerant."

"Cease your prattle!" Tancred said in a voice louder than he'd intended. This sudden sternness caused Timothy to pucker his face. Tears filled the baby's eyes, and soon he was wailing loud enough to bring down the walls.

Helena reached out and took the baby when Arianne sat back and watched in amused anticipation. Tancred was relieved to be rid of the squalling infant. He had little experience with babies. The frailty and tininess of them only served to make him feel cumbersome and awkward.

Helena, he noted, was quite at ease with her charge. She began to sing to him with such love and gentleness that the infant instantly calmed.

"I will surely miss her ways with Timothy," Arianne said softly. "She has been a wonder and pleasure to have in our care."

"I can see why," Tancred said with a smile. He could well see in his mind's eye a home of his own and Helena singing to his son or daughter. What man wouldn't count himself blessed to make that vision an actuality?

Helena stopped singing and smiled over her shoulder. "He is the pleasure. I have been healed of my mother's passing while caring for this one."

"I never thought of it being a benefit to you," Arianne confessed. "I was so pleased to have your companionship that I began to fear 'twas selfishness on my part."

"Never fear it to be so." Helena brought Timothy back, and before Tancred could protest, she placed the baby in his arms. "I love children, and I want an estate filled with them, or," she paused, "even a hovelful. It matters naught, so long as they are loved and made to feel wanted. The place, the wealth, the manner of life, none of it be as important as love."

"Love will not fill an empty belly," Tancred said, meeting her meaningful gaze. He was well aware of what she was saying to him.

"Perhaps not, but love will sustain a person through all forms of torture and heartache. I know this full well and will listen to no other on the matter."

Arianne grinned at her brother-in-law, who was now relaxing a bit with Timothy. "It would seem you are bested in this matter. I suggest a compromise."

"And what might that be?" asked Tancred with a grin.

"Marry the wench," Arianne said in a low-bred manner.

Helena blushed at Arianne's boldness, while Tancred sobered considerably. "'Tis not a matter that I may yet address."

Helena said nothing. Perhaps Tanny had no interest in ever marrying her. Would he do the one thing Roger had accused him of with Maude? Would he dally with her feelings and leave her to face life with a broken heart? Nay, that could never be.

Arianne was the one who spoke, and again the conversation played itself out as though Helena were absent from the room. "Pray tell, why not? Is her love not true enough?" the duchess questioned with the slightest hint of sarcasm in her voice.

"You know very well that is not the case."

"Then what? She has offered you a life of devotion. Should it seem so strange that you might take her hand in marriage?"

Tancred's voice took on a tone that warned the women he was not pleased with the turn of this conversation. "'Tis not a matter we should attend to at this time."

Timothy again found his uncle's voice overbearing and began to cry. Arianne took this as the perfect reason to excuse herself and got to her feet. "My son is hungry. I will take him to my chamber where we might rest. Feel free to reason this out together." Her words were spoken as a hopeful suggestion.

"There is little here that may be discussed," Tancred replied, handing the baby to Arianne. "I will, however, endeavor to clear what you have muddied." He wasn't truly angry at Arianne, and he relayed that fact with his eyes. The matter did need to be addressed, in spite of his desire to avoid it.

Helena watched as Arianne took Timothy and left the room. Her heart was in her throat, and she wanted to avoid Tancred's eyes as he got to his feet and crossed the room to where she stood.

"I am sorry if I have distressed you," he began. "'Tis not my desire to do you harm." He fell silent, wondering how his words would be received. "I have wanted to speak with you on this matter. Come, sit down and I will try to explain."

Helena allowed him to take her hand in his. It was warm and comforting to feel his large fingers close around her smaller ones. She wanted so badly to throw herself into his arms and plead with him to flee with her before Maude could do more harm, but somehow she knew the words to come had little to do with Maude.

Sitting, Tancred stared at her for a moment. Helena met his stare uneasily, and she fought to keep tears from forming in her eyes.

"Helena, might I be forthright with you?"

"Of course," she replied, fear creeping in to sour her tone.

Tancred eased back against the chair and chose his words. "I am a pardoned man, that much is true. The king realized that I am not the one to blame for my parents' death, but the matter is not resolved." Helena nodded so he would continue. "The fact is," Tancred paused and looked at her intently, "until my name is truly cleared, I cannot even call it my own. It still bears the blood of those I loved."

"Tanny, you know it matters naught to me." Her voice was soft. "I don't care what the whole of England thinks, I love you and always will."

"But it matters to me!" Tancred bellowed. He frowned intently at his manner. "I beg your forgiveness, but I am not a man of gentleness."

Helena smiled, and though she wanted to avoid anything he might perceive as confrontational, she shook her head. "You are wrong, my love.

You are a very gentle man. Tanny, the past has left its mark on both of us, but it needn't bury us as well."

"I have nothing to offer anyone, much less a wife. I cannot put my burden upon the shoulders of another. Especially one such as you."

"And what do you mean by that remark, sire?" She was clearly offended.

Tancred got to his feet and paced a few steps before turning back to face her. "You are a delicate blossom and should be cherished and preserved for all that is lovely and truly good in this life. I cannot give you those things, Helena. I cannot even give you my name, because I have no name. I have but the letters that form a word, and that word stands for nothing but pain and betrayal. Until I learn of the true murderer's identity, I don't even have my name to share."

"Bah! Purely talk of a man. Why say you this? Is a name so much more important than what dwells within your heart? Is God not the source of your light and life? Is that to be perceived as nothing?"

"Nay, of course not," Tancred's voice sounded in frustration. "Listen to me, Helena. You pledge life and love to a person you know nothing about. I've given this much thought and believe that you have fallen in devotion of a man who no longer exists."

Helena took a deep breath. "You cannot return my love and so you look to put my love away from you? Is that your game?" Her heart was aching at the mere thought of such a thing.

Tancred stared at her in confusion. He seemed to be trying to sort through the words. "You doubt I could care for you?"

"It seems you doubt I could live with such caring." Helena stood and crossed to Tancred. She did not reach out to touch him or even to offer him her hand. "You misjudge me, sir. I am more durable than you can imagine. I leave you, however, to your decisions and choices. I cannot be false to myself. I cannot pledge ignorance of my heart. Be it well with you or not, I am offering my love and life."

She walked away from him, leaving Tancred stunned. How could he explain to her what he felt, knowing that he must ask her to wait—perhaps forever?

Helena passed into the hall and lost her bravado. All of her courageousness was but an act, and here, alone, she could admit to herself that the outcome of their meeting left her frightened.

Helena slipped into bed early. She hadn't bothered to go down for supper, and when her chambermaid appeared with a tray of food, she'd sent the girl away without sampling a single morsel. Arianne had pleaded an audience with her, but Helena had begged her understanding and sent her away.

Her heart was heavy with grief and worry. How could Tancred consider letting her go away from him? Had he not proclaimed his joy at their finding each other again?

The wind picked up outside and made a howling sound against the window. The restless waters of the sea crashed against the rocky cliffs just beyond the castle estate and left little doubt in Helena's mind that a storm was brewing.

With the first flash of lightning, Helena steadied herself for the crashing response of thunder. When it came, she nearly missed the light-handed knocking upon her bedchamber door. She thought to ignore the sound but decided against it. No, best to answer it and make her excuses. Pulling on her robe, Helena opened the door to reveal a young boy.

"I bear a message for you, Lady Talbot." He gave a brief bow and handed her the rolled parchment.

Staring down at the parchment as though it was something foreign in design, Helena immediately recognized the DuBonnet signet in the wax. "Thank you," she told the boy and quietly closed the door behind her. What DuBonnet would be writing her a note? Was not parchment plenty precious? Could not any one of them simply come to her door?

Tanny, she thought. She broke the seal and quickly read the contents. *Meet me in the west tower. Hurry.*

There was no signature, but her heart told her the letter must be from Tancred. She glanced down at her robe and wondered if she should take the time to dress. There was no doubt precious little time, yet to appear in public without some proper form of attire was unthinkable. She quickly grabbed the surcoat she'd worn earlier and shed herself of her night clothes.

There was lighting enough to make her way unhindered through the castle. Helena felt her heart pounding in anticipation.

Tanny wanted to talk to her!

Perhaps he had reconsidered the matter and had a change of heart. Then again, mayhaps his heart was decided in a way she would not like. Maybe he had decided to go away and leave her.

With trembling hand, she reached out for the tower door and pushed it open. The spiraling stone stairs bore no evidence of life. Even the rats in their constant vigil for food had neglected this part of the castle.

With nothing but the lighted torches on the wall to guide her steps, Helena began her ascent. "Tanny?" She whispered his name into the shadowy confines, but no reply came.

The first level revealed only storage. There were wooden crates with unknown goods and stacks of materials on top of unneeded tables. In the corners of the room, spectral figures rose up and proved to be nothing more than rolled wall hangings. Helena shivered nevertheless. It was an unpleasant place to be, and she longed to find Tancred to ease her worried mind.

Progressing up the stairs, she squealed in fright when a fat mouse crossed her thin-slippered foot. The noise she made echoed in her ears.

"Tanny?" she called out a little louder this time but still heard no reply.

With one hand on her skirts and the other against the wall to balance her, Helena again trembled. The dampness of the cold stone seemed foreboding. Perhaps she should turn back.

A noise from above caught her attention. Quickly passing the unused rooms of the second level, Helena made her way cautiously to the third-floor room. She knew from here there were ladders that would reach the highest castle battlements.

With her right hand constantly feeling the way, Helena remembered that the stairs had been spiraled to allow defenders coming from the top to use their right-handed swords, while the attackers would be at a disadvantage with the wall at their right. After all, it was well known that only the truly evil were able to fight left-handed.

The third floor revealed a door slightly ajar and light coming from within. Helena reached to push the heavy wooden door open. "Tancred, are you here?" She stepped inside and searched the room with her eyes. The ladder to the roof stood in one corner, while the circular room otherwise bore no sign of life save the lighted torch.

The door slammed shut behind her with a resounding thud. Helena jumped and turned to find Maude staring at her with a malicious smile.

"So you got my message."

"Yours? I thought Tanny sent it." Helena backed up against the wall at Maude's advancing form. "What do you want?"

"I want a great deal, and with you in my life, I cannot have it." Maude stopped several paces away and looked Helena over from head to toe. "I cannot see what the fuss is about. 'Tis true you are comely, but not overmuch. Your hair is fine yellow, but your eyes are too pale."

Helena touched her unbraided hair. It hung in ringlets around her shoulders and down to her waist. There had been no time to dress it before coming to the clandestine meeting.

Maude continued taking inventory of Helena's appearance. "I cannot see that your figure is any more shapely than mine. Nor are you more graceful or capable." Maude seemed to genuinely puzzle over the younger woman's merits. When she turned slightly away, Helena ran for the door and managed to pull it open, but Maude saw her movement, reached over, and slammed her hard against the stone wall.

"You certainly are not as intelligent as I."

"Maude, what is it that you want? I did what you told me. I told Roger to take me home, and he is doing so in the morn."

"Cease! I will not listen to your lies. Tancred is also going with you. What spell did you weave to capture his heart? Is it the same one you used to wile away my father's love?"

Helena blinked and swallowed hard. "I never strove to put distance between you and Father."

"Do not call him that! You have no right. He was not your father. Your mother came into our house with you heavy in her belly. You were not my father's child, but the orphan of my father's friend."

"'Tis true enough that my father died upon the battlefield, but your father loved him dearly and saw my mother's need. With your own mother long dead and mine without hope, they formed an agreement and joined their estates. What possible fault can you find in that?"

"Dear Helena," Maude stated sarcastically. "Sweet, precious Helena. My father strutted about the house as proud as a peacock on the day you were born. What think you of my lot when that hour came? I was but seven years and had, until that time, held my father's heart in full. Even Roger loved me best, and I knew much kindness from the people upon our lands."

"That needn't have stopped on my account. You brought sorrow upon yourself with your bitterness and anger. You treated my mother badly, and your father could scarce stand to see her grieved."

"Do I not know this for myself? I oft wonder if my father did not love your mother long before their union."

Helena shrugged. "Mayhaps, but what can we make of that now? My father and yours were closer than brothers. Neither had kit nor kin beyond the offspring they were to give life to. It bonded them in a way that could not be severed. It seems natural that our mothers might also have been close. It matters naught."

"It matters!" Maude screeched. "You took away from me the only things that did matter. Every suitor—"

"'Tis not true!" Helena interrupted. "I but lost my heart to Tanny, no other."

"'Tis true indeed. You batted your eyes and flashed your smiles at the men, until even though you were but a child, my own courters were asking Roger about your betrothal arrangements."

"But I had no part in that," Helena protested. "I was but a friendly child. I simply enjoyed the company of people. I sought not to destroy your marriage plans."

"'Tis unimportant now." Maude stepped closer, and Helena slid against the wall, away from the door and her hopes for freedom. "You have the eye of the one man I want. Tancred DuBonnet is mine. He has always been mine, and I will bear no other becoming wife to him."

"Surely you jest," Helena said, suddenly feeling bold. "Tanny loves me. I know that he does."

"Mayhaps," Maude said, bringing a dagger up to Helena's face. "But will he love a corpse?"

"You mean to kill me?" Helena questioned, suddenly realizing just how serious this matter was.

"You stand between me and happiness," Maude replied. "I have but to rid myself of your existence in order to obtain that which I desire."

"And you believe Tancred would ever find it possible to love you? He knows how you played him false when we were younger. He saw your ways. Would he now look aside and wed the murderer of his own true love?"

"Cease this prattle! You have no claim on a love falsely taken. You stole his heart. It rightly belongs to me. You are a witch and have cast a spell over my beloved. I have but to put an end to your life in order to break the spell and have Tancred for myself!"

Chapter 19

Tancred found Richard in his counting room, reviewing the ledgers left him by Arianne and his steward.

"If this is a bad time..."

"Nay," Richard said, motioning Tancred forward. "I am finished. You can see the candle is burned nearly down. What is on your mind? Have you thought of something more concerning our parents?"

"Nay," Tancred said, taking a seat. "I have come on another matter." Just then thunder rumbled loudly.

Richard raised an eyebrow. "Roger and Helena?"

"More simply, Helena."

Richard grinned and stroked his beard thoughtfully. Arianne had told him of the two lovers and their devotion for one another. She had also told him of Tancred's worry regarding the matter. "My wife mentioned your interest."

Tancred smiled. "She would. There is not much that escapes that woman. She mystifies me at times and often reminds me of our mother."

"Aye," Richard stated in surprise. "I had not thought on it, but you are right. She's been wife to me for nearly a year, and every day I learn something new about her. But you did not come here to speak of Arianne. What of Helena?"

It was Tancred's turn to look thoughtful. "I have been pardoned by Henry, but nothing was said of returning my land or title."

"True. I never thought of it that way, but I suppose it is a grave concern of yours."

"Of course it is a concern. 'Tis not that I am not most happy to be pardoned of a crime I did not commit, but what is to become of me henceforth? I do not, in fact, even have full use of my name. It bears the stain of blood from the trial and consequent punishment that I endured. Many know the name of Tancred DuBonnet and believe that man to have been a murderer."

"I think I understand," Richard replied, suddenly seeing his brother's dilemma. "You love Helena but cannot offer her your name in marriage because you feel you have no name."

"Leastwise not one I would share with such a tender heart."

Richard nodded. "'Tis a difficult matter, but surely not one that is without hope. We will go to Henry and inquire of him about your land and titles. If you are reinstated those things, then people far and wide will know of your redemption."

"Aye, but that may well take years. I do not wish to lose Helena in this matter. I have come to ask a favor."

"Name it. I owe you that much."

Tancred shook his head. "Nay, there is no obligation here. Please hear me out. I seek only to ask for a home here at Gavenshire. At least until we can learn of my chances with Henry."

"But you have no need to ask that. I have already given you that. You need never feel obligated to me for a roof overhead and food in your belly. I denied you. . ." Richard held up his hand to stop Tancred from speaking. "Nay, 'tis truth enough, and I beg you hear me out. I denied you a home and your name because of my blind fury and desire for revenge. Tancred, I know I have your forgiveness, but I do this to offer you my heart. My home is yours."

"Thank you," Tancred said and hesitated for a moment before continuing. "But, what if Henry refuses to give me back my land?"

"Then I will bestow land upon you myself. 'Tis my right. This lot and more have been given to me through Henry and my marriage to Arianne. I will see you reinstated one way or another."

"I am happy to work at your side and do the service of a knight," Tancred said. "I will not be idly kept."

"I knew it would be so with you," Richard said with a grin. "You may come to regret those words."

"Nay, I think not. Still, there is another favor."

"Pray continue." Richard was now genuinely curious.

"I would like to beg a place for Helena as well. You see, I intend to take her as my wife. That is, if she will still have me. I was a bit brusque with her earlier this day."

Richard laughed and shook his head. "There is no doubting she will have you. She's defied her stepbrother and sister, and were Henry not sympathetic with his wife and Helena's mother, Helena would no doubt have challenged the king of England as well. I could very nearly envy the devotion you have in that woman."

Tancred nodded with a sober look of awe. "'Tis a wondrous thing, indeed. I have no mind for it. The love I feel for her is a newborn thing compared. I loved her as a little sister when I fostered in her home. I've dried her tears and played games with her, protected her from her overbearing nursemaid, but all in all, it was nothing.

"Through my years of misery I did not call her face to mind. If I had, 'twould have been the face of a child that filled my vision. Still, it is easy to give her my heart now."

"And why so?"

Tancred's face went momentarily blank, almost as if Richard's words were incomprehensible to him. "Why so? Because she fills me. My heart beats because she bids it do so. I cannot see the future without seeing her in it as well."

Richard laughed and pounded the table with his fists. "A love match! How rare, indeed! You are blessed, Brother, and why not? You have suffered through much, and now God gives you back in full measure, just as He did Job. Have no fear, I believe your lands and title will be returned by and by."

Tancred smiled. "Would that I might have your confidence."

"Where is that faith you boast, Brother?"

"'Tis here," Tancred said, thumping his fist against his chest. "But he is still a timid fellow."

"Then let him be bold. I give you and Helena my pledge. Gavenshire shall be your home until you desire it no more. Even then, I shall never close its doors to you and yours. Marry her quickly and be assured that even in your death, she will know my protection."

"Thank you, Richard." Tancred stood, and Richard did so as well. "I will go and speak with her on the matter. Roger has already given me his word on it. If Henry will but agree. . ."

"Never fear; I've a feeling Henry desires to right this wrong as much as I do. Henry will give you all that you ask."

Tancred left the room with a purpose. He would seek out Helena, even though the hour was late, and ask her to marry him. He would pledge his love and life and promise to make her a new home. Taking the steps two at a time, he felt his heart lighten in a way he'd never known. Helena was his. For the moment, it was enough.

The door to Helena's room was ajar, something Tancred had not expected to find. He pushed it open full and walked inside, fearful that something might have happened.

On the grate, a fire burned brightly, and on the rumpled covers of the bed, Helena's linen robe lay discarded. Wherever she was, Helena had apparently been drawn from her bed to be there. Perhaps, Tancred thought, Arianne had need of her service. It was possible that Timothy had been inconsolable and Helena had been fetched to sing. Still, there was no sound on the air, and always before, Helena's voice had drifted through the halls to warm his blood.

He glanced around the room again, hoping to see something that might tell him where she'd gone. It was then that he spied the letter. Near the door, on the floor, a pale flicker of firelight shone on the single page. Tancred bent and retrieved it.

Immediately his eye fell on the wax signet. His signet. His and Richard's. He opened the page and read. Helena was beckoned to the west tower, but by whom? Taking the parchment, he went below to confront Richard and, instead, met him on the stairs.

"Did you write this?" Tancred questioned, thrusting the parchment forward.

Richard strained to see it in the dim light. "Nay, 'tis not my writing."

"But 'tis our seal. I found this in Helena's room. She is not there."

"I did not send it, and I presume you did not."

"Nay, I did not," Tancred reaffirmed.

"We should go to the west tower and find her. This would seem an unsavory matter," Richard said, keeping his voice a husky whisper. "But who would have our signet ring to seal the wax?"

"Roger Talbot has a ring such as ours. I gave it to him eleven years ago." Tancred was getting an uncomfortable feeling in the pit of his stomach.

"Is it possible that Talbot would endanger Helena?"

"I pray not, but what else might this mean?" Tancred asked. Then glancing behind him, Tancred asked another question. "Where is Roger's room?"

"There," Richard pointed. "The room to the left of the stairs."

Tancred crossed the distance quickly and pounded upon the door. A sleepy-eyed Roger appeared, wearing nothing more than a linen chausses.

"What are you about, Tancred?"

Tancred motioned Richard to bring the note. "Did you write this?"

Roger pulled the parchment close to the wall torch. "Nay, 'tis not my writing."

"It bears my seal, and none save Richard and you have ever worn that ring, with exception of our father." Tancred's voice was edged in anger.

Roger eyed him for a moment before handing the note back. "It pains me to admit this, but I lost that ring only three days after you gave it to me.

'Twas among my things one day and the next it was gone. I searched but never found it again. Besides, why would I send you a note to meet me in the west tower? I have no reckoning of this place. I would not know the rooms or the way to them."

"'Twas not written to me," Tancred said, stuffing the note into his tunic.

"Then who?"

"I found it in Helena's room, and she is gone."

Roger didn't bother to ask for more information. He dressed quickly, and while pulling on his boots, a desperate thought came to him.

"Maude wrote that letter," he announced suddenly.

"What?" Richard and Tancred asked in unison.

"I believe that letter to be Maude's handwriting. She could well have stolen that signet those many years ago. She was determined to have you for herself, mayhaps she thought to use the ring to bear witness against you. Perhaps she intended to give it over to the king and declare it a symbol of your pledge. For whatever purpose," he said, getting to his feet, "I believe it is Maude's writing."

Tancred paled. "Then Helena is in grave danger."

"Why say you this?" Richard asked, now the only one who did not perceive the circumstance for what it was.

"Because the same hand wrote and sealed the letter that took me to our parents the night they died."

Richard and Tancred exchanged a look and then glanced to Roger. "Maude!" the men said in unison, and Richard motioned them out the door.

"The tower is this way."

Chapter 20

or all of my life, I have lived in your shadow," Maude spat hatefully. "You were always there to make my days unbearable, and when I could stand it no longer, I married a man I did not love. All, I might add, in order to escape the presence of you and your mother."

"Maude, be reasonable. Mother held naught but kindness in her heart for you, and I was a child of ten years when you married. I had naught to do with that choice or decision."

"I wanted DuBonnet!"

"I had naught to do with that, either. My love for him was not returned. Certainly the love of a grown man could not be given to a child. If Tanny had loved me, he could have asked for my hand. We could have been betrothed—others were at ages younger than mine. You speak false if you say I had anything to do with keeping Tancred from seeking your hand. He didn't know I existed."

Maude help up the dagger. Her face contorted in rage. "You spoke out against me! You told him I was unworthy of his love."

"Lies!" Helena's anger matched that of her stepsister. "I would have, but my mother would not allow it. She said 'twas a matter for adults to decide. 'Tis true enough that I wanted to keep you from Tanny, but I said nothing!"

"Then 'twas Eleanor."

"Nay! My mother would not have done such a thing. She would have happily seen you married off. What was it to her but to be rid of your sour face in her home?" Helena knew the feelings were more her own than those of her departed mother.

"It was my home first! You were intruders. You, who came into my house and stole all that would be mine. I dealt with Eleanor for her treachery, just as I dealt with Tancred. Now, I will deal with you."

Helena's eyes widened. "Tancred? Have you slain him already?" Her voice betrayed the anguish.

Maude laughed dementedly. "Nay, not until a priest joins us in marriage. I am not stupid."

Relief flooded Helena's face. "Then what speak you of having dealt with Tancred?"

Maude's face relaxed and a smile formed upon her lips. "Revenge has always been my closest companion. When others would not do my bidding, revenge served me well. Just as I make Tancred pay for rejecting my affections, so I will make you pay for stealing his love from me."

"I do not understand. How did you avenge yourself against Tancred?" The cold of the stone wall was seeping into Helena's body, but still she did not move.

"When Tancred would have no part of me, I decided 'twas only fair to exact a punishment." Maude toyed with the dagger, then waved her arms. Before she could speak, a noise sounded outside the open door and drew her attention. With a quick glance at Helena, Maude turned to investigate the noise.

Helena hurried to the roof ladder and might have made an escape, but her surcoat tripped her up and the ripping sound of material, along with Helena's headlong fall, quickly brought Maude back into the room.

"You cannot hope to defy me in this. The rats may make merry in the tower, but you will die this night."

Helena picked herself up and tried to hold the torn garment together. Her blond hair was wildly askew, and her breathing came in panting gulps. "How," she gasped, "how did you avenge yourself? I would know that much before I die."

Maude smirked at the younger woman. "He kept from me what I loved most, so I took from him what he loved most."

Realization suddenly dawned on Helena. "His parents!"

"Aye, his precious father and mother." Maude's eyes gleamed at the memory. "I sent him a message, much the same as I did for you this night." She moved the dagger to her left hand, and it was then that it occurred to Helena that Maude was right-handed.

So much for the left-handed being the only truly evil. Helena's thoughts were interrupted as Maude retrieved something from the pouch of her belt. Holding it up, Helena saw that it was a ring. "'Tis the DuBonnet signet. The same I took from Roger's room and kept with me unto this day. A simple thing, yet it yielded a way to trap the man who would not be trapped."

"You sent for Tanny and called him to his parents' home, but how. . . ?" Helena's voice faltered. She couldn't say the words.

"How did I arrange for them to be killed? 'Tis what you are asking, is it not?"

Helena nodded and shuddered. "Aye."

"I could not very well kill them myself. So I took coin and paid it to be done. I arranged it carefully so that when Tancred arrived upon his homelands, it would be a signal to those who lay in wait. The deed was done, and just as I had planned, Tancred arrived first upon the scene. 'Twas luck, plain and simple, that Richard arrived shortly behind to find the knife in his brother's hand." Maude slipped the ring on her finger and shifted the knife.

"But what of the witnesses?" Helena questioned, again backing up to feel the wall behind her.

"They were paid and later poisoned to keep them from telling their tales. The real murderer did not live long enough to be dealt with by me. He was killed the next day fighting over another man's wife. So you see"— Maude stepped forward in determined steps—"you are the only one who lives to tell my story."

"They will find me," Helena murmured.

"Perhaps, but not for a long while. Especially not if I play the details out properly. I will go to Roger and tell him that you were desperate to leave the castle. I will tell that you could no longer bear your misery here. He will look upon the road for you. No one will seek you here."

"But I left your letter in my room," Helena said, grasping at the slim hope Maude would falter.

"I will simply retrieve it when the deed is done here. No one will be the wiser."

"Roger knows," Helena finally admitted. She had to make Maude see reason.

"Pray tell, what does Roger know?"

"I told him that you were forcing me away from Tancred. Tanny knows, as well, and he will never be yours after this." Helena drew a deep breath and continued—afraid that if she stopped for long, Maude would refuse to hear her out.

"Tanny found me crying, and Roger insisted I tell the truth. He and Tanny waited with me until I explained it in detail. I told them you were forcing me away. I told them I had no desire to leave, but that you wanted Tancred for your own.

"They assured me you would be no threat to them. Roger planned this entire matter and arranged it so that you would stumble upon your own words. He knew it was your plan to remain here at Gavenshire, so he and

Tancred agreed that Tanny would accompany us. When you had played out your game here and returned to the manor, Tancred was to accompany me back to Gavenshire at the request of the duchess."

Maude's lip curled. "You are more deceiving and wicked than I gave you credit for. It matters naught! For this as well you will die!" She came at Helena with the knife, but just as her arm came down, someone pulled Maude backward. With a muffled thud, Maude hit the floor with her attacker. She quickly rolled away and found Roger springing to his feet. Tancred and Richard rushed to Helena's side.

"You have caused enough pain, Maude," Roger stated while Maude struggled to her feet. "You have lied and forced your will upon innocent people. Now I personally will see you before the king to admit your guilt in the killing of the DuBonnets and Lady Eleanor."

"Never!" Maude steadied herself and held tightly to the knife. "I will not be made the fool. You played me false, Brother, and you," she said looking hard at Tancred, who stood in front of a shaking Helena, "you played me a fool. You made me believe there was hope when there was none. You toyed with my affection and left me behind to suffer when it suited your purpose."

"The only hope you saw for a union between us," Tancred replied, "was one you conjured in your evil mind. I had no love for you and would never have thought to offer you my name."

Roger ignored Maude for a moment and stepped toward Helena. "Are you injured?" he questioned.

"Nay, my gown suffered more than I." Helena looked up at her stepbrother with gratitude. "'Twould have been much worse had you a slower pace."

"You have Tancred to thank for my pace. He awoke me and brought this matter to light."

Helena turned her eyes to her beloved. "Oh, Tanny," she whispered. Her heart pounded all the harder at the passionate emotion she saw in his eyes. "My dying gratitude to you, my love. It would seem that once again you have rescued me from trouble."

Tancred smiled down at her with pure pleasure. "Seems I am ever called upon to perform such tasks. 'Twould be only fitting that I make proper arrangements to keep you under my guard on a more permanent basis."

Helena raised a brow in question, but Tancred had no chance to reply before Maude let out a scream. All four turned to find her on her feet, dagger in hand, and face contorted in rage.

"He is mine! No other shall have him!" She rushed forward to stab at

Tancred, but Roger easily deflected her blows and sent the knife clattering across the stone floor.

"'Tis ended, Maude. You have spilled enough blood. Must I spill yours to still your hatred?" Roger growled.

Maude refused to cower, but her voice took on a frail air. "But I love him. I have always loved him. He was to be my husband, and—"

"I was never to be your husband, Maude. I never loved you and never will. You have no hope of a marriage with me. Not then, not now, not ever."

Maude lowered her head in complete dejection, and Roger exhaled a sigh of relief. "I am truly sorry for my sister's behavior, Your Grace. I would never have endangered your family had I known what Maude was fully capable of."

Richard shook his head. "There is no need for apologies, Talbot. You had no way of knowing."

"She murdered your parents," Helena said, stepping from behind Tancred to face Richard.

"Aye, we heard her confession." Richard's voice betrayed his sorrow. "At least it is put to rest."

"I am so sorry," Helena murmured, tears forming in her eyes.

Tancred put his arm around her and pulled her close. "'Tis no longer a matter for consideration. 'Tis finished."

"At least it will be when—" Roger's words were interrupted by Maude's sudden bolt to the door.

"I will not hang for this," she screeched and raced down the stairs. Before anyone could move, a terrible scream rang out, followed by a thud, and then ominous silence.

"Come," Richard said to Roger. "Tancred, you keep Lady Helena here."

"Aye," Tancred replied, feeling Helena trembling beneath his hold.

Helena gripped Tancred tightly and buried her face against his chest. It was all so ugly and heinous. How could any of them bear up against Maude's violence?

She wanted to say something. Anything. What words would show Tancred how much she grieved for him, for his loss? Nothing she said would bring his parents back. Just as there were no words that could bring back her mother. All three were dead because of one person's selfishness and twisted cruelty.

Tancred was smoothing her hair, and Helena relaxed against the rhythmic strokes. He was so strong, and he'd borne so very much. Helena knew she would always love him. Even if he could never offer her marriage, Helena would go on loving him from afar.

Roger returned to the tower room with a grim set to his face. "She is dead."

"Dead?" Helena choked out the word.

"Aye, she broke her neck in the fall. Her days of inflicting pain and suffering are finished."

Helena looked at Tancred and then to Roger, wondering what it all meant. What would happen now? Could they prove Maude was responsible for the killings and free Tancred from further humiliation?

Richard entered the room just then, and Helena noted that his expression was one more of relief than sorrow. "We will bury your sister and then go to the king." Roger nodded, and Tancred only tightened his grip on Helena. Richard continued. "I've instructed my men to remove Lady Talbot and see her to the priest. I will beg him to take pity on her and offer her a proper burial."

"You mentioned the king," Helena said, pushing back her long blond hair.

"Aye," Richard said solemnly. "We will go, your brother, mine, and myself. We will give Henry the facts of the matter and allow him to determine what is to take place from this moment forward. If you will excuse me, I must go speak with the priest."

"I will go along, as well," Roger offered.

When they were both gone, Tancred released his tightened grip on Helena and held her at arm's length. "You are truly unharmed?"

Helena nodded. She sheepishly held up the torn edge of her surcoat. "This is the worst of it."

"It is well. It vexed me sorely to imagine you had come here, thinking as you must that I beckoned you, only to be injured at Maude's hand."

Helena nodded. "How did you find us so quickly? I had not but come a short while before you entered."

"I had come to speak with you and found you gone. The letter was upon the floor."

"I must have dropped it in my haste."

"When I saw it, I could only imagine that someone meant to trick you. I knew I had not written it, yet it bore my signet. I thought I recognized the writing, and after learning that Richard was innocent of it as well, I presumed it must have come from Roger."

"You thought Roger had played us false and planned to harm me again?"

"That did cross my mind." He studied her hard for a moment, his eyes seeming to drink her in with an unyielding sobriety. "I feared that moment as I have never feared anything done to me."

Helena smiled and lowered her head. "'Twould seem you might care a bit for me. I am glad."

Tancred pulled her close, causing Helena to raise her gaze to meet his. His finger lightly stroked her cheek. "A bit? You think I might only care a bit?"

Helena's smile broadened. "I cannot guess more, sire. 'Twould be a dangerous assumption on my part. There has been little more to prove such hope."

"Then let this be your proof," he said and lowered his lips to meet hers in a passionate kiss.

Chapter 21

It was most trying to be left behind, but Helena and Arianne found themselves once again in that position.

"'Tis the lot of women," Arianne sighed when the second week had come and gone with no word from Richard.

Helena tried not to look too downcast as she nodded. "'Tis well there is much work to be about." She looked down at the tunic she was stitching and realized she would have to pluck out the thread on a good portion of the seam she'd just made. "Yet I cannot keep my hands and mind working together on this matter." She held up the material sadly.

Arianne laughed. "I know how it is." She held up her own piece, a linen coif for Richard. "This has borne my frustrations poorly."

"Will the king believe them?" Helena asked softly. She let the tunic fall to her lap.

"I believe so. There is really no doubt in my mind." Arianne's words were not simply given to encourage; they were heartfelt.

"Do you believe Henry will restore Tancred's property and title?"

"That is a matter I have no head for. Richard believes it so, however, and he is scarce wrong when it comes to his beloved king."

Helena nodded and got to her feet. "I'm going to the chapel. It would seem I feel best when on my knees."

Arianne put her sewing aside, checked on the sleeping Timothy, and joined Helena at the door. "Matilda and I have been praying as well. God will do what is best. Never forget this."

"I won't."

Helena went below and walked somberly to the chapel. She spent a great deal of time there in prayer, and when she entered the room, she immediately felt strengthened.

The chapel was empty; no other sole had come to pray, and the priest was in the village attending to matters there. Helena was glad for the solitude. She loved to look up at the stained glass of the chapel window and think.

Richard had surprised Arianne at Christmas with the window of deep scarlet, blue, and yellow. It was the likeness of an empty tomb, with a cross overhead. Richard said it reminded him that Christ's story did not end at the cross but began anew. The empty tomb, he had told her one evening in reflection, was one of the most hopeful symbols of all. It was there to remind us that we are resurrected in Christ, that just as He rolled the stone aside and walked away from death's grip, we, too, could do the same in Him.

Kneeling in the rushes before the altar, Helena prayed for some time, asking blessings upon those she loved. She asked that God would grant the king wisdom and mercy in dealing with Tancred and added selfishly her desire that He make Tancred her husband soon.

She was startled when someone knelt in the rushes beside her, and she opened her eyes to find Tancred.

"Tanny?"

He reached out to take her hand and kissed it lightly. "Your prayers have brought me home."

"In more ways than one this is true," she replied. "Would you pray with me now?"

"Aye, it would be most fitting." They bowed their heads, and after several moments of silent communion with God, Tancred pulled Helena to her feet. "Come. We must talk."

Pausing outside the chapel, Helena casually let her gaze travel the length of Tancred. Disheveled a bit from an obviously fast-paced ride, Tancred's hair begged her touch, and Helena could not resist.

"Do I meet with milady's approval?" he asked, grinning.

"Aye, very much so. You could stand a bit of grooming, but otherwise I find you perfect."

"Nay, it will never be so, but I am glad to find you satisfied with me."

"Pray tell, why?" She looked at him with little-girl innocence.

Tancred's grin turned roguish. "I could say, but I'd much rather show you." He pulled her into his arms and kissed her lips soundly.

Helena wrapped her arms around his neck, totally forgetting where they were. Her heart pounded from joy and passion, and she sighed a deep, throaty sigh when his lips traveled boldly from her mouth to the side of her face and then just below her ear.

"I most enjoy this talk," she teased.

"You are a hard vision to put from my mind," Tancred whispered between kisses.

"No more so than you," Helena countered. "Remember, I held your face for eleven years in my heart."

"And glad I am that you did." The spell was broken, and Tancred set her away from him just a bit. "Which reminds me."

"I know." Helena grinned. "We must talk."

"Aye, and quickly."

Tancred led her out beyond the castle walls. The brilliance of spring grass and wildflowers set a lively mood that infected Helena. Beyond the castle, a calm, blue sea awaited their review, while gulls flew overhead, searching for bits of food.

To Helena, it was as if spring had come all at once. "'Tis so beautiful!" she exclaimed and strayed from Tancred's side to do an animated jig. She hummed a song to herself and laughed when Tancred pulled her back to him and held her fast.

"You have not yet asked what happened with Henry."

"True." She sobered a bit. "Mayhaps you will tell me now?"

Tancred reached up and pulled the linen wimple from her head. "Pesky things. I rather fancy the way your hair was spilled out that night in the tower." He toyed with the wisps of blond hair that had come loose from her braid.

"'Tis pesky when a man would undress a maiden's hair without the right to do so," Helena said snidely. "If I had a champion, he would be called to defend me just now."

Tancred chuckled and tossed the wimple aside. "You have a champion in me, milady." He bowed low before her, making Helena giggle.

"I would rather have you for a husband," she stated boldly.

Tancred rose and shook his head. "It would seem that you and Henry agree on the matter."

"Oh, Tanny! Did the king give us permission to marry?"

"Aye."

He seemed quite pleased with himself, and Helena couldn't help laughing. "Tell me all!"

Tancred put his hand about her waist and walked toward the cliff edge with Helena snugly beside him. "Henry listened to all we had to say and made a full record of Maude's treachery. He was most satisfied that the matter was ended."

"Did he restore your lands?" Helena asked hesitantly lest she sound greedy.

"Nay," Tancred said softly in a reflective manner.

Helena frowned and looked up to catch his eyes looking out across the vastness of the sea. She squeezed his hand. "Alas, my love, 'tis of no matter. It will be well with us so long as we have each other. I care naught for the land or the titles, only for you."

Tancred gazed down upon her with such deeply felt love that Helena had to look away. "He could not restore my lands for they were given to the church and made into a monastery. He did, however, give me lands not far from these. I will not make a beggar's wife of you, my dear."

Helena gasped. "Lands here?"

"Aye, within a two-day journey of Gavenshire. We will join Richard's land on one side, while Devon's estate joins them on the other."

"How wonderful!" She hugged him tightly and was not surprised when his arms wrapped around her and held her fast.

"Marry me, Helena," he whispered.

Helena melted against him. "Aye," she murmured. It was the culmination of a lifetime of dreaming.

Pulling away, Helena turned her back to Tancred and stared out across the sea. "These waters once separated us, and for many years I cursed them and mourned my loss. But the same waters brought you back again, and I curse them no more."

Tancred pulled her back against him, nestling his face against her shoulder. "I pledge you that no one shall separate us again. There may come a day when I am summoned to do the king's work or attend to matters of my own, but here in my heart, we shall ever be one. I love you, Helena. I vow always to love you."

Helena felt tears upon her cheeks and wiped them away with her hand before turning to face her beloved Tanny. Her heart nearly burst at the sight of him. She opened her mouth to speak, but instead a song came to her lips. Tanny's song:

> *If my beloved were a king,*
> *I couldst not love him more.*
> *Were he a jester to make men laugh,*
> *My love I would implore.*
> *But, alas, my love is but a man,*
> *Of heart and soul so free.*
> *And I couldst no more break my vow,*
> *Than break the heart in me.*

Tracie Peterson, bestselling, award-winning author of over ninety fiction titles and three nonfiction books, lives and writes in Belgrade, Montana. As a Christian, wife, mother, writer, editor, and speaker (in that order), Tracie finds her slate quite full. Published in magazines and Sunday school take-home papers, as well as a columnist for a Christian newspaper, Tracie now focuses her attention on novels. After signing her first contract with Barbour Publishing in 1992, her novel, *A Place To Belong*, appeared in 1993 and the rest is history. She has over twenty-six titles with Heartsong Presents' book club (many of which have been repackaged) and stories in six separate anthologies from Barbour. From Bethany House Publishing, Tracie has multiple historical three-book series as well as many stand-alone contemporary women's fiction stories and two nonfiction titles. Other titles include two historical series cowritten with Judith Pella, one historical series cowritten with James Scott Bell, and multiple historical series cowritten with Judith Miller.

A Child of Promise

Jill Stengl

Chapter 1

The young lions do lack, and suffer hunger:
but they that seek the LORD shall not want any good thing.
PSALM 34:10

A light evening breeze with a lingering hint of winter rustled the fresh green leaves of ancient beeches, rowans, oaks, and hazels. Sunlight struggled to pierce hazy gray clouds; the wildflowers dotting a small clearing lifted their bright heads to find each infrequent ray. A red squirrel scolded bitterly from his perch in a crooked oak, disturbed by noisy intruders below.

"Oi! Go to, thieving beast!" a laughing voice echoed through the trees, intermixed with ferocious growls. A small, scruffy dog gripped one edge of a flat cloth hat between his sharp teeth while a young man, not long past boyhood, held the other edge with both hands. Round and round the forest clearing they spun, the dog growling and tossing his head from side to side. The hat's owner allowed the dog to tow him along, his arms swinging loosely though his grip was firm. "Thought to fool me, did you, Ragwort? Thought to catch me unaware? Think again, scurvy knave!"

Black, close-cropped hair lifted in the breeze as the man spun about. Strong white teeth flashed through his sparse beard. A coarse holland shirt lay open at his brown throat; its rolled-up sleeves revealed sinewy forearms. Gray woolen hose hugged long, lean legs; the lacings of his skirted jerkin hung loose. Rather like a lumbering puppy himself, the young man sported enormous feet and hands in keeping with a large, raw-boned frame. He radiated youthful exuberance and good health.

It was a ludicrous mismatch of strength, yet the tiny dog appeared to be winning. Another dog, a tall hound, squatted in the grass on the other side of the clearing, its sharp muzzle open in an apparent smile. "Do you also make jest of me, Laitha?" the man called, his tone gentle. The hound dropped to the ground and rolled to her back, wagging her entire rear half.

While watching her antics in pleased surprise, the man slipped on a crushed dock weed. He fell to one knee, then rolled over in the grass, his broad, bony shoulders demolishing more wildflowers. One hand still gripped the hat, and Ragwort redoubled his efforts, fiercely growling as he tugged the man's arm over his head at an awkward angle. The man laughed helplessly, allowing the dog to pull his arm back and forth above his head.

Suddenly the terrier dropped the hat and stared, ears alert. A low woof from Laitha brought the man scrambling to his feet. The greyhound stood like a sentinel, her nose pointing in the direction of possible danger—behind the man's back. He spun in place, crouched defensively, one hand reaching to the knife sheath at his side.

At the edge of the clearing stood a pony; on its back perched a girl. A gust of wind rustled the oak towering over her, scattering shadows across the child's white face.

The man relaxed, straightening. "Ah, well met, maiden. What do you seek here?" His voice was pleasant, though he inwardly berated himself for lack of attentiveness.

He presumed that she was of gentle birth, for she possessed a horse and her clothing appeared fine; but closer inspection caused him to wonder. The pony wore neither bridle nor saddle. Bare feet and skinny legs dangled below the ragged edge of the child's kirtle. The grime edging her pale face appeared to be of long standing. Bony wrists extended far beyond the gathered edges of her smock sleeves. Huge dark eyes regarded him with an expression of mingled wonder and apprehension. Was she lost?

"Are you a wicked man or a good man?"

The low question raised his brows. "A good man, I hope, though every man has the wicked sin nature within. Why do you ask thusly, child?"

Her eyes narrowed. "Are you a wizard?"

He sobered. "Nay, I have no such evil craft. I am a bond servant of Jesus Christ, devoted to His service."

"You are a priest, then?"

"Not so, maiden. I am but a simple craftsman. Harry the joiner, at your service." He flourished his rather moist hat and made a graceful bow.

"I saw you not ere this day. You are a foreigner—not of this parish. Do you have leave to encamp upon manor grounds? Sir David Marston does not take kindly to vagabonds." Her tone was formal and proud, and he wondered again about her station.

"I have leave. I am in Sir David's employ, maiden."

"What is your trade?" Genuine curiosity colored the question, so he excused her impertinence.

"I am a joiner, as I said. I craft woodwork. You are welcome to share my pottage, and I shall play you a tune upon my lute." Though but a child, she was company.

"I have supped." Belatedly she added, "I thank you," with a respect that had been lacking at first.

Ragwort had by now worked up enough courage to approach her pony and sniff around its hooves. The pony lowered its head and snorted. Ragwort scooted quickly away, barking shrilly. Another low woof answered, and the hound moved farther into the clearing, hesitant to approach.

"What ails your hound?" Bending over her pony's neck, the girl tried to gain a closer view of the dog's face. "It behaves strangely."

"Come near, Laitha." Harry the joiner bent to touch the hound's head as she slowly approached. At first Laitha cringed away, but as he continued to speak softly and stroke her smooth head, she leaned against his leg and heaved a grateful sigh. Her backside began to wiggle as though wagged by a tail, but no tail was visible, only a ragged stump.

Harry looked up to find that the girl had dismounted. Leading her pony by its forelock, she stepped over a clump of bluebells, her eyes glued to the white hound.

"Speak to Laitha as you approach; she cannot see you," he instructed, still stroking the dog's hard, bony side with one hand.

The child stopped a few feet away, horror twisting her face. "Why, she possesses neither eyes nor ears! What have you done to her?"

Laitha cringed, sinking down at Harry's feet. Empty eye sockets gaped with ghastly entreaty as she turned her slender muzzle to her master; pathetic stumps framed naked pink ear canals. "Nay, lass, the child shall harm thee not," Harry crooned, his hands caressing the dog's head, which had once been attractive, marked with brindled patches over each eye and ear.

"Last Michaelmas I came upon Laitha in Epping Forest, blood soaked and nigh death. I can only guess wherefore. Perhaps she angered a lord with timidity on the stag hunt; perhaps she made chase to a hare; perhaps she was simply too slow."

Dropping the pony's forelock, the girl sat down tailor fashion and reached out to the dog. "Laitha," she called, her low voice pleading. "Come hither, Laitha. I will harm you not." Patiently she coaxed while Harry studied her.

Her laced waistcoat and kirtle of cranberry red were torn and faded, the embroidered edging missing many threads. Her soiled cap slipped back to reveal greasy hair of an indeterminate hue. Was it red? Odd, with those dark eyes. Long, slender fingers wiggled as she entreated the dog to come to her. These were not the hands of a peasant child.

The little terrier made the first move. Quivering tail held like a pikestaff over his back, he took cautious steps closer to those outstretched fingers, his black nose twitching. Soon he was happily seated in her lap, his pink tongue lolling as she scratched his wiry back. Laitha still pressed against the joiner's leg.

"You have charmed Ragwort," Harry observed. "He has eyes to behold your honest face."

"Alas for Laitha!" she sighed. "Do you think she will e'er trust another?"

"I know not. Perchance in time you shall win her."

Ragwort's button eyes twinkled merrily. The girl's lips softened in the first semblance of a smile. "Ragwort pleases me."

"And you please him." Harry smiled. "Tell me your name," he ordered gently.

Her eyes flew to his face, alert and suspicious once again; but after a careful search of his countenance, the child replied, "I am called Maela."

"May Ella?"

"Nay, Maela." Her eyes narrowed. "Ishmaela Andromeda Trenton."

Under that challenging glare he dared not smile. "'Tis a pleasure to make your acquaintance, my lady." This designation must certainly accompany her surname. Trenton was the nearest village, and ancient Castle Trent dominated the local skyline.

But her lips curled. "I am no lady." Gently dumping Ragwort from her lap, she leaped to her feet and marched across the clearing, leaving her pony to graze at will. Harry looked from her to the pony, then tugging its forelock, led the obliging little horse after its mistress.

Maela headed directly for Harry's small camp and stood with hands on hips to survey it. An empty two-wheeled cart leaned on its shafts beside a crate of clucking chickens. A woolly spotted donkey lifted its head, letting out a raspy bray in greeting. Beside the makings of a fire rested an assortment of iron pots and utensils, a few wooden bowls and spoons, and a smooth board. A bucket full of vegetables waited where Harry had left it to chase Ragwort.

"You dwell here among the trees? Why not at the manor with other hirelings?"

"I prefer peace and solitude to noise and squalor," he explained. "I sleep alone and care for my own needs." Releasing the pony, he began chopping vegetables for his pottage, squatting beside the iron pot of water. The dogs flopped down beneath the cart, Laitha's head resting across Ragwort's back.

"You cook? Mend your own clothes?"

"What I do not for myself, I purchase or take in trade."

The child shook her head. "What manner of man is this? Never heard I of one such." She sounded disapproving, yet admiring. "You have need of nothing and no one."

"Nay, not so."

"What do you mean?"

"I have need of the Lord God. It is He that provides my every need, as He promised in His Word. Lions do lack and suffer hunger, but they that seek the Lord shall not want any good thing."

She did not respond. Those eyes watched his every move.

"What age have you, child?"

"Thirteen last January. And you?"

"Nineteen last March. I had guessed you at ten years."

"And I took you for a man grown!"

He frowned, though his lips twisted in amusement. "I am a man grown. I have been on my own these many years."

"You do rove about the land as a vagrant?"

His reply dripped with irony. "I do pause to lay hand upon work now and again. I made acquaintance with Sir David last summer while at De-Haven Park, Lord Weston's estate in Essex. I did, at that time, carve rampant lions atop the newel posts of the great staircase. Sir David Marston repeatedly expressed his desire of a carved screen for his minstrel gallery and frequently lamented the dearth of skilled joiners in his county—hence my presence in Suffolk. I move farther north, closer to home, with each position I accept, it seems. Soon I hope to visit my family. I have not seen them in many a year."

"Where is your home?"

"Near Lincoln."

"I would hear of your travels. Have you been to London?" She sat upon a handy log, obviously intending to stay awhile.

"Yea, I have even seen our queen at a short distance. Once she did stop and take the hand of a man near me and smile and talk to him. She is delicate and pale, like you, and yet," Harry frowned thoughtfully as he studied Maela's face again, "yet your features, though similar in color, are unlike."

Maela sighed. "And she is reputed a beauty. Tush!" she brushed it aside. "'Tis of little moment. Do you admire life at court?"

Harry chuckled. "Court life I know nothing of, for I move not in that sphere. I am a hired artisan, not among the gentry, Maela. And I care not for town life. The smells—faugh!" He shook his head in disgust. "And the plague! I took me off afore the worst of the plague hit, yet many a red cross I saw upon doors in the leaving."

Maela leaned forward, bony elbows upon her knees. "Have you beheld the Black One?"

"Eh? Which black what?" He picked up an onion and peeled off the papery skin.

"*Grandmere* says that when plague takes a man, the Black One takes his soul out the front door! She did witness it." The girl's slight frame shivered. "I dread this frightful sight!"

"Maela, the plague is but a sickness, not a curse. I believe 'tis caused by filth. If people bathed often and laundered their clothing, mayhap these illnesses would strike not."

The child gaped. "Surely you are mad! Bathe often? Bathing chills the lungs and brings on fever! I bathe only twice a year, as Grandmere bids me."

"I see," he murmured, and might have added, "so I smell," for an occasional ill wind had already told him that the child reeked. Her sentiments about bathing were not uncommon; Harry had met few people in England who shared his unorthodox views about hygiene.

"I bathe frequently," he informed her, "and I perish not of lung fever. In truth, I am seldom ill."

She was silent for several moments, watching his nimble fingers slice the last few parsnips and drop them into the pot. "You are a strange man."

Harry lit a pile of tinder with a few expert strokes of his flint. Blowing and carefully feeding the flame with dry twigs, he soon had a large enough fire to cook his pottage. Hanging the pot upon a sturdy framework, he suspended it over the fire. Still sprinkling herbs into the pottage, he casually asked, "Will you take a cup of milk?"

"Whence comes this milk?"

"A gift of love from Genevieve." He grinned.

"Genevieve?" Lines appeared between her dark brows. "I thought you slept alone."

"So I do. Genevieve sleeps with Samson, though they are merely friends." He uttered a short yodeling call, and an answering bleat came from behind the cart. With a scramble of legs, a small brown goat rose to its feet and bleated again.

"Genevieve—a gift from a grateful employer. Her milk is a wondrous addition to my meals. No longer must I drink only ale and beer. A kid shall birth come summer." He watched the child make acquaintance with his goat. It was abundantly clear that beasts were Maela's passion in life.

"Samson is the ass's name. What do you call the fowl?" She leaned over the crate to inspect his chickens.

"Sage, Parsley, and Rosemary. It keeps them humble."

A gurgle of laughter rewarded him. "You would not eat them?" She sounded slightly concerned.

"Nay. They provide eggs."

Harry rose to release his three hens and encouraged the girl to scatter their grain. She squatted down to stroke their soft feathers, pleased when the friendly birds allowed her caresses. "These also were gifts?"

"Accepted in payment for services rendered, more like."

"Do you not fear to lose them? Stoats, foxes, and thieves abound hereabouts, and you have little protection."

"The Lord watches over me," he assured her. "I own little of value, but I will fight for my possessions."

"Are you armed?" she asked, eyes widening.

"I am armed sufficiently." He smiled. "Few venture to accost me."

Her eyes flitted over his rangy frame from head to toe. "One would not. Two might try, and from cover."

"Leave them try. No arrow may take my life unless the Lord allows." Returning to the fire, he stirred the pottage, sniffing the steam.

Maela's small nose twitched like Ragwort's. "Truly, you do cook well," she wavered. "Grandmere's pottage lacks flavor. Have you enough for me?"

He looked down at the full pot, then lifted one eyebrow in her direction. "'Twill suffice."

Maela consumed an astounding amount of pottage, and Harry polished off several full bowls, yet the pot was still partially full when they had finished eating. Harry offered more bread, but Maela clutched her stomach, shaking her head. "Nay, I would surely burst. I have not eaten so well since. . ." She paused, then shook her head. "I cannot think when."

He indicated the waiting dogs. "Rag and Laitha would eat our leavings. You may give them sup."

The words were scarcely out of his mouth before she had refilled her bowl and placed it before the dogs. They ate together, one at each side of the bowl, while Maela crouched beside them, fascinated. Once the bowl was empty, Ragwort licked Laitha's muzzle with almost motherly tenderness. Unable to express her feelings with tail or ears, the hound whined softly, enjoying her friend's attentions.

"They have a great love," Maela observed wistfully. Firelight flickered across her face, for the forest grew dark.

Harry smiled at her. He was startled at the brilliance of the smile she returned, having grown accustomed to her sober expression.

"You will abide here, Harry Joiner?" she asked. "I may visit you again?"

The passion in her request took him aback. "Surely you may return, child. I shall wrap these soft rolls and a pasty for you to take and enjoy at your leisure. Dovie, the cook at Marston Hall, baked them," he remarked to lighten the conversation. "Do you know her? A comely maid and excellent cook."

Maela's face darkened abruptly. "I know her not."

Harry went on, thoughtfully stirring the fire, "I considered not my words. A lady of Castle Trent would not know a cook. You dwell at the castle?"

Maela nodded shortly, her expression guarded.

"Are you related to Sir Hanover Trenton? His son visited Fulbrook Manor in Hertfordshire where I carved the drawing room paneling two seasons past. A goodly lad he is, though harsh with his pony. Isaac Trenton. . ." he paused, finally noticing the girl's stiffened shoulders. "Your brother? Cousin?"

Maela abruptly sprang to her feet and flung herself at the grazing pony. Apparently used to his mistress's unpredictable whims, the pony hardly batted an eye, allowing her to scramble upon his broad back. She dug bare heels into his sides and wheeled him away.

"Maela, tarry! I would escort you home—" Harry leaped to intercept her, but he was too late. Thudding hoofbeats faded into the darkness. His arms fell to his sides; his mouth slowly closed. Attempting to track her in this strange forest would be useless. "Lord Jesus, bring the child safely home, I pray," he spoke softly, his face upturned into a falling mist.

He returned to the fireside, his eyes troubled. "What did I say to offend her?" Ragwort looked as puzzled as Harry felt; Laitha looked blank, her mutilated face revealing no thoughts.

Harry caught his sleepy hens, moved Samson's stake closer to the cart beside the goat, and banked the fire. "Tomorrow I shall inquire about the waif," he muttered, yet misgivings assailed him. With increased knowledge might also come an increased sense of responsibility. "Lord, what would You have me to do?"

He retired early, rolling into his blankets beneath the partial shelter of the cart. The dogs crowded under the blankets on either side of him. Misty rain fell all that night, but he paid it no heed.

Chapter 2

If any of you lack wisdom, let him ask of God,
that giveth to all men liberally. . .and it shall be given him.
JAMES 1:5

Harry woke early the next morning, to his mild annoyance. His face was cold, but warmth radiated from the dogs at his sides. Laitha snored softly and whimpered in her sleep, the probable cause of his early awakening. He wrapped an arm around the dog. Laitha suffered from the cold, her short coat affording little protection. She deserved to spend her remaining days by a warm hearth, dreaming of past hunts. A blinded sight hound—could anything be more pathetic? Never again would the great dog stretch her long legs to race through fen and forest. Mankind's cruelty to dumb beasts at times caused Harry shame—yet even more appalling was man's inhumanity to man.

Maela sprang to his mind. Though she was well-spoken and mannerly, the child's furtive expression, ragged clothing, and bruised face bespoke neglect and harsh treatment. His eyes drifted to the log, dimly visible in the morning half light, where she had perched the night before. Her slight figure and ethereal smile now seemed a figment of his lonely imagination. Yet, would he have imagined the dirt and the smell?

"Lord, did You bring me to dwell in this place for a deeper purpose than the carving of a gallery screen? I have questioned my wisdom in accepting the position—for this lack of proper accommodations is an onerous trial—yet I did believe, and believe still, that You desired me to take it." Harry often prayed aloud while alone. "Guide me, Lord, for I am at a loss."

After a breakfast of boiled eggs, porridge, raisins, wild strawberries, and a large mug of Genevieve's milk, Harry extracted his greatest treasure, a Coverdale Bible, from his small clothes chest. In the book of Ephesians he located the apostle Paul's concise description of a believer's behavior. It was difficult to read in the gray twilight beneath the trees, but Harry's memory filled in the blanks.

As he read, he prayed, requesting strength for the day to live as God pleased. "Let me not grieve Your Spirit with corrupt speech or wicked thoughts. Help me to forgive others as You have forgiven me and to walk in love. Purify my heart from filthiness and foolish, coarse talk, and fill me with Your goodness. I go before my fellow workers, the maidens, the gentry, and every human creature I meet today as Your emissary."

An unpleasant thought struck him. "Surely You would not have me to dwell among the servants, Lord. The manor garrets are crowded and noisome. I can function as emissary from here."

He argued aloud with the persistent, silent Voice. "Nay, I do not consider myself above them, but. . .Yea, I know You have commissioned me as salt and light to the world, and yet. . ."

His shoulders slumped. "Verily, I can deny You nothing; for Your sake I can endure even this. I shall move my possessions to the hall this very day."

This was a momentous surrender indeed, for Harry cherished his privacy.

Harry packed up his camp and cared for his beasts. After hitching Samson, he loaded the chicken crate and his few possessions into the cart.

"Come," he ordered the dogs and set off without a backward glance, walking at Samson's side. The beast seldom needed prodding; he enjoyed Harry's company. Genevieve, tethered behind the cart, trotted in its wake.

Marston Hall loomed out of the morning mist. Harry approached it from the rear, but the great manor house was impressive from any angle. Half-timbered with many glass windows, the magnificent hall blended aesthetically into the surrounding green fields and lush forest.

Dogs rushed to greet the small cavalcade as Harry picketed his beasts beside the carp pond. Laitha and Ragwort bristled, stiff legged and alert. Upon recognizing Harry, the manor mastiffs and hounds relaxed. Soon all tails wagged, noses sniffed, and invitations to play were issued. Harry smiled as he watched. It was good to see Laitha accepted as an equal, though she could not join their romps. Ragwort was dwarfed by his new playmates, but he didn't seem to notice. Harry hoped none of them would crush the terrier by mistake.

"Good morrow, Joiner."

Harry turned to see Marston's headman approaching. "God give you good day, Goodman Lyttleton."

"I bring news," Lyttleton went on without pause. "The master has requested you to abide in the woodman's cottage near the oak coppice rather than hide out in the forest like a bandit. It needs repair, but he will provide lumber and thatch, if you will do the work. There is grazing for your stock and room for a kitchen garden behind."

For a moment, Harry could only stand amazed at God's incredible sense of timing and humor. He recalled seeing the cottage, a ramshackle one-room dwelling, located not far from his favorite camp. "I accept this generous offer with many thanks."

Amused smiles flickered across Harry's lips as he worked that day. He should not have been surprised, really, for Sir David Marston was a kindly, generous country squire, and God was certainly never behindhand with His blessings. Had he only surrendered his will sooner, he might have been ensconced in the cottage by this time! Harry was eager to explore his new home. He felt ashamed, now, of his stubborn refusal to mingle with the manor servants, but God had made the best of the situation; and, Harry realized, had he dwelt at the manor, he would not have encountered Maela.

Maela. He had almost forgotten to ask about her.

"Have you met such a person?" was Dovie's answer when he questioned her at dinner. She did not appreciate his topic of conversation. For days, Harry had taken the noon meal in the cook's company, and he seemed to admire her; but always he seemed out of her reach in a way Dovie could not understand.

"Yea, of a truth, in the wood yesterday. She has the appearance and manner of gentry, yet her clothing is in rags. Has Sir Hanover Trenton a daughter?"

Dovie gave an affected giggle and spoke rapidly with great animation. Her hands fluttered about, frequently caressing Harry's arm or chest. "Do you speak in earnest or in jest? Sir Hanover has a son, not a daughter. Do you know that he is a courtier of the queen? He is an important man. The castle is but one of his many estates. He seldom journeys hence, for of late the castle has little to offer—yet I tell you plain, he comes within a fortnight. When in the vicinity, Sir Hanover lodges with Bishop Carmichael at Parminster Court."

"Indeed," Harry remarked. "He ne'er abides in the castle?"

"I think not." Dovie batted her big eyes and retied the drawstring of Harry's shirt. To her irritation, he wasn't even looking her way. He munched on a handful of walnuts and relaxed against the bench back. They were alone in a kitchen corner, hidden from the chattering maids and field hands by a row of tall milk cans.

"Is Castle Trent deserted?"

"Nay, it has a few retainers. Dobbin Titwhistle collects rent from tenants, and Hera Coats, the witch, watches over the keep. A few old servants remain in the outbuildings for lack of better position."

"Did you say 'witch'?"

"Yea, in truth. Every man fears to cross her path, though sundry seek her out for spells and potions. She ne'er attends church, yet no churchwarden dares demand a fine lest she place a curse upon him! She once gave our vicar the evil eye and caused his horse to go lame."

Harry believed her. The vicar had not so far impressed him with either intelligence or sincerity. He seemed the type to lend credulity to the curses of a village witch.

"I would have Mistress Coats prescribe you a love potion, for your heart gives me little notice!" Dovie leaned close, her eyes serious. "Leave off this incessant talk of castle affairs! Give me your full regard, for I would know you well, Harry Jameson."

Now she had Harry's undivided attention.

"I hear you have been provided a cottage, Harry. Couldst you use mine aid setting it to rights?" She playfully walked two fingers up his chest and cupped his bearded cheek in her hand. "I would accompany you hence at eventide." Heavy lashes fluttered as she lifted inviting eyes.

"Nay, I need no such aid!" Harry leaped up, nearly fell over the milk cans, and fairly ran from the kitchen.

Safely back in the woodshed, he berated himself for a fool. Dovie was obviously practiced at using those big cow eyes and her shapely body to entice men. He had been foolish to spend time in her company.

"You have removed scales from my eyes, Lord! It is well, in truth, that I shall not live at the manor. Dovie is unlikely to frequent the coppice cottage, for it is a fair distance. Indeed, You do all things well."

Tense and somewhat rattled, he felt in need of vigorous work. Simon, the ancient woodsman as gnarled as the oak trees he husbanded with tender care, discovered Harry behind the woodshed, pounding on a knot-ridden hickory log.

"Harry, you could better use your skills. His Lordship pays you to carve wood, not hack it to kindling," the old man chuckled.

Harry's mallet dropped to his side, and he jerked the adze from the half-split log. "True enough, Simon." He wiped one arm across his forehead. He had stripped off his jerkin to work in his shirtsleeves. It was not a hot day, but Harry was overheated. His chest heaved in a sigh; sweat trickled down his temples.

"Have you a burden upon your heart?"

Loath to speak of his misadventures with Dovie, Harry instead broached the subject of Maela. "I met a child, a gently born child in tattered raiment. She claims the name Trenton. I would learn more of her."

"A maid child, you say?" Simon mused. "Artemis Coats's daughter, no doubt."

"Coats! Is the child mad, then, to claim kinship with Trenton?"

Simon rubbed his rough hands together. "Did she appear mad?"

"Nay, she appeared intelligent and sane," Harry admitted.

"Her claim is valid, though not legal. I know the Coats family of old."

Harry nodded. "Continue."

"Sir Hanover Trenton has a wife who resides at another of his properties, near London. Notwithstanding, while lodging at Castle Trent, His Lordship went in unto the damsel Artemis, daughter of a servant. In time she was found with child, and Sir Hanover was filled with joy, for his wife was barren. His Lordship intended to make the child his heir, but alas! His wife also conceived a child. Artemis delivered a girl child, but the wife presented Sir Hanover with a son."

"Isaac Trenton," Harry murmured, suddenly understanding Ishmaela's reaction and the significance of her name. "Artemis named her daughter Ishmaela, knowing that Isaac was the child of promise."

"If you claim acquaintance with the child, she must yet live, though her mother died years since."

Harry's eyes were vacant. He was recalling Ishmaela's betraying statement, "I am no lady," and her evident hunger for love and friendship. "Poor little waif," he sighed.

"Attend upon me now, leave the wench alone, Harry. If Sir Hanover wishes me to think her dead, then dead she is. I would not cross the desires of the gentry."

But Harry's thoughts were far away. The afternoon was waning; soon he would be on his way to the cottage. Would Ishmaela return to the clearing? He would have to look for her, just in case.

Chapter 3

Therefore if any man be in Christ, he is a new creature:
old things are passed away; behold,
all things are become new.
2 CORINTHIANS 5:17

Marston made good his promise; stacks of lumber and thatching reeds awaited Harry when he arrived at the cottage that evening. It was, actually, little more than a pink wattle-and-daub shack with a small livestock shed and fenced clearing at the rear. Its rotted thatching had caved in at one place near the peak of the steep roof. No chimney emerged through the blackened thatch, for the cottage had no proper fireplace, only a charred depression in the center of its dirt floor.

Harry took a quick glance around the filthy interior. "It has. . .potential."

He left his possessions and livestock in the weed-choked yard and set out for the clearing with the dogs at his side. Ragwort barked for joy, and even Laitha let out a yelp or two. All day long they had watched over Harry's possessions, waiting beside the fishpond for their master to finish his work.

"No longer, my friends," Harry told them. "We now possess a cottage and garden. No more traveling to and fro; no more vagrancy."

If only that were true. For many months now, Harry had wanted to settle, to possess a free-holding of his own. He wanted a wife, children, and a community wherein he would not be always considered a foreigner, an interloper. He greatly missed his family—especially his mother.

At the tender age of thirteen, he had left school to be apprenticed to an itinerant master joiner. Three years later, in Lancashire, Master Wilson Tupper had suddenly died, leaving his apprentice to complete their current project alone. Harry not only completed the mahogany mantelpiece, he improved upon his master's work. Impressed and amazed by the boy's genius, his employer had recommended him to several friends. Never since had Harry lacked for work—indeed, he could not meet the demand for his exquisite carvings.

But a traveling artisan's life did not offer the stability Harry craved.

Ishmaela's pony grazed contentedly beneath a spreading tree. Lifting its head at Harry's approach, it whinnied, sniffing noses with Ragwort, who still kept a wary eye on its hooves.

"How now?" Harry greeted the friendly creature, patting its shedding neck. A cloud of chestnut hair rose beneath his hand.

"His name is Pegasus," advised a voice from above. Harry looked up into the branches of the oak but saw nothing at first. A pixie face peeked from around a huge bough, and Maela giggled. "Fooled you, did I not?"

Warmth welled up in Harry's big heart. "Yea, of a truth, you fooled me, child."

Kirtle hitched into her sash, Maela showed most of her skinny white legs as she nimbly scrambled down the tree. Harry averted his eyes, dismayed by her lack of modesty.

Retying her cap strings, Maela skipped up to him, then fell to her knees to greet the dogs. Ragwort covered her face with moist kisses. Laitha still hesitated to approach, though she showed some desire to meet the child who called her name in such caressing tones.

Maela looked up into Harry's eyes and smiled.

"Come hither." Harry held out a hand, but Maela only looked at it, then at his face.

"Do you not wish to see my new dwelling? Sir David presented me with a cottage this day, and it needs work aplenty ere I sleep in it."

Maela rose in a fluid motion but made no move to accept his hand. She called her pony, which came to her with bobbing head and a soft snort. Taking him by the forelock, she looked up at Harry.

Harry turned to lead the way to his new home, telling her the story of its acquisition as he walked. Maela strolled along beside him. She said nothing, but once when Harry looked at her she smiled again. He noticed that her teeth were straight and even, though as dirty as the rest of her. Why they had not rotted was the question.

Stopping before the ramshackle cottage, Harry gave a sweep of one arm. "You are welcome to my humble dwelling, but I commend you not to enter ere the roof be mended. The present thatch is occupied, I fear."

"You will need a canopy upon your bed." Maela giggled as she pushed over the gate to the livestock pen and herded her pony inside. Genevieve had made good headway against the weeds in Harry's absence.

He smiled. "No doubt, lest my slumber be disturbed by enterprising mice." Watching her fondle Samson and Genevieve, he wondered what subject to discuss next. He could not bring up the subject of her parentage unless he wished a repeat performance of last night's hasty exit.

Turning from the animals with a happy sigh, she inquired, "What would you have me to do? I would help you."

He floundered for a moment. "Uh, you may sweep rubbish from the yard while I replace this gate."

"Have you a broom?" Maela approached the cart. At his affirmative reply, she dug through his tools until she found the old twig broom, then proceeded to sweep the yard. Following her industrious lead, Harry set to work, building a new gate for the livestock pen.

Conversation would have been difficult, so Harry began to sing as he worked, filling Maela's wondering ears with ballads and hymns. His medium tenor voice was sweet and clear.

Her work completed, Maela busied herself with freeing the chickens, scattering their grain, and brushing the donkey and the pony. "May I milk Genevieve?"

He stopped filing for a moment. "Have you milked a goat before?"

"Never."

"I will teach you." Laying aside the nearly finished gate, he rose, brushing shavings from his hose. Lifting his elbows and flexing his shoulders, he stretched, groaning softly. "A long day," he explained to his waiting audience of one.

She nodded, looking sympathetic.

"I'll begin supper soon. Tonight we have a coney for our pottage. There was game to spare at the manor this day." He rubbed his belly, and Maela smiled, rubbing her middle in imitation.

Genevieve was more than willing to be milked. Harry tied her to one of the few solid posts in sight, then settled on a stool at her side. Placing a wooden bowl beneath her swollen udder, he showed Maela how to pinch off the teat, then push out the milk with her remaining fingers. Milk foamed into the bowl.

Maela clasped her hands at her breast in delight. "May I try?"

Harry vacated the stool but stayed close. Maela patted the curious goat, then reached for the firm udder. Taking one teat in hand, she tried to squeeze it off, but her small fingers could not reach, and only a trickle of milk rewarded her effort.

Genevieve stamped impatiently, narrowly missing the bowl.

"Here." Harry squatted and placed his hand on top of Maela's to pinch off the teat for her. "Now squeeze gently." He felt the warmth of her little body beside him. The foul odor was intense, but he bravely ignored it.

She didn't move. Glancing down at her, he was startled to see her eyes squeezed shut. Every muscle and nerve in her body was strung taut. "Maela? What ails you?"

With a suddenness that knocked him off his feet, she flung her arms around his neck and squeezed. For an instant, he thought she had attacked him, but when his hand touched her quaking shoulder, he realized that this was a hug, a sign of trust and affection.

Sitting in the dirt, he patted a protruding shoulder blade, not knowing what to say. She knelt before him, her arms squeezing tight, her dirty cap resting on his shoulder. Gently he reminded, "Genevieve awaits you, child."

Maela nodded, wiped her nose and eyes on one sleeve, and turned back to the goat. This time, with Harry's help, she managed to squeeze several good streams of milk from Genevieve's udder. With a satisfied smile, she surrendered her stool and watched Harry finish the job.

"May I milk her again next day?"

"Perhaps. 'Tis time to prepare our coney stew, lest we starve."

While Harry built the fire in a cleared space in the yard, then gutted and skinned out the rabbit, Maela made herself useful by washing and chopping the vegetables. Harry stole frequent glances at her intent expression as she worked. In spite of the dirt and the smell, she was an appealing creature. Those big dark eyes and black brows were startling against her white skin, and her turned-up nose gave her a saucy look. She seemed younger than thirteen, perhaps due to her diminutive size.

"Tell me about your family," Maela ordered, scooping chopped leeks into the pot.

"My father is the youngest son of a Spanish nobleman."

Maela's jaw dropped. "Indeed?"

"He was destined for the Roman church but could not accept its teachings, so he fled to England. King Henry was yet living at the time, and a Protestant Spaniard was acceptable company, even in Lincolnshire. He wed Susan Dixon, a yeoman's daughter, purchased property in the Wolds, and became a sheep husbandman. He is a fine, godly man, upright in all his ways."

"And your mother?"

Harry's expression softened. "My mother is fair beyond description. She did weep copiously at my departure, and that is nigh six years since.

Mine eyes ache to behold her lovely face once more."

"Why have you not hitherto returned?"

Harry chopped the rabbit into large chunks and dropped it into the simmering pot. "They cannot support me, and I cannot earn my keep as joiner there, for manor houses and fine churches are scarce." He rose to his full height, eyes fixed upon the distance, and revealed a dream, "I would settle in Lincolnshire someday on a free-holding of mine own. I had planned to depart hence this season, but I accepted Marston's offer. . . ."

"Had you traveled home, I would know you not," Maela mused softly.

Harry met her gaze across the fire. "God planned us to meet," he stated firmly. "He loves you, Maela, and He desires that you should know Him."

Maela stared at him, her expression quizzical but open. "Wherefore say you that He loves me? I know Him not. Grandmere says He is cruel and harsh and sends men to hell."

"Do you trust and love your grandmother?" Harry asked, wondering about her relationship with the "witch."

The child's shoulders hunched, and she cast frightened looks around. "I love her not. Should she discover that I am here, she would send plague upon you."

"Your grandmother has no power over me. My God is greater far than any power here on earth. He would be your God as well, and protect you. After we sup, would you hear more of Him?"

Maela nodded, one hand pressed to her flat breast.

Harry read to Maela by firelight that evening, seated upon logs beside the fire. Page after page he turned, until at last Matthew's gospel had ended.

Maela waited, hoping for more. "Is that all?"

"Nay, but 'tis sufficient for the night. Shall you be missed at the castle?"

Maela shook her head.

"May I accompany you home?"

Her hand fluttered to her breast again, a movement he now recognized as an attempt to calm a fast-beating heart. "Part way," she allowed, unable to entirely reject his offer.

Harry walked beside her pony along the dark road. Perhaps the darkness made her feel safe, or perhaps the late hour loosened her tongue, for Maela became unaccountably talkative as they walked. "When I was a child, my grandmere did watch me like a cat watches a mouse and screech at me for every fault, but since Mother's death, Grandmere frequents the wine cellar. She knows not of mine absence."

"And Master Titwhistle?" A name like that was not quickly forgotten.

"I allow not Dob to see me—ever. He twists mine arms and hurts me. I did not think a man could be kind until I saw you at play with Ragwort."

Maela shifted on her pony, swinging her legs forward over Pegasus's shoulders. "Men that laugh are wicked men—yet Harry is not wicked, and he laughs often. Good men smile not and hate childer—yet Harry is good, and he smiles oft and is kind to childer. I think, Maela," she addressed herself, "that Harry's God is not the god of Bishop Carmichael. Harry's Jesus makes him beautiful."

Harry spoke softly, half afraid to interrupt her soliloquy. "Heed yourself, Maela. Harry's Jesus can be Maela's Jesus and make her into a new creature also."

Maela was quiet for a moment. "I would hear more of Jesus on the morrow. Did you write the stories, Harry?"

Though amazed by her ignorance, Harry answered calmly, "Nay. Long ago, men who knew Jesus when He was on earth wrote the stories. They are true stories, Maela. The men who wrote them died for the truth when men that hated Jesus tried to make them recant."

Maela nodded. "They would die not for the stories had they invented them."

Her simple wisdom surprised Harry. "That is doubtless true."

"They were men such as you, Harry. I love them, and I love Jesus. Would that I might embrace Him as I embraced you!"

Harry's heart melted into a puddle. "Maela, you are the sweetest child."

"Do you love me, Harry?"

Taken aback, Harry stammered, "Why. . .to be sure. . .I am ever your friend, Maela."

"None has loved me since my mother died, Harry. I knew not that a man could love."

Harry knew he was treading on eggshells. "Your father?"

"He has a son to love and cares nothing for a girl child. When he comes from London, he brings me fancy clothes to wear while I play the recorder and dance for his companions. He will come again soon. Would that I could hide until they are gone away!"

"They do not. . .harm you?" Harry asked hesitantly.

Her voice was haughty at first, then died to a near whisper, "I let no man touch me. Nevertheless, they speak words I do not understand and laugh together. There is much evil in the castle when they are about."

Pegasus halted abruptly. Harry wondered how Maela signaled her pony without a bridle. "You must stop here. Dob would kill you should he discover you on castle grounds."

"You are safe, Maela?"

"Yea." Without another word, she cued her pony and cantered down a side road, vanishing into the shadows.

Chapter 4

The angel of the LORD encampeth round about them
that fear him, and delivereth them.
PSALM 34:7

While Harry shopped one morning several weeks later, a group of noblemen rode past the marketplace. Supremely ignoring the common folk surrounding them, they talked and laughed loudly. Their horses' hooves clopped on the rude cobblestones. Servants, more modestly clothed and mounted, followed behind. A pack of hounds trotted among the horses, wagging, yelling, casting about, soiling the already dirty streets.

Harry watched them pass. One of these men might be Maela's father. Harry shook his head slightly, finding it difficult to comprehend the connection between ragged little Maela and these gentry in their rich garb. Where would they be going this morning? On a hunt, most likely. The jolly group turned down a side street and passed out of his view.

Maela had not returned to Harry's cottage. He had hoped to see her at church, but she did not appear. No chestnut pony grazed in the meadow; no sprightly monkey climbed the ancient trees. While in town, Harry searched the streets for any sign of the girl, with no success. He could not seem to help worrying about her. Was her father treating her well?

In saner moments he admitted that quite possibly he would never see her again, and at any rate, her fate was out of his control. God would have to handle this one without Harry's help. Maela's situation was difficult, but far from rare. Many noblemen sired illegitimate children, and many of these children fared well for themselves. Perhaps Sir Hanover would arrange an advantageous marriage for his pretty daughter. Such things had been known to happen—but this knowledge gave Harry no comfort.

Around Harry, market vendors touted their wares in stentorian chant. People pushed, shoved, and cursed, vying for the finest wares, dickering for the lowest prices. Children on their mothers' hips wailed; donkeys loaded with bundles brayed. Chickens cackled and pigeons cooed from their cages. The stench of blood and flesh was nearly overpowered by the reek of rotting fruit, animal waste, and unwashed bodies. Market day—an adventure for the senses.

Feeling eyes upon his back, Harry turned abruptly but saw nothing untoward. A man staggered past him and belched loudly. Two large dogs circled beneath the fishmonger's table, hackles raised, teeth bared. Harry was glad he had left his dogs at the cottage. A house sparrow hopped boldly along the cobblestones, searching for crumbs.

Frowning, Harry resumed his business of selecting a fresh roast, brushing flies from a promising cut. "Are you certain the lamb was slaughtered this day?" he asked skeptically.

"Ye say full true," the butcher responded, looking affronted at the question. "This very morn at dawn."

Catching a furtive movement from the corner of his eye, Harry glanced toward the next stall and caught sight of a dirty little hand sliding a peach from a stack on the table. Hand and peach quickly disappeared from view.

"Wrap it. I shall return," Harry assured the butcher, then ducked around the booth in time to spot a flash of red petticoat whisking between the flowerseller's and the cobbler's booths. Harry could not squeeze between people and carts as easily as a child could, but his long legs overtook the girl behind an alehouse.

Gripping the back of her waistcoat, he hauled her to a stop. She screeched like an angry pig and kicked at his shins. Harry dodged those quick little feet, protesting, "Maela! It is I, Harry!"

"Leave me! Unhand me!" she screamed, flailing with every limb. A bulge in the front of her waistcoat told Harry where the peach had been secreted.

Hearing the genuine panic in her voice, Harry obeyed. She flopped ungracefully upon the dirty stones and stared up at him, eyes furtive, hooded. It was then that Harry noticed: her embroidered emerald green kirtle and waistcoat were new. She looked older, somehow, yet the clean garments emphasized her unwashed condition.

Pushing with both feet, she tried to sidle away, but Harry stepped on the edge of her kirtle and planted his fists upon his hips. He was about to berate the little thief, but something in her dilated eyes stopped him.

He dropped slowly to his knees at her side. "Little maid, I would not harm you! Have you forgotten your friend so soon?"

Her lips pressed together in an angry line. "If you were my friend, you would free me."

"Maela!" Words seemed to choke him. Questions filled his mind, yet he could voice none of them coherently. "I beheld gentry in the village. . . Are you at market with. . . ? Your raiment is new. . ."

Her expression grew darker still.

Frustrated with himself, Harry blurted, "Maela, I have missed your presence. You have become. . .dear to me, as a sister. I pray for you daily."

Those haunted eyes widened. "Verily?"

Harry wanted to touch her, but he knew better. In her present state she would inevitably misread his intentions. Words alone must suffice to convince her of his sincerity—but Harry, glib, loquacious Harry, could think of nothing to say. So, right then and there he prayed for his little friend. "Lord Jesus, I ask You to calm Maela's heart and teach her to trust You and me."

Now her eyes were so wide, he could see his reflection in them. "Does He hear you?" she whispered. Harry could not catch her voice over the market clamor, but he read her lips and nodded with a smile.

"I would give you aid, Maela. Confide in me?"

Hope flickered across her face, then faded. She sat up, scooting away from him. "You can do nothing for me. I am cursed from my birth."

"Not so!" Harry blurted without thinking. "You are blessed indeed!"

She made a disrespectful face. "How so?"

"The King of kings would adopt you for His child! What greater blessing can exist?"

The disgust in her expression brought blood to his face, but he persisted. "If you need aid of any kind, come to me without delay."

She looked him through and through. A little nod, and she scrambled up and out of his reach. Harry's last glimpse was of twinkling bare feet amid rampant petticoats. Another moment and she was lost in the milling crowds.

"Wench, more wine!" a slurred voice commanded.

Maela grimaced but could only obey. Defying her father was useless—and painful. She had discovered that fact long ago. Hefting the pitcher of red wine, she re-entered the great hall and filled cups around the head table.

It was a strange scene. An immense log burned upon the hearth and wax candles lighted the table, yet darkness seemed to hover just above the heads of the diners. Incongruous in the medieval hall were Sir Hanover and his debauched companions, clad though they were in jeweled silks and velvets. In Maela's opinion, they desecrated her castle's venerable stones.

True knights had supped at these very tables, great men of old. The castle's time had passed long years ago. Could these men not leave it to crumble in peace?

"Cease your gaping and come hither, Ishy."

Maela obeyed reluctantly.

"Hold up your head, filthy rag. Almost I shudder to call you mine, for you smell like unto a hog, yet you have your mother's features. Someday shall you mirror her form." Sir Hanover ran his big hands over Maela as he spoke, as though he were pointing out the finer points of a horse. She closed her eyes and tried to distance herself.

"Her music is pleasant to mine ear, Hanover. Entreat her to play another madrigal for us." A younger man with a golden beard seemed kinder than the rest.

"Nay, I have heard enough of her playing. What is the wench's present age?"

Maela quailed at the sound of that deep voice. More than anything in life, she feared Bishop Carmichael.

"Thirteen years, Titus. Your wait is nigh its end, surely. The child must ripen soon."

Maela gave her father a puzzled glance. "Am I a peach or plum?" she blurted without thinking.

"Silence, wench! You forget yourself." Trenton clouted her across the mouth. His frown cleared as he caught the joke. "My prize peach." The other men began to chuckle in lewd amusement.

"Indeed, a peach for my plucking," the bishop remarked, and the laughter faded. "I hope she will be worth the wait, for your sake, Hanover. I have no liking for childer and their prattle. The wench is quiet enough, but I would have more flesh and less bone. She must eat more ere I pay your desired price."

"I shall have words with her keeper. In the interim, Ishy, our vessels are empty once again."

This time when Maela made the rounds with her pitcher, the blond gentleman leaned close and whispered, "I like childer, Ishy."

For a moment, she believed him her friend, but then his hand slid around her waist in a distressingly familiar way. Blue eyes glittered as he moistened his red lips and tried to pull her down for a kiss.

Maela cried out, struggling to escape his degrading clutches.

In an instant, a sword point glittered at the blond man's throat. Bishop Carmichael's black eyes held the promise of death.

"Clayton, have done. Bruise not the bishop's peach before its time," Sir

Hanover said, attempting to defuse the situation. His slurred words were jovial, but the warning was real.

"Verily," another man jibed, "bruised peaches are of little worth."

The bishop's long fingers bit into Maela's shoulder as he hauled her out of Clayton's reach. Without another glance, he sheathed his sword and drained his tankard.

It was nearly dawn before the last of Sir Hanover's guests passed out snoring beneath the table. Their servants were likewise prostrate in the kitchen. Maela slid from her hiding place behind a fly-bitten tapestry and crept upstairs to her chamber. There she wrapped a few possessions in a frayed pinafore. Sneaking back downstairs, she tiptoed past the snoring servants and let herself out by the kitchen door.

This time, she dared not ride Pegasus. Someone would be certain to notice the pony's absence, and he would be easy to trace. It was a long, hard walk to Harry's cottage, but Maela was desperate.

A few tears escaped as she walked. Many times in the past she had believed that life was not worth living, but never before had she felt this low. In her father's eyes, she was no better than a beast, to be sold out of hand. Since her mother's death, Harry alone had shown Maela kindness and respect.

But Harry was a man. Instinctively, Maela distrusted men even while she yearned for a man's love. If Harry, her only friend, were to prove false... it was unthinkable. The memory of his kind eyes and voice had comforted her during many a dark hour since their first meeting.

Jesus. Harry's goodness came from Jesus. Maela spoke the name aloud, savoring its taste upon her lips. "Jesus. Jesus, I beg You to save me from this evil."

A Presence filled the emptiness surrounding her. She was no longer alone, yet she did not fear. This unseen Presence was the goodness she sensed whenever Harry was near. Jesus had heard, understood, and answered her desperate plea. Maela's heart pounded; a sense of awe filled her soul.

Maela almost did not recognize Harry's cottage. It was lime-washed, patched, and repaired, and a flintstone chimney emerged from its fresh thatching. Genuine glass windowpanes sparkled in the morning light. The yard was neatly cleared, its fences solid. A new jakes had been built beside the livestock shed, with a chicken coop in between.

Before Maela could knock, the door opened and two dogs rushed upon her, whimpering for joy. Harry stood in the doorway, blinking and tousled, wearing only his nightshirt and trunk hose. Patting the excited dogs, Maela tried to explain, "I...I had need..."

Her face felt hot. She hadn't, somehow, expected to surprise Harry. His nightshirt was unlaced, showing pale skin with a sprinkling of dark hair to match his adolescent beard. His feet and lower legs were bare.

"Down, Laitha, Ragwort," Harry commanded, his voice gruff with sleep. "Enter, child, and welcome."

It was her first glimpse inside. She dropped a small bundle upon the bench beside the door and turned to face him. "Your cottage is changed indeed. You have labored quickly."

"I had hoped you would approve." Harry indicated the neat stone fireplace set into one wall, the new wooden floor, and the lime-washed walls. "I did all but the roof. Sir David's thatcher obliged me there."

"It is fine work."

An awkward silence. Maela glanced around. Harry had acquired a feather bolster. It lay upon the floor in one corner, still rumpled.

"The dogs told me of your approach. I fear that I am ill-equipped to entertain at this hour. Is Pegasus in the paddock?"

"Nay, I did walk." Her throat felt tight. "I have come to you, as you bade me."

She saw Harry's eyes lower to her feet. "Wherefore, Maela?"

She tried to speak but could not.

Harry's arm lifted as though he would embrace her, then dropped. "Come, allow me to tend your feet."

Maela obediently sat upon the bench and let him examine her feet. To her surprise, they were cut and bleeding. Dark stains marked the place where she had been standing on Harry's new floor.

"I shall cleanse them," he told her. "Sit still."

Silently she watched him build up the fire, fetch water from the cistern, and heat it in a kettle. Harry talked to her while he worked, about Lord Marston's new stallion, the dormouse that had built its nest in Samson's manger where Ragwort could not get at it, and his suspicion that Laitha was carrying pups by one of Marston's hounds.

Then he knelt before her and lifted her feet into a basin of warm water. The cuts stung, but Harry's hands were gentle as he scrubbed her feet and ankles with soft soap and a cloth. The sensation was unlike anything in her previous experience.

"Tell me, Maela, why you have come to me." He patted her feet dry with a clean cloth. They looked strangely white. She was glad the nails were trimmed, at least.

Still kneeling, he looked up at her expectantly. Her memories returned with an unwelcome rush.

"Sir Hanover," she gulped and began again. "Sir Hanover plans to sell me to Bishop Carmichael. They spoke of me as a fruit that must ripen ere it is plucked. I comprehend this not. I do know that I am a slave, Harry—yet I am his child! How can this be?"

Harry swallowed hard, but she was not finished. "Sir Clayton DuBarry grasped me while I waited upon him. He said that he likes childer, but he intended evil. The bishop and Sir Hanover warned him away. I am to belong to the bishop when I am older; therefore, I must not be harmed. I cannot understand, yet I fear men; they are wicked!"

"God save you, child!" Harry blurted, shaking his head.

Maela's hand pressed against her chest. "In the market, you did speak a prayer. God has answered, for I trust you, and I trust Jesus. I would abide with you until Sir Hanover departs, two days hence."

It took a moment for her meaning to penetrate. "Here? With me?"

Maela saw varied emotions cross his face: embarrassment, suspicion, pity, doubt.

"You fled from me at the market, and today you entrust your life into my keeping?"

It did seem strange, she had to admit. "I do. I trust you."

"But can I trust you?"

She caught his meaning and flushed. "I would not steal, Harry. I know it is wrong. It. . .is no habit of mine."

"I paid the grocer for the fruit."

Maela felt dreadful. "Why?"

He rose abruptly, throwing his hands up. "I would not have you lose your hand as a thief! Maela, will not your father seek you?"

Her head bowed. "He will seek me not here."

"Had I an alternative, I would avail myself of it," Harry muttered. "But as yet I know not any brethren in this county. Yea, child, you may remain here with me."

Her face began to glow with delight. "I could go in disguise as a lad. Have you a spare jerkin and hose to lend me?"

He frowned. "Nay. You are a lady, and I would have you remain so."

She sighed in resignation. "Would that I were a lad and could wear trunk hose. 'Twould simplify tree-climbing."

Harry answered in a matter-of-fact voice. "You should wear drawers beneath your kirtle. My sisters and mother do wear them."

"Indeed? They do wear drawers?" Maela's delight was evident.

" 'Tis the Italian style. My mother would ne'er adopt a scandalous fashion, but drawers are modest and sensible." Harry's face looked flushed.

Speaking of drawers must be difficult for him, Maela concluded.

After they had broken their fast with toasted bread and cheese, Harry warned Maela to remain indoors while he was away. She was not to care for the outdoor animals in his absence, but she was free to amuse herself indoors with the dogs. She promised obedience, feeling somewhat frightened.

"I shall return as early as possible," he assured her. "God be with you."

All seemed normal at Marston Hall that day, until Harry entered the house to take measurements. Several gentlemen stood in a semicircle about the finished portion of Harry's carved screen.

". . .and but look at the rose petals. Are they not lifelike? And they of solid walnut!" Sir David Marston was saying.

Eyes widening, Harry turned to sneak away.

"Ah, and here is the artisan in the flesh. Joiner, I would speak with you. Tarry if you will, and come hither to greet my guests."

Harry squared his shoulders and turned. *Help me, Lord!*

The gentlemen regarded Harry with a mixture of interest and disdain. "Sir Hanover Trenton, Bishop Titus Carmichael, Sir Clayton DuBarry, and the Honorable Samuel Fredericks, meet Harold Jameson, joiner."

Only Fredericks showed interest. "Indeed? Well, Joiner, I must express myself enamored of your work. Would you take employ at my house near Norwich? Of a certain, I shall wait patiently until Marston's screen is complete," he added with a chuckle.

"But he shall have more projects when this screen is complete!" Marston protested. "Many days have I pondered the south stairs and have come at last to a decision. I would have dragons, or perhaps lions, mounted upon the posts at its base. And again, the great hall has need of a surround for the fireplace, something magnificent in walnut, I believe. Would you create this masterpiece for me when the screen is complete, Harry, my boy?"

Harry felt awkward, but he agreed to stay on.

The other gentlemen looked askance at Marston's friendliness toward Harry. Such camaraderie from a member of the gentry toward an artisan was rare indeed, but then Sir David's knighthood was of recent origin. Although Lord Marston was not extremely wealthy, the high-quality Norfolk sheep's wool produced on his farms sold for peak prices in nearby market towns, and he could afford to gradually decorate his new house with beautiful things. He was a kindly, jolly man who loved his wife, son, and three daughters and treated his tenants fairly. Harry liked him.

"This talk is all well and good," Sir Hanover interrupted gruffly, "but it answers not my purpose." He turned to Harry and pinned him with a stare. "Have you seen a small damsel about the manor? She is a slave, gone missing from the castle."

"I will look for such a damsel, sir." Harry bowed slightly.

"Repeat this to other servants, for I would have her returned promptly."

Harry nodded his understanding but made no promises he could not honor. He carefully kept all emotion from his expression, and the men noticed nothing amiss.

Sir Hanover was not a tall man, but he was trim and strong, with auburn hair, mustache, and pointed beard. His plumed velvet hat, embroidered silk jerkin with shoulder picadils, puffed trunks, trunk hose, and nether hose looked ridiculous in Harry's eyes, but he knew this attire was the height of fashion.

The other men were similarly attired, though perhaps with fewer jewels. Bishop Carmichael wore nothing but black, though his clothing was ornate in style. He was evidently a secular bishop—appointed his position and property as a reward for service to the queen. On the whole, he was not an ill-favored man, yet the idea of his owning little Maela caused Harry's fists to clench.

At last Harry was dismissed. The other men watched him depart—sans measurements. He would come back for them later.

"An outsize lout, is he not?" DuBarry sneered.

"I'd give a thousand quid to have such shoulders," Fredericks remarked wistfully.

Then the door closed, and Harry heard no more.

Her respite was over. All her life she would treasure the memory of two blessed days in Harry's cottage. Harry had treated her like a queen, serving her meals, attending to her every word and need, reading her Bible stories until late in the night. He had even given her his bed while he slept in the shed with Samson and Genevieve. She had never before experienced such luxury as that feather bolster.

But now Sir Hanover had gone away, and she must return to her prison. Before Harry arrived home from work, Maela gathered her few possessions, hugged the dogs in farewell, donned her soft new leather shoes, and walked home through field and forest. Tears streaked her cheeks and dripped upon her waistcoat. Already she missed Harry dreadfully, but she simply could not have bidden him farewell without crying. Maela hated to cry in public.

Her footsteps slowed as she approached Castle Trent. She stopped, trembling, beside the ruined gatehouse. At times she loved her castle, but now the crumbling keep seemed to loom over her like a malevolent entity. Black clouds roiled across the sky behind it. Thunder rumbled in the distance, startling Maela back into motion. She darted across the courtyard and pushed at the kitchen door.

Castle Trent had been modified during her grandfather's tenure. A wing had been added, connecting the kitchen with the keep. Sir Oliver Blickney Trenton had discounted the increased possibility of fire spreading to the living area, for modern fireplaces and ovens were much safer than the open cooking fires of earlier days, and besides, his castle had been modified structurally to withstand fire. Sir Oliver had proved more lucky than accurate, for during Sir Hanover's boyhood, a fire had, in fact, destroyed the upper bailey, though the castle's main living areas escaped harm. Maela's grandmother spent most of her time in the kitchen and scullery. Maela spent much of her time alone in the cavernous keep.

The kitchen door opened easily beneath her hand, and her hopes rose. She slid along the kitchen wall, her eyes fastened to the motionless form slumped over one filthy table. Perhaps she would not have to explain her absence at all! Perhaps her grandmother would pass off her escape as a harmless escapade and—

The slumped figure suddenly lunged into motion, and gnarled fingers gripped Maela's upper arm. "Where have you been, malapert knave? Your sire did hunt for you high and low, Ishy, and did blame your grandmother for your absence! Your grandmother, who tends you as a ewe lamb! Doltish lout of a wench! Did you think to escape my wrath?"

Maela writhed in her grandmother's grasp, to no avail. A horny fist clouted her upon the side of the head, making her ears ring. "This for my trouble, thou lousy lurdane! And this!" Repeatedly she slapped Maela's cheeks, ignoring her cries for mercy.

"Out upon you now, and should you sneak away again, I shall give you to Dob and let him punish you, errant wench!" Breathing hard, Hera released the child and sank back upon the bench.

Maela scurried from the kitchen, along a passageway, through an empty chamber, up spiral stairs, and along a gallery to the dismal comfort of her room. Tonight she would have no candle to relieve its stygian darkness. Shivering with shock and fear, she dropped upon her lumpy bed and heaved with dry sobs. "Where are You, God?" she whimpered. "Why did You not protect me from Grandmere?"

The door slammed against the wall, and Dobbin Titwhistle entered the kitchen. He loomed over Hera Coats, slapping a crop against his heavy boots. "Up, you drunken witch. What aroused your wrath? Has the wench returned?"

"Yea, and I have punished her," Hera snarled, pouring another tumbler of port from a flagon.

Dob snatched up the flagon and sniffed it. "I heard the master say that the port was low, and now I find you here soaking in it. What say you, witch?"

"I have earned it, as you have earned the rent you hold back from Sir Hanover," she mocked. "Threaten me not, fool. A pox upon you!"

Thunder rumbled outside, nearer this time.

Dob paled. "Repeal your curse, woman, I beg of you."

"For the present," she relented, grinning. The woman still possessed all of her teeth—an almost unheard-of feat at her age. Only a witch could have managed it, the townsfolk said.

"Where is the wench? I would have words with her," Dob explained more respectfully, flourishing the switch. His heavy brows drew together. "The master did lay her escape at my door!"

"No more than at mine," the old woman growled. "She is in her chamber." In spite of the whip, Hera did not believe he would harm the child, so she allowed him to pass. Sir Hanover had made it clear to all that the girl was not to be tampered with.

Hera dozed again until a flash of lightning roused her. Faint screams reached her ears just before thunder rolled over the castle. Hera bolted to her feet, blinking in surprise.

"The fool!" she exclaimed, along with more potent adjectives. Grabbing a poker from the fire, she hurried to the spiral staircase and laboriously made her way to Maela's chamber. Sounds of blows and cries of pain fanned her wrath. Opening the door, which fortunately Dob had failed to latch, she entered, brandishing the poker.

"Unhand her," she croaked. Dob turned to face her, saw the glowing poker, and froze. His grip on Maela's arm relaxed.

Maela scurried past her grandmother and crouched against the gallery wall. Her new clothing was shredded. Throbbing weals rose upon her back and legs; oozing blood stuck to her smock.

"You well know Sir Hanover's decree concerning the wench," Hera stated in her creaking voice. "Yet you would disregard it for a moment's pleasure! You are the doltish lout, Dob! This day I do place a curse upon Castle Trent: any man that enters herein before Sir Hanover's return shall be carried away by the devil himself!"

A flash lit the room in blinding white light with a crash that shook the castle to its foundations. The sudden roar of pouring rain on slate and lead sheet roofing filled their ears.

Dob's eyes widened until the whites showed all the way around. With a fearful screech, he rushed out the door, crashed into the gallery railing, passed Maela without seeing her, and thundered down the stairs. The front door slammed behind him with a force that echoed throughout the stone keep.

Cackling in delighted triumph, Hera Coats swept past her shivering granddaughter and slowly descended the stairs.

Chapter 5

*Likewise, I say unto you, there is joy in the presence
of the angels of God over one sinner that repenteth.*
LUKE 15:10

our days later, Maela had healed enough to ride to Harry's
cottage for an evening. Upon her arrival, she saw Harry's
reaction to her battered face, but he seemed to accept her explanation that she had fallen. Once she saw him perusing the fading bruises on her bare forearms and the patches on her new garments, but he said nothing. She did not stay long, neither would she sit down, but her eyes followed Harry's every move as though his presence sustained her life.

The bruises eventually faded, the stripes healed, and no further beatings ensued. Dob left Maela strictly alone, and her grandmother virtually ignored her. Sir Hanover did not return, and the bishop neglected Trenton parish.

Maela had ways of discovering how long Dob would be away from the castle each day. She had memorized his routine and easily caught any variation from his usual behavior patterns. On most days she could find an hour or two to spend at Harry's cottage, though not always while he was at home. Friday was the best day of the week, for Dob left the castle grounds early, visited every alehouse in the village, and generally did not return until morning.

Upon her arrival, Maela would free the chickens, feed the animals, brush Samson and Pegasus, pet Genevieve's twin buck kids, and play with the dogs while Harry worked around the cottage.

That first summer, Harry transplanted wild rosebushes to frame the front door, and Maela tended them lovingly until they adjusted to the change. "Imagine them in bloom," she murmured, smoothing a glossy leaf with one finger. To please her, Harry bartered for bedding plants with the gardener at the manor, acquiring perennial vines and shrubs in exchange for carved knickknacks. Before long, her flower garden nearly equaled Harry's kitchen garden in size, and in effort expended.

When inclement weather prevented outdoor labor, Harry built furniture: an oak table and benches, two armchairs, a bedstead for his feather bolster, a wardrobe, and a washstand. No cottage in the county boasted finer furniture, though it was rather crowded.

Not all of Harry's free time was devoted to the cottage. With Sir David's permission, he took Maela fishing on manor grounds, teaching her to construct a pole and line, dig bait, and prepare the fish once caught. Her acuity and aptitude prompted him to try new lessons; one thing led to another, and Harry soon found himself in the role of tutor. Ishmaela seemed determined to extract every drop of knowledge and skill from his brain, and Harry thoroughly enjoyed teaching her.

Once introduced to kitchen arts, Maela was enthralled with cookery. Harry taught her the basic skills and recipes he had learned from his mother. Maela mastered them, then branched out on her own. Many of her attempts were dismal failures, but the dogs enjoyed them. Harry tasted every experiment, though he might have wished that the hands kneading the bread dough and chopping the produce were cleaner—Maela still resisted his attempts to introduce her to hygiene.

The joy of learning was addictive, and Maela delighted her tutor with her rapid progress. Harry used his Bible as a primer, and Maela produced a treasure trove of writing materials from the castle: quills, ink, parchment, paper, pencils, slates, and chalk. Along with reading and writing, Harry taught mathematics, Latin, history, and music.

Best of all was scripture reading time. Maela soaked up knowledge of Jesus with every fiber of her being, begging Harry for more each day. He introduced her to Adam and Eve, Abraham, Moses, Joshua, Ruth, David—her interest was unquenchable.

Maela designed drawers for herself out of her mother's old flannel petticoat. They were both comfortable and convenient. Modesty had been a foreign concept to her, but now Maela did concern herself with it, since modesty concerned Harry, and apparently it concerned God.

One day in early December, Laitha's pups arrived. When Harry returned home from work one evening, he found the mother and nine pups settled, not in the whelping box he had provided, but in his best blanket at the foot of the bed. The blanket was ruined, of course, but he could not be angry with the new mother—Laitha's manifest contentment touched his heart. He gently moved the family to their cozy box, and the new mother reluctantly accepted the change.

Ragwort was confused. His best friend would have nothing to do with him; she snarled when he so much as approached her nest. He felt better once Harry sat down and let him hop into his lap. Harry tipped his chair back on two legs and scratched the terrier's belly. "We shall have little attention from our womenfolk these days, Rag. The pups shall receive all their love, I fear."

Harry ate a cold supper, assuming Maela would not come that night, for it was snowing and windy. But commotion outside warned him of company. Ragwort stared at the crack beneath the door, his tail quivering. Harry opened the door, and Maela stumbled inside. He caught her, staring aghast at her blue lips and frosty eyelashes. Only a threadbare shawl draped her head and shoulders. Her hands were like blocks of ice.

"Pegasus is stabled." She gave Harry a sheepish smile before seeking out Laitha's box. "The pups are whelped! I knew it! Oh, Laitha!"

Harry released her to run to the puppies. She must not be quite frozen, after all. Words of reprimand died upon his lips. She had taken a terrible chance, all for the sake of Laitha's pups.

To Harry's surprise, Laitha made no demur when Maela picked up her puppies and admired each one. The dog had seemed uneasy when he handled them. "Six males and three females. A magnificent family, indeed!"

"The sire is Sir David's prize staghound. These pups shall be valuable."

"They are already valuable to me. Oh, Harry, behold this tiny face!"

Laitha licked the pup along with Maela's fingers. She seemed delighted with the girl's attention.

"What is Ragwort's opinion of them?" Maela glanced back at the scruffy terrier.

"Not high, I fear. They are not his, of course; he is too small. However, there is a litter of terriers at the manor that bears his likeness. Lyttleton declares the pups are Ragwort's."

"Shall you take one?"

"I possess eleven dogs at present. I have no need of more!"

While Maela petted Laitha and cheered Ragwort by playing tug-of-war, Harry balanced on two back chair legs and his toes, his hands busy with a small carving. The growls and giggles ceased, and Maela reclined before the fire. Harry was relieved to see that color and warmth had returned to her face and hands.

Maela turned her head and stated bluntly, "Harry, I must tell you that

I am now a disciple of Jesus Christ."

Harry blinked. "I thought you had decided this long ago."

"Nay. I loved Jesus and wanted to learn more of Him, but I did not wish to repent of my sins. Now I have done so, and He has forgiven me. My life is now His."

She spoke firmly, but Harry heard a little tremor at the end. His hands fell to his lap; his front chair legs hit the floor. "This is a vital decision, Ishmaela. Never will you make a greater." A smile lifted his mustache. "Well done. The angels are rejoicing with you, as I am also."

Ishmaela nodded. Her eyes returned to the fire. "Does this mean that God has adopted me into His family?"

Harry wondered at the intensity of the question. "Indeed, it does. You are His child and my sister in Christ Jesus."

"You have read to me of Abraham, Isaac, and Ishmael. I had never heard the story."

She fell silent. "And?" Harry prompted after a long pause.

"I understand much now. . .about my mother, and. . .my name." She rolled over and looked directly at Harry. "I was not the child of promise, Harry."

"Not in man's eyes, perhaps, but in God's eyes you are of infinite value. Jesus laid down his life for you, Maela. There can be no greater love than this."

She stared into his eyes as though reading his very soul. Harry said softly, "His Word is sure, Maela. You are a child of His promises, and He never fails to keep His Word."

Silence fell. The gammon Harry had spitted over the fire dripped and crackled. He pulled it out and placed it on a plate for the girl, along with a roll and an apple. "Eat well, Maela."

She accepted the food, munching quietly, her thoughts far away.

"You have added flesh to your bones since spring. You are slender as a birch sapling, but a breath of wind can no longer bear you away."

Maela smiled self-consciously, still chewing. She swallowed and said, "You have fattened me well, Harry. 'Tis your provender which sustains me. Now, I must return to the castle, for Dob took the cob Orwell to ride this day, which means he will not stay away long."

As she rose, Harry produced from his wardrobe a woolen cloak and rabbit fur muff. "I had intended these for Christmas, but you have need of them now."

"Oh! Oh, Harry!" Maela clasped his gifts in her arms and buried her face in the fur.

"May I walk you home?"

Recovering, she shook her head and donned the cloak. It covered her slight figure from head to toe. "It is most wondrous warm. I shall depart now. Tend those pups with care!"

Sliding between mossy stones, Maela hunkered down to survey the castle grounds. In winter, her natural cover was sparse, consisting only of dry grasses, bare trees, and a few clumps of gorse. It was not yet noon, but Dob and the other retainers had left early to join holiday celebrations at the local bear garden and pubs. Grandmere had retired to her chambers with a large pitcher of spirits, leaving Maela free to celebrate Christmas as she pleased.

Maela scampered into the forest, taking her roundabout path to Pegasus's snowy, overgrazed pasture. The pony greeted her with his cheerful nicker. "Soon you will enjoy a full manger, my friend," she assured him, hopping upon his back. The sturdy pony seemed to have shrunk somewhat during the last year, but he still carried his mistress easily.

"Welcome! 'Glory to God in the highest, and on earth, peace, good will toward men,'" Harry called, rising politely as Maela stepped through the door. He had been ladling juices over a roasting fowl and turning the spit.

"Let us rejoice and be glad," Maela agreed. " 'For unto us a child is born.'" Harry's joy was contagious. Contentment flooded her heart. She dropped a package on the bench and pulled off her oversized boots and new cloak.

Ragwort sat on the hearth with his eyes glued to the dripping bird. Laitha lay in her box while the puppies nursed. She lifted her face to Maela's loving touch, but Ragwort barely acknowledged the girl's presence with a glance and a tail wag.

Maela could not blame him. The aroma was mouthwatering. Then an unwelcome thought struck her. "That is not one of our hens?"

Harry chuckled and hunkered back down on his low stool. His legs stuck out at angles like a spider's. "Nay, I would not slay any pet of yours, Ishmaela; I love mine own life too well. The bird was a gift from Sir David—also ham, pastries, and dried figs. Kind in him, was it not? The manor festivities upon Christmas Eve were grand indeed. We did eat our fill, field hands, house servants, and all, and played and danced until our feet ached and our voices failed. I wished for your presence, Maela."

"I am thankful enough for this day," she replied, peering over his shoulder at the chicken. The fire's heat made her icy cheeks burn. She could imagine Harry dancing and singing with a pretty maid on each arm. The thought gave her no joy.

"I have a gift for you," Harry said suddenly. "Turn the spit, and I will bring it."

"But my cloak and muff. . .they were my gift," she faltered, though her eyes brightened.

"Nay, 'twas insufficient."

Maela willingly took his place on the stool. Her kirtle settled around her as she bent to her task.

From a cupboard over the washstand, Harry retrieved his gift. Holding it behind his back, he approached her. Firelight twinkled in his brown eyes. Squatting beside her, he held out the gift on one callused hand.

It was the carving he had begun the night of the puppies' birth, a gracefully carved dove. Each delicate feather was carved in detail; the sweetness of the bird's expression brought tears to Maela's eyes. Carefully, she lifted it from Harry's hand, her thin fingers trembling. "It is the most beautiful thing. . .its breast looks to be downy soft, though it is of wood." The polished wood glowed in the firelight as she pressed the bird to her cheek and closed her eyes.

"It pleases you?" A redundant question.

Leaning over, Maela squeezed his neck with one skinny arm. "It pleases me." He looked satisfied.

Leaving Harry to turn the spit, she retrieved her bundle and placed it at his feet. "For you." She stepped back, hands clasped behind her back.

"I must rescue our supper first." Harry removed the chicken from the spit and set it upon a platter to cool—out of Ragwort's reach. The dog transferred his fixed gaze to the table.

Then, folding back the corners of a grayed and stained pinafore, Harry uncovered the gift, a needleworked pillow. He smiled in recognition. "It is Laitha and Ragwort. Smells of flowers."

"I did stuff it with lavender," she informed him eagerly.

A crude yet artful representation of the two dogs at play in a field of wildflowers decorated the canvas rectangle. Such detailed needlework must have required many hours of painstaking labor. Harry traced Laitha's curved crewel spine with one rough finger, then Ragwort's face. She had somehow captured Laitha's air of tragedy and the terrier's saucy, scruffy appeal.

Leaning back on his stool, he stared at the thatching overhead, fighting to control his emotions. His Adam's apple bobbed up and down beneath his beard. Maela watched him with tender eyes. Her bird was lovely, but Harry was the most beautiful creature she had ever seen.

"It is fine indeed. Nothing could please me more," he finally croaked, rubbing his eyes with his thumb and fingers. He turned to finish preparing the meal, keeping the pillow tucked under one elbow. "We shall starve while I forget my business here," he rumbled.

Maela caressed her dove, satisfied that Harry's reaction had been worth every stabbed finger, every ripped-out stitch. Her mother's training, not to mention her mother's supply of yarns and needles, had finally been of some use.

After a most satisfying feast, they settled around the fire. For once, Harry was not carving. He rubbed Ragwort's back, staring into the fire. The little dog's belly was tightly rounded. He sighed contentedly in his sleep, sprawled across Harry's lap. For a while, Maela sat beside Laitha's box, fondling and crooning to each puppy in turn. Then she scooted closer to the fire, closer to Harry, sitting tailor-fashion.

"Tell me of your mother," Harry demanded suddenly.

"Mother had golden hair and blue, blue eyes and white, soft skin. She taught me to dance and ride and stitch fancywork. She wore colorful gowns that flowed about her when she danced. . . . I was eight years of age when Mother fell ill of a fever and died in the night." Maela's low voice faded away.

Suddenly sitting up straighter, she proclaimed, "Grandmere loves me not. She has eyes that. . .I cannot explain. She has cast a spell upon the castle."

Harry's brows lowered. "Maela, surely you do not fear such things."

"Nay, but Dob does. Grandmere's witchery has helped me in this way."

"What do you mean?"

"Once last summer Dob was. . .cruel to me. Grandmere laid a spell around the castle, cursing any man that entered the keep ere its master's return. Since that time, Dob has troubled me not."

Muscles worked in Harry's jaw, making his beard twitch. Maela wondered what he was thinking.

"How do you manage to escape the keep without their knowledge?"

Maela's shoulders jerked. Just above a whisper she replied, "A secret tunnel."

"A secret tunnel," Harry mused softly. "I have heard of such things concerning these castles. How did you discover its existence?"

"I found it while playing. I doubt anyone living knows of it, save me. My one fear is that someday Dob will notice Pegasus missing and discover my secrets. Grandmere suffers pain in her limbs and drinks to excess. Because she never climbs the spiral staircase to my chamber without dire need, she knows not of mine absences. This morn, she started early upon a large jug of rum; therefore, I left earlier than my wont."

"Does she beat you?" Harry asked quietly.

Maela turned away from the fire, away from Harry. "Not often. She threatens horrors beyond imagining should her commands be disobeyed. I know Jesus will protect me from her evil spells; nevertheless, I dare not cross Grandmere without desperate need. She has excellent aim with a skillet."

"And does she work about the castle? Cleaning, baking, washing, and such?"

"She collects and dries herbs for her potions and prepares food for herself and for me. Dob and his like fare for themselves. I know not how. There is provender enough, but Grandmere does not trouble herself to prepare it properly, and she allows me not to try my hand. If you did not share of your bounty, I was like to have died of hunger long ago. Cleanliness is unknown to Grandmere. The bowls and such-like are scoured with sand ere we eat. That is all. Once I swept out the old rush matting as you have taught me, then sprinkled fresh rushes and herbs about. Grandmere was asleep, and I do not believe she noticed my handiwork when she awoke. I try to make things finer, but there is little to work with."

Maela looked troubled by her ineptitude, but Harry was touched by her efforts. "Make no excuse for your labors; they are worthy. I might come to the castle and help you. Often I behold its tower above the treetops and think of you hidden within. 'Tis no proper place for a child. Mayhap I could reason with your grandmother—"

"Nay! It can never be. I must depart. All thanks for my dove and for the bountiful feast." Frightened, Maela leaped to her feet and began to don the large boots she had scavenged from a bedchamber in the castle.

Looking startled and rather hurt, Harry held her cloak, then tried to open the door, but she ignored his good manners and let herself out. The two dogs followed her but turned back quickly. Daylight had gone, leaving frigid darkness, though it was not yet five hours past noon. A thick fog rose from the melting snow. Maela could scarcely see to the shed where Pegasus waited.

The pony was not thrilled to see her, but he made no protest when she led him outside and climbed upon his back. When she rode past the cottage, she was surprised to see Harry in the doorway, silhouetted against the fire. "God be with you," Maela called.

"Fare you well, Maela," Harry called back. He sounded strangely forlorn.

Chapter 6

The LORD is my light and my salvation; whom shall I fear?
the LORD is the strength of my life; of whom shall I be afraid?
When the wicked, even mine enemies and my foes,
came upon me. . .they stumbled and fell.
PSALM 27:1–2

A few weeks later, Ishmaela did not show up at the cottage for several days in a row. Harry philosophically accepted the first few days of her absence, for sleety snow driven before a knife-edged wind would keep most people indoors—though Maela was unlike most people. Laitha's bright-eyed, tumbling, fuzzy puppies were an irresistible lure to the girl. It was strange, indeed, that she did not come.

After six days of lonely, worried waiting, he could bear it no longer and prepared a sack of food and herbs. He let the dogs out, then shut them back into the house and set out toward the castle. Anything might have happened to the child. She could be sick or injured or imprisoned. . .

"It had best not be Dobbin Titwhistle," he muttered grimly. He had seen Dob about town, a burly man with florid face, bushy beard, and a large belly. The thought of the man harming Maela made Harry's protective instincts rise in full force.

"Wish I had a horse." Not for the first time, he imagined himself riding up to the castle gates and demanding entrance, then galloping away with Maela across his saddle. His daydream always degenerated into the more realistic prospect of riding over on Samson, his feet dragging on the ground as they jounced along. He gave a rueful chuckle. "I would find a place as court jester, more like."

He pulled his hood over his face in a vain attempt to shield it from the wind. It was no longer sleeting, but it was dark, with no moon or starlight to brighten his path. Patches of snow remaining beside the way took on a ghostly aspect in Harry's eyes. Wind whipped naked treetops into frenzy. Branches strewed the narrow road, swirling about as the wind caught them.

Harry heard and felt a crash somewhere to his left; a mighty tree had fallen before the storm.

He nearly missed the turnoff to Castle Trent, a black tunnel through the trees. A chill caused by neither sleet nor wind trickled down his spine as he entered it. Mocking voices in the wind screamed of doom and disaster. His flesh began to creep; the hair on his scalp lifted.

Harry stopped and closed his eyes. His cloak whipped and fluttered about his legs, but he stood like a rock in the center of the path. "Lord," he spoke aloud. "I ask Your protection and blessing upon this mission. Uphold Ishmaela with Your almighty hand; keep her safe. You are greater far than any power of darkness and fear, and all creation rests in Your hands. Help me to find Your little child this night, and give Your angels charge over us. In Jesus' name I ask this."

Shoulders squared, he strode down the path like a conquering hero. His armor was invisible, yet it was invulnerable. Now the wind sounded angry, defiant.

Castle Trent appeared out of the night, seeming to glow with a silvery light against the black sky. There were no castle gates; they had long since crumbled. Thus ended that fantasy. A moat had once surrounded the grounds; of it, only a grassy depression remained. Inside the moat's outline, piles of rubble overcome by moss, bracken, and brambles were all that remained of the castle walls. Only the tall stone keep and a few outbuildings remained intact. Few of the keep's lower windows showed flickers of light, signs of human life.

Harry paused beside the ruined gatehouse, sensing danger. His eyes darted from corner to dark corner, suspecting. . .he knew not what. One hand on his knife sheath, he walked into the courtyard where knights had gathered for battle one hundred years before. Almost he could hear their shouts, the clatter of hooves and clink of armor.

Nay, that metallic clank was of the present. . . .

Harry sprang to one side just as a pike pierced the air where he had been standing. His cloak billowed around him; there was a sound of rending fabric as the pike ripped it from his back.

Carried by the momentum of the thrust, a large body stumbled past, uttering a frustrated oath. Harry grasped the man by the back of his jerkin, hauled him off his feet, and kicked the cloaked pike out of reach. Whipping out his hunting knife, he held it to the man's throat from behind, pressing its edge to the skin. "Hold," he ordered, as though his captive could do otherwise.

Wheeling to look for other assailants, Harry held the man before him like a shield. The courtyard was empty.

"Slay me not!" the man begged through clenched teeth. "Who art thou?"

"One full willing to dispatch cowardly assassins such as you," Harry snarled, fear still whipping the blood through his veins. "Where is the child?"

He felt surprise ripple through the heavy body. "The child?"

"Lord Trenton's daughter."

"He has no daughter." The voice was unconvincing. "If you desire ransom, take the boy child from his home near London. I could counsel you how to accomplish it."

Harry's teeth clenched. "Foul traitor!"

"Nay, I am faithful to His Lordship," Dob whined, ready to butter his bread on either side.

"Less talk of your worthless loyalty," Harry spoke sharply. "Where is the girl child?"

"In the castle," Dob gasped as the knife pressed harder. "I've done nothing to anger you, lord."

"But for attempting to skewer me, I trust that is true."

"You should fear the witch Hera. She commands the powers of darkness; indeed, I know it." Genuine fear laced the foreman's gravelly voice. "She has placed a curse upon the castle so that no man dare enter until Sir Trenton's return."

"I give you fair warning, Master Titwhistle"—thick sarcasm colored the title of respect—"should any harm come to the damsel, your life is forfeit. She is under protection far greater than any witch could provide."

"How do you know of the wench? Are you a wizard?"

"I have means beyond your ken" was Harry's enigmatic reply. If Dob believed he was a sorcerer, so be it.

Apparently, this was exactly the conclusion Dob had arrived at. Who but a sorcerer could know of Sir Hanover's child or dodge a pike thrust with such perfect timing? Dob was no fool, but superstition clouded his judgment. Shaking with fear, he offered no resistance when Harry bound his hands behind his back using his own woolen hose. Rather than leave the helpless man exposed to the elements, Harry locked him into a storeroom, certain that he would be found in the morning. One hazard eliminated.

Harry freed his cloak but left the pike where it lay. The castle loomed above him, ominous, cold. Ishmaela's home? It was difficult to imagine his lively little companion dwelling in this gloomy fortress.

"Lord," he spoke softly while wiping clean his knife's blade. "I thank

You for Your protection this night. Hera Coats has allied herself with Your sworn enemies and will doubtless strive to prevent mine entry. I ask You in Jesus' name to defeat Your enemies and allow Your servant free access to Castle Trent."

With a raucous cackling and clatter of wings, a flock of rooks launched from the castle battlements, circled once, then headed north above the tree-tops, a ragged black cloud, tattered by the wind. Harry stared up into the darkness, hearing the noise but unable to determine its source.

Taking a deep breath, he shrugged his shoulders to relax them and headed for the keep, knife in hand. This time, he kept an eye on his back trail, not caring to be surprised more than once a night.

The drawbridge, rotted and treacherous to unwary feet, lay across the dry inner moat. The portcullis was up, set, and ready to cut off the unwary or unwelcome visitor. Within these barriers, stone stairs led up to an enormous oaken door set deep in the outer wall. It was a far from pleasant prospect. Harry paused at the base of the steps. He could not imagine Maela opening that door. Perhaps there was another.

Circling the base of the rectangular keep, he soon discovered the attached kitchen wing. A light glowed from within. He knocked on the door. No answer. Circling the castle once more, he studied its windows. They were too narrow to enter even if he should manage to climb up.

Returning to the kitchen door, he pushed at its iron ring. The door swung open with a low groan. Slightly rattled by this easy access, he paused in the doorway, brandishing his knife, but nothing happened. A short, narrow hallway lay within, dimly lit by a fire in the room beyond.

Harry stepped inside. There was a weird scream and a scuffle at his feet. With a startled yell, he flourished his knife and crouched in a defensive position—but it was only a cat rushing to escape through the open doorway. He must have trodden upon its tail. From the courtyard it turned to glare at him with glowing eyes and yowled again before gliding into the shadows.

Harry swallowed hard, blinked, and let out his breath in a puff. "Overmuch talk of witches makes me fear a little cat!" he muttered.

Flaring coals cast a red glow over the kitchen's tiled floor, filthy worktables, and a jumbled assortment of baskets, barrels, pottery, and cast-iron pots. A heap draped across one of the tables emitted a low rumbling noise. Harry silently moved close enough to recognize a human shape and to understand the significance of the empty jug at its elbow. He gently lifted one of the woman's shoulders, showing a lined, yellowed countenance with slack jaw and deep bags beneath the closed eyes. Greasy, grayish hair slipped from beneath her cap.

"Mistress Hera, I presume," he said and released her. "No fear of your evil spells. You have succumbed to an evil of your own making." It was difficult to imagine this sot as Maela's grandmother. Although the woman might have been handsome in her youth, it was impossible to discern beauty in her ravaged face now.

Taking a beeswax candle from the kitchen, Harry began to explore, checking chambers and hallways, softly calling Maela's name. Only scuffling rodents and echoes replied. Mildew and dry rot tickled his nose. He stifled a sneeze, then another. Wind moaned through the windows, lifting tapestries from chamber walls in ghostly waves. Harry's candle flickered wildly. Every sound, every leaping shadow caused his heart to race. Though he felt chilled, sweat beaded his brow. *I wonder*, he thought, *have I covered the ground floor, or have I traveled in circles? Each chamber looks like the one before.*

Near the entry hall he found the stairwell, dark and steep. Holding his long knife in his right hand, the candle in his left, he began to ascend. Eventually, the spiral stairwell opened into a gallery. He extended the candle into it while standing poised on the stairs. Three doors opened into the gallery; all were closed. Opposite the doors, at Harry's left hand, was a waist-high frame barrier, and beyond this barrier a vast, empty space. Casting wary glances over both shoulders and listening with every nerve in his body, he stepped into the gallery. Its wooden floor creaked ominously beneath his feet.

Before trying the doors, he held his candle over the barrier to see what lay beyond. Heavy beams supported a vaulted ceiling. Long tables lay below, lined with heavy chairs and benches. It was the castle's great hall. The gallery overlooked it from on high, a good two stories up. Leaning slightly against the barrier railing, Harry felt it give beneath his hand. Instantly, he backed away, thinking, *This place requires the services of a good joiner. . .but I shall not apply for the position.*

Harry paused before the first door.

"Maela?"

Silence.

He knocked at the next door. "Maela? Can you hear me?"

"Harry?" A guttural reply. It could be no one but Maela, though it sounded nothing like her.

He took a deep breath, gulped, and felt tears of relief prick behind his eyes. "Maela! Yea, truly 'tis Harry."

The door creaked open to reveal Maela's pallid face. "Harry, you are in danger here!" she barked, then began to cough.

The sound thrust a knife of fear between Harry's ribs. The candle shook in his hand that had been rock steady a moment before. "You are ill! I did fear it."

Maela shook her head. " 'Tis but a cough. I shall recover. Harry, you must go away! Should Grandmere discover you, or Master Dob. . ." Her eyes implored him, but he pushed past her into the room, his feet crunching on withered rush matting.

A tiny fire consisting of a few twigs flickered on the hearth but produced no discernible heat. No wonder the child was ill. The dank, dark chamber was perhaps six by eight feet, with a small doorway to the garderobe near the wall. Maela's bed was a straw pallet on the floor. Two moth-eaten blankets and her woolen cloak were its only coverings. From the corner of one eye he saw furtive movement near the hearth—a mouse, no doubt. The entire castle reeked of vermin.

He turned to Maela. Arms wrapped about her body, she shivered, clad in only her shift and red flannel drawers—no nightcap. Tattered sleeves dangled at her elbows. The sagging neckline revealed protruding collarbones. She had lost considerable weight. Dirty ankles and bare feet showed beneath her drawers. Her eyes looked dull, though firelight flickered in their dark depths. Her hair hung in a snarled, greasy mass that reached past where her hips must be.

"You must go away," she repeated weakly, choked, then doubled over again with racking coughs that seemed about to tear her delicate body apart.

"Dob Titwhistle is locked up, and Hera Coats lies snoring in the kitchen, past waking."

Maela's eyes widened. "Dob has seen you? Oh, all is lost!" Her lips trembled. "Now he will know! He will discover my passage." She began to sob softly, gasping for breath.

"Nay, he saw not my face. Should I vanish, perchance he will think 'twas a dream or one of Hera's curses come to pass. Your secret is yet safe."

Maela's eyes closed. Harry saw her sway. He leaped to catch her, and her weight was as nothing in his arms.

Maela awoke but did not wish to open her eyes. Her dreams had been so wonderful that even their memory warmed her. Harry had stroked her face and arms as he spoke tender words of love and encouragement. She heaved a deep sigh.

"It is well. You can breathe clearly now."

Maela's eyelids felt weighted, but she had to see if it were true. "Harry?" she whispered. His face came into focus. The room seemed filled with light.

"You are truly here?" Her hand groped in his direction and felt his gentle squeeze.

"You do not remember?"

"I thought 'twas a dream."

"I know not how I will leave you now that day has dawned, but I care not. Your fever has broken, and your cough is productive. I caused you to breathe an herbal mist while you slept. You have coughed up the congestion."

Maela thought this over. It sounded disgusting, but Harry did not look disgusted. "I dreamed. . ." she began. She lifted one arm into view. It was no longer grimy.

Reading her thoughts in her actions, Harry said soberly, "I rubbed your arms and face with wet cloths, Maela, to bring down the fever. I knew not what else to do."

Maela thought her fever must have returned, for her face burned. Harry rose to prowl about the room. "I feared you would hate me, as you would have no man touch you."

Far from feeling indignant, Maela wanted to beg for more. "Once you did tend my feet."

"Yea, but this time I did tend you without your consent."

"You have ever my full consent, Harry. I trust you. This castle seems a brighter place, for I have seen your face herein."

Harry brightened. "I hazarded your wrath to make you well and strong again. I cannot tell how I have missed your presence this past sennight. The dogs miss you, as well."

Maela smiled. "And I them. But. . .how did you come here? Grandmere. . .Dob. . .the curse—" Wonder creased her brow.

" 'Yea, though I walk through the valley of the shadow of death, I will fear no evil: for thou art with me,'" he quoted softly. "Your grandmother slept, and God protected me from Dob. I saw none beside the twain."

"But how will you escape?"

"The secret tunnel?" Harry suggested. "I wish not to leave you, but Dob will soon be discovered, and I fear your grandmother will wish to ascertain your continued presence. I have left bread, cheese, and apples here in this cloth at your feet." He pointed. "I brought you fresh water in a flask; it and two fagots for your fire are hid in the garderobe. Now, I must require my cloak of you."

Maela followed his glance and realized that she was wrapped snugly in his cloak. Slowly, she sat up and tried to unwrap its folds. Harry came to help her.

"There is a lever between two stones inside the fireplace in the great hall," Maela explained. "Reach up about thus far"—she showed him the distance on her arm—"and pull it down. It is on the left behind a black stone. Harry," she paused, flushed, "I must use the garderobe."

Understanding her implied request, he helped her to her feet and into the side chamber, then left the room to allow her privacy. Maela remembered to wash her hands afterward this time, though the cold water added to the draft from the seat holes started her shivering again.

She crawled between her blankets and tried to soak up the warmth of the fire.

Harry knocked at her door. "Maela?" At her bidding, he re-entered the room. She was nearly asleep already. Kneeling beside the pallet, he stroked her pale forehead lightly with one fingertip and watched her lips twitch into a smile. Through the night he had studied her face in detail while sponging away the grime. Someday she would be a prize whose heart any man would be honored to win. The unbidden thought brought him to his feet, frowning.

Quietly he closed the door of her chamber behind him. Slinking gingerly along the gallery, Harry peeked down the stairwell. All clear. Knife at the ready, he crept down the stairs and moved toward the great hall. Maela had told him it would be to his right, and sure enough, he stepped into the vast space of it a moment later. Somehow he had missed it during his explorations the night before. Far above was the gallery. He could just glimpse the top of the door to Maela's room. He felt less alone at sight of it.

The hall fireplace was immense. Maela must have been playing inside it when she discovered the lever, Harry decided. It was easily large enough for several children to play within. He searched for a black stone on the left side. There were several, but he soon found the right one. The lever pulled smoothly, and a narrow opening appeared in the paneled surround about two feet to the left of the fireplace. It had been invisible while closed. Harry couldn't help stopping to study it before entering.

Shouts reached his ears, and the sound of confusion. It was time to make haste. Slipping inside the tunnel, he slid the panel back into place and found himself in total darkness.

After a moment, his heart began to beat again, and he remembered that Maela used this tunnel frequently. He was unlikely to become lost. Groping his way along the rock walls, bending nearly double beneath the low ceiling, he felt the tunnel slope downward beneath his feet. He took many hesitant steps, unsure of his footing. Suddenly the rock wall to his left ended, and Harry nearly fell into what turned out to be a shallow alcove. In it he felt wooden panels. A door? Maela hadn't mentioned that possibility. Was it the door he should take? Shaking his head in doubt, he kept walking ahead, hoping for a glimpse of daylight. It seemed he had been walking in darkness for an hour when at last a trickle of daylight dazzled his eyes. It came from above, and in its glow he saw jagged stone steps up the rock wall. Climbing with hands and feet, he pushed his head through bracken and popped up from the hole like a rabbit.

Where am I? He dared not wonder aloud. He was in a forest. A small hill rose behind him. Brambles caught at his cloak as he lifted himself from the hole. This explained Maela's perpetually scratched arms and legs.

It was a gray morning, just past dawn. An icy, misty rain was falling. A bird chirped hopefully from a nearby elm tree, and occasional scuffles in the underbrush indicated other small creatures. Harry crawled forward, searching for a place to stand erect. Brush scraped his hat from his head. When he paused to retrieve it, he glimpsed the castle keep just peeking above the hill at his back.

Of course! The hill was part of the ruined castle wall. The tunnel must have been intended as an escape route during siege.

There was no path through the wood, in spite of Maela's constant usage. The child must take care to leave no marks that might lead anyone to the tunnel entrance.

Skirting the castle road, Harry made his way cross-country through the forest. Coming out upon the main road about a mile from the cottage, he brushed dead leaves and gorse thorns from his hair, hat, and cloak, then struck out for home. He would scarcely have time to break his fast and care for the beasts before church began.

"Lord," he prayed aloud, "I thank You for Your protection, guidance, and assurance of Your complete power over any enemy, visible or invisible! And I thank You for Maela." His heart held far more, but he could not express it in words—or even in thought.

He broke into a jog, his breath forming frosty clouds.

Dob caused a minor stir when he was discovered and released. Old Balt, the nearly deaf and blind smithy who stayed in the castle stables, eventually heard him kicking at the storeroom door and released the latch. As soon as he was loose, Dob ran to the keep and shouted outside the kitchen door until Hera staggered to open it, bleary-eyed and prickly as nettles.

"An intruder! Did you fight off the intruder in the night?" he panted from the exertion of his short run.

Hera glared at him. "You are surely mad." Vitriolic epithets spewed from her tongue, but Dob ignored them.

"A man, a giant and powerful lord—nay, a wizard—wished to take the wench for ransom and demanded her location! He locked me in the store-room, and Balt only now released me. Is she safe?"

Now somewhat concerned, Hera closed the door in his face and shuffled away. Dob waited on pins and needles for her return.

He did not wait long. "You dolt! You doddering idiot, to send me up those accursed stairs on a fool's errand! The child sleeps, and all is well within. You dreamed, or were in your cups."

Baffled, Dob took himself away to rehash the night's events. At length, a plausible explanation dawned upon him.

" 'Twas the curse!" he told Balt firmly. "The rooks took that sorcerer! I heard them in the night, then a frightful scream; now, as you can see, they are gone. 'Twas the powers of darkness come upon us!" He crossed himself vigorously and pulled out his dried frog, a charm against witchcraft, to rub between his fingers.

When Balt eventually understood the gist of Dob's story, he also stared wide-eyed at the vacant battlements. Rooks had nested atop Castle Trent for many years. Now they were gone. There could be no other explanation.

Chapter 7

My son, preserve sound judgment and discernment,
do not let them out of your sight.
PROVERBS 3:21 NIV 1984

Although Harry treasured his time with Maela, he also took pleasure in other activities. Sir David Marston threw feasts and dances nearly every holy day; the parish church was an excellent place to meet people; and Trenton village held frequent concerts, pageants, meetings, and competitions. Harry participated in many of these. He and his dogs were well known figures in the town.

Sports were more to his taste than the quieter pastimes. Harry romped with village boys and men, playing at football, ninepins, or battledore and shuttlecock. Fist fighting, bull-baiting, bearbaiting, and cockfighting seemed cruel sports to Harry, but he did appreciate an occasional dramatic play staged in Trenton's bearbaiting hall. He also participated in frequent archery matches and the required drill and weapon practice of the village militia. Along with every other man in Trenton between sixteen and sixty, Harry marched, lunged with a pike, clashed swords, loosed arrows, and fired an harquebus.

One hot summer afternoon in 1566, more than a year after Harry's arrival at the manor, two female servants from Marston Hall brought drinks for the militia. While the men drilled, the women rested beneath a willow tree near the riverbank outside Trenton village and watched.

Waiting for his turn at the archery butt, Harry chatted with friends. Many of the men had already discarded their armor lest they faint of the sun's heat. Harry unbuckled his thick leather breastplate, dropped it on the grass, and heaved a sigh of relief. "I sympathize with the fate of a turtle," he jested.

"Oh, what a goodly man it is!" a freckled housemaid sighed as her dreamy eyes followed Harry's every move.

"Waste not your time a-dreaming of the joiner, Lottie. He is over-religious and a doltish lout. He delivers abhorrent sermons to all and sundry. Surely you have not escaped unscathed from his double-edged tongue!" Dovie rolled her eyes in disgust and lay back on the grass.

Lottie looked doubtful, her eyes drinking in Harry as he drew his long-bow, aimed, and shouted, "Fast!" His first shot just missed the bull's-eye.

"But he is strong and brave!" Lottie protested. "His skill at arms impresses even the men."

"Remove your eyes from his fine limbs and goodly countenance, Lottie. They conceal a man whose character is beneath your notice." Thus saying, Dovie allowed her own eyes to follow Harry's second shot. The arrow struck an outer ring of the target. "They say he despises women. No honest man will abide near him—therefore, he lodges in the coppice cottage."

"I cannot believe this slander! Not only does Harry speak oft of God, he is exceeding kind and good. I cannot believe that his nature is evil. Your two charges lie at odds with one another!"

"Please yourself. I gave you fair warning."

It was Lottie's first week at Marston Hall. She welcomed the break from household chores, for this had been her worst day yet.

Lottie had been assigned to pour drinks at dinner. After enduring sly winks and pinches from the field hands, which she had been unable to repel while holding a large pewter pitcher of ale, she had welcomed Harry's respectful manner.

"Have you any new milk?" he asked, refusing the double ale.

Opening her mouth to make a sharp reply, she met his gaze and stopped cold. " 'Twould pleasure me to fetch it for you," she fluttered, and hurried to the dairy house.

His smile had rewarded her when she returned with the jug of milk, but to her dismay, she had poured too fast, deluging his arm and lap. He had quickly leaped to his feet, brushing off his clothes. Not one word of blame, not one oath escaped his lips. He had refused her offer of help, claiming that the sun would soon dry him and that cold milk was good on a hot day—though he had never before applied it to his exterior. Lottie had gaped at him in silence, her blue eyes glazing over.

Palpitations of the heart seized her even now as she watched him hit the edge of the bull's-eye with his next shot. She clasped her hands at her breast. "Oh, well done, Harry!" Hearing her, he touched his helmet brim with a smile.

Another man heard Lottie's praise. When it came his turn to shoot, he picked up his bow, aimed quickly, and in rapid succession sent three bolts into the bull's-eye, dead center. He checked to make sure Lottie was watching, but her eyes followed Harry. The tall man frowned and retrieved his arrows with shoulders hunched.

"Impressive, Fleming," Harry remarked. "You do show us apprentices how it should be done."

Fleming acknowledged the compliment with a nod and watched as Harry joined the women under the tree. "Come hither, friend, and rest with us," Harry invited the older man, but Fleming pretended not to hear and drifted toward town.

"Please yourself." Harry pulled off his helmet and leather jerkin. Sweat drenched his body and trickled down his face; his hair was plastered to his head. His yearning gaze turned toward the river. "A swim would suit me well this day."

"Have a cup of ale?" Lottie offered, already dipping from the bucket. "We brought it for your refreshment—and that of the other men."

"With pleasure." Harry drained the dipper in one long draught. He wiped his mustache with the back of one hand and smiled. "I thank you, maiden. You are ever ready with a drink when I thirst, it seems."

"I hope so," Lottie simpered, finding it difficult to breathe. Only sixteen, Lottie had little experience with men, but she was eager to learn. Other sweaty weekend warriors gathered round, slaking their raging thirst and flirting with the women. They distracted Dovie, but Lottie saved her attention for Harry.

Dogs romped on the grass nearby—Laitha, Ragwort, a bloodhound, and two of Laitha's adolescent pups. One pup still belonged to Harry, the other to the town beadle. Laitha's pups had brought Harry a sizable profit. In a way, he missed them, but the cottage was certainly more comfortable without them! The one pup he kept, a large, brindled male, was Maela's dog, Dudley.

Harry lay back at Lottie's feet, clasping his hands behind his head and gazing up into the willow's flowing branches. He took a deep breath, wondering how it would be if Maela could join him at these social activities. In his imagination she was clean, prettily clad, and enthralled by his athletic prowess. The admission brought a smile to his lips.

Lottie stared at him, not at all repulsed by the large damp patches on his stomach and beneath his arms. Adolescent acne still marked his complexion, but Lottie focused upon his many fine features. Thick lashes and brows framed his pensive dark eyes. Shiny hair fell back from his broad forehead. One long leg was bent, the other stretched upon the grass.

Plain woolen trunk hose stopped at his knees. He had opted not to wear nether hose—probably due to the heat.

Lottie perused his recumbent figure once more from toe to head and, upon reaching his face, was startled to find Harry's eyes upon her. "Do you think we are ready to fight the Irish should the queen require?" he asked.

Lottie immediately gushed, "Yea, of a truth, you are prepared for anything!"

"The local militia fought in Ireland in recent years, so 'tis unlikely we will be called up soon."

George, a Marston Hall field hand, remarked, "I once heard that Sir Hanover Trenton's grandfather received his knighthood after brave fighting in Ireland under Henry the VII."

"Indeed?" Harry propped himself up on his elbows to listen. "And when passed the castle into Trenton hands?"

" 'Twas taken by the crown after a siege and awarded to the first Trenton. He was a good manager, unlike the present master. All know how Dob Titwhistle fills his own purse ere he sends the rent to Lord Trenton." George swallowed another dipper of ale.

Lottie felt left out. "Why does Lord Trenton not suspect?" She leaned forward to pick a burdock from Harry's hair, letting her fingers linger. His hair was damp with sweat, but soft, as she had anticipated. She began to brush leaves from the back of his shirt, but he sat up and moved out of her reach.

George chuckled. "He takes not the time to learn what monies he should receive. He has other properties, and likely other dishonest assessors. The castle itself falls to ruin, and he cares nothing for it. His mind is taken up with Good Queen Bess and international affairs."

"Does he court the queen? I hear she has countless suitors," Lottie inquired. Romance of any kind fascinated her.

"He is a married man, else he would likely top the list of hopefuls. That Austrian archduke has given up hope of her. The Frog king, though half her age, has hopes—or perhaps they're his mother's hopes. The Earl of Leicester holds our queen's heart, 'tis rumored, but she should ne'er marry him."

"Why not?"

"His wife died in suspicious circumstances. It can never be proven, but should he marry the queen, many would say he murdered his first wife to make himself free. He is beneath Her Majesty in birth, rank, and all else, yet she favors him. His fine figure and comely face hold her fancy, though she loves him not enough to make him king. Nevertheless, Parliament pressures her to marry and provide an heir to the throne."

"I pity her," Harry remarked.

"You pity Her Most Royal Highness, the queen of England and Wales?" George scoffed. "I would take her place."

"I would not. She fears to marry, I think, lest she lose her power and the love of her husband. Mind her sister's fate. Queen Mary's marriage brought heartbreak and disaster—and no heir."

" 'Tis noised," Dovie jumped into the discussion, "that the Scot queen's husband, Lord Darnley, has murdered her secretary, David Rizzio."

"Of a truth?" Lottie's eyes were enormous. "For what cause?"

"Jealousy, if talk be true. The queen did love the man."

Harry pressed his point. "Her cousin's unhappy marriage cannot encourage Queen Elizabeth to seek a husband."

"Yet the Scot queen has at least provided an heir to the throne," George observed.

None of them dared voice the thought aloud, but all knew that Mary, Queen of Scots, was a threat to Elizabeth's sovereignty. Although the Protestant government of Scotland was continually at odds with their Catholic queen, many in England considered Mary Stuart their rightful queen. Elizabeth's position as legitimate heir was in serious question. Her parents' marriage had been declared invalid many times over the years. Was she the rightful queen? It was a ticklish situation, at best.

"Harry, the purpose of this is unclear to me." Maela obediently stirred the kettle of hot fat while Harry poured in the lye, but a frown wrinkled her brow. " 'Twould surely profit me more to pursue my studies in Latin this day. What is the purpose of making soap? Can you not take some in trade if it is needed?"

Harry glanced up long enough to appreciate her little pout. "The soap will be of use to us."

"Of use to us, indeed. You wish to smell pretty for that housemaid. I have beheld her with you at militia drill."

This arrested Harry's attention. "You have witnessed the practice sessions?"

"It pleases me to watch. But it pleases me not to see that. . .that wench with you!"

Harry chuckled. "Do I hear the rantings of a jealous woman?"

Maela's face was already as flushed as it could be while she worked over the boiling soap, but Harry saw her cringe from his words. "Maela, I do but jest. Once I beheld the exquisite visage of a maiden—but, alas, this day her beauty is veiled from my sight. I would see her face once more, and this soap may aid me toward that end."

Maela looked narrowly at him, suspecting a hidden meaning. "Do I know this maiden?"

"You have heard me mention her name—Maela, the soap thickens." Harry changed the subject, hoping to distract her.

Since Maela's illness, he had not seen her hair; she kept it bundled beneath a cap. He wondered how long it had been since she combed it out, but he never dared ask. Most people were undismayed by fetid body odors, for they all stank alike, but Harry came from a family that valued cleanliness.

Harry not only wanted Maela clean for his own sake; he also worried about her health. Maela was seldom close enough for her body odor to bother him, but he worried about parasites. Some people took lice and fleas for granted; Harry was not among them.

Maela was not to be distracted. "It is that Lottie. She haunts you like a spirit, I trow, and you enjoy her worship."

"Cease this foolish babble. Lottie is a silly child, no more. Have you spied upon me at the manor as well, wench?"

Maela glared at him. "Upon occasion. If she is a child, what am I?"

"A younger child. Nay, in truth, she is your inferior in understanding, Maela, though superior in years. Envy her not. Your jealousy is wasted upon her."

"You are too kind and gentle—her affection thrives on your kindness."

The soap thickened into sludge. Harry was not sure what to do next, for in spite of his boasts to Maela, he had never made soap before. He began to ladle it into pots and pails while Maela watched. "Her interest thrives on air. I give her no encouragement," he grumbled. Lottie's hero worship had begun to annoy him long before Maela pointed it out. "To be sure, she makes no indecent proposals, unlike others. She is a chaste and worthy maiden."

Wondering about this comment, Maela asked, "What indecent proposal might she make?"

"Why...uh...she..." Harry dithered, then busied himself, awkwardly pouring the soap. It slopped over the top of one pail, then another. He was creating a slimy mess in the yard of his cottage. Evidently, he had not given the location of his soap-making project enough forethought.

Maela dipped a finger into the cooled product and lifted it to her nose. "Will you place this foul stuff upon your body?"

"I shall add lavender scent to it," Harry assured her.

"When?"

"Now." He sprinkled a liberal amount of dried lavender blossoms into each container and bade her stir it in. Maela obeyed, grimacing at the result.

"Now it stinks and has flowers in it. What will you do with this...mess?"

"Wash my raiment and my body with it," he asserted bravely, though a closer examination gave him pause.

"Keep it far from me!"

Chapter 8

O Lord, thou preservest man and beast.
Psalm 36:6

One September morning, Harry awoke to find that a wild creature had broken into his chicken coop. Feathers littered the yard; Sage and Rosemary were gone. Only poor Parsley perched atop her ravaged house, squawking distractedly, and would not allow Harry to touch her. The dogs had failed to sound an alarm at the crucial time. Ragwort snuffled and snarled around the coop and made short dashes into the forest, barking a challenge, but the damage was already done.

Harry left work early that day and started repairing and strengthening the coop. It would not be difficult to replace the hens; he was more concerned about Maela's reaction, for she was deeply attached to every one of his animals. Selling the buck kids had nearly broken her tender heart, though Harry had avoided mentioning their probable fate.

Harry glanced over his shoulder and was surprised to find Maela standing behind him. "Good morrow, child. A sorry day is this." After tapping a peg into place, he tried to stand up and bashed his head on the low doorway of the coop. "Ahh," he grimaced, rubbing the sore spot.

Maela stared at him, her face pinched and sober. He squinted at her out of one eye. "A stoat or weasel carried off two hens, some creature small and strong. Parsley alone is with us still."

The girl nodded, her lips pressed together.

Harry noticed a lack. "Where is Pegasus?" he asked, glancing around the yard. "Did you walk this day?"

Maela turned away, her slender shoulders quaking, and lowered her face into her hands.

In two steps, Harry stood before her. "Dead? Ill? What has become of him?" he demanded.

"I know not; only that his pasture is empty," she gasped. "I believe Dob has taken him and the cart horses to market." She burst into tears, something he had never before seen her do.

Harry swallowed hard. He patted her shoulder awkwardly, uncertain how to react to her tears. Spinning options through his mind, he finally stated, "Today is market day in Hently. I shall attempt to find your horse. Care for the others in mine absence."

He took more than the price of a pony from his hidden store of coins and stuffed it into the hanging pocket tied to his belt. Tossing his cloak over one shoulder, he bade Maela pray for success and struck the road toward Hently, a market town north of Trenton.

Hours later, he believed himself on the right trail. One merchant recalled seeing a burly stranger with a chestnut pony and two cart horses for sale, and he pointed Harry to another merchant who had talked to the seller. This merchant directed Harry to a farm some five miles to the southwest, where he believed the pony's buyer lived. It was a long walk for an uncertain outcome, but Harry was willing to try.

To his surprise, the directions led him, by a circuitous route, to a farm near the outskirts of Marston Hall property. The bleak outline of Castle Trent keep was visible above the treetops as Harry approached the farmhouse.

A slender, pleasant-faced yeoman emerged from the barn. "God give you good day," he greeted respectfully. Harry had seen the man before but did not know his name.

"And you," Harry replied, bowing in return, then extended his hand. "Harold Jameson, joiner at Marston Hall."

"Well met, Jameson. I know you by reputation and have seen you at church. I am called Jonas Fleming. May I give you aid?" Fleming had a firm handshake.

"I trust that you may. I seek a chestnut gelding, nigh eleven hands, no markings, sold this day at market. A merchant told me I might find it here."

"Verily, my son purchased such a horse this day. His mother did wish for a pony to drive. Is it stolen?" The farmer's face was troubled.

"Nay, but I know the horse well and would have purchased it had I known 'twould go to market. 'Tis a child's pet and well loved."

"Ah, indeed." The yeoman scrutinized Harry's youthful face, wondering about this unknown child. " 'Twas Master Dob of Castle Trent that sold it, you know."

Harry nodded. "But the pony belonged to Lord Trenton's daughter, and she consented not to part with it." Something prompted him to trust Fleming with Ishmaela's secret. "I am her tutor and friend, unbeknownst to

Dob Titwhistle or Mistress Hera. The child is a believer, and greatly in need of friends, Master Fleming."

The farmer's bearded cheeks creased in a wide smile. "I thought you had the look of the redeemed. Might you take an interest in our Bible study meetings? Many church members meet independently to search the scriptures each week."

Before Harry could answer, a younger man emerged from the barn, laid eyes on Harry, and stopped short. "Jameson?"

"Fleming! This is your abode?"

"Indeed."

"You are acquainted?" Master Fleming observed with pleasure.

"Militia," Lane explained. "Jameson excels at broadsword."

"And you are expert with the longbow." Harry grinned. Despite his best efforts to be friendly, he had never exchanged more than two or three sentences with Fleming, for the man was painfully shy.

Before long Harry was seated at the farmhouse's rough board, sharing his life story over a tankard of milk and a loaf of bread. Lane Fleming sat opposite. He was a clean-shaven man in his late twenties, as long and lean as his mother was short and wide.

Mistress Rachel Fleming was fascinated by the story of Ishmaela Andromeda Trenton, filling in a few gaps for Harry from her own memory. "I knew Hera Coats many years ago, and her daughter Artemis as well. Old Reuben Coats was a fine tailor and a decent man, worthy of a better wife. Hera was a comely woman, but Artemis's beauty surpassed her mother's by far. Like the goddess of her name she was, white of skin, formed to perfection, with hair of spun gold. After Reuben's untimely death, Hera saw opportunity in the lass and put her in Sir Hanover's way. Being the carnal man he is, His Lordship was overcome by desire and made Artemis his mistress."

Harry was accustomed to crude speech from kitchen maids and field hands, but blunt speech from this wholesome farmwife embarrassed him. He wished she would not speak of sin with such apparent relish. He glanced at Lane, but the other man did not bat an eye. Of course, he must be used to his mother's active tongue.

"Sir Hanover was a well-favored man with flashing dark eyes. Artemis was flattered by his attentions and believed herself in love. She was soon found to be with child. Overjoyed at the prospect of an heir, Sir Hanover showered her with gifts and gave her proud standing in the community. Most knew of his previous marriage, however, and secretly despised Artemis for throwing her virtue away with both hands."

Mistress Rachel finally noticed Harry's discomfiture. "I do abash you, lad? Are you married yourself?"

He gave a quick shake of his head. "Nay."

Her rosy cheeks crinkled when she smiled. "Not for lack of takers, I'll wager." She patted Harry's shoulder as she rose to refill his tankard. "Lane, here, is besieged by local females, and you, too, are a fine figure of a man, Harry the joiner. More milk?"

"Nay, but I thank you." He covered the tankard with one hand. Wishing to resume the former subject, he inquired, "Have you seen the child Ishmaela?"

"Nay, but Jonas would have it that you know the maid."

"That I do, and well. It was a year ago last May that I met her first. The pony was hers, though how she manages to ride it daily without Dob's notice is a puzzle."

"Dob notices little beyond his nose," Lane observed through a mouthful of bread. "The man cares solely for his own comfort. However, he is deadly with the longbow." For a moment, he lifted vivid blue eyes to meet Harry's gaze. It wasn't exactly a smile, but an amiable expression flashed across his craggy features.

Harry's brows lifted. "I shall keep that in mind."

Rachel calculated in her head. "The maid is nigh unto fifteen years of age. Do you think to wed her, Harry?"

Heat flooded Harry's face. He couldn't manage to close his mouth for a moment. "She. . .she is but a child, mistress."

"Fie! Do you love the maid?" It was more of a statement than a question.

"Yea, verily, she is dear to me." Strange emotions rippled beneath his conscious thoughts. Rachel's smug smile irked him.

"I would see this child of Artemis and Sir Hanover, this Ishmaela Andromeda." She chuckled at the mental image such a name invoked. "Will you bring her to us?"

Harry hedged, "Perhaps." The last thing he needed was a nosy old woman to plant suspicions and ideas in Maela's innocent head!

"I am sorry to lose the new pony, but of a certain he must be returned. The child has little else to call her own. Lane shall find me another." Rachel beamed at her son, who did not respond. Harry deduced that Lane simply tuned out much of his mother's prattle, though he did speak to her with respect.

In the end, Jonas and Lane accepted a reasonable price for Pegasus and agreed to keep him in their back pasture, where Ishmaela should be able to collect him easily for her daily rides. The Flemings were husbandmen, but they also raised fine Suffolk cart horses. Pegasus would never want for company, though he would be dwarfed by his companions.

Walking home late that night, Harry whistled cheerfully. A more generous answer to his prayers for help could not have been imagined. Maela's pony was presently tearing mouthfuls of grass from a rich pasture in an ideal location—with Dob none the wiser. Harry also carried a burlap sack full of two clucking pullets; a certain softhearted farmwife couldn't bear to think of a child losing her pony and two pet hens all in one day.

As an extra bonus, Harry had received a personal invitation to attend Bible study services. During his sojourn at the manor he had attended the village church as the law required, making do with the small amount of spiritual sustenance he gleaned from the vicar's dry sermons. Now he had opportunity to worship with other committed believers. He liked the Flemings, in spite of, or perhaps partially because of, Rachel's nosy, motherly ways. Jonas was a pleasant man, and Lane seemed to be an interesting personality.

Harry's cottage was quiet, though smoke trickled from the chimney. After depositing the pullets in the repaired coop, he opened the cottage door quietly. Maela lay curled up on the hearth before the flaring coals with Laitha as a pillow, Ragwort snuggled against the small of her back, Dudley in the curve of her legs, and Parsley peacefully roosting in the crook of her arm.

Dudley's tail whacked the floor as he lifted his head in greeting. Harry squatted at Maela's feet, searching her face in the dim light. His tender smile faded into a frown. What would become of the two of them? This idyllic existence could not continue forever.

"Ishmaela," he called softly. "Ishmaela, I have come home." A pang shot through his heart. This was his home, but only because she was here. "Maela, wake up." He tickled her cheek.

Ragwort stretched and hopped into Harry's lap. Laitha quivered but did not rise. Parsley gave a protesting gargle when Maela rolled to her back and sat up, rubbing her eyes with the back of one hand. The girl blinked; then her eyes grew wide as memory returned. "Harry! Did you find him?"

"Yea, of a truth I found your pony and redeemed him for you."

"Oh, Harry!" She burst into tears for the second time that day and flung both arms about his neck. Harry sat down with a thump, then fell flat on his back with his knees in the air. Maela fell upon him; Ragwort narrowly escaped being crushed by her. He yipped in protest and tugged at Harry's sleeve. Laitha sat up and whimpered. Dudley barked. The chicken fluttered across the room, clucking in fright.

Harry laughed helplessly. "Such a to-do! Why do you weep, child? I tell you the pony is found, and even now he grazes in rich pasture. You shall have him on the morrow; I'll take you to him." Harry patted her back uncertainly. She was heavier than he remembered. Her head rested in the hollow of his shoulder, her cheek pressed to his chest.

Suddenly Maela sat upright, her tear-streaked face averted. "I must go home," she mumbled. "I thank you, Harry."

Before he could say a word, she had dashed out the door and vanished into the night.

Chapter 9

*Therefore I say unto you, What things soever ye desire,
when ye pray, believe that ye receive them,
and ye shall have them.*
MARK 11:24

Maela's new pullets, two red hens with shining feathers, settled quickly into the repaired chicken coop and thrived under her tender care. Within months, they were each producing at least one egg a day. Maela named them Thyme and Pepper.

Harry saw the Flemings at Bible study and at church each week, but, as yet, he did not feel comfortable bringing Maela. One evening, Rachel cornered him. "Harry, lad, when will you bring the lass to meeting? She needs fellowship with other maids; and I perish to meet her."

"I. . .I am uncertain," Harry stuttered lamely. "She has little experience in society. Her raiment is tattered, and. . .I fear that once her existence is widely known, 'twill make her life difficult."

"I am certain that the brethren would be prudent, Harry. We would show only kindness and acceptance to the child. Not one of us lacks sorrow and sin in our past lives. We have no cause to judge a child for the sins of her parents."

Harry remained unconvinced.

It was spring again, a chilly spring that year of 1567. The weather dampened many spirits; yet in at least one young girl's heart, thoughts of love predominated. Lottie's devotion could not be quenched, and Harry's steadfast rejection of her overtures brought about unforeseen results.

One afternoon when Harry arrived home, Maela exploded from the cottage door in a whirlwind of excitement. He laughed aloud at her capers. "Child, I know few other maidens who come aflutter over a fishing venture. To be more accurate, I know of none beside you!"

"Then other maidens lack wisdom and interest," she retorted, skipping about like a rabbit.

"I'll not argue that point," he admitted. "Now hark; I shall return quickly."

Harry entered the shed and emerged with fishing poles and a wicker creel. The jolly pair hiked down the river path with the dogs leaping at their heels. Once Laitha turned back and growled softly, but they took no notice of her. Maela boasted that she would catch the largest fish. Harry assured her that she was mistaken.

At last the pair settled upon the riverbank. "I do enjoy the spring. Snow is gone; the air is cool and delicious—like wine should taste, but doesn't. Have you ever tasted wine, Harry? A dire disappointment it was to me. From here we can see for many miles. The land is like a plowed field—it undulates. Is the sea like that, Harry? Ever have I wished to look upon the sea. Is it like the river, but much more broad? The river is high this day, Harry. The rains have swollen it. I like not how the brown water swirls about these tree trunks. Our customary fishing spot is under water."

Harry managed to slip in a reply. "Indeed, the river is high. The current runs strong, though not fast. We shall remain in this shallow place and cast out into the deep. Bait your hook, Maela, and lower your voice. I care not to have you frighten the fish."

"The water roars far louder than I, Harry."

"But not so rapidly."

Maela wrinkled her nose at him but obediently baited her hook and cast her line. It was a windy afternoon. The sinking sun occasionally peeked between rushing gray clouds, casting its golden light upon gently rolling terrain. Trees wore a pale green glaze of newly budding leaves, while delicate wildflowers peeked through soggy mulch.

Maela's line went taut. She threw off her cloak and pulled with all her strength. The lissome rod bent nearly double. Harry propped up his rod, stood behind her, and together they gave a great jerk. A flopping fish flew over their heads and landed in a wild rose bramble. Maela laughed at the sight of Harry wading into the prickly bushes to retrieve her fish.

"You do laugh like a fool this day, Maela!" Harry chided her. "Calm yourself, child. The county shall be up in arms to defend against this lunatic in our midst!"

She tried to gain control but still giggled occasionally. Harry relented and smiled at her. She did have a contagious laugh, and it was good to hear the once sober child laugh freely.

She admired her gleaming trout as it lay, twitching feebly, in the creel. "It shall give us a sumptuous feast this night."

Then Harry's rod jerked. "What ho!" he shouted in delight. It was a powerful fish. Harry slipped upon the wet grass and accidentally sloshed into the shallows, still fighting that fish. His boots filled with water. Maela followed him without considering how cold the water must be. She gave a yelp at its icy bite but, undeterred, reached for the line, trying to grasp the fish before it could pull free. Dudley stood behind her on the bank, barking in excitement.

"Go to, child! I can do this," Harry protested. "Have a care; the bottom drops off steeply just beyond you there." He grasped the line and hauled in his fish, a magnificent tench that still fought to be free as it dangled from his hand. "Now, who has caught the largest fish this day, eh?"

He looked at Maela, but her startled attention was focused behind him. Ragwort barked hysterically—a piercing scream rent the air—something came crashing down the bank. Dudley dodged, tail between his legs.

Harry pivoted, but his boots would not move. He barely had time to see a body rushing toward him before it barreled past, collided with the tench dangling from his hand, and hit Maela with an ugly thud and a splash. Harry sat down in the water, losing his boots entirely.

He quickly scrambled up, shouting at the cold shock. The fish was gone. His pole was gone. Rising from the water beside him was Lottie, drenched and wailing. Maela was. . .

"Maela?"

Harry spun about and could only watch in shock as Maela surfaced several yards away, sputtering, arms flailing. Her eyes entreated Harry, but her open mouth only took in water. Weighted by her sodden skirts and boots, she was again pulled helplessly under, caught by the relentless current, and swept away.

Harry left his boots in the mud and sprinted barefoot along the bank, crashing through shrubs and saplings as he kept his eyes upon Maela's bobbing figure. At last he caught up and passed her, then launched himself into the river in a wild dive. He thought he had missed her, but then his hand connected with fabric. He grabbed hold and pushed for the shore, pulling her along with him. At this point the river was not deep. Harry found his footing, lifted Maela's limp body into his arms, and sloshed heavily ashore.

Lottie trudged along the bank, wringing the edges of her sodden kirtle. "Is she dead?" Lottie gasped. "Who is she?"

Harry had no breath to spare for explanations. He pressed his ear to Maela's chest and thought he heard a faint heartbeat, though he could not be certain. Placing her facedown, he turned her head to the side and began to push rhythmically on her back. Her mouth hung open; her eyes were closed. She was white and cold.

"Oh, God, please," Harry choked, gasping for his own breath. Still he pushed, but there was no response. Rolling her suddenly to her back, he pressed upon her chest and stomach, striving to push air into her body. He thought he saw movement in her face, but then she was still.

He turned her facedown again, almost fell upon her in his desperation, crushing her beneath him and pressing, rolling. Tears poured from his eyes, but he was unaware. "God, grant me this boon! Oh, God, I love her so! Spare Maela, God, I beg of You!"

Lottie watched with wide, unblinking eyes. Ragwort and Dudley stood beside her, ears pricked, expressions worried. Earlier Laitha had been wandering in the woods, but now she appeared, looking concerned, though she could neither see nor understand the crisis at hand.

Then Maela choked. Water trickled from her mouth, her body convulsed, and a gush of water poured forth. She coughed, retched, vomited, and writhed upon the ground.

Harry was ecstatic. "I thank You, O my God! Your goodness is everlasting!" Rocking back on his heels as he squatted beside Maela, he lifted his hands to the skies and wept now for joy.

"Harry?" Maela croaked. "I'm so cold!" Her teeth chattered audibly. Her face was ashen.

Harry scooped her into his arms and marched back to their fishing spot. He wrapped her in her dry cloak, donned his own cloak, picked up the fishing rod and the creel with Maela's fish and handed them to Lottie. "Carry these."

Lottie grimaced but dared not quibble.

Harry bent down and swung Maela over his shoulder. Her cap was gone, lost in the river. One of her boots was missing. Her bare foot swung high in the air as Harry shifted her weight more evenly. Maela was too weak to protest, though her fingers grasped at his cloak.

Harry did not intend to be rough, but his tangled emotions preoccupied him. Gratitude for Maela's recovery, fear that she would become ill, anger with Lottie, embarrassment at the intensity of feeling he had displayed, worry about the future, exhaustion. . .

He determined to take Maela to the Flemings. Rachel would know how to care for her. She needed a woman's care; Harry was out of his depth.

Not until they were walking along the road did Lottie dare try to explain her presence. "I followed after you, but then a wolf did howl in mine ear and I ran to you, but the bank was steep and I could not stop. I did not intend to knock this. . .person into the river."

"Yonder is your wolf," Harry nodded at the terrier trotting briskly ahead of them. "His bark is greater than his stature. You did deserve your ducking, spy. Almost I hope you fall ill of a fever." His voice sounded flat.

"The dog sounded large; indeed, it did. And I am most dreadfully cold!" Lottie shivered daintily. She wore no cloak, and her damp kirtle kept wrapping about her legs, making it difficult to walk. She hitched it up into her girdle, leaving only her smock to conceal her legs. Light brown curls escaped her cap to bounce upon her shoulders. "Who is this maid, Harry? I know her not." She glanced behind him. "Has she no comb? Never have I seen such filthy hair."

Harry could hardly blame her for noticing. Maela's long hair swung in a heavy, dripping, matted clump. It was disgusting, but Lottie's comments were cruel. He felt Maela flinch.

"Have done!" he growled. He had frequently noticed that Lottie was no sweet-smelling rose herself, but he did not say so. It was nearly dark, and the wind was rising. It whipped through Harry's cloak, slapping it around his boot tops. If he was this cold, how must Maela feel? His back and shoulder aching, he paused to switch sides. She didn't make a sound, just let him drape her over his other shoulder. Heavy though she was, he walked faster. Lottie puffed along, trotting at times to keep up.

"Where are we going?" she demanded. "This is not the way to Marston Hall."

"We go to the Fleming freehold. I would have Mistress Fleming care for Maela's needs."

He felt Maela stiffen in silent protest.

"Wherefore did you follow me, Lottie?" Harry would have the truth of the matter.

"I. . .I came to discern if Dovie told the truth about you."

Lottie glanced at Maela. "Is this wench your lover?"

Harry's voice was dry. "She is but a child. I have no lover; but had I a lover, 'twould most certainly be my lawfully wedded wife!"

"I would marry you, Harry," Lottie offered hopefully, her teeth chattering. "I would be a good wife to you."

With surprising strength, Maela began to struggle. Harry hurriedly set her on her feet. She took two steps, fell in the road, scrambled up, and tried to run again, but he grasped her cloak, pulled her back, and held her, squirming and grunting, her back against his chest. Not this time would Maela run off to the castle!

"Ishmaela, you did but narrowly escape death this day," he reminded firmly.

"Release me!" she ordered. Were tears clogging her voice?

"Nay, I will not." Harry's voice gave no quarter.

"I would return to the castle." Her voice was stony.

"I take you to the house of friends who will care for you." Hearing anger in his own voice, he drew a deep breath and added quietly, "Give them opportunity to show you love, Maela. They are brethren in Christ and of your grandmother's age."

Her little figure went limp. She nodded in surrender.

Harry scooped her back over his shoulder and started walking.

Lottie had not lost her train of thought. Trotting up beside him, she asked breathlessly, "Do you not think I would make you a good wife? I can cook and clean, and I would give you many children."

"I need no wife at present," Harry growled, panting in near exhaustion. Much though he loved her, Maela was a dead weight. He could hear her teeth chatter, and she shivered convulsively.

The Fleming farmhouse reached out to them in welcome. Its windows were warmly lighted. Smoke drifted from the flint chimney.

"Rachel?" Harry called out between puffs. His great chest heaved; his heart pounded.

The door opened before they reached it. "Harry the joiner? Wherefore do you stroll about at this hour—"

She broke off abruptly. "Who is that with you? What are you holding?"

"These are Lottie Putnam—from the manor—and Ishmaela Trenton—who is nigh drowned and freezing. I bring them to you for aid!" he explained between pants.

With many exclamations and much clucking, Rachel ushered all three inside and bade them sit before the crackling fire. Harry carefully ducked through the low doorway and set Maela on her feet, this time holding her upright until she regained her balance. She would not look at him.

Lottie held her hand out to the fire's warmth and hitched up her skirts to warm her legs. "I knew not how cold a body can be," she tried to joke.

"Lane!" Rachel called out the door. "Tell Longwell to bring the washtub inside." She bustled about, giving orders to her hapless maidservant. "You need hot baths, all. The maidens first, of a certain."

Rachel ordered them all to strip, so Harry went into the sitting room for privacy. It was cold, for no fire burned upon its hearth. He handed his clothing through the door. "I remain here while the maidens do bathe," he insisted; though Rachel argued that he would surely freeze. He'd been right to come here; Rachel had things well in hand.

The blanket she had given him itched terribly, but at least it was dry. He bundled into it, lay down upon the wooden settle, and fell asleep.

Lane entered the kitchen. His curious gaze swept the room, taking in the two blanket-shrouded females beside the fire. Rachel hastened to explain and introduced the young women to him. Maela only nodded, too tired to speak. Lane took one look at Lottie and started visibly. She met his eyes and smiled in her friendly way.

"Good even, Master Lane Fleming."

His blue eyes brightened. "Charlotte Putnam. Well met."

At this interesting point, Rachel chased him from the room. "The maidens must bathe. Out with you!"

"A quiet man. He is. . .unwed?" Lottie asked with interest. She tested the water.

While hanging Harry's clothing to dry upon a trivet and a chair, Rachel examined the girl critically, then seemed to approve her. "Verily, Lane is our only living son. He is, as yet, unwed."

Lottie climbed into the steaming tub and settled herself with a sigh. "This is a fine house, and your son is a goodly man. I have heard your name noised in town."

Rachel followed her thoughts with no trouble. Lane stood to inherit the family farm—an enticing prospect to many a single female. "And your family is located where?" she asked the girl.

"Beyond Hently. My father is husbandman on the land of Sir Giles Thorpe."

Bending over Maela, Rachel pulled aside her blanket. "Ah, the poor maid. She sleeps. She is the picture of her mother, though dirty and unkempt. I shall soon make a thing of beauty from this rough fabric." Turning, she asked, "Do you need soap, Lottie Putnam?"

"If you please."

"Harry, waken!" Rachel insisted, shaking his shoulder. "Your bath water awaits."

Harry jumped and sat up, rescuing his blanket just in time. His brain scrambled to recall why he was here.

He blinked groggily at Rachel. "Maela?"

"She sleeps. Lane has escorted your other maiden to the manor, for she must not neglect her work. A buxom lass, that one, and fair. Do you admire her?"

Harry smiled fleetingly. "Lane may have her with my blessing. Maela is not ill?" He returned to his major concern.

"Not as yet. A long soak in hot water did she require ere her skin warmed to the touch, and I did soap her hair three times ere the rinse water ran clear. It would not comb, so I cut a length of it from her. You are welcome to stay the night, Harry, you and your dogs. I'll prepare a pallet for you nigh the fire."

Rachel and Jonas retired to their bedchamber while Harry bathed. Maela was already settled in the loft over the kitchen. Harry's dogs snored contentedly beside the fire.

He bent to rinse his hair with the pitcher. Soapy water cascaded over his face and dripped back into the tub. His knees jutted nearly under his chin, but at least the water was hot and the soap didn't have wilted little flowers in it.

Chapter 10

*Shout for joy, O heavens; rejoice, O earth; burst into song,
O mountains! For the LORD comforts his people and
will have compassion on his afflicted ones.*
ISAIAH 49:13 NIV 1984

Maela felt like a new girl. She pulled her hair over her shoulder and studied its color and texture. Spreading her fingers upon her kirtle, she smoothed it over her hips. Standing in the doorway to soak up a brief patch of early spring sunshine, she twisted her hips back and forth to make the borrowed kirtle swirl about her legs.

She seemed to have taken no permanent harm from her near drowning, and though her chest ached if she breathed too deeply, the pain grew less with each passing hour. Her memories of the day before were fuzzy and troubling.

But for now, she was happy. Her borrowed smock was clean and white. The blue linen kirtle had lain in Rachel's wooden chest since the death of her daughter seventeen years ago; now it hugged Maela's slim waist and swirled about her legs in a satisfying way. It smelled strongly of lavender.

Rachel smiled as she watched the girl preen. An amazing transformation, she congratulated herself. Having seen the matted, greasy mop that once topped the girl's head, Rachel would never have guessed that her hair would be of such remarkable color and texture. Dark red without a hint of curl, it flowed smoothly over the girl's shoulders, gleaming like heavy silk.

"Mistress Rachel," Maela spoke quietly, looking at Rachel with almost reverent eyes. "Did you know my mother?"

Rachel stopped kneading the bread dough for an instant, then resumed her work. "Yea, I did know her better than some. She was of an age with our youngest daughter, Agnes, whose kirtle you wear with such pleasure."

Maela nodded, having already heard Agnes's sad story. Of the Flemings' seven children, only Lane had reached adulthood. A small family cemetery lay behind the Fleming barn. "And Agnes did know my mother?"

"Many's the time I did hear the twain chatter like starlings as they drew water and washed clothing together. Your mother was surpassing fair, yet not so wise as Agnes, for she did like men overmuch. Hera, her mother, did push the maid to be forward, to her great cost." Rachel sighed.

Maela's eyes were sad. "I was that cost?"

Rachel started. "May God forbid that you should think such foolishness, child! You were your mother's joy and comfort amid sorrow. I doubt not she did love you greatly and desired you to know the truths that she came to know too late. Artemis was lovely in her heart, as you well know. 'Twas her bane and her blessing to be among the fairest of women and to take the fancy of Sir Hanover Trenton."

"Beauty, therefore, is a bane? But I so desire to be beautiful to please. . .to. . .to. . ." Maela's cheeks flushed crimson.

"Nay, 'tis not wicked in you to desire to please your man, and he shall be well pleased in you, child. Like a flower you are, in appearance and in scent. These things do please a man."

"Lottie is. . .is round where I am. . .not. He does admire her, I know. I hate her." Maela's dark eyes smoldered.

Rachel said nothing, but a little smile tugged at her lips. She shaped the dough into round loaves and left them to rise.

"It is wicked to hate," Maela reminded her as though prompting a reprimand.

"I think your sin is envy, not hatred, and you do waste it upon a poor maid." She chuckled. "You will cause weeping and gnashing of teeth, child. The maidens shall cast one look at you and despair!"

"But why, Rachel? I understand so little. What is it that maidens do desire of men? What is it that makes my breath come short when Harry smiles at me? He cares for me yet as a child, and such kindness is to me as bitter gall! I cannot comprehend this change in me, and I know not what to do! Surely I cannot speak of this to Harry; yet I know none else in the world—save you."

"Oh, innocent child, bereft of your mother! Surely I shall counsel you in any manner you desire. Come and sit beside me, and we shall speak privately of many things."

Rachel was true to her word and generous with her time. While the bread rose, great mysteries of life that had puzzled Maela for months were at last resolved to her complete satisfaction.

The girl quietly pondered the information she had been given, while Rachel braided her hair. Color came and went in Maela's smooth cheeks, and smiles flitted across her lips. "Shall Harry come here this night?" she asked. "I wish to speak with him. Yet, verily, I must return to the castle, for I shall be missed. I would not cause you trouble."

"You are no trouble, child. 'Tis many a long year since a maid did come to me for advice and training. I enjoy the duty. You will often return to us, Maela? I would have you as companion, for I no longer have a daughter."

"Oh, but you could not keep me away!" Maela assured her. Kissing the older woman's soft, wrinkled cheek, she whispered, "All thanks to you, Mother Rachel. Indeed, you are good to me!"

Rachel dabbed at tears with her apron. "Now, now! Enough of this. Jonas has gone to the smithy with an ailing horse. He would wish to bid you farewell."

"I shall not depart until his return. Presently I wish to visit the kittens in the barn again," Maela announced and skipped outside. "When Harry comes, please tell him my whereabouts."

Shortly after noon that day, a courier arrived at Marston Hall. To the surprise of all, he carried a letter not for any member of the Marston family, but for Harold Jameson, the joiner. Sir David's youngest daughter, Dorcas, delivered the missive to Harry and watched with interest as he broke the seal and opened it.

She saw him stiffen, and all expression erased from his countenance. "Harry, is your news unwelcome?"

He glanced up. The letter in his hand shook. "Yea, Dorcas, 'tis most unwelcome." He stared blankly at her until the little girl backed slowly from the room and ran to tell her father that Harry was stricken. Never before had she seen Harry without his smile.

Harry struggled to work that day, but in spite of his valiant efforts to keep control of his emotions, his eyes blurred and his hands shook. He spent most of the afternoon sanding and polishing—two tasks that trembling hands could accomplish.

He wanted to see Maela. He needed her. He closed his eyes and was overwhelmed by the memory of her cold, deathlike face and clammy hands. Fear smote him again, and he broke into a cold sweat. Although she had not drowned, Maela might be sick and dying at this moment—she might succumb to a deadly illness, like. . .The tightness in his chest constricted his breathing.

"Harry, lad," a kindly voice startled him. He dropped his cloth and straightened, brushing one hand across his eyes. Sir David Marston stood behind him. "Dorcas has told me of your letter. 'Tis dire news of your relations?"

Harry nodded, his eyes upon the floor.

"Alack! My heart sorrows for you, my friend." He lifted a hand to Harry's shoulder, stretching up a little to reach. "I would do all in my power to aid you."

Harry nodded again, unable to speak. Finally he rasped, "Thank you, sir."

"Do you plan to go to your family?"

Harry coughed softly. "Yea. My mother has need of mine aid. I would complete my work here apace and go to her." He indicated the nearly complete fireplace surround, a masterpiece in walnut, depicting the English countryside.

Sir David's eyes caressed the carved foxes, deer, rabbits, butterflies, trees, and flowers, amazed anew at its intricate detail. "In future, your name shall be noised abroad as Master Joiner, Harold Jameson. I tremble and stand amazed before your workmanship."

" 'Tis a gift from God, Sir David, and I must use this gift for His glory and honor. 'Tis an awesome responsibility."

"Then God must be greatly pleased with you, my son. Your work is masterful, and your repute beyond praise at the manor. All herein speak of you with respect and kindness and do marvel at your impeccable honor. I would know more of your creed, for mine own satisfies not my soul. I faithfully attend services and hear scripture read, but Latin or English, I comprehend it not. I have heard you relate the scriptures with alacrity, as though 'tis quick upon your tongue, and you live the life of a saint with joy. Would you take time to tell me of your faith?"

Sir David drew up two chairs and bade Harry join him. For two hours, Harry spoke with him of Jesus, His life, death, and resurrection, and God's power manifested in the daily lives of His people.

"There can be no salvation without Jesus Christ?" Sir David inquired. "What of indulgences, sacraments, and the like? The varied reports between churches oft confuse me. How can a man know which to believe? Men have died for their beliefs on either side, convinced of the truth—yet their beliefs widely differ! How can these things be?"

"I know not, sir. I only know that Jesus claimed, 'I am the way, the truth, and the life: no man cometh unto the Father, but by me.' Churches are composed of men, and men can err. God's Word is our sole immutable source of truth. 'Tis by God's grace we are saved, through faith—and that not of ourselves. It is the gift of God, not of works, lest any man should boast; the apostle Paul wrote these words to the church at Ephesus. Sir, I would invite you to a Bible study. It is composed of brethren who wish to study the scriptures, share thoughts, and encourage one another in the faith. The meetings are unsanctioned by the vicar and bishop, but there is nothing of sedition in our discussions."

Sir David nodded. "I trust that you speak truth, Harry. I cannot explain the joy, the hope you have given me. I feel. . .I feel like a starving man which has been offered a feast." He cleared his throat, swallowed hard. "I know the risk you have taken in extending this invitation. I feel the honor of your confidence and shall strive to be worthy of your trust."

He extended his smooth gentleman's hand, and Harry clasped it firmly.

Harry's heart was still heavy when he left the manor that day, but he was at peace. He had discussed his future with Sir David and felt no anxiety about his imminent departure—the man had been kindness personified, doing all that lay in his power to alleviate Harry's burdens.

Now Harry could think only of Maela. His fears for her had eased, yet he still longed to see her safe.

Before heading toward the Fleming farm, Harry stopped by his cottage for the dogs. They needed a good, long walk. Laitha trotted calmly at his side, while Ragwort darted into every thicket, itching for a good hunt. After spending the day inside the cottage, the terrier was bursting with energy. Dudley vacillated between following Ragwort and sticking close to Harry. The young dog was powerful and fast, yet somewhat timid by nature.

The Fleming barn appeared over a rise, its thatched roof gray with age. Harry scented wood smoke above the blended aromas of plowed fields, new growth, and the early red campion blooming near the tumble of rock wall beside the road, yet the sights and scents gave him little pleasure.

Harry called out as he approached the house. Maela herself appeared in the barn doorway and returned his wave. His heart lifted; his step quickened. She was well and strong as ever!

Yipping with excitement, Ragwort dashed ahead of Harry. "How now, Ragwort?" Maela called cheerily and bent to greet him.

But Ragwort barreled past her and pounced upon a kitten that had followed her from the barn. Two quick shakes of his head and the kitten went limp.

Maela stood as though frozen. Ragwort dropped the dead kitten and wagged his tail at her, grinning happily.

"Shame, Ragwort!" Harry cried, breaking into a jog. He was too late, but perhaps he could rescue other kittens.

Ragwort's stiff little tail drooped. His ears dropped, and his mouth closed. He looked crushed.

Suddenly, Maela snapped into life. Her hands lifted to clutch her head, and she screeched, "Get you hence, monster! Wicked beast! Never shall I forgive you!" She kicked at the dog, but he dodged, tail between his legs, and ran to Harry for protection.

Harry placed his hand on Maela's arm. She jerked away. "How dare you bring that beast hither? He has slain my favorite kitten! Get you hence! I do hate the sight of you!" She burst into tears, scooped up the crumpled kitten, and rushed, sobbing noisily, into the barn.

Laitha squatted just inside the gate, waiting quietly. Failing to receive consolation from Harry, Ragwort went to her for comfort. She nuzzled him and allowed him to press against her side. Dudley rollicked around them, oblivious to the tense atmosphere.

Harry bowed his head and pinched the bridge of his nose. *Lord, grant me wisdom—and comfort Maela's heart. I know not how to make this right with her.*

Inside the barn, Maela sat upon a bench with the kitten in her lap. She stroked its soft fur, but her eyes stared vacantly across the barn.

Harry stopped before her. He pulled off his cap and fiddled with it. "I cannot tell you with words of the regret in my heart," he said quietly. "I would help you bury the cat."

Maela nodded. Harry selected a spade from a peg on the barn wall, knowing Jonas would not mind, and led the way to a corner of Pegasus's pasture. He dug, and Maela watched in silence, shivering with cold. Harry stopped digging long enough to shift his cape to her back. She accepted it but said nothing. When the hole was deep enough, Maela tenderly laid the kitten to rest. She walked back to the barn while Harry filled the hole and laid stones upon it.

When Harry rejoined her in the barn, she scooted over to give him room on the bench, though she did not look at him. A tear trickled down her cheek; she smeared it with her fist and sniffed. Harry offered her a handkerchief and she honked her nose into it.

"You should not have brought that dog," she stated coldly. "You know he does hunt small creatures."

"I knew not that he would kill a kitten," Harry admitted.

His gentle tone took some of the starch from her back.

"I hate death, Harry. It is cruel!" She ended in a wail and fresh tears.

Harry said nothing.

Footsteps approached from without, and Jonas entered, leading a limping cart horse. "Good even, Harry lad. How is it with you? And Maela, dear maid."

"Well enough, Jonas. And with you?" Harry rose respectfully, patting the horse's rump as it passed him.

"I find nothing to complain of." Jonas smiled. "God is good. Farley, here, has a bruise on his sole, nothing serious. I feared that he was ruined, but all for nothing." He patted the horse's thick chestnut neck. Tethering it in a clean stall, he began to brush it down.

"Harry's dog slew the spotted kitten," Maela told Jonas, like a child in need of a father's condolences.

"I am sorry," Jonas said sincerely. "You may have another as your own, if you wish it. We lack not for cats."

Maela considered the offer. "I would fear for its safety in the castle. It would find mice aplenty, but I fear that Grandmere's tom would kill it. I think I must leave the kittens here where they can be most happy," she decided regretfully. "Death is cruel, Master Jonas."

He nodded in agreement. "Nevertheless, it is part of life. Until Christ's kingdom is fulfilled and He ends sin and death, we must accept the reality of death in this world. Just as we rejoice at a birth, so we mourn at a death. 'To every thing there is a season. . .a time to be born, and a time to die.'"

"Is that a quote?"

"Yea, from Ecclesiastes, written by the wise King Solomon. Perhaps at meeting you can hear more of it."

"Mistress Rachel has told me of these meetings."

Harry turned and walked out of the barn. "Harry, where. . . ?" Maela began, but he was gone. She turned her puzzled gaze to Jonas.

"Harry has a sorrow, Maela. You did not observe it?"

"Nay, I was absorbed in. . .mine own sorrow. What is it, Jonas?"

He shook his head. "I know not. You must discover for yourself."

Maela found Harry behind the barn, seated in the bed of a wagon, elbows propped on his upraised knees, watching horses graze in a back pasture. Hopping up beside him, she scanned his face. He would not meet her gaze. "Harry, tell me your sorrow, I beg of you! Forgive my selfish anger—'twas foolish in me, I trow."

He only sighed softly, blowing through his lips. She heard the catch in his breath. Hesitantly, she reached out to him, taking his hand in hers. His hand was cold, lumpy with calluses, and rough as she held it between her own warm hands. He must be cold, for she still wore his cloak. That was just like Harry—always thinking of others, never a thought for his own ease.

Harry turned to her, really seeing her for the first time that day. He had seldom beheld her without a cap, and never with clean hair. A gust of wind pushed clouds away from the setting sun, allowing a beam to rest upon her head, turning her hair to fire.

His free hand reached into his jerkin and pulled out the crumpled letter. Maela released his hand to take it. "This arrived at the hall," he explained shortly.

She read it quickly and gave a horrified cry. "Your father, your brother and his wife, and their children—all gone! Oh, Harry! I wept over a kitten, while you. . . Can you forgive me?"

Then she was crushed into his arms and felt his entire frame shaking. At first he was silent, but as his grief continued to pour forth, it escaped in racking sobs. Maela had never before heard a man cry—she felt as though her heart would break with his sorrow. She wept with him, wetting his jerkin with her tears while he dampened her neck and shoulder. When his weeping subsided, she wiped her face and his with Harry's handkerchief. It was quite moist by this time.

His reddened eyes and swollen face cut her to the quick. Wishing to console him, she reached up to pull his head down and kissed his forehead. "Harry, what shall you do anon?"

"I must repair home. My present work at the hall is nigh completion. I shall finish the surround, then depart. Sir David knows that I must go, for my mother has need of mine aid. He has been exceedingly kind."

"And what of me?" Her voice sounded small.

"I shall return for you, Maela; I know not when. I am now the eldest son; after me came five sisters—four yet living—and my eldest brother is but eleven. Mother expects another child in autumn and cannot farm alone. Her father, my grandfather, abides with them, but his strength is limited."

"How long shall you remain here at present?" Seeing him shiver, she removed his cloak, secured it around his shoulders, then crawled beneath it and snuggled against him with only her face peeking out. Almost absently, he wrapped his arm around her shoulders.

"A fortnight, at most. Maela, I would have you attend church and fellowship with the Flemings. These friends shall support you during mine absence."

"Mistress Rachel said that she has long besought you to bring me to worship. Are you ashamed of me, Harry?"

Put on the spot, Harry floundered. "Ashamed, nay, but. . .afraid. I feared alteration in. . .the special way we are together. . .or were. 'Twas selfish in me, I know." He could not look at her.

"Not selfish, Harry, for I feel the same. I have ever been jealous of your time and attention."

"We did spoil one another, mayhap." Harry smiled but felt even more uncomfortable. Their friendship had but rarely included physical contact, and her infrequent caresses had never discomposed him. Could this be the same fearful, wary maid who had shunned any man's touch? Why did she now nestle against his side as though by habit? And why did hot blood rush to his face and disquieting thoughts possess his mind?

"I am thankful for your introduction to these good Flemings. Mistress Rachel has taught me how to clean my teeth with a broken mint twig and how to dress my hair. Is it not pretty how she has bound it? I am clean everywhere—and I must at last admit the truth in your assertions that cleanliness is good. I feel. . .wondrous fine. Mistress Rachel sprinkled my hair with rosewater, and she has given me a bottle of mine own."

"You are a new creation without as well as within."

"May I come with you to Lincolnshire?" She sat up straight and looked into his eyes.

Harry could not move. He vividly recalled the scented softness of her hair against his face. Heat swept through him, and a frightening desire to take her as wife, come what may. His eyes closed as though in pain. "Greatly though I desire this, it cannot be, Maela."

She stiffened and pushed herself upright. "Mean I nothing to you?"

He tried to swallow but could not for the dryness in his throat. "I would not leave you, but I must! You are Sir Hanover Trenton's daughter. Never would he consent to such a match."

"We could marry without his consent," she begged. "We could, Harry! I want nothing more than to be with you all my life. Surely this is God's will, for He brought us together." She flung her arms around his neck.

"We would ever live in hiding. As criminals we would run from the law." Harry held her tenderly. "Your father would leave no stone unturned, for you have value in his eyes. Should we then be found, I would be hanged, and you would face worse than death. It cannot be so, Maela. Such a life cannot be God's plan for His children. 'Twould be misery, and you would soon learn to hate me for bringing you into it for mine own selfish gain."

"Nay!" she protested into his shoulder. "Not for your gain, but for mine! The bishop desires me not as wife, but as his slave! Surely you know. . ." She faltered and stopped.

Rachel's lecture had finally solved some of the puzzles in Maela's brain, and not all of these completed puzzles were pleasant to contemplate—such as precisely why the bishop would have her as his slave. But she could not speak of such things to Harry. Realizing how forward her marriage proposal must sound to him, she fell silent, blushing deeply and thankful for the falling dusk.

Harry could only shake his head as he allowed her to pull from his grasp. "We must wait upon the Lord, Maela. He will preserve and defend us in His time. We must not take matters into our hands and attempt to work our plan in His name. Suffering would come of it; of this I am sure."

She drooped. He tried to think of something comforting and loving to say, but his mind was blank. He climbed off the wagon and helped her down. She allowed him to envelop her in his cloak, and they walked back to the house, side by side.

The Flemings invited Harry to remain for the evening meal; afterward he would escort Maela back to the castle. Rachel wished to spend every last minute with Maela, and Jonas absorbed Harry in conversation about biblical principles and obscure scripture passages.

Lane had wandered over to the manor that night, undoubtedly to visit Lottie. Rachel was delighted with her son's budding romance, for despite her claims about his popularity, he had always been too shy to court a woman. She and Jonas had nearly given up hope of ever becoming grandparents.

At last Maela stood before the men with a sack of clothing in one hand, a loaded basket in the other. "Rachel has sent a propitiation of biscuits and strawberries to my grandmother, hoping to ease my way. I know not what has occurred in mine absence, but I do know that Grandmere will be angry."

"You are prepared at last," Harry observed, rising slowly and smoothing his jerkin. "I thought perhaps Rachel had persuaded you to remain for aye."

Maela flushed and dropped her gaze to the floorboards. "Verily, I am tempted to remain."

"One last kiss, my child," Rachel requested, folding the girl into her arms. "Come to us if ever you have need."

"I will," Maela agreed. She then hugged Jonas and kissed his leathery cheek. "Extend my farewells to Lane upon his return."

Maela's path from the Fleming's back pasture to the castle was difficult to find in the dark. Harry tripped over hidden obstacles while Maela seemed to glide along like a ghost. He could see her when occasional breaks in the trees allowed moonlight to silver her white cap and face, but her expression was unreadable.

"I have come to the castle only once ere now," he observed, "when you were ill. Remember? 'Twas a stormy night, and cold."

"I recall as though it were last night," she answered. "I feared for your safety, but God did protect you."

"I used your secret tunnel. Do you plan to return hence this night?"

"Nay, I shall walk through the castle door. Mine absence is no secret, and my return must be open or Grandmere shall wax suspicious."

"And Dob?"

"You are with me. I fear not Dob with Harry at my side." She sounded both timid and brave. "Grandmere is more to be feared. She did beat me the last time I stayed away overlong. But then I was a child and had no strength." Harry watched her lift her free hand and clench her fist as though to show off powerful muscles. Knowing how slender her arms were, he was not reassured.

"She had best not lay hand to you while I'm near," Harry muttered grimly. "Come to me straightaway if she tries it." He shifted Rachel's heavy basket of food to his other hand.

"Mistress Rachel has instructed me that I must no longer go alone to your cottage. It is not seemly, since I am no longer a child."

Harry had feared as much, yet he knew Rachel was right. Unfamiliar feelings now stirred within him, powerful feelings that might prove difficult to control.

"May I visit you at the castle?"

She immediately shook her head. "I dare not attempt such boldness, Harry. Grandmere would dislike it. I did promise Rachel this day to attend church. I will see you there, and perhaps we can meet at their home."

She turned and continued on toward the castle. Harry followed in her wake.

A dark blot appeared against the starry sky—the castle keep. Minutes later they stood before the kitchen door. It was locked. Harry pounded with closed fist.

"What shall I say?" Maela squeaked, now that it was too late for planning.

"The truth, though not too much of it," Harry advised.

They heard nothing from within until the door creaked open. "What is it?" Hera Coats asked, holding a candle up to light their faces. "Who are you? We take no lodgers at Castle Trent. Away with you!"

"Grandmere?" Maela quavered.

Hera's bloodshot eyes opened wide. "Ishy? Whatever. . . ? Wherefore came you to be out with this stranger? I did believe you sick abed!"

The realization that she had not even checked on her granddaughter's health roused Harry's wrath, but he held it in check. The old woman had a gray pallor upon her cheeks. Perhaps she herself had been ill.

"I did fish her out of the river yesterday. The Flemings took her in and cared for her. Mistress Rachel Fleming sends you greetings, Mistress Coats."

"And these biscuits and berries," Maela added, taking the laden basket from Harry.

Hera's mouth opened and closed a few times. "And how did you come to be in the river, blaggard?" she snapped at Maela.

"I did sneak out," Maela admitted, truthfully enough. "I intended not to fall into the river."

This turn of events had evidently shaken Hera Coats. Reaching out a clawlike hand, she grabbed Maela's arm and dragged her inside. Two berries fell to the floor and rolled into bleak darkness beyond Harry's view. "To your chamber, wench. I shall settle accounts with you later."

Then her cold blue eyes pinned Harry to the spot. "What do you want of the wench? She is not for a commoner—she, the daughter of a great lord. Begone, knave, ere I call the guard."

Thinking of his last clash with "the guard," Harry restrained a bitter smile. He saluted the old woman respectfully, saying, "Fare you well."

He marched away without a backward glance, though his heart cried prayers for Maela's protection.

Chapter 11

And, lo, I am with you always, even unto the end of the world.
MATTHEW 28:20

'T hey that wait upon the Lord shall renew their strength; they shall mount up with wings as eagles,'" Maela quoted softly as she stood upon a rickety table, leaned both arms on the narrow windowsill, and gazed across the countryside. "Ever have I loved the prophet Isaiah's words and sought to hide them in my heart. Now they shall comfort me in my sorrow. Jesus is with me always, though Harry cannot be."

Setting her jaw, she stated, "I shall strive to please Jesus with my thoughts and actions. When Harry returns, he will be pleased with me. I shall attend church and learn more of the scriptures and of God, with or without Harry the joiner." Hopping down from the table, she whisked across the chamber and opened the door with a flourish.

A search through one of her mother's old chests had produced a treasure trove of clothing, scented soap balls, and a tortoiseshell comb and brush set. Most women possessed but one set of garments; Maela now owned seven, not counting Agnes Fleming's hand-me-downs. This was wealth, indeed.

Clad in one of her mother's embroidered smocks and a puce kirtle and waistcoat, she tied a white cap over her neatly bound braids, hurried downstairs, and marched openly through the kitchen. "Grandmere, I go to church this day. I shall return late." Before Hera could do more than stare in reply, she was gone, running down the road like a deer.

She was too late for the regular church service, but Harry had thought she would prefer the Bible study meeting anyway. It usually took place Sunday afternoon. Master Tompkins, the vicar, seldom audited the doctrine being taught; he preferred his afternoon nap. This was fine with the attending believers; the vicar's sermons tended to lull his flock to sleep.

National church leaders would have frowned heavily upon the meetings being held in the stone church building, but Master Tompkins did not wish to cause trouble, and the bishop was seldom around. Therefore, Trenton parish flourished and grew in knowledge of the scriptures of its own accord with little fear of reprisal.

People squeezed together on the benches, women on one side, men on the other. A hush fell over the crowd when Harry entered with Sir David Marston. Many eyes widened, glued to the nobleman's flushed face. Sir David had always attended the liturgical service, never the Bible study. Lane Fleming scooted over to make room and waved to them. Harry nodded his gratitude, and the two men settled on the bench.

Maela knew Harry had not spotted her, for Rachel sat on the end of their bench, hiding her from view. She had not seen him for three days—it was difficult to keep from peeking around Rachel for a sight of him, especially since his remaining time in Trenton was dwindling rapidly.

The Bible teacher was a wainwright from Cambridge who had come to work in town for a few months, supplying dung carts and a few wagons for the local populace. He opened the huge Bible and began to read aloud from Isaiah. For two hours, he read and spoke of God's compassion for His people, of Israel's perfidy, and of God's anger and forgiveness. It was a new passage for Maela, and she soaked up the scripture with a rapt expression.

Sir David was not the only newcomer to create a stir. Several young girls tried to examine Maela without turning their heads. A few young men were equally interested in the new maiden, casting their eyes across the aisle. Though her bright hair was hidden beneath her cap, her face was sufficient to capture their attention. Maela was unaware of their scrutiny; Rachel noticed and was pleased.

After the service, one of the girls introduced herself as Hepzibah, daughter of the coppersmith. Maela felt shy, but she listened while the other girl chattered, and she soon began to relax. It was another novel experience for her to spend time with girls of her own age. Two other girls soon joined the group. One of them was married and held a baby on her hip. The baby fascinated Maela. She had never seen anything more amazing than this tiny boy with his soft brown curls and dimpled arms. Maela forgot to look for Harry. She forgot everything but the fun of companionship and girlhood.

Sir David was also welcomed into the family of believers. Yeomen, husbandmen, merchants, and craftsmen alike welcomed him as their brother when he professed his faith in Jesus Christ. Joy radiated from his countenance—none could doubt his sincerity.

While the men talked, Harry watched Maela from across the room as she took the baby from its mother and cuddled it close. She looked mature in her new clothes—too mature. Had Rachel given her that embroidered smock with the scalloped neckline?

Yet it was good to see the girl clean, blooming, happy, healthy. . .lovely. . .and no longer in need of him. He could no longer provide for her, so God had removed her from his hands and placed her, in a sense, with a proper family. It was right and good. So why did he feel as though he had received a fatal wound from a well-driven halberd?

"Harry, have you heard about your little friend? The red-haired maiden—your fishing companion? Lane tells me she now dwells with his parents." Lottie stopped to chat while dusting the hall.

"Come again?" Harry was sanding down the last portion of his masterpiece—a magnificent red deer, carved with its antlers thrown back, its mouth agape as it bugled a challenge to its foes.

"The maid you rescued from drowning—I cannot recall her name. 'Tis a frightful scandal about town; I cannot believe you have not heard of it. Hera Coats was found dead, and the little maid found sanctuary at the Flemings. Dob Titwhistle has disappeared, and rumor indicates he headed for Parminster Court. The bishop likely enticed him away with higher wages."

Harry decided it was time for a break. Climbing down from the ladder, he picked up his tools. His mind ran in circles.

Lottie followed him to the door. "Lane made this known unto me last evening as we walked out together. Shall you take your leave soon despite these happenings, Harry? I believed you did love the maid."

"I must repair home. My family depends upon me." Harry felt like tearing out his hair. This exigency would surely bring Lord Trenton to his castle in a hurry, and then what would become of Maela? She was now "ripe" enough to tempt even the bishop.

He could not deny his hurt that Maela had run to the Flemings for aid, not to him. And yet, it served him right. He would soon be leaving her in her time of great need.

Harry simply told Master Lyttleton, "I have emergency business of a personal nature. The carvings will be complete tomorrow as planned." And he left.

It was a cool, dismal morning. Fog lay thickly in shallow vales and drifted haphazardly across the road. At times, Harry could scarcely see his hand before his face. He felt his spirits drooping and fought to keep them high.

The Fleming farm looked deserted and dreary, though smoke trickled from the chimney. Pegasus grazed near the roadside fence; he spotted Harry and whickered a friendly greeting. Harry took a moment to ruffle the pony's thick mane. Pegasus was getting older, like Samson. His face was sprinkled with white hair.

Another horse joined them at the fence, hoping for a treat. It was an immense gray, dappled beneath and nearly white above. Its mane and tail were dark at the roots and white at the ends. Heavy white feathering made boots around its black feet. Its skin was dark gray, and its eyes looked very dark upon that white face. Harry had never seen such a horse—the top of his head scarcely reached its withers. Its coloring was unusual and quite handsome.

"That gelding shall be yours," Jonas said from behind him, making Harry start.

"Indeed! I have not the means to pay for such a beast. It looks strong enough to pull your barn from its foundation. It must stand eighteen hands!"

"Verily, it is strong indeed, but contrary, high-spirited, and ever hungry. My Suffolk horses pull well enough, are calm in spirit, amenable, and eat half as much. I must let this fine beast go. I bought it at market some months past, captured by its handsome face and impressive muscle, though it was in poor condition at the time. Not a sennight passed ere I knew 'twas a mistake. Its will is as strong as its neck, and it cares not to pull a plow. Even Lane confessed himself out of patience with the beast."

"And it is to be mine for the agreed-upon price?" Harry could scarcely believe his luck. "It has the aspect of a warhorse, a charger."

"No doubt that was its origin."

"Is it broken to saddle?"

"Yea. Should it displease you, you may freely choose another. I would not cheat you, Harry."

"I know that. I trust your judgment, Jonas." Harry patted the horse's shoulder and suddenly remembered. "Maela! Is she here with you?"

"She is in the barn," Jonas answered simply. "You did come to see her?"

"Has she departed the castle for aye?"

"I know not. Only that she came to us in her need, and we shall keep her while we may. Do you wish to ride the horse? Its saddle is in the barn. I will prepare it for you."

Harry couldn't resist. "If you would."

Jonas walked with Harry to the barn and picked out a large head collar. "I shall call when he is saddled."

Harry nodded and waited for Jonas to leave before inquiring, "Maela, where are you?" There was no sign of the girl.

"In the loft."

Harry climbed the ladder and hauled himself up. He waited for his eyes to adjust to the dark. Something scurried amid the mounds of hay. There was a thump, a squeak, and a large tabby cat appeared along the wall with something dangling from its mouth.

"Is that the mother of your kittens?" he asked.

"It is the father, I believe," a quiet voice replied from his left.

"I did not bring the dogs with me this time."

She didn't answer, so he went on. "I heard of your grandmother's death. Lottie told me this morn. I came straightaway to find you."

She crawled toward him slowly, for her smock entangled her legs. Her kirtle was looped up and tucked into her leather belt. When she reached him, he took her hand. "Tell me all."

Maela's low voice trembled. "Grandmere went outside. I heard her shout and Dob shout, and then silence. I suspected no tragedy, for they often fight. But then I heard Dob enter the castle—he has entered it not since she laid the curse. Somehow I knew then that she was dead. She has been ill, but I knew not that her death was near. I ran and hid myself until Dob quit searching and calling for me. Then I packed up my raiment and fled here. I wanted you, Harry, but. . .I may not have you."

"Maela," Harry blurted in dismay. "I am ever your friend! Conceal not your troubles from me."

Jonas called from below. "Your horse awaits, Harry."

"Your horse?" Maela echoed.

"Perhaps. We shall see if it will be my horse. I must not make Jonas wait." He descended from the loft, then waited for Maela to follow.

Seated at the top of the ladder, she peered shyly down at him. "Away, Harry. I shall follow in my turn."

He obediently turned his back and waited until she slipped her hand into his. He gave it a quick squeeze, then dragged her outside toward the gelding, which pawed the ground with a hoof the diameter of Maela's head. She pulled her hand away and retreated to the barn doorway.

"The giant gray," she breathed in awe. "Can you ride such a horse, Harry? Have you ridden before?"

"I have oft ridden, but I shall not know whether I can ride this horse until I try it." Harry took the horse's reins and let Jonas give him a leg up.

Once he was in the saddle, the horse danced in place, an impressive sight. Its neck, shoulders, and haunches bulged with muscle, and its mouth gaped and slavered as it champed the bit. It snorted and shook and rattled its tack, making far more noise than Maela liked.

Harry's face shone. To Maela's surprise, he apparently enjoyed this display. He slapped the animal's neck and laughed aloud. "Grand fellow!"

"I would advise you to ride first within the pasture," Jonas said calmly, opening the gate for Harry and the horse.

Harry guided the horse through the gate, then gave it rein and requested more speed. The great horse nearly reared as it leaped into motion. With the sound of thunder it pounded across the field. Harry's hat flew off; his hair lifted in the breeze. The pair disappeared into the fog.

Maela looked at Jonas. He smiled. "Fear not, child. Harry manages the beast well. I was not certain of this horse for him, but now I know that it will do."

The earth shook, and horse and rider loomed out of the fog. "Would you ride with me, Maela?" Harry asked. His eyes were sparkling, and his white teeth showed through his dark beard when he smiled.

Maela hesitated, looking at that awesome creature. But when her eyes returned to Harry's, she could only nod. He reached down, Jonas boosted her up, and she flew to the horse's back. They were off again, racing through the silvery mists. The pasture sloped slightly downward. Maela wrapped her arms tightly around Harry's waist, closed her eyes, and hid her face between his shoulder blades.

"He is incredibly strong," Harry exulted. "He notices not your weight. To him, you are a feather!"

"What will you call him?" Maela shouted, then gulped when the horse hopped over a small ravine.

"I have not decided. Do you like him?"

"I prefer my Pegasus."

She felt Harry's chuckle. He slowed the horse to a walk. Maela could scarcely believe how wide her legs had to stretch to straddle its vast back. She was going to be sore after this ride.

"I never dreamed that I should possess such a beast. He shall carry me to Lincoln within three days! He is not so very fast, but ever so strong. He will never tire, I believe."

A great knot formed in Maela's chest. It had become a familiar knot during these past weeks, forming whenever thoughts of Harry's departure recurred.

"Thursday, I head north," Harry told her bluntly. "I would not leave you, but I have no choice. I shall return as soon as ever I may. You may write to me. I will write to you."

"I know not whereof to write, and I know not how to send a letter."

"Jonas would arrange delivery for you, I am certain. Write to me of

Samson, Pegasus, the hens, and the goats. Tell me of Dudley, for I shall leave him here to protect you. Tell of your meetings with the brethren, of friends you have made. I would know your thoughts and feelings, as ever, and I would share mine own with you. I would tell you of Laitha and Ragwort and of this horse."

"Saul."

"Come again?"

"I suggest the name King Saul, for your horse stands head and shoulders above his fellows."

Harry laughed. "Indeed he does. I accept your suggestion with gratitude. Saul he shall be from this moment."

He leaned forward and slapped the horse's shoulder. "Saul, my fine fellow, we shall return to the barn now, if you please." He nudged the horse's sensitive sides, and King Saul obligingly burst into a rapid trot.

"Oof," Maela protested, so Harry asked for a canter, and the ride smoothed dramatically.

Wednesday afternoon, Harry collected his pay and took leave of Sir David Marston, his family, and the servants. He was gratified by the sorrow shown on his behalf.

"If ever you return to Suffolk, my house is open to you—our finest guest room for my beloved brother in Christ. No fee, no honor can repay the debt I owe you, my friend."

Harry flushed, abashed. Sir David chuckled, shaking his hand vigorously. "Or, should you prefer, we shall find work for you, Harry. Lady Sarah desires a carved bedstead."

"Indeed, I do, Harry!" his wife agreed.

"The coppice cottage shall ever be open for your use—you have improved it beyond measure during your tenure."

"I am hopeful of return, sir, and I thank you for your surpassing kindness. 'Twas an honor to serve you. God bless you and your house."

"Return to us quickly, Harry!" little Dorcas called.

George, Lottie, Simon, and others of Harry's friends were equally sorry to see him go. He was touched by their kind words and wishes for his return. He had never before realized how many friends he possessed at the manor.

He cleaned out the cottage and closed its door for the last time. The roses climbing around its door were budding; in a day or two they would burst into color. Maela's flower garden would be desolate this year; the kitchen garden would fill with weeds. A lump caught in Harry's throat as memories flooded over him: Maela lying before the fire with her head on

Laitha's back, milking Genevieve, laboring in her garden, romping with Ragwort, toasting bread and cheese over the fire. Together, he and Maela had turned this old cottage into a home. He was sorry to leave it.

That night, he sat before another fireplace in a ladder-backed chair that creaked ominously beneath his weight. His hands, for once, idle, he stared into the fire, his mind busily mapping out his route to Lincolnshire. Because he must skirt the marshy fens and good roads were infrequent, he estimated three long or four shorter travel days. Considering Saul's stamina and strength, Harry hoped for three days.

Maela sat at Harry's feet with Ragwort in her lap; she and the dog had reconciled days before. Dudley curled around her bottom like a pillow, his long head on Harry's foot. Laitha lay stretched upon the hearth, kicking slightly in her sleep. Rachel and Jonas also sat before the fire—Rachel knitting, Jonas polishing tools. Lane was out with Lottie again.

As the fire crackled, Maela's hair shimmered like an autumn wood in sunlight. Harry's eyes rested upon it.

"At what time shall you take your leave come the morn, Harry?" Rachel asked.

"I set out ere dawn. I shall try to make Cambridge on the morrow, Stamford the second day, and home, nigh Scamblesby, the third evening."

"I packed a bag of food for you—bread, bacon, fruit, vegetables, and the like. Plenty to last you a day or two. Have you fodder for the horse?"

"Jonas has seen to that."

Rachel shook her head sadly. "Maela shall pine for you, I doubt not."

"And I shall sadly miss her company." Again he looked down at the girl. Long lashes fluttered against her pale cheeks. She would not look at him.

"You shall have your family and many other young companions to fill your need of fellowship, as shall Maela. Now, as to accommodations this night: Lane will share his bedchamber, or you may repose here upon the kitchen hearth. The sitting room is chill."

"This hearth is adequate for my needs."

Rachel nodded. "I shall find you a blanket."

Maela gently put Ragwort from her lap, rose, and walked to the ladder. Without a backward glance or word, she climbed to her loft bedroom. Harry turned puzzled eyes upon Rachel. Why was Maela again leaving him alone with no explanation?

Rachel only smiled, then rose to find the promised quilt.

Harry lay awake long after the *couvre-feu*, the metal dome that protected embers during the night, was in place and everyone else in the house had retired. He had rolled up his cape to pillow his head. Laitha and Dudley lay full length against his sides, snoring softly. Ragwort curled between his feet.

A rustle came from the loft. Harry thought he saw movement at the top of the loft ladder, but thick darkness made him uncertain. Stealthy footsteps confirmed his suspicion. Maela was climbing down. Did she need to use the jakes?

Her feet padded softly in the fresh reed matting. Harry saw her as a dim white figure approaching. His stomach clenched into a knot.

"Maela?" His whisper made no sound.

She knelt down beside him. Laitha whimpered and sat up, placing her paw in Maela's lap. Maela wrapped her arm around the dog and bade her hush.

"I could not let you depart without a word, Harry," she whispered. "I could not look at you this night lest my tears begin to flow, for I fear that I shall not look upon your face again until we meet in heaven. You are my greatest blessing next to Jesus Christ, and I will love you ever."

Harry tried desperately to think of a calm, controlled answer; but when Maela's soft lips touched his forehead, he could not check his startled gasp.

She jerked away. "Harry, I thought you did slumber!"

He sat up, dropped his face upon his upraised knees, and groaned, "Would that I did."

Silence stretched long between them before Harry said, "Go back to bed, Maela." Without a word, she returned to her loft bedroom.

Harry lay awake for a long time. *Lord, I need Your comfort and strength, for my heart is sore afflicted!*

Harry's departure seemed almost anticlimactic. After helping Lane, Jonas, and the hireling with the morning chores, Harry ate heartily of Rachel's wheat cakes and honey, fried salt pork, dried fig compote, and fresh milk. Rachel had insisted that he take a meal before departing. She bustled about at the fire, rosy and bright no matter the hour.

Maela did not appear until Harry had nearly finished eating. When she did clamber down her ladder, she looked as though she had been crying throughout the night. Her eyelids were swollen, her cheeks blotched. Hair had pulled loose from her frazzled braid and dangled around her face.

She looked desperate until her eyes lighted upon Harry. "Oh, I feared you had gone and I had missed you!" she gasped. Her hand quickly covered her lips, and color crept into her cheeks.

Harry gulped a bite of wheat cake without chewing it well enough. It hurt all the way down. He took a drink of milk and wiped his mustache with the back of his hand. "Would I depart and not bid you farewell?" he growled. "What manner of man do you consider me, Maela?"

She looked abashed. "I did but fear it in my dreams, Harry."

It was time to leave. Rising, Harry thanked Rachel and Jonas for the lodging and board. "You are kind friends indeed," he said haltingly. "A man could not ask for better. I cannot tell you how thankful I am that Maela may stay here at your house."

"Your horse awaits you at the gate," Lane said from the doorway. He had saddled King Saul while Harry ate.

"Let us ask the Lord's blessing upon your journey," Jonas suggested.

They joined hands in a circle and bowed their heads as Jonas requested God's traveling mercies for Harry. Maela's little hand was cold in Harry's grasp.

"All thanks to you, Brother Jonas." Harry heartily shook Jonas's hand, then embraced him. "I shall miss your quiet wisdom and generous nature."

Lane shook his hand. "God give you good journey, Harry."

"Harry, my boy!" Rachel hugged him. She was very soft in his arms, like a warm, living feather pillow. Tears trickled down her round cheeks as she backed away. "Come back to us."

Harry felt tender toward her. "Mistress Rachel," he said softly. "I honor your kind heart."

Maela held back at first, but when Harry looked lovingly at her, she threw herself into his arms and sobbed. He held her close and pressed a kiss upon her head. "I shall love you always, Maela."

Chapter 12

*Wait for the LORD: be strong and take heart
and wait for the LORD.*
PSALM 27:14 NIV 1984

"You are lost in your mind again, Harry," Rosalind Jameson chided her older brother. "Do you dream of your beloved?"

Harry blinked and resumed scratching Ragwort's back. "Perhaps," he allowed. He sat upon the doorstep, looking out at rolling hills. It was mild for November. Evening sunlight streamed across the hilltops, leaving the vales in shadow.

"In your mind, you do kiss her?" the girl teased unmercifully. Rosalind was lately betrothed to a local tanner, and her mind was consumed by thoughts of romance. Harry often found her company tiresome.

"Rosalind!" their mother intervened. "Have done! Harry pines after the damsel enough without your taunts to remind him of her. I would have you finish the laundering, maiden. Your idle hands give me no aid."

Standing in the doorway, Susan Jameson smoothed her apron over her shrinking belly. Her baby boy was now a month old, bringing the total of living Jameson children to nine. Four had died in childhood, and Horace, the eldest, just last winter, along with his wife and two children.

Even more difficult to bear was the absence of her beloved husband, Rolf Jameson, born Raoul Inigo Diego de la Trienta. Only days before their twenty-fourth wedding anniversary, he had dropped dead in the field while sowing corn. Yet the Lord had given Susan a joy to ease the sorrow of great loss—baby Rolf was the picture of his handsome Spanish father.

Turning up a pert nose at her older brother, Rosalind flounced off toward the river. Harry found it difficult to believe that his sister would soon be wed. She was younger than Maela and seemed too immature to consider marriage, though her pretty face and figure attracted hordes of admirers.

"What news weighs heavy on your mind, my son?" Susan sat beside him on the step.

He glanced sideways at her. "News from London. Nothing to concern you, Mother."

"If it brings this scowl to your face, it concerns me."

Harry smiled acknowledgment, though his eyes remained worried. "I hear that Sir Hanover Trenton has fallen from grace. It is noised abroad that he made adulterous dalliance with one of the queen's ladies-of-honor, and Her Majesty is justifiably furious."

"And?"

"He has disappeared, most likely to the continent. There is a reward for his capture. I expect he would face the block."

"Wherefore does this hapless nobleman's plight bring a scowl to your face, Harry? You have minded little the executions of other nobles."

Harry sighed. "He is Maela's father."

"Your Maela? The maiden you love?"

He nodded.

Susan blinked rapidly in surprise. "You have temerity indeed to aspire to a nobleman's daughter. Why did you keep these particulars hidden from me these many months?"

"She is his natural daughter, Mother. He cares for nothing but the profit she may bring him. And I purposed not to conceal the matter; 'tis simply that your mind has been occupied with more pressing matters than one son's marriage plans."

His mother pondered in silence, far from pleased but unwilling to hurt Harry. "She has written you, I recall, but not since summer. Have you proposed matrimony? Are you certain quite that she has no plan to wed another? Her father might already have contracted a match."

"Maela would ne'er consent to wed another, and I cannot but think that friends would have sent me word had the bish—" He broke off, then resumed, "I hope that soon Maela shall be my wife."

Susan reached a work-worn hand to touch his hair. "I would have you near me, Harold, but I would rather have you content with your lot. You have left all in order to aid your kin; you have given freely of your strength and skill for our benefit while enduring your own loneliness. We can now survive a short season without you, for the fields are harvested, the sheep marketed or pastured, and all is well in hand. I believe the Lord shall richly reward you for your faithful labor and patience. You shall ride forthwith, settle your affairs, and return with your bride ere the new year begins."

He glimpsed a twinkle in her eye as she gripped his upper arm. "You are grown soft and lazy from dreaming of your love."

Harry couldn't help but smile. He looked into his mother's blue eyes and saw her pride and love for him. "You will love her, Mother. She is. . .very dear."

Susan leaned against her son and reached up to stroke his neatly trimmed beard. "I shall love her because you love her. When will you depart?"

"Soon." He wrapped his arm around her and squeezed gently. She was a sturdy woman, but to Harry she felt little and soft. Strange, that his mother should seem small when she had once cradled him in her arms. "I shall not keep long from you again, Mother."

"I know. You have a tender spirit toward women, as do few among men. You are akin to your father, and you well know how I did love him!"

"That I do know." Harry pressed a kiss upon his mother's forehead.

"Is Lottie not a comely bride?" Hepzibah Wheeler asked, tossing rice at the newlyweds as they climbed into the rented carriage.

"In truth, she is," Maela answered warmly. "Lane adores her, and his parents greatly approve the match."

"We thought Lane Fleming would never wed. Many did attempt to catch his eye, but no maid could bring him to speak!" Elizabeth Goddard giggled, shifting her toddler higher on one hip. "It needed Lottie to snare him—a maid both bold and unabashed!"

"Will you remain at their house? I know you are friendly with Lottie, but. . ." Prudence Foster held her pregnant belly with both hands. "I would little desire an unwed maid in my household."

"Prudence, that is unkind!" Elizabeth chided. "Lottie is not jealous of Maela, I am certain. They have regard one for another."

"Nevertheless, were I Lottie, I would place no other maid before my husband's eyes—at least for a season or two. What has become of the joiner? We did all believe he would wed you, Maela, but it appears his attraction was fleeting." Prudence's pale blue eyes held little warmth.

Blood rushed into Maela's face. "I received a letter from him only a fortnight past. He shall return for me." Her voice sounded tight.

"I am certain he shall," Elizabeth soothed. "Harry was besotted with Maela, Pru, and no wonder, for she is gentle, good, and fair. Make no doubt, he will return as soon as ever he can." The plump, kindly girl-mother patted Maela's arm.

"Hmph!" Prudence gave Maela a disdainful glance and picked her way down the church steps.

Once she had passed out of earshot, Elizabeth said, "Prudence is only jealous, dearest. Your Harry never gave her a second glance, and she did esteem him greatly. She wed Clarence Foster as second choice, and he cannot make her happy."

"Make haste, or we shall miss the procession," Hepzibah reminded them. "Lottie's brother carries the cake, though I fear he has too oft partaken from the bride's cup!"

Leading the wedding guests into town, Melvin Putnam followed after the bridal carriage, bearing the heavy cake on a great platter atop a short pole. The crowd gasped in horror as he reeled, nearly impaling the cake upon a tree limb. The portly young husbandman did, indeed, appear cheerfully drunk.

"'Twill be a miracle if we taste that cake," Elizabeth remarked as she started down the steps. "I believe 'tis not long for this world."

"I care little." Hepzibah lifted her kirtle and skipped down the steps. "Dancing shall continue, with or without wedding cake. I shall dance every dance with Joseph Clark this night!"

"The next wedding party shall likely be yours, Hepzibah." Elizabeth smiled at the exuberant girl. The three young women had been friends their entire lives, and Maela appreciated the generous way they had allowed her into their circle.

"Join us, Maela? We shall be jolly the whole night through!"

"Nay, though I thank you. I shall remain." Her eyes followed the chattering, giggling women, but she felt no desire to join the procession. Dancing held no attraction, and the thought of plum cake made her feel ill. Prudence's thrust had sunk deep into Maela's tender spirit.

When no one was looking, Maela wandered across the churchyard, threading her way between gravestones. Her mother's grave was not here, and neither was her grandmother's. They had both been buried in a common graveyard on the outskirts of town, with beggars, criminals, and other no-accounts. Maela stepped over a stile and kept walking. She missed Dudley. He was usually with her, but not today, not during a wedding.

"Lord God," she prayed under her breath, walking faster and faster. "I have striven daily to surrender my life into Your hands. I long to be the woman You have created me to be, yet I fail dismally. Ever within my heart is an ache, a longing for Harry. Shall it ever be so? Must I give up my desire to be his wife?"

Tears overflowed as she walked and prayed, wrestling with God. At last, she groaned, "I will surrender him, Lord, but I must have Your love to take his place. I cannot live without love!"

Blindly she walked, not knowing whither her steps led. "Rachel and Jonas love me, as do Lane, Lottie, and other friends, but they can do very well without me. I want someone to love who needs me, Father!"

She was obliged to stop, for a stream blocked her way. Glancing around, she realized that she was thoroughly lost. This did not distress her, for she knew the area well. *I need only find a clearing, look for the castle, and I shall be oriented.*

A strange feeling crept over her—the feeling of being watched. Wise in woodcraft, Maela dropped to the ground and tried to slide into the bushes, but rapid, crunching footsteps told her she was too late. She tried to scramble to her feet, but a hard hand clapped over her mouth, and she was bodily lifted from the ground. "Silence, or I shall slit your throat."

She nodded, and the hands loosened. Her assailant gripped her shoulders, turned her about, and Maela gasped, "Lord Trenton!"

"Ishy?" Shock turned his dirty face gray. "I did not know you!" He released her so roughly that she staggered. Striding away, he seemed lost in thought. Then he turned, a smile spreading across his face. "I thought you dead or gone away. 'Tis a pleasure, indeed, to find you well and"—he gave her an assessing look—"in remarkable appearance."

"We envisioned you escaped to the continent, sir. There has been no sign of you, though the queen's soldiers search diligently." Maela's feelings concerning his return were jumbled. She was thankful to see him alive and well, but not here.

"Have you seen the bishop?"

She shook her head warily. "Is he yet friend to you?"

He chuckled grimly. "He should be, for his hand was deeply in the pie along with mine. His head shall roll alongside mine if I go to the block!"

Maela shuddered. "Is the queen also angry with him?"

"Nay. Her Majesty knows only of my part in the matter, not of his. The silly trollop admires him and said nothing to the queen of his guilt—only of mine."

Though she pitied Trenton's plight, Maela's heart lightened at this news. Perhaps she need no longer fear Bishop Carmichael. Should Harry return, they could marry and be free of worry. Her father was in no position to object.

"Come." Trenton gripped her arm and dragged her along behind him.

"Where are you taking me?" she cried in alarm.

Minutes later, she discovered for herself. Taking Maela straight to the opening of her hidden tunnel, he climbed down and dragged her, stumbling and panting, after him into the darkness. Instead of entering the great hall, he opened the door in the side of the tunnel and pushed her in before him. Immediately, she blundered upon a short, steep flight of steps.

Climbing, she was surprised to find that the passageway was not completely dark. Small slits let in daylight from high above. She seemed to be in a very narrow passageway within the castle wall.

At the far end of the corridor, Hanover opened another door and shoved Maela inside. Without another word, he closed the door and latched it from his side. His footsteps died away.

Horrified, Maela stared at her dim surroundings. Large casks lined the walls of the chamber. She tried to figure out exactly where she was in relation to the castle and decided she must be somewhere near the great hall or the entry hall.

The only way to be certain was to look out one of those air vents. How could it be that she had never noticed them during all her years of exploring the castle? She clambered to the top of one row of casks and peered through a crack. Only dirt lay before her. She tried to get a better view, but the horizontal slit was angled down.

She tried the other side of the chamber. These "windows" gave her a view of flagstone flooring, but at least she could see a few feet to another wall. This must be the entry hall. It was dimly lighted, as an indoor hall would be. Her guess had been accurate.

Maela paced the floor until her feet ached. Would anyone notice her absence during the bustle of wedding celebrations? It was highly unlikely.

At last she heard her father at the door. He entered, carrying a rush-light holder, blankets, and a laden sack. Maela's heart sank. It looked as though she was to be a prisoner here.

"But why? Wherefore hold me captive?"

"You are my means of escape. I was obliged to fly from London with little blunt and had no means of obtaining enough to purchase my passage. My wife would gladly hand me over for trial, and I have nothing to offer in exchange for aid. Titus shall pay handsomely for you, as agreed upon many years since, and subsequently I shall arrange passage to Calais." He seemed smugly pleased with himself.

Yet, for the first time, Maela noticed how threadbare his clothing was. His recent trials had marked his face and grayed his hair. He looked the part of a wanted and desperate man.

"How will you notify the bishop of your plans?"

"He will come. I know Titus well, and he will come after you. He is. . .insatiable."

Maela shuddered. The bishop's burning eyes were fresh in her memory.

Trenton made two more trips, bringing fresh water, a chamber pot, and a straw pallet. "At night I shall allow you to walk about the castle, to wash and perhaps cook, but the risk is too great in daylight."

"Where do you lodge?"

"In finer quarters than these," he grumbled, "yet ill fitting my station. It suits me to have conversation with you; mine own company grows tedious. You shall tell me what has come to pass here, for I confess myself amazed at the changes wrought in mine absence. Where is the witch? And that toad, Dob Titwhistle? He owes me a considerable sum, and I descry no hint of his whereabouts. I did arrive to find my castle deserted, my holdings unguarded. Even the stables and outbuildings stand empty! Why has neither word nor payment come to me since spring?"

Maela sighed. *Lord, what is Your purpose in bringing me here? I asked You for someone who needs my love, but this is not the answer I did envision.*

Chapter 13

And he said unto me, My grace is sufficient for thee:
for my strength is made perfect in weakness.
2 CORINTHIANS 12:9

Whoa, Saul." Harry reined in his horse before the gates of Marston Hall. It seemed strange to be back after nearly seven months' absence. "Do you recall this place?" he asked the dogs. Ragwort perched before him on the saddle. The little fellow's legs had long since given out.

Harry clucked and nudged Saul's sides. Marston's dogs rushed to meet them as they entered the drive. Laitha was quickly surrounded by old acquaintances, and Ragwort barked greetings from his perch. Tired as he was, King Saul shied and bucked a little while dogs swarmed about his legs.

"Harry!" a young boy shouted in excitement as Harry neared the stables. "You have returned! We nigh despaired to behold you again."

"Well met, Ned," Harry called back. "Come, hold my horse, and I shall reward your courage. Saul is kindly, though the dogs have made him mettlesome."

The boy took Saul's rein as Harry swung from the saddle. "Shall I walk him for you, Harry?"

"Yea, and give him drink when he has cooled. You are a good lad, Neddy." Harry thumped the boy companionably on the shoulder.

Word of Harry's arrival spread like ripples on a pond. Before he had even reached the house, Sir David burst from its doors. "Harry! Harry Jameson! How is it with you, son? I have craved the sight of your face these many months but had begun to believe you would never return." He gripped Harry's hand heartily, clapping him on the arm. "Enter, sir, and welcome."

Harry followed his former master through the great front doors and into a parlor. "I came first to see you, sir. I have just ridden into town and would ask—"

"Has noise of Lord Trenton's disgrace traveled even unto Lincolnshire? 'Tis a sad business. Hanover was my friend, though we seldom spoke these many years. And now this disappearance of his natural daughter! I know she was your particular friend, so—"

"What is this?" Harry demanded, stiffening. "What of Maela?"

"Ah! You had not heard? I am indeed sorry to bear these tidings. The maiden disappeared nearly a month since. She attended the nuptial celebration of her friends, Lane Fleming and my former housemaid Lottie. Afterward, she vanished and has not been seen since. They set dogs upon her trail, but it had rained and frosted in the night, and the trail was cold."

Harry's face was ashen. His thoughts ran wild.

Sir David was still speaking. "Were I not a Christian, I would believe the Trenton line cursed. First the son's death, then Hanover's title and holdings stripped from him. Now the maiden has disappeared. The castle is a ruin, and the tenants pay no rent since that ruffian absconded—what was his name?"

"Dobbin Titwhistle. Trenton's son has perished?"

"They know not what took the lad. It came of a sudden. One day he was in health, the next, gravely ill. He had fits and spasms, they say, and went rigid. The mother said the lad had trodden upon a horseshoe clamp some days before and punctured his foot deeply; but the wound had healed and the doctor thought all was well. They leeched and drenched him, but to no avail. 'Twas a sad business, from start to end."

Harry was only half listening.

"I must find Maela. I ask, sir, for use of the coppice cottage. I would pay its rent."

"Nay, it is yours to use, Harry. It stands vacant. These calamities have stricken you a mighty blow, I can see. I sorrow for you, my son. You are foremost in my prayers until your maid is found safe. I would do anything to aid you; if you have need, come to me."

Harry expressed his appreciation and soon took his leave.

The cottage looked neglected and lonely. Harry realized in one glance that its small paddock and shed would never do for King Saul. He must find other accommodations for the horse. The cottage also seemed small and dreadfully empty. Excited, Laitha and Ragwort inspected every corner, sneezing at intervals. Ragwort killed a rat near the chicken coop. He tossed and caught it cheerfully.

Leaving his pack on the dusty bench, Harry hurried back out to his waiting horse and set off at a canter. Saul's great hooves splatted in the road's muddy ruts. Laitha loped nearby on the grassy verge. Ragwort stood before Harry on the saddle, his small forepaws planted upon Saul's crest, his black nose drinking in scents. Harry held him by the tail.

The Fleming farm looked neat and prosperous, as always. A sizable addition had been built on one side of the house, undoubtedly for Lane and his new bride. Jonas appeared in the barn doorway.

"Jonas!" Harry shouted, waving an arm over his head as Saul trotted up the lane.

Jonas returned Harry's wave with vigor.

The two men met in the barnyard. Harry swung down from Saul's back and clasped Jonas's arm, then hugged him. Typically, Jonas turned to the horse, slapped Saul's sweaty neck, and said, "The gelding looks well. He has served you faithfully?"

"There can be no better horse. He desires a good rubdown and—nay, Jonas, I shall care for him. I did not intend that you should do my work," he tried to protest, but Jonas waved him off, leading the horse toward the barn.

"I shall tend him. Go to Rachel in the house, lad. We have much to tell you. I shall join you shortly."

Ordering his dogs to follow, Harry headed for the house, his cape swirling behind him in a stiff breeze. Rachel burst into raptures at the sight of him, laughing, hugging him, and wringing her pudgy hands in turn. She dragged him into the house; he bumped his head on the lintel. "Dogs, come as well," she invited the animals. "Does your head ache, Harry? Let me take your hat and cape, sir. I say 'sir' for you have changed so these months. Tush! You even have a sword! Have you been in a duel?"

"Nay, I did carry it for defense upon the road," Harry tried to explain, but she scarcely paused for breath.

" 'Tis a grand man you are, Harry Jameson! Sit here now. They have fed you well and worked you hard, though I detect no fat upon you." She prodded his chest and stomach as she spoke. Harry meekly allowed her motherly inspection, thankful to have no audience. His dogs settled on the hearth, panting audibly.

Rachel took his chin in hand and frowned. "Your trim beard resembles that of a high lord. Maela shall—oh!" She clapped one hand over her mouth, her eyes wide and worried.

"I know of her disappearance. If you would, relate to me the facts."

As soon as she uncovered her mouth, the words flowed again. "Oh, if only you had come sooner, mayhap the child would yet be here! 'Twas the morning after Lane's wedding—did you hear of it? Lane did wed Lot—"

"I did hear of it. 'Tis glad tidings, indeed. What of Maela?"

"She did not attend the festivities; her friends saw her last at the church. Jonas raked the countryside for her, and our brethren searched likewise. Nothing has been seen of her."

"The castle?" Harry's voice was deadly calm.

"It is deserted. They have searched it, to no avail."

"Where is Dudley? Did he not guard her?"

"He is with Lane in the fields. Of a certain, Maela would not take her dog to church for a wedding, though some do. Lane set Dudley upon her trail, but the dog became distraught. He has shadowed Lane since her disappearance."

"Did Maela take anything with her? Clothing? Food?"

Rachel shook her head. "Nothing that we could discover. Even her kittens are here."

It was a silly remark, but Harry did not notice at the time. It did not seem strange to believe that Maela would have taken kittens along had she been able.

Harry ate the evening meal with the Flemings. Despite his distress, he smiled to see Lane and Lottie together, evidently well matched and happy. The tall yeoman had gained poise since the spring. His craggy face had softened, and his blue eyes twinkled.

"I feel peace concerning Maela, Harry. You will find her. God will protect her." Lottie's round face was sober, yet calm.

Harry nodded, unable to reply. Strange, how people he had once counseled and ministered to now offered him comfort and counsel. First Sir David, and now Lottie.

"Do you need lodging this night?" Jonas inquired after a long silence.

"Nay, I dwell at my old cottage, but King Saul has need of your hospitality. I would pay for his feed, for he does eat hearty, as you will recall. On the morrow I shall ride in search of Maela. I take leave of you for the night."

Harry lay awake for many hours, staring into the thick darkness, listening to night sounds. His feather bolster smelled musty. "Where is Maela? God, I know not where to look. I am helpless," he whispered. "You alone know the whereabouts of Your little maid, and You alone can save her from evil."

He held Maela's needlepoint pillow against his cheek, his eyes closed against the pressing darkness. "Guide me to her, Lord, if it is Your will for me to find her. I can only lean upon Your knowledge and strength, for mine own are as nothing."

Chapter 14

*A horse is a vain hope for deliverance; despite all its great strength
it cannot save. But the eyes of the LORD are on those who fear him,
on those whose hope is in his unfailing love.*
PSALM 33:17–18 NIV 1984

Early the next morning, Harry returned to the Fleming farm,
rested and eager to set out. He had decided to begin his search at
Bishop Carmichael's estate, Parminster Court, at least a half
day's ride away. The bishop was highest on his list of suspects. Exactly what
he would do once he reached the ancient abbey he did not know, but he
trusted God to give him wisdom at the proper time.

The sky was streaked in glorious sunrise when Harry arrived; Jonas had
just emerged from the house with Dudley at his heels. Harry called out a
greeting, and the dogs rushed to meet one another, tails wagging. "I would
collect my horse and set out in search of Maela. I intend to begin my search
at Parminster," Harry explained in passing.

But to Harry's shock, his horse was pacing in circles, sweating pro-
fusely and looking sorely distressed. "Saul, are you ill?" The symptoms were
clear: colic. Harry began to lead the groaning horse around the barnyard in
wide circles. Saul frequently cocked his tail, but to no avail; he had a painful
blockage. The great horse was helpless. His dark eyes looked to Harry for
relief, but Harry could do nothing to help aside from keeping him on his
feet and walking, hour after hour. Jonas offered to help, but Saul pinned
back his ears and bared long yellow teeth. In his agony, he would allow no
one but Harry to lay a hand upon him.

Harry could not be angry at the hapless horse, but he fretted inwardly.
Once, when they stopped for a moment, Saul rested his enormous head
upon Harry's shoulder and blew out a heavy sigh. Leaning his face against
the horse's sweaty face, Harry closed his eyes and tried to be calm and accepting. *I did ask for Your help, Lord. When am I to receive it?*

Lane had gone to town that morning. He returned at noon, riding his roan cob at a rapid clip. Dismounting, he left his horse standing and ran to Harry's side. "I bear tidings of great import, Harry! The village is rife with talk about Bishop Carmichael. He has arrived without notice, and our fellowship shall surely suffer his wrath. The Reverend Master Tompkins has informed him of the believers' activities, of Marston's involvement with Puritan leaders. The bishop now resides at the King's Head Inn, along with a large retinue. It would appear that he has come to conquer, not to direct our manner of worship. The townsfolk are greatly disquieted."

The two men absently circled the barnyard. Saul's big head bobbed faster above Harry's shoulder as their pace increased. Lane added, "Armed men wearing Carmichael livery have visited—some say raided—nigh every freehold, husbandry, and business in the parish. They appear to search for something of value. Could it be Lord Trenton they seek? Or Maela? Would the bishop know of her existence?"

At last Harry spoke, his voice deep with repressed anxiety. "He knows, and desires her for his own. At least we may know that she is not already in his power."

"I have further news," Lane continued. "Dob Titwhistle has been sighted at the King's Head. The man is clothed in velvets and furs, and while in his cups, he did boast of his connections with sacred and influential personages. There is little doubt that he is in the bishop's employ!"

"Dob!" Harry blurted, then fell silent. This alliance was unexpected; he had discounted the rumors, but now they proved true.

"I must now inform my family," Lane excused himself, and Dudley followed him into the house.

And still, Harry could only walk his horse and pray for patience. Saul groaned in relief when the rapid pace slowed. Harry rubbed around the gelding's twitching ears. "Forgive me, my friend. I forget your pain while dwelling upon mine own."

At last, more than two hours past noon, Saul relieved himself. Harry gave a fervent prayer of thanks, for aside from his need of Saul, he was greatly attached to the horse. It had troubled him to see his friend in distress and be helpless to give aid.

Lord, I apologize for my former arrogance. Your will be done on earth as it is in heaven. Had I ridden to Parminster Court this morning, I would have missed Lane's vital information.

Saul seemed subdued, but he was himself again. He bunted Harry affectionately with his Roman nose, pricked his ears at Ragwort, and even nibbled at the hay Harry offered. "He shall recover," Jonas diagnosed. "Back to normal in a day or two. He is of a kind that recovers quickly."

Harry rubbed Saul's soft gray nose, smiling when the horse threw his head up in annoyance. Saul disliked having his nose touched, but sometimes Harry couldn't resist. Saul's big lips flopped together noisily as he reached for the carrot Harry held just out of reach. Harry gave him the treat and hugged his warm neck.

Jonas smiled as he watched. "You two are well matched."

"How so?"

"In appearance you are like, both large and powerful beyond others of your kind, comely of face and form, and boisterous by nature, capturing the notice of all whether ye will or no."

Harry tried to hide embarrassment with a joke, "And we two consume fodder beyond others of our kind!"

Jonas wryly acknowledged, "True." He reached out to pat the gelding's neck. "I know that Saul's illness has caused you to chafe. The Lord will have His way in this, Harry, if you allow Him to lead."

Harry nodded humbly. "I asked for God's guidance, and He leads by strange paths indeed. Jonas, will you watch over Saul? I shall walk to the castle. I know that you have searched it, yet I must see with mine own eyes."

The dogs cruised the area around Harry as he walked toward Castle Trent. He found the castle courtyard devoid of life. No rooks perched upon the battlements.

Harry tried the kitchen door and found it unlocked. Ragwort trotted on in, scouting for rats or cats. Harry was surprised to see kegs, baskets, and cooking utensils arranged neatly against the walls or hung upon hooks. The supply of fagots was low, but tidily stacked near the hearth. The floor tiles were cracked and stained, but clean. The last time he had seen it, this kitchen had been in total disarray.

Wiping the table with one finger, he pulled it away free of dust. He checked the scullery. The supplies were low, but fresh. A side of bacon, a barrel of coarse flour, turnips, apples, carrots—plenty to feed a maid and her captor for many a day.

Moving on into the entryway, Harry felt that he was being watched. He spun around, half expecting to find Dob upon him with a pike, but the hall was empty. Only Laitha stood beside him, her nose working overtime. A barely audible whine escaped her. "What is it, lass?" Harry whispered, but Laitha merely cocked her head toward him.

Ragwort rushed past, wuffing eagerly. Harry and Laitha followed him up winding stairs to the gallery outside Maela's old chamber. There was a splintered gap in the gallery floor; a board dangled beneath, hanging by one peg. Below, the great hall stood empty.

Harry's skin crept. He did not believe in haunting spirits, yet his fear could not be denied. "Lord, I need Your strength," he breathed aloud, "for my courage does falter!"

Tentatively, he stepped into the gallery, momentarily expecting its floor to give way. It held, protesting with creaks that seemed deafening in the silence. Harry opened the door to Maela's bedchamber. The room was empty, the hearth cold. No skinny, dirty figure greeted him with glowing dark eyes. He swallowed hard. Laitha bumped against his leg, then again turned her head and growled.

Other rooms were just as unrewarding. The master chamber was thick with dust, its rich bedstead cold and deserted. Other chambers showed signs of decay, though they had once been rich indeed. Covered furniture resembled ghosts of odd shapes and assorted sizes in the fading light. Surprisingly, there was no evidence that the castle had been looted. Fear of Hera's curses still held the superstitious at bay.

Mounting the battlements, Harry looked across the county, awed by the view. Almost he could imagine himself a baron of old, scanning the countryside for approaching enemy armies. . .but that romantic era had passed away. Unconsciously, Harry sighed.

Suddenly Laitha bristled and snarled, facing the staircase behind them. Harry glanced around but saw nothing. He peered down the stairs; they were empty. Ragwort had vanished.

Awkwardly drawing his new rapier, Harry descended the steps. The tower stairs were open, giving him a clear view down to the bottom step; while below, in the living quarters, the spiral stairwell was enclosed and dark. At each landing Harry brandished the sword, his eyes darting back and forth.

There was no further sign of Maela. Had he been mistaken? Perhaps others had straightened the kitchen since Hera Coats's death. Or—Harry inwardly winced—perhaps the bishop had already taken her. He had not previously considered that possibility. She might even be—

Nay, I will not regard it. Shaking his head, Harry hurried to the great hall. He had not yet examined it from ground level.

Loose, dry rushes rustled as he strode into the vaulted room. Its walls were hung with rusted rows of iron helmets, crossed swords, and battle-axes, trophies of an earlier day. The head table was empty, filmed with dust. High-backed chairs lined it on one side. Crude benches lined the lower tables, their rotting wood scarred by knives, swords, and axes. Harry tried to visualize the room filled with fighting men of old, but the aura of decay impeded his imagination.

Laitha sniffed along one wall and began to quiver and whine as if she had found a rat hole. The hound did not usually bark and yammer about vermin—apparently, the castle's eerie gloom had affected even her.

Ragwort was also barking somewhere, a shrill, frantic bark. He must have cornered a rat. Harry whistled, but he knew the dog would not respond immediately. Ragwort's barking and Laitha's whimpering strengthened Harry's urge to leave. Approaching the fireplace, he considered using the secret passageway for a hasty exit. He wished for a torch. "Come, Laitha."

She did not come.

"Laitha! Come hither unto me," he snapped.

Reluctantly she obeyed, looking cowed, as though he had whipped her. "Ragwort!" Harry called and whistled again, waxing impatient as his desire to depart grew.

Silent drafts wafted the mildewed, tattered banners overhead. The hair on Harry's nape tingled. The castle's ghostly air of desolation had vanquished even his bold insouciance. "Forget the dog," he growled. "He can find his own way home."

Harry drew his sword again and reached for the lever. Laitha whimpered and growled. She pressed against his leg, looking nearly as confused as Harry felt. What was she trying to tell him?

He pulled the lever, and the secret door slid open.

Chapter 15

Unto thee, O LORD, do I lift up my soul. O my God,
I trust in thee: let me not be ashamed, let not mine enemies
triumph over me. Yea, let none that wait on thee be ashamed:
let them be ashamed which transgress without cause.

PSALM 25:1–3

Maela sat up, feeling stiff in every joint and muscle. "Sir Hanover?" she questioned, forgetting that he was no longer a knight. Her only answer was the scuffling, squeaking fight of rats in a corner behind the casks.

It was midafternoon, she deduced by the light from her ventilation holes. Her father usually released her at night, allowing her to wash, cook, and clean, though twice she had been denied the privilege when someone came to search the keep by night. Trenton watched her vigilantly, but she had made no attempt to escape.

Rising, she rolled her head and shoulders, trying to ease their stiffness, and walked the perimeter of her prison chamber. Not only had her father known about the secret tunnel, he had also known of, and used, this hidden wine cellar. He fondly believed that he alone knew of the tunnel's existence, and Maela never dreamed of telling him that she had betrayed its secret to an outsider.

Over many years, Hera Coats had drained Castle Trent's store of inferior wines and liquors; all the while, Trenton's extensive collection of superior vintages had lain safely hidden in its secret chamber. He often consoled himself thereby during his enforced exile, imbibing until his problems faded from memory.

There was a crunch, a rattle, and the door to Maela's prison slowly opened inward. Trenton entered, rushlight in hand. "Ishy, fill this jug from that keg there," he ordered, closing the door. "I wish to speak with you."

"Of what, sir?" she asked, obediently filling the jug with a dark liquid. Some spilled to the floor before she could stop the tap.

"Wastrel!" Hanover shouted, seized the jug, and clouted her shoulder. Maela fell back against the kegs, bruising her back. She said nothing.

Her father took a long draught from the jug, then gave a satisfied sigh and belch. "Ishy," he began, wiping his mouth with one stained sleeve. "You are a comely wench and, as was your mother before you, well suited to warm a nobleman's. . .er. . .heart. I have chosen well for you. Titus will supply your every desire."

Had these days of selfless service been for nothing? The kindness she had lavished upon this undeserving man must have soaked into barren ground! "Do you care so little for your only daughter that you would sell her as a slave?" she asked, managing to sound calm.

Trenton choked slightly and spilled brandy down his shirtfront. "Come again? Did you say 'slave'? Was your mother a slave, chit? She did enter into my house willingly." His mocking tone faded at the last, and a pensive frown wrinkled his brow. "She was fair beyond expression, and love welled in her eyes at sight of me," he mused. "Ah, Artemis," he shook his head sadly.

"My mother did love you ere she entered your house. I love not the bishop. I despise the man!"

"Wherefore? Titus is considered well favored, handsome of face and figure. Ladies of the court find the fellow fascinating."

"He repels and frightens me! My heart belongs to another, a man far exceeding the bishop in every particular. In his keeping my heart shall remain until my death or his."

"A nobleman?"

"He is noble in spirit, bearing, and countenance, if not in title. His father was a Spanish exile of noble blood, his mother a yeoman's daughter."

"Indeed? You had not claimed a lover ere now, which was wiser of you, for I shall discover the blackguard and skewer him ere dawn." He hitched his sword into a more comfortable position. "Then your heart will be free once again. Who is it?"

"Sir Hanover. . .Father, have you no mercy in your soul? I would no more betray him to you than. . .than I would harm you with mine own hands! Where will this killing end but in your own murder?"

He scoffed. "Preach at me again, will you? I weary of your tirades. Do not the scriptures speak ill of a nagging woman? In truth, I expect to die by the sword, as I have lived. 'Tis an honorable death. I shall be disgraced by female baggage—of high or low station—neither to hang nor to face the block! I have done nothing worthy of such a death."

" 'It is appointed unto men once to die, but after this the judgment.'"

Maela quoted. "Take thought for your eternal soul, my father, before your hour is upon you. I would not have you go to judgment unprepared."

"You speak as the very devil!" Trenton protested. "I am a good enough man; I support the church with my tithes and give every man his due. Of late, God has cruelly removed from me all that I valued on earth. Surely He will be merciful to me in the end."

"There can be no mercy from the Father unless we come to Him through the Son, Jesus Christ. This He has stated clearly in the scripture. The church cannot save you. Your good works cannot save you."

Trenton's eyes narrowed. "I have not heard this nonsense before. 'Tis heresy, for the queen's church alone gives absolution. You shall burn at the stake should your heresy reach less merciful ears than mine own."

"I beg of you to listen, my father. I fear not death, for to be absent from the body is to be present with the Lord, and my Lord is my light and my salvation."

Hanover could only stare. "How have you learned this heresy?"

"I learned it from the Bible, and I learned it from the man I love and intend to marry."

Slowly, Trenton rose and pulled his rapier from its scabbard. He twisted it, watching the light reflect from its polished surfaces. Approaching Maela, he touched one edge of the blade to her throat. "Recant, thou recusant witch. I would as soon slay you as see you wed to any but a man of my choosing. You are useless to me unless you follow after my will."

Maela did not flinch. "Then slay me, sir, for I shall recant neither of my love for Jesus Christ nor of my love for Harry."

"Harry, is it? Stubborn wench." Hanover tickled her throat and collar-bones with the sharp point of his weapon. "Like your mother you are. Your eyes are mine, however—dark as sin. Except," he paused, "there is strength in your eyes, and goodness. You have a stronger character than your mother's, and more virtuous by far than mine. I do believe you would face death with courage, Ishy, for I could easily have killed you just now, and you know it well. I have killed before. Yet, the daughter of Hanover Trenton, a commoner's wife? I cannot allow it. You would perish of labor or boredom. You were raised to court life, wench."

"You know not how I was raised, sir, for you were here but seldom. Of late, I have lived as a yeoman's daughter. I did clean, bake, sew, reap, winnow, and all other tasks the life does require, and I am the stronger for it. You have seen me labor for your comfort and ease in this castle these many days—did I appear to suffer at it?"

"And is your lover worthy of you?"

Maela was uncertain whether he mocked her, but she answered, "Harry is worthy of the highest and best in the land, sir, for a better man I cannot imagine. He is God's humble servant and the servant of all mankind. No man alive has a more generous heart. He did take into his care a dirty, bitter, hopeless child and, expecting nothing in return, did give her freely of all he possessed. Through his love, I learned of God's love."

For a moment, she saw a flicker of human feeling cross his face. "A veritable saint, this fellow—" He paused abruptly, still pointing his sword at Maela's bare throat. His eyes lifted to the ventilation cracks. "I did hear a dog bark. Intruders storm the castle yet again." He swore softly, and his eyes hardened. "Keep still, wench, or I shall slit your throat with impunity, for my life is more to me than yours."

"Father," Maela said quietly as he headed for the door.

He stopped and turned slowly. When his eyes met hers, she saw in them a new expression, a softening. "What, Ishy?"

"You are my father, and I do honor you."

For a long moment, he showed no reaction. Then he strained as though attempting to swallow with a dry throat. At last he simply turned and slipped silently through the doorway.

As the door swung shut, Maela stopped it short. This time, her father was too absorbed in listening for sounds of the intruder to notice that the latch did not click.

She heard the tunnel door open and close at the far end. Venturing into the narrow passageway, she felt her way along the wall. The light from outside was dim. She could see little.

A snuffling sound from above startled her. Peering at the wall to her right, she saw a long crack near the ceiling with a series of foot and hand holds beneath it—a peephole. She immediately climbed up. That sound had not come from a rat.

Her assumption proved correct: a dog's black nose sniffed at the crack. It pulled away for a moment, and Maela dimly caught sight of a patched face and empty eye sockets.

"Laitha," she dared to breathe. The dog began to tremble and whimper happily, but she could not understand Maela's position within the thick wall. "Tell Harry where I am," Maela choked. The knowledge that Harry must be near almost reduced her to tears.

Laitha disappeared from Maela's sight. For a minute more the girl waited, then lowered herself with a hand on the far wall. Did she dare try to escape? Where was Trenton? At the end of the passage Maela descended the few stairs to the wooden door, but she could not open it. Its latch must be on the outside. She hurried back to the rock ladder and scrambled up, bracing herself with one foot upon the outside wall.

She caught a glimpse of Laitha across the great room and heard what sounded like a man's voice. Was it Harry? Dared she take the chance that it was? Should she be mistaken, her father would most likely kill her and leave her body forever undiscovered within the castle walls. But if it were Harry and she said nothing, she could lose her only chance!

Suddenly she heard strange sounds, a clash as of metal upon metal, and men's voices shouting. She could not understand the words but thought she recognized Harry's voice. "Harry! Harry, I am here!" she shouted. Her voice was lost in the clatter.

As soon as the panel slid open, Harry had known he was in for trouble. Laitha had tried to warn him, so he was hardly surprised when Hanover Trenton leaped through the opening, thrusting a sword at Harry's head. He barely had time to fall away before the older man was upon him again.

Harry lifted his sword to parry the thrust, finding it difficult to maneuver while seated upon the floor. Laitha helped him by getting in the way. When Trenton tripped over her cringing form, Harry seized his chance and crawled beneath the head table, between chair legs, and out the other side. The disgruntled nobleman shouted curses, but he did not harm the dog. Laitha yelped and scuttled blindly into the tunnel, seeking peace and shelter.

"Come hither and fight, coward!" Hanover Trenton shouted. "Thou blackguard! How did you know of the passage? What evil arts revealed it unto you?"

"No evil art, Lord Trenton, but your own flesh did reveal it. Ishmaela told me of the tunnel. Where is she?" Harry asked from the other side of the table. He was now upon his feet and had his cloak wrapped around his left arm as a kind of shield.

Their voices echoed from stone walls and ceilings. Hanging banners rustled like whispering voices of long ago. The setting sun, released by a passing cloud, suddenly poured light through the hall's cross-shaped windows. Brilliant golden crosses appeared across the walls and floor, one spotlighting Trenton. Harry saw fatigue and strain in his opponent's lined face.

Hanover stepped out of the light. "Let me conjecture—you are the esteemed Harry, the man my foolish daughter professes to love more than life itself." As he spoke, he casually reached into the fireplace and pulled the lever to close his secret tunnel. He would not allow Harry to escape by that means.

Harry's eyes flickered, but he did not lower his guard. "I am Harry the joiner. I was privileged to tutor Maela through her childhood and have become her mentor and friend."

"Then you love not the wench?"

Before Harry could reply, Hanover leaped atop the table and fell upon him with a flashing sword. Far from comfortable with his narrow rapier, Harry did well to parry the varied thrusts of his enemy, let alone launch any form of attack.

One vicious encounter breached his guard; with lightning speed, Trenton's rapier slashed down upon Harry's left shoulder. Harry dodged, but he was not quick enough; the sword sliced into the muscle of his upper arm. He made no sound, though his face whitened and sweat beaded his forehead. His sleeve darkened rapidly, feeling hot and damp against his skin.

Another cloud obscured the sun. Once again, the hall fell into grim shadow.

Trenton stepped back to catch his breath. "Ishmaela is pledged to Bishop Carmichael. In the abbey, she shall be treated as a veritable queen, wanting nothing. What life would she have with such as you? A hovel in the countryside or a hovel in the village, twenty children, and never enough to eat. The daughter of Hanover Trenton deserves better than your dirty hands upon her, joiner man. Come and let me slice those cursed hands from your limbs!"

Harry's teeth clenched against the pain and fury. Should this. . .this scoundrel kill him, Maela's doom was sealed. Would he, could he, allow himself to be cut to ribbons in this way? He would not.

God, I ask Your immediate aid! The situation is dire, indeed.

Letting go of his injured arm, he walked boldly toward Sir Hanover. Sweat dripped from his nose, but he gave it no heed. The sun broke through, again flaming cross signs throughout the hall. Harry's upraised sword caught a ray that turned it into fire.

"You think not to—" Sir Hanover began, then Harry was upon him. Pounding and battering, he made the smaller man use his sword as a shield against the attack, giving him no time to set himself for fencing thrusts or lunges.

The tables were turned—for as long as Harry's rapier did not break. Ignoring his wound, Harry used his superior strength to advantage. Trenton was soon bleeding from several nicks and cuts; his breath wheezed from his lungs.

"Slay me quick," he panted, staggering back from another of Harry's assaults. "I beg of you, turn me not over to the queen, but slay me like the man of honor I have ever been!"

Harry stopped abruptly. Echoes of clashing swords still rang among the rafters. "I would slay you not, sir!" He sounded astonished at the very idea. He stood with his back to the entryway, his chest heaving. Hanover Trenton drooped against a table, gasping for breath.

A voice bellowed, "Nay? But I would!"

The shout was followed by a swish-thump, and Hanover staggered back with an arrow in his left arm. His agonized cry rang in Harry's ears.

Both men stared wildly about, then heard a laugh from above. Dob Titwhistle stood upon the high gallery, longbow in hand. "The next shall pierce your wicked heart. Long I have dreamed of the moment when our fortunes would reverse, Hanover Trenton—the knight that was! And thou, joiner—a sorcerer, indeed! I would give you trade—the baseborn wench in return for this! It did bite me upon the leg and deserves not to live." He pulled Ragwort from a sack and suspended him by the scruff of the neck. "Work your sorcery now, if you can!"

He drew back his arm and tossed the wailing dog lightly into the air. Before Harry's horrified eyes, his beloved pet spun, legs outspread, high above, then hurtled downward. Without conscious thought, Harry dashed across the room, hurdling tables and benches. His rapier clattered to the floor. With his one good arm outstretched, he flung himself face-first and caught Ragwort only inches from the stone floor. He skidded along the floor on his belly and stopped just before the fireplace.

Dob leaned against the gallery railing to watch Ragwort's flight, but the rotted wood could not bear his weight. With a grinding crash it gave way, and Dob plummeted, screaming, headfirst into the floor. The fate he had wished upon a dog came to him instead. Boards and splinters continued to rain upon his body in the dreadful silence that followed.

The last gleam of sunlight disappeared, casting the hall into shadow once again. Harry watched as Trenton, with clenched teeth and a deep groan, drew the arrow from his own arm and threw it down. One-handed, he wrapped a handkerchief around the wound.

Then Trenton limped across the room and squatted beside his former retainer's body. A table blocked Harry's view, but he heard a satisfied grunt. "I take only what you did owe, traitor." Trenton rose, still stuffing something inside his jerkin, staggered to a table, pulled out the bench, and sat down, exhausted.

Harry scooted up to lean his head and shoulders against the wall and cuddled his trembling dog. Ragwort seemed to be in shock; he clung to Harry's neck like a baby to its mother.

"I have no longer any war with you, Harry the joiner. You are, indeed, a noble man. Take the wench and Godspeed." Trenton's voice was tired, but relieved. Retrieving his fallen sword, he made as though to sheathe it, but at that moment there was a rush and clatter in the doorway, and several men-at-arms entered the room and lined the wall on either side of the door. Each held a lighted torch and a crossbow.

Bishop Carmichael followed his men into the room. His dark eyes quickly assessed the situation, showing some surprise at Dob's violent death. "I see that my faithful dunce has met an untimely end. 'Tis fitting, no doubt, that one of so little wit should unwittingly cause his own demise."

The bishop cut a dashing figure, clad in black from head to toe: velvet hat with a long aigrette plume, slashed doublet and trunk hose showing gold satin lining, muscular legs in tight nether hose, jeweled buckles upon his shoes, and a satin cloak with velvet lining flung over his shoulders. His black goatee was neatly trimmed; heavy hair curled above his starched collar. A handsome appearance he made, but no beauty marked his expression. He approached Trenton, but eyed Harry. "Introduce your recumbent companion, I pray you, Hanover."

"Bishop Carmichael, may I present Harry the joiner, lately employed by Marston, as I recall. I have long expected you, Titus. The sight of your face brings me pleasure." Trenton rose to greet his friend and bowed politely.

The bishop smiled slightly but did not return the courtesy. "Your pleasure shall doubtless be short-lived, but let us enjoy it while we may. And this Harry the joiner is. . . ? A relation of yours, perhaps?"

"Nay. He prowled about my castle, and I did apprehend him here."

"Indeed." The bishop appeared to dismiss Harry as inconsequential. "Let us not linger here to no purpose. Hanover, where is the wench? I have come for her, you perceive, though I never imagined myself so fortunate as to find you here as well. For too many days I have endured the propinquity of that"—he waved a lazy hand at Dob's corpse—"in order to locate the wench. Almost I discarded this repugnant accomplice, but here, at last, my Christian forbearance has been remunerated in full. The odious Dob did serve me well ere he departed to his reward."

Trenton stared blankly. "I comprehend you not. You have come for Ishmaela?"

"Of a certain. Tales of her exquisite pulchritude reached even unto Parminster Court, and I did deduce thereby that my protracted wait need quickly end. I would have her, sir. Kindly divulge her location." A salacious grin showed every tooth in the bishop's head, but his black eyes were like death.

"I regret the trouble you have endured, Titus; and all for nothing, for my daughter has—"

The bishop interrupted dryly. "I receive ample reparation for my trouble. I shall delight in the wench's charms at my leisure, but equally gratifying will be the spectacle of your head upon the White Tower wall. I shall behold your rotting carcass in a gibbet yet!"

Harry watched Hanover's jaw drop and felt pity for the friendless man whose entire world had crashed into ruin. He stated for all to hear, "None that wait on the Lord shall be ashamed: they will be ashamed which transgress without cause. Place your hope and trust in God, sir. He alone is always faithful, just, and merciful."

Trenton heard him and turned. For an instant, his eyes met Harry's; then, before the men-at-arms could react, he lunged straight at Carmichael with sword out-thrust. In the blink of an eye, the bishop was impaled upon the rapier's point.

"Be merciful to me, Jesus Christ!" Hanover shouted. Leaving his sword, he fled through the door. Chaos and confusion ensued—some men stopping to load their crossbows, others bounding in pursuit of the knight, a few gaping in horror at their fallen leader. Two rushed to tend the bishop, but there was nothing to be done. Trenton's blade had pierced his heart.

While their attention was diverted, Harry scrambled to his feet, reached into the fireplace, quietly pulled the lever, stepped into the passageway, and closed the panel. He was surprised to find that the tunnel was not entirely dark. Trenton had left a rushlamp upon the floor. It still shone brightly, though the rush was burning short.

Harry picked it up. "Maela?" He spoke softly lest the men in the great hall hear him.

A low woof was the only reply. Harry followed the sound to find Laitha waiting before the tunnel's side door. Ragwort struggled weakly, and Harry set him down. The terrier limped over to Laitha and cowered against her. She licked his muzzle, sensing his fear.

"Is Maela in there?" Harry asked. He pressed the latch and pushed at the door. It groaned in protest but gradually gave way. Harry's head began to swim. The wound in his shoulder had drained his strength. His sleeve was blood soaked and stiffening. He placed his right hand over the cut to stem the blood flow and, putting his good shoulder to the heavy door, soon gained entrance to another tunnel. A set of very narrow steps led steeply upward. "Maela?" he said again.

"Harry!" Footsteps descended the stairs, and Maela threw her arms around him.

Chapter 16

The LORD God said, "It is not good for the man to be alone.
I will make a helper suitable for him."
GENESIS 2:18 NIV 1984

She was trembling, sobbing for joy. Harry kissed her hair, marveling at her sweetness after so many days of bondage. The dogs whimpered and danced about them. Maela's appearance had done wonders for Ragwort's morale.

"We dare not tarry here," Harry warned. He wanted to sound loving, but his lips and tongue felt wooden.

Maela nodded in agreement. "Let us hurry. My father may return at any moment."

"I think he shall not return," Harry said slowly. His voice sounded mushy. "I think he is dead."

"You killed him?" Maela wailed. "Alas, but I had only just told him of Jesus! And now you have shed his blood?"

"Nay," Harry managed to tell her. "I slew him not. I—" He staggered back, unable to support Maela's extra weight.

Maela gripped his arms, and her right hand came away red with blood. In startled understanding, she took the rushlight from his weak grasp. "Sit you down."

Harry almost collapsed upon the sandy tunnel floor.

"Harry! Oh, my beloved, do not die! I will not have it, do you hear me?" Kneeling beside him, she pressed her ear to his chest. His heartbeat was steady, but it was not strong. Examining his wound, she found that it still bled. She began to rip up one of her already-tattered petticoats to provide a bandage. Once the wound had been bound, she felt better.

"Come, my Harry. We must hurry to Rachel. She is skilled at healing."

Blindly, he staggered after her. At the outside entrance to the tunnel, she climbed up to check the surroundings, then dropped back down. "Night has fallen, and no enemy is in sight. Climb out, and I shall push you from behind."

Harry obeyed without question. He crawled a few feet away from the tunnel and dropped.

Maela crawled to his side and checked his shoulder. The wound had bled again; her petticoat strips were soaked through. She tore off more strips and wrapped them around the others. Ragwort supervised her every move; his cold, wet nose was everywhere her hands needed to be. He was not about to let Harry out of his sight again that day. Laitha lay between Harry's outstretched legs.

The night was cool, and Harry shivered. He could travel no farther. Maela moved to his uninjured side, leaned against a tree, and pulled him into her arms until his head rested against her shoulder. She felt his heart racing weakly.

"Maela?" he croaked, surprising her. She had thought him unconscious.

"I am here," she soothed, pressing her lips to his hair. "Conserve your strength, Harry, and pray. God will send aid, I doubt not."

"Leave me not," he begged.

"Never shall I leave you of mine own accord, Harry."

"I never wished to leave you. I was obliged. . ." His voice trailed away.

It was cloudy, but no rain had fallen that day. Nevertheless, dampness seeped through Maela's cloak and chilled her to the bone. She worried that Harry would survive his injury only to die of exposure. He was asleep, breathing roughly through his mouth.

Absorbed in thought, she almost missed Laitha's low growl of warning. Ever vigilant, the greyhound pointed her long nose away from the castle, into the woods. Ragwort lifted his head from Harry's chest and whimpered. Suddenly, a large shape barreled into them, and Maela was swarmed by a licking, whining, wagging, bristly hound. "Dudley!"

"Maela?" A quiet voice spoke from the darkness.

"Lane, we are here," she answered in the same guarded tone. "Harry is injured."

Lane and Jonas appeared and knelt to examine the unconscious man. "We must make haste," Jonas said. "He is poorly." They lifted Harry between them and carried him off, moving quietly. Maela ran to keep up.

"The woods are filled with armed men, searching." Lane gave her a quick glance and added, "Welcome home, Maela. We did greatly miss you."

Rachel washed her hands with soap and took a sharp needle out of a bowl of strong spirits to thread it with gut. Lane and Jonas lifted Harry upon the table, and Rachel set to work. Lottie had promised to pray in another room, for she could not bear to watch. Maela's job was holding Harry's head still. The men held his legs and arms. He had unfortunately regained consciousness.

Rachel unwrapped the wound, which immediately started bleeding again. She pried open the slice and poured alcohol inside upon the raw flesh. Harry let out a shout that nearly lifted the thatching overhead, then clenched his teeth, determined not to cry out again.

The razor-sharp rapier had made a three-inch slice down the meaty outer portion of Harry's upper arm. Instead of stitching a mere cut, Rachel had to hold the slice in place and sew around it. Even if the wound healed well, the muscle would never be quite as strong as before.

While Rachel stitched, Harry looked up into Maela's eyes. Instead of observing the surgery as she had planned, Maela returned Harry's upside-down gaze. She knew he needed her as a kind of anchor in the storm. Her thumbs caressed his stubbled cheeks.

"I approve your neat beard," she told him. "You are a goodly man, indeed."

He closed his eyes, then looked up at her again. "Thou. . .art well?" he gasped as Rachel made another stitch.

"Well enough. It was cold in that chamber, but I had sufficient food and water. Sir Hanover allowed me freedom within the castle each night. He was not unkind."

"I thank God," Harry whispered. His face looked almost green. It frightened Maela. She laid her cheek against Harry's forehead, feeling the chill of his flesh. "Lane, he needs a blanket. He will not kick while you are away, I am sure. Find a blanket for him, I beg of you!" Lane obediently found some blankets and helped Maela cover Harry's shivering body with them.

Jonas had been quiet throughout the ordeal, his eyes closed in silent prayer. When Rachel at last stepped back, Jonas breathed, "Amen."

The shoulder was neatly bound with clean cloths, and this time very little blood seeped through. Harry was given a drink, then placed before the fire to rest and warm up while the others ate a late supper. Laitha pressed close to Harry's side, seeming to understand that he was injured. Ragwort sat beside Maela at the table, shamelessly begging for scraps. Though Dudley seemed happy to have Maela back, he lay at Lane's feet.

Harry slipped into a restless slumber.

Bright sunlight streamed through the open doorway and disturbed Harry's sleep. Blinking, he lifted his hand to block the glare.

"Harry, you are awake!" Maela hurried to his side and bent over his pallet. His blanket had slipped when he moved his arm; she tucked it back around his chest.

"More or less so," he admitted. "It is morning?"

"Nay, 'tis past nooning. You have slept the day away." She settled beside him on the floor, her kirtle and petticoats fluffing out around her. "Do you hunger or thirst?"

"Yea, for sight of you." He smiled weakly. "You are a sight for sore eyes, and mine are, of a certain, sore."

Rachel walked in. "Ah, I see that our Harry has awakened! Does your shoulder pain you, lad?" She took Maela's place and began to unwrap the bandages. Maela hovered near his head.

"It pains me little. I would rise and eat, Rachel."

She regarded him with pursed lips. "Your color has improved, and there is no fever as I had feared. You may rise, if you wish to. Maela, fetch me Lane's shirt from the line. Harry's shirt is stained and rent."

After replacing his bandages, Rachel helped him pull a clean shirt over his head and slip his good arm into the sleeve. The other arm was bound against his body. Slowly, giving his spinning head time to clear, Harry sat up, then drew his legs under him and rose. All went dark, so he simply stood still, waiting for his vision to clear. Slowly, awkwardly, he tucked the shirt into his woolen hose. A jerkin could wait; for now, he was at least decently clad.

He blinked at Rachel. "I hunger."

"I might have known," she chuckled. "There is provender aplenty. Cold mutton, cheese, apples, and bread baked fresh this morning."

Harry tucked in with a will and felt much stronger once his belly had been filled and his thirst slaked. His shoulder throbbed, but he could ignore it. Despite her protests, he helped Rachel clear away the mess from his meal.

"Where has Maela gone?" he asked.

Rachel answered calmly, "Lottie did require her aid at the laundry."

Slowly, carefully, Harry walked toward the pond where the two women bent to their task, pounding soggy garments upon rocks and rough boards. Harry could hear them talking together: ". . .and whatever shall I do without your company, Maela? I do love Rachel, but she is not the friend to me you are."

"The Lord shall supply you friendships aplenty, Lottie, dear sister. Women of our age are abundant in the fellowship. And, of a certain, Lane shall be your dearest friend, as Harry is mine." Maela dunked Harry's shirt into a bucket of clean water. The extensive bloodstain had faded into a dull yellow patch.

"I do love Lane, but our conversation is limited. He speaks of field production, labor ills, and the imminent foaling of a favorite mare. I speak of village gossip and the furnishings of our home. 'Tis a sad— Oh, Harry! I heard not your approach!"

"Harry!" Maela sat back on her heels, shaking her reddened hands. "You should be abed! Does Rachel know of your escape?" She jumped up and caught hold of his arm with those icy hands.

He nodded. "She knows I could remain abed no longer. I am on the mend and would have private speech with you."

Maela's eyes widened at his serious tone. She glanced at Lottie, then nodded. "In the barn out of this wind, perhaps?"

Harry let her help him to the barn. Inside, they sat upon a bench and leaned against the wall. Two kittens scampered over to greet Maela. She picked up the calico kitten while the tabby playfully attacked her skirts. "There were four kittens when I left, but Lane says the tom killed two. I don't understand why." She snuggled a kitten against her face. "They are so innocent and dear."

"Though Ragwort has sworn off kittens, I do not believe we can take them with us," Harry said slowly. " 'Twill be difficult enough to travel without them."

"Travel?" Maela's chin jerked up. Her dark eyes bored into Harry. "You are not—" Then one word sank in. "We?"

He looked surprised. "We travel to Lincoln as soon as we are wed. My family does expect us ere Christmastide."

Maela looked dazed. "Wed? I heard nothing about a wedding." She released the kitten to join its sister.

Now Harry looked puzzled. " 'Twas understood that we would wed except for your father's objection. Now that is withdrawn, and we are free to marry."

"My father. . .is not dead, so far as we know, Harry. He has eluded capture."

"Praise be to God!" Harry exclaimed, his face lighting up.

Maela was confused. "You are glad of this news? He can no longer sell me to the bishop, who is dead, but he is unlikely to approve our—"

"Your father gave me his blessing ere the bishop appeared last night," Harry announced.

"He did? I cannot conceive of it!"

"Nevertheless, it is true. I have your father's blessing; now I need only your consent." Harry was beginning to wonder. Maela did not seem particularly overjoyed. "Will you become my wife, Maela? Or has your ardor cooled during mine absence?"

She looked into his worried eyes and smiled. "Foolish man. As though such love as mine could cool!"

"It is well, for I could not do without you. Only anticipation of return has enabled me to bear our parting. I doubt not that my sisters shall regale you at length with tales of my distraction." Harry smiled sheepishly and picked up Maela's hand. Their fingers twined together, and each of them felt unaccountably shy.

"Uh. . .when shall we wed?" Harry blurted. He could hardly keep his eyes from her but feared she would find his dazzled observation rude. It was difficult to equate his beloved little tree-climbing monkey Maela with the lovely young woman at his side.

Maela immediately shifted on the bench to face him. "As soon as you are mended; we must arrange affairs with the vicar immediately. I would not have a great festival; the simple ceremony would please me more. I shall wear my mother's finest silk gown. It is green like the corn in spring and patterned with leaves and flowers. And Lottie shall design my hood. She is gifted in this way."

Harry nodded, watching each animated expression light her face.

"I suppose we must have cake to distribute. Rachel baked Lottie's cake, and it looked well, though I never tasted it."

While Maela chattered on about wedding details, Harry stroked her cheek with one fingertip. It was as soft and smooth as it appeared. The finger trailed down to trace her rosy lips. At last Maela stopped talking.

"Harry." She reached up to hold his hand and pressed a kiss into his rough palm. "You are. . .most distracting." Delight and irritation blended in her voice. She met his gaze and stopped, inhaling sharply.

Harry kissed her parted lips and ended all discussion of wedding plans for the time being.

Chapter 17

How delightful is your love, my sister, my bride!
How much more pleasing is your love than wine,
and the fragrance of your perfume than any spice!
SONG OF SONGS 4:10 NIV 1984

Harold Jameson, joiner, and Ishmaela Andromeda Trenton exchanged vows December 3, 1567, at the Trenton parish church, Suffolk. The Reverend Master Cecil Tompkins performed the ceremony, and Sir David Marston, at his own insistence, gave away the bride. Lottie and Lane stood as witnesses.

The young couple honeymooned in the coppice cottage for six days. They wavered between wishing to be alone together and wanting to share these last few days with their friends. The Flemings and Sir David wisely left them alone to work out the dilemma together. They ended up spending afternoons in the company of friends but usually returned home before the evening meal.

Maela was both thrilled and frightened by the prospect of their imminent journey. "I cannot imagine what it shall be like. Never in my life have I left the vicinity of Castle Trent. Shall we sleep beneath the stars, Harry?" She tipped her head back to look into her husband's face.

Harry stroked the red braid that draped across his lap. They sat before the fire, as of old, but now Maela rested her head upon her husband's leg and Laitha snuggled against her side. Ragwort, displaced, curled up on Maela's belly.

Harry shook his head, pursing his lips thoughtfully. "Nay, we must find shelter each night. We shall be several days upon the road, for I would not exhaust you with a hard pace. We dare not give opportunity to highwaymen, Maela. Much of our way lies through thinly settled country, rife with brigands."

"I fear not, for few would accost such a man as my husband." She reached up to caress his shoulder, carefully avoiding his still-tender arm.

"We have little of value to tempt a thief. Did I not hear you say that your savings was safe at your home?"

"Verily, after purchasing your steed, I have left only sufficient coins for our board and lodging; but the horses, our provisions, and you would prove ample temptation for many a villain."

Maela digested this information in silence. Changing the subject, she blurted, "And we cannot take Samson or Genevieve? I understand the necessity of leaving the poultry, but the beasts are. . .are like family to me, Harry!"

Harry sighed. They had already discussed this problem more than once. "Be thankful that Pegasus will join us, Maela. Samson is too old for such a journey, and Genevieve would delay our travel. I have goats and sheep aplenty for you at your new home, my love. The Flemings promise our beasts good care and kindness all their days. We cannot ask more than this."

"I have given Dudley to Lane," she said quietly. "He shall be happier here, for his heart is Lane's as it was never mine."

"You have Laitha and Ragwort to love."

She nodded. "I regret that I trouble you over the beasts, Harry, but I love them all so. . ." Her voice caught. "I must leave my kittens as well, and at times my heart aches. . ."

He sighed. "I would transport them all for you, if it were possible."

"I know it well, Harry. You are exceedingly good to me." Brushing away her tears, she smiled up at him. "Truly, I need none but you to love, Harry. I shall be content and complain no more."

Maela's new cob, a chestnut gelding called Abner, cheered her considerably. She vacillated between excitement about her new horse and feelings of regret. "Pegasus will think me fickle," she mourned, scratching her pony's furry neck. "I have never ridden another horse in his presence."

"He will adjust to your betrayal." Harry chuckled at her nonsense. He was loading the pony's pack, testing its balance and adjusting the contents accordingly. "He receives enough attention to make your husband sore jealous."

"Tush!" Maela slipped her arms around her husband's waist. "Demanding, you are."

Later that morning, George arrived from the Hall with a message. "Lord Marston requests your attendance upon him this day, Harry. It seems urgent." The stocky field hand had recently married Dovie after a somewhat rocky courtship. He seemed content with his lot, but Harry did not envy him such a contentious, conniving wife.

Harry cast a regretful glance at his wife but obligingly accompanied

George to the manor house, leaving the dogs with Maela for protection. He returned a few hours later and resumed his packing and preparations. Maela thought he seemed somewhat distracted. "Harry, what said His Lordship?"

He glanced up, startled. "Sir David? He. . .uh. . .wished us a safe and pleasant journey." Quickly he delved into a new subject. "Have you considered that we have no ladies' saddle for you, Maela? And I have not the funds to purchase one."

She brushed this aside. "It is of no moment. I have ridden astride since my childhood and see no reason for change." I shall wear my drawers and a full-skirted gown, and none shall know that I ride astride until I dismount. I care not what people may think as long as I shame you not."

"You could never shame me. Maela." To Harry's relief, she did not return to the topic of Marston.

At last, the day of departure arrived. A small crowd clustered in the Fleming barnyard to wish the travelers Godspeed. Maela felt confused—uncertain whether to laugh or cry. For so long she had dreamed of seeing new sights and meeting new people, but now that she was leaving her hometown, possibly forever, she felt bereft. Familiar faces had become extremely dear: Jonas and Rachel, Lane and Lottie, her girlfriends at church. And the knowledge that she would never again see the familiar battlements of Castle Trent against the horizon brought tears springing to her eyes. She allowed Harry to lift her to Abner's back, but her shoulders slumped as she adjusted her reins.

"Farewell, my dear one," Rachel held her foot and kissed her hem. "I shall pray for you daily." Tears streaked Rachel's plump face, and her chins quivered.

Maela nodded, unable to speak. Jonas held Abner's bridle. He winked and smiled at Maela, but she spotted tears in his bright eyes.

Lottie was sobbing, clinging to Lane as they approached Abner. Lane reached up to take Maela's hand. "Lottie desires me to tell you of her undying love and gratitude. We shall miss you greatly, Maela child."

Maela and Lottie had already exchanged several weepy good-bye hugs. Maela smiled through her own tears at Lottie's dramatics. "And I you."

Sir David himself had ridden over to bid Harry farewell. The two men had been speaking in low tones while the Flemings clustered around Maela, but now Harry reined Saul up beside his wife's mount. "We must away."

Maela was ready. Side by side they trotted down the lane and into the road. Pegasus followed on a lead rein, and the dogs loped along behind. Maela turned to wave one last time.

It was not until that afternoon, when they had passed through Bury

St. Edmunds and headed toward Newmarket that Maela noticed Harry's unease. "Wherefore do you look back so often, Harry? Are we being followed?"

He glanced over at her, his expression unreadable. "Perhaps."

A twinge of fear pinched Maela's heart. She began to pray again for God's protection, and for a while she distracted herself from the pain in her backside. Unused to spending hours in a saddle, she felt blisters forming on her inner thighs. Abner's saddle was poorly finished, and its rough edges abraded Maela's skin. Harry had insisted that she wear high boots to protect her lower legs, and now she was grateful to him.

She glanced back. The rolling, forested terrain concealed any possible pursuers. She sighed, thinking that travel was not as exciting and wonderful as she had dreamed.

Maela was exhausted by the time they stopped for the night at an inn on the outskirts of Newmarket. She waited in the saddle while Harry arranged lodging for the horses, then nearly fell into his arms. He half carried her into the inn and up to their room. She was unaware of anything going on around her.

Later she awoke to total darkness. Laughter and singing rose from the pub beneath the floor, and the room smelled strongly of ale and unwashed bodies. Maela sat up gingerly, very much aware of her aching legs. She felt for the blisters and was surprised to discover that they had been salved and bandaged. Dear, considerate Harry!

Laitha and Ragwort lay across the foot of the bed. Ragwort rose and staggered across the blankets to snuggle into Maela's arms. "Where is Harry?" she asked the dogs. Exhausted, Laitha only snored on. Ragwort sighed but made no answer. Maela considered rising to search for Harry, but that would involve too much effort. Surely he would return in good time. She lay back down and quickly dozed off.

It was still dark when she awakened to Harry's kisses. Feeling warm and loved, she began to return his caresses, but he pulled away. "It pains me to wake you, but we must away, my dearest." He was already dressed and ready, to her dismay. "The horses await us outside. I left you to sleep until the last possible moment. We shall break our fast in the saddle."

Shivering in the icy air, she donned her waistcoat and full kirtle, drawers, hose, and boots. Harry helped her brush her hair, then watched as she braided it and bound it upon her head. Tying the strings of her cap, she announced, "Let us be off!"

To Maela's delighted surprise, Abner's saddle was now padded. Harry had somehow acquired a feather pillow and fastened it upon the hard seat.

"Harry," she began but could not think of adequate praise. She simply gave him a quick hug and allowed him to boost her up.

For the next two days, they kept the same schedule, stopping at convenient towns for their meals and lodging. The horses appreciated the leisurely pace and were full of life each morning. Not even little Pegasus seemed tired, though his pack was heavy. Harry had packed it carefully, evenly distributing its weight. Ragwort generally walked in the morning and rode with Harry after dinner. Laitha trotted easily beside the horses. Maela's blisters still pained her, but they did not grow worse.

They lodged on the third night in Stamford. Maela was excited when Harry told her that they were entering Lincolnshire. Another day of travel and they would be near home.

"Queen Elizabeth's minister, William Cecil, has a manor near here. Your father has frequently sojourned there. He is well acquainted with Cecil, though not on the friendliest of terms."

"How do you know this?" Maela asked, her eyes narrowing.

The Jamesons were dining in a pleasant inn alongside the Welland River. The proprietor had gifted Laitha and Ragwort each with a knucklebone, and the dogs were pleasantly occupied thereby beneath the table.

Maela watched Harry's face redden. "He must have mentioned it to me."

"I was unaware that you had spoken with him on a casual basis."

Harry made work of chewing his tender beefsteak. He could not meet Maela's eyes. After a moment, he sat back and sighed. "I cannot deceive you longer. Your father follows us to Lincolnshire. I have met with him each night while you did slumber."

Maela sat like stone. "How long have you known?"

"Since Sir David told me, before we did leave Trenton. I was sworn to secrecy ere I knew what I was about; I would ne'er be party to deceit otherwise. Your father wishes to take ship at Boston harbor, where no troops shall lie in wait for him. Marston gave him a letter of introduction to a merchant there who will provide safe passage to the continent."

"He said he needed funds from the bishop to pay his passage. This was why he held me captive."

"No longer. He acquired Dob's purse, filled with Trenton rent money. It was his own by right and full sufficient for his need. This is why he gave me his blessing, Maela. He does care for you, in his way, and planned to sell you only to provide for his exigency."

She grimaced. "Had he truly loved me, he would have found another way to resolve his dilemma. The bishop was a nefarious man, and my father knew it well. Real love places the loved one's needs first."

Harry gave her a long, sober look. "Your father had not the Spirit within to teach him such love. 'Love beareth all things, believeth all things, hopeth all things, endureth all things.' Have you demonstrated such love to him?"

Maela's face puckered. She pushed her plate away. "I did try, Harry. You know not what I did endure..." She covered her face with both hands and sobbed.

Harry wiped his face with the tablecloth, and rose. Lifting his wife by the shoulders, he led her to their room. Laitha followed, carrying her bone, but Ragwort could not lift his. He remained under the table, gnawing frantically.

Maela slept little that night. Ragwort awakened her by scratching at the door—he had finally finished with his bone. Harry was missing again. After opening the door to the let the dog in, Maela lay alone in bed, staring fixedly at the low ceiling.

"Lord, I desire to love my father, though he has cast my love back into my face countless times. I know that You did instruct us to forgive seventy times seven, but I fear I have surpassed that amount already! You have promised me love and forgiveness despite my willful ways; help me now, in the same manner, to forgive my father and truly forget his sins against me. I did not know how hard was my heart, until now."

At last, when Harry slept beside her, she snuggled against his warm side and slept peacefully.

Chapter 18

My little children, let us not love in word,
neither in tongue; but in deed and in truth.
1 JOHN 3:18

aela remounted after a rest stop, groaning as her tired back-side hit the padded saddle. Abner pawed restlessly and shook his head, anticipating her command. Harry, Saul, and Pegasus waited at the roadside.

"Better?" Harry asked solicitously.

"Verily, I thank you. You are indeed good to—" She stopped, staring at Laitha. Whimpering, the hound trotted ahead along the road, nose in the air. Suddenly, she dashed off, heading back the way they had come. Her white figure vanished around a curve in the road.

"Laitha!" Harry shouted fruitlessly. Ragwort followed a short distance, barking, but quickly gave up and returned to Harry, requesting his after-noon ride.

Harry and Maela exchanged glances. "She shall rejoin us, I am certain," Harry said, ignoring the terrier. They waited for a few minutes, though the horses chafed and fidgeted.

There was crackling of brush, and three armed men leaped from be-hind trees and into the road. They were filthy, skinny, and ragged, miss-ing many teeth. "Ho, there, guvna'," one shouted, aiming his bow at Harry. "Tarry a season. We would have business with you."

The other two grinned, eyeing Maela and the horses greedily.

Harry struggled to keep Saul still, repeatedly ordering, "Stand." Calmly, he asked, "What business have we with you, my good fellow?"

Maela silently prayed, squeezing her eyes shut, peeking between her eyelids.

"Grafton's my name, and daresay I ain't so very good! Dismount, sir. Hawkins, get me the gray," the leader ordered.

One of the men approached King Saul, but Harry warned, "Have a care! He has a wicked kick and would readily bite."

This was news to Maela, but she kept quiet. The horse did look danger-ous. His mouth gaped and foamed; he pranced ponderously, ears flattened, eyes rolling. Harry seemed unable to control him.

Hawkins looked to his leader questioningly, but at that moment there was a thunk and an arrow appeared in Grafton's breast. Eyes popped wide, he dropped his bow and grasped the arrow with both hands, then crumpled in his tracks.

Hawkins fumbled to load his bow but stopped when something sharp pressed against the nape of his neck. It was Harry's hunting knife. Drop-ping the bow and arrow, the would-be thief lifted his hands in submission. "We're lost, Becker."

Laitha sniffed at Becker's worn boots, growling. The thief looked from her to Harry, then beyond Maela, and his hands also lifted.

Maela turned. There, not ten paces away, stood her father with an ar-row at the ready, aimed at Becker's heart. "Your company was greater than we knew," Becker observed. "I like not these odds."

"Coward," Sir Hanover observed without malice. "Shall I shoot the rabble?"

"Nay," Harry replied quietly. "Disarm them and let them go."

"They shall assault another company another day," Trenton remind-ed him.

"That is not my business. We shall alert the constable at Bourne."

The two men disarmed the thieves and let them go. After obsequiously thanking Harry for sparing their lives, Becker and Hawkins disappeared back into the woods, bearing their leader's body between them. Maela held the horses, allowing them to graze at the roadside while Harry and her father discussed plans. She had never before seen a man die. Had she not been obliged to hold the horses, she might well have lost her dinner. Only gradually did awareness of her surroundings return.

"I must collect my horses," Trenton was saying. "When your hound came to me, I ascertained your need and hastened to aid you. Unwilling to alert your assailants, I tethered the horses a short way off and skulked through the trees. I am acquainted with these woods, having hunted here in the past. Thieves abound herein."

Harry thumped Laitha's bony sides, praising her to the skies. "Wise, most excellent dog! You have done us great service this day. Thanks be to God for His timely intervention by means of a lowly dog!"

"And a lowly scoundrel father." Turning to Maela, Trenton lifted his eyes to meet hers. "I desire to make amends to you, Daughter. My heart does rue my past behavior toward you and toward others of my kindred. During my convalescence, I spoke often and at length with Marston about the duties of a father and of my duty to the Creator. For many years, I did give all to Isaac, believing him my child of promise; yet he did spurn mine attentions. Thou, Ishmaela, child of my true love, I did neglect and disdain. I would ask your pardon, my dearest, most undeserved child."

A great lump formed in Maela's throat. Pegasus tugged at his rein, giving her an excuse to look away. She did not know what to think of this humble speech from her father, though she wished to believe him sincere.

"While I held you captive at the castle, your forbearance greatly impressed me; and yet I would not confront mine own heart and see myself as I truly was. I have abused you, humiliated you, neglected you, and intended to ruin you, yet you have returned unto me only honor and loving-kindness. I have purposed to make restitution unto you in any manner possible. I observed your nuptials from hiding and blessed them in my heart; I attempted to guard you during your travels, though your husband has proven himself proficient. He would have outwitted these brigands unassisted in a matter of moments had I not intervened."

Trenton turned to Harry. "A masterful exhibition of horsemanship, I must say, Jameson. Your steed would have flattened that rogue ere he knew what hit him."

Harry smiled acknowledgment but remained silent.

Maela's father continued, "I have learned, though late, that God promises fulfillment and love to those who repent and give fealty to Him. With my remaining days upon this earth, I desire to seek His face. I can only trust that His promises are true."

Brows knitted, he gazed at Maela. "You have little reason to trust my word, my daughter, but perhaps a deed will convince you of my sincerity. Not least among my trials of penance has been the safe conduct of two creatures, which, I have been assured, are dear unto your heart. Why this is so, I cannot imagine, for they have occasioned me labors incalculable these four days."

Trenton looked into his daughter's wondering eyes and smiled. "Tarry here. I shall quickly return." He hurried into the woods.

Harry took Saul's rein and slipped an arm around his wife's waist. "He hungers after your forgiveness, Maela. Truly, he has endured much for your sake, as you shall acknowledge upon his return."

Still feeling shaky, she leaned against him. Harry was easy to love, always so considerate and gentle. But did she dare forgive her father and trust him with her love? He was violent, volatile—just now he had killed a man and seemed to think nothing of it! Maela knew she would see Grafton crumple in her nightmares for many nights to come, just as, countless times, she had relived the cold edge of her father's sword at her throat. And yet. . .he had called her dear, apologized humbly, and actually seemed to crave her forgiveness and acceptance.

Hoofbeats upon the road warned them of Hanover Trenton's return. Maela faced her father, allowing Harry to take the horses' reins from her. She was acutely aware that these approaching moments represented a turning point in her life.

Trenton dismounted, then carefully lifted a sack from his packhorse. Strange noises emanated from it, almost like. . .

Maela gasped in startled anticipation. She took the proffered bag and loosened its string. Two wobbly heads emerged; enormous golden eyes gazed up at her, then around. "Daisy!" She barely caught the tiger kitten before it sprang to the ground. Giving it a hug and kiss, she shoved it back into the bag and caught up the calico for a moment. "Oh, Lily, my dear!"

Harry helped her confine the frightened kittens once more, then took the bag from her. His smile, overflowing with love and assurance, bolstered her resolve.

Maela approached her father and looked up into his hopeful eyes, seeing her face mirrored in their dark depths. "My father," her voice cracked. She swallowed hard and tried again. "You have my full pardon. I love you unreservedly, as Jesus Christ loves me."

A moment later, she was crushed in strong arms, and a husky voice repeated her name over and over, "Maela! Maela, my little child!"

Harry watched, smiling, swallowing hard. Then Hanover Trenton lifted one arm and thumped his son-in-law's shoulder, exclaiming, "God is indeed good! As He has promised, so He has done!"

Chapter 19

Praise ye the LORD. O give thanks unto the LORD;
for he is good: for his mercy endureth for ever.
PSALM 106:1

Standing on the quay, Maela wept into Harry's jerkin, shivering with sorrow and cold. Chill winter winds cut through her cloak; only when Harry held her close was she warm. The ship had passed out of view, and with it her father. After eight weeks of blessed fellowship, work, and fun spent with Harry's extensive family and his own daughter, Hanover Trenton had taken ship for the continent. He could no longer endanger his loved ones' lives by remaining with them.

Harry murmured into his wife's ear, "Let us return to the inn. We can sup and speak more of this in comfort."

Maela managed to tuck away a creditable supper, finding that she did, after all, have an appetite. After finishing his supper, Harry handed meaty bones to the two dogs. Contented growls and crunchings emanated from beneath the table.

"Our home will seem empty without my father," Maela observed, apparently determined to be gloomy. "I am exceedingly grateful that he stayed on past Epiphany and truly fellowshipped with us, but now I shall miss him terribly."

"I am certain we shall not suffer from loneliness. My mother appreciates your value as willing child-minder, and she certainly enjoys your company. Now that Rosalind has married and gone to town, Mother needs your listening ears, my dear."

"I do love your mother." Maela smiled but still seemed distracted. "Harry, I must tell you something of import." Her expression was deadly serious.

He waited, then prompted, smiling, "Which is?"

"I believe Laitha again carries pups by Lord Marston's staghound."

Harry chuckled. "Verily, I know it; but when shall you tell me of our own pup?"

Maela gaped, uncertain whether to laugh or cry. "Wherefore did you discern it?"

Harry smiled lovingly. "You have been violently ill each morn this past fortnight and believed I would suspect nothing?"

She flushed. "Are you pleased?"

"I could not be more so. My dearest love. . ." He glanced around the crowded room. "Let us hasten to our chambers and discuss this privately." Together, the young couple and their hound left the dining room.

Under the table, Ragwort tugged at his large bone, stopped to stare at it, sighed, then abandoned it to follow his family upstairs.

Jill Stengl is the author of numerous romance novels including Inspirational Reader's Choice Award- and Carol Award-winning *Faithful Traitor*. She lives with her husband and youngest son in the beautiful Northwoods of Wisconsin, where she enjoys spoiling her three cats, teaching high school literature classes, playing keyboard for her church family, and sipping coffee on the deck as she brainstorms for her next novel.

A Bride's
Agreement